ALNILAM

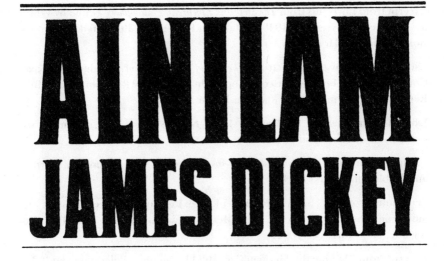

ALNILAM
JAMES DICKEY

DOUBLEDAY & COMPANY, INC.
Garden City, New York
1987

Library of Congress Cataloging-in-Publication Data

Dickey, James.
  Alnilam.

  1. World War, 1939–1945—Fiction. I. Title.
PS3554.I32A78 1987   813'.54   86–19699
ISBN 0-385-06549-3

to Deborah, Christopher, Kevin, and Bronwen

And next I will speak of the air which is changed over its whole body every hour in countless ways. For whatever ebbs from things, is all borne always into the great sea of air; and unless it in return were to give back bodies to things and to recruit them as they ebb, all things ere now would have been dissolved and changed into air.

—Lucretius

May I not clearly and distinctly conceive that a body, falling from the clouds, and which, in all other respects, resembles snow, has yet the taste of salt or feeling of fire?

—*David Hume*

Where am I, or what? From what causes do I derive my existence, and to what condition do I return? Whose favour shall I court, and whose anger must I dread? What beings surround me?

—*David Hume*

*　　　*　　　*　　　*

The wind pulled back, the sound of a huge, emotionless suction outside the head, and then, at a distance fairly far off in day or night, caused itself to be circling and milling, a strange tilt to it. Direction came, and it started once more toward him, gaining a velocity that made him hunker down under the three quilts as all the breath of the world burst apart straight onto the corner of someone's house, failed this time to retreat, and died spinning. He lay there in the gold shuttle, wishing for the dog-head.

After he was relaxed and warm enough for the next surge—surely from a different wind, one with a whole new range of movements and tactics—it did not come. Under the covers he unballed his fist in the fur-lined glove, took off the glove, and touched himself between the eyes, in the exact middle of the wild-flying shuttle, the gold sparks hurtling with an awesome, silent force that gave a new meaning to the words speed of light. He was getting used now to seeing them fly endlessly, night or day, whether he slept or woke, whether he sat or said something or ate. They wove themselves; they could not form anything solid. A few among them now and then floated, traveling across the screen; these were tinged with pink. He lifted his lids and there was no difference. He closed them again and rested, his thumb and second finger on both lids where he could feel the ceaseless jerking of the eyeballs as they tried of themselves to follow what could not be followed. A clock below him created time in what must have been the hallway of the house; there were two sounds of metal, spaced distinctly apart. He knew a little about where he was, and now, pretty much, when.

"Zack," he said.

He heard something that could only have been the rising of fur from the floor. Between the gusts of wind there was a bristling, off, as he judged, about ten feet. The click of toenails—leisurely and sure—came toward him, until animal breath flowed over his face. From under the cover as though from his real self, he lifted his right hand, and the dog-head was there. With his thumb he felt for the eyes.

Slowly, through the nose hair, his thumb came to rest on the shape of

1

sight. The dog-eyelid fluttered gently, under the tentative and protective pressure, but Zack did not move away. Then Cahill felt the soft, batlike ears, and came down the line of the jaw. The teeth were clamped; the way they fitted together, with the huge incisors set in the bone as deeply as stones in the rock of a mountain, was as reassuring as the word of God.

He ran his palm down the thick side of the dog, and, in addition to the continuous sparks of his blindness, he was pleased to feel that certain sparks of the electricity of dog-fur might have entered into the ceaseless fires that diabetes had given him three months before.

His bladder was building up.

"Lie down, Zack. Right where you are is all right."

He turned, and tried to take refuge in the possibility that sleep, if he could reach it, would do something about his distress. But it did not come. He sat up, and his underwear clung to him, clammy with tiredness.

He swung slowly, pivoting to his right, and put his foot down toward the floor. He must have hit Zack, for a low tentative snarl came from the room; a cave-growl.

Where was the door that enclosed him in whatever safety there was, and now threatened to explode his lower gut? He stood; there was a slight sensation of things moving around him in curious patterns. He put his hand in front of him and took a step and then two, then three. The wall was on his hand.

It was cold and pitted, and it had to have the door in it. Three months ago he had had no idea of how much sensitivity the human fingertip could contain, nor how much power it could command. Unhurriedly he moved both hands along the wall, using the forefinger nail of the right hand and swinging the left forward at waist height. He found the crack that separated the wall from the door and the doorknob at exactly the same instant, and a wave of power and assurance went through him. The gold shuttle of meaningless sparks wove themselves blinder, and for a second he believed that the intensity of their wildness would explode, split the darkness from his eyes, and that he would erupt back into the world of seeing: would see the wall and the door, would move confidently to whatever window there was and then behold—not see— the winter moon of North Carolina. He framed the door with both hands, and turned the knob. The door was locked.

"I did that," he said aloud, "stupid son-of-a-bitch that I am. What in the fucking hell am I afraid of? Anybody come through that door, Zack'd tear 'em apart like a rotten crocker-sack."

Click of beast-nails on bareness: the movement at the name.

He found the lock and pushed it until it clicked.

"Hey, hey," he said to the big dark and to Zack, "I did it! I have no more goddamn idea of where there is a bathroom in this place than a snake has fleas. I'm gonna try for the open, just to see what will happen. If I can't make it I'm gonna pee all over their floor. And you can do the same thing, my man."

Cold underfoot. Probably linoleum; not wood.

"You know," he said, "I ought to get my overcoat, or at least a shirt or something on, but I'd just as soon be cold. It seems like it's that kind of a time. Come on Zack, and let's go get 'em."

Through nothing but underwear, any part of air could get at him; he kept waiting to be reached; with the wind heaving at the house, the illusion of being blown one way or the other in perfect stillness was strong. He opened the door and moved forward.

His right hand was on the wall, and he twined his left in the fur somewhere along Zack's spine; he could feel the forward-moving bone. A door passed under his hand, and then the wall came back, chill and uneven. Another door, and Cahill's step picked up confidence, going toward the stairs.

The next door. Zack growled, standing. Cahill held to the body-fur.

"Let's go," Cahill said. "Let's *go.*" The nailless wall flowed under his hand; Zack bristled and padded.

No wall, now suddenly. He had hold of right-angled wood. He turned loose of Zack's fur, hearing the dog breath newly, and extended his left hand into the abyss.

"It's just a boardinghouse," he said, "just a boardinghouse in North Carolina."

A large-house updraft caught his underwear, and he billowed slightly at the top of the landing. The cold was not fatal, and when he shivered it was inside the something he had that made him invulnerable. A very faint indoor wind came to him, and he was sure it had in it the layered sense of stairs, rising to him. Still with the wall and the dog he started down, remembering that there was a landing, but whether twelve steps or fourteen from where he began to descend, he did not remember, and he told himself to fix the number in his mind, going back.

For four months he had been developing techniques; those of permanent darkness. Barefooted was better on stairs, but even with shoes you could test the edge of each step by a down-curling of the toes. The golden shuttle of flashing sparks that would never leave him was somehow confirmed by the fact that he could bend his toes over the forward end of a step, and thereby take the next one.

"This is enough now," he said, as he sat down cautiously on his last step. He believed that he was no more than three stair steps from the landing, where he would use his left hand to guide him to the ground floor, and then would go by dog-fur alone to the front door, down a few more stairs and into the openness that meant the uncrushing of his bladder, the freeing of the human water into night and snow.

"We're winnin'," he said. "Nobody can stand against us. Let's go on down."

But for a moment he sat there, his attention on the wild shuttle of light, the thing that had been given him by his blood sugar: that had destroyed his retinas and substituted for his personal vision of the world a darkness through which played, in an unpredictable and fascinating way, a literal infinitude of golden javelins. These were his.

He stood up. "We got to go to the left," he said, and he did. Levelness was under him. Right foot or bare left foot could find no way to fall; he would not fall.

The new door, locked or unlocked, was a factor now. A few more steps, probably slick with ice, and then the snow, and the moon, if it was there.

The knob was his, engraved, almost as big as an artichoke; he turned it and went through.

Wind died and he and his dog stood together, only the man shaking, and full of stone water.

He went slowly, for there was a slickness too deep to crackle. The air around him held what felt to be the ultimate zero of outer space, except that it moved slightly from time to time. Where was the wind? Where was all that wind?

Barefooted, he stood in the snow. The night was covered with a golden shuttle which had nothing to do with the universe. There was something about coming down, under his condition, from the last ice-covered human-made step onto the snow-skreaking ground that sent a strange thrill through him. This was the zero point: but he felt the breath of the dog, also, in the stunning air. Where he stood did not really matter to him; it was somewhere in the world; that was enough. It was somewhere in the world in the snow which made his feet lose their existence, and there was the sound of an animal beside him. He imagined that there were stars, for he could feel no snow coming down, and the weather might have cleared.

"Zack, my man, I came out here to ree-lease the water."

He flowed from himself, and his coupled hands could feel the steam rise from the snow.

He began to turn, spraying himself over the white landscape in a slow ritualistic movement known only to the new-blind. The snow crackled and burned around him for no reason but his will. Blindness entitled him to anything; why not?

"Zack," he said. But the dog was moving, somewhere in the burnt-out snow. Then there was his fur once more under his hand.

Through him came a bitter and familiar throe.

"How lucky can you get?" His bowels were suddenly filled with necessity, and he pulled down his shivering drawers and squatted, the weight of food—but very little of it—forced itself through him to the snow. He wiped himself with his hand, then cleaned his fingers on snow and reached for Zack again.

"You're more interested in my shit than you are in me," he said.

When he stood up he was lost, and knew it. His willful and senseless spinning—that of a big red-faced man wanting to face all directions the dark could show, and put his mark on it—had lost the house, and, though it was no more than five yards away, Zack could not find it for him. He opened his eyes wide, and the eyeballs shuttled frantically, filling his inner vision with the billion gold meteors of nothingness. Over the country rooming house, the emergency way station, the stars blazed and were no use.

He felt with his toes for a stair, any stair, any house, tried again with the other foot. He was wrong both times, both feet; the house had gone. Slowly he began to wander in the field, Zack following, and then coming up on Cahill's left side.

"They'll find me, out in all this purifyin' mountain air, if they don't find my carcass first."

He knelt on one knee in the snow, broke the crust with his fist, and swallowed mouthfuls of feathery water. Temporarily it took the place of the ice cubes he was always chewing on, whenever he could get them.

"We can get back, God damn it. Which way is the house, boy?"

He found Zack by his breath, then by the fur.

"Let's go home, Zack. Home."

Zack stood motionless, awaiting a command he knew.

"All right," Cahill said. "I'll try to figure it out. I've been holdin' back on my legs, so we must'a been goin' downhill."

He took a step, held back, and turned carefully 180 degrees, as nearly as he could estimate. The first step seemed up. At least it was not down. They ascended together by small degrees, Zack stepping easily, Cahill foot-feeling forward.

He slid a little on something soft. Once more Cahill knelt, again on one knee, then on both, and felt in the snow. He raised his fingers to his nose.

"That's shit, my man. Put your long nose down here and tell me if that ain't shit."

Zack whined, sniffing eagerly.

"Now what we need is an angle. I'm gonna try it right like . . . *this* way."

He put out an arm as in a salute of some kind.

"Just to see what might happen. Just to see."

The wind, gusting again with tentative force, was now as strong at times as it had been. There must be a difference, he thought, between wind blowing over the bricks or boards of a house and the open wind of a field. He stopped, and he believed he knew. There was a sense of strain in the air above him, perhaps a sound of obstruction, of being cut-into, perhaps even of dividing and going-around. His foot hit the first wooden step with a knocking of hollowness, and he fell to the ice, which came to meet him face-on out of such a depth of malice as he could not have imagined.

Numb-headed, he groped up and down, back and forth. He was evidently at the left side of the steps, for there was no ice to the left; there was nothing. He fingered between his eyes, found his blood.

"We got it, Zack. It cost us, but we got it. Let's go in."

He crawled from ice into the country of splinters, and stood up. "Hot damn," he said loudly. "I could go to London and make a million dollars of that London funny money. Over there it gets so foggy that people go lookin' for blind men, and payin' 'em to get 'em where they're goin'. Bein' able to see is bad in all that fog. You *know* it is."

He found the knob, and was in the cold hall, which held only a little of the air's movement. Arriving at the stairwell was absurdly easy, and he started up, one hand on the wall and the other deep in Zack's neck-fur. His steps came out level, and he was on the landing with the clock. The spaced, leisurely ticks came to him at very close hand. He stood facing these for a moment.

6

No bell from time, but one way or the other it would have to come. And there were people, here; they were around him.

Again, the travel was easy. He felt along wood, counting jambs and doorknobs, and on the fourth knob he opened and went in. Identification was in his shoes and the placement of them, and in the fact that there was no one in the bed. He piled in and found his syringe case beside the pillow. Under three quilts his old lonely arrogance returned.

"You show me," he said loudly, "anybody else who could'a done what I just did." He touched the drying place of his head-blood and his penis at the same time. To both organ and wound he said, "You ain't never gonna give down. Not now, or not ever. None of us."

Using the main two locations of himself, Frank Cahill began to drift, slanting through the insane hailstorm of golden slivers toward the last place he had seen.

Until the time of total blindness four months ago—and even now, for he had someone to operate the place for him—Cahill had owned and run a small amusement park in Atlanta. The complex was built around a three-section swimming pool: a children's pool, a diving tank, and a long, thin Olympic-length pool where he held swimming meets and various kinds of contests in season. There were a dance pavilion, a skating rink, a game room, and an elaborate half-completed mazelike building he was constructing himself, both to save labor costs and because he considered himself a good, almost a master, carpenter. The maze, called the Honeycomb, he worked on under a gigantic tent rented from an awning company just before the war. He had measured, fitted, and hammered in vile summer sweat in which he lost close to twenty pounds because he wanted no one but himself to know its architecture and what it contained. The Honeycomb was the hardest part of the park complex to build, and had taken him six weeks of working by arc lamp, mysteriously, in sunlight, to get it to the point it was now.

One hot June day, when he crawled out to get another hammer and a bag of nails and stooped back through the door of the labyrinth with a flashlight, he first became aware of something peculiar about the way he was seeing. The lamp was in a low wooden tunnel, and before he switched it on he turned off the flashlight and bent, watching. From left to right ran an odd gold streak, much like the line passing across a laboratory tube in a science movie, like Frankenstein. It came again, pulsing and gaining speed. He closed his eyes and shook his head, then reached down for the lamp and turned it on. He closed one eye and then the other, but the line continued to draw itself whether his lids were up or down. Also he was very thirsty, though he had just had a long drink of the springwater that ran beside the Honeycomb. He needed to piss, and his crotch burned with itching. He realized now that the thirst and the night rising had been with him for several years, and maybe more, but he was not much interested in small physical details, and he was satisfied to put up with these things because they seemed to go along with a surprising loss of weight without his having to diet. Where formerly he had weighed two hundred and forty pounds, his weight had come to an even two hundred, and he was now big not in bulk but in frame only; his wide shoulders made him look top-heavy, but he had lost most of his gut, and could walk among the bodybuilders who used Willow Plunge as their headquarters without feeling quite so self-conscious as before.

He turned, and the lamp, in the intense other darkness, caught by its cord and nearly jerked itself out of his hand.

"I guess I better go look in on my friend up here," he said out loud, and snapped the flashlight back on. He climbed seven rungs and came out through a trapdoor into a small room with three doors. None of these led anywhere but into dead-end cubicles. Suddenly, as he stepped into the cubicle on his left, a buzz began, getting stronger. A panel sprang up the grooves of a slitlike window. Through this, when the tent was not up, light was supposed to slant and fall on a huge rattlesnake in the strike position, reared back to throw its head before the heart could beat again. A door snapped closed behind him. Cahill picked up the snake in the flashbeam and went over to it.

"Just had to check you out, Buster," he said, as he pushed down on the snake's head with a finger. The fanged head bobbed, nodding. "You like it here?" Buster nodded, less vigorously, yet still in favor: "We're gonna cover these floors with virgin-pee: right?" He pushed hard, and the snake so agreed that the coils themselves separated, and Buster showed his coiled springs in the beam.

Cahill refixed the window, unlocked the door, went down the ladder and out, where he stooped under a willow and drank again, rapidly and long, from the spring there.

"It's good water, but it ain't doin' enough for me," he said as he straightened and watched a high school boy turn a half gainer with full layout from the high platform.

"Good one," he said to the boy's head in the pool. "Want you in the meet next Sunday."

"I'll be there."

He walked past the platform toward the park's office building, spoke to the lifeguard, and went into his office. Cahill himself could not swim.

Ruíz Alonso was filling out profit-and-loss forms and entering these into his account books according to a system of his own. It was not very accurate, but effective enough for the needs of an employer who did not care much for money, and had few personal expenses and no dependents.

"How we doin', bullfighter?"

Ruíz looked up, his eighteen-inch biceps stretching the rolled-up sleeves of a T-shirt he had bought a half-size too small, so that the definition of his almost brassiere-worthy pecs would be inescapable.

"Good," Ruíz said, nodding. "This is gonna be a mighty good summer. Wartime is good for swimming pools. Lots of soldiers, and more coming. All looking for girls, and the girls looking for them. We get good weather for the next two weeks, this'll be the best we done since I come here."

He was a Mexican-American boy of around nineteen or twenty, with a 4-F punctured eardrum. In addition to his main duties, he operated as groundskeeper and odd-job man. For a while he had lived in the office, sleeping on an army cot, but had since moved to a small apartment near Cahill's. He had been working for the park three years now, and though Cahill liked him as much as he liked anybody, he never saw him anywhere but at the park. He was willing and affable, very useful, and did not at all object to coming out early, checking the equipment, pulling out the drowned dogs that showed up now and then in the pool, taking care of the big purifying units, hauling and stacking fifty-pound sacks of diatomaceous earth. He could swim like an otter, never lifting his dark sleek head, and Cahill liked to see him swim at night, when he was green-lit from the sides and dark as a shadow from above unless the moon was full. His physique and his water skills made him especially useful at the little catch-as-catch-can water carnivals that Cahill put on every other Sunday. There were age-group swimming and diving contests, and an event called Silverspout where Cahill flung up handfuls of nickels, dimes, and quarters, spraying them into the air like a man casting seed, and the whole pool erupted with the geysers of thrashing legs driving down toward the scattered treasure. There were also beauty contests—though not many beauties—and weight-lifting and physique contests. The men's dressing room always carried a strong smell of the linseed oil and machine oil with which the contestants greased their shaven vein-wired bodies; they looked as though they would hum like harps if you flicked them with a fingernail.

One of the perennial contestants walked out of the locker room, not a hair on his body and very few on his head. He was usually a third-place physique winner, and spent several hours a week at the pool perfecting his tan and his poses.

"Guess who just came by," Cahill said.

"The pride of the Lockheed night shift, Karl Kesmodl, if I ain't mistook. He usually shows up about this time. We better get outside."

They stood by the lifeguard's chair, where a thin freckled boy in a pith helmet and zinc oxide on his nose was reading a pulp magazine.

"Better put your library down, Darrell," Cahill said.

"Lord, Frank," Darrell said, "why do you make it where these greasy freaks are always around? They look like fireplugs been run over by a oil truck."

"Because they all bring girls," Cahill said, "and they all spend money. And I get it. And I pay you with it. They think the girls come out on Sundays to look at 'em, and just try their god-damned best to get their hands on all that slick muscle."

"Well, I can tell you for a fact they don't," Darrell said. "I never met a girl who liked those guys. Queers, yes. Girls, no."

The squat lifter passed beyond the diving board, muttering to himself. The board was used as a posing platform; Karl put his towel carefully on the grass behind it, walked with clenched fists to the end of the board, took a deep breath, and clamped down the force of all his workouts to date on his sparkling body, one fist raised before his profiled face and the other at his hip. Darrell put his hat on the seat and stepped down.

Karl turned and slowly tried out his next pose. But the turn had made the board nervous, and Karl's pose crumbled like a sand castle. Little by little he went, looking as though he might even to the end get his balance back, but it wouldn't come. With the explosion of a depth charge he disappeared, feet up and backward.

"An earthquake throwed you, Karl," Darrell yelled.

"Y'all go drag that clumsy goon out of there," Cahill said with a long sigh.

Ruíz stripped off his T-shirt and broke the two steps toward the pool in one motion. He was curving from the air when Darrell launched.

They swam easily side by side, as though strolling, toward the only threshing water of the calm pool, in the center of which was Karl's fist, still clenched for his last pose; they reached him and circled for an opening.

"Let him swallow a little more of the damned pool," Cahill shouted. "Then he might learn how to swim."

Alternately pushed and pulled up the ladder, Karl was laid on his face to drain before his next pose. The others came back to the chair.

"Jesus," Darrell said, "that's the third fucking time this summer."

"I count four and a half," Ruíz said.

"Frank," Darrell said, "I got an idea for a new event. Drive 'em crazy. Call it the Underwater Greased Pig Contest. Karl could be the pig."

"Too dangerous," Cahill said, smiling. "If that monster ever got hold of you, he'd drag you right straight to the bottom. He'd drag you *through* the bottom."

"No, he wouldn't," Ruíz said. "All you have to do is hold his head under water and let him panic; then he'll turn loose right quick. He panics easy."

Darrell climbed into the chair and picked up his magazine. A girl carrying a Guatemalan bag passed them in the direction of the dressing rooms. Cahill and Ruíz went back in.

"Regular six to one?"

"You got it." Cahill took out a dollar and laid it on the desk, while Ruíz peeled a five and a one from the cash register.

His eyes shooting the strange spear-marks, Cahill drew aside a dark brown curtain. It had covered a very clear pane of glass; clearer than any ordinary window. Through this showed a bare plank dressing room; past the half-open door Guatemala ambled along disguised as a college American, head down and musing.

"You lose," Ruíz said, reaching for Cahill's dollar.

Cahill put up an open hand and flexed the fingers. "Not yet."

"OK," Cahill said reluctantly. "You left all the other doors open. What the hell chance does that give me?"

Ruíz, his eyes on the glass, said, "No I didn't. But I don't forget the time you *locked* all the doors. Except this one. Looka there; you done won after all."

The girl was closing the door and turning on the light, now trapped in warped wood and invisible watchfulness. On the far side of double-sided light Ruíz and Cahill sat down as at a movie.

The girl undressed neither quickly nor slowly, hanging her sophomoric clothes thoughtfully on the hooks.

Ruíz clicked his tongue.

"Shut up, stupid," Cahill said. His gold rays swept through the sweating female body. She was looking around now, her bra off, fingers crooked in the elastic of her panties, preparing for the one gesture, the necessary denuding stoop, that no woman can look graceful performing. After a moment's unsatisfactory bareness, she pulled on a blue tank suit and went out.

"You crooked son-of-a-bitch," Ruíz said. "You did it again. You took me. All right, the next time we're not gonna leave yours open."

"We do that, the odds are going to have to go up. That open door and the mirror, they're the only things I've got going for me. That way, they know for sure there's not anybody else in there."

"All right, boss," Ruíz said. "I need the job."

"Go check the doors if you want to, Ruíz," Cahill said. "Go check 'em. Somebody'll probably call the cops, and tell 'em we've got a genuwine peeping Tom, right here in broad daylight. And if nobody else calls 'em, I will."

"Kiss my ass," Ruíz said. "But I know damned well you locked all the other doors when me and Darrell were pulling the sea elephant out."

"You just got unlucky. You know it and I know it."

"Tell the truth," Ruíz said, "I don't think I was all that unlucky. That's the best thing we had come in our little box of pine all summer. Let's wait'll she comes back. I like to see 'em with the water running down 'em. That's the thing; that's the good thing."

It was their only game. Cahill could have put in one-way mirrors in all the booths and seen every female body that came to the pool, but chance, anticipation, and the gamble would have disappeared if he had done so. Though both watched as often as they could, Cahill had won only a few times, and the girls and women by means of whom he won were so disillusioning that he thought of removing the glass and returning to fantasy, which was better, mostly. But this girl was valuable, even though only in contrast to the others, and he decided to go on with the game, peering into the sexual future.

He liked women—everything about them from skin to mind—and the older he became the more he liked them. This was partly the reason for his wife's having left him nineteen years ago, when he had been seeing more of a woman who worked in a loan office than he had of her. She had been pregnant at the time, and though he had written a few letters asking her to come back, he was honestly glad that she did not. When she told him that she never wished to see, hear from, or hear of him again, he was glad to comply. Neither of them had ever remarried; she lived in Memphis. He knew this, but he did not know what she did there. Her brother had told him that he had a son, but Cahill had never seen even so much as a photograph of him. That was best, he was sure whenever he thought about it, for he considered himself a man alone; self-sufficiency and the control of the elements of his life were as valuable to him as food.

But the gold streaks continued to run, to split, to come together, to range from the top of his vision to the bottom, and then begin to climb again, sometimes out of phase with each other, sometimes in perfect unison. They overlay and underlay everything toward which he turned his head, caging it with the hurricane blank flight of meteors.

"Ruíz, will you do something for me?"

"Sure, if I can."

"Come over here and look at my god-damned eye. The right one."

Ruíz squinted carefully, from a foot away. His face came even closer, and the darting flames cut it to pieces.

"Well, what is it?" Cahill asked impatiently.

The other hesitated. "It just sort of seems to be kind of . . . kind of jumping around."

"Just the right one?"

"No, the left one too, but not as much. Can you see OK? Tell me, now."

"Yeah. I saw Karl Kesmodl fall in the pool, didn't I? I saw that girl in the blue bathin' suit, didn't I? What do you mean, can I see? You're fuckin'-A I can see."

But he said nothing of the locked lights that went through, of the pierceless javelin cutting through Karl's huge back as he teetered on the board, or of how a gold streak had traversed the girl's forehead, and, as he leaned forward to make her out more clearly, through her neck like a sun-slant come from red stained glass, then through her navel as she pulled her bathing suit over it.

"Sure, I could tell you saw her, but you were looking like you didn't see her enough. Why don't you go see a good eye man? I know one; he got me some glasses I don't ever wear except when I'm by myself. Anyway his name is Dr. Ghil. He'll tell you what's making that little jumping-around. It's probably nothing but all the work you're doing in that crazy house. It must be awful hot in there. The house is so crazy your eyeballs are going crazy. Most likely that's all it is: too much heat and too much craziness."

"I don't think it's that," Cahill said, with deliberation now, ready to level. "I'm seein' things I know ain't there, and they seem like they're comin' from way deep down. I keep seein' these sparks go by: there must be millions of them, and I don't know where they're comin' from, or where they're goin'. Right now, right this minute, from where I stand, you're smack in the middle of a whole lot of 'em. You got more light on your head than a angel."

"The first and only time," Ruíz said. "God didn't put it there, I can tell you."

"No," Cahill said. "I can tell you He didn't."

"I regret to inform you, Mr. Cahill, that you have diabetes. And even more regrettably, you have a very bad case. Even at the age of fifty-four, you have what is called early-onset diabetes. This is the kind that usually develops in children and teenagers and people on up to the age of thirty. Early-onset is the bad kind, and almost always requires regular insulin injections, a strict diet, and a quite regular schedule of eating. A man of your age, if he develops diabetes, usually has a much milder form; it's almost as though it were a completely different illness. With late-onset the person can usually get by if he watches his weight and his diet, and he doesn't need to inject. But your case is extreme. I'm surprised that you haven't blacked out at least once. You are one of the fairly rare exceptions. Your fasting sugar is the highest I believe I've ever seen. Diabetes has come on you like a hurricane: a hurricane of sugar."

"What do you want me to do?"

"Just let me go on for a minute, and I'll tell you. I want to talk about your eyes just a little bit. But first, why in the name of all the gods of the Islands of Langerhans didn't you come in sooner? Didn't you know something was wrong with you when you first noticed this terrible thirst you tell me about? Didn't you know that your kidneys were not operating as they were used to doing?"

"I work in the sun a lot," Cahill said, piecing the past together under a new interpretation, grudgingly. "That makes a man thirsty, don't it? And then he drinks a lot of water, or beer, or whatever wet he can poor down his gullet. Right?"

"Did you feel weak?"

"Hell no," said Cahill. "I've never been weak a day in my life. And even if I did, it'd just be that, like they say, I'm not gettin' any younger."

"Do you know anybody who is?" said the doctor, with an easygoing conspiratorial grin. Then: "How about your skin problems?"

"I have an everlastin' case of jock itch. I work around locker rooms a lot. My balls are always on fire on the outside, and that ain't the good way."

"No indeed."

"Can you give me somethin' for it? I'd burn it out with a blowtorch if that'd get rid of the stuff. So give me somethin' or other: somethin' that'll clear it out and keep it out."

"Here's your jock-itch medicine," the doctor said, handing across the desk a snap-lid kit that looked made for high-quality, small, expert gear, probably from Germany. "This'll put the below-the-belt fire back where it belongs. It's also your thirst medicine, and your runaway-bladder medicine."

Cahill handed back the case without having looked inside it.

"But now the eyes," said the doctor. "A Niagara of sugar is pouring through your system every hour. We can hold that at bay with the insulin"—here the doctor took a syringe from the kit, flourished it dramatically until it ended in a fencing pose—"but you'll have to walk a nutritional tightrope: one that balances you between insulin and sugar."

Cahill nodded; any challenge was good. He felt a bounding impulse to get started on the whole new life.

"In addition to these streaks, does your vision show anything else you're not accustomed to?"

"In a way, I guess," Cahill answered. "If you can follow me, I'll try to tell you about it. Supposin' you had yourself a sheet of black paper, and on top of it you was to put a crossword puzzle. And suppose you was to take out, every now and then, one of them little squares, so that there was only black where the square was. Wouldn't be no letter there, no place for a letter. Nothin' but a black square. This keeps goin' on. And then pieces of fire keep shootin' through the puzzle all the time."

"Some puzzle. Each one of those pieces is a part of your eyesight dying. Why the pieces are square in your case, I'm damned if I know."

"They're square, but don't nobody but you and me know it."

"All right. But at least *that* doesn't matter."

"It does matter."

"Have it your way."

"What I see right now looks exactly like a crossword puzzle takin' on more and more black in little pieces. But I don't have no words."

"There is only one word that will solve that puzzle, Mr. Cahill," the doctor said gravely, in relief at the metaphor that enabled him to make the point he had not been able to come to.

"What word?" Cahill asked, watching.

"Blindness."

"That's a mighty hard judgment. Are you sure?"

"I'm sure. I wish I weren't, but I am. The ophthalmologist, Dr. Ghil, tells me that the retinas are just about gone, both optic nerves are affected, the eye muscles themselves are deteriorating. Two to three months, I'd say. You let it go too long, and now you're headed for the Big Dark, the solution to the universal puzzle." He paused, smiling resignedly. "None of us gets out of this world alive, Mr. Cahill. There are plenty of dead folks. Remember: you are alive. And you'll stay alive, if you do what I say. Alive is a lot."

"Maybe. We'll just have to see."

"You'll be seeing in other ways, now," the doctor said, picking up on the word. "Your other senses will become far more acute. You'll be able to hear a baby cry through a stone wall. Music—*any* music—will have so many levels it'll be like whole buildings, floors of sounds. And your nose, that you likely never used for anything but farts and flowers, is going to be an entirely new implement. Whatever's in the wind, or in the air of a room, you'll know, and the others won't."

"What's your point?"

"A new kind of life is my point. Diabetes can be devilish. But if you have guts, it can help you live longer than you otherwise would have, and know more and feel more. What people want in their lives, and almost never have, is meaning. That, the blind have, and it's with them every second. Everything means. I'm not one of these doctors who go around saying to patients 'You're going to have to learn to live with it.' That seems to me the wrong approach. No; I'd like you to look on what's coming to you as a kind of *adventure:* one that's never going to end. There's a lot of diabetes around; sometimes it's good, sometimes not. Depends on the people who have it. Incidentally, did you know that diabetes is the second-largest cause of blindness? Only accidents cause more."

"How about wars?" Cahill asked.

"They don't count."

He explained to Cahill the use of the syringe, the dosage he wanted him to use, and cautioned him always to have several sugar cubes or a candy bar with him to guard against overinjection.

"I want you to enroll in a school for the blind. Check in before you go to black. You'll be that much ahead."

"I'll think about it. But I prob'ly won't go."

"You sure are a hard man to deal with, Mr. Cahill. You really should take the course. It'll save you a lot of trouble later on."

"I'll handle it."

"And you ought to get a dog. That's a fine relationship; one of the best. Those seeing-eye mutts can do everything but sing 'White Christmas.' "

"I'll get my own," Cahill said. "I want a one-man dog. I'll train him myself."

"I'll figure to see you splattered all over the street, then. And not long from now, either."

"You figure this, I figure that. I don't reckon he's gonna want to get run over any more than I do. That's enough for me."

Cahill stood up.

"Good-bye," said the doctor. "Let me know what you need."

"Just don't look too hard at my blood on the cement, specially if the sun's shinin' hard. Might put your eyes out."

Cahill went back to his apartment and needled himself for the first time. After a week his bladder filled less quickly and the terrible thirst died, but the flying sparks stayed on.

Through the half-black the shuttle wove, so that he believed, before long, that the rays would still be shooting through themselves when he was in his grave, with his eyes either open or shut.

He sat in the office on the last day of the pool, before the dressing-room window. Ruíz was beside him in his desk chair with his hand on Cahill's arm. An enormous bronze-nosed German shepherd lay on the other side of the chair, facing the other way, its head on the floor and its ears down. It was dead quiet in the room where the only motion was that of Cahill swirling in his eyes, being drowned in the tails of comets. His look was something like that of an Asiatic conqueror examining prisoners or slave girls. Sweat stood on his face but did not run. The soaring mesh in which his head was caught was still penetrable.

"I can still see," he said, his face fixed into the glass. "Some. Not much. How about handin' me one of them spring grips?"

17

Ruíz handed it to him, taking care not to *put* it in his hand. Cahill's fingers felt the air until the grip was his.

The room was arranged. There were zinnias from Cahill's ex-lover, now married but in contact. Among these Ruíz had placed Buster, the snake from the Honeycomb. He had also arranged accoutrements and paraphernalia from the pool and park around Cahill's chair, as though he had been an interior decorator called on for an impossible but challenging assignment. Sets of barbells were crossed and piled around the chair. Spring cables were stretched to their maximum tension and nailed to the wall, where they twisted and strained the faint September light to its breaking point. Ruíz had wanted to nail them in the shape of a cross, but Cahill did not want that. Rakes were standing on all sides, their teeth intermeshed.

"I can still see," Cahill repeated. Almost all of the lightning that had ever hurtled above the earth and not struck, all the flame-streaks from silent guns, all the children's sparklers since the beginning of industrial amusement stormed his eyes. Methodically he squeezed and released the metal exerciser. His big forearm flared and subsided in the silence.

"Everything here?" he asked matter-of-factly, low-toned.

"Everything's here. I got it all fixed up for you."

"Buster here?"

For answer, Ruíz leaned into the zinnias and activated the snake's electric rattle. The dog lifted its ears and head.

"Zack don't like that," Ruíz said.

"Don't do it again, if you can help it. I want everything quiet. This is important to me."

"Look, Frank, there's nobody out there. Nobody's coming; nobody's been coming. It's getting too cold. There's a boy and a girl sitting on the grass up by the diving board; I didn't even make 'em pay to get in. I'm going to close this place up tomorrow and drain the pool."

"Somebody'll come. Somebody's got to come. In a way, this is the end of the world."

"Frank," Ruíz said, his voice lifting, "listen to me. Even if somebody did come you'd still only have one chance in six."

"I'll take it, as long as I can see. That's the way we set it up."

"I'll go out," Ruíz said with last-ditch patience, "and get you one. I'll drag her in off the street if I have to, and throw her down and rip her clothes off for you and hold her up in front of the mirror."

"No."

"What is all of this supposed to prove, Frank?"

"I don't know."

Through the blazing shuttle a figure seemed to dim out the dressing-room door.

"Yes," Ruíz said quietly.

Cahill could make out only the outline, but not the girl's face.

"No," gasped Ruíz, "no. Oh no."

The girl unstrapped her right leg at the knee, and, sitting on the empty bench, pulled on her suit. She hopped toward the mirror and fixed her hair, smiling gently at what she thought was herself. Hot from his last buzz, Buster rocked his drawn-back rubber-deadly head in the red flowers, saying yes. Ruíz was crying. As she turned and moved in small bounds toward the door, Cahill squeezed with the whole strength of his body on the spring grip just as she hit the sun in a wild billion of stratospheric sparks, exploded it into its atoms, and disappeared. The world was somewhere else.

A gentle wood-stopped thudding came through the cold covers. Zack's head rose, and his ears partway.

"What is it?" Cahill said, finding himself already more awake than not, in the last of his sleep.

"Time to go," a boy's voice said. "Let me in and I'll help you."

"No, thanks," Cahill said. "I can get myself together all right. But come in, anyway. What the hell would I be lockin' up?"

Zack propped on his forelegs, starting the first tone of his full animal thunder, as Pfc. Tim Sistrunk entered. He was a pale, good-natured twenty-year-old Armored Force draftee from Allentown, Pennsylvania, returning to Fort Bragg from a three-day pass to Atlanta, where he had gone to visit a girl met on another bus. That was all Cahill knew about him: all that north Georgia had given in the late afternoon and twilight, and more than the western half of South Carolina and the beginning of the mountains of North Carolina had given, when everything was quiet until the bus had broken down.

"Lie back, boy," Cahill said to the dog. "On down, now. Down. This is a good 'un here. You know a good 'un when you see him. He don't mean nothing. He ain't bothering nobody. Down, Zack. Keep it down."

As Cahill went through his few effects and dressed with slow, quick-touching matter-of-factness, Pfc. Sistrunk stood uncertainly just inside the door, watching how things were done in a situation he had never thought about before. Cahill worked on the small, intense details of his operation with a certain grim pride; his lips made a faint resemblance to

19

silent words as he armed himself into his shirt and buttoned it, looped and knotted his tie with a skill that Sistrunk would more likely have associated with a musician, sat on the side of the bed and pulled on his pants, then tied his shoes with his face turned first in Zack's direction and then toward the door.

"They tell me they've got us a new bus coming," Tim said.

"That so? About what time?"

"Supposed to be pretty soon. Might already be here. They can't leave without us."

Cahill reached under the pillow and took out the syringe case. Tim's eyes narrowed, and he was aware of the deliberateness of his breath as Cahill sterilized the needle, fumbled out a matchbox, and, working the syringe from one hand to the other, passed the needle through the flame.

"This is just extra," Cahill said, as the match died. "No doctor ever told me to do it this way. But it can't hurt none."

He hiked up his shirt, pinched up some of the flab of his stomach, and injected himself. "That's an all-day run," he said. "If it's too much juice, I got sugar." He held out two wrapped sugar cubes on the flat of his hand. "Balance. Blood balance. That's what the little man said."

Tim for a moment did not reply, then said, "We might as well go on down."

Along what was now for him night's creaking North Carolina country hall they went to the stairs whose numbering Cahill stubbornly remembered. With no word or touch from Tim, they came correctly to the clock, and hesitated.

"What time is it?" Cahill asked.

"Quarter to seven."

"You ain't got the guts to say 'first light,' have you? How're you goin' to kill anybody? Ain't you ever seen a blind man before?"

"Yes, I have. And I don't know how I'm going to kill anybody. I hope I don't get asked to. I'm a mechanic, or I will be in six weeks. That's all I know."

DARK	LIGHT
The porch opened him, and he sensed it as solid with invisible landscape. No stars now, or the last ones. He was supposed to be	A step below Cahill and Zack, Tim steadied his eyes on the low forms of the hills close about them, holding snow in patchy

among hills; he willed the sensation of being surrounded and placed by risings of land and irregularities of height, and concluded that the air in his nostrils like piano wire had come down slopes and lifted to him from the near ground still full of far-off trees and bushes, bringing to the porch the snow they held as they hovered motionless in clean, dissolving light. It was that cold; things must be that way.

forms. Two silver-and-blue commercial buses were pulled up on the near side of the highway, and their sack-bodied drivers appeared to be arguing with different aspects of steam; their heads were barely visible amongst the milling of their breath. Passengers shifted from foot to foot about them, and shifted suitcases from hand to hand.

"God," a man's voice said behind them. "Look at that, would you?"

"Smell it, you mean."

Two men went past and down. "That big dog must've come out here and shit," the first one said.

"Well, what did you want him to do? Shit inside?"

"Jesus."

So you might say, Cahill murmured to himself in the same soundless word-shaping with which he counted steps, and in which were all the distances he wanted to remember, either temporarily or for the rest of his life. Back in Atlanta, next to the blue-green and side-lit underwater of the diving pool, the sun flashing off human forms, it was fifteen steps from the willow-hung grass to the dark of Buster's room; he had hammered the steps nail by nail; he could go there now, night or day, and spring the door to the rattlesnake's alcove; the coiled buzz he had invented would be there, and be home. So what? Maybe something, maybe not. But he had that situation, and there would be others that depended on him. They would come, and they would be enough. As Tim had said, they can't leave without us. Can't leave, and can't live.

The three of them came down, Zack patient and wary. The passengers parted for them. Both drivers turned.

"This is your dog. Right?"

"Right," Cahill said. "Everybody's on the same bus."

"Well, you can't take him on this one."

"Why not?"

"Because it's against regulations. I can show you."

"Now just how in the hell are you going to show me?"

21

"Somebody else will tell you. The other driver can tell you: the one you came with. Or you can take my word for it."

"No, thanks."

"Take him," the first driver said. "Bend the rules a little. Why not? Nobody said anything till you did. This man's blind. What do you figure to do with him? Leave him here?"

"I don't give a damn what happens to him. But this bus is not leaving with that dog on it. That's all I'm gonna say. That's *it*."

"No, that's not it," Cahill said. "He's not goin' to hurt you, unless I say so. He'll just lay down in the aisle by my seat till I get off at Peckover. That's all. And I can guarantee nobody's goin' to stick up this bus while he's on it."

"Come on, come on," one of the men from the porch said. "We done got helt up enough already. Let's get on with the damned thing. Let's go, dog or no dog."

"You-all get on," the driver said, motioning to the passengers. "All except you and your dog. You can send back for him later, maybe."

"Won't work," Cahill said. "He won't stay here, and I'm not goin' to ask him. I'm goin' to get on your god-damned bus, and so is he. If you want to report this, file a claim, sue me, you go right ahead. I'm goin' to Peckover."

The passengers had boarded, and those at the window seats stared into the unhurried smoke of the voices, trying to make them out.

"He's not going," the driver said, with what was meant to be finality. The driver of the first bus drew back, putting his hands under his armpits.

"He's goin'," Cahill said, "unless you want to tangle with him."

"Stay here, then."

"Don't move, if you want to move more than once."

A foot scuffled and squeaked; a crunched step ground.

"Look. Look here now," said the first driver, coming back, pushing the fog away from his face with elbows. "This is my run. Why don't I take this bus and finish out? You can call the company to send somebody after you. Get this clunker fixed, go back home, and forget about it."

"All right. There's gonna be hell to pay back in Atlanta, though. I'll make sure."

"All the hell you want. But not like you just now come close to gettin'."

22

The older driver faced Cahill toward the door, gently. He climbed and entered, Zack following.

The driver settled; the door closed and fitted.

"Right here, Mr. Cahill," Tim said. "Take it slow."

As they turned out into the landscape, the passengers moved for a time into association; reasonable talk began a little to form. Those on the aisle seats believed that the snowed-down pines and bushes held an image that would free them from the slavery of travel. Those at the windows knew this was not so; they took a single look outward, but mainly kept their eyes fixed halfway down the seat in front of them, though with the long gaze that should have been going over the flat snow-forms and brown earths, far off to the stogged woods and the hills pointed at them but angling past.

"Made it," Tim said. "Good."

"I've got to get where I'm goin', like everybody else," Cahill said. "Only there's two of us doin' for one of us; me and Zack."

"Makes it a lot harder, huh?"

"Not all that much harder. Some people try to make it seem harder than it ought to be. You have to know how to deal with 'em; that's all. It takes a little more trouble to train people than it does dogs. You have to romance 'em a little more."

"You mean you'd'a let this dog kill that asshole driver?"

"No; not kill him. Knock him down, though. I never would'a let him go in on him. Take somethin' more than that before I'd ever really turn him loose on anybody. I don't want to hurt a man, a woman, a cow, a German, a Jap, a snake, or Jesus or God. I just want to finish the ride."

"He likes to ride, don't he?" Tim said, craning cautiously toward the aisle.

"About like I do," Cahill said. "About like you do."

"How long you had him?"

"Three . . . four months now. He was no more'n a big puppy when I got him. I seen him when the lights was goin' out. Nothin' but legs and teeth and tail is all I remember. But he filled out real quick. Me and this other fellow—a fellow that works for me—kept feedin' him all the time. He'll eat anything that gives off the meat smell, or anything that's scared of him, or anything you can make him think is scared of him. And he'll also get after anything that's not scared of him. It don't make no difference."

"How much does he weigh, you reckon?"

23

"Between a hundred and fifty and a hundred and sixty, I'd guess. Maybe more like a hundred and sixty."

"This about as big as he's gonna be?"

"I don't know. Prob'ly is. He may pick up a few more pounds, up in the shoulders. Could end up a hundred and eighty."

"I didn't think you-all—I mean the kind of *citizen* you are—"

"Blind men."

"—I didn't think you were supposed to teach these kind of dogs to get after people."

"That's them other dogs."

"Did you buy him from one of those places where they train dogs to go around seeing for you?"

"Zack does his own seein'. He'd do it anyway, whether I was with him or not. We kind of walk around together. That's all."

"Where's his harness? Ain't he supposed to have a harness?"

"You see any harness? His harness is in the same place where my cane is, dipped in the blood of the Lamb. I can't see myself fiddlin' and fussin' around with no walking cane, tappin' on the sidewalks and the streets, beatin' on the door of the shithouse, punchin' people in the belly or the ass. Next thing I'd be gettin' myself a tin cup. I can't play a guitar, so I guess I'd have to have a thing to play records around my neck. That ain't my way, soldier. I say fuck that. I don't use no cane, and Zack don't wear no harness."

"How can he . . . how can you tell . . . ?"

"All he has to do is lean against my leg, one way or the other, easy or hard. He's got his ways of gettin' through. Sometimes I reach down. I don't have to do that much anymore, though. Between my listenin' and his seein' and leanin', we know all we need to know. Works out fine. Has so far, anyway."

Settling back, he let his hand down onto Zack's fur, where it grazed lightly along the hair tips, and then went deeply amongst them; he could feel the dead bumps of the highway come up and to life in the animal flesh, and the curves through which the bus passed transfer themselves into the still, solid backbone and seem to straighten there. The dog's first-seen form was in his mind now, and its last. It had belonged to Ruíz's brother, and Cahill had never known or asked about its parentage. He and Ruíz and the brother had walked through long, wet afternoon grass to a single tree set among bushes, and, through the strengthening cross-rain of his vision, Cahill had watched the dog

24

waver toward clarity, throbbing in and out of sight as though riding on pulse beats, frilled and arrowed with hopeless gold. It was the angle of the head that Cahill most richly recalled, holding as it did every possible condition except servility. The long black muzzle and slightly oriental eyes—the slant shaped by the same forces as a wolf's, surely—floated in the grass outwaiting him; it was not until later that he noticed the long legs and the great length of the awkward, unintimidated body. Twenty-five dollars had bought him—already him, not it—and he had walked with Cahill and Ruíz from one tree into the new life.

From the first, living with the dog had not been at all hard. Cahill could still see well enough to shop and otherwise look after himself, and it was not much extra trouble to buy cheap meat, including horse meat—which Zack particularly favored, and Cahill himself came to like —to keep a pan of water in the kitchen, and to take the dog out a couple of times a day. Zack slept on a mat of newspapers near the front door: newspapers from which the print was being withdrawn, fading from the war, even in its largest headlines relayed from the deserts of northern Africa. His coming life in darkness, in the total explosion of the sun, was the only condition in which Cahill took interest. Zack's body and face— especially the hazel eyes that might have been tipped up from gazing over endless tundras and through the needles of lost forests of spruce, on the migrations of caribou through deep valleys to barren ground, toward but never reaching Asia—were the center of the world which was enclosing him more and more each day in storms of stars: storms of a centerless universe through which the dog prowled and prisoner-paced, full not of longing but alert patience, lying at night and bristling —Cahill's pulse quickened when his palm felt Zack's back-fur do this, and he slept more deeply whenever it happened—or delicately pawing the door whenever Cahill approached it from the other side. At first when they went out together Cahill had used a chain, and had let Zack range and explore, but pulled him back when he felt like it. Before long, though, he found that the dog stayed close to him naturally, and would come back if he went off. Since he needed a name to serve as a command, or as the alert to a command, Cahill reasoned that the name should be short and sharp, like a gunshot. Though he had never shot a gun, the idea pleased him, and at first he had shouted a simple "Crack" at the dog, who came quickly to respond to it and the force of Cahill's harsh voice. The command had gradually changed into Zack; there had been a local politician, much on the radio denying implication in graft, who had that middle name, and it did well enough.

When the pool and the rest of Willow Plunge closed, Ruíz usually came by and together they would work with the dog. From the beginning Ruíz had insisted on Zack as a protective force, and Cahill was not reluctant to attempt his "training" in this way, although two or three of the retired couples in the building were terrified by the situation and complained of it. But Cahill was going blind, blind beyond all help except what he could give himself, and that placed him beyond or to one side of the law; he knew that everyone who came into contact with him, from acquaintances to strangers, would sense this to be the case; it was proveable, and he was living it.

They began with the horse meat, sold by groceries for pet food, and with any scraps of animal matter that Cahill did not eat. Ruíz would have to be the villain and the victim, and their parts were always cast that way: Ruíz as the tormenter and frustrater, snatching the meat from the dog, teasing him with it, kicking him, at first lightly and later with more and more force, hiding from him and leaping over the gutted gray furniture of the apartment with Zack crashing over stools and ottomans to corner him, snarling and craving, and Cahill always as the benefactor, the rewarder and comforter, the being who spoke in sharp, explosive commands, and, producing food, dropped his voice and sighed, throaty with false compassion, as Zack ate, letting the meat fall from his jaws and snatching it up again, his eyed narrowed for Ruíz's first move in the sweaty light. At first Ruíz wore only his veined T-shirt, but as his forearms showed more and more cuts and scratches he put on a light jacket of artificial silk; after a weekend when the sleeves were left spotted with teeth of blood, he went to denim. The night sky of Cahill's vision packed its hurtling sparks closer and closer together, Ruíz snatched, grappled and fled day after day, and the summer heat began elsewhere to fail, though it still poured like stone-channeling water from Ruíz's cheeks and forehead, for by this time Zack was after him in earnest. Laughing quietly, Ruíz adjusting new garments on himself and, Cahill helping, discovering unexpected resources in fingers and palms, they swathed the Mexican boy in old blankets and ragged oil-dense mats, pulled from under cars in the apartment garage.

Now, feeling the highway curves waver and lodge in Zack's spine, Cahill thought of Ruíz and the muffled beating he had taken in the shredded blankets as he fended off Zack's rushes. A few days before his blindness was completed, they had finished Zack's indoctrination, not because of neighbors disturbed by the floor-shaking savagery of sound, but because Cahill—though not Ruíz—was afraid that Zack's jaws would really close with the strength of the full-grown dog, and no such proof was needed. It was better to wait, now, in a new calm in which Ruíz became a friend once more, cautiously taking off the weeks of bullying and mocking at the same time that he unwound the chenille blankets from himself, and the oil mats slid back beneath the cars.

It was time: time to pull loose the necktie and breathe more. "What's the matter with this damned thing?" Cahill said.

Tim's sleep failed as his armpits dampened. The bus was much hotter than it had been; the others were writhing. "Somebody open a window," he said. Then, "I'll do it."

A form rose from beside him and thumped and cursed at something beyond. There was a sudden grating slide, a slotting, stopped noise, and

"Good Jesus! JESUS! Now I've sure done it. I've *done* it! God damn *Almighty.*

"What is it?" Cahill said, drawing back.

"I caught my fucking thumb in the fucking window," Tim said in a low, choked-back scream. "I sure did. God DAMN! Look! Ripped it up pretty good."

"Sit down, son," Cahill said. He could say it. "How bad . . . ? I mean . . ."

"No bone," Tim said with underpowered control, but assessing. "Just about, though. "It's filling up and starting to run. Pretty soon my hand's gonna be all over the place."

"Why don't you go ask the driver if he's got some kind of first-aid kit? They ought to carry those things."

"No," Tim said. "I'll be all right. You got a handkerchief?"

"Sure. Two of 'em. Let me see, son."

Tim put his hurt hand, clasped by the fingers of the good one encircling the hump-boned wrist, carefully on Cahill's thigh. Beginning at Tim's wrist, Cahill felt cautiously toward the base of the thumb. When

27

he first reached blood, he stopped and began to feel in the pockets of his coat. From among coins and a crush of paper money he brought up the handkerchiefs.

"One clean, one sort of clean. All right with you?"

"Got to be."

"The clean one first. Washed it in my kitchen sink yesterday, and ain't had my nose in it yet," Cahill said. The cloth passed twice around the webbed V, and Cahill did what he could to draw it tight. When Tim's leg tensed against his, he stopped pulling, and held what he had. "I think we caught the fellow," he said. "At least most of him. I don't believe any more of him's gonna get out. Now if we can just hold him, we'll all be fine. You can see the base doctor, soon as you get in."

"You're fucking-A I will. That's good duty. There's been many a Purple Heart give to some joker over something that ain't this bad. They tell me the war's full of 'em."

Cahill tied the used handkerchief over the other, his fingers moving in the small moves that the knot required. These little operations are the rough ones, he thought: and here's going to be a rule about *that:* when my sense of feeling gets better than this, that's when I'm going to have a real advantage: that and the way I hear things. And they're both coming to me with everything I do, everything I listen to. There's not any end to the new way: anybody who can't feel and hear like a blind man just can't do what he can do, or know what he can know.

They rode that way, the boy's hand in Cahill's lap, the blind man projecting himself into the future, coming to stand in a room at first empty, then with people, where he could hear the distances on all sides, the echoes of ordinary sounds taking on their own kind of measurement as they reversed themselves at walls, bodies, and objects and came back to tell him—and no one else in the same way—where they were, what they had for him. Or he might find himself one day in some woods that hung on him a thin smother of rain, and a limb would fall, somewhere: would he hear it? He would hear that sound; he and the developing power of his ears would make it good: the tree it fell from and the woods themselves. The hand now on his leg would contribute, he was sure, to the sharpness and the correct imagination of his sense of touch; he had hidden its blood, buried it in his own cloth, and now he was keeping it safe, moving somewhere toward noon. His guess of time must be true, for into the stifling bus, through the tooth-hissing whee-dle of the stuck window with its splinter of an opening, another kind of warmth, a down-shining one, rested on the back of his hands and wrists, delicate as the hairs that must be—used to be—growing out of them. The glass heat on his skin and the clothed ball of blood he held were now and again passed over, like a chance flutter of space-dark, by nervous fleeting shade, an intermittent reasonless shadow, and in this slatted and shuttering dance of temperatures he dozed off, sometimes alive in a dream of performing surgery or undoing complicated knots, and again in the deepest and thinnest rain of woods, listening for the limb to fall, in his hearing, into its only place in the world.

"This is you," Tim said. "Peckover. And don't ask me what side of the road it's on. I might as well tell you, though. It's on the door side."

"How's your thumb feel?" Cahill asked, lifting Tim's hand from his lap to the boy's.

"Numb. But it'll be all right."

"Sure. Keep the handkerchiefs. Dip 'em in the Rising Sun."

"I will, if they let you fight with pliers."

"Fight with what you got."

Cahill and Zack went forward unhurriedly, down and then out. The driver handed him his straw bag.

"Thanks," Cahill said. "I hope I get you next time."

"You just might. I'll look for you. When will it be, you think?"

"I don't know. Two or three days. Maybe a couple more."

"Like I say, I'll look out."

"Don't make a point of it. I'll know you."

He and Zack stood quietly, waiting for the way in which the town would say it was surrounding or facing them, and for the engine to die. When it did they still did not move, and stayed waiting in the cold, sunny silence that might have been that of one of the fields they had come through. No hinges, no doors, no metal-clank, no voice, though they faced a small two-story hotel that was also the bus terminal. Still they waited, four ears, going outward and alert, breaths steaming and eddying. After the doze of his images, Cahill half expected a far, discreet crash, or a near object crunching in snow. Surely if they stood long enough, something, a step or a branch, would reach the ground. If nothing did, they would take steps in whatever direction was forward from where they stood.

He took these, and whistled, hoping for the walls of a building. Instead of the banked-off return of sound he had hoped for, music appeared in his ears where he had expected something solid; this was part of "The Beer-Barrel Polka," and not from the open.

A press of warm air, already chilling as it reached his face, held a few voices not concerned with him. A slushy shuffle of movement ground underfoot, then gritted hesitantly before him on ice and concrete. "Hello," Cahill said, for the mixed voices had been closed off as the cold settled back, and there now must be someone outside with him, ready for what he would say.

He listened, on and on. No one said anything to him, and he thought it was probably because of his dog, pressed now against his leg with no feeling of impatience in him, waiting for Cahill to move.

On both sides of the bus about equally, the town stretched out to its visible ends. The point that Tim had brought up about the side of the road the town was on was one that this town could answer with no trouble: on the right if you're going north, on the left if you're heading south. Except for a feed store and a deserted, poorly steaming filling station, its two levels of gasoline caged in the wire of its pump tops, there was no town across the highway. On the station side, for three blocks apiece up and down, were a café, a palmist's, a small jewelry store, a dry-goods store, a grocery, and a pawnshop. When he turned his head to the north to listen with his better ear, Cahill's dark glasses flashed and glittered with the nervousness of bayonets and knives struck through the pawnshop glass by the low sun concentrating there. Through the station door a civilian in a red-and-white mackinaw came forward and stood before the blind man, the suitcase, and the dog, whose breath was heavier and more composed in the air than that of the men.

"Hello," Cahill said again. "Who are you? *Where* are you?"

"Well," the other said, "I'm right here. This is the bus station and the hotel, and the rest of Peckover, North Carolina, is up and down from here but not back and forth. What can I do for you?"

"I'd like to stay with you for a few days."

"You can. We got three upstairs rooms, and you can have the one with the bathroom. You just look after that big dog, and you can have anything I've got for five dollars a day."

"He'll be all right," Cahill said. "He'll eat just about anything. I'd like to get him some meat every couple of days, if I could do that."

"We could fix that up, for sure. How long you plannin' to be here?"

"I'm not quite sure. No more than three days. Maybe four."

"The reason I asked you is that they're having class graduation out at the base on Sunday, and some people'll be coming up to see their boys take off and fly out of this froze-up chicken track of a town for good. But don't worry. You come on in, and I'll take care of them when the time gets here."

They went in, and, though no one or nothing touched him, Cahill felt himself crowded; there were a lot of voices. "Farmers and soldiers," the other man said. At the counter Cahill spread the pages of the book placed under him and followed his name across the paper, writing, he believed, very legibly. A boy, not a Southerner, was arguing short-temperedly with a woman's slow, self-righteous, and sullen tongue, which told him that his money would take him only to New Mexico but not to California; he reckoned that he'd risk it and hitchhike the rest of the way, because anybody these days would pick up a soldier, especially if he was carrying a guitar, wasn't that so.

The room had a big sagging bed, like the one he had just come from. He sat on the edge of it, talking and listening for spaces and objects.

"I got to apologize for the smell downstairs," the manager said. "Seems like nobody ever takes a bath no more. It's just awful in the wintertime. Can you smell 'em up here? I can."

"No, I can't," Cahill said. "I didn't pay no attention." He touched his nose at the bent bridge, which looked as though it had been sideswiped by a large, unremembered object, or pushed aside, but not contemptuously. "My smell's in and out. Sometimes it's damn good, when I pay attention. But mainly, too many car wrecks. Too much bad luck in the mills; once I got hit in the face with a seven-hundred-pound swingin' crane. Too many fights; too many fists comin' at me, all right at my nose. You can keep your soldier-stinks, your barracks and latrines, you can keep your frozen mule turds. What do *they* smell like, anyway?"

"They don't smell."

Cahill grinned. He liked this; the guy didn't embarrass. "Good," he said. "That's one thing I learned today."

"You done been playing in bad luck, buddy."

"Not so bad," Cahill said. "I can still taste. Some, anyway. I'm gonna work on my smell. I can hear good, and I can guess. And I can feel." He flexed his right-hand fingers. "Come here."

In the space above his lap he held out his hand and turned the palm up. The midsummer sun of Willow Plunge warmed it, burning from memory. "Put your hand in here," he said. And, "What's your name?"

The manager became conscious of the size of his tongue, which was larger than he had thought, and the relation between it and the whole act of eating and smelling. "My name is McLendon," he said. "Boyd McLendon. Some of those people you couldn't smell downstairs call me Boysie. Some but not all." He looked down into Cahill's big half-opened hand and its tracks; another's existence and whatever had made it. "What do you want me to do?" he asked.

"Just hold on," Cahill said. "Hold on for a second or two." He took the other hand, almost as large as his, and came slowly together on it. The sense of his physical strength, an undeniable thing, first given but mostly made, struck every vein in his body like snake poison; the barbells and spring grips of his park fed into his arm, and that arm alone.

"No, I ain't," Cahill said, another kind of strength, equally calm and equally deep, in his voice. He bore down; there were no limits; the huge sun filled his muscles as though they were Ruíz's after a workout of bench-presses and curls and a swim, his arm solid with meaning, world authority. A low sound came from Zack; dazed with himself,

McLendon's hand began to give back force against Cahill's. "I see what you mean," he said, offering to pull away. "You ain't ready to give down yet, old man."

McLendon threw all of the force he had in his body, all he had ever had, into his hand offered first as an act of accommodation, then of pride, but now of survival. Nothing helped. The knuckle-sinews quit bracing; they popped and gave up as McLendon gasped and struggled to get away. "Wait, now . . . good God, that's . . . THAT'S . . .

Cahill was startled to recall that one growl was all that the dog would give. He let up his grip. "No, Zack. No, boy. Get down. Down. Down. We're just playin'. Down, big boy. Take it easy."

"That ain't so," McLendon said, holding his hand and feeling it in several positions with the other. "Playin', my ass. How come you to bear down on me like that? I don't see no reason. You do that every time you meet somebody?"

"No," Cahill said. "I'm sorry; it's not somethin' I do very much. And I'm sorry Zack scared you, if he did."

"I ain't gonna die," said McLendon, putting Cahill's bag by the scaling dresser.

"No, we won't die," Cahill said. "At least not today. Can you get sugar?"

"Sure I can." McLendon hesitated and said, "As much as I get rationed. Enough for me and my family and the soldiers and field hands down at the fountain. Maybe a little more. Why?"

"Cubes?"

"Yeah, I can get cubes. How many do you need?"

"Above a dozen would be all right. I only got two with me." He pulled the syringe box from his pocket and opened it. "I need sugar to fight this thing with. The needle and the sugar fight it out in my blood, see? Every day I can't let neither one win." Suddenly he shivered and clasped his elbows to his sides. "New match coming up pretty soon; I'm starting to sweat."

"Maybe it was the shit-assing around we was doin'."

"No; it's a different kind of sweat."

"If you want to stick yourself, I'll go on downstairs, and check back with you later on. Or you could call, whenever you want me."

"Stay on, if you've got a minute. I don't mind if you don't."

McLendon stood respectfully as Cahill went through the ritual of sterilizing the needle, filling the syringe, pulling up his shirt tail and injecting himself in the stomach, his head turned slightly as though it were looking into the hard, pale sky of the window.

"How can you tell when you've got the right shot?" McLendon asked, mildly interested.

"I can't always," Cahill said. "Have to wait a little while. That's where the sugar comes in. Or it might."

"How do you feel?"

"Feel OK. How far is it to the base?"

"Ten, fifteen minutes."

"Good. I might as well get on out there."

"I think you owe me something. If you can't give me back my fingers, you can at least tell me what you're doin' here. Then I'll drive you myself."

Cahill put a hand to his throat, held it there for a moment, facing McLendon's sound-position and the middle of him, then reached into the breast pocket of his coat and drew out a telegram. "This is what I'm doin' here," he said.

McLendon took the warm paper and unfolded it.

NEXT OF KIN JOEL WESLEY CAHILL PFC AVTN CADET
A/C 2027858 MISSING PSMD KILLED TRAINING ACCIDENT
ONE THIRTEEN NINETEEN HUNDRED FORTY THREE
STOP PLEASE CONTACT STOP DEEPEST REGRETS STOP
        HOCCLEVE, COL USAAC RES
        COMMANDING
        LATHAM AAC PRIMARY TRAINING
        PECKOVER, NC

McLendon gave him back the telegram. "So that was him, huh?" he said with a constraint he seldom used.

"It was. You-all must'a heard, around here. What happened? I guess they done found his body by now. This is the fifth day."

"I don't know what happened. Somebody said he went down in a fire; there was a big one twenty-five or thirty miles from here, just before it snowed. I don't know whether they found him. Nobody said anything to me about it. They'll tell you out there, whatever they can. But I sure do feel for you, big man. I sure do. He your only boy?"

"He was. The only live one; the only dead one."

"Let me know when you're ready to go."

"I'm ready now," Cahill said, as though this should have been obvious. "Why not?"

"Don't you want to hang up your stuff?"

"No need; it looks better baggy, they tell me."

"OK, come on, then."

"Come on, Zack," Cahill said. "Let's git 'em. Ho."

The three of them made their way down the stairs, leaving Cahill's door unlocked, and came out flat among the small group gathered at the ticket counter.

"Just a minute; I'll get you some sugar," McLendon said. He came back and nudged Cahill. "Where do you want to keep these?"

Cahill took the envelope and shoved it into his overcoat pocket.

"Let's go on around out back," McLendon said. "Won't take a minute. I want to sh . . . I'll introduce you to something you may not know about."

They went out and moved along the building. McLendon made as if to take Cahill's arm, but Cahill shook him off. "No," he said. "I'm with you; just go on."

They turned the corner and left the highway as a pickup truck pulled out onto it.

The air was perfectly still, and as Cahill passed it through his nostrils it drew itself very fine, as though being made into wire. Instead of holding his usual contact against Cahill's leg, Zack drew apart; Cahill half crouched and felt for him; the dog's hair was rising, and his body was tense with the vibration that came before a growl.

"What is it, boy? What's getting to you?" There was a faint jangle of cold keys, then an uncertain slide, a grinding rotation, a click, a withdrawing, and a dangling thunk against larger metal.

Cahill stepped forward into a closed chill not like the wired air

They were moving toward a kind of hood, a galvanized shed. Like many buildings in the country it had a kind of slapdash mystery about it: something of the garage, something of the storehouse, something of a place where an object or event had been long hidden and either forgotten or had ceased to matter. Anything at all could have been inside; without knowing, one would most likely have thought of bales of rusted barbed wire, old highway signs full of bullet holes, two work shoes that were not matched nor of the same size, and, somehow, a ruined hat from another climate.

"Come into my house," McLendon said. "This is where I *really* live; this is where *it* lives: what I want you to meet."

he had become used to. This was an underground feeling; he thought of stone, and around that, deep earth. Zack swayed now against his leg, growling with hard, arched shudders, and barked sharply once; twice. It was not stone that the sound returned, but the less deepseated resonance of steel or tin.

"I've been hunting all my life, and I've heard about these things but I've never seen one before this. Here, feel."

His hand aided by a light touch, Cahill groped downward: the back of the head of something. Cautiously he explored, losing the head for a descending maze of curving forms, graceful but sharply pointed at the ends. Following them now with both hands, Cahill traced a stiff, branching web in the air, and then stood up. "That's a right big buck," he said. "Eight points? Ten?"

"You ain't through yet. Feel this here other'n's mouth, now."

His touch again guided, Cahill ran the tips of his fingers along a ridge of hard bristle, then, directed more closely, reduced his hand to the forefinger and traced out a vicious, hooking semicircle of what must surely have been bone. Cahill stood in a testing crouch, forming the animal in his mind. "Lord," he said, "What is it?"

36

"Now, right here," McLendon said. "Feel this other jaw. How'd you like to get your balls caught betwixt them things?" Holding Cahill's finger on the tooth, he put the blind man's back on the antlers.

"You ever heard of a jackalope? Combination of a jackrabbit and a antelope?"

"No," Cahill said, grinning a little. "This is a mighty big rabbit."

"It ain't a jackalope. This is a wild doar."

"Door?"

"Combination of a deer and a boar. Some call it the original North Carolina Buddy'ro. You and me are the only ones ever seen one." He broke off. "I shot the buck in a cornfield day before yesterday. The hog was in a whole swamp of ice. Two other fellows was running him with dogs, and he come right by me. Sun was going down, and I couldn't tell what he was, but there was an awful lot of shooting at him, and so I shot at him, too. Before I dressed him out, he weighed four hundred and fifty pounds. If your big dog can wait, he can eat on him in peace." He paused, looking at Zack. "I'd sure like to have him for a catch dog. He'd run him down and hold him good, I'd be bettin'. But I reckon you wouldn't want to take a chance on your dog getting chopped up."

"There's not many things around that would want to try," Cahill said. "You better not live to see the day when he gets after somethin'. You wouldn't like to see it, even if it wadn't you he was after."

"I see what you mean," McLendon said, for Zack had put his head inside the gutted body cavity of the boar, and his muffled growls, still at the point of exploding but not yet quite out of control, gave the interior of the shed the choked and savage fury of a thunderous anger no one could expect to stand against.

With some trouble dragging him by the side hairs, Cahill backed the dog away from the boar, voice last. McLendon locked the shed, and they went back to the highway and the car.

"Don't play with no echoes," Cahill said to Zack, as McLendon opened the rear door for him.

"What? You talkin' to me?"

"Don't pay no attention; I was just mumblin'."

It was warmer now, as they drove. The lifting and falling fields around them were thawing; the snow would probably be off the ground, or mostly, by sunset. Now and then there was a stand of trees near the road that Cahill could hear in a quick solid whoosh, but there was mainly the sound of space, and once an aircraft engine that vied briefly with the car-sound and faded. But in the above-noise there had been something like a flurry of menace, a suggestion of pursuit, even.

"That's what we don't like," McLendon said. "Nobody's used to the noise. Same as with deer, you know: they never look up; they don't have no enemies above 'em, like in trees. Since they put in the base five months ago, everybody's been a little scared; the whole thing's so new. This town is just *here*. Nobody likes it especially, but we use it and we're used *to* it. All that's changed now. Everybody's nervous. The people at the base, the Corps of Engineers and the Air Corps, told us that all this would be fine for the town, but we don't really want their money, and we can make do without all them kids in uniforms. All we want to do is what we've always done—farm tobacco, go to church, go to Fayetteville shopping every now and then, drink a little, hunt a little, look at the fields, look at each other, and sleep whenever we feel like it, especially in the wintertime. Now all we do is keep lookin' up, and waitin'." He paused. "The accident with your boy was the first thing like that we've had. Now . . . I don't know where it's all gonna end. Some of the town ladies'a tried to set up a kind of cadet club back a ways from the station, and the boys come in and drink beer on the weekends. But there's only a few girls here in the high school and some more that work in the cotton mill back between here and Union City. That's about all the social life there is. It ain't good; none of it is any good. I'm more or less stuck here with high blood pressure, my restaurant, and my rent-rooms. I hunt, I sell bus tickets, listen to the planes at the base warm up in the morning, and look up when I go out, and sometimes when I don't."

"Well," Cahill said, thinking slowly, "your huntin' must do a lot for you."

"I like to go out by myself," McLendon replied. "I'm sorry I—well, took advantage of you about my deer and pig. And I'm sorry it bothered your dog, too; I shouldn't'a done that."

"There's nothin' to worry about," Cahill said. "Tell you the truth, it worked out fine; it was friendly, and that's how I took it. A little out of the way, maybe, but when you're blind, you get used to things like that. At first, everything that you thought you knew, and could use without no trouble, has got another side to it that you got to learn. But what goes out with colors, and all that, comes back in your ears and your hands, mainly. You start to put things together in another way and, just a little at a time, but more and more, you come to the notion that you can have the world be anything you want it to be, because it's all in your head anyway. You're all right, as soon as you tell yourself that you'll keep on drawin' the line between what you can use and what's liable to hurt you and this other place in your head that could be anything and *can* be anything; then you've got yourself a pretty good situation." He sat forward and turned toward the other man. "You just gave me a new animal. I can still feel his horns and his tushes, and, far as I'm concerned, they go together and make up the same critter. If you hadn't told me, I would have throwed out my old seeing-eye judgment and wouldn'ta had no trouble believin' that the thing was what you said it was—some critter with big horns and long teeth. I can make a whole world for that thing, and put him in there with the others I've got. I like this . . . this doar partic'ly because, even when I could see, I believed that there was animals like that. Down home in Georgia there's somethin' people claim leaves a crazy track in the mud alongside of rivers; they call it a hog-bear. He's with me, too, but I've never felt him, so he's not as much with me as that thing you got hangin' up in your shed. The doar has just been made up, and made; he's true, now."

"Well," McLendon said uncertainly, "that's one way to look at it, I guess."

"Yeah," Cahill said, nodding. "It's the way I've got. I'll be ramblin' around in it and buildin' it up for the rest of my life."

They rode silently for perhaps another five minutes. Cahill was not a talkative man, but since his blindness he had felt, much against his will, the necessity of conversation. His usual tone was one of sullen banter; it would not have occurred to him that his continual bad-humored teasing was a means of self-protection, for he actually feared nothing, certainly not physical pain. But a great deal of the life of the blind is lived through talk, and must be; information is crucial, and Cahill had come to find that his truculence, by irritating his informants, interfered with his knowing what needed to be known, and made his day-to-day survival that much harder. He welcomed the boredom of riding silently, for by now he was tired of the defensive muttering that he still used with strangers, not wanting pity or any show of it. Dislike was better. For that reason he was a little surprised at the way he had just opened up to McLendon—all that about the creation of a new and private animal. Had he meant it? The bumps and irregularities of the highway became both comfortable and strange to him as he concluded that he could very well have meant it: that suddenly he was right about his situation and its possibilities, its forms of secrecy and power. He pulled his latissimus and trapezius muscles tightly about him, and gave himself with new confidence to the hidden flow of concrete.

Into a setting of scrub brush and a thin creek, he was looking downward and inward out of early morning. The pines and bushes could have come from anywhere in the South, and the creek, which flowed from him toward the center of the thicket, might have been somewhere in the foothills of the Blue Ridge Mountains, where his father's family had lived before moving to Atlanta. He was invisible; delicate light shaded from him into the pierced and murmuring tangle, and he rested in attentive relaxation, in his mind flexing his fingers for a renewal of the touches which had taken place half an hour before within McLendon's gutted and hanging dark; his real hands, however, did not move. Whether with his will or not, the light strengthened, and somewhere in the knitted spikes—no, distinctly to the left of center, where the brush suddenly went denser without seeming to change—an almost ladylike twin pink glittered splinteringly back at him, gone fierce or mad, and shone into his high place of concealment. He drew on the scene, and the gaze began to define itself as part of a horned form either terrified or infuriated; he could now make out a long jaw, an open mouth into which Cahill's whole being of the moment poured, blazing on the wild and perfectly matched curvature of tusks. Cahill waited; he had done enough. Now it—

"Here we go," McLendon said. "Here's the base, or what there is of it up to today."

They stopped and McLendon got out, walked over to the freshly painted guard box, and spoke to the enlisted man there. He came back.

"They're sendin' somebody down in just a few minutes. You'd rather ride than walk, wouldn't you?"

"No, I don't think so. How far is it?"

"I'd say about a quarter of a mile."

"I'll walk, then. Blind people don't get enough exercise, and neither does Zack. Besides, it feels like a fairly nice day."

"Yeah, it's real clear. This is pretty land, through here. It's flat, with hills all around it just barely . . . well, you know, just barely *there*. This used to be a tobacco farm. Most of the buildings they're using for classrooms, offices, and the other stuff are old warehouses. The Corps of Engineers built the hangars right quick. Then the Air Corps flew in the airplanes, drove in the trucks and jeeps, the people came in from every which way, the first class got here on a troop train from Pre-Flight

School in Montgomery, Alabama, and they had the whole base set up in no more than a month. They're still workin' on it: listen—all that banging is them putting up the rest of the fence."

It was true; a racket of hammers, set in a line going away from him, hit steadily, some in rhythm and one or two others finishing off, the nailheads going to the wood. "I could show that nearest guy somethin' right now," he said, half to himself. "He's missin' more licks than my grandmaw."

Around the near turn in the base road a jeep with two men in it came out of a graceful stand of low pines such as might have been part of the rough of a suburban golf course.

"Here's your ride," McLendon said.

The jeep pulled up; the hammering fell away from Cahill's attention. A neat corporal got down, looking mainly at Zack.

"Mr. Cahill," he said, "would you like to come on with us? Colonel Hoccleve would like to see you."

"I'd be out of luck if he didn't, now wouldn't I?"

"I'll be happy to wait for you out here," McLendon said. "You got any idea about how long this is gonna take?"

"No idea. You go on, and I'm sure they'll get me back. That be OK with you?" he said to the corporal. "Can you take me back to the bus station?"

"I'm sure we can, sir. That shouldn't be any trouble," said the corporal.

"Don't worry, Mr. Cahill," said the other soldier, still sitting in the jeep. "We'll take care of everything for you."

"Well, first off, you can go ahead on with your jeep. Me and my dog and this first boy will walk on in."

"You sure?" asked the airman in the jeep uncertainly.

41

"I'm sure. Tell the colonel I'll be right along." Cahill put out his hand toward the highway, and McLendon took it. "See if you can get hold of some meat for Zack tonight," he said.

"Sure. I'll carve up part of that boar and thaw it out. Might have to use a chisel, though. Does Zack like a gamy taste? What I call a 'green' taste? My wife never did like it."

"I don't know he's ever had it from anything that was wild," Cahill said, "but he'll prob'ly like it, if it's meat. Ain't but one way to find out."

"I'll look for you when I see you. Just come on in; station's always open."

After McLendon had gone and the jeep had gone, the corporal stood sideways to Cahill. "This way, sir," he said, pulling timidly on Cahill's sleeve. Instead of stepping forward, Cahill took off his glove and stooped, picking up whatever was underfoot. He straightened, running his thumb over the substance in his palm. Snow or sand? Sand, though as cold as snow. He pitched it away and started in the direction he believed he had been shown. Zack moved to his side, and lightly against his leg.

"Did you tell me your name?" Cahill asked, entire in the clean air; sight did not seem particularly important.

"My name is Phillipson, sir," the boy said. "I'm permanent party here; I work in Colonel Hoccleve's office, in the records section."

"You don't do no flyin'?"

"No, sir. Wish I did. I know something about it from listening to the cadets, but I don't fly. I've never even been off the ground."

Almost directly overhead an aircraft engine built its strong broad unified buzz. Then suddenly without any warning it went through a change that stopped the heart: it was as though its bull-throated roar had

been violently twisted, over-turned, convulsed, corkscrewed.

"Snap roll," Corporal Phillip-son explained. "Not too bad; he came out on a point. He's too low, though; that'll cost him."

Cahill primed himself for the sound to come back, but the en-gine faded and disappeared, and there were others, from several directions; these were farther; they wove or swayed with dis-tance. Closer than the engines, now, were also the voices of men, young surely, excited, given as though out of running.

"We're just at the end of the last PT period," Phillipson said. "For the first twenty minutes they do calisthenics, and for the rest of the hour they kind of break up into groups and play basketball or touch football. Some of them box, and some of them just do laps. They'll quit in a few minutes to go get ready for chow."

"Can we stop and let me listen a little?" Cahill said.

"Sure," Phillipson said. "Colonel Hoccleve is very easygoing about things. Take your time."

Going by were many feet, and beyond these inside the tram-pling were voices that yelled to each other and against each other. There was a shuddering rattle overhead, and the live glancing off of (surely) a basket-ball. This or something else bounced nearby: feet ran toward it, or toward Cahill. "Sorry," a hard-breathing Northern voice said. "I rimmed it off." But the other remained where he was, for Cahill could hear his breath, still quickly caught, evenly, though urgent yet.

"Mr. Cahill," Phillipson said, remembering both names and glad he did, "this is Aviation Cadet Harbelis."

Cahill put out his hand, and the chill flesh of thin, medium-sized bones closed around it, but for once there was an impression beyond those given by touch. The boy's breath was being withheld; before it took up, Cahill listened more intensely. Within the flicker of suspended time, someone outside it threw something, grunting explosively, and Cahill waited for it to come down among the more distant ghostliness of feet and voices.

"Well," said Harbelis. In another long silence the cadet's large, dark eyes first widened and then narrowed under a single heavy eyebrow.

"I guess we better go ahead in," said Cahill. "I don't want to try the Air Corps's patience any more than I have to."

"Maybe I'll see you when you get finished," Harbelis said. "I could use a couple of more laps; I like to run in this kind of weather. Reminds me of Pennsylvania."

"I don't know how long I'll be," Cahill said.

"We've got an hour before formation; I'll stay out as long as I can, and be looking for you."

"Sure," said Cahill, puzzled. "Do that, if you want to."

"Maybe you could help me do something."

"I will if I can."

44

"If we've got enough light, maybe you could time me on a windsprint or two."

Harbelis unexpectedly held up a stopwatch looped to his wrist, then thought twice about it, shoved it under the waistband of his sweatpants, and jigged with cold. He turned and ran. The feet and the ground carried their rhythm, now striding, into the sound-blend of the young field.

"Stairs," Phillipson said clearly.

"How many?" Cahill asked.

"Seven . . . eight."

Cahill felt for a railing, which was there, climbed, and ended as his eighth step leveled into a platform. Here he turned toward the rattle of basketball metal, the slow unison steps of joggers, the sharp cries for recognition, and the grouped laughter that traveled from one unexpected direction to another. He wondered how many boys must be out there; a guess gave him a hundred or so. When Cahill thought of voices younger than his own, he had got used to their being those of the swimmers and sunners of Willow Plunge, the stenographers and weight lifters, and with the slight Spanish-American accent of Ruíz, both overearnest and cynical. With the voices there had always been explosions of water, and, after his blindness had come, the sensation of waiting for a body in midair to descend and burst apart the pool. But here the only sounds that were not voices were those of engines sighing to an

Phillipson opened the door and stood waiting. Behind him the porch was perfectly still. The blind man and the dog were facing out over the field, and Phillipson was not sure of what he should do. He wanted to show his concern, but he had no clear notion of how to do it except by his voice, which had nothing but information, and the silences he hoped would be taken as understanding. Still with the door open, he too gazed out into the playing area, not moving his eyes from the long central space of the football game off to the groups of basketball players nearer the hangars, or to the runners both almost underfoot and far off among trees. He saw all this four times a day, but now there was an intensity in the scene that he had never noticed. The calm and sightless human body beside him, hovering over an ordinary part of his world, passing judgment on it, absorbing it for rea-

end behind him, fulfilled against the play taking place on the ground. *"Here. Here."*

sons never to be known, was unnerving and without precedent. Despite his broad view the corporal found his gaze now going farther and farther from him, moving through the pines with the few runners who appeared and disappeared among them with lonely followings of breath. "This way," Corporal Phillipson said softly, again taking Cahill's sleeve.

He sat at the end of a backed bench where there was an armrest, comfortably, listening to two typewriters, and wondering about military furniture. Most of it would have to be cheap and functional, but would it generally include, as this armrest did, a slight sweat of varnish? He took his hand from the wood and put it in his lap, then shifted his weight; the wood pulled at his pants a little. Four steps came through the light nattering of typewriter keys. Corporal Phillipson's voice said, just loud enough, "Colonel Hoccleve would like to see you now."

For a moment Cahill could not put off the notion that he was back in a doctor's waiting room, and got to his feet as the usual reactions of impatience, apprehension, and defiance rose with him. He stepped forward with Zack; Phillipson touched and guided him to a door. Cahill went through, stopped with his feet together, and held out his hand into blankness. There was a quiet blockaded flurry, for the colonel was seated behind a desk. He got up, circled quickly, and took Cahill's hand.

Cahill would have welcomed a stronger grip against which, even though tentatively, he could have asserted his own. But the long, fragile bones—bones with the feeling of *distance* in them—which his fingers held were not as noticeable to him as the unexpected brush of his sleeve by something else: the officer's other hand; it could not

Remembering the slenderness and the long-jawed elegance of the son, the eyes almost always narrowed and never direct, the colonel was not prepared for the father's solid, bulky immobility: the foursquare appropriation of space, the big, stooped body, the florid beaten face which looked as though it were still only half healed from some injury many

46

have been anything but. What was this supposed to mean?

I am not just some poor creature dragged in out of the cold, he thought: beginning right now, I am the center of this thing. While I am here everybody who had anything to do with my boy will have to come to me and tell me whatever he wants to. I am wide open; I am waiting: I am waiting in my park, my penned water, my master carpenter's maze, my rubber rattlesnake, the sun, and my muscles. Let anything that wants to, come on. The familiar sideways rain of gold streaks picked up speed, as at a command, almost solid, shimmering and radiating, giving a hidden and crackling brightness to whatever was there.

"I know you are," Cahill said. "I know you must be. This is not easy for you, either."

years ago, and, above all, for the truly startling power that flowed from his grasp into the colonel's whole body. He peered closely into Cahill's dark glasses;

there was, or could have been, no concealment, no evasiveness there. "I'm sorry," Hoccleve said. "I'm truly, truly sorry. I realize—"

"This is the first accident we've had here," Hoccleve said, leaning forward and speaking slowly and with extreme distinctness. "I mean, it's the first in which someone was killed. You know, there are not many fatalities in primary training. These aircraft we use are just about as safe as anything you can find. They'll practically land themselves. The only way a person could possibly be killed or be seriously injured short of flying straight into the ground, is for two planes to run together." Out of habit he showed a collision with his hands in front of Cahill's glasses. "There has to be a considerable impact, caused either by contact with another aircraft, or with an object, or with the ground."

"You mean he ran into somebody?"

"No. He hit the ground."

"How? Why?"

47

"He was flying over a brush fire, a very big one that had lasted almost a week. There's been a lot of wind lately, and until the snow the other day, the weather has been very dry. The land over across the river is mostly woods and brush. No one seems to know how the fire got started, but it may have been that one of the farmers over there was trying to burn off some of his property, and the fire got away from him in the wind. That's not really important, though."

"No, it's not. At least not to me."

"Flying over fires of whatever magnitude is strictly against regulations, Mr. Cahill. Your son was where he was not supposed to be, for some reason that nobody knows. There is a great deal of turbulence over a fire. In addition, the visibility is bad, and the situation is altogether a very dangerous one, particularly for an inexperienced pilot with less than sixty hours of solo time, flying a light aircraft. As far as we can tell, he must have been at no more than five hundred feet, which is regulation minimum altitude, unless you're actually taking off or landing. The plane must have got away from him in the turbulence, and he went down. Before we took the plane out, I walked in there with some of the other officers and had a look at it. He hit pretty hard, but he was not actually killed outright."

"How do you know that?"

"A farmer who was trying to dig a firebreak between the main part of the fire and his house heard him come down and impact, and pulled him out. He managed to get your boy to the house, and he and his wife tried to do what they could for him. From what the man said, Joel was bleeding pretty badly from head wounds and almost certainly had sustained internal injuries. He felt that Joel was too badly injured to be moved, and he left him to go for a doctor. While he was gone, Joel came to and attempted to leave the house. The wife tried to calm him down, and even struggled with him, but evidently your son was so deeply in shock that he couldn't be reasoned with. He got away from her and started off toward the fire. She ran after him, and almost caught him when he fell, but he recovered and disappeared into the smoke, heading toward the river, which is about half a mile away, through a part of the fire that was just about burned out but still giving off a lot of smoke. After that, we don't know anything. It was two hours before we got in there to look for him, and there was no indication that he'd ever been there, except for the plane and the blood on the farmer's quilt. Personally, I think he must have stumbled off into the river; we've been

48

dragging for him ever since the accident. I don't see that there's anything more that we can do."

"I reckon not."

"We've sent the report in, and listed him as missing."

"Couldn't be missing in action, or something like that?"

"No; just missing in the line of duty, presumed dead."

"Presumed dead," Cahill repeated softly, as though to another part of himself.

"Yes, and until—or unless—we find the body, that's all there is to be said about a very regrettable situation." He paused. "The rest is up to you. If you like, I can arrange for you to talk to some of the people he knew up here: his flight instructor, some of the Air Corps pilots and other personnel, other cadets. Just about everybody here knew him, or knew about him. He had a kind of following; some of the boys admired him a lot. But they'll tell you about that. Let me know what you want, and I'll set up some interviews for you."

"That might be a good idea," Cahill said. "Could we do some of this tomorrow?"

"Sure. Whenever you like. How about nine o'clock?"

"Good. You want me to meet you here?"

"Yes, I'll send someone into town for you at nine. You're at the bus station, right?"

"That's where I am."

"I assume you'll want to go through Joel's personal effects, since you were named next of kin."

"Yes, I think I should do that."

"I have one item here with me. Something you might like to have." He opened a drawer, came around the desk once more, and placed a folded object in Cahill's hand. "He left these behind; they were found on the floor of the farmhouse after Joel disappeared."

Cahill weighed the object in his hand. Two chill curves faced each other, and gritted lightly when he moved them. He ran his

49

thumb over the bulging surfaces; one of them held a shape of cracks. With his free hand, Cahill touched a lens of his dark glasses. "Are these— You mean he had these—"

"Yes; those are the goggles he had on, regular Air Corps issue, but for some reason there's a big B.V. initialed on the strap."

"You sure these are Joel's?" Cahill said, stretching the tough elastic.

"I'm sure. They were issued to him brand-new."

Cahill put the goggles into his pocket. "Is it all right if I keep these?"

"Sure," Hoccleve answered. "That is the least we can do."

"Thanks," Cahill said. "I appreciate it."

"The tactical officer, Lieutenant Spigner, has Joel's personal effects. You can see him tomorrow. I can make up just as full a schedule as you want; it just depends on how many people you want to see and how long you can stay with us."

"I'd like to see as many as I can," Cahill said. "The time don't make no difference."

"Would you like to stay until Joel's class graduates on Sunday?"

"Well, I might. It just depends on what happens. I'm open."

"So are we," Hoccleve replied, trying to keep down his sense of relief. "I imagine you'll want to be getting on back on to town pretty soon. I know from experience that these wartime bus rides can wear you out pretty good, as the boys say."

"They're not all that bad. There's nothin' about 'em I mind."

"All right. Corporal Phillipson will see that you get back."

"Tell him to come on out after me in about ten or fifteen minutes," Cahill said, rising. "I'd like to talk to one of the boys playing ball out in your yard, here."

Cahill worked through the front door, felt for Zack, and straightened. The railing, not quite solidly planted, came under his right hand in one pass. He made it down the eight steps to the ground, moved out of the way of anyone needing to use the steps, and waited for Harbelis to

50

come. From the far pines, now truly beginning to mass with darkness, a single figure bounced slowly toward him, weaving through the defensive backfield of the football game. Harbelis drew up, running in place, and smiling broadly. "Made it," he said. "Now I've got to do just one more thing. Or maybe two. You want to help me out a little bit?"

"Any way you like," Cahill said. "Have at it."

"My flight's been losing out to some of these jokers in the relays we run around here. We really ought not to lose those, because we've got some fast guys. If we can win tomorrow, we might get Thursday open post, which don't mean much, but it's better than nothing around here."

"What do you want me to do?"

"I want you to hold this watch on me, and see what my time for the hundred has done been slipping back to."

"Somebody else could probably do better for you on that. I've got some disadvantages you might not'a noticed."

"No, I'd like you to do it."

Cahill shrugged. "OK," he said. "I'll do what I can with what I've got. I'll try not to mess you up too much."

"Let's move on down over by the trees," Harbelis said. "That'll give me a good shot at ten-six, which wouldn't be bad in tennis shoes, and on this sand."

They walked for a few minutes past the football game, which was now at the far end of the field.

"This'll be OK, right here."

"I don't run none too well in this overcoat," Cahill said. "Maybe you and Zack can race."

"What I want you to do," Harbelis said, "is to take this stopwatch. I'll go down a hundred yards and give you a holler when I'm ready. Put your hand up in the air, and then drop it and start the watch at the same time. When I come past you I'll make a noise, and you push down on the winder again. That'll be all; then I'll come back and take a look at the bad news."

As Harbelis's light steps left him, Cahill found his attention moving away again to the far wall of voices. The only sound now was a low murmur, fading; there was no surprise, no wild appeal, no individual voice. For whatever reason, he noticed, catching himself doing so, that he was listening also for engine sounds over the game, over himself, for the moment seemed to contain an element, an incompleteness, that only a kind of return could satisfy. He fixed in his mind the sight of an airplane almost touching the ground, and was beginning to be bothered that no engine blew into life in his ears to confirm it when, instead, words floated to him saying, "Ready. All ready."

Slowly Cahill raised his free hand and pressed on the grooved knob of the watch with his fingertip. A sense of wonderment at how he must look under these conditions struck through him quickly and passed off. He dropped his arm and closed his fist; the watch bit and clicked.

Breath and steps: he had set them going, and Cahill listened with new commitment, especially since the voices of the game, blurred with distance, had no single focus, sent him no true cry. Then, as though made by hands instead of feet, a lonely but persistent and increasing applause, a line of delicate pats developed toward him; he could hear in them a lunging of strain on and on, the battle for both traction and speed that bore now definitively into the ground, and shook it under Cahill's feet. The one breath came almost in his ear, bursting, saying "Now." He clenched the stopwatch and released.

Harbelis entered his running form, rising slowly through the crouch of the first few bunched steps into the full pickup stride. Seven and a half feet was comfortable for him, and even in this uncertain footing he knew by his acceleration that he had reached it at least two steps before he usually did. He pounded hard into the field, aiming at the black figure with the animal beside it, leaping from side to side in Harbelis's jolted eyes and shuddering with all the power Harbelis could direct toward it, driving all out, shocking the sand as cruelly as he could for more stride, turnover, more speed, more meaning. He gasped with his finishing stretch and passed beyond.

Harbelis came back, blowing passionately. He took Cahill's hand and turned the watch to the light. From all the playing fields at once a great ragged cry went up, and Cahill momentarily thought that this was connected with Harbelis's run, but it was not; the training period was over, and the cadets and their instructors were talking and jogging toward the now-lighted barracks.

"Ten-eight," Harbelis said. "Not so bad. It'll have to do, anyway."

"Sounds like everybody's leaving us," Cahill said. "You maybe ought to be gettin' along."

"Stay just a minute," Harbelis said with a new, serious tone. "That wasn't really what I wanted. Just stand here talking for a minute, and then we'll go on over to the courts."

"Whatever you want. I'm about out of questions. The colonel's got 'em all."

"This'll just take a minute." Harbelis led Cahill and the dog to the nearest basketball court, and stood them together in a position roughly that of a foul shooter. He went to a canvas-covered container and came back with a basketball. "The goal is right in front of you, maybe twenty-five feet. See if you can knock one in for me."

"How come?"

"Just for the hell of it."

"This ain't one of my games," **Cahill said, taking the ball, "but** **it won't hurt, I guess." He** **weighed the ball in his hands,** **brought his thumbs together be-** **hind it, and raised it ceremoni-** **ously overhead to stretch both** **his overcoat and his muscles.** **Then he carefully imagined an** **angle, a curve, brought the ball** **quickly down to chest level and** **launched it into the arc in his** **mind. In the brief silence that** **followed his release, he poised** **with his arms up, fairly sure that** **he would hear the ball either hit** **the ground or fall into hands. In-** **stead, there was a sharp, startled** **ring of metal.**

Under the basket, Harbelis narrowed his eyes at the dark figure and the squatting dog. There was an air of calculation in the blind man that filled the runner with tense and compressed excitement, and as the ball lifted into the lighter span of the sky, Harbelis stepped under the basket and through the rim and the strings watched its hanging fall. The shot was off center, but looked remarkably true until it actually hit the rim and bounced off. Moving quickly, half into his sprinter's stride, he intercepted the ball and returned it.

Wordlessly the ball was given **back to him. Again he went** **through the routine, reflecting** **that most basketball players** **could probably shoot foul shots** **almost as well blindfolded as** **not. This time there was no re-**

The blackened figure shot once more, this time the ball, hardly able even to seem round in the air in which a few faint stars had now appeared, fell both wide and short. Harbelis fielded and gave it back.

sponse of either basket or backboard. Harbelis handed him the ball.

A little irritated, Cahill repeated the stages of his newfound process and lofted the ball not with more care but with a good deal less. Yet the instant the ball left his touch he could tell that something remarkable was happening in the next twenty-five feet of air. He gripped his hands quietly, and as the fingertips met the palms, there was a definitive stir of cord, frontal, as at his forehead.

Cahill felt sure that he would say something else.

"One more time," he said. Harbelis barely had time to return to his position and sight through the basket before the ball, a growing blotch, showed above the rim and came through without touching. The net side-swiped and whipped; Harbelis caught the ball without moving. He ran it back to the container and returned to Cahill, who had folded his arms. "Good. That's good." Harbelis paused.

"That's it."

Lights were around them now, in the Administration Building and in the cadet barracks facing it across the assembly area, and a few, strung on long wires apparently by chance, came on between the hangars and the cadet mess. Corporal Phillipson, who had returned in time to watch the last shot, stood respectfully in the at-ease position. "Are you ready to go now?" he said.

"I'm ready," Cahill replied.

"Do you think you might like to have dinner with us?" Harbelis asked, touching Cahill's sleeve.

"Would that be all right?"

"I'm sure it would, sir," said Corporal Phillipson. "Just give me a minute and let me go ask the colonel."

He had been moved, without moving, to the edge of a great number of quietly spoken, excited words. Group by group, this language drifted toward him and stopped. From the opposite

The neat, two-story buildings across the open space were giving out one group after another; these moved through the friendly, residential pines out onto the packed sand of the yard, the boys maneu-

54

direction came purposefully stepping feet with Phillipson's voice.

vering unobtrusively, each talking to another and then another until he reached the place awaiting him in the formation.

"The colonel says he's delighted to have you stay for chow," Phillipson said.

"Come on, then; we'll just go over here while they run the flag down," Harbelis said. "It won't be but a minute or two."

Cahill allowed Harbelis to take his arm, for he was already interested in the glimpse of conversation that he heard beginning to surround him as he moved with Harbelis and Zack through the thickening of boys. "I was over the other side of the reservoir. You know I was never . . ." "He told me to keep . . . I mean he told me and *told* me. For some reason I just couldn't . . ." "If I get that son-of-a-bitch on a check-ride, I feel like I'm already sunk. I'm already on the train to . . ." "I found out a good thing today. On a snap to the right, when you kick in the rudder, don't bother to L the stick but jerk it right on into . . ." "A little dog-fight . . ." "Don't talk to me about that . . ." "A lot of northeast wind . . ." "I remember the first time I killed the engine, up there by myself. How quiet it was. Could I spin it? I couldn't. Not without the instructor. I still . . ." "It was about angels five, I'd say . . ." "Right into the sun."

By now the intense language— essentially a foreign language, familiar as all the words were— had left him more or less behind; Cahill could not catch any more words. There is never room in the world for a complete quietness, he thought. Real silence is impossible. Even the dead must hear something, maybe a faint ringing or an echo that only bone can hear: a head made out of a bone. That's what you hear with, when you are not anything but bones. Not anything. From

"I'm going to take a quick shower and throw on a uniform. Just hold what you've got. When the formation breaks up, I'll come get you." Harbelis had stationed Cahill in a group of pines beside the door of the barracks. Here, he did not stand out, for no light from the building fell on him, and his overcoat and hat were dark. To the flicker of expectant, half-military eyes that touched him or fixed momentarily and by chance upon

55

the ground he tightened his legs, and they were satisfyingly firm amongst the drifting descriptions of flight that were mostly all turned away from him and probably disappearing into the cold young clouds of voice-breath above the groups. I ought to walk more, he said to himself. Yes, I will do that; I will leave behind everything to touch and feel for, all places that give off sounds, and see what happens. I will even leave Zack, and go in a line for an hour, and stand wherever I come to.

Unexpectedly a broad casual note of an utterance like music, statementy, forthright and carrying suggestions of a human voice which could speak with clear directness only through the intricate coilings of a machine, stood forth, spread, and with bold finality descended. Despite himself, Cahill found his

him, he was only a figure not usually there, and worth some conjecture, but not much; his mystery was slight.

The shifting assembly tightened now little by little. Those nearest the platform landing of the Administration Building were as brightly lit as figures in a prison lineup, as were the faces of the cadets in the spotlight slanted toward the mess hall. In the direction of the road to the gate, however, the uniforms and features were less and less distinct; those farthest from the building stood in no more than ghost-light, and the last of all in darkness. At the flagstaff beside the stairs two cadets prepared the descent of the colors, which wavered resignedly in the half existence afforded by the hooded off-glow of three strong beams. A short blond boy raised a horn. Keeping the tremors of darkness that stirred at the top of its mast, the flag slid with proper hesitancy down the staff. Halfway it hitched and stalled; one would have thought it had done so in order to discover and outroll, with a gesture lost and deeply found in mid-air, most of its length, developing in the steady strange light a stun-

body bracing in anticipation against the started shimmering layers of brass, the ranging, directed tones stepped-down to stand through him and on behind. It was the ordered fall of sound that he liked, and the sensation of eagerness he shared with the long mass of boys as in the impossible cleanness of pronged phrasing he also, among trees, held his place.

Inside the following silence, a small lulling drone grew from nothing until it was knowable as electronic. Borne by this, a vast movement and suspension of air, so unthinkably huge as to belong over wastes as barren and regardless as the Gobi Desert or the moon, dwelt in preparation. It was a single breath, and Cahill was sure, though he did not quite know why, that it came through nostrils instead of lips.

ning reality made more disturbing by the captured and serene nature of its struggles. Among the cadets there was a single gasp as one of the flag detail flicked a rope respectfully and the now-blazing cloth lapsed into hands. The oncoming intensity of colors was not so much blinding as riveting; Harbelis, in from his late-come post in the front rank, thought he had never experienced such red.

Before Colonel Hoccleve spoke, he was conscious of his enlarged breathing, with a suggestion of springs or of tines poised to embody it, forming to go up from him and down, to go around him and others in a brooding and machine-enchanted circle, an emanation vast and necessary, free of any human throe. He kept his voice level, and sent it, hushed with concentrated space, already foreign to him.

"Just a few announcements," the floodlit voice said. "Air Corps Cadet Colonel Shears will have some information pertaining to the current status of classes and events, and particularly to the graduation ceremonies on Sunday. For those of you who have relatives and friends coming in for the weekend, I'd like to remind you again that accommodations in Peckover are extremely limited; if any of you have made acquaintances in the area whom you know and like well enough for you to feel comfortable in asking to put up your visitors for a day or so, it would alleviate our situation here if you would contact them tomorrow or the next day." The colonel shifted, preparing again. A low-hanging hum came from the posted speakers, and then increased toward an intolerable pitch, a chill, needlepointed squeal that seemed intended to drive bafflement, rage and perversity through the human head, until a hidden adjustment foiled it, and again the colonel ranged and sparked over the yard.

He stood solid in the form of his natural force, as limitless and established as magnetism, the presences in the space about him probably trees, an opening and closing to his left surely what it was, a door, and behind that a framed fluttering that must have been panels of glass or a single very large pane that caught the splintered feedback between the public words. Volted with authority, he listened against the blocked and membraneous shuddering behind him, to the crisp Northern voice into which came the multileveled speaking of his name.

A running, overtaking murmur passed in front of him. For a moment it seemed to belong to the

"This evening we are privileged to extend the courtesy of the Army Air Corps's Latham field facility to Mr. Frank Cahill." The colonel paused; the speakers stuttered and readied. "Mr. Cahill is the father of Aviation Cadet Joel Cahill, who was, as all of you know, involved in the unfortunate accident we had here last week. He has come from Atlanta to spend some time talking with the officers and the other trainees who shared our experience with Cadet Cahill, and . . . well . . . to get to know us here, a little." The mounted squealing returned to the microphone, and the colonel's monologue turned intermittent, ridiculous, and dissolved in the stiff racket, a crackling of wilderness straws, in which some of the half-lit cadets smiled on the dark sides of their faces, and farther off in night, nearest the moon, an actual laugh almost developed, then ceased.

In the likable wave that swept gently along the top of the formation there was a discreet but spir-

low commotion proper to a market, though there were no clanks, no striking of metals; everything—all whispering, all silence—was felt to be sane and relieved and tentatively hopeful. Then this was changed for another hush, kept and adjusted once more, with a new prickling of static, which descended and came to rest somewhere below.

The new voice was a half tone lower than the first, graver and not as rapid. Though formal it was seemingly friendly, but it was also unwaveringly conclusive, no matter what it said; Cahill wondered what had happened to the youth of it. For the last twenty years he had heard many young voices and the water-sounds they lived among when he heard them, and, not completely realizing it, had let them become so much a part of his consciousness, as it came to rest in, depend on, and expand more and more into hearing, that they now belonged with the

ited tossing of glossy brims, as though in a crosswind this time traveling lengthwise, an unsuspected force that could understand laughter and take it anywhere.

From among the older men stationed with the light of the building front, a tall form stepped forward and into part of the broad-air darkness where the long mass of boys reestablished its military geometry, settling firm. From the front rank, Harbelis looked upward to the face of the raised figure whose feet were at the level of his eyes.

"Early this afternoon . . . a major defeat . . . and a major victory! Early this afternoon, like the forces of radiant, rebellious youthful light over the humdrum, cloudy army of official power, in a culinary battle of champions on the dusty basketball courts of proud Peckover, Shears's Suns of the Morning, the Cadets' Ba-

dawning of blindness itself, and were as integral to the merciless hurtling gold of his world as those lights themselves, and their afterglowing parabolas. That web now played over the darkness in front of him and took in the voice of the cadet colonel as one among those at Willow Plunge. In his loom of orbits, he began to listen carefully, half expecting the springboard-shudder, the pause and explosion of a dive, a scatter of unowned coins flung broadly, the afterfall of invisible water. In this he missed a little of what was being said.

Backward and forward, a wordless murmuring materialized, blown along the formation not as though in rows but picked out at random, like certain leaves on a deserted building side that are stirred when others are not. Fugitive, anticipatory, reversing back the way it had come, the whispering fell away, leaving for the official voice an excited and wondering void.

nanas, defeated, by a score of forty-six to forty-one, the aging but gallant, the balding, the gray brigade, the offscourings of the typing pool and the Physical Training Staff, the outclassed and overdone Warneke's Wieners."

". . . I have not met him yet . . .

. . . but as Colonel Hoccleve has told you, he's here."

"I am told that he has just come in this afternoon, with his dog, and he'll be with us for several days, and maybe even on through graduation. I hope he'll stay. But whatever he decides, remember that we want to do right by him, as right as we can, all of us; we want to give him whatever we've got it in us to give."

60

There was something he should be thinking when it came. A daring authority as to what should appear at different times among the phantom storms of blindness had come to be working in him, and now concentrated on being delivered of something ultimate as he listened and chose. There were two forms hanging in the dark—iron dark he could smell with one nostril—and one of these had horns, and the creature made a sighing as it then passed overhead, over a running boy being timed as he fought through winter brambles. On the other side of a playground grill a single sweaty child moved toward him with a beaten ball in her hands, looking straight at him for some reason other than the reason he was there.

He began to take on her quality of unthinking assurance . . . something could happen . . . but with the awaited word she vanished, as uncorrected light and whole darkness collided and fused, beyond reason, on the primed snake of the Honeycomb, inwound through a barricade of sparks that should have been humming but were not. The long pane of the barracks tremored at his back as the word "blind" flashed in a high-tension center-bore through his breastbone. He stubborned and tensed, drawing strongly on his

"Mr. Cahill is blind."

61

muscles to hold the rest together beyond correction, and from that vantage began to beam himself forth in earnest upon the others and the rest of his surround.

He relaxed and waited, still feeling himself go forth, wander at will, stand and move on, but now without tension or any sense of deliberate thrust.

Though he had no precedent for comparison, Cahill could tell, even so, that this tone was not usual for the voice. And yet, through the softly banked rows of boys that stood between him and the speaker, there sifted a curious other sound, the barely audible brimming of a possible echo; he tuned himself to make it out, but could not quite, until the last word.

The address system boiled and fuzzed anew, patient between voices, but within the expectancy the phantom afterhang of

"I don't think I need to tell you there's a lot of evil machinery around this place. Well, not evil: dangerous. So . . . we want to watch that. Mr. Cahill is going to be with us where he wants to be. It's up to us to watch, and to do. We want to watch the engines for him. We want to watch the jeeps and six-by-sixes coming in and out. The wheels of airplanes. We don't want him getting dirty with any of our grease. We want to keep him, and we want to tell him. Whatever, and wherever. We are going to give him a schedule, so that he can know whatever we know, and do whatever we do. But he may decide that he wants to play it another way, and so he may just show up anywhere: on the flight line, in the hangars . . .

in the classroom . . .
on the ball field . . .

on the courts . . .
in Supply . . .

in the Administration Building . . . at the flight surgeon's . . . or anywhere, at any time. So be ready. Keep the grease off him . . . and the wheels . . . . . . and the propellers."

the word "propellers" united like a last stirring of low air, not corded, not clear and not electronic. After it, a massed and unsteady rustling of bodies within clothes ebbed for the return of official speech, which could now be heard, indrawing.

"We can break and go in, now," Colonel Hoccleve said. "Be sure not to touch Mr. Cahill's dog. He's not used to us." He paused. "Just as a last rundown: Flights D, F, and G on the line in the morning. Section marchers show up here at seven-thirty. At ease."

A short, granted pause, in which nothing stirred. No ease was in it, but anticipation.

Cadet Colonel Shears stepped forward again. His voice was slightly more than too loud, and brought somewhere out of machinery a rattle as though of a loose wire unnecessarily electrified. "Ten—hu*uut.*"

A splattering, summarizing crack of heels, like something, an assertion, a unison, achieved in a dream, now centered. In his shoes, not his feet, Cahill felt a perilous, strict impulse toward temporary perfection, gave to it and stayed with it.

"Dismissed."

Behind him the wall of glass fluttered and eased off, then solidified and ceased to matter. In the large space of boys between Cahill and the platform one body separated from the position it had occupied between two others, and in this movement a general breakup was repeated and spread outward to vague limits left and right. Through the courteous murmuring drift Phillipson and Harbelis wound resourcefully to Cahill, and halted, so that the unbroken gaze of his dark glasses stood squarely between them as though directed into the region beyond, where other boys moved in small groups toward the low flat building and into its suppression of hard light.

"It's liable to be getting hungry, right about now," Harbelis said. "That the truth?"

"Whatever it is, it could eat," Cahill answered. "Me and Zack. We could eat."

"Can he stay with you, till we finish?" Phillipson asked guardedly. "We'll give him something afterwards. Would that be all right?"

"Sure," Cahill said.

"All set, then," Harbelis said. "Let's go on in."

Phillipson touched the cloth of Cahill's sleeve, and the three turned gravely, as though over great depth, into the territory now losing its boys. No one looked back at them; they were alone as they reached the low wide stairs leading into the mess hall.

"We go up, here," Phillipson said, kicking the wood of the first step. Cahill nodded and slid his foot forward. From the beginning of his loss of sight he had had an image of himself that depressed him, and he had resolved never under any circumstances to allow it to take him over: that of pawing the air with a leg meant to climb an object that existed in the world, but not where he had supposed. When he toed the step, he shook off Phillipson's hand and mounted, counting and concentrating. The last board went solid with sound and feel; a whole building existed, balanced, and opened.

It was warm; half of his head unstopped, and with it he smelled a strong standing of fried food—probably chicken—on all sides more and more around him as he went forward. The breathing was that of a crowd, but the spaces for it were wrong. To one side and the other he reached though he realized that these gestures were, in their oddness, almost as humiliating as the pawing with a foot would have been—but he could not come into contact with anything on any side; yet nothing seemed to withdraw. He was in a kind of vastness in which many objects, many people were packed, or distributed in certain ways he could not image. The collected tenseness he was sure was there caused in him no sensation of being crowded or pressed upon, or indeed any of weight at all. Instead there came quickly—stayed, went, strove and barely stayed—the presence of an intricate force field around him, developing more and more as he bulked among the tables and along the suggested aisles. The air was full of obstacles: one continuous obstacle, in fact: a coil, made of nothing but coiling itself—no, made of wire, something that could cut, could wring your neck, slash your running legs out from under you or leave you hanging, dead, your feet an inch off the ground: wire, coiled, and massed in space, one endless strand of it, looped so hugely, in so ingrown and haphazard a way that it shook continuously, alive with itself, a haze of purposeless danger. In this, in the middle of it, and on down into the utter and innermost tangles of it, he edged forward, with the conviction that he could never touch any part of what enveloped him, though his hands and knees, particularly, were nerved for discovery. With all his hatred of groping and missing, he found himself with a

Expectant, poised but not stiff, most of the cadets made certain their lips did not touch each other, as the big half-stooped form in black worked through them with his dog, and with two soldiers they had once known.

powerful impulse to reach suddenly, to snatch, to whirl and
strike out, for contact with something seemed necessary and
would restore him. For a while
he had had fears that nothing in
the world existed—at least for
him—except by contact. He had
first noticed this in his apartment a few days after total blindness, and had dropped a coin,
and had not been able to find it
anywhere on the floor where it
should or might have been; but
he had heard it run: yes, run on
the hard floor, and even strike
something perhaps metallic, and
stagger and fall. It was the running that had filled him with anxiety and helplessness: the perversity: the coin had run, and there
was no way to tell which way or
how far. It lay beyond him; or it
lay nowhere.

Step by step he concentrated
on the yellow lights moving before his mind. All these others
are here, he thought. Wherever
they were, in whatever position,
at whatever distance, he played
over them: it must be happening.

No sound came from the arranged
boys, holding to the long shapes
of their tables.

They were standing. Not so much over them as through, an irregular
line of intent and expectation rallied and swayed, passed and came
back, through the fresh, warming, high-colored, and undamaged faces.
This might have been in some way connected with the passing of
Cahill's unseen and limitless mesh of lights over them, but however it
might have been, they stood as in a loft, and as though they had all just
taken off helmets, and then bathed, and come together into the subtlest
and most private groups, in animal remoteness and presence; here, in

intense clumps, there, in isolation; on a few there was a light sweat that curled hair.

"Here," Phillipson said. "Right here would be all right."

Cahill put out a hand, and found a chair back. Very slowly he pulled his overcoat off; Phillipson took it, and the hat. Cahill leg-felt himself into the chair. Food spread out before him, perhaps on and on, a difference of steams, and at first the surface that contained it seemed to progress and diminish beyond thought, for there was no way for him to limit its extent; but something scraped and rapped at the far end of it; there was a faint shaking in the oiled surface under the heel of his hand, and from it a quick tingle—almost electric—sprang also into the tines of a fork on which his thumb had come to be resting, tensing it with life, as though it might mean to pierce.

"You want me to serve you a plate?" Phillipson asked. "Do you like chicken all right? How about some peas and potatoes? And the bread's coming around."

"Good," Cahill answered. "That's fine; as much as you can spare."

Below the glancing interclash of metal, pottery, and food, Cahill stooped with his arm and tingling finger, at once found Zack between the shoulder bones, and slid his hand deep within the heavy fur. As he reached the dog's neck the head came up like a snake's, and he soothed and pushed it down, bent farther, and lightly worked along the long frontal bone of the nose to the muzzle breathing moisture and tenseness. He spread his forefinger and thumb tip for a moment on the eyeballs, holding them both and joining them in his hand, and then, with a private thrill of seriousness, lifted the saw-edged lip and ran his finger down and back along the deep teeth, set in the jaw as solidly as anvil studs, curved with delicacy and purposefulness.

"Here's the best we could get out of the cows around here," Phillipson said, guiding a glass of milk into Cahill's free hand.

"He's right," Harbelis said from the other side. "No matter how sorry it is, the Air Corps gets the best."

Cahill lost himself in food, and in one glass of milk after another. He was sure he tasted stone in it, and whatever there was in snow that was essential to it from the standpoint of color, but could not be extracted. The snow around the building where he sat was now mostly gone, he had been told, but from the basketball court he could still recall the creak and dead stop under his soles as he let go the ball, and he remembered also the changes in sound in Harbelis's shoes when he had sprinted past; he knew from only this one time, he believed, the difference between snow and sand underfoot, at least when someone was running.

"I wouldn't know what to do with a radio on my head," someone across from him said.

"It's just a whole new bunch of techniques," a lower voice answered. "You'll start getting some of that in Basic. If you can talk on the telephone, you can talk into a mike in an airplane. You tune them in, they tune you in. You say what you need to say, and so do they. It all goes back and forth, and you get somewhere, or come out somewhere, or do: you know, *do.*"

Cahill tuned, and for a moment formed replies, for he felt himself at no disadvantage. He had no more idea of what one might say from an airplane—to another airplane, to someone on the ground, to the light, or to his own ears or to the air itself—than these boys did, boys who were after all learning to be pilots, and for that moment, in that one fact of brute assessment, he felt himself their equal, and absorbed himself in their fragmentary assertions and exchanges on that basis. None of them knew what to say from an airplane, or how to say it, because the how had not been given.

". . . but right now you've got your instruments. That's all you need. You've got them, and you've got a visual on what you're flying over. And you've got the feel. We all ought to have a pretty good feel of the thing now, after sixty hours. I believe I do, anyway. I believe I know where the damned thing I'm in is at, all the time, and what it'll do if I do this, and what it'll do if I do that. I don't need to tell anybody about it, over any radio. Not now. That'll come later; we'll learn all that."

"I wish I could be as sure as you are," Harbelis said, unexpectedly at Cahill's side, where he had been forgotten. "I feel the same way most of the time—some of the time—but there's always a little something . . . especially . . ."

"Well, it's so cold. *Cold.* I come from Michigan, and I've never been as cold as I have here. It wasn't so bad, at first, up with the instructor. And when you first solo. You can't believe there's not anybody in the plane with you. You holler, you sing as loud as you can, you try to talk yourself through, but then you find yourself talking about something else: all kinds of things. Then you get back to singing. Did you sing? What did you sing, Stathis?"

" 'Rambling Wreck from Georgia Tech,' " Harbelis said. "I'm from the South, too, you know. South Pennsylvania."

"South of Macedonia, maybe," said another crossing voice.

"It's all different, when you turn out of the pattern," said the first voice. "All. Everything. When you make that one turn out, that one turn that sets you completely free, and then you look out . . . you just look, and see what you've got. What's coming right at you, and going on under. You've got it all to yourself: all that air. All that space. Wind. Everything that the wind can do, you can do."

"Seems like I've heard that before," a new quiet voice said.

Cahill tuned, waiting. This was another thing.

"As I came through the desert."

"Amen. As I came through the desert."

He understood the outlines of the table now, from the depth and placement of the voices, and the sounds of other eating. But his name had now been used, and he bent a little forward in its direction, as it was repeated.

"Mr. Cahill," said the auburn-haired boy who had brought up the desert, "I ought to explain to you what we're talking about."

"You see, Mr. Cahill," the boy hesitated at the word 'see,' and then went on. "There's a flight pattern, called a traffic pattern, around the field. If you could imagine . . .

. . . if you could just imagine this table lifted up, lifted right up from here . . . on up . . . on up and up, through the roof and all, and then at five hundred feet in the air, you know, stretched out, but keeping itself . . . its . . . its shape, kind of: well, that would be it. That's what gets us free of this place, the field, and that's what gets us back in it. We fly by the numbers."

Cahill submitted himself grudgingly to the abstract pattern—

69

surely rectangular, as most tables are—and rose into the night sky dead and inflexible, holding his shape.

"Is it clear tonight?" he asked the cadet to the right of him.

"Yes, it is," the boy answered. "Clear and windy. Some stuff may blow in later on, Weather says. I don't believe it'll be much, though. Couldn't be."

He remembered the winter stars as being intense, or rather as becoming more intense while one watched: an intensification not of cold but of remoteness, and with the striving to become something other than they were, or to cease. Why did he feel this? Like an animal, all his life he had seldom looked up, but his quick reverie did so now, and invented a rectilinear pattern of stars that he believed might actually exist. "Clear, you say," Cahill picked up and said.

"Yes, sir; seems clear. It just now was, at formation."

"I used to . . ." Cahill began. "It may be I used to remember . . . Isn't there a big . . . some big section of stars that's more or less in that shape, already?" Something from the night sky was left, or might have been.

"Yes," someone at a sharp angle to him said. "Yes. Right." Then, a little more boldly, "It's out there now . . . or maybe I ought to say 'up there'; anyway, it's getting up there. It's a real big constellation,

70

real strong; it's the biggest and prettiest thing in the sky, this time of year. You can't miss it, and you can't get out from under it. The name of it is Orion; supposed to be a hunter. Just looks like a big box kite to me, though."

Again, he made an effort to visualize, for the point seemed important to the boy. There might have been, also, he believed he sensed at once, a subtle change in his hearing pattern, a closing down of movement-noise, and at least one clink of glass or china muffled; touched, then held, perhaps. Quite still, he strove for a remembered pattern of any night sky of his life, through the sideways headlong sleeting of yellow lines, but he could fix nothing there: nothing that carried any impression of intent or design; a few vague points overhead, maybe, a suggestion of insanely shaken and dead-stopped powder, waste material timid and powerless, a strewn hesitant vastness. It occurred to him that he had never seen an entirely open sky, and that most people probably hadn't. There remained only what he had glimpsed through trees in clearings during hunting trips, or among roofs, or out of windows: what was up there took those shapes. In one of the few times he actually remembered looking up deliberately the recollection was oblong: that of the pool complex, where he sat tilted back against the wall of the dressing rooms, just out of the light of the lifeguard's chair, neither really looking or thinking, as he now found himself, and as he remembered he could not be sure the stars were not themselves tinted with green, with the otherworldly wool glow of side-lit underwater. What pattern the stars had was of summer; it was oblong; yes, over Ruíz's haunted and effortless swimming they had been there, as the boy lay forward in the fresh water, swaying onward side to side in his dark earthless muscularity, projected, underlain. There had been, Cahill remembered with a vicious pang like terror of some sort, the impulse—no, the compulsion—to glance upward, while the blank wall of the building buzzed with insects and pulsated against him with quiet machinery.

Yes, summer: the warm dark and the buried lights, and the boy upcast into himself like a strong shadow from below. But there was also the grim Atlanta midsummer sunlight, and Ruíz again, still in the pool, but the concrete bare and empty as he scrubbed with a brush on a long

71

pole, shoving and singing. From underfoot his naturally vibrant voice, rebounding from far and near walls, took on the qualities of its own echo. It was unplaceable, haunted and happy. As Cahill walked by the pool, now and then giving instructions, the voice would reach him through the shoes. In the slant, the light, blinding green of paint, Ruíz sang in Spanish. He sang very emotionally, like an Italian, Cahill thought, and sleepily, with nonchalant power, in vibrations that shook him through concrete, and with a sense of the most profound confidence and promise.

There seemed to be no breathing around him, and Cahill heard his own. Alone among these boys, he wondered why he had not brought Ruíz with him, then. He could have, easily. It was off-season, and Ruíz had little to do at the compound beyond keeping leaves and branches out of the empty pools and making minor repairs on the pumps and purifiers. But now, surrounded by this strange silence of boys and with the side of his foot against Zack's side, remembering the hanging animals in the metal cold of McLendon's shed, he was sure he had been right to come alone. He felt gathering in him the strength he believed he could call on more and more in the sightless realm which still contained everything that existed in the world, but that now was there only by hearing and touch; but deep and new-made, with him at the center. Ruíz was better off where he was. The closed park would keep for a week; there was little to vandalize; the skating rink was solid, and of close-grained wood almost impossible to burn. No one would be likely to steal the weights; the idea of a thief or several of them running off with barbells—*running* with them—was ridiculous: metal is cheap; anyone who would steal barbells would steal them because he wanted them, out of some commitment to an idea of his body and its improvement, and this was not likely. No bodybuilder would risk getting caught in the combined awkwardness and furtiveness of such an act; it would be better to be caught than be seen doing such a thing, or even worse, photographed. Ridicule is the one thing that the self-improver could not suffer. As for the Honeycomb, it was padlocked. Buster the snake would rest and rust on his coils, under the tarp where he waited, and after his return from New Mexico, where he might have gone to visit relatives, Ruíz would overheat the little office and work out, his T-shirt tuned to his skin with sweat, going transparent. Beside his old cot of clean rags, pliable with the washing he did himself, he would be working on his reverse curls, mauling sheer heaviness, the body distending and contracting with deep breaths in deep weights, rooted, straining into the mirror for expansion, the little-by-little growth of power, staring straight into its utmost effort. Weight lifting muzzled you, Cahill thought. Some of the more operatic lifters grunted, but Ruíz made no sound except the catches of breath which the changes in position and intensity of effort brought on. Purpose silenced him, and the effect was that of a self-sacrifice, a half-perverse burial in one's own body. Cahill had spent much of his adult life in the company of bodybuilders, lifting not fanatically as Ruíz did, but when released from the odd and demanding lifelessness of known metals he drifted; there was no other outlet. Ruíz also had singing, and it came from his bunchy sun-stained body with great resonance, a booming thunderous and foreign glory, demonic and human. Cahill's mind kept going back to this; the voice came most truly from the empty pool, from the reinforced underground; it was something from beneath, a human sound from an unknowable center, the tone of inhabited rock, invisible streams, the dead still alive.

The boys still waited, and he still strove for them, with them, because of them. He had only looked upward out of confined spaces; this occurred to him now for the first time in his life. And kites, yes, he had made them, as most boys have at one time or another; one boy had mentioned kites. The main thing in his memory was their color; the shivered reds were redder, far redder now than before, and the greens were more vivid, intently green; the kites beat in the air, yawing and nodding, confined and rising, trailing rags, neckties, oddments of old clothing whipping loosely underneath them as the sheeted sticks backed upward over the neighborhoods, over houses sometimes several blocks away, over the streets and the deadly wires, bravely, raised over their writhing ballast. And now, without his willing it, the sensation of a string lay through his fingers, going from him and at the same time feeding back into his hand with enthralling intimacy, with gigantic and secret involvement, with small quick lateral plunges, personal and nervous. The bare hand had been plunged into a whole new element, responding and attempting to control by instinct but not by understanding, by reflex, by the sense of fragility within the power of the air itself. And there was the falling that was always part of it: he invented rather than remembered how they fell. One of them, a dime store red, came down, world-forces failing it in some way, and everything was gone. The whole air slid wrongly; perhaps a strange setting of the hand was called for, but under the table he did not have it, and he watched

73

the triangle of banana-oiled fabric plunge out of sight into south Atlanta. He could not remember anything so obviously doomed, so vivid, so helpless, so silent in its disappearance.

"Box kite," he said. **"I'm not sure . . . I'm not quite sure."**

"Yes," the boy across from him said, "that's what it's like, if you look at it that way. The whole thing is like, well, like the shape of a box, a little lopsided, but a box, all right. It's got a couple of lines of stars inside it."

"Lines? What are those?"

Next to him, Harbelis said, "Those are supposed to be, kind of like a belt and a sword, you see. The whole thing is supposed to be like a great huge hunter up there, though if you ask me, you got to have a lot of imagination for it to be like that." A small boy down the table, speaking with conviction, said, "Those are probably the same people that tell you that you're supposed to be able to make the Big Dipper into a bear. But it just looks like a dipper."

A box kite; no, he had never seen an actual one. But now that the image had come up he remembered seeing the plans for one in a *Popular Mechanics* magazine, for he had collected those during grade school and high school and still had wired bundles of them in the boiler room of the swimming pool. He liked plans of all kinds; there was something about a blueprint, for example, that always filled him with an instant mixture of fear and hope; it was the color, perhaps. He had once heard the word *nightshade*, and without knowing what it meant or having any notion of the connection in which it was used, had since applied it to the color of blueprints. There was that night *thing* about that color, and the pale, fragile lines, the ghostliness that was at the same time the indication of the actual dimensions of an object: that might have *been* it:

an object that could by these moonlit lines be caused to exist: that could be caused. The box kite had looked very awkward, though; it took an effort to imagine that such a thing would fly. Somehow it must, but it still did not look like it should be able to; with no tail, but with an extra dimension, an inside spaciousness, that seemed a kind of mistake: that what should be a room should be at the end of a string, flat against the air, backing from the long front of the wind—it seemed more like something discarded or escaped from a house, from the basement or attic, a closet wrongly afloat in space. He had returned to *that* page of *Mechanics* all during his boyhood, however; though not for the box kite. Opposite the box kite were the plans for a rubber-band-powered twin-pusher model airplane. The curious shape of it fascinated him: the dragonfly skeleton of the wing and the long, delicately woven, criss-crossed V of the body, with the point of the V supporting the small flat tail to be thrust forward by the long graceful propellers, spread by the separation of the V just wide enough apart to clear each other. If he could see such a thing fly, a thing of such elusive lightness and strange-ness, he would build one now, at his age, even, if he could go back and find the magazine. At this idea, the loss of the possibility of it, a bitter rush of impotence and self-hatred, one of the few authentic ones he had had since his blindness, reached him, for at the same time he remem-bered that he had once seen such a plane, not exactly like the plans but at least a twin-pusher model, a very large one. Now this came back, and the part of life that surrounded it.

After graduation from high school, Cahill had wandered Atlanta, working at whatever carpentry jobs came along. The wandering, the aimlessness, were right for him; carpentry took care of the rest; that and the saving of money; it kept piling up, for he had nothing to spend it on. He had met Florence Acree when buying flowers for his mother's funeral; she was the one who had tried to become more than simply an interruption in his existence of measuring, nailing, wandering, and looking without thought.

The main color of Cahill's life had been gray. In memory he was surprised that there had been such striking other colors in it at unex-pected times, and that it was these that kept coming back. The cemetery was just outside the limits of southwest Atlanta, and the suburb nearest it was the grayest gray of all grays in the world. The street where the florist's was located was gray, except for the one store. The color of flowers in the window, especially the yellows, had been of such vivid-ness that he felt intimidated, but he had gone in and bought a wreath, awkwardly specifying which flowers were to be twisted amongst the wire mesh, picking up interest from his own directions.

It was Florence's unsmiling compliance that had impressed him, and something she had said about his hands. In his mind this came to a very strong focus now, and he sat among the hushed boys looking down in his mind at his hands among circling flowers. When she had remarked on the size and power of them, he had involuntarily tensed one of them, and the forefinger tendon had risen slightly among the swarm of colors, ready for anything, very solid, gray, very strong.

He had had plenty of time, and they had spent some of it together at meals, at movies, enough to indicate that they might be able to get along, for there were no particular difficulties—personal or family-related or financial—to overcome, and when he had taken her to the land he had bought for Willow Plunge and showed her the blueprint and the parts of it he had already begun to build, there had been another such moment as in the florist's shop, and they had agreed to marry. He had asked her among boards, and he saw her at the best she had ever been for him between slants of timber and new nails: her strong, listless face had remained with him surrounded forever by a bright evening haze of nailheads in fresh boards that gave off a sheen like metal gauze, a soft inhuman glimmer.

They had married and he had continued to work on the park, choosing his carpenters, plumbers, and engineers as though they formed a true elite. While Florence had got them into an apartment and furnished it, he had dug and rooted, joined and nailed, measured and sawed and directed. Once he had torn down almost everything he had put up because the plan was not large enough, and rebuilt the whole complex from the weathering lumber. The first construction had been too timid; it had lacked the two qualities he found he wished the place to have, height and secrecy, and he realized that it could have as much of these as he could conceive, draw, finance, and build. While the earth-moving crew dug the pools to his specifications he put in a high chain-link fence around the acres of temporary men, tractors, graders, and cement mixers, and day after day toiled upward on boards, raising two wooden towers, perhaps like those in minimum-security prisons. Climbing board by board, setting his feet where he had securely nailed the evenly cut planks, was exciting for him, and when he had finished he was sorry that he had not planned four towers instead of two, or that he had not made those two higher. In the sun, while he worked, he enjoyed the heat of the boards on one side of the structure and equally the shade on the other, the roasting bag of nails slung to him, and the sense of setting his feet on positions he knew were firm, the steadying of the new plank under the heavy spell of his hammer. There was something about nails and nailing that struck a very deep response in him. The long twenty-penny nails that went into the wood with one sound and changed it when they were all the way in, and had no more length but would hold, were unique and fascinating to him, and when he came down from the structures after each day of hammering, the even matched points on their west sides held in their symmetry a hard patterned brightness of accomplishment; they burned with a structured and separated fire, and he walked away from them into a satisfied and probably a deeper sleep. Now, as he pushed back from the mess table, he could in a sense feel the flight of the nails in his towers, and the physical force that had raised them each nail: the first lick that started the metal into the wood, the effort of the other arm to hold the plank perfectly in position, the preliminary lift of the heart, the new set of the brain with an essential rightness when the nail point touched then entered the second board, the increase in confidence as the holding power became stronger and the final filled-in, fulfilling sound when the nailhead was flush with the wood and then sank into it farther with the last blow, standing deep-centered in the hammer bruise: these were parts of a sequence he believed in with total bodily involvement; he experienced them day after day, and in the towers at height after height, leaving a sense of permanency in the level sun, fronting the air in tiny parallel flame heads, and as stable in the dark as any structure he could make. At night the air in those two places was solid with wood; this too was a fact. He had a camp chair in each of the towers, and sometimes would climb into the southwest one and read there by the single un-shaded bulb, or turn it out and sit listening to the distant traffic, and the human, antihuman noises that came up from the sump of tract houses across the suburban woodlots and weed fields beyond the undeveloped spaces of his land and the western reach of his fence. On these nights he would listen in an uninvolved way to the far traffic east of him, to the flurry of a night bird, to an occasional owl between him and the houses. His own solidity underlay him as he watched the moon come up and spread its image on the gently riffled water of the long main pool and mix there with the green light from underwater, minted, jelly-jewel-like. Once, for some reason, he had laid his carpenter's level on the railing before him, and watched the stillness of balance in the bubble hanging like quicksilver. The moon trued in the bubble, absolute trembling stability. That seemed to say something, and at that time he remembered the full of the sun, the last stroke of the hammer as it drove the nail beyond argument, and shook the building against him with the fury of his exactitude. At night the labored solidity of his concern was absolute, and when he came down by flashlight and drove home it was with an increasing irritation, over the months of his marriage, at the situation to which he would return. He had had no idea at all of what marriage would be like, but it was not long before he realized that he had very little to offer either his wife or anyone else under a permanent arrangement. Neither he nor Florence was talkative or demonstrative: both were matter-of-factly listless, she with resignation and because listlessness was an important part of her nature, and he because he genuinely did not like company of any kind, and because getting through stretches of time was difficult for him. There were very few incidents and images that were valuable to him, though there were a few that recurred unexpectedly, and seemed uneasy with meaning, strong and self-willed. He lived a couple of miles from the pool, and he spent most of the year of his marriage working out the details of the construction. From the beginning the project had the feel of success. Atlanta had nothing resembling it; as a point of fact had few swimming pools of any kind, and these were connected with public parks—one even with the city zoo—and would appeal to no one really interested in swimming, diving, or even in having a good time, with plenty of room and plenty of water. He wanted his spread to have an atmosphere of freshness, openness and uniqueness, secrecy and he felt that there would be an attractiveness about the place that would consistently fill its grounds during season but not crowd them. Even when he was home in the apartment with Florence, he still worked on plans and budgets, coordinating the board feet of the skating rink against the money he had borrowed from the bank, and shading and patching figures with a slide rule from trigonometry class in high school.

He and Florence seldom went out together. She was a good and reliable cook; he ate a lot of meat and candy, and often ate the dessert first. On weekends they sometimes listened to comedy programs on the radio, but the bursts of laughter from the studio audience bothered Cahill, for he had no sense of humor; the closest he came to laughing was whenever Molly would say to Fibber, " 'Taint funny, McGee," and Cahill would agree, his face near smiling. The peculiar battle of sex, in the bedroom of the thin-furnitured apartment, brittle with hard colors, was mainly a form of staring, as Cahill, propped on his rocky forearms, worked matter-of-factly, his jaw strong, the muscles there bulging from the double wad of gum he chewed while lifting weights, deep inside his wife, his body subject to the needful movements of buried work; he yet remained outside and above, clamping down on his teeth while she looked up steadily into his blue-gray eyes with an expression of questioning, an incomprehension that would finally turn to affirmation as her flesh took the matter of resolution away from her. Neither had stared down the other; if the consummation was a standoff, it was neither fulfilling nor frustrating; he would lie beside her for a while before sleeping, or, more than likely, get up and go back to his plans.

Only once had there been anything more, and this had nothing to do with Florence. On one of the side ladders of the intermediate pool a girl had slipped climbing out and peeled back the large toenail on her right foot. Cahill, who had been reading, he remembered, *G-8 and His Battle Aces*, whose cover showed G-8 in a Spad taking heavy fire from a red tri-wing Fokker piloted by a skeleton, had put the magazine down and circled the pools in response to Ruíz's calls and the assembling crowd of swimmers. He had looked down for a moment through the pink dry shoulders and the wet brown ones onto the writhing girl, her hands trying separately to get at her foot, but restrained by the lifeguard Darrell so that Ruíz could get a better look at the injury, and had, before he knelt beside her, glanced at the pool and seen, thinning out of sight, a pale swirling of blood, going everywhere into nothing. The girl was very freckled, fair, pale, and hysterical. When he concentrated on her toe, Cahill saw that the nail could go either way; it could either be torn off or bandaged back, though there was not much likelihood, he was sure, that it would regrow. Dropping among the others he had rested on his knuckles beside the legs of the pain-heaving teenage body.

"Just hold her for a second," he had said to Ruíz. Then, to the girl, "Bite down hard, honey. Bite down and grab onto something. It's just a little twitch." Before she had responded, he had torn the nail off, she had screamed and someone was wrapping the foot in a towel. Ruíz and Darrell and others had helped her back around the pool, sat her in Darrell's raised chair, and doctored her with Mercurochrome, gauze, and tape. There was iodine in the emergency cabinet, and Cahill thought of using it, but Mercurochrome would do, and as the girl sat with Darrell doctoring her the expression on her face, coming under control and yet tentative, was of such vulnerability that Cahill stood watching, quite silent, waiting for the tears to break and run, but they did not, either from the girl or from himself; there was that balance, and over everything the whole sun hovered newly, entirely fragile and human in a way that any light ever known could scarcely maintain.

Weeks later he still thought about it. Though he saw the girl again, now clear and bright, moving up the same ladder and walking over the same place she had lain and twisted, it was not this, but something different, something that still stood where he had been between the surrounded girl and the pool. Increasingly he was troubled by the strange vibrancy there in his place between the girl's body and the faint image of her blood dissolving in the water, the serene disappearance of it, the faint coils, lessening, like smoke, but not yet gone, for before that happened he had turned. At least once a quality akin to thin metal being wildly unbearably tuned came to his body, and this when he was deep inside his wife, and for an instant it entered the staring between them: a quality so frightening, so full of remote and baffling urgency that he had nearly buckled and given over the strong mechanical throe familiar to him, and lost its conclusion, and was beginning to fear that this would happen to him for the first time in his life when he realized that it had already taken place.

When the work on the first phase of his park complex was finished, Cahill had no reason to be gone from the apartment as much as he had when he was building the towers, hammering upward and truing the level, or waist-deep in red dirt going over the plumbing plans with the contractor. He took to walking to and from his park, even running a little, and on the way back would stand and wait, thinking that he could go in any direction he wished, up poplar trees, into any house.

In the apartment the silences had set in, worse and worse. He ate a lot, but the weight lifting, the walking and running kept him at an even two hundred pounds, ungainly, uncoordinated, but with the strength of will and stolidity underneath, his measurements increasing all the time, impressive, slow, and silent. The fact that his wife was pregnant was not important in any way: not mysterious, not part of him. Though he tried to go through the motions of sympathy and interest it was quite clear to her that he had none. The gradual remaking of her shape was something coming from somewhere else; from her not him.

He had supposed that people, when they had children, were able to remember their own childhood and from that, summon up or invent a common bond, but he had disliked himself intensely as a child, and could think of no good thing from that period that he might bring to bear and make work for someone else's good. He had grown up in south Atlanta, within sight of a tall square building that made bread and cake, and his sense of smell was still filled with sweetish smoke, part of the settled dimness of the neighborhood. School was mainly a blank, except for the marble games at recess and in the afternoons. His heaviness of leg and the slowness of his reactions had unfitted him for football, basketball, and baseball, and until he had been introduced to weight lifting in the last part of his thirties he had had little to do with his body and with organized sports. Stillness was the best, truest part of what he did; though he loved quick movement and speed, they were not natural to him. The position of marbles in a ring and his careful drawing down on them, the flick of the taw from his thumb, the ringed explosion, the picking off of the last marble, were things he missed when he left grammar school; in fact, he would like to have played now, were there any way to justify it. And yet he had a yearning for motion, if not of his own running, then of riding. The three bicycles he had had, and the several pairs of skates, were as present to him now as they had been when he was on them. Skating: that was close: that was near running. Alone, he had skated the streets of south Atlanta, swinging from one leg to the other along many streets, through rich and poor neighborhoods, past communities, stores, unknown schools with their frazzled poplars and empty playgrounds and the brick chimneys of their power plants. He remembered once going with a strong wind, and a piece of wax paper that had blown beside him, a foot off the ground for a whole block, the fragile paper twisting at his side like an obsession, its crackling drowned out by the rolling of his feet. There was his hour-long, five-time encirclement one day of the sewage-treatment facility, orderly and blank with hopeless water; most of his long forays through Atlanta were over level pavement. But toward the northwest part of the city the land steepened into little hills, and around his steady and driving sweep larger houses and grounds arose, and through these he would move, afternoon by afternoon, his feet planted in long splaying strides out-angled, split, dealt like cards from a hand. Sometimes, in these northern suburbs, he would be completely alone, and, trees on some streets closing almost over him in spring, he would power through that freshness in what might have been the strong swings and balances of a powerful sleep. That was best. On one rich road there was a tall house, off so far from the street that it seemed, except for the driveway, not really to belong to it but to another place altogether. A long blue-black car had pulled out of it once, just after he had gone by. Slowly he had wheeled and gone back to the driveway; the deep down-bellying hollow of it came toward him off a steep grade—a thrilling steepness, just to look at it—and rose again with short abrupt upsweep to the road. At the low part of the dip a creek ran under the drive, and with no feeling except a sense of necessity he had crossed it and with short, dogged stabs of effort gone up the drive, through the thick rich trees, to wherever it led, to come down. Where the concrete leveled at the top, he was still among trees, and could not see the house, and he listened for cars he could not have heard, so far off and down and leaf-screened they were, then sighted down, lined himself up, crouched on his heels, and dropped. His balance was good, and in the second before he was going so fast that he was swept into a really dangerous velocity, and could have fallen or shot into the bushes, or even grabbed one to save himself, he knew that he was centering into a condition he needed, and in the pressed fall of speed through green cloud and bloodless with urgency, he swung up from the heft of the earth and felt it fall away; when his sound changed at the creek he had hooked upward into the last rise, come clear of the ground, and seemed not able to return. When he hit, halfway across the deserted street, he had shot into another driveway opposite, this time only a gentle lift, spread his feet and spun on himself as he knew how to do, low-positioned, contained, self-solid with whirling.

There was something *in there* with him, something drawn into the most central of his spinning, from the outside world, from anywhere and everywhere, as from an infinite and ever-present waiting, an enormous hovering without air and without anything of the mechanical or the lawful, and he spun, as though enclosed in a live stone, dangerous, containing all fragility, impregnable with speed, then wheeling slowly down, restoring the trees and mailboxes to their places.

For some reason he had never tried anything dangerous on a bicycle, though he liked to ride almost as much as he liked to skate. But the larger wheels were not as intimate; he did not feel the road as cleanly and variously through rubber as he did through shoe-steel. The over-floating he did feel was another thing; he associated it not with a dangerous solidity but with detachment, ghostliness, disembodiment. He could not imagine or remember a bicycle in blazing sun; it was a thing of twilight, the thin, strong indirect penumbras of streetlamps and houses not so much quiet as hushed, and by some common consent, all gliding. He wished to be as quiet as they were, and, pedaling home from high school, he had made up a way to come, depending on the lights over the streets, which lit up in late fall at the time he started for home. Between Oak Street and Preston, on the corner of which lived a boy named Kytle Chesnutt, the first lamp came on in Cahill's distance. There were evenings when there was no traffic at all, and he could take over the middle of the street, directly under the lights, and move from one toward the next. The rest of the way was a preparation, the renewing and dying of his shadow; the first intensity of its blackness under the scalding lamp, the crouching, huddled intensification when he and the shadow were the same, then the throw-forward of the shadow-head, the lengthening of the image, the long faint stretching, the disappearance into new light, the far body waiting again on the distant cement.

The trips home were seldom interrupted. He generally circled his high school once or sometimes even twice to be sure the city public lights would coincide with his homing. In spring they came on later, and once he had stopped on the rise above the football field and track, and watched what was there: now one of the scenes came back, again for no reason. There had been—or was now, in his mind, at least—a peculiar importance to early twilight. A tall boy named Weeks was carrying two vaulting poles toward the distant gym, a building into whose roof a concentration of all the Atlanta gray was set, but in his recollection it seemed also to glow, as with a fire inherent only in gray. His school colors were blue and gold, and the gold trim on the trunks of the last boy on the track, one digging starting holes in the uneven cinders, was of an unnatural brightness; something about the sharpness of the gold was troubling; it was as if it had been drawn around the boy's legs and up the side of his hip by a living needle so sharp that the color it defined was too accurate to be possible, or to be understood, too sharp-edged, too thin, too bright to be logical. The boy came to the get-set position, his balance rising, his spine bowed and level, and waited. On the bank above, leaning on his bike against a telephone pole, Cahill waited with him, his eyesight grown just bearable with expecting the same signal. In the position of extreme tension, the boy's forelock above his eyes increased in heaviness and importance. Nothing shook; everything hung savagely at the highest point. Then, with an effect of fulfillment or outrage, the runner leaped. His first strides were choppy and to Cahill seemed slow; the leg muscles were too bunched and blocky for a sprinter—this would seem to anybody to be the case—but after the slow start and the stomping pickup, the acceleration in a totally unexpected way was remarkable; Cahill would not have believed it could happen, but he understood at once that he had not reckoned on two things that the boy, in the still position of tension, did not show: the enormous live power in the solid thighs, and in the curious, spurning back-kick from his ankles that slung the loose cinders spattering behind him. As he moved nearer and for a furious split second was level with him, it seemed to Cahill that he was in the presence of a new intensity. The sprinter came down with much more force on his left leg than on the other, so that he was not so much running as galloping, in a stepped-up lurching, splaying urgency; his animal-like motion, like one member of a terrified herd, was so riveting that Cahill felt, even now, in his mid-fifties and blind, that he could reproduce it pretty well himself, given enough space and an open track. The boy's speed peaked, and then peaked again, and then again; when he seemed to have attained the utmost of which he was capable, as much as, more than anyone could have asked, he made yet another demand, the leg beat increased, the gallop became more necessary, grotesque, and unstoppable, and Cahill felt that from his bank he should scream something out: encouragement, delight, consternation, or cry out to tell the boy that the insanity of effort was too much to be borne, that, like the slashing gold of his trunks, it was something that should not be in the world: something the world was not prepared to sustain, and should not be asked to witness. In his mind there was no end to this image; the height of the acceleration was what mattered, and Cahill barely remembered that, at what must have been its true utmost, the boy had leaped slightly as though shot in midstride, and with astonishing grace, come down, done several little hitch-kicks to slow himself, and with his hands on his hips and his bullish head down, had come to a walk, very solid, earthbound, flat-footed even, as Cahill wheeled into the traffic and into the self-shadows of the home route.

And another; there had been another episode like this. Dim with smoke: Atlanta had been dim with smoke, half blanked out. What should have been the vivid white of the dogwood flowers in Piedmont Park was as gray, in April, as anything else in the city. And yet he belonged there, he was more or less sure; he had rather be there than any other place he knew, among the huge Atlanta parks, the playgrounds and their games of lonely dodgeball, the baseball games where a ball was sometimes knocked from one diamond into another, or between the tennis courts, where the players were older, and sent the ball back and forth without sound, without communication. In these places in which he did not figure, in which he passed through like a ghost through walls, he felt his strongest sense of self, and moved for hours at a time, usually late in the afternoon when the leftover light seemed perfectly matched to the long stretches of well-tended vacant fields, like gigantic pastures with no cattle, no other creature, and especially no shadow fleeing across them. One could not hide; perhaps that was it. The sense of openness in the middle of the city was one he felt he understood, though it might have been bothersome to someone else. The far sound of the streets of Atlanta was barely heard in most of the places he traveled, but in what seemed to him to be the absolute center of the largest park of all, Piedmont Park, it would have to have been a very loud shout or scream even from inside it that reached him, standing in the midst of the enormous short-grassed freedom which faced away on all sides toward buildings so hazed and toneless with distance that they seemed to belong to another life that did not so much recede but kept an indistinct space between them and anyone who cared to look. Parks are made for old people, and if he had wandered there at the age he was now—in an air-cadet mess hall in wartime—he would not have seemed out of place; the larger the park, the older the men who should be wandering in it. He had seen many old men, some of them many times, but among them he was the only one not lost, the only one with no sense of futility and waste about his wandering. He felt right doing it, with the city opened wide above and around him; he liked the staying-open of it. It might have been that there were many possibilities in that free space; he was sure this was true, for on one of his Sunday walks he had come on a single boy, perhaps five years younger than he was, winding up the rubber bands of a twin-propellered pusher-model airplane with a kitchen eggbeater. The ingenuity of this appealed to Cahill: the using of an object efficiently for a totally different purpose than it was intended for; as he neared the boy he also saw that the plane was in design if not in exact scale the same as the one he had noticed years before in *Popular Mechanics;* it struck him that he had never seen one of these fly. This was one of the few coincidences in Cahill's memory, and though he was not inclined to mysteries, there was something about this situation which seemed to him more than mere chance. The two of them stood in the darkening openness of the city, and the boy asked Cahill to hold the body of the model while he wound.

He took the plane and turned it so that the boy could hook the eggbeater into one of the rubber strands. Its delicacy was extreme; yet the power and purpose of the shape were also impressive; one did not get to hold a thing like this every day. The V-form made by the two main struts was disturbing in its assurance; it was like a geometric abstraction, with the gaunt purity of a vector problem, the tension of a harp.

The booms were braced apart by an intricate crisscross of struts, and between these was strung, almost filigreed, a webbing of the thinnest piano wire Cahill had ever seen or touched. A kind of scientific gut-thrill was built into the thing, a combination of excitement and a mysterious fear; in spite of its arrogance, the whole craft was so lacking in weight, so easily threatened, so vulnerable that Cahill even now remembered that he took care not to close his eyes lest he inadvertently close his hands with them. But he did neither, and the model throbbed intently with the metal hum of the beater as the blades twirled and the long rubber band braided on itself and hitched into lumps. "I'm going for triple knots this time," the boy said, and Cahill nodded, holding, as he must. When the knots were set to the boy's satisfaction, he switched to the other strand and began again. While he did this Cahill looked quickly and entirely at the boy, now whirling the other band, turning his fist evenly over and over. He was tall, slightly studious, smiling; especially at the corners of his eyes and lips was an expression of glad purpose, of driven gaiety so wholly alien to Cahill's temperament that he was afraid he might end up staring at the other out of nothing but incomprehension, and had then looked down at the second set of knots. The new, fulfilled tension in the aircraft was as deadly and creative as electricity, and as the boy hooked the straining bands to the big light prop, Cahill was afraid that the massed pull of the elastic might crumple the frame, but it did not, and the frail cross-struts and wires waited in tensile patience. The boy took the whole craft from Cahill and faced into the red-gray light of part of the city.

The day was dead still. For a second he and the boy looked at each other, and at the contact the boy's youthfulness, studiousness, and eagerness increased. "This one just might do it," he said, tentatively raising the plane, his left hand under the middle of the body and the other holding the lower ends of the propellers. "There's one thing I forgot to do, though," he said. "Wind. I should have checked it." Then, "Could you do us a favor? Wet your finger and hold it up." Cahill, with a sense of strange rightness, licked the end of his forefinger, and then because of something else, some other element in the situation strange to him, slowly ran the whole finger into his mouth, withdrew it, and held it up inside the great open surround.

"Where is it?" the boy asked, his eyes moving toward different parts of the far city.

Cahill concentrated. On the knuckle side of his finger there was an almost imaginary sensitivity, a hint of movement so undefinable that it was more likely in the skin than in the air, but he pointed with the other hand and said, "I think that way. It's coming from there."

"That's good," the boy said, nodding. "That's the best. If we're right we might get a whole minute in the air; we might make it all the way out of this park over into the other one; over the lake, even."

Toward the glitter of the far lake the boy lifted the sharp prow of the aircraft and set its angle into the air. "Pray," he said, took two steps into the imagined wind, and, with a controlled slow-motion heave, let go the propellers and pushed. As Cahill moved to one side against the catch of his muscles that sought to fix him in place, the wings nodded and dipped to left and right, trued up, the propellers spun evenly, and the plane hovered upward more and more, with a strange look of penetration, of drilling-through. How long would those jammed rubber muscles last, Cahill thought; the twists and knots we put into that thing? And what did it matter? Yet, as quiet as the other standing beside him, he gazed into the flight, the tension across his shoulders and down his arms strong; the underside of the big model hung upward on the round shadows of the propellers, one yellow wing and then the other sheening, touching the low sun, balancing, rising smaller. It sought a level, then lofted from it; all rocking stopped, and the craft settled into a course so certain of its intent, its thrust of direction, its assigned altitude, that there was no way in which eyes could be taken from it. The V-shape began to be lost, and then was lost; the model was now pure wing, and that too was dissolving. As it disappeared for good Cahill had the impression that it had already begun to descend, so distant, so utterly destined and uncaring, so self-sufficient that the frame of air as he had held it with the knots muscling into the rubber, when his eyes had moved along the severe lacquer of the wing as though with a kind of perilous touch, a sense based on sight, but other, seemed something he should never have let go of, never have allowed to be taken from his hands; the starkness of design, the matchless and merciless fragility, the illusion of mindless purpose, held him, would hold him.

"One minute," the boy said. "One minute and seven, until it went out of sight. One minute and thirty now, but it's down. It's down now. I'll go see if I can find it." He walked off, and Cahill watched him to his bicycle, and part of the way along the park road and into the thick line of the lake, the browed glitter.

The old food was gone. He had eaten some soft and some hard, all to some degree salty,

now cleared from under him. On the metal tray something un-metal was placed. He picked it up and without groping found a spoon, lifted, his lips cooling, hovered and fed himself.

It was ice cream. The sweet-ness and coldness, the taste, un-freezing, was as thrilling as alco-hol; rough and feathery, grainy, reminding of snow, it might even have come from a home freezer.

A chair near him pushed back, and Cahill assumed that this was to give him and Zack more room, but before he could readjust himself a light touch on the arm stayed him, and he now under-stood that if he leaned to that side he would be moving into someone else's space, filled out deliberately.

"This is Malcolm Shears, our ca-det colonel," said Harbelis from above. "But nobody calls him Malcolm. He's either Cadet Colo-nel Shears or Shears."

"Well, which is it?" Cahill said, half smiling.

"Shears," the other said. "Or Mal-colm would be all right. It would be better than that."

"You knew my . . . you knew Joel, did you?" The closed si-lence between Cahill and the standing boy rarefied and deep-ened; nobody who was certain of a thing would have taken so long to answer, Cahill thought, and began to think of something else to say.

"I did," said the other. "I sure did. He was here."

Into his hand, which had just put a spoonful of ice cream down on the table, another came, about the same size as his, but with smaller bones. The strength was not equal to his, but it had reserves; at least some. Cahill imaged him as at least as tall as he, though probably not as heavy, thickset, and pulled together, perhaps a football player from the center of the line. Because the voice came from far back in the throat the eyes might also have been recessed. The chin would have to be strong. From these guesses, and as the details of the image strengthened, he imagined curly hair, coiled, close to the head, and twisted into itself by vitality. That would do; from now on that would be Shears.

"Maybe we can talk some in the next couple of days. I don't know when, though. I think the colonel and some of the others have got some things planned for me. But there ought to be time, somewhere."

He was shorter than Cahill, and even more physically powerful than Cahill assumed. His hair was dark blond, loose and light on his head, with a tendency to flop. His eyes were clean and grayish, and not inset deeply. About the chin Cahill was right, though not about the abruptness of its cleft, which was almost as though incised. His teeth were even and small. "Well," Shears said. "This is good. I mean, sir, it's good to have you here. We're all glad you came. I mean, if we could . . . if I could say it that way."

Since formality did not seem natural to the boy, Cahill was a little surprised at the "we will" instead of "we'll"; it did not seem to fit. But then, what had he

"We'll make it. Just leave that to us. We will show you."

89

expected? What would have
been right?

"They'll keep me in sight," Cahill said. "The colonel and
them."

"So will we," Shears replied.
"You can bet on it."

The chairs scraped and began to still, the general rising and standing
changed all relations in the room, Zack got to his feet, and Phillipson
and Harbelis guided Cahill toward the main aisle between tables. As
they moved, Zack patient and pressed against his leg, Cahill felt himself
given forward and into the narrowing pressures of a funnel, where the
bodies around him dropped away until there was just one boy ahead of
him and one behind; as though from under, a sense of quiet propriety,
of secret justice, came through him: that his son, though unknown to
him, had done this, had moved here, had known these boys, and that a
mortal war surrounded them all. His boy was dead, and many of these
would be dead as well, surely, here or somewhere else, but some of
them were laughing. This was strange, in this dark: this particular one,
with its blankness, its gradations. All were moving forward, and somewhere among them he was, also. It came as a heavy shock that this was
so; it was actually so. Something battered and then swung, and he
fronted into the other temperature, where weights, bodies were stepping downward, and hit the cold face on as it stood just there: immediate, lasting, penetrable, without anything against him.

This time there was no dream, as he lay heavily and peacefully. His
dreams were usually vivid and active, but this time, all night, nothing
had happened. It had occurred to him that dreams and memory—
especially dreams—were now his only form of sight, but in these his
vision was strong, full of sharply defined, quick-moving shapes and
primary colors, as though colors themselves were a kind of luminosity.
When he did not dream, and lay at rest, he looked in memory for
something to sustain the moment. His body, especially the power of his
hands and forearms, his stance as he stood or sat staring into sparks and
darkness, talking to someone, could do only just so much; the strain of
being, of existence on his terms and no other, was physically exhaust-
ing, and he longed for freedom from it. He welcomed his active sleep,
in which he ran, bicycled, and skated, and knew people who liked him.

90

"Zack," he said. He listened for the dog to stir, for the sense of balanced weight moving over the floor, the click of nails. But there was another sound here, and he began to pay attention to it. You can hear a long way in cold weather, he thought. Sound comes well through cold, and the more merciless the cold, the more the sound stands out. This must be dawn, he guessed, or before it, for that is an engine, probably an aircraft engine, and therefore at the base. He remembered now that it had started a short time ago, in the last of his sleep, and he wondered why he had not made some kind of dream of it, for he sometimes felt that a part of his mind had the ability to do things of this sort. The sound had begun as an abrupt puffing cough, a splintering shot, like a rifle, a small unexpected blast, and then it lifted into confidence, rising with challenged effort, and at the same time riding savagely, being given off as though something were being held to another thing, as a chisel to a grindstone, a rasping, uncompromising statement. Another such sound joined the first, tuning, failing to tune to it, sawing up and down, in and out of the first thin, guttural roar, but increasing it. Cahill had heard a noise like this before; several times, in fact, when on one of his bicycle rides near Southwest Atlanta he had for some reason, perhaps because he did not know the area, gone past the Ford assembly plant there, and had heard from several blocks away the hemmed, intense humming of hundreds of machines. There was something about the closed-in condition of the sound that was deeply disturbing to him, and he had gone back once or twice to hear it, at first to keep it and then to get rid of it, to forget it forever. But he had not forgotten it, and here, as a third engine joined the first two, and then a fourth, perhaps, and then others, he felt once more the motion of the unfamiliar leafless streets under the wheels on his feet, and turned away from the factory, though it followed him. But the engines to which he was now listening did not have the trapped, buried, sleepless sonority of the mill; it was open, free, and, remote as it was, necessary, adventurous, powerful, and self-deciding. His heart responded, and his brain cleared. "Zack," he said again. With his outside hand he touched the floor, and felt the change in it as Zack approached, the unhurried slight room-tremble, the distributed balance, moving. "Come here, big boy," he said. "You big, heavy-headed devil. How're you doin'?" He put his hand out into the room, away from the bed, wherever it would go. But nothing touched it; instead, over one side of his open face, a slight heat developed, as though the air were closing and sweating. The warmth lessened, was renewed, not heavy, but coming from a body, rhythmic, patient, not striving, expectant. How alone this place is, how very far from everything, he thought, and here I am, as blind as the dead, not even knowing why I am here, and yet my face is warm with the breath of this thing, of this big dog I brought with me, that I don't even know very well. "But what a head you got on you," he said, and felt between his own face and the breath, to the nose, and then back over the skull until the flat of his hand spread over as much of it as it could. He had never been so sure of himself. The far engines seemed to be a part of this moment with the powerful animal, to bring into the situation of which he was the center the outside world as well, and because of this he believed that he had an authentic image—a vision full of power, certainty, control, and delight—of aircraft lined up in the gray distant openness, held back, eager, sending the sounds of their engines amongst each other in a defiant ongoing accord.

Into this he rose, and with Zack crossing with him, and one hand out, went a few steps toward the sound, feeling tentatively for wall or window. He anticipated board or chill glass, and was unprepared when he touched a substance that gave, that rustled and rattled. For some reason the shade was down, and he fumbled for its bottom, pulled down and rode the sheet up in his hand, and then on impulse turned loose and let the shade whip onto the roller and bat and battle there until it was still. This is glass now, sure enough, he thought, and touched in front of him at throat level. It was glass, the pane in-sweating.

He remembered now the perfect innocence, the involvement and self-complicity, of drawing with his finger on a winter window, where nothing could be subtle, or made of strokes that were not broad, and the childishness and harmlessness of doing this. With the tip of his forefinger, idly, imagining the drops running downward from his movements, he drew first a circle, and then went over the same area, with a circle inside the first, as he believed.

He pulled back, thinking of

Intently, with his breath going onto the pane as he drew, his face closer to the glass than he thought, Cahill marked out an oblong figure whose ends did not connect. Before it was complete, his breath closed over it, and he drew, where it had been, a smaller

magic. It had been a long time since he had drawn on a windowpane, but it seemed natural now. In his mind he drew, and saw what he drew, and the sparking gold shot through the frozen, crude circles he imagined. Again, it was like his childhood, a place and time he seldom went back to, except in a few images in which he could not help it. But now, with blindness growing longer and longer behind him, he remembered more; he remembered now: the house off Moreland Avenue, hardly more than a shed, a kind of squatters' shack so close to the other two larger houses on either side that there was only a two-foot space between them. He remembered the red rim of the stove lid in winter, and the curly hair of his older brother, Perrin, who fought semi-pro, welterweight, under the name Kid Tanazian.

and almost perfect circle; this disappeared also into his breath.

He stepped back and put up his hands, as Perrin had showed him. They had gone through the moves of his fight in slow motion, and Cahill went into the motions again, backed off a little from the window. He pushed out a left softly into the air, as in a free dream of constricted but determined motion. Stepping into it, he crossed a right. His heart increased, and the sparks of his blindness, it seemed to him, turned slightly red. He moved back; he moved from side to side.

He crouched a little, he weaved

like Dempsey, he stepped forward, he went in, and, a little faster than true slow motion, he speared with the left again, toward his brother's good-humored face, where Perrin, on his knees to equalize the heights, grinned and left himself open.

The glass kicked and rattled. He had touched it, but only at the end of his jab. He went forward and felt; it was not broken, nor cracked. Perrin was dead of Graves' disease at twenty-five.

"A hole in something," Cahill said aloud to himself. Before him now what must have been the intense and almost fiery gray-white of the window frost seemed to him somehow visible, an opening into the world, and in which there might actually be visions, reality a truth you could see.

He closed his hand to one finger, and drew downward on the pane; and again. His mind rushed with early memory, then blanked. Again and again he drew, pressing harder on the downstroke, then changed and slashed across, helplessly moving with fury. Something came from this; leaped suddenly to him from nothing. The dead cinders of the track beside the downtown Atlanta high school extended the splattered birdlime of its lanes and the stocky sprinter charged down them, his

What little there was of a pattern disappeared quickly, as clearness showed through, smudge by smudge, rubbed into existence as through clean sweat. The few stores of Peckover stood left and right, all as though held in the far sound of engines.

brutish head forward, solid as a buffalo, and, as memory enlarged him, came down to only the slashing and shock-livid gold stripe of the side of his trunks.

Across the street a man in overalls and a red-and-black checked hunting cap silently rattled the front door of a hardware store. A little boy, hatless, but his light hair moving with his own motion as though by wind, went by him.

He turned, and felt the room square around him. He understood it; he learned such things quickly. Facing the door, he knew the bed to be on his right, against the cold wall that nothing could change. To the left was a dresser, in the top drawer of which lay his shaving gear, and the instrument case having to do with his disease. The small bathroom was next to that, and, feeling for the one chair he had not yet completely mastered, because, earlier in the room-space, he had moved it and was now not sure where, he went to the dresser, took out the case with the insulin bottle, hypodermic, and disinfectant, and came along the wall to the bathroom. Working with concentration, and using the sink as an assembly point and base—after first having found and placed the chained drain plug in its socket—he drew out by feel and by the length of the plunger a dosage of insulin. He straightened, bent, swabbed an area of his stomach next to the navel with disinfectant, pinched up that part of himself, and sank the tiny braced pain of the needle, concentrated as a wire, between his thumb and forefinger. Dropping his other thumb back to the plunger head, he drove the chemical down.

Since he had first been on insulin, he had always felt cheated that there was no positive effect on injection; or afterward, either. "The effect is that there *isn't* any effect," the doctor had told him. "It's just that you feel all right, and until the next injection, if you hold your balance and eat what we tell you to eat, you'll go on feeling all right. That's all there is to it." That's all there is to it, said Cahill, pulling out. He repacked the implements, put them back in the dresser, moved across the room toward the bed, met the chair, which he now placed definitely at the head of the bed, between it and the closet, dressed, and with Zack following without command opened the door and began the eight steps that would fall away into the staircase, but would also produce the solid slant of a railing. Finding these, he went down almost as though he could see. Voices came to him, and the chink of metal and china. When he was partway down, a swath of cold air touched him in the hands and face, as someone opened the front door, coming in or going out.

At the bottom of the stairs he waited quietly, sure that the people at the counter and in other parts of the room were either looking directly at him or were swinging, at this second, in his direction. Conversation tailed off; the nearest voices dropped, until McLendon's, which he recognized readily, spoke with no special pains, but as to anybody.

"You all right?" McLendon asked. "The room all right? Is it too cold up there?"

"Yes," Cahill replied to the first question, his head correctly set toward McLendon's; they were the same size. "Everything's fine. It's not too cold; I like it a little cold, at night. If you have plenty of blankets, that's the best way to sleep. You're looking at the proof."

"That's good," said McLendon. "The only thing's that the shade don't work right, but . . ." He broke off.

Cahill picked up. "I know what you mean," he said easily. "I did fool with it, and it jerked away from me. I just left it."

There was great silence around them; McLendon said, "I just thawed out some pig meat, for your dog. If you want to come on with me out to the kitchen . . ."

"Sure," Cahill said, "That'd be fine. I don't want to run you short."

"That won't happen," McLendon said. "He's a lot of pig; takes a lot of whittlin'. We're a long way out from the bones; *any* bones, except the tushes."

"This is sure nice of you," Cahill said, and meant it. Then, "Could I beat you out of some of them sugar cubes I done asked you for, on back a while?"

"Sure you can. I've got some, and I know where to get some more. People who run restaurants—and I mean *any* kind of a restaurant—can get holt of it. Maybe not later, but we can now. How many do you need?"

"I'm not sure," said Cahill. "Three or four would be all right, I think. I ain't never had to use 'em, and I don't plan to. But if you've got some, I'd feel safer. Or at least I'm supposed to feel safer."

"Here," McLendon said. "You want me to put 'em in your pocket?"

Cahill held out his square hand and took the papered cubes. McLendon very gently put two fingers on Cahill's left shoulder, as though to turn him; Cahill turned, and stopped when the touch left him.

"Straight ahead," McLendon said. "I'll get the door."

Cahill and Zack moved forward along the grouped men at the counter and the empty seats between. Nothing touched them. Cahill waited for the change of airs to show when he passed into the kitchen. The new one came, with warmth, steam, the smell of bacon, onions, toast, eggs, meat, coffee, grease.

"Do you want something, yourself?" McLendon asked, a little embarrassed at having thought of the dog first.

"Yeah, I sure do," Cahill said. "The way it smells in here, I could eat up the whole place. How about some kind of a bacon sandwich? Since it seems like there's more bacon around here than anything else."

"You got it," McLendon said. He went somewhere near, quickly, and in a moment stepped back and tapped Cahill's hand to get him to raise it.

"Here you go," he said. "Now we'll get your black wolf some bait. Come on out here, just a little ways."

He took the sandwich, and biting through soft bread, crisp salt, he moved with Zack out through another door into the half-cold of a latticed porch.

"He knows where it is," McLendon said. "Is there something you have to say to him, to get him to eat?"

"Not always," Cahill said, as Zack, who had been whining, confused by the smells in the kitchen, now bent his head, snarling as if to fight, toward the shallow bowl with the big fistfuls of meat. "Go ahead," he said, tilting his face down. "Go ahead and eat, Jughead. Eat it up."

He had fed Zack many times, on almost everything he could think of, including leftover vegetables mixed with dog food, on table scraps, even on bread dipped in gravy. But now as he listened there was a fury in the dog's feeding that was like an attack. The scraping, the sense of headlong scrambling that came back to him reminded him how secure he was, in the isolation of his gold-shot void, from such feverish participation. There was

Zack picked up a chunk of meat, dropped it, picked it up again, chewed with his whole body, his muzzle kicking the oval steel pan this way and that. McLendon watched him, his arms folded, his

97

not only the comfort of his remoteness but an assurance also in the fact of savagery itself; it was like the sound of the far engines a little earlier: there was nothing he could do; there was no connection with him; he was invisible, and could enjoy the unstoppable and doomed parts of the world, the savage and foolish frenzy outside, wherever it might be, however far or near. The shuffling and scraping of the dog moved away from him, and then back. It might have been that the floor was uneven, or the bowl top-heavy or lopsided; he would have sworn that there was even an instant or so of spinning, and again he thought of the engines, and what he envisioned as the circles he had made, the crystal wheels on the cold window, then of the meat itself, the woods-meat, and the boar as he had felt it in the shed, the hanging tusks and the solid, stiff-haired body. He wondered where this meat had come from; the thigh, probably; as McLendon had said, far from any bone: in the frozen shed now, the boar with its congealed snout-blood, and the iron wound. The metallic angling underfoot continued this way and that; he wondered if Zack would be able to corner the bowl somewhere, finally.

eyes alert and sympathetic. He glanced at Cahill, who rubbed his chin, as he seemed to stare through the lattice, mysteriously and eagerly.

McLendon continued to look at the blind man, as his blank green eyes watched the lattice.

"How did you like the base?" McLendon asked.

"Well," Cahill said, half smiling, "it was all right. I can't really give you much of an idea, but I listened to it the best I could. There's a lot of noise around, out there. All kinds."

"A lot of noise and a lot of boys," McLendon said helpfully.

"A lot," Cahill repeated. "How many, do you reckon?"

"I've been told three hundred. I've never been out there, but there's supposed to be some sort of air show on Sunday, and I might go out then. Maybe we could go out together."

"Could be," Cahill said. "I'll have to see what happens between now and then. This is all new to me, you can believe."

"It'd be new to most anybody, I'd think," McLendon said. "I'm damned if I'd know what to do."

"Well, I don't," Cahill replied. "I don't have no idea. But the people there are tryin' to do what they think *they* ought to do, and I'm just followin' along with them. Me and Zack."

"Did you meet the head man? The colonel? The commandant-y?"

"I met him. I met him first of all. Of all the officers and such, anyway."

"What did you think of him?" Again McLendon caught himself speaking as though to someone who was not blind. This was not only easier, he was surprised to notice, but more natural.

Cahill thought for a moment, and as he did so his right arm rose a little, involuntarily, as he remembered extending his hand for the colonel's expected handshake. Then, drawn toward its own body, the hand felt for his coat pocket and went down into the cloth there, no darker than any other dark.

The elastic of the goggles was first, he looped it over thumb and forefinger and tested; it pulled to bring his fingers together; live resistance. With care he picked up one eye plate into his palm, and felt, through the splintered powder still coming away, the diagonal crack, splintered, like a shape out of lightning.

"I've only met him once," McLendon was saying. "I didn't get no very clear impression, neither." He hesitated, then went on, at first with hesitation and then with conviction. "A lot of people don't seem to like him," he said. "I don't know what it is, exactly. It's not just that he's from outside. Hell, most of the boys are from up North, too, or from out West somewhere. But the colonel has got . . . has got that way about

99

him, of saying things that's . . .
well around here, nobody's used
to hearing anybody be that *definite*
about what he says. You know
what I mean? I mean it's just
something about the way he tells
you a thing."

"You mean he's an asshole," Cahill said, and for the first time really smiled. "Don't you?"

"Well," McLendon said, glancing to one side, "I don't know if I'd put it that way, exactly. To me . . . well, to *me* . . ."

"I just met the man," Cahill said, "and I don't know for sure whether he's an asshole or not, but I'd bet on it. And if you think so, that clinches it."

"Clinch it, then," McLendon answered with relief. "He may be doing fine out there. Them planes are in the air all the time, and that's supposed to be what it's all about. As far as I know, the job's gettin' done, and like you hear all the time, there's a war on. But he's too sure of everything, when he talks to you. And he looks a little too much right at you. That ain't natural."

Cahill swung as though to look right at him, took his hand from his pocket, made a fist, and punched deliberately, with friendliness and some force, finding McLendon's chest, as he felt he probably would.

"I've got to go back again today, and meet some other people." He waited a moment. "This must be crazy for them, too, you know. They don't know what the hell to say to me, and I don't know where to start in, either. It's kind of an unlikely situation, and I've got an idea I'll just be movin' around—that they'll just be movin' me around from one place to another, from one person to another, and I'll just sit and listen, I guess. Then I'll go on back to Atlanta in a couple of days. There's some things to do there."

"You go ahead and talk to 'em," McLendon said with his eyes both mystified and brightening. "I'd like to hear what they tell you. You seem like you're a real good listener," he added, fearing too late that he had made one observation too many.

"You can see why that might be, I reckon," Cahill answered. "I don't think that people who ain't blind can really know what things sound like. I mean *really*, the way they *want* to sound, from the middle. I don't think I ever heard the wind, till about three or four months ago. Not the *wind,* not the wind when there's nothing to see blowin': nothin' of it but the sound. There's the feel, too, but sometimes you don't have that. It's the sound: *all* of the sound. There ain't no way I could explain it to you."

"There should be plenty of wind out there," McLendon said. "Used to be, two families owned all that land. Old man Trexler owned part of it, the part that backs up on the reservoir, and Corley Pettigrew had the part where the airfield and the buildin's are. I used to be out there all the time with my own dogs, runnin' rabbits. It's real strange, but the whole place never had many trees on it; it was all empty, just weeds and wind. It was so wide open and flat. We're used to hills around here; the land has a nice roll to it, mainly; a nice easy roll; you can live with it. But up on old Pettigrew's place—I never went on Trexler's because I didn't know him, and he didn't come into town much—I used to tramp around in the fall and on into the wintertime, about like this here, until the cold and the walkin' done tired me out. Pettigrew's place was just one big field. He had a couple of dozen head of cattle, you know, and enough corn for the stock, but in the winter there wadn't nobody there but me and my dogs, movin' around thisaway and thataway. So *much* field seemed like it bothered 'em; they was always runnin', and never come up with anything. I killed three rabbits in ten years, and all it left me was worried and nervous. The way the dogs sounded was not quite right; their carryin' on over nothing—no rabbits, no nothin'—was more than it should'a been, and there wadn't no place you could go, except back to the highway or the dirt road up to Pettigrew's house. When you first come into the field and knowed that it was all there waitin' for you, and that nothin' would happen, there was somethin' terrible about it, and you couldn't hide from whatever it was. All this I might just'a made up; it's all changed now, with so much racket and activity, and the planes, and all. But there was one thing that might'a caused me to remember it like this, I recollect. It seemed like the thing that should'a happened to anybody who was to go out there by himself, when it was as cold as this, and dark almost like the first part of the night."

Cahill nodded, smelling bacon freshly placed in grease, the hiss and the smell connecting.

"I can squeal like a rabbit," McLendon said matter-of-factly.

"You can?" Cahill asked with interest. "Why do you do that? Why would you do it?"

"No, see—it's like a varmint call. Things that eat meat; if there's any of 'em around, they'll come see—they got to come—see what it is."

From a low tone, found as though merely somewhere unnoticed in the uneven press of voices, fed only on itself and lifting through pitch after pitch, a scream so thin and pale, so lost and desperate, so penetrating, so hanging, so echoing and beseeching that Cahill touched his glasses in appeal from it, developed, rose with a shrillness that shook and all but broke tooth metal, and was there, for its own purposes, between Cahill and McLendon. Cahill beat the air with his hand to calm the cry, something in him violated, gone-beyond, outraged.

"That's enough," he said, as the scream broke off. Against the side of his leg Zack appeared, his barrel tense with uncertainty and body force. "That's enough of *that*, for a whole lifetime. My life, anyway."

"That's a rabbit," McLendon said. "You'd never think that anything so little and skinny as these rabbits around here could make such a racket. But they do, and that's when the varmints will come, as quick as they can get there. It's somethin' they know. They know it, and they been knowing it. This one time I was telling you about, I was doing what I just now done."

"Don't do it again," Cahill said, half bantering, but only half.

"Don't worry," McLendon said. "You don't think I want this place filling up with foxes and weasels, do you?"

"Okay, so what happened?"

"It was gettin' along in the day, a day a lot darker than this one, and about as cold. There was nothin' in Pettigrew's big field, and the wind was down. I remember feelin' like the place didn't really belong to nobody, and there I was right in the middle of it. I thought about what I might do, just for the hell. I had my gun and my two redbone dogs, and I thought, since my old man taught me how to make the squeal a long time ago, that maybe I just ought to do it, to see what would come. There was things that was cold and hungry around there, and they had to have meat. Anywhere there's woods—they was maybe a long ways off, but all around that big field, they was there—anywhere there's grass and weeds, they're there." He paused, "You know, you'll do some strange things when you're by yourself, even when you're right in the open, that anybody that wanted to could see you do. I looked around at the cover, any place that a fox might could hide, or come up through. There was a thick place full of briars and beggar lice, and I turned that way, took a good close look at it, and then squealed one long time."

"Hold back," Cahill said. "I'll take your word for it. So will Zack."

"I made it loud, and high as I could, and then I felt like I could do a little more, if I tried, so I went at it harder, and tried to make it higher, and it was workin'. You know, what you're tryin' to do is to make it sound like a rabbit with somethin' after it, that's hemmed up and can't get away, or a rabbit that somethin's done got hold of, or one that's hurt real bad. The more scared and hurt and high and dyin' you can make it sound, the more and quicker the meat hunters are gonna come after it. That ought to tell you somethin' about the way things are put together."

"Did a fox show up, finally? A weasel, maybe? What?"

"Nothin' on the first try. I was watchin' the brambles, about fifty yards off. I figured that if I could call him out of the tangle and get him to come a little ways out into the open, I was pretty good. It was my idea to get him to show himself, commit himself, like they say, and to see how far I can make him come. Then when he wouldn't come no farther, I thought I'd probably shoot him. But that's not what happened."

"All right," Cahill said, picturing the gray field and the low light, and the frightening, breathable openness around the single figure. He had it. "All right. Go ahead."

"Somethin' just *paralyzed* the air right behind my head. That's the only way I can explain it. Somethin' just took it apart. It was so quick I thought maybe somebody had shot me, but all I heard was one big soft *blash*, a kind of a rammin' whoosh, like a couple of big thick feather dusters beat together. Then it went on by, and up."

"Owl, maybe?" Cahill ventured. "Owl blindsidin' you?"

"No." McLendon shook his head. "It should have been a owl, if it was anything. But it wadn't. The shape was not right for a owl. It was either a great big hawk . . ." He broke off. ". . . but I will swear to you to this day that it was bigger than any hawk I ever seen, and there's a lot of hawks around here. If it was not a eagle, I'll eat it. Or I would, if I could'a caught it. I stood there and watched that thing go on up, on those wings that were so long and broad that there wouldn't be no picture or movie, or nothin', could ever give you a real notion of what they was like; I never heard nothin' but that one beat on the air right next to me."

"That's *somethin'*," Cahill said, finding nothing else to say.

"It is, I guess. But it still ain't the main thing."

"What do you mean?"

"I mean that thing went on up and started to turn, and right there I knew there was a connection. I mean a real connection that I could make."

"So what did you do, then?"

"I squealed again, and he circled and come down. He come down, and he come down some more, and *on* down. He wadn't confused, because the right noise was there; right for him, something he knew. He came down to about ten feet over my head, and went around twice't. You never saw nothin' like it; I turned right around with him. And then I quit, and he rose on off and left."

"You quit? Why? You had somethin' goin', I'd think. Why'd you quit?"

"I don't know. It was too strange, I reckon. I was afraid of what might happen. He wouldn't give up, while I was soundin' off. He couldn't believe that nothin' was there, nothin' was hurt. Nothin' was dyin'. He couldn't believe it was not somethin's last breath that had done called him in. It seemed to me like the wrong thing to do, to keep goin' on too long."

"And that's all, huh?"

"That's all, but if you could'a been with me, you'd'a knowed somethin' new about the real sound of things. That's one you would remember, I can tell you. Just that one big soft rammin' lick. The rest of it was just me, makin' a squeal, and him goin' around, and me turnin' around with him twice't, and comin' out right in line, again, with the brambles. That's all. I shucked the shells out of my gun and come on back to town. I left my scream out in the field. By God, if you'd'a heard it out yonder, you'd'a believed that anything could hear it, anything would come, no matter how far off it was. But I left it there. Far as I'm concerned, it belongs to that field now. Let the people who believe in ghosts around here listen for it, when the wind falls off."

"They might be surprised," Cahill said, thinking about listening in large fields. "News right from the almost-eagle."

"Sure. The almost-eagle and the no-rabbit. That's where they are; out at Pettigrew's. Listen, from behind your head, if you can hear it amongst all them engines. It's just a puff, like a soft sandblast, right behind you when you're thinkin' about somethin' else. I can sure remember that thing, just that one second. It was different. It was, you know . . . it was what it made the air do. You know, *do*, what somethin' *else* could make it do." He waited a moment, looking up the line of men at the counter. Corporal Phillipson was coming along it toward them. "Here comes your boy from the post. He looks friendly."

"All right, Zack," Cahill said to the floor. "Get your head out of your boar bowl. Let's go hunt 'em."

When Corporal Phillipson withdrew, Cahill waited with his hand over Zack, expecting the door to close. He did not like the uses of thin wood, and he would have preferred the ill-fitting sound of it to be over and done with, and to be enclosed in the room with the colonel and the other person who was in it with them; whose feet were standing, and scraped nervously or eagerly. But the door did not close, and he sat as though in a corner of a large office, with typewriters a part of it, voices of men talking about the cutting of orders, plans for a weekend party in another town, the weather, the progress of the present classes.

From the creak of a chair, a rolling of casters, a spring-release of weight, Cahill guessed that the colonel had risen, and would probably be moving toward him. Slowly, first pressing Zack's head down, he got up, took off his hat with his right hand and put it in his left.

Cahill waited; someone must speak.

Cahill stayed with the words, the information. But his interest was in the man who had not yet spoken. He turned his head from the colonel's voice; the third man was somewhere else. He had come to assume that such apparent inattention to speakers on the part of the blind was not necessarily considered impolite, and he no longer worried about it. He put out his hand, and it was taken.

There was force in the hand, and Southern-country in the

Three of them were standing and facing.

"This is . . . I want you to meet Instructor . . . Civilian Instructor McClintock McCaig. He was Joel's instructor, the . . . the whole time." Colonel Hoccleve grew less hesitant as he went over actual facts he knew. "Instructor McCaig—the boys here call him Double-Mac—was with your son in the air more than anybody else was. Anything you want to ask him about that, he can tell you."

"This is somethin'." McCaig said. "I didn't have no idea. I

voice. At first the voice seemed affected; the most curious mixture Cahill had ever heard of the thin-nosed, assertive, half-defensive tone of Appalachia and of the one or two Texans he had met, and the soft, considered accents of old-family Southerners, which he had heard a few times in banks.

He said "col-yum," Cahill noted. That's a rich man's word; you don't hear it all the time.

Cahill invented him, putting together an image, adding to it, changing it. Around thirty-five or maybe forty, he made Mc-Caig. The voice and the hand were both confident, and the overeagerness was explainable. From the tone of some of the words he sensed also a leanness of body; it would not have been the way of a fat slow man to speak. He waited, listening to what the image said, though the figure in his mind did not move

mean we just . . . this is somethin' that . . . well, I just didn't have no idea. I'm glad you could come up. We're all so sorry. We're just so sorry. Me, I'm the sorriest. Nobody could feel as bad as I do."

"It was just one of those things," Colonel Hoccleve said. "It happened, and nobody will ever know why. These things are so final, though. There's not anything that anybody can say. We know that. But if you want to talk to the people here about Joel, this is the man to start with."

"The first time I ever saw him," McCaig said, "he was in the middle of a column of threes, going out to the flight line. He had a scarf on. Bright white, and I wondered if I was going to get him in my section. I got him—this was the first day, just orientation—and we were out there on the line, standing beside a Stearman. 'This is an airplane,' I told 'em."

"That's the way I usually start with a new bunch," McCaig said, who was ruddy and gray, with hair of great vitality and disorder. "I start real basic, with somethin' that they ought to know, that anybody could see. That's the only thing I ever say to 'em that I memorize, except when one of 'em asks me how good I can fly. I always had *that* ready, from an old James Cagney–Pat O'Brien movie, when somebody from the Air Corps asked Jimmy Cagney, who was an

its lips, but stood respectfully. Cahill did not try for the other's clothes; he imagined only the frame and the eyes, which were brown.

He had not seen the movie.

There were this man, the one Cahill had just made, and a boy standing beside an airplane, like one of the planes on the cover of the magazine that his lifeguard, Darrell Cochran, used to read at the pool: *G-8 and His Battle Aces.* Two wings? Or maybe three? The boy had his back to him, and was listening closely to the man. Cahill listened closely.

"Such as what?" Cahill asked, feeling that he should come in, now. Airplanes, he thought; let me make one up, so that I can follow this. He tried, mainly newspaper photographs, stories of Lindbergh, pictures of planes from the Wright brothers and those he had glanced at, as other

old barnstormer like Lindbergh or Wiley Post, how good *he* could fly. 'I can fly the boxes they come in,' Cagney told him. I just used that one time, and that was with your boy, Mr. Cahill. He asked me, and I told him, just like Jimmy Cagney, and that was the beginnin' of it."

"The first day is just wings, engine, and tail. The big thing is to tell 'em that the body of the airplane is called the fuselage. Most of 'em don't know that, and if you can get that over to 'em, you're coming out ahead on that first day. I remember the way your son looked things over, Mr. Cahill. He was a lot more relaxed than I was. Usually when I get finished telling 'em all this preliminary stuff, I let 'em ask a few questions, to see which ones have ever been off the ground, and which ones might be tryin' to get me to think they know more than they do. Then I ask *them* some things, usually. But I didn't say anything to your boy, because, from lookin' at him, I was more or less afraid of what he might say back."

"Such as I didn't have no idea. But I think I was right, because when I got to know him, some of the things he used to talk about, and the way he got things off, might have been confusin' to them other boys, standin' out

107

Americans had, in the pictures of the beginnings of the war. He saw wings and wire; these dropped from places higher up, where they had been, or they did loops, with a rounding of sound, in newsreels.

But this was a sitting craft the other was talking about; one surrounded by boys, among which, in a white scarf —"bright white" —was his son, who, according to this voice, might have said anything, and had not spoken. In the cold the plane stood; he put two wings on it, though Lindbergh's had only had one. Two wings; most of them, he believed, had two. At first it sat there in wings and many wires. From years back he began to bring boys, and put them there: the blocky, buffalo-headed sprinter with the slashing gold stripe up his thigh, and the young student from the openness of Piedmont Park with the pusher V-frame model. He felt the knitted, perfect tension of the frame in the boy's hand, and the knots muscling into the rubber, building what would be flight.

Meaningless as these images were, Cahill tried for them, half because they might take on meaning, and half to kill time. He reached into his pants pocket, found the spring grip there, and squeezed it a couple

there in the cold around that skinny airplane."

"Orientation don't really take very long," McCaig said, his gray eyes on Cahill's glasses. "It's not a good idea to do anything to confuse anybody. Those kids want to make it so bad, they're just so anxious and nervous, that you don't want to make it any harder on 'em than you have to. So we work—or at least *I* work—work 'em into the idea of flyin' an airplane just as simple as I possibly can. When they first get up and sit in the plane, and I just point out the simplest little things to 'em, they're so overanxious that they can't hardly take it in. The next day I do that, show 'em where things are at. I had your boy sit last, and I showed him what I showed the others. He touched everything he was supposed to touch—the stick, the rudder pedals, the throttle, the trim tab, the ignition switch—and called 'em back to me, real relaxed. He looked like he belonged there, doin' what he was doin'. He just went right with it. He could'a been in a Spitfire in North Africa,

of times, then quit when he imaged himself standing there pulsating for no reason anybody else would have been able to figure out. I don't need that right now, he thought, and tried again to relate to flying, making a cockpit out of his memory of driving an automobile. His dead boy was sitting there for the first time—Cahill could not figure any reason that it might not the first time—and saying nothing back to McCaig, who was now talking to somebody else about something else. The plane was supposed to be in cold and wind, in the open.

The only thing he could make out was the scarf, in the wide cold. It was bright white, sure enough, white in the mind; he wondered where he had ever seen anything as bright, as white, as he believed he made it, as bright as it had come to him from the words. But the face—the calm face, as the instructor had said—would not come to him either from living people, or from the dead, or from imagination. He had only a hint, a glimmer, when someone—a regular lifter's mother—had sought him out at the swimming pool a year or two back with a speed-confused photograph of a basketball

with fifteen thousand hours behind him. I was interested in him right off, because he had a good chance of ending up in combat. More than I do. To fly for the Air Corps I'd have to come back and go through this whole damn program myself, and I'm too old. They wouldn't take me. Would they, Colonel?"

"*I* might," said the colonel, with usable friendliness. "I don't know about the Air Corps, though. They've got their own rules. It'd be up to them."

"Anyway, I could already tell that your boy could handle himself, and that most prob'ly he could handle the airplane just as easy. Just sittin' there, he looked like he was in the right place; he looked good doin' it. He sat for a while, lookin' straight ahead, and then, I remember, he folded his arms and waited for me to make the next move. You could feel a lot of reserve was in him. I didn't know what to think, to tell you the truth. Then, after a little while, before I could tell him that that was all, that we could all go back inside the ready room and get warm, he pulled his goggles down, and turned around and winked at me. What he meant was, I guess, is that we were goin' to fly that

game. "This is your boy?" he was asked, and it was. He tried to think; he had not kept the picture; in fact, it had not been given to him.

"I might could," Cahill said. "We'll see."

Cahill felt for the arm of his seat, and went into it slowly, dropping his hat to the floor. It was now warm in the room. His overcoat was heating, near over-heating, and on his hands and one side of his face a steady burning was planted; he realized that it was what the sun could give, at this time of year, and in this place. The huge comfort of it was agreeable, and he listened with close to full attention.

thing. And we did." He broke off, half apologetically.

"I'll tell you all about that later. You want to stay here on through graduation Sunday, don't you? Can you do that?

"Let me try to persuade you," McCaig said. "You know these boys—why don't we just sit down a minute, Mr. Cahill. You're not in a hurry, are you?" McCaig made as if to squat, then went to the side of the room and came back with a chair. He sat and leaned forward like a football coach, leveling the faces, while the colonel stepped to the door and spoke outside.

As McCaig spoke of the layout of the base, of the flight line, the classrooms, the athletic field, doing his best to build a picture that might be useful in some way, he could not help looking at the double image of the sun in Cahill's glasses. Green, closed, and violent, the concentrations of light came back at him. When the colonel, left behind them, went back to his desk, McCaig did not even notice, as he went on talking about the flight line, the dirt strip, the distance of the field from the reservoir, with the feeling of himself and another in a situation of great uncertainty, and yet of some natural balance. Behind the double sun there could have been anything; McCaig, an excitable man with steady nerves, touched his own forehead at one point, half surprised that there were no glasses there, and realized that nothing an ordinary man had could match or contend with the blazing detachment of the blind in sunlight: the *beyond*-position, and above all the mysteriousness of reception. Where is it going? he wondered, listening to himself trying to explain. What is being done to what I say? Where will it end? What might it come to? What is the good of it?

And yet he continued; he was explaining now about the graduating class, and where it seemed to him, from what he knew, most of the cadets would end up. "We've only had one class before this one, so we can't say for sure. The ones that graduated are all in Basic now, and we really don't know where they'll go from there, the ones that get through there, and Advanced. But the call right now is for multi-engine stuff, B-17 and B-24 co-pilots. And some for ATC pilots. Fighters are where they all want to go, though. Being a fighter pilot is like playing in the backfield."

"This is all lost on me," Cahill said. "I don't know one airplane from another."

"Your boy would have gone to fighters, if anybody would. He had the feelin' for it, and he would have been better in somethin' that would move fast and turn quick. He had the whole-air feelin'; he could have done anything with it. But . . ." He slowed and thought. "You can't tell. You go where they need you. I can see him in a bomber squadron, too, and he'd do plenty of damage to whoever was down there, if his people would do what he told 'em to. I can't think of 'em doing anything else."

Cahill tried to visualize, but could see neither planes nor son. Nor enemy, either, he thought. The Germans? The Japanese? Who would that have been? Who was the enemy?

Someone fronted on him again, and Cahill tilted his chin to receive.

"Mac's going to take you around to some of the places on the base, and let you meet some people," the colonel said. "I've got a suggestion or two, and Mac has some ideas of his own. Do you need anybody else? Phillipson can go along with you, if you'd like. He's a good boy."

"Yes, yes he is," Cahill answered gravely. "He's a lot of help. Is he right around here, someplace?"

"No, but I can get him."

"That's all right," Cahill said. "Don't bother, don't pull him off whatever he's supposed to be doin'. Mr. McCaig and me and Zack will just go along, and see what happens. Don't worry about Zack." Cahill smiled. "He just hangs around."

Cahill rose, pulled up his collar, reached down for his hat and went right to it, put it on, and stood up, his hands going into his pockets, fastening on the spring grip in one, fingering the slivered goggles in the other.

"All set," he said. "That's my approach to Air Corps lingo. Does it work?"

"It could work," McCaig said. "We know what you mean." He touched Cahill's sleeve to turn him toward the door. "In lots of situations, it could work."

Now, he thought; now I go into it and make out the secret. I stand here and I key in; I tune myself to it, to whatever is here, on all sides. What is the first thing?

Once more, wind, this time as though made of many concerted small points, varying on his face except on the glassed-off eyes. He wondered what things were being picked up in it, perhaps whirled and lifted, or somewhere sustained, held off the ground, without weight though still in some dark form or shape. These were shapes of space, and to himself he phrased it like that, and agreed that it was so. Inside, amongst the wind, some changing and some steady, there were engines, and before he tried the stairs, though with a hand on the rail and its trembling from another source, he projected toward them, listening for their position in deep space. There were two kinds, one on the

They stood a moment on the porch, to the left and behind them the flight line and the strip, to their right the athletic fields: basketball courts back-to-back, and behind them a big worn field on which anything could have been played, or several kinds of games at the same time; boys were playing them: softball and touch football. Before them, across a white-sanded assembly area, were the main cadet barracks; beyond and to the right of them, down a pale track like a logging road, were a swimming pool with board chairs and a small building that served as a cadet club.

"This place has to do with flyin'," McCaig said, and then, taking confidence in his own lead, "it has to do with a lot of boys flyin', and a few of us tryin' to teach 'em how to do it. We go up, and we come down and talk, then we go up and come down and talk some more. Then *they* go up, and we stand around and watch, and

ground, vibrating in the railing and in the planks he stood on, as from something rooted, perhaps coiled and touched like a buried tuning fork. Something in his breastbone responded without questioning, and the image came to him again, as from the same sound early that morning, of a fierce fronting of eager and fragile machines. There was again the line of them imagined through the glass of his room, and the cast of his breath that must have been on the pane, that he had slicked away with his hand, trying to possess what he had called up.

"Where do we go first?" Cahill asked.

"I came up from the highway, walkin'. I thought snow at first, but now I'd say sand. There was a lot of people, off to the left, seemed like playin' games, maybe one big game, but prob'ly different ones. I don't know. Me and Zack and the other fellow just crunched on in. I listened around."

He was glad not to feel himself enveloped, and to be standing free just before going down a rail. He could not hear trees, though he listened far, and

hope to hell they don't forget what we showed 'em. We don't hope that they won't forget *somethin'*—some little thing we showed 'em. They all do that. We just hope they don't forget *everything*, and just get up there and blank out. Some of 'em do, you know. They can't handle what they've got, and then it's dangerous. It's real dangerous. We try to get those out; get 'em out of it, into somethin' else."

"Let me see, now," McCaig said. "We could break it down. You done come out here twice't. Where have you already been?"

Only the near end of the road was visible from the door of the Administration Building, but McCaig had been over it many times, and he wondered how the difference in sound might have been for a blind man, for he himself had always been changed a little, in coming off the rigid concrete onto the pale yielding road which—it seemed to him—could just as easily have been straight but curved one way and another with likable perversity through a single large stand of virgin pine, a graceful, dignified and somehow orderly crowd of thick-bodied long-nee-

wanted to move in that direction, for their hush gave the background against which talk, information, took on a conspiratorial tone to which he responded, and in which he felt the strength of his command. Among trees, he was sure, the presence of the dog at his side was awesome, more than symbolic, especially with the going so silent, the sand, the hidden surface over which one moved toward something unsuspecting, which could not hear as well as he, and did not know. There is a self in the open, where things are stated, he thought; there is open hearing, and there is closed-in listening, also, no matter how large the space is that is closed.

He keyed in human voices, and again he was in openness he understood. Even in this little time he could cut the engines in and out of his attention, and listen through them toward woods,

dled trees which gave off a steady church-dark and enveloped whoever entered or stood among them with silence and an atmosphere of cunning, stalking; some quick, final thing about to happen. There, everything was muffled, felted, a sanded wilderness, a quiet surround that must be whispered in. McCaig glanced down at the huge restless dog at Cahill's side. Get him off this porch, McCaig thought: get him across the open place and on back into those trees, and he'll change into what he ought to be, what he came from. McCaig had never remembered seeing a wolf in a zoo, or even a picture of a wolf, that looked as wolflike as this dog. His idea was that wolves were gray, and had slanted green eyes and thin legs, but he changed this now, for a live, aggressive, compact and high-strung black, as powerful in the legs as in the body and light brown in the eyes. A pack of those could sure tear you to pieces in a hurry, he thought; but this 'un wouldn't need no others; it wouldn't take a pack.

It was the unity, McCaig thought, the entire secrecy of the fir trees, the compacted quiet that changed you as it took you in; because of it any sound had a poignancy and consequence of terrifying resonance: haunting, prophetic, not lost. The cries of players on the big scurfy field all had

buildings, even the far highway, which he believed he would be able to reach without practice, and with no conversation he must take part in. The voices were always coming past the engines, or coming out of them: boys talking and going past, or standing still with each other, and the distant fighting and panic of their games. Now he heard a boy shouting rhythmic numbers, and a scuffle of many feet that could have been one person, but the steps were too heavy for that. I am where I want to be, he said to himself. The openness and the woods and everything here including the air over it all is an enormous net organized around me; I move, it moves, takes shape and changes shape, changes its distances and forms and volumes, its loudnesses and fadings, but it all flows in on me: an army of boys, on the ground, in the air overhead; they will come to me, any way I ask; they will fall to me from the air I am breathing.

this quality as they came to you there; some were of sudden penetration and abandon, some had overtones of pain or hope, of questioning and disappointment. But it was the aircraft that were the most changed by the sense of the forest. It was because of the trees, which always seemed to be thickening among themselves, that engines are so strange here, McCaig thought. According to the wind, they came toward, came at, came into the woods from many angles. McCaig always paused, turning off the highway, and looked out over the pines for aircraft, as they descended with a great sense of ease and homing, their blades whickering, falling, lilting a little, as though each one sank, sighing, into the heart of a forest, and since no sound of a crash, no flame or the smoke that one expected, came, it seemed to belong there, disappearing without question. McCaig never tired of this; the planes and their homing in the dense green was gratifying, more and more fulfilling, every time he watched and listened. He was—had come to be—aware of a sense of privilege, for the secrecy of the field inside the forest was his own secret, he felt, more than anyone else's, and each plane falling into the still and dignified green confirmed in him the conviction that such places should exist, such things go on.

"What we'll do," McCaig said, "is to go down and around to the left, for about a hundred and fifty yards. That'll take us on past the mess hall, and we can walk along the edge of the flight line to the hangars and the ready room. There'll be some people there you might want to talk to. I expect you can get some of the feel of it, of what goes on around here." Cahill took the rail and nudged Zack.

"Let's go down, Anvil-head," he said to the dog, "one more time."

On the open sand they worked slowly toward the hangars, keeping together by talk. It was important to McCaig that he not touch the other; already he knew that Cahill would resent it.

He was easy in this walking, and easy, already, with the other man. It did not matter whether he was able to catch and interpret everything that McCaig told him, for the accent of the voice and the forthright confiding quality of it was enough, no matter what it said. And yet what it said was evidently being given with the conviction that it should be registered, and Cahill, because the registering of it was his excuse for being here, began to listen. But this was being made more and more difficult, for with each step the machine sounds increased. Cahill kept feeling that he was walking into an engine: the engine itself, not just into its propeller but through it and into the inner, necessary, and hidden part of it. Then the central sound flagged, fell more, moved off; another took its place. This was at first a low, grinding noise of rotation, grating with a circle in it; the pitch yawed and yawned up-

"I don't know how long it's been since you've seen your boy," McCaig said, talking slowly and increasing volume to maintain his meaning over the heavy ratcheting of the flight line.

"I mean, I don't guess you've seen him since I have. And I don't know if he ever struck you like he struck me; there's no way I could know that. I do remember he told me," McCaig went on, as though not to a blind man, "that he planned to have you come up here before he left for Basic. He told me a couple of times, and the other boys expected it, too. Some of 'em." He glanced at Cahill, and continued looking at him for a few steps. He was no longer unnerved by the fixity of Cahill's face, but it seemed to him that something more should show on it than showed when the subject of his dead boy was put to it. It's not the glasses entirely, McCaig thought; that's not the whole thing.

"Like I was telling you back in

ward, a discordant and urgent grinding of metal forced toward its highest point. Near the point something whucked, exploded, and caught, and another engine had come in; toward this, too, they were walking. They passed it—left it, or it left them—and were now where there were multiple other sounds: hammering, trundling, ringing: an area of difficult weights being moved around with effort.

For the first time he felt Mc-Caig touch him, and turned, and, reaching down, turned the dog.

Any sort of work space was familiar to him, and though these were the sounds of metal rather than wood, and though they were more reverberant than he was used to, he was sure that, making allowances, he could tell almost exactly where he was in relation to any situation that produced sound, particularly if it were regular. The only danger lay in the feet, and he began to slide his steps a little, remembering that other people left things around: wrenches, boxes, bolts, screws, nails, gloves, glass and, anywhere work went on, cloth of all kinds, long and short.

In front of him, space not so much gave way but boiled open: the confusion of humanity, loud, questioning, explaining, begging, was everywhere with him,

the colonel's office, you couldn't tell the difference in him right away; you wouldn't pick him out at first, and then you would. You would pick him out, just as soon as he said something to you. I didn't have no more idea of what he would do when I got him into a airplane than, well, no more idea than nothin'." McCaig's voice was very loud now, and high, and needn't be; he brought it down. "We're goin' along the line side of the hangars now," he said.

"We can go in here," McCaig said. "This is the main hangar. What you hear is the guys workin' on the planes. The maintenance on 'em is fairly easy, but somebody's got to keep on top of it; we don't want nothin' to happen because of malfunction."

Quickly he glanced at Cahill again, and down at Cahill's feet. "Most of these kids we're goin' in to see are scared of the airplane at first. They're scared of the engine, they're scared of the controls, they're scared of the instructor, most of all they're scared of the air." He broke off, then coached, talking Cahill through. "Watch yourself, now. There's one step up. I'll get the door.

"Remind me to tell you what I was going to tell you," McCaig said. "You'll understand it better later on, after you've been in here with these boys a little while. This is the real way it feels, the ground

and as he advanced, around him; he was among boys again. They then subsided, and in the new silence, the heated smell of leather, fur, and sweat, the hothouse breathlessness of packed enclosure, Cahill spread his feet and rooted, swung his gaze of solid rock from left to right, then back.

part of it. Hot and loud and confused, is what it is."

Where they were they stopped, boys and young men packed around them, all sizes clumsy and bearlike in their huge scuffed-leather clothes, some with breasts and suspendered pants torn open and flapping and hanging loosely, some zippered and sweating, some just down and out of the cold, an excited and fresh pink, those yet to go, pale, eager, and uncertain. The two boys nearest to Cahill moved away, turned back toward him and stared with the rest. Only one cadet looked at another, but the glance was brief, and the boy fixed again on Cahill and the brutal powerful alertness of the dog. A man older than the boys, but not much older, an instructor with a white scarf undone and uneven, slowly took his hand from a blackboard on which there were wavering parallel marks and three emphatic arrows. He looked not at Cahill but at McCaig, and started to say something.

"You see," McCaig said, "this here's where you see—you can prob'ly tell—that there are . . . that there are a lot of people in here. Good Lord," he said, fixing on a real truth, "you can prob'ly smell 'em! You could prob'ly smell 'em from way out yonder on the flight line." Cahill moved his head in the direction of McCaig, but said nothing. Again McCaig was not certain how to go on, but he could not resist, at the mention of smell, glancing at the dog, now sitting on its haunches but leaning its head a little forward as though toward something of interest or importance.

"Anyway," he went on, "some of these patriots and heroes and ace-makers have just come in off the first flight, the nearest thing we have to a Dawn Patrol, and they're talkin' with each other about what they just done."

"Go ahead," Cahill said suddenly. "Go ahead with what you're doin'. We'll try not to bother you."

The lieutenant at the blackboard pulled down the short end of his scarf until it was more or less even with the other. He tapped on the blackboard with chalk, and turned to a short dark-haired boy with his helmet and goggles in his hand, his unpacked hair shining with sweat.

"Your trouble is with the wind," he said. "Look here. When I tell you to keep this eight-pattern on the road more or less uniform, I mean more rather than less. Do you know what uniform means?"

"Yes, sir," said the boy, working as best he could with an enormous wad of gum. "It means the same. It means one circle like the other."

"And it also means," the lieutenant said, back to normal now, and forgetting Cahill, "it also means each *half* circle like the other. You have around twenty-two hours now, and you ought to have a whole lot better feel for the wind than you've got. Some people never get it, and maybe you won't, but if you're going to get it, you'd better get it fast. I'll pass you on this one. You made a pretty fair landing, and you did all right on emergency procedure. And you didn't get sick. You can get rid of that stuff now."

The boy respectfully took the large knot of pinkish chewing gum from between his teeth and dropped it into a trash can, his eyes not leaving the blackboard. Beside one of the longer arrows the lieutenant drew an even longer one, and put two points on it.

"The wind is coming from here, Yearwood. It's coming out of the northeast, blowing down from the intersection of the North Carolina-Virginia line and the Atlantic Ocean, toward about the middle of the southern part of the Appalachian range: range of mountains. How far down that way it will blow is not of any interest to us. But right through here, right through those farms and those fields—those very fields you and I were just over, Mr. Yearwood: *that* silo and *that* creek and *those* poplar trees and *that* little road and that *other* little road that came across it at a right angle, the one we were using as a checkpoint: right where we were, the wind was coming out of the northeast, and pushing the plane *this* way. Now you knew all that, didn't you?"

"I sort of knew it," the boy said.

"Now," said the lieutenant, "the wind is pushing on the plane like this," he drew a third arrow beside the others, and tapped on it. "When you turn the wings of the airplane, the airplane you're in, the airplane you are supposed to be controlling, Mr. Yearwood, and give the wind—from the northeast—more surface, more *purchase*, on your aircraft, you're going to have to do something about the way you fly the airplane when you do this maneuver, when you try to make this eight-pattern

119

and keep the loops more or less the same. What are you going to try to do?"

"I'm going to tighten up the turn on the downwind side, and have it not so tight on the upwind part."

"Why didn't you do that, then?"

"I thought I did," said the cadet. "I didn't think it was all that bad."

The lieutenant turned to him squarely. "It was not all *that* bad, Cadet Yearwood," he said. "The question is, whether it was all that good, and it wasn't. This is a maneuver that depends on two things, or rather on three things." He lifted three fingers up and turned them down theatrically one by one with the forefinger of the other hand as he talked.

"First, it depends on visual references, and your ability to relate those to your position and the attitude of the aircraft, and thereby to translate such knowledge into a controlling of the aircraft so as to perform the pattern as it should be performed. This means that you must be able to translate, either mechanically or in some way known only to you, the visual references into a reading of the direction and force of the wind. The second is a *feel* for the wind, for that part of air, for the part of it that you and the plane are in. This is like a sixth sense; in some people it can be developed, but some people never get it; they are like people who are color-blind, and those are people we have to get rid of. You are about half color-blind, Mr. Yearwood. You are just hanging there in the wind, knowing a little bit about what to do, and maybe enough, but only just barely."

"You said something about three things," Yearwood said, doing what he could to steer the lieutenant onto something, anything, else.

"The other is just the control of the aircraft, the hand-foot control that makes these other things come out together: the wind, the aircraft, and you, and the pattern. Here's what you did." He drew, over the neat symmetrical pattern of an eight lying on its side, a lopsided exaggeration of it, with the loops on one side long and irregular and the others irregular and short.

"On the downwind side of the road the wind blew us nearly into Tennessee; on the upwind side you still turned at the same rate, and just got us a couple of hundred feet past the road. As soon as you got halfway round the starboard turn, we got blown right back past the road, and you still didn't tighten up. Tennessee is still where it's always been, but I don't plan to go there anytime soon. Not with you, anyway."

He pitched the chalk into the trough. "I'll give you a bare pass, and hope I don't see you the next time."

McCaig stepped quickly to the lieutenant, and drew him back toward Cahill.

"Mr. Cahill, I'd like you to meet Lieutenant Purcell Foy, one of the Army check-riders here."

Cahill pulled the glove off and put out his hand slowly and automatically.

He held the small grip for a moment, and wondered why he was making everyone he met blond. The other hand was chill and steady, small-boned, with almost no muscle between the thumb joint and the inner bone of the first finger. He believed this to be a sure gauge of the muscularity of a person; Ruiź and he and the other lifters and bodybuilders at Willow Plunge considered it a personal secret, a personal device of judgment between them: that the degree of muscular development of a body could be judged by the thickness of the pear-shaped muscle in that part of the hand; it was a more accurate indication when the thumb was deliberately clamped against the finger, but even so it was possible to tell a good deal from a simple handshake. Small and not strong, he thought. Not athletic, not active. But again, blond, though no real reason for this; and maybe balding.

Lieutenant Foy, holding the big hard hand, looked at the unseeing face, and tried to think of something to say. There was no precedent for the situation, as far as he knew. He had only been out of cadets four classes, himself, and perhaps through no fault of his own, but perhaps through some, he had been involved in the crash-landing of a B-25 in a Transition Training Unit which had given the authorities on the accident board reason to believe he was perhaps better suited to an instructional position in an early phase of pilot training than to a fighter or a bomber squadron. Though there was still a slight boyishness to him his face was deeply lined. The top of his head was almost flat; the straight thin rusty hair combed across it lay like something open on a table. Even in the flapping garments there was a slender slightly seedy elegance about his body, and carriage; the scarf seemed both pretentious and called-for.

"I'm very sorry about your son, Mr. Cahill," Lieutenant Foy said, glancing quickly at McCaig and getting nothing back. "It was a real shock to everybody. Have you talked to Colonel Hoccleve?"

"Yes I have," Cahill said, putting his glove back on. "He don't seem to know what happened, either. There was somethin' about a fire, he told me."

"For some reason unknown to anybody on the base, surely not known to any of the instructors or the military personnel, he was flying over a brush fire about twenty-five miles east of here, on the other side of the reservoir. He was evidently below altitude, and the turbulence got him, and maybe the smoke was part of it. Anyway, he never made it across the fire; from what we could tell, he was flying almost due south-north, but he never got out the north end of the fire."

Cahill remained facing into Foy's voice. Several cadets, maneuvered, listening, and the lieutenant motioned them away.

"There was nothing anybody could do," Foy went on. "Everything he did was against regulations, but when you take one of these planes up by yourself, there's no way for anybody to stop you from doing anything you want to do. If you want to go fly over a fire, under minimum altitude, and if there's a fire, you can go and do it, just like some people —some of the kids in the RAF—fly under bridges and under high-tension wires; I heard of one pilot who flew a B-17 under the Golden Gate Bridge, and maybe it was worth it, worth it to the people who did it. But bad things can come out of that attitude. So much is a question of attitude, Mr. Cahill. So much of it is. If these boys won't pay attention to us, and do what we ask them to do, and not do what we ask them not to do, we can't help it. It's very bad to lose somebody in training, Mr. Cahill. Everybody suffers. But to lose somebody like that—I mean in a situation like that—is so useless. It's just so useless. But what can you do? Nothing, is the answer. You can't do anything. This was a bad thing, a bad situation, and I'm sorry. That's all I can say."

"Did you ever fly with him, Purcell? I don't believe I remember that you ever did," McCaig asked.

"Yes," Cahill said, "I'd like to know about that. I'd like to know what you thought about him, and about how he might have done."

"No," Lieutenant Foy said, "I never did fly with him. He was in another section, and I came here too late to fly with him when he was in the first part of the course. McCaig, here, can tell you more about that than I can. I never did know Joel very well; just talked to him a few times. And I used to hear about him from the other boys. He was the first to solo here, you know; the first in his class. A lot of the boys looked up to him. He was not ordinary."

"Do you know—what is that Greek boy's name, Instructor? That runner?"

"Harbelis," McCaig answered.

"Do you know Cadet Harbelis?" Cahill asked, directly front.

"Yes I do, sir," Foy replied. "I do know him, and I've flown with him. He started out kind of shaky, but he came on. I think he'll get through here all right, and probably all the way through graduation from cadets. He'll be overseas in a year, somewhere or other. He'll make somebody a good man. He's steady, and he's got good control of himself. He doesn't have any great natural talent, but he'll listen to you, and he doesn't mind learning. Tell him a thing once, and he's pretty much got it. About thirty or forty more hours solo and he can sure fly my wing."

McCaig's eyes narrowed a little at this, but he said nothing; by now, though he had not known him long, he felt that he was able to anticipate Cahill's reactions, and he was not surprised when Cahill did nothing to continue.

"I've got to be going along," Lieutenant Foy said. "Everything here is on schedule, and I move around like the rest of them. If there's anything I can do while you're here, let me know. McCaig can probably take you to the boys that knew Joel the best. Harbelis was a good friend of his; I used to see them together. How about Shears?" he asked McCaig. "Has he met Shears yet?"

"Yes, I have met him," Cahill said. "Just barely. I didn't get a chance to talk to him very much."

"Well," Foy said grudgingly, "he's good. He can fly. He's an impressive boy. If every cadet colonel after him could be as good as he is, we'd win this war a lot sooner."

"Right," McCaig replied. "Sure would."

"I've got to go now," Lieutenant Foy said. "I have some things I need to do over in Administration. If there's anything else I can help you with, just tell Colonel Hoccleve, and he'll run me down."

"I don't know what I might want to do, yet," Cahill said. "I might want to talk some more, later on."

"Sure," Foy said doubtfully. "Maybe I could give you some opinions, if you'd like that."

"That might be good," Cahill said. "You can't tell."

"You want to go along now?" McCaig asked.

"Yes, all right. It's a little hot in here." Then, to the dog, "Come on, Zack. Stay close."

Cahill, the instructor, and the dog stepped down out of the room from the sprung planks onto the solid and large cement floor of the hangar.

It was dead cold again, and Cahill rooted in his overcoat pocket in his gloves. The opening of any space had come to be exciting to him and, though he knew himself to be enclosed still, his awareness increased, now that he was out of the packed room. Here there were no voices, or only a few, far off, one-worded, and indistinct. Instead, there were metal-whines, the screwing or spinning of one hard substance into another; in the midst of these, with what took him as steady human force, something was being nailed. He fastened for an instant on the nailing, listening for the last stroke—the finishing stroke and the certifying one just following it—involving the plank. This came, and a new nail was started. As they walked, he kept listening to it, and for it, from far off and perhaps a little above. It was the only right sound in the confusion of the rest of it, in which he could identify only a few sources: a long slither of what could only be chain dragged over itself, a piece of thin metal being cut by high-speed friction, the high nasal rising of a drill,

McCaig looked around him, taking account of what was going on between him and the far end of the hangar. He wondered what the blind man might be making of all this, and did what he considered an honest best to respond to the scene as if he couldn't see it, even closing his eyes momentarily. When he reopened them the familiar area was present with an increased authenticity and strangeness: the round engine near at hand, full and tight in a tremendous vice with the cylinder heads naked and half a dozen of the greasy cylinders on the workbench beside it, another engine in chains, hanging, isolated, ten feet from the floor, a squat platform ladder with a clean towel over the top rung. Beyond it was a whole Stearman, and two mechanics in lumberjackets were working on the guy wires between the wings on one side. Farther off stood an engineless aircraft, awkward and raped, and beyond that, two others, intact, unattended. In the farthest curve round of the humped building a man was on his back on

like dental work, and the reluctant down-spinning of the freed drill bit. He longed to be free of wherever he was, now, for in spite of the variety of noises that told him that the space through which he was moving was large, there was still the sensation of enclosure, for every sound shook with a beaten-back resonance, the caught-down vibrancy of entrapment, and he could not forestall the image of the workers being chained to their tasks and their materials. He shook his shoulders, loosening up, and folded his arms across his chest. He stepped strongly, listening-in: into what was around him, the reality and the creation, powerful with his presence, with drama. If I can keep in the center, and keep people and things relating to me, I will be all right. I will be all right for the rest of my life, and when Zack dies I will go on by myself, for by that time I will know how, no matter where I may be. All I need from people is a little give, a little concession; most of them will let me have that, and when they give it, I will know what to do with it.

A fair way off was a springing resonance, like unexpected sheets of water: a live battering. Cahill was suddenly thirsty, and for the water he was hearing. He wondered what it would take for a high platform, nailing upward. He was securing lights, beneath him, in a heavy ghostly sheen of radiance shed by the lights already installed, an AT-6, markedly different from the awkward, dragonflyish bodies of the Stearmans, planes for boys or Boy Scouts, McCaig thought, stood wide-stanced, solid, and privileged; as he watched, a civilian worker hosed down the faceted canopy in an explosion of splintery lights. This place is something I should look at more, McCaig thought. There is a whole lot here that you don't see just any time. As they passed he looked again at the cylinder heads of the engine locked onto the bench, particularly at the top one, behind which was a bulb in a cage. From one step to the next, like glancing through a set of cards in a rack, he saw directly through the fins of the head into the light, and for that second was seized by a preciseness of split metal, a cloven and shaved stone, which made in his mind an inevitable connection between light and metal and air. He glanced with intent from the locked engine to the one hanging free in space, not swaying or turning but unprotected, heavy and terrible. There seemed to him something religious about it, churchly, though there was no slant ray of light on it, or on the links of its twin chains. It was odd, he reflected, and use-

him to leave McCaig—and Zack also—where they were and make his way toward the pouring and splattering: whether he could get there, what might be in his way, what he would look like when doing it. There were people, now hammering and twisting with pliers, shunting heavy objects around, drilling, bolting, and he had no doubt they would stop, and all those on a level with him would watch silently as he passed by them, passed through, until he reached where he was going, and at least one would look down from wherever he was nailing. He took this other's position, and saw what the other would see: a blind man in an overcoat open his mouth to a spray of water coming to him from somewhere he had reached.

less thinking, but he had been struck in this way, and it was disturbing that if such feelings were part of the scene for him, the engine in the vice, though displayed on the workbench as on a kind of altar, did not have this quality, did not provoke in him the wish to stand before it—or even under it —silently watching and waiting or, yes, the desire to bring it down from its exposed position, to keep it, care for it, hide it.

They were approaching a small door in the great building; a rigid sliver of winter sunlight stood down one side, and as McCaig pulled it back and open to the full cold and sun, he took in the whole hangar again, as hose water at the far end burst forthrightly and with great shimmering-power against the near side of the colonel's AT-6, filling the dark air around its focus of lights with a haze of drops thick as atoms, muffled and enchanted.

His wife had made good picnics, and for the time they had been together this had been very nearly their only common ground, except for occasional clashes of strong uninvolved sex from which they both turned with relief and quick attention to other things. But, as with flowers and plants, she was good with food, particularly cold food; she believed in her version of the country and the forest, and could make a surprisingly enjoyable occasion of a meal in some remote place. They never carried one basket but two, and he felt a genuine touch of approval on remembering the times when they had walked from dirt roads up over the nearest rise and found—she could usually find—a creek or a pond somewhere she had never been. There was always shade, and he could not remember that insects had ever bothered them. He would sit there and eat, and listen to creek water run, passing on and on. He could have eaten a whole chicken ranch of her fried chicken; though there was always plenty of it—thick-battered and more golden than brown—there was never really enough. Her potato salad was also delicious; the slaw was coarse and bulky, like part of the field growth itself made palatable. And he had never taken a single preliminary bite of one of her deviled eggs, but put the whole half into his mouth, appreciatively and with a sense of justice in doing it in this way. She liked cherry pie for dessert, for she took a special pride in her crusts, but cherries were the wrong sweetness for him; devil's food cake was right, and righter than right. The cake part, however, served only to hold the icing, which he stripped from the layers carefully and ate as though it were a particularly rare kind of fudge, rolling up bits of the layers into balls and pitching them into whatever stream was there. Afterward he would lie in the grass and close his eyes and listen, and perhaps have one more beer in the sun. At these times his life and his marriage seemed not so bad; he could see a short and livable way into the future, in which there would be more such times: more fields, more wild, soft-spoken water flowing by, more potato salad, more icing, more chill spicy eggs, inhaled as much as eaten.

Fields were one resource; woods were another. Florence was not afraid of snakes, and this was unusual and much in her favor. It meant that they could get as far off into trees as they could walk, as he could carry the heavy baskets full of meat and bread and bottles. Though grassy fields were good, overlooks were better, and on weekends in good weather—early spring and midfall—they would often drive into one of the three hilly national forests not far from Atlanta. These were real forests, and once around the first turn of any path away from the road, the walker was in woods as deep as woods had ever been in that place; the Indians who had lived in it hundreds of years ago would have noticed no change. These trips took a different form from those in which they sat in fields under the shade of a single tree. Woods and their quality of the unknown and unexpected caused him to wander, and after the meal he would usually set off for half an hour or so, while she slept or read a movie magazine. Though he liked openness better, there was a side of him that took to the oppressiveness, the closeness of woods also, though not for long periods. In spring especially this was true; it was the intensity of *light* green that drew him farther into it; there seemed to be no reason for it to be the way it was, and yet the pervasiveness, the uncompromising and utter assertion of growth seemed a sort

127

of assurance, a condition with which he could not argue, but might move through wherever he could find footing.

Some of this had been among wet rocks, and toward a roaring that held—the nearer he climbed toward it through ferns and moist roots—three or four different sounds: one a steady hanging pour, another a splattering, a pelting, and a third, a hoarse, deep reckoning whisper, as of some terrible disclosure attempting to be said in sleep, not able to break its own outcry into parts, or make enough silences for syllables or words. Suddenly the track through the stones leveled. He could step forward, and he did. In front of him the woods had gone off, had distanced into a single color. Two more steps would have brought him to the end of a thin solid spur of rock. He took one of these and then part of another, caught up now in what had been a complex roar as he approached and now was so pervasive that it seemed no different from silence; it was the sound that should have been there, filling the deep hollow below him with luminous mist which floated above some end, some limit that could not be seen from where he stood. The view outward and downward was so compelling, so insistent on placing him at a high and curious vantage point, so walled with far, light porous green, so fraught with drop-off into peaceful and phosphorescent mist above some final danger hidden beneath it, that it took him a short time to refocus—without moving even his head, but composing his mind in a different way—and to take real notice of what was nearest him, on both sides. This was lifted and silver water going past, a split downpour that held him exactly in the dry center of its upper falling. The few ferns on the rock glittered with drops, hardy and delicate, and slowly, as he did nothing but be there, he felt building up an exhilarating sense of new authority. It was like the space beneath him, the nothingness under the rock, the effortless disappearance of himself into bright cloud, into the thunderous and fragile foaming of air, should he move slightly in any direction but back. He thought of what he might do, other than edge back into the woods and return to Florence. He was sure there was something remarkable involved here, in the randomness of his poise in such a place, in the sense of irrevocable falling that built under his feet and did not come, yet expanded from the mist beneath as though to include everything he could see. The thought of his disappearance straight down between two shafts of water that seemed as much to be standing as falling was one he took some pleasure in rejecting, particularly since he felt none of the impulse to leap that he had heard was a part of heights. Still, he thought, I have not done enough here. He had no camera, and doubted he would have used it if he had. There must be something else. He raised one hand out from his side into the thin near edge of the split falls, and then his left into the other, and closed his eyes.

There was no downpouring of himself, no doubling, no revelation, but yet another renewal of power, this time through the wrists, as the drops shed sideways off the vertical headlongness of water, the plunge beyond everything into fine-spun whiteness, struck his hands and wrists, each drop with the full force of the whole tonnage of water going past him, beating steadily on his upturned veins. His whole body fed on hooded necessity and suicidal freedom, as though on a closed current running through it. He stood in a mixture of water and air, inhaling moisture like cold, heavy steam, and the pressure from the rock thrusting upward to hold him seemed unnecessary, accidental. He had not forgotten the uniqueness of the sensation, which kept coming back to him at unlikely times, disturbing, challenging, and necessary. Suddenly, now, he understood what was central to the situation, and to the memory: it was that beneath the rock on which he had stood with his arms out and his wrists catching the hard drops of down-driving water, there had been nothing, nothing but air smoky with exploded water from invisible rocks many feet below, in uncommon and turbulent cloud. He had projected himself out over this, over air and water, unwitnessed in cold assurance, and he felt that he had partaken of the unstoppable quality of the double falls, the uncaring and irrelevant reality. This, and the thought that he could disappear into the whiteness below him—that his control of the situation was absolute, no matter what he did—had become as valuable to him as anything that had ever happened in his life. At first this had not seemed to be so, but since his blindness the other images from his former life had come to revolve around this memory of himself in the cold spring woods, completely alone, near death—above death—in a kind of pose that had in its odd theatricality a quality of rightness; it had become his main personal resource. The strongest images from the time when the images were made—his brother Perrin's sparring, the fast heavy boy on the track with the slashing gold stripe down his thigh, the hurtling green of the high driveway in North Atlanta as he came down it on skates, the stillness in the wedged ponds of the water works—had come to depend on this one, and gave way immediately when his mind turned toward it. He had had no body there, between the light, hard-falling double whites; had felt no weight in himself; none—but there had also been the sense of his body as his alone, something that could not be made again; either Cahill could have risen from the rock.

Through the double hissing fall at his sides, the stunned roar uprising to him through weightless and brilliant cloud, came a soft whickering murmur, a resolving overturn, as though breath might be made in some way to whirl: that spokes could be made to turn through it.

A hundred and fifty yards away a PT-17 was thirty feet above the runway on the final approach, the front cockpit empty, the figure in the rear one upright and rigid. Too high in its approximation of a landing stall, it free-feel the last few feet, and hit hard.

"The poor son-of-a-bitch dropped it in," McCaig said. "Damn near busted his ass. If he'd'a been up about twenty or thirty feet more he really would have busted it. But that ain't one of my kids. Thank God." Then, to Cahill, "I just thought. Would you like to go into Supply? We're right here at it. There's a civilian worker that I think knew your boy. Would that be any good to you?"

"Who knows?" Cahill said. "I don't have no rules about any of this. There prob'ly ain't any. There prob'ly ain't any. Sure, let's go see whoever it is."

"Whoever it is, is Lucille." He hesitated, but with relish. "I don't know Lucille's last name, but she's around. I mean, *around.* If you get what I'm sayin'."

"I get what you're sayin'," Cahill said matter-of-factly.

"She's one of the civilian workers on the base. I'm not sure, but I don't think she comes from town, here. Maybe some other little town, out in the county. Anyway, she's been around here for as long as I have. She took up with the colonel for a while, and she may still be takin' up with him. It don't make no never mind to me, what she does. But she gives out with the flying boots and sheepskins and the rest of the equipment, and it would be kind of strange if she didn't remember Joel, because you couldn't be around him and not know that he was something different from just somebody you'd meet anywhere. You'd know that without him sayin' a thing. But usually he'd say somethin'. If he did, to her, she'd remember, sure enough."

With light touches McCaig guided the blind man and the dog around the corner of the hangar, and down a short walk half snow and half gravel. He opened a door close-set into the building, and guided Cahill through.

One or two steps forward, with the door closed behind him, brought a surround to which Cahill knew it was going to be hard to adjust. The air in it was wrong, though cool and not unpleasant. There was a closeness, an inertness to it that suggested its being held between heavy, soft substances, batting or wadding.

The voices of McCaig and a female were a little muffled, and did not seem to want to carry. Zack stirred against his leg, smelling and being bothered. Cahill felt held there with the dog, as though both were encased in substances—or one substance, maybe—meant to protect them, but also indifferent and murderous. The odor was fresh and musty at the same time.

The voice was aggressively country; there was no other way for Cahill to embody it except as

There was only one light in the huge high room, packed from the floor to levels requiring a ladder to reach, with leather-and-wool jackets, pants, boots, helmets and gloves. The hooded bulb over the counter allowed only a small amount of this to be seen; the static, hushed, and vaguely sinister atmosphere of insulation came from the rows and racks of wool going back far into the dark.

"There are a lot of sheeps in here, Mr. Cahill," McCaig said. "I don't say sheep; I say sheeps. There's a lot of 'em in here. All dead."

"Hello, Double M," the woman behind the counter said. "What can I do for you? Done wore out your wool? Need some more?"

Anyone's last impression of the girl would likely be the same as the first. She was flat-faced and small-mouthed, with dry rough two-toned blond hair and high color, but another would hardly notice this, for the attention, particularly the male attention, was drawn to her obvious and powerful breasts, tight and upthrust through a blue rayon blouse over

a waitress in a truck stop, with savage nails and bright caked lipstick, or as one of the munitions workers—a lady welder, as they called them—like the kind Karl Kesmodl and the other weight lifters brought out to Willow Plunge on Sundays. He saw Karl and his last date, whom his lifeguard had described as "rougher than a night in jail in south Georgia." Stocky, he remembered, with plenty of ass, and lipstick so purple it was almost black. That seemed to be in line with the compressed deadness of the room, and he went with it.

which she wore a heavy porous white sweater like a man's. Her breasts gave her a pouter-pigeon look, as though she were meant to rest her chin against them. She was working on a form, which she finished and placed on some other paper.

"My wool's all right," McCaig said. "I've got what I want." He nudged Cahill. "I got my own place to pasture my sheeps, up there in the clouds, in that great sheep wallow in the sky."

The girl looked up fully from the counter, and stood waiting, glancing at the dog, which was throwing its head uneasily from one side to the other, sniffing different directions.

"Lucille," McCaig said, "I want you to meet Mr. Frank Cahill from Atlanta. His boy was the one who got killed up here a few days back. You know about that."

"I do," she answered. "I'm real sorry, Mr. Cahill. Everybody up here is real sorry. He was a very good-looking boy. Everybody liked him."

Cahill drew the pair of goggles from his pocket, feeling a slight unexpected sting of pain in his middle finger. He put the goggles on the counter and felt for the splinter of glass with his other hand, pulled it out, and licked the finger before speaking.

"They tell me these were Joel's, and they also tell me that they came from you, from here, from in this place. Am I right so far?"

"Yes, you are," she replied. "They're standard issue; everybody wears the same." She looked at the glasses without making any move.

"Do you know who B.V. is? Or what it is?"

"I don't get you," she said. "I don't believe I know what you're talkin' about."

"Look on the strap," he said. "Don't it say B.V.?"

She hesitated, then turned the strap so that the letters were visible.

"It does say B.V., but I don't know what that could mean. Right off, I can't think of anybody around here with them initials. I can't help you."

"Could they have belonged to somebody who had 'em before him?"

"No; these were new issue; new with his class. I could show you the forms." She caught herself, and went on. "I could show *him* the forms," she said, indicating McCaig. "Joel Cahill must have put those initials on his band, or somebody else did, after he drew the goggles. That's all I can say. I don't know no more."

McCaig moved as if to pick up the goggles, but Cahill kept him in place with a forearm, then ran his hand over the cold surface until he found the goggles, folded the splintered glass parts together, and put them back in his pocket. He was ready to leave, and McCaig saw this.

"Lucille, thank you. Don't feel bad. Mr. Cahill just wanted to ask. He's talking to a bunch of people."

"No," said Cahill, "don't feel bad. I don't reckon it really makes no difference who B.V. is. It just seemed kind of an odd thing, that he would do that. I would think it must have some meanin' to it, but we won't never know what it is, most likely. And that's prob'ly all right, too."

"Maybe you will," she said. "Maybe somethin' will come along."

"Sure," Cahill said.

"Lucille," McCaig said, brightening a little for the farewell, "I'm sorry I didn't give you a better introduction, with your whole name and everything, but it just now come to me that I don't know what your last name is."

"My last name is Wick, Mr. Two-Mac. My name is Lucille Wick and I come from Stancill, South Carolina. I was born there and moved here. And you ought'a have that in all your introductions from now on."

"I won't forget," McCaig said. "I'll tell all the people. I'll tell 'em that you live with hundreds of dead sheeps, and send 'em up into the clouds."

"You do that," she said. "It's true."

"And I'll tell 'em that you wear a man's sweater around, and that you look good doin' it. Who does it belong to?"

"A man," she said. "That suit you?"

"It suits me," said McCaig. "We'll see you later on."

"I'll look for you. It was nice to meet you, Mr. Cahill."

"Yes," Cahill said. "Thank you for talkin' to us." They turned and maneuvered outward. When the door had closed behind them and they were walking again in the air, fresh, clean, and moving, carrying again the sound of engines both on the ground and above it, McCaig said startlingly, "Did you like that?"

"What? What do you mean? Did I like what?"

"Did you like that in there? I didn't like it. I didn't like it, and I don't like her. One of these days I'll tell you about that one."

"All right. You might as well. It won't cost you."

"Right. I might as well tell you," said McCaig. "She's the first of her kind around here; she's real popular. She came here to fuck, and there's many of these boys has taken up with her. Also the colonel has taken up with her. Also I've taken up with her, but not for long. She's rattled and bounced around this base for the whole time I've been here, and God knows what she was doin' before that. She gets all over you, and she's hoping to get *to* you, but you'd be damn foolish if you let that happen. I don't know what Colonel Hoccleve is doin' about her, or with her—that I don't want to know; I don't even want to think about it. But everywhere I go and see one, I see the other. It must be that the colonel's wife, who is real nice, especially to the boys and the instructors, and don't deserve no bad time . . . it must be that she either don't care or knows she can't do nothin' about it, but I sure wouldn't want to be her. Or him, either. And I sure wouldn't want to be Lucille; that would be bad. That would be the worst of all. She's got some nice tits, and plenty of natural fire, for a few years. After all that's gone, she's not goin' to have nothin', and anybody who ever fooled with her is gonna have a real bad taste in the back of his mouth, and is not goin' to feel right about himself, especially if he ever has children, and gets around to lookin' 'em in the face."

"Maybe you're makin' too much out of it," Cahill said. "There's plenty of them kind around. I run a swimmin' pool, and a swimmin' pool will attract more sluts and shits than any other place you can think of. Some of 'em turn out all right, and get married, and the rest of it. Some of 'em even marry each other. Think of that, why don't you?"

"You think about it," McCaig said. "I'm already married." He waited a moment. They were moving across an open space, cutting between the jeep road that led in a long curve from the cadet area to the flight line, heading in a vague direction back toward the Administration Building.

"My connection with flyin' has to do with makin' things come up out of the ground," McCaig said. "I came into flyin' off the farm, and the whole thing has got that kind of relationship, don't you see? I was raised in a hardscrabble situation, about half red clay and half sand. I was the oldest of six of us, and the strongest by a long ways. I was lucky whenever I could get a day in school; any day my daddy told me he didn't need me to work, I figured that was my good luck; either he had forgot about it or somethin' good had happened that I didn't know about. Right now, Mr. Cahill, I could take on anybody head-to-head with a posthole digger. Every time I close my hands, I get another grip on the ground, and pull it up, pull it out, and lay it down. If it didn't make you so tired so fast, I would have got to like it, because you're grabbin' down deep in there, and when you get a good holt of the underground—I mean *in* it, deep down inside of it—it's different from just bringin' it up with a shovel. But, like I say, it gets old. It gets old, and you get old and tired, fast. I was fairly well bent over when I was seventeen, and it could'a well been that I was lookin' for somethin' to straighten me up. I got into flyin' the easiest way you could do it, I guess. We had bad grasshoppers through here. The worst you ever saw. It was the second time we had 'em. The first was when I was a little boy, and I was out there beatin' 'em off the soybeans with an old coat, my little sister's. My daddy sat down in the field and went to cryin', and after a while I sat down, out by myself where I was, and just watched the grasshoppers stripping them plants. I never seen nothin' like the way they went after 'em. At first I watched a whole bunch of 'em, and then I watched just one, for about fifteen minutes. That's somethin' you don't forget. There was nothin' that could'a stopped that thing from eatin', except to kill him. And you'd have to kill him mighty dead. The grasshoppers, they ruint us that year, and when I was sixteen it looked like they was fixin' to come at us again. My old man went in with some of the other farmers around and hired a crop-duster, and he come and done us some good. There was still some damage from the hoppers, but not nearly so much; it wadn't nearly as bad, the second time around. But the main thing was that I got to talk to the pilot. I can still remember his name; his name was Prentice McBrayer, and he was about ten years older than me. All the rest of the kids used to hang around with him and drink Coca-Cola, and try to get him to take 'em up, but he never would. But before he left he did sneak me in, and I never have got over it yet. When we left the ground, and we went into that other thing, where you don't have no holt on anything anywhere—not with your hands, not with your feet—but are just sittin' there kind of jiggling inside a whole lot of noise and wind; well, that was *somethin'*, for a country boy. That was something *else,* as they used to say around home." He slowed. "Have you ever been up, Mr. Cahill?"

"No," Cahill said. "I never have. One time I helped some young boy crank up a model airplane and fly it, back in Atlanta. That's the nearest I ever got. I thought for just a second that I might'a had some kind of notion of the feeling of it, but no, I ain't never been up. I can't think of no time when there might'a been any reason."

"I got awful sick, that first time," McCaig went on. "These boys around here that get sick before they get used to it, I know how they feel. But I ain't never in my life been so happy and so sick at the same time. We were up above our farm, which was in the middle of three or four others, about seven hundred fifty or a thousand feet, where there's just a change in things on the ground that you know makes a lot of difference: makes all the difference. It hit me right off: you could make things change their angle; if you wanted them to, the creeks and the fences and the barns and silos would slant any way you said; everything would tilt, and it would come to you or go away from you; you could go down to it, or on up away from it; it would do everything and anything you had a mind for it to. I sat there and watched the controls make them little moves. We was in a old Waco, not too much different from the planes these kids is flyin' in. I was sick and happy. I still had my connection with the ground, with the farm, with the fences and creeks and dirt roads and the fields and the hills and the rest of it, but there was somethin' else to it, now. I could leave all that in a different way, and I could come back to it, and keep what I had done seen and how I had done felt, and have it with me while I walked around, knowin' that the whole thing wadn't really solid, and had another side to it that most people didn't know but I knew."

"How did you actually get into it?" Cahill said, involved beyond his wish. "How did you learn to fly? Don't that take a lot of time? Somebody has got to pay for it, I'd think."

"Well, there's ways you can work it out. Once I had that first time up off the ground, I had somethin' that I'd go through a lot before I'd turn loose. I was already out of school, and I moved to High Point, by myself, and got a job changin' tires in a Shell station, and bought me some lessons—as many as I could—until I got a license. Then a little at a time I worked into dustin', myself. That suited me. I like to be close to the ground, to fly near the ground; near the ground, and still in the air. In this-here war, they tell me there's a lot of low-level work. One pilot who'd been in England, who came through here in a P-51 and refueled, said that the Germans've got pilots who come in under them new electrical systems the Limeys've got for warnin' 'em, flyin' so low you can't pick 'em up; they fly instruments six foot off the water."

This meant nothing to Cahill, but he went on listening. He was walking in no particular place, feeling outward with his leg from time to time for Zack, but there were no obstacles, nothing to step over or go through, no stairs here. He settled into the temporary condition and tried to pick up on what McCaig was saying. It was only when he did so that he realized that the other man was not saying anything, and that he apparently was not near him, either. He slowed, stopped and, not wanting to seem foolish, turned slowly toward where he had expected McCaig to be.

McCaig was thinking of something else; it grew on him and then stopped him. He saw Cahill and the dog walk on, slowly and with a look of patient and relentless exploration. The gloved hand on the side with the dog reached down once to feel for the dog and touch it, but the other was in Cahill's pocket, and McCaig realized suddenly, and with sickening force, might have been closed on the dead boy's goggles. The thought shut off what McCaig had been saying, had been planning to say, and, as he stopped speaking, the knowledge he thought he had of how to walk beside the blind man and the dog fell away from him. But it was not silence that was needed; the horror of their curious parade moving through the nondescript field edge without communication, stepping slowly and wordlessly along, the blind man so far down and in, so remote, so taciturn and impenetrable, so reserved and hard to talk to that McCaig would have taken any other possible situation, was not something he could allow, so long as he was part of it. McCaig moved, jogged a few steps, and came up.

"Listen," McCaig said. "Listen, I just want to . . ." Cahill swung toward him.

"I just want to make some . . . some comments on my own, that don't have nothin' to do with these military people around here, or the civilians either. These boys, I don't really know none of 'em very well. I try to do what I can for 'em. But most of 'em really don't have no business flyin' airplanes. There's not really anything in the air *for* 'em. Some of the other instructors tell these boys that flyin' an airplane is just like drivin' a car; that if they can drive they can fly. But the boys that go into it with that attitude are mighty lucky to get through here, and they'll be lucky to stay alive, whether they get shot at or not. An airplane is not like a car; it's a lot more like an animal of some kind, a bird, a big one. You see what I mean? You're . . . you're ridin' it, and it *feels* everything, up, down, and to the sides. It feels everything that's in the *thing* it's in, the air, and you feel it through the plane. The air is different from the ground. The way you move is so different. And the different ways you can be in it, the angles and all. It's . . . it's *personal.* For somebody who's got this kind of feelin', who has just got it because it's his nature to have it, can fly an airplane, and he gets more out of doin' it than anybody else could do. These boys here, they take whole notebooks full of the things we tell 'em, and they try to fly, right by the notes. You take one of 'em up for a check-ride, and you watch the needles, and you see that they make a starboard or a port turn out of the traffic pattern at exactly five hundred feet, or as near as they can get to it. That's what we've told 'em to do, and that's what they do, if they can. And it's what they ought to do, because a lot of flyin' depends on watchin' speeds and altitudes, needles and different matchups of instruments. They should know that part of it, but it's not the real nature of flyin'; it makes flyin' like ridin' a stuffed horse that runs on batteries or winds up with a big shiny tin key. Somebody who's got the . . . the instinct for the air—like your boy did—is doing somethin' and feelin' somethin' and bein' somethin' that these windup fliers like most of these kids—and some of the instructors too, like that Foy back yonder in the ready room, talkin' to that boy about the wind like he knew somethin' about it—don't have and can't get. I fly with 'em and get paid for it, but they don't see it my way. It was a whole lot different with your son, and I'm not tellin' you this just to make you feel good. You let him get into the air, you ride with him, and you know right fast that he's got a different lick from the others: from *any* of 'em. Inside of twenty hours he could do anything in an airplane that I could do, or that I can do

138

now. He was not reckless, but if he wanted to do dangerous stuff, like flyin' under some of these high-tension lines around here, he could'a have done it with no trouble, and with him it wouldn'a been dangerous. He had a kind of control of these little crates that you would have to see to believe. About fifteen hours out he did a perfect slow roll with his eyes closed: came out right on a point; never got off the point. I didn't look at him to see if they was closed, but he said he did it, and I believe him. Just two or three days before he was killed, him and me went up one afternoon and really wrung one of these things out. It'd be hard for me to explain to you some of the stuff we did, but I was hard put to it to think of anything I could do that he couldn't. At the end of the hour, after I'd make some kind of maneuver and he'd do exactly the same thing, and then do another one, I just let him have it; turned loose the controls and just rode, and if I ever had the feelin' of being in an airplane that was flyin' itself, it was then. Everybody who knew him could tell there was somethin' not real about him, and there was. Not real, but better. I'll tell you what he used to do, and I know this for a fact because I was one of the ones that seen it. People say they seen it, but I really did see it. I asked him about it, and he said it was true."

Cahill, puzzled, waited, now very cold, and suddenly conscious that he was standing there suffering.

"What was it? He did what?"

"He'd take a plane up solo, and then go off somewhere toward the edge of the general area we fly in around here, and he would get down in the cockpit, down on the floor, and just control the plane with the trim tab, you know, with just little moves with his hands, and fly along, back into the main area. I was up with another cadet one day, and I seen this Stearman come by with nobody in it, or at least as far as anybody could tell. It was the goddamnedest-lookin' thing, a plane just flyin' along with two empty cockpits. Like I say, I really did see this, and some others did too, but not everybody who said they saw it, did."

"What was the point of that?" Cahill asked, interested and irritated. "He couldn't see where he was going, could he? Ain't that dangerous?"

"Sure it's dangerous, and I don't think he did it but a couple of times. I asked him about it, because I was afraid somebody would get hurt with him foolin' around like that, and he just said he wanted to see what people would say when they saw an empty airplane go by. It had the effect he wanted, though, I guess. The boys and everybody else on the base talked about it a lot, and nobody ever identified the plane with him, but everybody knew it was him and that he'd done somethin' else in the air that nobody but him would'a thought of. Turns out, nobody got hurt. At least not from that."

Cahill broke from his frozen position and moved toward where he had been going. Before McCaig could say anything else, Cahill spoke into the weak, fluttering wind he bowed into.

"This is the way you find out stuff when you're blind," he said. "You keep movin'. You keep other people movin'. I plan to do a lot of walkin', up here. Can we go some place where it ain't so cold?"

"We sure can," McCaig replied. "We can walk on over to the cadet club, and get a Coke, if you want to. Or maybe a Coke and a sandwich. I've got to make an outside phone call, and I usually use the phone in there. These military phones make me nervous; the whole business in the Administration Building makes me nervous. We'll go to the club. Some of this base used to be a little country club, and they got as far as puttin' in the swimming pool, and I think they had just about laid out the golf course, at least on paper, but they never got to build any of it. All the graders and backhoes and road scrapers they were goin' to use to build the sandtraps and bunkers got used to build a airfield. As a airfield this is a pretty fair golf course. No; I take that back. It's not a pretty fair anything, but it's the best the Air Corps could come up with, so fast. They tell me eventually they'll put in a mat runway, but I don't think they will. Primary trainin' needs a big open place like a cow pasture, like this one, so the boys can get used to what the wind does at different times, get used to the traffic pattern being set up in different directions: learn to match the plane to the air just at that time when they're going up into it, and coming down out of it."

Cahill plodded forward, cold space planted on his forehead, reaching down for Zack every few steps. Ruíz had asked him, and so had Darrell and others at the pool in Atlanta, why he didn't put a harness on the dog, or devise something with a handle by means of which he could be in contact without having to bend over and feel continually, but he had resisted them because he liked to believe that the bond

They were heading on a slant course for the space between the mess hall at the end of the flight line, with several aircraft nearly touching its baseboards and shingle, and the Administration Building. They cleared into the packed sand and lightly snowed assembly area between the Administration Building and the main cadet bar-

140

between Zack and himself did not need to be physical, something artificial, but that the dog would do, as a matter of course and its instincts, what needed to be done, and that, whatever this action might be, it would also include Cahill's own safety: it pleased him to keep Zack's strength and quickness unbound, close and free.

They were leaving one of the two main sounds with which Cahill had come to identify the base, and coming into another, moving slowly from the flare and whicker and sighing of engines into the confused and excited voices of what seemed to him perpetual play, an endless game of some sort, or perhaps of many sorts. There was a sense, now, of mighty and strenuous breath over large space, from many distances, many tones of delight, urgency and uncertainty. All at once, nearer to him than most of the other voices, there was a wordless explosion, a strong grunt which could only he thought have gone into a throw: a throw as far as someone could manage; Cahill paused, turned toward the field and the sounds, waiting for the sound of the reception, the completion, or whatever would tell that the thrown object had come down. Far off he heard this happen, or something like it: someone's racks, passed the long low structures, and moving casually but carefully, came opposite the great playing field where a football game, like an encounter between two large groups—no, armies—of boys was going on. There were forty or fifty players on each side; the scrimmage line was thirty yards wide, and as McCaig watched, the ball was snapped to a small figure with his back to them. It seemed to McCaig that the whole playing field erupted into one tangled mass of rushers and blockers, some of them hitting pretty hard, he thought; hard enough for pads; surely too hard for a game of touch. The small boy with the ball retreated toward them, side on to the line, looking. He moved aside quickly, out of the path of a tall, balding, fresh-faced rusher, started to his right, changed his mind, then leaped and fired the ball, out into anything; it hung as the passer was swamped. He fell, but an opponent steadied and righted him. The throw looked as good as a football in the air can look; the spiral was so smooth that the ends of the ball seemed not to waver from the axis. In the distance a lean figure picked it off; it seemed to have been thrown directly to him, though he was one of the enemy.

flesh—hands—smacked not together but on another thing, the voices loudened, there was a tremendous lift of excitement, and many feet running from him. He believed it was football; he was satisfied it was.

In this space he was willing to wait, and it seemed better to say nothing, to ask nothing. The voices and collisions of the game were remote, and he faced them with no feeling, but with a slight interest to listen, turning his better ear. Sound was his distance, and as he tuned to it there was a change. The far shouts, like sharp whispers with wrong high tones in them, had suddenly taken on a note of surprise, appeal, warning, a kind of panic. The pelter of feet reappeared, bearing toward him; quickly he could make out the curious trudge-and-sprint shuffle made by runners on sand. His uneasiness, at first nothing much, began to increase. There was now so much noise, so much yammering and tussling, so many yells that seemed all to one purpose but at the same time all against each other, so much turmoil and heaviness and skewing sand-squeak of feet, that it was impossible not to feel pursued, stampeded, just before being stomped, overwhelmed, left dead. The man beside him leaned against his arm, and he

For a moment the far figure with the ball did not move, but leaned to one side, as though listening. Then with a quick shift of weight it broke, leaped in the opposite direction, slanting through the nearest clutch of boys like a gangling shadow, knees high and wide apart, slender, swaying, bulkless and graceful. Though he had never been an athlete, McCaig felt himself drawn onto the field, into it; this and more as the ball carrier came involvedly toward him, fronting and faking, giving and taking away, lost among clumps of boys and appearing through them with quick shifts and spurts, until McCaig could not believe that the runner was not gifted in some way with a quickness beyond that of the others, some form of intuition, anticipation, by which he drew his course in one direction, slashed or swiveled through them, their moves wrong for the new vector, on which he flared and from which he changed again, naturally and without thought, a lone, lean creature designed to run through herds of men, never breaking free and never touched. In contrast the

started, then braced himself anew. Nothing had touched him yet; he had not been overrun: as he thought suddenly, boys are on the ground coming at me, they are in the air over me, they are every which way I could go; but these here, he thought, setting his face with his body, will just break apart on me; they will just split and go around.

Now they were almost on top of him, milling, looming, seeming to lash and flame, glancing off, air of all kinds driven from bodies and exploding in cries beyond words, in curses and near-sobs like shock waves. There was a terrible mass wheeze and intake of breath, a violent shift in sand, one muffled and breaking impact like a hammer striking a flour sack, and another, lighter one.

other boys on both teams swirled in a pillowy chaos of sweatclothes about him, turning, leaping toward him, changing direction as he changed, but a fraction late, some unbalanced by their efforts, some undercut by blockers, all milling and clashing softly, with pained cries.

The whole game neared, and against so much bundled chaotic flesh, so much weight and brute confusion, McCaig moved without thinking toward the blind man, who stood on solid legs, one hand down toward the dog, with fingers spread but not bending his body. Like a statue, McCaig thought as he glanced, but knew immediately that this was wrong. Cahill's face was not set, but had a look of remote vigilance; if he was like a statue, it was a statue that saw, that watched something far off and important.

The weaving runner and his pursuers and blockers were very near now, and just as McCaig turned back to the field, a heavy boy with tight curled black hair threw himself into the sand under the feet of a defender—which were off the ground in a leap— and over his ankles, more than humanly alive in his vivid swerve, the runner hooked his own foot and went down, rolled once on the ground as though this were part of the run, and came up to them, pitching the ball to one of his players.

"Good," McCaig said, meaning it. "Very good, Shears. Too bad you can't fly like that."

"I can," Shears said, panting. "I do it all the time. When are you going up and wring one out with me?"

"Sometime," McCaig answered. "You showed me somethin' on the ground, though. You went through them other cadets like Ex-Lax through a werewolf. You was in three or four places at once. How do you do it?"

"I do it," Shears said. "What you have to do is to get their feet set the wrong way. Always be going the wrong way, for them. That just flashes 'em off you, backward and wrong-side out. They never knew what went where."

"It looked like you was bringin' all them boys right down on top of us, like a herd of turtles."

"Well, I did see you standing out here, and I did more or less home in on you, because I was going that way anyway. If you said you were the center of my control, you wouldn't be far wrong." Here, strangely to McCaig, Shears glanced at Cahill, and the instructor was almost sure that he winked or did something conspiratorial with one eye, or both. McCaig looked more intently at the boy, whose chest was lifting and falling less strongly, but strongly, his color pulsing a high delicate deep rose with exertion and cold.

That is some good-looking boy, he thought. How come he seemed so delicate and skinny and tall out there dodging those other boys, he wondered, and so blocky and solid now? There was no way to tell, but as the three of them stood breathing together he noticed something about Shears that he had not been aware of before. The expression on the face, youthful and alive beyond any life McCaig felt a human being could afford or should ask for, was a little fixed, almost as though glazed; the eyes were vivid but flat, as though they did not belong to the body now slowly calming its breath and turning from them.

"Will you be going into town tonight?" Shears asked then. "I get open post, and I could meet you somewhere."

McCaig hesitated. "I don't know what Mr. Cahill might want to do," he said. "I got to go on home and take care of some stuff." He turned to Cahill. "What do you think you might want to do, later on?"

144

Cahill brought his ungloved hand from his pocket and touched his chin twice, thinking. "It depends on how I feel, then," he said. "Usually I try to get tired enough to sleep. I can tell when I get that tired. Where I'll be when I'm ready to go to sleep, I don't know, but somebody'll be with me, to get me home. I told that Greek boy I would talk to him sometime today, and if I go anywhere tonight I'll prob'ly go with him. So don't worry about it."

"Tomorrow," Shears said. "We'll see you tomorrow. That's for sure. Out here."

"Out here," Cahill said. "That'll be fine."

The game tattered and dispersed, its moment gone, and its focus. Cadets, looking ordinary, heavy, and let down, trooped off, with the mutter of aftermath.

"Would you like to sit in on some ground school?" McCaig asked. "It prob'ly won't make any sense to you, but it's all part of what the boys go through. We're between classes right now, and if you want to we could walk on over to the classroom buildin's and listen to somebody talk about the physics of flight, or maybe about DR navigation, or about fuel octane ratings." He relaxed, planning what he would say and how he would say it. "You drive a car, don't you?"

"I used to," Cahill said, smiling a little. "I'd play hell drivin' now."

"Do you know what octanes are, in gasoline? And how they get that way?"

"No," Cahill said. "I don't have the slightest idea. And I don't give a shit."

"I don't either, but it's part of what them civilian ground bunnies try to pass on to our young fellows here, and if you want to listen to 'em, we can go on over and listen."

"We could sort of start movin' in that direction," Cahill said. "We might think of somethin' else on the way. If we can, we'll do it, and if we can't we'll go listen to 'em talk about gas."

"We could stop off at the cadet club and have a Coke. Are you hungry? Would you like a sandwich?"

"I could eat," Cahill said, "and maybe we could get somethin' for Zack. He likes sandwiches. He eats more bread than any blood-dog I ever saw. Can't get enough."

"I thought he was mean," McCaig said. "He looks mean. I been keeping you between him and me."

"He can be mean." Cahill raised an arm and pointed off. "Move out yonder about five or ten yards, and do what I tell you."

"Listen," McCaig said sincerely, "I don't want no demonstrations. I believe you."

Cahill went on, into it. "If you stepped out there, and then made a quick move and was to come at me, you would wish you hadn't. And if I told him to get after you . . ."

"What do you mean, 'get after'?"

"I mean kill you. He would kill you if I said one word. He would kill you, or you'd have to kill him."

"What's the word?"

"That's between us. It's a deep word. It works, too."

"I don't have no doubt of it," McCaig said, glancing around at the openness they stood in.

"Zack!" Cahill said suddenly. The dog stood up, ears high, tail tense.

"Don't show me *nothin'*," McCaig said. "I believe you right up to heaven and on down to hell, and all around and in between. Don't sic that dog on me."

"I won't sic him on you. Look here," he said, bending his head down. "Sic him, Zack. Sic him." The dog waited intently, and moved his tail once.

"I told you," Cahill said. " 'Sic him' is not the word. 'Sic him' is for them other dogs." He grazed McCaig with a big hand. "Just don't make no moves like you was comin' after me with somethin', or trying to beat on me, or even push me. He don't like that. *I* don't like it, but he don't like it twice as much. That's the only other thing that'll trigger him. Besides that, he's just a big old boneheaded wolf that eats sandwiches and likes mayonnaise and other stuff that ain't even manly."

They took up where they had left off, keeping the same relations and the same distance from each other, the dog with his tongue out panting grayly, and the men stepping considerately as little by little they left the now empty field, and followed the last of the sweatsuited boys back toward the central area of the base, with its wide buildings and stands of long-needled trees. They passed the Administration Building, and between it and the barracks continued through the assembly area toward the road that led to the highway. There was little sound; sand, when not made to squeak by violence and effort, is quiet; one walking in it lowers the voice, as Cahill and McCaig now did, on the soft road.

At the first curve McCaig waited for another of his rewards, like the aircraft homing into trees. The base cadet club came to them through the low limbs of firs bit by bit, as was right, for it was a charming subtle place, not obvious, not military, but cottagelike, resembling a golf clubhouse or the headquarters of a real estate company which sold lots in "natural locations." It was shingled, and the windows and door-frames were white, trimmed in green almost the color of the surrounding trees. A gravel walkway led to it from the road, past a swimming pool now low in water and slush, skimmed with ice; two chairs made with attractive clumsiness out of thick boards and grayish with white paint sat at curious angles to the pool, one near the diving board and the other facing away from it toward the flight line. They went in, McCaig holding the door respectfully for Zack.

Cahill's body, particularly down the sides and in the feet and hands, responded gratefully to the warmth, and in spite of himself, he was even grateful to be among people, some of them near enough to touch, should he choose. With his left hand he took hold of the spring grip in his pocket, and tightened it three times, satisfied when his face tightened as well. He concentrated, to learn the scene his way, and own it. The voices—young, always, and this time with one female among them—were nothing he wished to keep, nor was the music some yards away, which had mentioned a paper doll two or three times already, since he had been inside. What caught him was a series of bounces and clicks, which at first he could not identify, but he listened, for there was both rhythm and uncertainty in the repetitions, all with a suggestion of fragility and lightness.

"What's goin' on?" he asked

McCaig shook out his arms in their sleeves in the pleasantness, for he had been holding them close to his side. Just inside the door they were at the edge of the current group of cadets using the club between classes, before or after flying. A few were reading or looking over notes, but most were standing, restless, nervous and enthusiastic, clean-shaven, neatly combed, in the dark drab olive uniforms—again, almost the color of the trees and the trim of the clubhouse—and always the incessant freshness of their winter color, not just in spots of brightness on each but in every case taking the cheeks fully, whether the complexion was dark or light. There was a soda fountain, where a girl bantered shrilly and sexually with a couple of cadets in country terms with much animal imagery, and a Negro sandwich-maker in a white paper hat sliced steadily, put the sandwiches on plates, and pushed them away from him along a wooden counter.

McCaig. **"This where we get somethin' to eat?"**

"Well," McCaig said, "it's a right lively scene this time of day. Over yonder Colonel Hoccleve is playin' Ping-Pong with a red-headed cadet, I think his name is Appleby. The colonel does pop check-rides every now and then, and it looks like he just rode with Appleby. Appleby must'a passed." McCaig looked down at the dog, and resisted patting its head, which he had nearly bent to do.

"I'll get you a Coke and a couple of sandwiches. Any special kind?" he said.

"Anything with meat," Cahill said. "Bacon or ham. Zack likes bacon. And mayonnaise. You don't believe it, but he does like it. I wouldn't shit you." In the new quiet that had been coming on them, Cahill was already sorry that he had said shit, for he kept forgetting the seriousness of his being where he was, among these invisible boys and in their world. He might even have said "Excuse me," but knew without thinking that it would only make things worse, and tightened again, for what they would make of it.

McCaig came back with a large Coca-Cola in a crisp paper cup and two sandwiches on a limp plate.

"Bacon and mayonnaise," he said. "You didn't say nothin' about lettuce. I don't reckon he likes lettuce, does he? I could'a got lettuce on one of 'em. Still could."

"No; that's all right. We'll go on outside and eat."

"Don't you want to stay in here where it's warm?"

"No," Cahill said. "It's a little too close in here for me. I warm up fast. And I don't like to hear too many people talkin' all together, real close to me. Makes me nervous. I never do know what to say." He swung around to go, knowing he had come only two steps inside the door and sure he could find it; he believed the main door opened inward—it would have to—but was also reasonably sure there was a screen. Concentrating, he moved, reaching for Zack's collar. McCaig followed with the drink and sandwiches, letting the blind man do what he intended.

With Cahill seated in the chair by the diving board, McCaig put one of the sandwiches into his hand, and sat the Coke on the wide board of the chair arm.

"I've got to go make a phone call," he said. "I'll be back in just a minute, and we'll go on to class. If you get up, don't step straight ahead, or you'll end up in the swimming pool."

"I'll stay put," Cahill said. "This ain't my pool."

He turned up his collar again, settled his big coat around him and closer to him, felt for the cold paper cup, took a sweet biting drink, replaced the cup, and putting the hand back in the pocket began to eat the sandwich, the bread, slightly stale, the salty bacon, and the slick mayonnaise. He felt normal; I must be doing the insulin business more or less the right way, he thought; I'm not thirsty, I'm not pissing a lot, I'm not craving sweets, I'm not sweating, and I don't feel weak. He finished the sandwich, and slid that hand into the pocket, curled the fingers around the goggles, which were doubled, eye over eye, by the small space. With his thumb he tested again for splinters, and for the first time let his mind fix not on the goggles but on whom they had belonged to, what they had done, where they had been and what had happened to them. No imagery came from this, though he began shyly to think of thinking of fire and smoke, and was even at the point of

From the classroom building area, cutting through on no path, a trim wool-collared man emerged and walked toward the pool. He stopped, almost dandyish, and regarded Cahill. He stood watching all the time Cahill ate, then came toward him and stopped again when he saw that the blind man was talking to himself. Slowly he made a half-circle behind Cahill, as though hunting, on an open-country stalk. His expression was bemused and slightly professorial. Finally he went to the chair facing the flight line and gently began to work it loose from the ice that froze it to the cement deck of the pool. When finished, he stood his nearest to the blind man, with one hand on the chair, staring as though at an object which fascinated him more than any other in the world, and in which he could not completely believe.

149·

imagining what kind of head the goggle strap had been around, and what kind of eyes might have been looking through them at the time of death, and before. Something heavy gritted to him across concrete. Someone sat down a yard or so away.

"Mr. Frank Cahill," said the other man, who wore a wool jacket not like those of the cadets, but which seemed made more for dress and appearance than for flying.

"That's you."

"That's me," Cahill said, not surprised. "That's me, and this here's Zack. Just sit still and be cold, and talk, if you want to. Would you like some of my Coke? You can have it all because I'm watchin' my sugar. Got me into trouble once."

"Frank Cahill from Atlanta. That's you."

"Yeah, that's me," Cahill said, wondering at the repetition. "I guarantee it. Who are you?"

"My name is Lennox White-hall," he said. "I am a captain, and I try to teach these boys a few things fast. I have been in the Southwest Pacific, I have had a full tour of duty in B-17s, and a few extra missions in B-25s. I am not a pilot. Nobody here calls me Captain Whitehall, or gives me any kind of military title. I am known around here to the boys, to the instructors, and to the nitshit military personnel only as the Navigator. I am the only one here. I am the only one on the base who can take a celestial sight, but that's not especially valuable since there's not a single sextant on the base but mine and none of these boys is ever going to need to know what to do with one."

"Well," Cahill said, feeling forward in his mind, "if you don't teach 'em that, what do you teach 'em, then?"

"I teach them navigation, but not celestial. The only one here who was interested in that was your boy, who had his own reasons. He could use a slide rule, and you can work out some of the mathematics, some of the trig of celestial, with that. I don't think he got very far with it, but the times we talked, we talked a lot. He picked up on it right away."

"The other boys here, though, what do they . . ."

"I teach them pilotage, which is just looking down and seeing where you are and where you're going, and dead reckoning, which is just plotting on a map and working with course, speed, distance, time, wind and fuel. It's not hard, really. I have to string the course out over two months, and try to keep them from getting restless at so much repetition."

Cahill had hold of enough of him by his voice to begin to visualize; it did not matter whether or not he was wrong, or even if he came close. He had not yet tried to make out anyone's features by touch, though he knew that blind people—or some blind people—did this. He felt no need for it, however; the intimacy of it would be wrong; he did not know anyone well enough to try it with except Ruíz, and Ruíz he had deep in memory, face, voice, and body. He was sorry he had not brought him, but not entirely.

The other man he pictured as being average size; he would be sitting there in his uniform and overcoat. He would have a humorous mouth, probably wide. He would be about thirty-five, to be a captain. He was not a Southerner.

The Navigator folded his suede-gloved hands in his lap and sat deeply and slantingly back in his chair, crossing his legs in their grayish-pink pants. His elegance was the opposite of military stiffness; he seemed moneyed, privileged, and a little condescending: pale, with extremely fine-spun thick hair which, unlike most thick hair on men, grew out of a high forehead. He extracted a pair of issue Ray-Ban dark glasses from under his combed-looking wool coat, put them on, and stared at the sky again.

"What are you waiting for?" the Navigator asked. "Who?"

"A fellow named McCaig, who used to be my boy's instructor. He's in there making a phone call."

"He's all right," the Navigator said. "Who else do you know around here?"

"I met the colonel, the head man. Is he all right?"

"Maybe," said the other. "He hasn't been out of the States, but maybe he'll go later on. Yeah, I'd say he's okay; all right for this job, anyway. Who else?"

"There's a Greek boy, and I met the fellow who bosses the other boys around."

"They're beginning to come to you, are they?"

"Who?" he asked, surprised in spite of himself to hear it put this way. "I've just met them and one or two others. One lieutenant and a few other boys. I'll prob'ly be here till Sunday, when Joel's class gets through. Then I'll go back to Atlanta and hole up for the rest of the winter, till my swimming pool opens up."

"Your boy was unusual," the Navigator said. "He put things together fast, and he could put a twist on them. He was good with figures. Mathematicians—navigators, maybe—are supposed to be cool heads.

Detached. And so on. I said so; he said not. He said that precision leads to impulse, I remember. He was all for impulse. But the utmost precision first. That locates you. Then, wherever that puts you, you can sing, dance, eat, fuck. Whatever. He was for abandon. I never got that far with it, myself. But you know Joel. You know what he was like. He was a cool-headed demon. Nobody knew what the hell to do with him. But you talk to these instructors around here about his doings in the air. They swore by him; they were proud of him. They'll tell you that he was one in a million, a born natural. He might have traded on that, a little."

Cahill could not take in what was being said. He sat, trying to coordinate the sudden information, realizing what a crude mechanism of identification and assessment blindness forced him to use. What little he had managed to imagine about his son now left him; everything about the boy was so different from himself that he could not imagine how Joel could have come by such attitudes, or how anyone could.

"Location, he used to say," said the Navigator. "Universal location at every minute, every second. All you have to have is the key."

"What key?" Cahill asked.

"A key like spherical trig, for one thing. If you can work it, and sight on some things up there in God's heaven, the universe will tell you where you are, and will not fail to tell you. It can't. It's locked around your key. All you have to do is turn it. It's complicated, but it works. The mystery comes out of the numbers, which are kind of like a spell, you might say. It comes out of them and it touches you right between the eyes, and tells you where you are. Not who, but where."

"Is that so?" Cahill said lamely.

"Yes, it is. It was the mystical part of it that he thrived on. Anything he got hold of, he would immediately give a name to, and you usually remembered it. Mathematics, and especially astronomy, he called precision mysticism. That's not bad; I've felt it."

"What do you mean?" asked Cahill.

"I've felt it in clouds of rain, and of sand and dust, and on clear nights, when the numbers match up, and you get there. When I came to this little crackerbox place a couple of months ago, this boy—your boy —told me exactly what it was like. He described the inner feeling of the matching up of the numbers and of all things working for you, according to a mystery. Location: it's not just a thing for fighting wars with, and bombing people. There is something more to it. A lot more. When I came here, Cadet Cahill was not exactly on to something, but he was *getting* on to something. He was excited; there was excitement everywhere he went. Even when he was walking tours, everybody's eyes were on him. People followed him around. The instructors wanted to fly with him, not even logging the time. When I talked to him about celestial, things seemed to come together for him. I got hold of a star map, and we went over it. He knew a little bit of mythology, and he learned more, and he came back and asked me about the mythological figures, and I told him what I knew, which is not a whole lot. 'What is centered?' he asked me. 'What is the center, the dead center of something? Something big? Something in the winter sky? The night sky?' "

"What is?" Cahill asked.

"The star at the center of the belt of Orion, which is the most obvious of the winter constellations in the Northern Hemisphere. But, I told him, it has to be a moving center; the whole thing seems to move; move across. The central star is cailed Alnilam, which somebody told me means string of pearls in Arabic. I remember he said, 'That doesn't throw me. The moving center. I like that. It carries you with it, and yet it's always the center. You follow. Everything follows, and holds together.' He did like it, too. He liked it in the way that only some strange kind of boy like him can like a thing. He was unusual, I tell you." He hesitated, then said with conviction, "They'll come to you, these other boys around here. Don't worry. They will."

"Well," Cahill said, "what can I say? Most of this I don't have no idea about." Something occurred to him to ask. "People keep talkin' about him, when he'd get into these . . . what would you call 'em? Enthusiasms, maybe? I'd like to . . ."

"Yes, it's not something you'd forget. There was some craziness in it, though maybe I ought not to say it that way. To you, anyway. But there was. He did not really have hold of me like he did the cadets, because I didn't know him that well. I only saw him a few times. But I can tell you, he sure had hold of these boys, or some of them, the ones he knew best; it was more or less like he selected them, but exactly what his principle might have been, I don't have any notion. That Shears, that cadet colonel, was one of them. He was around Joel all the time. I hardly ever saw one without the other, except when Joel was on the carpet for something, walking tours, which he did a lot of. Sometimes Shears would walk with him, when he didn't have to. It was funny. Cahill didn't resent it, even when it was open post for everybody else, walking those punishment tours. He did tell me that this military life was not for him, though. It was not military enough. One time he mentioned something he called 'the higher military,' whatever that might mean. He had a lot of phrases like that. They meant something to him that I never could figure out. Maybe Shears or some of these other people could tell you."

Cahill took his hands out, and softly hit into an open palm with his fist. I am very nearly on to something, myself, he thought with some surprise. Things are linking up. Now I need to go talk to Shears, and ask him about some of the things this fellow said, and see what happens. And there's a lot more, here, right here, right in this conversation, right while I'm sitting here.

"You said something about how . . . how he would look, how he would look at you when he got to talkin'. Then we got off on somethin' else."

"Well, it's hard to describe. The first time I saw him, he was interested in my navigators' wings. There were not any others like them around here, and now that I think of it, it may be that he had never seen them before. There are not that many navigators, in all, compared to pilots."

Was this of any importance? Cahill asked himself. But he was in this place, and talk was going on, and he was part of it. "There's some kind of a difference?"

"Yes," the Navigator said, taken with a sudden and very real rush of pity, wanting to help if he could. "See, pilots' wings are a kind of shield with wings branching out from it. Bombardiers' wings have a little bomb in the middle, and a gunner's wings have a big bullet. The navigators' are like . . . like a little copy of the world, with a line through it for the equator, and a lot of other little lines going around it every which way, for different arcs of celestial bodies, like the sun and moon and stars. Only it's not really supposed to represent the world, but the celestial sphere, which is a projection of the world out into space, like the universe was a kind of big version of the world. Can you follow all this?"

"No," Cahill said. "You lost me."

"It really doesn't matter," said the Navigator. "It was just somebody's idea. But the way you do celestial navigation is to imagine the world at the middle of the universe. The exact middle, as though all the things in the sky were the same distance away. Then you project the angles and the math out against the universe, which is all around the world like another big ball we're inside of, and you make your calculations out of that. The angles and the math don't change, no matter what the distances are. That's the amazing thing. The whole idea of the celestial globe is . . . what can I say, is just a figure of speech, a comparison, a metaphor, I guess you could call it. There's not any celestial globe, but it works. And that's what I wear around. That's what I've got on my chest, under this here overcoat, as they say in North Carolina."

"Let me see," said Cahill, rubbing his right-hand fingers with his thumb, as though asking for money. He held up a thumb and two fingers, awkwardly, in the direction of the Navigator's voice. The other chair stirred, and a light grasp came to his hand. He let his fingers stay a moment on the half-chill emblem, and then cautiously spread his thumb and middle finger along the ridges of the wings, until they ended. Then he felt for the globe at the center. He had to press a little to bring the lines to focus in his fingertip, but he did so, and in his mind he saw them, or something like them. They made the figure of a cold cage, a wired circle.

The Navigator drew his chair closer, and leaned forward, opening his coat. He hesitated, having no idea how to go about such a thing, with the blind man's hand extended toward him, in a gesture no one on earth could possibly refuse. He took the hand with the utmost gentleness he could command, and more gentleness, even, so that Cahill's fingers rested on the wings above his heart. Whitehall then felt that heart, and in a way he had not done in many years, as the blind man's fingers spread with the wings, then centered in one finger on the webbed globe.

"And that's what it's like," Whitehall said. "That's what we've got to work with. Everything and nothing. A design. That's what I wear around. The thing's bound in, don't you see. It can't be any other way than it is. You ask the right question, in the right way, and the universe has got to give you the answer, and there's not but one. It's where you are, where you stand, where you sit, where you're flying. There's no other place for you to be than right there, because the numbers line up, just like in a slot machine; they come together, and they put you right in your location, no matter what you're doing there. That doesn't matter; it could be anything. What matters is complicity, the connection: your complicity between you and the big thing, the biggest of all. When you have that, you can do anything you like. Your boy used to say it's like a right-handed fighter throwing the punch from his right heel. The ground gives you the force to knock the ass off the other guy. It comes all the way up through your leg and body and out your arm, and if you hit him, he can't stand. The universe has established you; you have a base. The main thing is that you know it, and you know you know it, and you know *how* you know it. It's a collaboration, really; the thing is built in, and it turns on what is, really, a mystery, an unknown thing that's right."

"This is high talk," Cahill said. "I don't understand it no more than Zack does."

"That your dog's name?"

"That's his name. Some asshole was runnin' for office in Atlanta; I didn't like him, but I picked up on the name. You were talkin' about my boy's face. What about it?"

"I was," Whitehall said, "and I've been trying to get hold of some sort of way to tell you about it, because you probably don't remember him like he was when he was here."

"Well," Cahill said, "I'd like to know what you think; what kind of impression he made on you. He must'a—must'a changed a lot. It's like you're describin' somebody else, a different person." Can I get away with this? Cahill asked himself. But the other voice did not indicate disbelief, or pause, but went on, more and more caught up.

"I ran into him in town," the Navigator said. "There's not much social life in this place. A big lot of fun is to go down to the Shell station on Saturday night and watch them change tires. I was having a beer with two or three of these civilian pilots, and as I remember I was thinking about how I might write to my wife and tell her there's no reason for her to come to Peckover, North Carolina, because there's nothing to do. There are just some places that you can't make any kind of a life in, and Peckover, North Carolina, in the middle of a war and the middle of the winter, is one of them. All you can do is talk, and my wife is not that talkative. She would go crazy, and she would drive me crazy. It's better for me just to get into a day-to-day routine, and try to teach these boys a little about time, speed, and distance. What I'd really like is to ship out to some place like Lackland, in Texas, some real navigation school, where I could teach celestial, and there'd be some good heads around. Or I could try to get back overseas. But I don't really consider that seriously. I remember New Guinea with a lot of good feeling, but I don't want to go over Germany, and I sure as hell don't want to go out to the Pacific again. The Pacific is bad news, and the weather is bad. I done been there, like Huckleberry Finn says. I'd just as soon read about it in *Stars and Stripes* or *Yank*, where they've have some good cartoons."

He just goes on and on, Cahill thought. I'm not really interested in all this. "You were saying somethin' about meetin' up with my boy. Where was it?"

"It was just in some juke joint in town, the Boll Weevil is the name of it. He was with a bunch of other cadets, and carrying on about something; maybe it had to do with wind; the feeling in the aircraft, and the wind. I think it was then that he said something about the inner air, and about force, and about balance. I was in the next booth by myself, and I knew some of the kids from ground school, and I just sort of gravitated into the conversation. They made room, a couple of them shoved over, and I sat down across from him. The rest of them fell back from talking, but not Cadet Cahill. No more than a couple of words and I was in it with him, and I was fascinated, and I was lost. His mind did not seem to work according to any logical pattern. Everything he said was some kind of comparison or other. He kept talking about the 'laboratory brain,' about the 'concealment' of mathematics.' He seemed to believe that everything went along according to some secret plan, and when he began to talk about the night sky, and I corrected him on a couple of points, that just changed his vector a little, and he went right on from that point, wilder and farther out. I don't know if you remember this, but he had a kind of high color when he began to ramble; it was just like a girl's, one of these English girls, if you've ever seen one, that are so pretty and delicate because of all that cold and rain over there, all that cold rain." He glanced hesitantly, and then strongly, at Cahill to see if he were being misinterpreted.

"Don't get the wrong idea, Mr. Cahill; I'm sure you won't. But he had this high flush to his face, and if I could say that he looked like the ultimate man, the ultimate male kind of thing, raised to a higher degree, the ultimate young guy who had hold of something, or who was had hold of *by* something, and was not only carried away, but was more or less *blown* away by it, you might have some notion of what it was like. He was like a person on some kind of fire, and the contrast between him and the other kids was so huge that I was a little embarrassed to be with them, and be like them, and not like him. There was not any way I could be like him; I couldn't come up to him, and I didn't want to try to fake it. But it did seem to me then, and it seems to me now, that he was a kind of judgment against the rest of us; he was not sitting in judgment, he *was* a judgment. He was involved more with his own mind, he committed

158

more to it, he threw himself more into it, and he was more willing to go all the way with it, than we were, or than we could. I had the feeling, just sitting there in the Boll Weevil, that he was far *more* than me; I felt as though I had never really seen a human being at full potential before; at absolutely full potential. Which is to say," Whitehall concluded, "that I had never really seen a human being before. Any human being, especially not in the mirror."

"Do you think this might have been put on, some?" Cahill asked. "Kids that age have a lot of whims; they put on a lot. I never did, myself, but I could always tell the ones who did. I've been around weight lifters and bodybuilders a lot, and it's all for show. I don't mean some of it is for show; I mean *all* of it is."

"It didn't seem like that to me," the Navigator said. "If I've ever seen a person caught up in something that nobody but he knows about, it was Joel Cahill, just before he got killed. That really shook me. It shook my back teeth, and they're still loose. When I heard that a cadet had been killed, right away I knew that of all of them it wouldn't've been him. But it was him." He sighed, settled his coat around him, and slanted deeper into the boards of the chair, as though backing himself into a deep box. "It was him, and it *is* him."

"Do you know any more about what happened to him than the colonel and these other people?" Cahill asked.

"I sure don't," said Whitehall. "In fact, they probably know more than I do, because most of them have been up and flown over the area, and I haven't. There was a big fire east of here, and your boy went down in it. Nobody knows any more about why he was flying over the fire than they knew why he did anything else that he did, or why he talked the way he did, or why he was the way he was. It's all gone now, it's all up in smoke, as some stupid asshole might say. But if I could borrow a little bit from Joel Cahill himself, I would say that fire was the right thing for him, the right way for him to go. Smoke, and all that, no. That's just airborne dirt. But fire, yes. If there's any such thing as predestination, I would say that your son and fire met, like it should have been."

"That's just talk," Cahill said, and meant it. "Nobody wants to die. Nobody dies because of some comparison."

"You're right," Whitehall said. "You should stick to regular ways of thinking. That's the best. You shouldn't side with the wild man."

"No, you shouldn't," Cahill said, out of his depth and irritated.

"Not even if he's right," said the Navigator. "Not even if he's beyond right, and in some new place. I can't say 'not even if he's your son,'

159

because I don't have the right to say it. But if I had the right to say it, I would say it."

"You just said it."

Whitehall stood up to leave, stretching and putting his dark glasses back into the case. "That's too easy, though, you know," he said. "I'm really on the other side, but I can't get there." He put his knuckles down on an arm of Cahill's chair, and Zack's head rose from his paws; his ears came up and his lips parted questioningly.

"I'll see you again, before Sunday," Whitehall said. "Maybe I can think of some other things. I've got an idea that I'll remember more, not when I get to thinking about it, but when I'm doing something else, or about half asleep or half drunk. We've got a couple of days; something will come." He took a step toward the assembly area. "Is all this any help to you?" he asked.

"You can't tell," Cahill said. "I don't know exactly what to expect. 'Mission' seems to be a big word around here. I've never been on a mission exactly like this one, or anything like it, at all." Then he added, "But who has? A blind man and a dog lookin' for somebody in the air. If you people who walk around seein' everything and not thinkin' anything about it can't find out what the situation is, what happened to one insignificant little boy in a army of millions of people, how am I supposed to? You tell me."

"I can't tell you," said Whitehall, "but if you don't mind my saying so, you're as unexpected as he is. Let them try to get to the bottom of *you*. That would take some doing. Let them get to the bottom of you, before you disappear on Sunday. I'll see you before you go, and tell you what comes to me, whatever it is. 'Key' was a big word with Joel Cahill. I remember him saying that the secret was not in the structure of the lock, or what he called "the swarm" of the lock, but in the key; the way the key is made, the design of it, but also just as much in who had it and how he got it."

Cahill sat again alone, thrown back in the big solid chair; he shifted his hips to the side each way to test the pull of the nails, and nothing gave; the boards were well put together. He reached down for Zack's head, and went into his best stillness, which he could now maintain for long periods, beyond thought, beyond his heartbeat.

With the spring grip he had done sets of fifty, forty, and thirty repetitions with each hand, working in the coat pocket with the left hand and squeezing the stout steel in the open air with the other, not wanting to touch the goggles while straining, when McCaig came back and stood over him.

"I'm sorry I took so long. I had to call home, but the main thing I was tryin' to do was to get hold of that farmer out there where Joel crashed, because I thought you might want to go out there and see him. The colonel has got a report on what he said about the accident, but if you want to go out there, I'll take you, and we'll talk to him. His name is Bledsoe, Luther Bledsoe, and his wife is named Adele. They have some kids, but I don't think they were there at the time. They don't have no telephone, but I think I've got some fairly good directions from some people I know over on the east bank of the reservoir. I'm pretty sure I can find it. So"—he looked carefully at the blind man—"if you think you might want to go out there, say like tomorrow afternoon, we'll do it. I think you could maybe, well, find out more, if you was to go see what they have to say."

"All right," Cahill said. "I'll come out here to the base again in the mornin', and we'll go lookin' for this fellow after lunch. I don't think anything else will come up, so we can more or less count on the afternoon, and just see what happens."

"Right now, what would you like to do?" asked McCaig. "How 'bout another sandwich?"

"No," Cahill said. "I'd like some gin, to put in the rest of this Coke. But I can do without it."

"How about gasoline instead of gin? We can go over to ground school and sit in on the Fuels section. Engines used to interest Joel a lot. He really didn't know much about the actual parts, as far as I could tell, but he had a great feel for just what an engine would do, and what it wouldn't. We would do orientation work in the big hangar, and one of the mechanics would be showin' an engine part, like a piston, say, and he would look at it and make some crack about the whole engine's bein' different from the parts: as being somethin' completely beyond the parts. He said he was sorry for the parts, because they was beautiful in themselves, you know, just as objects kind of, but they really didn't have no reality till they was 'taken up into the engine'; he seemed to think it was like they had to be *passed* on, somebody or somethin' had to certify 'em, like Saint Peter, before they could get into the engine, like it was in a way going to heaven, or some great place, some *other* place."

Cahill stayed quiet; these remarks had nothing for him.

"Well," McCaig said, "however you feel about 'em, gasoline is what makes 'em run, and gasoline is what they're fixin' to talk about, over yonder in ground school, in about ten more minutes. We can go or we can not go. If we go I'll get you a drink afterward, and we'll have lunch with the boys."

"Good enough," Cahill said, and rose from the seat as from a hole, leaning heavily on his hands, his forearms and hand-backs tense and healthy with spring-grip repetitions.

"I'll tell you what we can do," McCaig said. "This might interest you more. I think there's a Principles of Flight class we could go to, and then if that part of ground school hits you right, and if you maybe meet some people you'd like to talk to, we could go right next door to the gasoline class. It might work out better that way."

"Yes, Principles of Flight. What the whole thing's about, I guess. I never saw anything fly except birds, and a few airplanes I never did even bother to watch."

"Well, flyin' is flyin', no matter who does it or what does it. The air is big. You breathe it, but to get up into it, off the ground with your whole body in it, that's another thing. You've got to find a way to do it; you've got to be took up into it, and when you get in everything is changed. All this your boy used to say. He'd look like a little child when the subject of the air came up. He would go on about it for hours, and you'd think that anybody who talked such a good game—even if I never could understand a lot of what he went on about—couldn't fly, but when he got his feet on the rudders and the throttle in one hand and the stick in the other, everything he said seemed like it was true. There was nothin' he couldn't do, when he got airborne. Mr. Cahill, you've prob'ly heard this from some of these people, but I'm not shittin' you just because your boy's dead: I've been flyin' most of my life, and I've taught lots of people to fly, but I've never seen nobody like him. I don't get tired of saying it, to anybody who wants to listen: he was one in a million. I doubt if Lindbergh was any better; I doubt if he was as good."

"Let's go along," Cahill said. "For one time I've done had enough of the outside. Air, okay, but this particular air is a little cold for blind men, right now. I need to move."

"Walk on down this way with me," McCaig said. "We're goin' along beside the pool, and you wouldn't want to step down there. First step is too long, and there ain't nothin' but slush and ice. Nothin' to do, down there."

"I wish I could see it," Cahill said, "I own a swimmin' pool in Atlanta, and we have to watch things in the wintertime, crackin' and all. But I don't think it gets as cold in Atlanta as it is here. Sometimes we would have a little water, maybe just rainwater, in the pool, and it'd freeze, and catch things in it, and it was interestin' to see 'em—leaves, and twigs, and once a mouse—in just that position; you know, just that one where they was. Dead leaves are pretty, like that. I never did take the trouble to look until last year, when my sight first started to go to the bad, just a little. But there was a sprig of a pine tree froze up in the ice of the deep part of the pool, and it was the prettiest thing you ever seen; so delicate, and all. And you couldn't touch it, not and for it to stay where it was, and like it was, just in that one position, closed in, and so far from you, and so delicate. It was way off, and way in."

"There's not anything like that here, I don't think," then, "yes there is, too. There's one dead leaf I can see. It used to be spinnin', you can tell from the way it sits. You know, there's an acrobatic you can do in a Stearman, called a Fallin' Leaf. It's not standard, but it's right pretty; it's a long kind of rockin' motion, back and forth and down, like a swing. I've heard that some pilots can do an inverted Fallin' Leaf—upside down." McCaig turned his hand over and made a lilting downward motion with it in the sign language of pilots, cadets, and other air crewmen, then dropped his arm, embarrassed again, hoping nobody saw. "The Fallin' Leaf upside down, though, was one maneuver your boy and I never did get to try out, though he'd'a been for it. I'm not quite sure why we didn't, but prob'ly it was because I'm not all that sure I can do it, myself. Not upside down."

They left the concrete and started through the thin sand, not on any road or path, but working toward a gap in low bare bushes that seemed also to open at about the same width through trees, these heavy with needles. They made their way through, and then into a building through a door not much higher than Cahill's head; inside, the ceiling was no more than three or four inches above the jamb; everything was crowded, and tunnel-like. They were between classes, in a hall; cadets were talking with quick low voices. The heat was too sudden for Cahill. He took off his overcoat, put it over his arm, and waited, loosening his tie and pushing his hat back on his head, where the sweat would break very soon.

"Let's go in here, and kind of edge around toward the back, and let 'em fill in around us." They moved into the classroom, Cahill feeling for the dog and pulling on his collar a little, until they reached the back corner, and sat down, the blind man in the corner itself with Zack next to him, and McCaig moving his chair to give them room. Cahill felt backward for the wall, and shoved his chair against it, and also against the wall to his left, so that he was truly wedged.

"Ah, shit," McCaig whispered. "We're in the wrong place. This is gas."

A slightly stooped pale young man with thinning, tightly curled red hair had come into the room; he sat meditatively on the edge of the front desk. He reached behind him, took a chalk stick from the trough under the blackboard, broke a piece of it off, and tossed it up and down. He was not ill at ease, but perhaps faintly bored, and it occurred to McCaig that he seemed not really to belong there, amongst the cadets in their prickly olive drab, wearing his uniform of civilian instructor, which did not impress anyone as being a real uniform, but was more like an outfit in a high school musical comedy about the military, or like an usher's.

"How long have we been at this?" the instructor asked, getting up and putting the chalk back in the trough. "I mean," he said, "that's a real question. We've been in here for three whole weeks, the last half of this particular phase, and I've seen only a couple of you take any notes. Any notes at all."

With a slight shifting of chairs and uneasy frictions of coarse wool against itself—arms and legs crossing and uncrossing—the class steadied for interrogation. The instructor came around to the front of the desk, lifted an arm and played it over all heads. He went row by row, silently, all the way to the rear corner, where Cahill sat, relaxed and immovable, sunk into the building, his hand loose in Zack's fur. McCaig watched carefully, as the instructor half closed one eye as though to intensify his vision, like a man reading fine print, or taking an eye test which he must pass, and shook his head just barely perceptibly, not quite ready to believe. Breaking out, he moved past McCaig, back down the last row, and reaching behind him, scrabbled lightly with his fingers and picked up his roll book.

"Cadet—ah, Cadet Sheplow, tell me what you know about the light and heavy ends of gasoline. Any gasoline."

McCaig looked for Sheplow, and couldn't find him. Nobody said anything.

"Is Cadet Sheplow here?" the instructor asked, his voice with an edge, but wanting to know, to resolve an actual point.

"I'm here, sir," Cadet Sheplow said, turning out to be a thick ash-blond boy three-quarter face from McCaig, toward the window. "I remember you talking about it, but I didn't really understand. Could

164

you go over it again?" Sheplow reached under his seat and brought up a notepad and pencil, and so did several others, but not all.

"How far back do I have to start?" asked the instructor. "Do you know what gasoline is, Mr. Sheplow?"

"Sure I know," said Sheplow. "I know enough to use it, when it's put in an engine, if you show me how to work the engine."

"That's good," the instructor said. "Do you know the power cycle of a piston and cylinder? We went over that, too. You ought to have known that before you got in here. Anybody ought to know that."

"I do know it, I think," said Sheplow with rising confidence. "And I did know it before I came in here. You've got intake, combustion, and exhaust."

"You'd be in a hell of a fix, if that's all you had," the instructor said. "It's a four-phase cycle. Would that help you? What's the other thing?"

"I don't remember, to tell the truth," Sheplow said. "I know there's something else. But the explosion is the main thing. Isn't that right?"

"They're *all* the main thing," the instructor said emphatically. He scanned the class again. "Come on now. Anybody. Give me something. Don't let's just sit here."

"Compression," McCaig said suddenly, not able to resist. The cadets turned around, all of them, and a great laugh of relief and complicity went up. The instructor broke a wide grin, and was suddenly very likable and accessible.

"You don't count, you son-of-a-bitch," he said to McCaig over the faces of the boys, but addressing McCaig as much for them as for himself. "You come in here interrupting my class again by displaying a little knowledge of the subject, and you're going to create a major disruption." He was still smiling, and the cadets enjoying the asset of their ignorance, and the instructor's acknowledgment of it.

"But I can get you out too," he said. "Do you know what 'heart-cut' means?"

"No," said McCaig. "I might know what it means . . ." Three or four cadets smiled almost enough to laugh. "But I don't know what it's got to do with gasoline. Heart-cut. Are you sure you're talkin' about gas?"

"I am definitely talking about gas. Heart-cut gasoline is aviation fuel, or rather aviation gasoline is heart-cut. If all of you want to get this one distinguishing feature of aviation fuel, which might just incidentally come in handy to you at some time in the future—God knows how and God knows where—any of you interested in taking notes can put down that the lighter the gasoline components are, the faster the engine starts and the faster it warms up in cold weather. The heavier the components are, the better the gas will burn, but the heavier they are, also, the more unreliable they are. There are more carbon deposits, and the flow is not as even. Too light, you lose a lot of fuel from evaporation, and when it's real hot your engine is liable to vapor-lock. If your gas is too heavy, you're going to get a rough-running engine, and your fuel distribution is not going to be as good as you would want it. Now," he looked at the class with genuine eagerness. "Which kind of gas do you want in an aircraft engine? Light or heavy?"

"Both of 'em," said one voice, a Southern-country voice.

"Neither one," said another, perhaps Midwestern.

"Both and neither," the instructor said. "Is that possible?" Then, into the general silence, he laid the essential Fact. "Aviation gasoline is not as light, at the light end, as the gas you use in your car; at the heavy end, it's not as heavy. That's what we mean when we say that fuel for aircraft is heart-cut. That doesn't mean that the heart has been cut out of it, but that both extreme ends have been cut from it, *leaving* the heart. The heart is intact. That way, your engine will work; things will work out."

He paused, while the few boys wrote. "Now don't think I'm not sympathetic with you; don't think I'm trying to pick on you or show you up. A lot of you don't give a damn about this classroom stuff. Your grades go on your record, but you and I both know that what gets you through this place, and on through Basic and Advanced and Transition and RTU and on out into combat is your flying. If you can fly, you can get through this place. You can score a hundred percent on every ground school test, and if you can't fly you'll go out of here, all right, but it won't be to Basic. You'll never vibrate in the Vultee BT. You'll be going to Cooks and Bakers School, or maybe to Gunnery School, if you still want to fly. A few of you math geniuses may have qualified for Navigation, but if you were math geniuses you'd be there already." He paused, scanning again, some of his good humor gone. Realizing he ought not to let it die, he brightened at first by will and then actually. "Me," he said, "I've never been up in an airplane in my life. Did you know that?"

A new general relaxation came in. "Up to now, I've been going the other way from you," the instructor said. "I went from the beets to the coal tunnels, hoping eventually to get to tungsten. Do you know what tungsten is, Cadet Quow?" he asked a cadet on the first row whose name he remembered, perhaps from its oddness, and from the boy's position in the room.

"I don't have the slightest idea," Quow said. "Does it have anything to do with flying?"

"Not one fucking thing," said the instructor. "Do you know what fucking is?"

"I'm finding out," said Quow, and the class laughed. McCaig, smiling, glanced at Cahill, whose laced fingers were at the bridge of his nose, though not, McCaig believed, in deliberate concealment; he was sure that Cahill was amused.

"I come from Minot, North Dakota," said the instructor, "land of the big beet. It is flat up there, and all the fields are running red, Cadet Quow, not with blood but with beet juice. My way out of it was down, not up. I went to the Colorado School of Mines as a chemistry major. Underground is my territory. You come down from flying, and I come up, and we meet at ground level." He changed his thought and came back. "Now about your problem, Cadet Quow," he said.

"What problem is that, sir?"

"Your sexual problem. I'm interested."

"I'm afraid I can't tell you very much, Mr. . . ."

"My name is Asbill, Mr. Quow. Bradley Asbill. Remember it, because you're supposed to put it on your exam, when the syllabus says I've got to give you one."

"Like I say, Mr. Asbill, I can't tell you very much about . . . about what you want to know. I'm just a young fellow these days. Just learning."

"Do you know any good phone numbers, Cadet Quow?"

"Not around here, I don't. You have to go to High Point or Greensboro." Quow smiled. "So they tell me."

Asbill sighed and hitched himself onto the desk, leaving a foot on the floor. "To tell you the truth, I don't feel much like talking about fuel anymore right now. You don't care anything about it, and I don't care anything about it either, but I know about it; for the past few years I've known a lot about it. And when I go back to civilian life I'll know a lot more about it; underground is my way; that's where it all comes from, down there with the old dinosaur in the Sinclair ads. And where you're going, up there in the wild blue yonder, it would be better for you to know at least something about what's holding you up there. Sheplow, do you know anything now you didn't know before you came in here today?"

"Yes, sir. You can't get any ass in Peckover." He paused for the certain laughter, which was strong. "At least Quow can't."

"Anything else?" Asbill said, grinning sunnily, with real sun.

"Don't cut the heart," another cadet directly in front of McCaig said.

"*Do* cut the heart," Quow said.

"Both right," Asbill said. "Cut the light and heavy ends off the fuel. Light, you get quick starts, fast warm-ups. And what else?"

"Vapor-lock, when it's hot," another cadet said. "Evaporation."

"How about the heavy end?"

"It heats up more, but you get carbon, and the flow's not steady."

"That's enough for today," Asbill said. "That's all I want. We can make it up next time." He started toward the door. "This is the way you can remember about fuel properties: Cut the heart, and leave it." He walked out, and the class rose with many sounds of wood, paper, and wool. McCaig and Cahill were the last out, and waited in the hall with cadets going by them thickly in both directions.

"You game for some more?" McCaig asked.

"Sure," said Cahill. "I don't see why not."

"You want to drain out some stuff? How about your dog?"

"No, we're all right. He's not restless. What's the other class about?"

"It's called Principles of Flight. Or maybe Theory of Flight, somethin' like that. I think this guy's been off the ground; I seen him down at the flight line one day, all dressed up like he was goin' somewhere. Anyway, he'll be talkin' about airplanes, and not chemistry."

A small man wearing captain's bars and curious wings slowed from the passing lines and stopped in front of Cahill and the dog. He had put his crushed cap back on between classes, for he was still adjusting it, but as he peered up slightly into Cahill's black glasses, at this moment reflecting no light at all, he took it off again. He was aggressive and slight, with such a heavy beard that darkness shone through his just-shaved pale face as though the skin were translucent.

"This is Captain Faulstick," McCaig said. "He's an officer trainee, and he's doin' okay." Faulstick continued to stare at Cahill, waiting for him to put out a hand, which he finally did. Faulstick took it, and his expression changed as Cahill held him.

"You're the one, are you? You're the one who lost the boy up here."

"I'm the one," said Cahill, letting go.

"He was all right," Captain Faulstick said. "These kids around here swore by him. Nobody knows what the hell happened. You been talking to these other people around here?"

"Some of 'em," Cahill said. "Whoever knew him."

"I didn't know him, really, I just used to see him go by, with all those kids following him around. I don't think he was interested in bombardment."

"Captain Faulstick was in it in Europe. He's been there. He flew bombardier in 17s. How many missions did you have, in all?"

"Just under fifty," Faulstick said. "And that's plenty. I'd rather do what I'm doing now."

"I'd like to get together with you," Cahill said. "You were in what my boy was goin' into, and I'd like to get to know about it."

"Well, the air maybe, and the war. But not bombers. That was not for him. If the Air Corps had any sense he would have been in fighter transition just as soon as he got out of Cadets." He turned to McCaig. "That right?"

"Right," McCaig said. "If he'd been in heavies, he would'a been flyin' 'em like fighters, anyway. Just as well have him where he belongs. Should'a had."

"Are you in this next class?" Cahill asked Faulstick.

"The flight class? Yes, I'm in there. All about the forces that keep the wings up in the blue yonder, and you with 'em. If I took all this stuff seriously, I doubt if I could get one of these things off the ground. I just get in it and go. Isn't that right, Mac?"

"That's what I done told you," McCaig answered. "Let's go on in and hear him tell his side of it."

Most of the cadets were seated, this time in a room without windows. Toward the weather side the cinder-block wall was dewed with light moisture, some of it running and crooking downward. Cahill sat next to it.

Used to the building, now, or so he thought, Cahill sprawled a little, and gave himself to his creation of the scene. No one was facing him; the whispering went the other way. Against the back of his left hand the porous solid block was damp: he turned the hand, touched the surface with his fingertips, and palped the sweat; in it there was a suspicion

The instructor came in, narrow-shouldered and athletic, light and a little stiff, with a nose so pointed that it was impossible not to think it had been deliberately sharpened. His hair was very dark gold, not delicate gold but cheap and plentiful, and though parted low on one side had no comb marks in it, but sat on his head like dark wood. His glasses were so thick

169

of grease, and because of it Cahill began to dislike being there. He shifted and reached with both feet forward, until his shins found the lowest rung of the chair in front of him. Hat in his lap, he listened, and bore down to create.

He searched for something in the air, something with the force of air, dependent on it, and brought back the kites. At once the whole neighborhood over which they flew came to him, their shapes and colors against the dense blue charged with striving: one kite green with a long ragged tail, another cut in a vague bird outline, fat, clumsy, out of shape, riding over a sandy filling station, and again the box kite, earthless light red, ghostly, its sides almost transparent like a small room climbing higher and higher with nothing in it, but still a room, the shape of a room. A handkerchief with a hook on it was climbing the bellied string toward the red kite, a small weight—a rock, a nail, a bolt—dangled under it, swaying and jigging as the handkerchief shoved upward. Fascinated, Cahill stared as he had rarely done before his blindness. I could have it go up at any speed I wanted, he thought, but it is going slowly. Very, very slowly, but

that his eyes appeared to thrust from the face a little into the room, a clear, practical, large blue. He started immediately.

"What's the highest you've been in these Stearmans?" he asked anyone.

"Ten thousand feet," a small cadet said. "That's all the higher they'll go. And you're hanging on the prop then."

"Why are you hanging on the prop?"

"Because the air's thin," the cadet said.

"It's thin for *you*, but it goes on up a long way. Hundreds of miles up. At sea level, the air exerts a pressure of about one ton per square foot. That's a lot of weight, pressure; a lot of force. You're flying very light aircraft, and every time you go up you can feel the air shifting around under you, shifting around with you in it. The air is always balancing itself. You remember last time we talked about pressure areas. Cadet Thomasovich, what happens when air moves from high-pressure areas toward low pressure?"

"Wind," Thomasovich answered. "It makes wind."

"You got it," the instructor said. "The air balance is upset. The shape of the wing—or the wings, in your case—creates a low-pressure area over the wing and a high-pressure area under it. The

it is going; soon it will be there. And then they'll shake it loose, and it'll come down. Somebody will find it and not know what it is.

But, nearly to the kite and barely visible, it did not shake loose, for at the word "pushed," where the instructor hesitated before he went on, the red kite, the handkerchief, the strings and other kites disappeared: the city as he had just seen it disappeared, spread out in a circle from around him and stood off from him on all sides, leaving an enormous space above where he stood, and twilight in it. The other figure beside him was not distinct, but the delicate craft in memory in his own hands pulsed with the energy being given it by the young shadow he remembered from that past because of the feeling that came back into his hands as the instructor talked on, more or less meaninglessly now. Briefly Cahill looked into *Popular Mechanics* once more, where the pusher model lay with its cross struts and wires, the blueing-and-spiderwork of a blueprint, and then became actual in his fingers as the rubber bands ticked and the tight knots wound into the body of the aircraft. A terrible fear sought Cahill as the yellow of the sleek wing came back to him, intense enough almost to burn: the arro-

air under the wing pushes up on the wing, creating energy; we call that 'lift.' But for the aircraft to develop lift, it has to move *through* the air: either be pulled like a glider or pulled or pushed— whichever way you want it—by an engine. And your impelling force makes it come out so that the lift of the wing is greater than the weight of the airplane *plus*"—he made a plus sign with his forefingers, held it above his head, and shook it emphatically—"the pull of gravity. That's your magic moment: that's when you leave the ground, and you're one hundred percent in the air, whatever it does, and whatever your plane and you do. It's all physics. Everything about the plane comes out of physics. Every part of the design of the plane and everything in it or concerning it is a classic physics text." He enumerated on his fingers with the thumb of the other hand. "Lift, thrust, drag, gravity. Lift and thrust are working for your flight, and drag and gravity are working against it. The air is uncertain, but there's a lot of it. It can be calm, it can be devastating. It's all a question of balance. You learn the physics and apply it, and you'll do all right. But you can't do without it, and it can do you in if you don't understand it."

gance and fragility were more than he knew what to do with. The soundless lift-away he remembered, and the unearthly and perfect circles of the propellers, rising out into the huge closing dark.

There was a new principle to his life now, he recognized slowly, as he sat with the back of his hand once more against the wet wall, the hard verticality warming with him, a sense of complicity developing between him and the concrete as his images, in their locked, endless field, took on qualities they had not shown. Up until now they had been static, more or less like substanceless photographs, bright with primary colors, and meaningful, but unchanging. Now, with the loft of the handkerchief-parachute thrust by the wind—more like being drawn—up the pure string leading into the sky, to the tiny red room of the box overhead, the surge of confident power that results from entering a new dimension, of coming on a new resource, limitless, full of possibility and secret authority, opened everything he knew. Now the coins in the air above the pool at Willow Plunge did not merely hang in the sunlight, bright flecks through which shot the endless gold streaks and smears of his blindness, but fell, and from the

"In physics, you need terms, and in applied physics you need applied terms. One of the most confusing terms you're going to find, when you talk about flying, is something we call the 'angle of attack.' " He was sure he had fooled them; he relied on it. "But what you're already thinking is wrong, naturally. You're thinking about coming in on an ME-109 or a Zero, or some other enemy aircraft, and opening up on it with a lot of imaginary guns. But that's not what we mean: we mean the angle at which the wing of an aircraft goes through the air. When you fly, your angle of attack changes: the smaller the angle, the less lift, and up to a point, the more the angle increases, the more lift the wing develops." He peered around the room, not yet ready to fix. "You'll notice I said *up to a point.*" He stopped, flatted his hand, rotated it, slid it upward at a small angle, and stopped, turning back to them. "Most aircraft, including the Stearman PT-17, stop developing lift after the angle of attack gets beyond twenty degrees, give or take a couple of degrees on either side. Af-

four rims of the pool many figures leaped, with much noise, confusedly after them. Eagerly he flung up more coins, and the surface was a white and light green thrashing of arms and legs. He pulled his view around to look at his own face, and there he stood, smiling with an involved friendliness and eagerness that he knew he had not shown in actuality. He had on a wide-brimmed straw hat with a blue-and-red band of cheap cloth, like a tourist's, and as he watched himself, the figure dug into its pockets for more coins and flung them high over the pool with both hands, the hat bristling with light. All memory filled with movement and interest, from the sight of himself shattering the coins out over the water with amiable involvement. The pool water itself could in an instant be changed now, and Ruíz could be—was—swimming in the woolen glow of sunken sidelights, arm over arm, a muscular shadow in the lightest green held by the earth, unhurriedly moving down the long racing pool to the sound of his own reverberent voice, his underground singing when he hosed down the empty pool, that made the soles of the feet on cement tingle with something the body had not known it could feel.

ter that, the air doesn't go over the top of the wing smoothly; it gets rough, and the more you pull the nose up, the more confusion, the more turbulence you get over the top of your wing. What's happening to you then, Bergman?" He centered with disconcerting suddenness on a cadet near the door.

"You're going to stall," Bergman said. "You're already stalled."

"That's frightening, Bergman. That's a frightening word. You're just beginning this stuff. Does it bother you to stall an aircraft, Cadet Bergman?"

"Not as much as it did at first," Bergman said. "But I still don't like to feel the thrust going out of it."

"Nobody does," said the instructor. "We want to keep on; we don't want to feel the aircraft mush, we don't want to feel it being pulled down, we don't want to see the nose drop through the horizon. But you're not as scared as you were, Mr. Bergman. Not one of you is as frightened as you were the first time, when you did this solo. Why not? Why not, Rothell?"

"Because we know what we're doing, better. We know more about the airplane, how to . . . to make it *do.*"

"You could have said it better," the instructor said. "But that's es-

And now more sun, again, very bright and through the water—it was the intermediate pool this time—a substance that Cahill did not immediately recognize, strung and rounded, filling him with a mixture of fear and excitement. The right color came into it, at first little by little and then subtly and starkly; it was blood, the blood of the teen-age girl who had lost her toenail on the ladder. He cut down the distance between it and him, so that there was nothing in his mind but a large center of pale water, its own color having little strength, and through it was the uncoiling redness, giving off threads from itself, neither fed-into or decreasing but twisting into itself by some strange means, as though trying to un-tangle. Like someone wrenching himself from a dream, Cahill willed to change his mind: willed some image of spectatorial sex— that was it, the one-legged girl at the transparent mirror, but after an instantaneous clouded flash of her, the whole scene of which she was a part rearranged itself around him: the closed office, the dying slats of sun, the miscel-laneous papers and dim loops of adding-machine paper on the desk, Ruíz weeping into his hands, begging the girl to be mi-raculous, the dog passing from sight into touch, the spring-

sentially it, and maybe you couldn't've said it better. Some of the most necessary parts of flying have to do with the control of what you might call the negative elements of flight. A landing—any landing—is an application of the physics of the stall: it is a con-scious bafflement of the equip-ment: a controlled frustration." He smiled slightly. *"That's* not bad, if I do say so myself. A con-trolled frustration of the wing.

"Now," he paused, mock-dram-atizing and enjoying the involve-ment that at least a few of them showed, "imagine yourself in your landing frame of mind. You want to learn to like your weight. You can't land without it. You like it and you're *using* it. If you stall the airplane up in the air, at low speed and high angle, your plane is not properly controllable, and you have to recover it. That is, if you have enough altitude, and you better have it. But when you land you shoot for a kind of ideal situa-tion: a full stall just as you touch the ground. Or just barely above. You stall it, see, but instead of the nose falling through, the ground, the runway, intercepts you, meets you, and you're on it. And every-thing's okay. Nothing has hap-pened that shouldn't've hap-pened. You look around you, and everything is real. The ground is solid underneath you, and you keep the stick all the way back, like

tensed rattlesnake bobbing its head as though intolerably put upon. His breath coming faster, Cahill labored in the dark, under tarpaulins of his secret house. With no more warning than he gave the swimmers, weightlifters, and other patrons, the shutter flew open on him—blew apart with superhuman light—ordinary summer sunlight, noon light—and, deadly in every scale, its sprung mouth more vivid with pale crimson than any photograph of a striking snake has ever been, its rattle buzzing uncontrollably, the snake he called Buster shook in the middle of the room Cahill had nailed together for him.

He pulled his feet, which had gone dead, from under the rung of the chair, and sat gradually upright, resting only the back of his head against the wall. He rubbed the brick sweat from his hand with the palm of the other, and there seemed to be a double moisture. With as much premeditation as he could, he put a hand into his pocket: not the one with the goggles, but going for the spring grip, which he turned to suit him and bore down on, counting silently, his jaw muscles tensing with his forearm, still breathing more than usual, but relieved, getting blank, going back to the familiar gold lines tinged with pink, crossing him forever, and only him.

your instructor told you to do, and you go into your taxi procedure, which is something else again. Timing is not nearly so important any more. The supreme moment of your timing is in coordinating everything, and *feeling* that aircraft into the full stall, just as you hit. You do it right, and I guarantee you, you'll never have a better sensation, no matter what you do. An airplane has something about it that gives you a little extra-special reward when you do just right with it; it gives you back just a little something more than you gave it. And your fear is gone. Isn't that so?" Not waiting for an answer, he went on. "Your fear is gone, maybe not for good, but for then, and something you like a lot has come in where it used to be."

Outside, the keen wind very welcome, Cahill said good-bye to Captain Faulstick, stretching and putting on his gloves.

"I told you it was simple," Faulstick said. "Very elementary. All you have to do is do it. That's not so simple, at least not for me. I may go back to the front of the airplane and drop bombs, or instruct, out in the desert somewhere, with big bags of all-purpose flour."

"I still didn't understand what he was talkin' about," Cahill said. "But it's not all that important. I ain't gonna be doin' it."

"Maybe we could have a drink," Faulstick said. "If they don't know where you are, Double-Mac can run you down, later on."

"Sure," Cahill said. "I don't know exactly what they figure I can do, but we can sure talk. We still got some time."

Faulstick moved away, arming on his overcoat, and Cahill, who had not taken his off, turned his head in the direction of different sounds.

"Is it that way?" he said forward, to McCaig, who was just behind him.

"Not quite," McCaig said, taking Cahill's pointing arm and swinging it gently toward the mess hall beside the parked aircraft. "Not quite, but you almost had it. Just about three points to your right, and we'll go straight to it. We'll get somethin' to eat, and I'll turn you back over to the boys. Harbelis is over there already, prob'ly."

Used to each other by now, at least in movement, they walked the seventy-five yards to the cadet mess without speaking, McCaig matching the other's stride with no self-consciousness, and Cahill putting his feet down soberly, setting them in the sand and picking them up a little reluctantly as he listened for the stairs he had been up and down once before; there were three, and they wouldn't change.

Since they were the last to go in, or almost, McCaig was thinking of what he would say when they came to the steps, but before he could imagine it, a big boy, sweeping his cap off, leaped up the stairs without touching the middle one, opened the door and was gone inside, but even as he did so Cahill knew he had vanished somewhere above them; had guessed the leap, and heard the boards creak at another level than his own.

They worked into the center of the large, low room, Zack winding under tables and joining them. Harbelis had two end seats for them, and saw to it that Cahill was placed with his back to the main aisle. Cahill pulled his overcoat off his shoulders and arms, and waited among them. There had been no more stir when Zack and he entered; he could concentrate on eating; he was not making anyone nervous.

"I guess some of you," Cahill said, ". . . I guess some of you I don't know yet, and if that's so, I do now. I'm not very good at names, so we don't need no introductions. Go ahead and eat, and then maybe, if you want to, I can ask a couple of questions, and you can tell me some things. If that'd be all right." Then, "What have we got to eat, this time?"

"Collard greens, turnips, big hominy, and some kind of meat," somebody said.

"Dinosaur meat," said the boy next to Cahill. "That's as close as I can come. About sixty million years." Cahill ate some of the greens, bitter and watery, picked up his slab of meat, bit off part of it, and then without concealment reached the rest down to Zack, who took it from him at once, with no sound. Most of the boys were finished, and, waiting a moment until he was more or less sure by lack of repetition of the clicks on the dishes, Cahill said, "If any of you knew my boy Joel, I'd appreciate you tellin' me what you remember."

"I never did know him," one boy said. "I just knew about him."

"I did know him," another cadet, a florid, almost bald one, said. "I was in his barracks in Pre-Flight, at Maxwell Field. It seems like a long time ago, but it was not but a couple of months."

"What can you tell me?" Cahill asked.

"I can't tell you very much," the cadet said. "He was just like all the rest of us. I don't remember that he ever got into any trouble down there. He played on the squadron basketball team, and I thought he was real good. I remember he had a double-handed overhead shot that he used to take whenever he was open, and it was a strange-looking move, and very pretty. But he didn't hog the ball. He passed off, and set the plays up. The other fellows all liked him, but there was not anything so special about him. Not like—"

With his intense concern for the qualities of silence, Cahill backed off mentally from the conversation and sat behind his glasses, aware that something had happened. When he had been able to see he had been in situations that had the same feel, when someone had farted in company, or worse, had told the truth among others when none of them wanted it told. He was at the center of a dead calm, growing thicker, until no one could break it unless he were desperate.

Harbelis was desperate; in his voice it was obvious. "Some knew him better than others," he said. "Dobson, well, he was just around." He turned to the pink cadet. "You're just *around*, Dobson. Maybe you shouldn't have said anything. You confuse everybody."

"I don't know why," said Dobson. "I just told what I remember. I'm not trying to shit anybody. I was not close to Joel Cahill. He was in my flight, in my barracks, and he always looked lean and good, in shape; he looked like he knew what he was doing all the time. He was a good basketball player, what they call a money player. He played guard, and brought the ball down. He could play the clock real good, and get the last shot, or get it in to the Big Man, and let him take it. I liked his double-handed overhead. That's all I know. I'm sorry he went in; I'm sorry he was killed; he would be the last one I'd think it would happen to. But you can't tell."

"You sure can't, Dobson," said Harbelis. "And that's the truth."

One of the KPs brought ice cream, and it was homemade again, and just as good as before, the rough, feathery taste from somebody's home freezer. The silence around Dobson gave way to something less temporary. Cahill felt Zack's head come up along his calf, and could hear the dog's long intake of breath, and then the head turned questioningly, sniffing. The house Cahill was in was taking on something, was stealthily being shaded. Over and around all voices, the ticks of metal and crockery, the single footsteps, there was a hooding, a new insulation. Cahill leaned toward Harbelis.

"Am I right, Harbelis?" he asked, listening more.

"You're right," Harbelis said. "God damn. It's snowing, and coming on."

"What do we do now?" Cahill asked. "I've been to about all the classes I can take. I believe I'll go on back into town and rest up a little. I may make a couple of phone calls home, or see if I can get hold of Joel's mother in Memphis. Do you reckon you could get me back to McLendon's place?"

"I'm sure the colonel will lend you his jeep, and Corporal Phillipson ought to be able to drive. Is he okay for you?" Harbelis said.

"Sure, he's okay. Why wouldn't he be?"

Harbelis leaned toward him. "Would you like to walk around some with me, sir? I have some things I want to talk to you about, and I can't think of any other way to do it."

"Well, we could do that, I guess. Where do you want to walk?"

"There won't be any flying this afternoon, so I'm off from that. We could just go down through the woods toward the highway, around the traffic circle, and come out at the administration building, and Phillipson could take you on back into town. It won't take long."

"We'll do 'er, then," Cahill answered. "It's all the same to me, just as hard and just as easy."

The meal broke up around them and Cahill inventoried, touching Zack in the side, checking his overcoat pockets for the spring grip, paying no special attention to the goggles this time, and then the pockets of his jacket for the syringe, insulin, and the sugar cubes he had got from McLendon; in his pants pockets he had some coins and the key to his room, and his wallet buttoned into the seat. He put on his hat and stood up, turned, pushed the chair back, took a step. Harbelis came to him. They walked up the mostly empty aisle and out the door, descending into the new snow, delicate and penetrating. As they reached the middle of the assembly area, behind them a beating whisper developed, and after it passed in silence there was an unexpected engine bellow that seemed in some way to be turning.

"Jesus, *he* was sure lucky to get down. That's got to be the last one. I sure hope it is. I've been up there when I couldn't get down, but I've never been lost in weather: not when the ground was whited out, or when I couldn't see anything at all. That would be bad. We don't have any radios in these things, you know. You don't get those until you go to Basic. With us, it's just by guess and by God. You can't land on nothing but a compass and an air-speed indicator and an altimeter and a tach. You can't find anything if you can't see it."

"Is that what you call flyin' blind?" Cahill asked. Then he added, knowing he should not, "I could do that as good as anybody, I'll bet." To his surprise, Harbelis laughed.

"You have to be equipped for it," he said, "one way or the other. Birds, I don't know, maybe some of 'em could fly in this. But the bat is the only thing with wings that wouldn't have any trouble at all. He could fly all day and all night in a snowstorm—in a lot more snow than this—and never touch a single flake, or let any of them touch him. The bat is the only mammalian body in the air, and he knows what's what. Joel used to say that. Did you know that McCaig was thinking of going to Canada and getting into the RCAF, and maybe going over to England?"

"He said somethin' about it," Cahill said, touching his face, which was beginning to lose sensation and burn within the numbness. "He may even have mentioned bats, and about flyin' at night; some kind of new system."

"Nobody knows much about it," Harbelis said, jogging a little for warmth, lifting his knees. "Double-Mac heard about the new RCAF program somewhere; the bats he got from Joel. They're the ones

179

who've got it knocked. The rest of us have to fly blind, at least some of the time. We're just about doing it right now, on this road; we're going into the woods."

"Is this where you run?" Cahill asked, the small snow hitting his lips and tongue, stinging and tasteless.

Cahill opened his mouth and snow flew into it perfectly, air and cold themselves, substance and cold but the essence of it was air. The substance was no more than temporarily frozen shadow, invented, forged, grated, ghostly, particled, and fiery emptiness; there were no grains in it, no seeds of anything. Nothing stayed; everything kept coming.

An intimation of gold came to Cahill, not from the snow or the substanceless touch of the flakes, but from what Harbelis was saying, and the recollection of his first meeting with him, when Harbelis had run and he had timed. There was now the sunny landscape of a track, and the plunging ram-headed sprinter he had watched from his bicycle his senior year in high school. The boy's terrible strain, his efforts to double and redouble his speed were still as impressive, as awesome and frightening to Cahill as they had ever been. Such effort seemed to him beyond all sense, insane, and the boy in a kind of involuntary state, a hammering spell, like a long, convul-

"Sometimes," Harbelis said, "we've got a lot of trees here. There's a big long circle through 'em, and a little traffic circle. It's good to run on sand, because you have to work real hard, like running along a beach in about a foot of water. I've run in this sand on this road ever since I've been here, and I do believe I'm in the best shape I've ever been in in my life. I'm not sure whether I've cut down on my time for the hundred, but I'd bet you I've dropped off a couple of tenths, maybe even half a second on the two-twenty. I hope this war ends before I move out of this age. Sprinters are no good after about twenty-three. That leaves me four years. Four years in the sand."

Though among the trees the wind had fallen off, Cahill and Harbelis still leaned as though into it, the boy watching for their new steps to break into the purity of the road; he glanced behind to see where they had been, and Zack crossed the road like a low ghost, in two leaps, from woods into woods.

"I try to hang on to all that,"

sive sexual throe. The gold line of his trunks slashed like an obsession. Deeply committed to the scene, much more than when he had actually watched, he noticed that there was breathing in it; the boy beside him here in the snow, was breathing hard, trampling and panting.

Harbelis said. "All that training. I was born pretty good at short distances. I don't have a whole lot of wind, and I don't have a long stride, but I turn over fast. And I like to be hard on myself. If I get through the war, I'll be right back on the track. I like to run, and run fast, and faster than that."

"Do you think Zack might like to play around in the woods some more?" Harbelis asked, when the dog came back to them.

"He might," Cahill said. He bent down and patted the dog's side. "Go on now," he said. "Take off. Go get us a rabbit."

Zack looked up uncertainly, then bent his head to the snow and left them.

"He won't get lost," Cahill said. "Other people worry too much about a man losin' his dog. And he won't bother nobody else, so don't worry about that either. It's just when I'm around that he gets excited. Me and another fellow tried to train him as a guard dog—make him mean, a one-man dog—but I don't know whether we did it right or not. Prob'ly not, but he's mean some of the time. And some people he just don't like. I don't know why. He knows why, because they're always the same ones. He ain't never been lost, though."

"Lost? *I've* been lost. I got lost the second time I was up solo, and it's not like anything that ever happened to me before. You talk about being afraid: I've been scared a lot in my life, but I've never felt anything like that. When you can't get back to the ground, when you're just *up* there . . . well, you don't forget it."

"You want to stand here or walk on?" Cahill asked. Harbelis started to move, but stopped and pulled Cahill by the sleeve, afraid his feet would not make enough sound for Cahill to follow. Cahill started forward.

"Walkin' is always better for a blind man, when he's with somebody else. I'm not against it. A lot gets said that way. You can stand with a blind man and not say nothin', or you can sit in a room with him where can't nobody think of anything to talk about, but you can't walk with him and not talk. You'll never see a blind man—or a blind anybody—walkin' with somebody else, and them not be talkin'. I'm goin' to do me a lot of walkin' up here, with a lot of people. Or some people, anyway."

They were on a road between heavy pines on which there was no mark at all: no foot track, no tire mark.

"What happened when you got lost?" Cahill asked.

"It was about six or seven weeks ago. I soloed in fourteen hours, which is about average, and it was a good solo. I flew by the book, I matched up the needles and the altitudes and just flew one hundred percent by procedure. If I had been sitting on a log, and the log had been made so that it would do what I told it to do, the log would have flown around the traffic pattern at five hundred feet and come in and landed, all the time with me on it, doing what you're supposed to do when you go up in the air on a log. That's what it was like. But in a couple of days, when I was cleared to turn out of the traffic pattern, that's when things changed. That's when I got lost."

"What happened, son?"

"I turned out of the pattern," Harbelis said, involuntarily demonstrating with his hand, half-smiling then and putting it back in his pocket, "and lifted on up. I was supposed to figure the wind and fly through a couple of the exercises they give us—one of the first ones is that you pick out a spot and you make a kind of a figure eight, and try to make the circles more or less even, which is hard to do when there's any wind. There's another move called a Chandelle, which is to gain altitude, and is kind of a nice motion to ride through, and very pretty to watch, too, when it's done right. But I didn't do any of that, didn't do any practicing that day. It's such a great emotion to be up there by yourself, you know. I had just met Joel, and talked to him a couple of days before. He was the first one in our class to solo; he was so far ahead of the rest of us that some people thought he already had a lot of experience, but he hadn't. McCaig said he could have soloed with no more than an hour of instruction, but they won't let you do it that fast. But he was the first, and that was when people began to look up to him. I sure did. He was so proud-looking, you know, and so sure of everything; you just couldn't help wanting to be around him. I was real nervous before I soloed, and all he said to me was 'Don't worry, you black Greek. The air is with you.' That's all. And the air was with me. Getting lost was my fault. But, really, it was the fascination. As soon as I was out of the pattern, and had all this huge power, I felt that I could do anything in the world I wanted to. There was a railroad track, and the sun was just sliding along it, going along under me, like a real delicate knife. I followed that for a ways, just because I could. I loved being out there in the wind, up there in all that open space. The colors are so

182

beautiful. I couldn't describe them to save my life, but the whole land is a sort of haze; nothing is a hard, sharp color, a pure color; everything hazes into everything else. That gold needle of the railroad tracks kept going along, through one haze after another. Finally I turned around, flying east back along the tracks, going by what my instructor had told me: that if you start out flying west and then make a one-eighty you'll eventually see the reservoir, if you don't miss the north end of it and go by. If you're south enough, you'll see it, or if you're too far south, you'll see the river running into it, and if you can find the reservoir, the field is just to the west. That seems simple enough, but it didn't work. At least not for me."

"What happened? What did you do?"

"It came on me little by little, and then it hit me all at once. I didn't know where I was. I didn't have any idea. I didn't have a map, and it wouldn't have done any good if I had, because I didn't recognize anything on the ground. A compass don't do you a damn bit of good when you can't read your visuals. I knew I had started west, and I knew that I had been flying west for such and such number of minutes, but when the panic first came on me I had already come back east for longer than that; a lot longer. I figured that I had missed the north end of the reservoir, and that what I should do was to make a long circle to the left and try to pick it up. That was all I knew to do. And it was getting dark. I started in on a circle, or part of one, moving from field to field, from one farm to another, where I might land if I had to. But the fields were fading out, the farms were going; I was losing them little by little. I couldn't think; I couldn't do anything but sit there and look down over the left side of the plane, where there was absolutely nothing I could use, nothing I'd ever seen in my life."

"The air was with you, was it?" Cahill asked. "You were prob'ly not all that sure, right then."

"It was not the air, Mr. Cahill, at all. I felt right with the plane; I felt right about flying. I had just made a stupid mistake. But it all turned out fine. The sun came around in front of me, low and red, and it flashed up off water, right in my face through the prop: the whole reservoir; nobody could have missed it. From being scared shitless, I came down off the flight with about twice as much confidence as I had before it. I had screwed up and figured what to do, how to cope with it: I had balls *and* sense; I had beat my panic, and when I got down I couldn't wait to get back up the next day. That one flight broke it for me. I was ready for anything off the ground, high or low."

183

Cahill was satisfied that he said no more, for he was returning into himself, this time without memory but simply into his own shape and what it was doing. His face could tell that the snow was thickening, and the thicker it got the lighter it was. His heartbeat increased with excitement as he approached complete isolation. If Harbelis were not with him he would be lost beyond any lostness yet in his life, and the prospect saddened him; he did not even know whether Zack would answer him, or could find him. The important thing was the development of a new kind of footstep, made possible as he made it, made it of snow, of what came underfoot from the air. There was almost no sound, but the feel was of the utmost stealth, of invisibility, of the all-power of a ghost. Where am I going? he thought. Where am I ever going? I am supposed to be on a road through some woods, but I could be in an open field with nothing in it but me, no other people, my dog gone, nothing but the next step, silent, seen by nothing, heard by nothing. He pulled up his pectoral and trapezius muscles, and they were as hard in the wordless snow, the small-ticking flames in his face, the endless curtain-hang through which he was going, as they had ever been in sunlight, with Ruíz beside him on the pressing bench, drops of pool water mixing with sweat on his good-natured straining body. It came to him, then, out of the recall of effort and sunlight, that never in his life had he looked upward into snow, and seen it coming down to him. He imagined that it would not be white, but some kind of dark, an enormous shadow in millions of pieces.

"Here," Harbelis said. "Here, take this."

"What do you want?" Cahill asked, stopping in the complete secrecy of his last step.

"Just take this," Harbelis said. "I'll explain it to you." He peered, not sure of Cahill's reaction. It was hard to tell anything about someone else without being able to see the eyes. The mouth was next best—it was all he really had to go on—but Cahill's hardly ever changed from a sardonic set grimness. Even in the short time he

He held out his right hand, as for the flakes to fall into it. Instead, there was a hard flat object, light, as he weighed it. He brought out the other hand and ran it over what he held. It was oblong—the better part of a foot but less than a foot, he judged.

The middle part was round, close to being an exact circle but ridged at either end, and through this was a long leaf of some sort; he pulled on it, and it slid.

"Well," Cahill asked, "what is it?"

had known him, Harbelis had come to realize that he could read nothing from the expression on Cahill's lips, and he was more or less comfortable with the fact; he found himself dreading to see the blind man smile.

"It's a flight calculator," Harbelis said. "It's called an E6B flight computer, and it's coded. Joel coded it." Cahill turned the computer over again and felt its inner circle on both sides, and the long slat through it.

"He did what? I'm not pickin' up on you."

"This is something we all have," Harbelis said. "Every cadet has one, every instructor. Just about everybody who flies an airplane has one of these, whether it's issued to him or not. This one is issue; everybody got one when he came here. They're all over the place. But there's a difference. There's a difference now in how they can be read."

"What difference? I'm still not with you."

"I know you can't tell just by feeling it," Harbelis explained, "but this whole thing is covered with numbers, and you can get all kinds of information from it if you know how to match them up. One of the best classes in ground school is on the uses of this thing; there are a lot of 'em. I won't go into all that now, except to say that if you know where you've been and how long it took you to get from there to where you are now, you can tell when you're going to get where you're going. You can tell what your speed is, over the ground, which is really the only speed you're interested in, as far as navigation is concerned. You can tell what the wind is doing, and how to use it, and not let it screw you up, and blow you all over the map. Most of the things about DR navigation—dead reckoning navigation—you can handle with that-there object—as they say down here in North Carolina—you've got in your hands. All the air crews in the Air Corps can read one of these the regular way. But Joel Cahill figured out another way to read it. Later on, if we have time, I'll show you how the code is set up. The numbers on the E6B decode into another language, a special language, that only we know about."

"We?" Cahill asked, in irritable confusion. "We? What 'we'?"

"Some of us," Harbelis said. "A few. There'll be more later on." He changed the subject back. "You can send E6B problems around through the mail, like you're explaining things to somebody, like people send chess problems back and forth. Joel believed that you could even send them through APO zones, send them out of restricted areas, or from one combat zone to another; even if intelligence figured out there was a code involved, they still couldn't get by the language problem: what the E6B decodes into. That's ours; we're the only ones who have it. We can reach any of our people with it, no matter where they are."

"I'm freezin'," Cahill said, wanting out: out of the snow and out of all efforts to understand. "I think you done froze my brain. Let's go back." He held out the computer and Harbelis took it.

They completed the traffic circle, on which they had been standing, and headed toward the invisible buildings through trees paralyzed with lightness; moveless, picturesque, and faint.

"Zack," Cahill called out. "Come on, big boy. Come on here." As they left the woods Zack joined them, blurred with flakes. To Harbelis the dog seemed full of joy, an oversized romping puppy, leaping against Cahill's thigh, following alongside now, looking upward at Cahill as he plodded. When at last they climbed back into the Administration Building, Corporal Phillipson, from behind his desk, stepped immediately to them.

"Mr. Cahill would like to go back to town now," Harbelis said, and then to Cahill, "Isn't that what you said you wanted to do?"

"Yes, if it's not too much trouble."

"I'll go get the jeep," Phillipson said, and left.

"How would you like to have dinner tonight with two real, honest-to-God combat men?" Harbelis asked.

"Which two?"

"Captain Faulstick and Captain Whitehall. You met both of them today. They'd like to take you to dinner, if you feel like going."

"I may," Cahill said, considering. "Tell them to call or . . . just tell 'em to come on. I'll be ready any time."

"Then, after that, we could go on by the cadet club, the town one. The old class gets open post tonight, and you can meet some of the other guys. They'll be a lot easier to talk to, off the Base. I'll come by McLendon's and see how you feel, and you can tell me if you want to go to the club. It's the best place around."

When he stepped from the snow onto the hard floor at McLendon's —slick, not as bare wood, with humps and cracks you could find, if you wanted to, with the edge of your sole, but the treacherous evenness of linoleum—and was in the heat and confusion of voices he associated with the place, Cahill balanced for a moment or two, getting solid, setting up the dimensions and relationships of the room in his mind. He felt very tired and dirty, as though he had sweated heavily in the snow. More than anything he wanted a bath, and turned in place for the stairs, then moved forward, his hand out for the wall.

"This way, just a smidgin," a voice said; hands were guiding him from behind by both shoulders.

"Straight on, now, and you'll have everything your way."

"How're you doing, Mr. McLendon?" Cahill asked. "You been missin' me?"

"I sure have," McLendon said. "I've been wonderin' about you. Not worryin'; wonderin'. Would you like to come into my back settin' room and have a big glass of whiskey with me? Tell me all about it?"

"I would like," Cahill said. "I thought I'd have a bath quick as I can get it. I didn't know snow was so dirty."

"Have the whiskey first. And what we don't drink, you can take up with you."

"You sold it," Cahill said. "Lead on."

"You go on along," McLendon instructed, "and I'll be right behind you, tippin' you this way and that way, until we get there. It's down the counter; when we clear the counter we turn hard right and go down the hall a ways, and then in. Do you like blended whiskey?"

"Not much. What kind?"

"Four Roses. It's all I've got, and all I can get. After the first swallow lands on you, or maybe the first couple, you won't care how bad it is."

After the open snow and the wind of the jeep ride—there had been much through the roof—the room was so close that Cahill broke a sweat within his other sweat, half dried and itchy. The smoke hurt his eyes and, though his sense of smell was not keen, it bothered him that the one pervasive smell was unpleasant, and that this time he could not distinguish any of the foods which made it up. The voices tailed off behind him, and with no prompting he turned right, found the wall on his left and walked forward, anticipating the door, which he reached before he was ready. McLendon's hand came under his arm and pushed the door open, and Cahill and Zack went in, Cahill's feet testing for obstacles. When he found none, he stood cautiously in place and took off his coat and hat; McLendon hung them up on a rack and guided Cahill to a chair where he sat, the material so soft his buttocks were only a couple of inches off the floor when the sighing cushion finally held him in one place.

It was a room full of tassels: long fringes from the arms of the brown sofa like those on a cheap cowboy vest; beaded tassels from the two floor lamps with piecework stained-glass shades; there was a table with a radio of arched wood. McLendon poured two full drinks in stout pantry glasses, added some ice, and gave one to Cahill. He pulled up a bare wobbly kitchen chair and sat on it with its back to Cahill and his arms on it, as he had once seen Buck Jones do in a movie.

"What did you do? How do you like the field? Are you doin' any good out there?" For the first time, leaning over the chair-back and scrutinizing as closely as he wished, McLendon really looked at the blind man in detail, his coat open, his tie pulled down and collar unbuttoned, his feet crossed at the ankles. He is pale and tough, McLendon thought. Very pale, very tough, and probably very sick.

"I met some people, some of the boys, and Joel's instructor. I don't have no lock on what it was about him that struck everybody so much. He must'a changed a lot, since the last time I—since the last time I saw him. Also," he hesitated, "I got the idea that some of 'em didn't like him."

"You goin' out again tomorrow?"

"Yes. There's a lot I don't know. I can't find nobody who'll really open up. Maybe they're afraid of hurtin' my feelings, or somethin'. Or maybe that's not it: somethin' else; some other thing."

"Where is your family?" Cahill asked then.

"Everybody's dead," McLendon said, slowly but not bitterly. "My wife, Shirley Dell, died about six years ago. She cut her hand openin' a can in the kitchen—right back yonder—and it wouldn't heal up. She had a bad time; they finally had to cut her whole arm off, and she never

188

did come out of it. She bled to death in the hospital. Before that I had twins, a boy and a girl, but they died fast. The girl lived for two days, but the little boy didn't make it into the world for very long; he never did get past the third breath, or the fourth, or the fifth; that was the only time he was with us. I was goin' to call the girl Dell, because I like that part of my wife's name, and not the other part, and I was goin' to name the boy Tal, because my brother is named Talbot, and he'd'a been a real good uncle. I believe in uncles; most of 'em are better than fathers. Mine was. You can do more for a little child if you're not with 'em all the time, but just come in and out. Then they'll do what you say, and they want to be with you. That way they love you a lot more. Or that's what I think, anyway." He straightened and eased his back. "Dell and Tal. That was goin' to be them. But it didn't work; everybody's dead around here but me. And you can have another drink, if you want. I'm goin' to get myself one."

"You bet," Cahill answered. "Let drive on me."

McLendon came back with the glass heavied and chock with ice. Cahill took a sip, and then a swallow; he liked to drink deep of whatever he had. McLendon went to another armchair farther away, and sprawled as Cahill was doing. He continued to look steadily at Cahill, fixing on one thing after another: the strands of speckled hair drawn over the head, the heavy strain lines across the forehead, the pale skin that looked as though it should be weathered, or had been weathered and lost the color, the thick shoulders, the powerful gut that did not seem that of a fat man—fat was not the word to use, but heavy, blocky, solid—the legs, with the pants drawn across the thighs by Cahill's position showing as beefy as a defensive lineman's, and—the part of Cahill that McLendon kept coming back to, from the face, from the legs and shoulders, from the summer-weight khaki pants and slouching, hairy tweed coat of brown checks, country-come-to-town—the hand that lay palm down and open on the arm of the chair. He had never seen such broad fingers, or broad nails, close-clipped and almost without convexity, as flat as windows. The width of the hand was also remarkable, and McLendon anticipated with great interest each time Cahill shifted in the chair, which caused him to take hold of the arm; when he did this, and pressed the thumb inward for the grasp, between the base of his thumb and his first knuckle there came to be a mound of tissue— muscle and veins—lifted and rounded, as big as half an egg, the wrinkles gone with the tightness, so that the skin over the muscle shone in the lamplight as though varnished, a big vein riding on top of it and branching toward the wrist.

"I've been askin' around," McLendon said. "Your boy wrecked his airplane on a farm over on the other side of the reservoir. There are three farmers right in there together." He took a piece of paper out of his shirt pocket. "One of 'em is named Tuttle. He's got a couple of hills and a flat. I don't think it was him. There's another family named Coffey which is north of him, but I don't think that's where it was, either. If you go over there, the one you ought to see is a man named Bledsoe. He's been in here a few times; I'd know him if I was to see him. If I was you, I'd go to his place first. His name is Bledsoe. Luther Bledsoe."

"Joel's instructor said he thinks he can find him," Cahill said, nodding. "I believe we'll go over either tomorrow or the next day."

McLendon shook his head. "Them's poor people, over there. Got nothin' at all." He sat back, drank, and smiled. "This is the damnedest thing, Mr. Cahill. I ain't run into nothin' as crazy as this since the eagle liked to have took my head off, before he found out I wadn't a rabbit. What do you expect to find out? You don't mind me askin' you, do you?"

"No, I don't mind," Cahill said. "I don't blame you, whatever you think. If I was you and some blind guy came in here and started drinkin' my whiskey and talkin' about goin' out into a burnt-up field where a airplane crashed, I wouldn't believe it neither, or I'd think I was having the DTs. But I'm up here, and I'll find out what I can. This was my boy. I want to take somethin' back, no matter where I have to get it."

Is this true? Cahill asked himself, as though someone else had asked him: as though the question were automatic, urgent. If it is not true, then what am I doing here? he asked in answer to the possible other. There are things I ought to admit to myself, before I go any further; I ought to get certain things straight. But what more can I tell this other man, this McLendon, who's giving me sugar and whiskey, who feeds Zack on boar meat and deer meat, who seems so interested in all this? I can't tell him any more than I've already told him. My boy is dead; that's the truth. I am blind: that's the truth. I came up here by myself, when I could have had somebody with me—could have had Ruíz with me. But I came by myself. That's the truth. I've talked to some boys and a few men. I can put together a little of what they told me. My boy was proud and a good flyer. He had some kind of hold on some of these other boys. I have four more days in this place; that's probably the truth. Will I go out to the farm where he was killed? I will. Will I eat with those two captains tonight? I will. Will I go on afterwards with that Harbelis boy? Damn right I will. Why not?

He stood up, tired and dirty but resolved and oddly satisfied. "I'm goin' up and soak for a while. Forget everything for a few minutes; you know, lose it."

McLendon rose and picked up the bottle of Four Roses, half full, and handed it to Cahill. "I know how you feel. I'll walk you back down the hall."

"Not needful. It's thirty steps—thirty of *my* steps, I don't know about Zack's—down the hall, then fifty-three to the end of the counter, unless somebody stops me, fifteen to the first step, and twenty-three steps up. And six more to the middle of the room. A little finaglin' from there ought to put me in the tub, and that's where I aim to be, fast as I can step."

"Good evenin' to you," McLendon said. They shook hands; Cahill pocketed the whiskey and began his count.

The door, the room opened inward, and he was prepared for the desolation. It was there, it was always there for the blind, no matter what they did, but now he was always ready for it: ready with routine, with slow meticulous activity, with finding and placing things, with control, with his body. He sat, now, untied his shoes and took them off, leaving his socks on temporarily, not wanting to put his bare feet on the cold linoleum. He footed into the bathroom, closed the door to hold the heat that would come, found the faucets, and sat on the side of the tub, his shirtsleeve turned up, adjusting the temperature of the water with one hand and testing it on the inside wrist of the other. He ran the water hard; the little room boomed and splashed; there was a slow urgency of filling, of water with heft, the weight of increase. In the deepening sound, the thresholding sound, he got up and methodically stripped off everything, the dark glasses last. He gripped the side of the washstand, and felt for the mirror before his face, passing his palm over it, imagining what it was giving back. He put a thumb and forefinger tip on his lids as if it were magic, withdrew his hand, opened his eyes and blinked into the new darkness, and smiled openly into the mirror, thinking that anyone who saw him would be delighted at such an open, outgoing individual; so friendly, so easy to talk to you wouldn't believe it. Before getting into the tub he listened through the door to determine if Zack were moving around in the outer room, but the dog had evidently settled himself, perhaps gone to sleep from the cold, the snow, and the running. He put the whiskey on the floor, and, holding on, stepped and felt into the tub, his eyes closed, sat on the end and slid by degrees down the smooth enamel, consumed by fiery water, his feet going for the far wall where the tap still ran thundering in on him, as in a cave. He leaned forward and quieted it, and lay back with finality, almost floating, his muscles lengthening, his bones separating, breaking a facial sweat, waiting for nothing.

In unopposed arrival, responding as though called wordlessly by his whole body, like the opening of all his veins the snow he had just left came to him, a directness, a seeking-out of piercing darts of flame which at the same time glanced off and disappeared, not being head-on when most head-on: small parts of a flock, of an enormous sheet, each meaning to be forthright but dying, as if in a touch the essential fire that made it were leaving it. He had been wandering with Harbelis in a kind of wall, an unhinged blank, a shadowed flocking, unballasted, hooded, hovering, unfurling, failing, and oncoming. It was the right kind of scene for secrecy; the snow had something to do with a code of some kind. Also with an instrument; also with his son born Joel Wesley Cahill twenty years ago in Atlanta, Georgia, and raised in Memphis, who had gone one year to a small college and had been, until recently, in this town.

He stirred the water, a turbulence in depth unguessed in the deepest seas of the world, reached over the side, picked up the bottle, hauled it in, and tilted into his throat four strong swallows of the hot sick-tasting sweetness. He did not dissolve. He drank again, and finished it all, the warmth around him in steam now and leaving the water. The presence of snow was also leaving: the ticks of flame in his face, the scatter as of hooded coins, the released and compulsive swirling about, the seething, the hiss from all sides, the in-ranging, the suggestion of hammers and anvils, paper-thin bells, forge-fires, the peltering of sparks, the bee shower, the vague quick coals dying instantly, and the sense of disclosure there in all that hoodedness and numbness and unlikeliness—was that gone? What had Harbelis meant? Was he supposed to pick up on what it might have been? Guess it? Build a meaning that he could add to, when he went back to them tomorrow? He shuddered, now helpless, the whirling envelopment of the snow gone except as a memory of discomfort temporarily dispelled, but returning as the water cooled. The cold room outside the door waited also, with linoleum ready to frost the brain through the foot-soles before he could lump into bed, and beyond that the town purposelessly feathered and draped in whiteness, half stunned, frozen in midair and skidding underfoot, and beyond that the countryside, and the field with its silent aircraft, having nothing, not even their engine noise, to defend them. They are parked in rows, he remembered, preparing to get up from the tub floor according to routine, as he did almost everything, envisioning aircraft in a long line stretching away from him out of sight, and the top wings— McCaig had said they had two—formed, from his angle—which could have been anywhere but was here—one single wing all the way to the horizon, a wing of snow, pure wing, ready for unimaginable flight when the weather cleared, or ready now. He rose to both feet, steadied and slow-hurdled out, tried to find a trash basket for the bottle, couldn't, backed it into a corner, left it, and toweled off. He felt himself out into the other room, turned the bed down, stood over it like a land-mass, got in, and went down.

McLendon woke him, knocking sharply on the door. "Eat! Eat! Eat here, on me. There's two Air Corps captains down here waitin' for you. Come on down and eat. And drink some more. They both brought bottles. Stuff I can't get."

Cahill injected himself tentatively, knowing he would probably drink. He was still not sure about insulin; not certain of what balanced what. Liquor was supposed to be bad for him, and his doctor had given him a complicated explanation of the relationship of alcohol to blood sugar, but he had made maybe not enough of an attempt to understand. What he had learned to do, he did, and so far as he could tell his body indicated his condition and his ability to function. Until now he had had no trouble, and had even once left off the injections for two days, but at the end was so weak and dispirited, so exhausted from thirst and urination that he had been glad to charge the needle once more and thumb the drug into his stomach fat. He had never overdosed, and had no idea, except what the doctor told him, of what to watch for. He had been told that at first he would most probably be aware that his thinking "was not quite right," and then he would start to sweat. Sugar would cure him quickly, would bring him back, bring his blood sugar to the level it should have been; he would know this immediately, or almost, when it happened: he would stop sweating, his mind would clear, his reasoning would be logical, and along a line. He had not used any of McLendon's sugar, but he patted his pocket, reassuring himself that he had it with him as, healthy-feeling and strong as ever, clean and still optimistic with liquor, he woke Zack and went downstairs, not even counting. At the bottom of the stairs McLendon and the two captains were waiting.

"Here comes the man himself," McLendon said, "and his dog, out of the devil's own kennel. I bet he killed the devil. Did your dog bite the devil in the ass, Frank Cahill?"

"No," Cahill said. "I'm the devil. He'll bite you in the ass, though, if I tell him to. You and anybody with you."

"Don't tell him that," Captain Whitehall said. "Ain't we been through enough?"

"War stories," Captain Faulstick said. "He's going to tell war stories. Do you like war stories, Mr. Cahill?"

"I don't know any," Cahill said. "I can't read."

"Faulstick thinks he's in combat," Whitehall said. "Every time he goes up in one of these little PTs he's got all his emergency equipment with him. What do you carry with you, flying over these farms, Faulstick? Your .45? You got your .45 with you? Extra clips? How about a knife in your boot? How about some emergency rations, in your pants leg? How about a blood-chit? Nylon map? How about dye-marker? String? How about fish hooks?"

"I'm waiting," Faulstick said. "You finished?"

"I'm finished."

"Mr. Cahill, don't pay any attention to him. All navigators are like that: obsessed with inventories. They're like office people, you know. In 17s we call the navigator's compartment the office; it's not because *we* want to call it the office, but because it *is* an office. Navigators are always surprised that they're up in an airplane, that they've been up in an airplane. It's all the same to them; they'd be doing the same thing on the ground; they probably *do* the same thing on the ground. They do stuff with figures. Can't get enough of it. And they inventory things."

"I'll give you gentlemen a choice," McLendon said. "We can eat in my own place, back in the back, or we can do it in my conference room: like they say in hotels, you know, 'a place for conferences and special groups.' I got one, God damn it. Damn if I don't."

"Let's try to be a special group," Captain Faulstick said. "I expect we could qualify. I doubt if there'll be anybody more special than us tonight."

"All right," McLendon said, pleased. "It's already set up in there."

They moved through the counter space, with its usual noise and smells, and then into a hall running the opposite way from the one in which McLendon had his apartment. McLendon stepped through a doorless jamb and turned on a light, a shaded bulb over a table that looked like one put there for gambling, conspiratorially round, covered with a dark blue cloth. Four places were set with chipped, clean china, unmatched cutlery, and heavy-sided glasses that angled the overhead light into the middle, and onto a metal pitcher of ice. The room was square, of wood so dark that it seemed almost black, suggesting oak, but it had the sprain of pine, painted and lacquered over several times, pulling apart in places; somber and subtly ramshackle, it had always seemed to McLendon serious: a place for serious conversations, though there were few.

"Raymond will be in here in a minute with somethin' to eat," he said. "I hope you like venison and hog. This is about the first and the last, but if you like wild meat, this might just be good. Zack's had some, and nothin' happened to him. But I'm afraid to let it hang out there any longer. Might hang out there for a while, after tonight, but I won't eat it. I'll eat it tonight, though. You all can have all you want." He stretched back and put his arms over his head.

"How do you like my private room? Shit, it's more private than my own room. Not only have I not been in it more than two or three times since I painted it, but nobody else much has been in it, either. Every now and then they have a mill party—some people from the silk mill, out of town about fifteen miles. They rent it and I clean it up."

A thin boy of about eighteen wearing a heavy black and white checked shirt with the sleeves rolled up one turn from the wrists came in with two plates of meat, went out, and returned with a bottle of Jack Daniels.

"That's good, Raymond," McLendon said. "If you can get us some beans and bread, we'd be in the good way."

This was done, and they shared the dark whiskey, passing it around. Cahill poured for himself, carefully, testing the level with his forefinger. He drank without water; the forthright fire-taste appealed to him, especially after the sickly Four Roses. Cautiously they speared the meat, Whitehall helping Cahill to both kinds.

"This is all right," Whitehall said. "And we do thank you in advance, Mr. McLendon. This is what you call a good interlude. We didn't even know this place was in town. And we thought we knew it all; you can find out everything about this town fast. That's what we thought."

"It beats what we've got in the way of a BOQ," Faulstick said. "When I first came to North Carolina I didn't know what the hell I was getting into, and I still don't. Here I am, twenty-eight years old, come in here from Molesworth, East Anglia, with a wife and baby in Coos Bay, Oregon. I look around me. I see little airplanes. I dress up in funny furs, leather cracking all over me, and I get in one of the little airplanes. I freeze my ass off in a cackling little piece of shit that we could have stuck in the bomb bay of a Fort. I come down, and I'm back in the third grade. What on earth am I doing, doing what I'm doing? I don't have any great desire to be a pilot. At least I didn't when I came here. It was just something they told me I could do if I wanted to, because they had this program, and they said I was eligible. Even North Carolina would be better than Molesworth. I thought so then, when I signed up. Now," he said, smiling around, "I'm not so sure."

"I know what you mean," Whitehall said. "Pretty much the same thing happened to me. I don't know why I'm wandering around among these boys. This is not my kind of flying. What I try to teach them about navigation they could learn in maybe four hours, if they concentrated and learned the principles right. They're very simple principles."

"Whitehall was in the great Rabaul raid of last May. Weren't you, Captain?"

"I was. What great raid were you in?"

"I was not in any that big," Faulstick said. "But I was in the first strike that the Eighth Air Force got up out of England. To a place called Rouen-Sottville, just into France. It was a kind of experimental raid; there were only twelve planes in it. High level, and most got back. There's been plenty of them after that, and they tell me it won't be long before we're going over Germany. A lot of people have been killed, though, because of that mission. We put up twelve, and pinned the target pretty well, or so Photo-Recon said. I was not in the lead ship, but except for a couple of seconds I had a good run. I hit the freight yards, I think. There was a lot of smoke, though, and I really don't know who hit what. Part of the idea of the mission was to try to find out if we could bomb and return with not many aircraft losses, because some people believed that the B-17 carried enough armament to keep the fighters off us, especially if we held formation and concentrated firepower. We didn't pick up a lot of opposition that day, but since then it's been different. I read about it in *Stars and Stripes*. That's where I get my combat information, ever since then."

Cahill could make nothing of this. He stirred uneasily, realizing that he was supposed to be the focus of attention, supposed to concentrate, in some sense to join them, participate, create in his head a whole sky of men trying to kill each other, shooting from one aircraft to another, dropping bombs on cities he could not begin to imagine, sweating, burning alive, spinning thousands of feet to crash in huge explosions of flame. These two men were survivors of all that; though it was awesome, he was not awed, and was suddenly glad for his position behind the dark glasses, his set face, and even his dog, which told the world that he was not responsible for any of this, or was even a true onlooker. Still, there was the problem of his relation to these two. They had come here, to this hot room, this whiskey and meat, because of him. He rallied to himself as he had always done since the total of his blindness, as the center, the reason for the disembodied voices that called themselves humanity, wherever he was.

"You like this meat, Cahill?" McLendon asked. "Which do you like best?"

"I like both," Cahill said, chewing slowly and sipping ice-raw fire. "Part of it has that gamy taste more than the other."

"That's the venison," McLendon said. "A wild hog don't taste much different from a domestic hog. But deer meat has got that gamy taste to it, that some people don't like. Up here in the hills and flats we call that a green taste. I might'a told you. It's wild; has to be, because there's not any domestic deer; at least to eat, there's not."

"What we need," Faulstick said, leaning forward, Whitehall thought, as at a briefing, "is a long-range fighter. Real long-range. We need to get more and more heavies up, and far out. If we eventually go over Germany—all the way to Berlin—we've got to have some fighters, a lot of them. We've got to have a lot of bombers in the air. Hundreds, maybe as many as two or three hundred. If we could get that many heavy aircraft up, and that many long-legged escorts, we could take it to 'em. We could finish it in a couple of years, and just blow Germany away, the whole thing. There wouldn't be any more Germany, and no Austria. Not one yodel."

"We never used much fighter protection in the Pacific," Whitehall said. "The Nips didn't have as much up after us, I guess. Losses haven't been as heavy in the war out there. It's bad enough, though. The distances over water are so long, and the weather is bad for a whole half a year. I wouldn't want you to have to do it."

"I wouldn't want to have to do it, either," Faulstick said. "I liked the 17, though, didn't you?"

"I liked it all right," Whitehall said. "It was reliable; it could take a lot of punishment."

"It's funny," Faulstick said, "After that raid on Rouen, I flew forty-nine more, one right after the other, up and down France, on into France. I saw fighters coming at me from every which way, but the closest to getting killed I came was not in that first raid, but the second, which was right near the first one, close to Rouen. Parts of the other ones tend to blur into each other. I can remember a fighter from this one, a glimpse of the ground from that one, the bomb line, the settings on the bombs, who got killed on one raid or another, who didn't, a little bit here and a little bit there. The first mission made some kind of history, I guess. I don't remember all that much about it. But the second mission is something I can tell you about from now on until the cock crows. I've got some guilt feelings about that first mission—I admit it—but I can also tell you why we need a lot of fighters up. The bombers are going to end the war over Europe. If the British can hold on at night and we keep stepping up the day attacks, we can take them out, take Germany out. The heavies are the key to it, but the fighters are the key to the heavies. They've got to get some help up there against the ME-109s, and that new boy, the butcher-bird, the Focke-Wulf. The Wulfs can't get at you at much over twenty thousand, but they're bad news anywhere else. We need the fighters, and we need the right pilots for them. That's what these instructors are looking for; that's what Hoccleve and these other training-command jokers want to turn out. They don't fool me any. They're not looking for truck drivers, or flour-sack droppers or stargazers or bullet pitchers. They want cowboys."

"Well, maybe you'll be one of them, Claude," Whitehall said. "Do you have the killer instinct?"

"I'm not sure," Faulstick answered. "But I might be getting it. You may think these little planes are funny, but they're not all that funny. The first time I went up solo in one, I thought I was flying a P-38. Here I was, actually flying an airplane, when I had spent three hundred hours riding around in one, looking through prisms for a few minutes every time, and once or twice blasting away with a waist-gun, with which I hit not a damn thing but the bloody blue sky. The navigator had a home in the Fort. The bombardier don't have any home. You've got a station where you sit around, and a few little duties, such as arming the bombs, and getting one of the waist-gunners or the co-pilot to help you with them, but except for the bomb run you just as well might not be there. If you can get warm enough, though, you can sleep. Not everything up there is fighting. Not much of it is, really. Most of it is just trying to keep warm and more or less comfortable until you get back to base. There are some bad exceptions, and you wish to hell it was quiet enough for you to get bored again, but mostly it's just boring for us, for what we do."

"That's not my job," Whitehall said. "It may be boring, but I'm working. There's not any let-up."

"You've got an office, sure enough," Faulstick said. He turned to Cahill. "It's a real, honest-to-God office in the airplane, Mr. Cahill. He's got a little table, he's got a drift-meter, he's got all his instruments, and tables, and maps, and compasses, and plotters, and God knows what-all. All I've got is the bombsight in a bag. I know how to get it out of the bag and into position, where I use it for a few hellacious minutes. Then I put it back in the bag and we go home."

His voice changed. "The first mission had everything. I did every-thing right, and everything *went* right. The second one was when I almost got killed, and the man over my head got killed. Just him."

"Over your head?" Cahill asked, picking up on the first detail he thought he might understand. "You mean in another airplane?"

"No," Faulstick replied, and his voice changed again, taking on a detached wonderment. "I mean in my airplane, just a few feet behind me, and up from me." He broke off, started again. "I didn't have the least bit of fear when we started out. I was not in the lead ship. We hadn't lost a lot of aircraft; only a few had been killed, in other outfits, and I didn't know any of them; I had just heard. We took off and droned on out over the Channel, and I leaned up against the bulkhead with my hands under my arms and went to sleep. It wasn't bad. I could sort of halfway look up through the bombardier's station, where I was going to be when it got time, and the view out there seemed beautiful to me. I remember closing my eyes just as we were passing over a cloud bank— just grazing it—and I thought I had never seen such a beautiful pure color. Over the Channel I kept hazing in and out of sleep, and I got the oddest sensation that I was not in an airplane at all, but just floating along like a ghost, a spirit of some kind, or some damn thing. One part of my mind kept going over the mission, and what I would do when we got to the bomb run. The lead plane would go on to AFCE, just like the first time, which means that the bombardier would fly the plane through the bombsight, and when we saw his bombs go, the others, including me, would just toggle off the bombs. That's what I did on the first strike, but this time I had a different notion.

"I wanted to bomb, myself. I wanted to line the target up and hit it with my training, you might say, what I had been taught to do, what I knew how to do. When we got on the run, I left the sleep—as beautiful

199

as it was; I wish I could go back to it now—and crawled up into the fishbowl. It was the middle of the afternoon. It was another kind of floating, there in that naked Plexiglas: no protection, no body armor, wide open, sitting out there. The flak started to open up around us. I didn't have any idea what it was, at first, any more than the other time. There were just these black puffs in the air, like a quick smear, popping open and then drifting. They just appeared, they were just there, no explanation; you couldn't hear anything. And then something like a big chain hit the side of the airplane, which hadn't happened before. I never will forget it. We dropped back from the formation, and then we made it up, and were back in, in our box. I saw the first fighter, an ME-109 yellownose, flash past. As it turns out, we hadn't got to the worst flak, but we were starting the run, with me sitting out there in the open. It was like anybody could see right through me, especially anybody with a gun, flying, or grounded. I mean, I was *there: out* there. They told us in bombardier school—they tried to train us—not to look around, but to concentrate on the problem: to get into the knobs and calculations, and if you were toggling off on the lead ship, to keep looking at it, but to check back and forth—traveling them, they call it—between the lead ship and the bombsight, because if you were ever in the lead ship, and set the pattern, you had better have had some workout on the sight; as much as you could get. So I tried to do that. The ground, twenty-three thousand feet down under us, moved along through the hairs—the calibrated crosshairs—and I moved the hairs. The plane jolted, and I could hear parts of the big chain hit us, but nothing hit me; I was looking through that clear Plexiglas for the lead ship to turn loose the first bomb, and then I would do what my instructor had kept drilling into me: get back into the sight. Get into it, and into your problem; don't worry about anything else. I would do that, then come up and look at the lead ship. I looked down through the sight, and then looked up, and the lead ship was gone. Gone. Just gone. Nowhere. Unconsciously, I guess, I had been thinking about the other Fort as protection, although that was not necessarily so; the ninety-millimeters could have hit us as easily as they could the one in front of us. But that's the one they hit, and Big Chicken was . . . was just not. Big Chicken was the name of it; the pilot was Major Lengel and the bombardier was Harold Eismann, who was first in my class, out in New Mexico, and came over with me as a replacement. He was not in the world, from that second. The plane was hit while I was trueing-up the sight, and Harold and everybody else went right back over us before you could even think. It was a good thing I had been setting up the problem, because my aircraft was the lead ship now, and I was the lead bombardier in our box, and it was up to me to hit something. I checked through on the AFCE, and I had the whole thing. I came back out of the air and into the scope, the instrument; I steadied down. After evasive action, it was dead on-line from then on through the run. I had it all; everything there was was in the sight, in the bomb settings, in the dials and gears and hairs; and all mine. The jolts didn't matter, the big chain didn't matter. The ground under us like a problem, a map, like a composition, like a mock-up, changed from grayish-green to gray; just gray. I had a good visual on the rail junction we were supposed to hit. It came right to me. I toggled off at exactly the split second when I should've. If I had learned what they taught me, there was plenty of United States hellfire on the way to the rails of that one spot in France where they crossed, and to whatever else was down there. The plane jumped when those four two-thousand-pound GPs went out of it; jumped like upchanging gears. I didn't stick to standard procedure after that. You're supposed to say, 'They're away,' or the old 'Bombs away,' or just 'Away.' But I said something of my own, like 'Done,' or 'It's done,' but I still can't be sure if it wasn't even 'They're done for,' or 'You're done for.' Probably it was something like that. We held on attack course for another minute, and I gave it back to my pilot, Jerry Nellermoe, and he turned us out. I sat there for a minute, bare-assed in the open sky; the sight might as well have been gone; it was just shrewd metal and gears and glass, not even that. I was just a man sitting out there in space, able to think again about my guts that might have been all over the inside of the airplane, myself in pieces blowing back through the plane in a wind stronger than a thousand Mack trucks, the plane gone in one puff, my eyes gone, my brain gone, my blood crystallizing in the air four miles up. I started to get back down out of the fishbowl, and looked up and out one more time. And that's when."

"What then? What was it that happened?" Cahill asked, pulled into the words.

"I saw, as fast as I ever saw anything, in just a quick blink like being killed—I thought I had already been killed, just by seeing it—an ME-109 yellownose coming at us, collision-course, straight into us nose-to-nose, and I was just sitting out there in my body. The rate of closure was so fast that I never got anything but that one blink at it, and as I blinked open he fired. I saw the spark from the nose cannon, a very tiny spark, a very pure fire, the purest fire that could possibly be, that anybody could possibly know, electric and fined down, like a needle point; it's the only time I ever really saw fire: the reality of it, the heart, the seed, the essence of fire, the meaning of it. The nose of my aircraft kicked up, and everything in it changed. But I was there, the Plexiglas was there, clear, looking out onto cloud now, very silent and beautiful, and the cold had got really terrible. I could hardly get back into the aircraft, the metal of it. The top-turret gunner's legs—one of them, the other one sort of— were hanging down. One leg was down and the other one was kind of around it, you know, like it had been wrenched. As soon as I saw Stynchcomb's legs I knew that something terrible had happened to him, up in that other Plexiglas. One of the waist-gunners—Sergeant Karst—came up and helped me with Stynchcomb. He was jammed into the turret. The glass was gone, the whole sky was blowing in on us. I could tell we had slowed way down, maybe as much as sixty knots. I had pulled loose my intercom jack; I couldn't hear anything but wind. Sergeant Karst worked Stynchcomb loose, and I got out on the floor and guided his feet, so that we could lay him down, just forward of the waist position. Blood was dripping out of the turret and freezing; there were these red crystals all over the place, freezing, drying, flaking off and blowing, spinning around in little whirlwinds. We got him down. His head was blown off, and both arms at the elbows. He had been firing, pouring his twin fifties into the ME, and that was probably—that might have been—what saved my bare ass. The ME's fire went over me, and took out the top turret, and Stynchcomb's head with it. He didn't do it to save me; I know that. He did it because he was there to do what he was doing. He was firing, the ME was firing at him, and what happened, happened. He was not a friend of mine; I only saw him a few times. I hardly know what he looked like, except down there on the floor of the airplane, with everything I might have remembered, gone, somewhere else; nowhere. He was not there to save my life, but he did save it, as it turns out. Don't ask me; I don't know what it means. These thoughts were just beginning then, and now they're in North Carolina in the dead winter, drinking whiskey. That's what the thoughts are doing. I looked at Stynchcomb's body, lying there in those wired-up issue clothes, no head, arm bones, and frozen blood, amongst all the spent shells from the waist-guns. Karst and I put a tarp over him, from a couple of ammunition boxes. I plugged-in my jack again, and got back into the mission. We were out of formation, off course, pretty much of a straggler, without protection, no fighters, no real firepower, a sitting duck, not even a top turret. But after we left the target we didn't get any pursuit, and we staggered on home back to East Anglia. And that was that, until the next time."

"And that was just one mission?" McLendon said softly. "And you had to go up there again the next day, and do the same thing?"

"Well," said Faulstick, "I don't know if it was the next day, or how much longer it was before I went back up, but it was soon. Some of the missions were pretty rough, but as I may have told you before, I think I told you before, *that* one stands out. I was lead bombardier on the last sixteen I flew, but I never had the same feeling of such exact pluperfect rightness as I did on that run over the rail-port near Rouen-Sottville. In just a matter of a couple of minutes the best and the worst thing that had ever happened to me, happened. I held to the exact procedure on the bomb run, and everything came together better than any textbook, better than any mock-up problem, better than . . . better than anything could be better than. I had that great, that total sense of vulnerability, which is almost sexual, and I beat it and made the run, we got the bombs off the racks and on the tracks, and I saw the beginning and the end, the pure, the essential grain of fire, coming at me from the Messerschmitt in that one blink, and Sergeant Stynchcomb got his head blown off. All, right then. I still can't believe it, but it's what I've got. It's what I've got."

"You're lucky to be here," Cahill said lamely.

"Amen," said McLendon. "I don't see how you do it. I don't see how you ever did it."

"Neither do I," Faulstick said. "People talk about a man growing up real fast in a war, but that's not what it is. You find out that there are not any emotions that ought to belong to what happens. You can see the most horrible things, like Ham Stynchcomb's blood whirling around in the air over the bomb bay, and somewhere in it there's humor, something is funny about it; somewhere somebody's laughing, and you're not really surprised when you find out that it's yourself." He drew in a long breath, and it was obvious to McLendon that he had said all he wanted to on the subject, or almost.

"The image of that body, that's a bad thing to have. No head, no arms. Psychiatrists in every base hospital in this country, every field hospital over yonder, are having a fit trying to explain that it's normal to be happy that the other fellow has been hit and not you. I felt that; you'd feel it; anybody'd feel it. I recognize it for what it is, and I can live with it. It's not positive or negative with me, any more. I don't worry about it. But that one blink from that nose cannon, it looked to me like right at me, right down my mouth, *that's* got a charge on it, and the charge is positive. I like remembering it. And I don't think it's because I thought I was seeing what was going to kill me, maybe what had already killed me. It's more like I saw backwards, into myself, in some kind of way, saw the spark out of which my own brain was made, out of which everything, the world, the universe, was made. I remember from some course at Oregon State the professor telling us that there was one law of nature that is absolute, and that is that there can't be creation of something by nothing. What's the term?" he asked Whitehall. "You probably know it."

"*Ex nihilo.* It means what you said: out of nothing."

"That one blink from a nose cannon of an ME-109 was exactly what that was, as far as I'm concerned. I get a real strange thrill, every time I think about it. It has nothing to do with God. The *ex nihilo* spark: it proved everything, it disproved everything. It couldn't be and it was. And I'm here. That's proof enough for me. The airplane that made it is gone; it just dissolved around the spark, just left that one little wink of light, so intense and penetrating that it could cut through tungsten steel, or anything else. It's the original spark, with no meaning; just a kind of impulse, but there's no way for it not to be. It made the world, and if the world was made in any other way than that, I can't imagine it. It scares me to death to carry it around, and I don't know what I'm ever going to do with it. But I do have it." He paused again, sat back, and picked up his drink. "And I'm not going to die in these little trainers, either. I can tell you."

"You know," Captain Whitehall said, "you probably wouldn't believe this, but Faulstick and I were born to do what we do. All the Air Corps tests prove it. He went right out of classification to gunnery school and then bombardier school, and I went to navigation the same way. A lot of navigators are washed-out pilot trainees, and most bombardiers are."

"About the same," Faulstick said dryly. "Don't try to sell these good people on the notion that you're a member of the intellectual elite, among all the other clunks and airborne misfits. We had some washouts, but so did you. Navigation is full of them."

"Good enough," Whitehall said. "I won't argue. We shouldn't argue, should we? After all, we owe everything to the same airplane. Did you all have the 'E,' the one with the tail stinger?"

"We did, and did some stinging with it. I always wanted to sneak back there and man that thing, because you had a good angle on the enemy fighters; you had the full sweep of the pursuit curve, and I was death

204

and damnation on that thing in gunnery school, in the mock-up. I banged away on one or two missions with the waist-gun, where you just get to snap-shoot as they go by: throw out a fire screen and let them fly through it. But the pursuit curve was fun; it was skill, Art. I never got to see an enemy fighter drop his inside wing and come in after me, where he'd have to slide down a wire that I knew all about, and I could ride down just in front of him with the gunsight. Three rads . . . two rads . . . one rad . . . point-blank just before he breaks off and down. That's classic. That's what they taught us, and it worked. If I'd had that I might have understood that second beginning of the world, that electric spark that I got from the ME yellownose, but I never did. I never made it back to the tail. I was always in the up-front, from the time we got in the plane to the time I bundled up the sight and took it home. Some of the same things, we had, Whitehall. But after those, that's where the stories get different."

"The sides of the world are different," Whitehall said. "That may explain it all. That and luck, bad and good."

"Tell me," Faulstick said. "Tell me your side."

"After I finished navigation at San Luis Obispo, I stayed and instructed for one class. We had only three boys to wash out; I did my best to keep them, but they were better off somewhere else than in a long-range aircraft. They were all right, mathematically, but not consistent enough. When the others went, though, when they graduated and went on to combat, I knew that there was no way in the world I could stay in California and send other people out. I could tell what was going to happen to me if I stayed. Even with one class I was developing too much anxiety about those fellows, some of them older than I was, and the little mistakes they might make: a wrong reading, the misplacement of a decimal point, a fuck-up in arithmetic—in very simple addition and subtraction—looking up the wrong date in the Almanac, a sloppy calibration of the sextant, missing a few seconds of a time estimate. There were a million things, there are a million ways you can get yourself killed by the numbers. That's what you might call the silent death, the most irrevocable one of them all: by a decimal point in the wrong place, or the mistaking of one number into another, a miscue that a fourth-grade child wouldn't make. The numbers will work for you, but you can't give them any leeway. If they're against you, if you don't understand them, if you don't control them, they will kill you. There's no coming back from any mistake you make with them."

"Our math was not nearly as hard as yours," Faulstick said. "The sight was maybe more complicated, mechanically, but we didn't have to figure as much as you did; if we had, I wouldn't have been able to do it."

"It's not all that hard. You put your factors and your numbers together, estimate the wind, match up a few needles, set the compass heading, and look at your watch, and you'll get there, if the plane holds out."

"I'm talking about that stuff with the stars and the planets, and all that."

"That's a little more complicated. All celestial navigation is spherical-trig problems, figuring out the sides of particular triangles. But the tables do all that for you; all you have to do is a specialized form of addition and subtraction. The logarithms are all built into the tables. I could show you how to do it in a couple of weeks; or do *at* it, anyway. If you wanted to pinpoint one of those tiny little islands in the Pacific, though, you'd have to have more time than that. But I could teach you the principles and the procedures in a couple of weeks."

"Even me?" Faulstick asked with theatrical surprise. "I'm dumb."

"Even you," Whitehall said. "If you got past the third grade. I could teach anybody here."

Cahill noticed that Whitehall said this with some deliberateness, and though he could not tell why, he was pleased.

"You talk about your experimental missions," Whitehall said, "I know what you mean. They're trying to turn the balance of power—of air power—around, over there in the Pacific, just like they are in Europe. They haven't turned it yet, but when I was in Australia, where I first started out, we had hardly anything in the air. We had about two hundred and fifty fighters, but not much over half of them were operational. It was so hard to get first-echelon maintenance on aircraft over there, especially after we got up to New Guinea; in-line engines were hard to keep up. The P-40 was our main fighter; it was good, for its day, but we needed something with a lot more performance. Some of the fighters we junked and robbed for parts, to keep the others going. I don't think we had any light bombers on go, and we only had about forty mediums in shape to fly, and about the same number of heavies, and some of them were, like they say, questionable. I was at Mareeba, not far from Cairns, which is a pretty little place, on the east coast of Australia, and very friendly, at least it was then. We didn't know what the hell we were doing there. We used to spend a lot of time, me and the rest of the crew, the rest of the squadron, in Cairns, looking for girls, while General Kenney and the others got together and tried to cook something up. The Nips were coming at us from their big base at Rabaul, up in the Solomons. They were hitting us pretty good, all with land-based units. Their fighters, Zeroes mainly, were coming in and strafing the north coast, and would hit Darwin and Cairns pretty often. Their Bettys were over Moresby dropping stuff almost every day. These were all coming out of Rabaul, and General Kenney figured, I guess, that if they could come to us, we could go to them. Around in July, the Nips started moving into places like Buna, because the Navy, further out in the Pacific, had messed them up on an invasion of Moresby, and as far as anybody could tell they were going to try to come over the Owen Stanley Mountains and hit Moresby from the rear. That would have been real bad for Australia. I talked to one old lady in a bun shop in Townsville who went on most of one afternoon about the horrors of an oriental invasion of Australia: what would happen to the Australian girls and women; even her, at the age of about eighty. Port Moresby is about due north of Cairns and less than a thousand miles. Townsville is not far south of Cairns, and if the Japanese had been able to set up an air base at Moresby, they could have given all that part of Australia a fit. Everybody was scared to death; they were sure the Nips were getting ready to invade, and they would have, too. If Moresby had gone the Aussies would have had to fight in the streets, and wherever else they could on their home ground; Grandma too."

"I wish we had a map," McLendon said. "All this is kind of vague to me. If we had a map, I could get into it more."

"No," Whitehall said, smiling slowly. "You don't want to get into it any more than you have to. I sure didn't. I had a pilot, Major Red Mathis, I liked, a co-pilot named Hinchcliffe I didn't like, three gunners I didn't even know, a flight engineer who was a Methuselah and could hardly get into the airplane, and a crew chief who had robbed half the aircraft in Australia to keep ours operational. He didn't want anybody to die; we were grateful for that. For some reason or other, maybe because of the condition of our one aircraft, maybe for some other reason, we were the lead ship, and I was going to have to plot the mission and get us back. No," he said directly and softly to McLendon, "You don't want to get into this too far, even just trying to imagine it. You might wake up from this peaceful whiskey and wild meat and find yourself getting into a patched-up aircraft in Mareeba, Queensland, Australia, bound for Port Moresby, New Guinea, and then for Vunakanau Strip, Rabaul, north of New Guinea, where nobody should ever have to go."

"But you went, though," McLendon said, his clear countryman's eyes looking at Whitehall intently and with direct admiration.

"We went. We refueled at Moresby, with all of us and everybody else, the ground crews, the armorers, and everybody, looking at the sky all the time. We were supposed to put twenty aircraft up, but we couldn't do it, to save us. We got, I think, sixteen Forts into the air. One crashed on takeoff and two others turned back on engine malfunction. The rest of us went over the Stanley Mountains and homed in on Vunakanau. I was in the office all the way to the target. We were on DR—dead reckoning—and pilotage all the way. I worked out the course the same way I would have been doing in ground school, taking classes or instructing. They had just raised my office to twenty-five thousand feet, that's all. There was not much wind, and it was more or less constant, so that we didn't have to correct a lot. I hardly used the driftmeter. The E6B was enough for me. I would check at the waist position whenever the map gave me anything I could identify visually. The plot on the map looked like a perfect geometry problem. I wish I still had it, because it was a nice design in itself; an art museum would have bought it. It got us there, although I was told afterward that our firepower was not optimum; nobody was used to flying formation. About a hundred miles from target the Zeroes began to come in on us, and we lost one aircraft; I saw it go down out of the box very slowly and kind of lazily, smoke coming out of the number three engine. I was up at the waist-gun, feeding the belt into the fifty of one of the sergeants, and I just happened to see Pease get hit and spiral down out of the formation. Just before I lost sight of him the port inboard wing tank caught, and a big bonfire ripped back all the way to the tail, just like a long flag of fire, and Pease was gone. The rest of us went on in, laying the wood to them, mainly to the runway and the fighters on the ground. They were lined up, none of them in revetments. We kept a whole bunch of them down for good. Some said twelve, some said seventy-five, but we gave Rabaul a bad time; as bad as we could. We turned back—I was still up at the waist-gun position, banging away at anything that didn't look like a B-17, but I didn't do any real damage; I just let short bursts at a couple of quick colors going by; no pursuit curve; that's in the tail position, like you say, Faulstick. Billy Strohecker got one back there, or he said he did; he got credit. His name means 'straw-ass' in German, he used to tell us. How's that for a tail-gunner?"

No one could think of what joke might be there.

"Just as soon as we turned back, as soon as we made the one-eighty,

208

the wind hit us, and hit us wrong, out of the southeast. There was no more firing; I could feel the whole plane, and all the other eleven planes beginning to concentrate on my plot sheet and the map under my light. I couldn't get enough of a visual—to figure drift—on anything in New Britain. I could tell something about the wind direction, but not about the force; I had no way to tell how much wind there was, so I just allowed for course correction by guessing; I made it two degrees' compensation, which is a lot. I knew it wasn't right, but it was the best I could do. We drove on over what I guessed by the clock was the Huon Gulf. I had the map blocked off in time segments according to the airspeed, which the pilot could give me. But what you really want is ground speed." He put his hand on Cahill's forearm just as Cahill raised it to drink. "Ground speed, Mr. Cahill, is the speed you're actually making over the surface of the earth, whether it's land or water, just as if you were in a car on a perfectly straight road that went from the place you left to the place you were going. That was the trouble; I couldn't get the ground speed by DR, and I didn't know the force of the wind, or even the exact incoming direction. My E6B was knocked out, no use. Unless I could get some kind of a position reading, with it weathering in more and more all the time, we would be hard put to get back to Moresby. With the Owen Stanleys ahead of us, we couldn't let down below twelve thousand, and even that would have been risky. We cruised back at fifteen thousand, and I penciled off the miles according to time and airspeed. That's a different kind of fear from yours, Faulstick; knowing that your figures can't be right. I looked at my instruments, the maps and the plotters, the chronometer and the dividers, the almanac tables, all meaningless figures, because there was no key to them. I began to get that sickening helpless feeling that comes from not knowing what to do, and my whole mind changed color when we got over what should have been the New Guinea coast, going toward the Stanleys; it turned green with the jungle that was under us—mountain jungle—and the notion that we might all have to bail out eventually, and take our chances down there. I am not an outdoor type. I had a .45 and one clip, I had a dull GI knife, a bayonet knife, I had a C-ration can in one leg pocket and an emergency kit in the other. I had my flying suit, jacket, and infantry boots, and that was all I had. I couldn't've eaten a monkey or a wallaby if I'd been able to catch one. I was thinking about nothing but snakes. Enough of that kind of thinking and I was sure that we were all going to have to bail. I got my sextant out of the case and stared at it. It was a beautiful thing; all that precise engineering, all those angles and mirrors, those numbers that match up on the sun and the planets and stars, and on the moon, and give you your lines of position. None of that was any good; the weather had us, blue-black all around, and almost completely black down under us. Major Mathis kept asking me for estimated positions, and I kept telling him my guesses. When we were over the mountains, as I thought, I called in that I was disconnecting the mike and going up into the dome, to try to get a fix. See," he said again to Cahill, "in a B-17 you have a little place, a little glass bubble in the top of the airplane where the navigator can stick his head up and sight on whatever he can see. It's not Plexiglas, not like the place in the plane that Captain Faulstick uses, up there in the nose, what they call the greenhouse. The dome is not Plexiglas, but it's real good-grade glass, so that there's no refraction. Lord, I'd hate to put my life on any sight you took through Plexiglas. Anyway, I poked my head up there and looked around, all the way around, to find something I could use my tables on, use my math on. It was clear black-gray around us, very solid.

"You can't imagine how you feel when you're sitting, supposedly in the airplane, with just your head riding up there, out there, outside the ship. You can't get clear of the notion that you're cut in two, that you've been halved, that you'll never get back together. You look down into the ship, into the place your life depends on, and everything is far-off metal, it looks like it's hundreds of feet away, except that you can see all the *dreck* there: spent shells from the waist-guns all over, the seam bolts of the bulkheads, metal ridges, chest chutes, mats, ammo belts; I even remember a K-ration box. That's reality, that's life. But outside, up where your head is, in that perfect glass, it is so serene and untouched, there's no way to describe it. The engines are faint, compared to the way they sound in the rest of the plane, and you feel completely detached and disembodied. You're like a spectator of something awesome and serene; you're not only the only one who's been allowed to see it, but the only one who will *ever* see it. I had such a view, a *view*, a three-hundred-and-sixty-degree view of nothingness, just a few inches away from my face, and every which way I could look, that all I wanted to do was keep looking at it. The drift problem faded away from me. There was no way we could have been on course. We were somewhere to the right of our true course, and probably a long way. I had the numbers, but I had not been given the key to the numbers. Without the key, I couldn't live; I was not going to live, and neither was anybody else on the mission. I was going to end, there in that close-by grape-blue, clean, solid nothingness a few inches from my face. Waiting for it was all I had, and the feeling of privilege at being allowed that clean, delicate, solid view. It made things easy, and as pleasant as I could ever have wanted. I had just a little vague uneasiness; the rest was new pleasure. And I used to call those boys down all the time, in that one class at San Luis Obispo, for daydreaming. Navigators can't do that. They sure shouldn't, but some things can hypnotize you. I was even getting sleepy. I knew somebody would come pulling at my leg and get me down before much longer, but I just hung on up there, with my head in the walled-off weather, holding my sextant like you'd hold a cat by the neck-skin."

"Who pulled your leg, finally?" Captain Faulstick asked.

"It never did get to that. The cover started to tatter, just a little. I could see a little greenish sky. It was coming on for twilight."

"I'll bet that made you happy," McLendon said, happy himself.

"You'd think so," Whitehall said. "It did and it didn't. It meant that I had to start doing something again, figuring, trying to get a position for us. It meant I had to start worrying again. To tell you the truth, I felt like I had been done out of something, taken advantage of. My mind-set was the other way. I had given everything away to circumstances, to the weather, and to bad luck. Now, if we didn't make it to Moresby, it would be my fault. I still had time to do something. I saw a star, an easy one. It was Deneb—Tail of the Swan. I cranked it into the bubble and took down the angle and the time. With that, I had an LOP, as soon as I got back to the office. Not enough, but better than anything that the beautiful grape-colored nothing had been giving me. I began to get excited. I saw what I was damned sure was Altair, in Aquila. Means 'the Star.' The Star in the Eagle; I swear it. I had two lines. They were close enough to exactly four minutes apart for me to take the last part of the gamble. I couldn't see any more stars. But I was full of purpose. The stars were going back into the books, and I knew the books."

The others waited, very still.

"Come on, Vega," Whitehall said, rhythmically touching his fist into his palm, not looking at any of the others, but past. "Come on, come on, come *on,* " he said intently. "I know you're there. I know where you've got to be. Come on, Vulture. Come on, you falling buzzard."

"How come?" Faulstick asked. "How come *him?*"

"Because Vega means him, in Arabic," Whitehall said, turning to Faulstick impatiently, taken off his course. "They taught us some of that stuff, so we'd remember the names. Nobody forgot that one." He went back where he had been, and regained his rhythm. " 'Come on, Vega,' I said, just like now. I know you're at fifty degrees true azimuth. I know you're fifteen-to-forty elevation. Just move the god-damned cloud off you. Move the cloud. Move just a little of it. Fall out of the cloud. Climb out of the cloud. Outrun it. Let it pass you. Come to me. Come on, you falling vulture. Come on. I looked at fifty degrees, nearly as I could tell. About east-northeast. Nothing. I looked fifteen-to-forty, up and down. Fuck-all. I looked at my watch. I still had thirty seconds. Twenty. Fifteen."

"What then?" McLendon asked. "Something: right? What then?"

"There was a tatter. Then there was another one, quick-moving. Closed right over, but I saw what was in it; I saw the damned thing, bluer than anything I could have thought; bluer than blue. Blue, blue, blue. In just that flicker. I pulled the sextant up and put the bubble where I'd been looking, dead-on. The cloud tattered again. I made one move with the sextant, a couple with my fingers on the knob, and I had it. I just held it there in the bubble for a second longer, to keep that balance between me and it, and I tell you, that thing was alive. Vega hung in the bubble, and the bubble trembled just a tiny bit, and then steadied down, like one, you know, in a carpenter's level, when the level is sitting on a plank, a floor, a piece of a building that is absolutely trued-up. That's the way it was, and the falling buzzard sat right in the middle of it, just as steady as the bubble, full of me and my situation, inevitable. I had it, I had it. Quick as I could I looked at my watch, and got the time down, deep in my mind. Drilled it. Set it on fire. Then I tried to pick up the star again. I wanted it. I wanted the angle and the blue. I wanted the bubble around it. I wanted my eye to hold it all, one more time." Whitehall spread his hands and dropped them in his lap. "But it was gone."

"Too bad," McLendon said lamely. "I guess those things happen."

"No," Whitehall said. "It was just as well. I might have messed up my figures, fooling around. They were pure, just like they were. I had my triangle." He waited, and came back smiling, a little. "Blue as a marble, though," he said. "It sure was. Blue as ice."

"And what then?" McLendon asked, crossing his feet and leaning forward. "What did you do then?"

"I came down, down from my high view, my high head, and sat down at my office table, working the lines of position for a fix. I came out with the smallest triangle I have ever had, even when I was showing off in front of my students at San Luis Obispo. I laid it on the map. We were almost four degrees off course. I plotted from my fix to Port Moresby, computed the ETA, had all my information in front of me. Then I connected my intercom jack and called the major."

"And everything was all right, after that?" McLendon asked.

"It was better than all right. I sat back and enjoyed the rest of the ride, knowing that I was going to live, at least long enough to get the next day's mail. Some kind of change had come over everything: everything that I could see from where I was sitting; everything I could reach. All at once the map seemed incredibly wonderful to me, like a work of art, but better than any work of art. I saw that the coastline of East New Guinea had—had had, all the time—a shape of so much delicacy that it would be impossible to say anything about it, except that it was there, and those were the real indentations, the curves and the loops, the places where the rivers came in. I had a smaller map of New Guinea—the whole thing—taped to the bulkhead; it was there instead of a window, and I kept looking from the map I was using over to the total shape of the island, like a dragon or something, and I could not see any way to believe that New Guinea had not deliberately been put there in that dragon shape. The head even has a mouth, drinking McClure Gulf, about to eat Ceram and the Halmaheras. In just a few calculations—the right ones—New Guinea had got to be like it was my pet, like a dog or a horse: that map dragon was *mine:* I knew its secret, and it knew I knew." Whitehall broke off. "I know this is real silly, and don't matter a damn. I'm just going on and on. It doesn't have anything to do with the war; it's just something of my own."

"No," McLendon said. "Go on. I'm with you."

"Well," Whitehall said, "there really isn't much more. But yes there is; there is one more thing." He hitched himself upright in the chair, put his drink down, opened his hands, and spaced them before his face, as to indicate a frame. "Here I was, sitting there with my implements, with the big area map in front of me and the little map of big New Guinea to one side of me, with the Weems Plotter across the map, with the E6B, the compass, the dividers, the driftmeter, everything giving a kind of glad light, giving it back off me, as though I were shining, and they were reflecting. I had taken my helmet off again; I had no communication with anybody but myself, and I didn't want it, no matter what in-flight combat procedure was supposed to be. One of the gunners stuck his head into my place, and signaled for me to put my helmet on, and I figured I had better do it. I did, and Major Mathis was on the horn. He asked me to come to the flight deck, but when he did it didn't sound like

213

routine stuff, at all. I remember looking at my watch, and we had come down to just three minutes before my ETA for Moresby. I did what he told me, and Major Mathis took me by the arm, real light, like he meant it, and pointed out ahead of us. At first I couldn't see, but then, when I could make out a little, I knew what I had been sitting with all along back there in the office since Vega had come into the bubble: everything I had already been knowing, like I say: there it was, Moresby came clear: the home base sort of—how can I say this—Port Moresby, the base, the strip, everything just kind of *dawned,* there at the very end of daylight. It dawned on me and the others, who were going to live, because I had turned the key right. Major Mathis looked at me without saying anything, and gave me Moresby. The stars and the books had got together; the stars had gone back into the tables. They were something you could understand, at least in some way; the only way that mattered."

"The others surely must have loved you after that," Captain Faulstick said. "Anything you did from then on would be all right. They would have followed you anywhere, I reckon. I wish we'd had you on some of those early strikes out of Anglia."

But Whitehall had turned to him, both astonished and angry. "Love me? Do you think that really comes into it? Gratitude? Respect? Awe, maybe, even? You're kidding when you say love, Faulstick, but you may just be right. The people in my aircraft, and the people in the others on the mission, may have felt something for me that you could call love; gratitude might just have passed over into something like that, temporarily. It's not impossible. But I can't say that I loved them. I loved my instruments and my straight lines. I loved the grid over the map, and my east coast of New Guinea, and the delicacy of the coastline; I loved my big New Guinea dragon on the little map. But the other fellows on the strike, I didn't think about. I just wanted to get down out of there. No; I didn't love them." Whitehall picked up his drink. "I didn't, but I do now."

"Why is that?" Cahill said, but not because he wanted to. "Will you ever see any of them again?"

"I doubt if I will," Whitehall said. "But that's not the point. The point is that they believed that I could do what I was supposed to do, what I was trained to do. They believed in me as being able to function in a certain way, and I did function. Luck was part of it, but not all. About eighty-five men owe me their lives, and if you don't love them for that, then you don't love them for anything; you can't love anybody."

"Wait a minute," McLendon said. "Wait a minute, Captain. Are you talking about you or them?"

"I'm talking about me. I saved them, and I love them because of that. Their gratitude—love, maybe—is nothing like as great for me as mine is for them, no matter who they are and no matter where they are. They were there at the time when everything came together for me, and it involved them. All of them were up there in that night sky, over those Stanley Mountains and those mountain jungles. Everything was riding on me. And here I am. I turned the key that was already in my hand. Vega broke out and came into the bubble, and we all lived." He smiled broadly and shrugged, easing the tensions of philosophy. "I got promoted, too. Not just like that, but the promotion came along. I also got the DFC for that one mission, and a cluster for all the others after it. The oak leaves of the hero. It's funny that they should be oak," he said. "I wonder where that idea came from? There are real leaves on real trees, you know. Oak trees. They're not all on medals."

"Those are for anybody," McLendon said. "I could have all of those I wanted, just walking around where they are, green in the spring, brown in the fall, dead in the winter. Your kind is for heroes, Captain. You are one, you know. We've got all kind of heroes in this room. Ain't that right, Mr. Cahill?"

"Sure," said Cahill, not knowing what he meant exactly. "I'm proud to be sittin' here with a couple of them. I hope you appreciate it as much as I do, Mr. McLendon. It ain't just every day we get this kind of company."

"I sure do appreciate it," McLendon said sincerely. "I don't think it would be too much to say that it straightens some things out for me."

"What things?" Cahill asked.

"That you don't try to back off, that you don't try to get out of doin'. You just try to do, as best you can. Especially when you've got other people. And sometimes you get lucky. But if you're not already in there tryin' to do, then the luck won't mean anything. In other words, that one star—I can't even pronounce it—came out just when it did, and it told this one guy, this captain right here, what it had to say to him. It would have come out just the same, no matter what. And it wouldn't've made no difference. Nobody would have even seen it. But it did come out when it did, just when he was lookin' for it, when he needed it, and it was the last piece of the puzzle. It's amazin'; it amazes the hell out of me."

"What does all this lead to?" Faulstick said. "I mean, is there anything in it for the rest of us? I got that one spark out of the air, out of the nose of an ME-109. I learned something from it, but it's private. I see everything through a bright piece—a very bright piece, the brightest—of my death, or it might be my beginning, the beginning of everything, or both. But very bright it was, that one little blink. But it doesn't go anywhere. It stays with me. Right out of the snoot of that yellownose it came to me, but it might as well have come out of the asshole—if there is one—for all the good it'll ever do anybody else. I'm just left with it; that's all. I'll die seeing it, but so what?"

"There is a difference, maybe," Whitehall said. "Maybe. I don't feel closed in nearly so much any more. I know you're closed in, Faulstick, up there in the forward part of the greenhouse with your sight. But you were never any more closed off than I was, in that office space that everybody else thinks is the safest place in the aircraft. I couldn't see more than eighteen inches in any direction. I had the maps and the instruments and the tables. For a window, I had New Guinea, another map. But there seemed to be some kind of extension out from amongst the bulkheads, out into the other airplanes: out into the dark—or the dark coming on—but having to do with the other planes and the other people. I couldn't take any error on myself. I was supposed not to make any mistakes, but I sure could have. I could have made the one mistake; the *only* mistake. When your life depends on numbers, the numbers are the first to get confused, if you do. Whole rows of them just stand there without any meaning at all: figures—decimal points: the decimal points are the most mysterious of all. The numbers seem to run all over each other, and the decimal points have absolutely no explanation. They've just been put there to drive you crazy." He looked around among them. "But then your principle of order comes back into it, if you get hold of yourself; and if you keep hold of yourself, the order holds up."

"As I take it, all this was your duty to begin with," Cahill said, though he had never used the word in his life, and he recoiled from it as he spoke. It must be all the propaganda you hear on the radio these days, he thought; that must surely be where I got it: they slipped it past me.

"Duty, I guess," Whitehall said quietly. "The Air Corps'll tell you all about that. But that's not what I came out of it with. I'm glad I did my so-called duty, to the Air Corps, to my country, and all that. I really am glad; I'm surprisingly glad. But that's not the main thing; duty is not the main thing, whatever it is, whatever you think it is, or the Air Corps thinks it is. At least not with me."

216

"What is it, then?" Faulstick asked. "I don't think it's duty either. I don't know what it is."

"I can't just come right out and say it," Whitehall answered. "It's more like it was a sort of dependence that we had, there. I can't say it, I don't believe, but I can see it, do you know what I mean? I can imagine it."

"What do you see, Captain?" asked McLendon, leaning forward.

"I see those aircraft strung out, holding visual contact as long as they could, holding to my figures. I see twelve B-17s on the same course, which is the right course at first and then not the right course, because of the wind, and because the lead navigator can't get any visuals. I see us having some luck. I see the stars in the bubble—I see Vega as bright as that ME's nose cannon must have looked to you, Faulstick, must look to you right now, when you think about it, or when it thinks about you— I see the map and the new course lines. I see my hand drawing from the alternation point to Port Moresby. The hand is not shaking because it's afraid; it's shaking with excitement, the excitement of discovery, you might say. I see the dark come on us, and those aircraft go line astern. Now you can call it what you like; you can make out of it whatever you would like to make. It's not brotherhood, it's not teamwork, it's not *esprit de corps*. It's just eighty-five men in big airplanes up there in the dark, more than half lost, and it's one guy with a few instruments and a set of tables, up there with them. I was the guy, and they were the others, and we didn't die. We went out to kill people, and we must have killed a good bunch of them. We're lucky in the Air Corps, come to think of it; we never have to see what we do, except in the recon photographs, and they don't have any more humanity to them than a map does. What happens to the people we blow away, we never see; there would be no way to do it, and no use. Maybe that's one reason you don't think about death when you're on a mission, except your own, and the main feeling when you're on the way back is life; it's a life feeling. You could endow a hospital if you were rich, you could sing and dance in a Broadway show with lots of colors; you want to become a doctor, or a saint. You want to do good for little children. You want to make the rounds of the orphan asylums. You don't want anybody to be lonely or scared."

"Are you going to do any of that?" McLendon asked. "I mean, when the war's over? Are you going into medicine, maybe? You ought to put all this to work, seems to me."

"You could stay in the military," Faulstick said. "You were lead navigator on a break-in mission in the Pacific where the enemy held the balance of power. That took some doing. They should have given you the Silver Star at least." He grinned. "Get that wit? Get it? The Silver *Star.*"

"I get it," Whitehall said. "I don't need any more medals. My star is Vega. The Vulture. That's what saved us. The Falling Buzzard that rises on time. My star is Vega, from now on and for good."

"They look up to you around here," Faulstick said after a moment. "They really do. You're the one who's been there. You and I are the only ones in Peckover who've been in combat. You teach 'em out of the real fire, the lion's mouth, or maybe the New Guinea dragon's mouth. But what do I do? I'm just another trainee. I'm no better than these boys; I'm just as liable to wash out as they are."

"I don't know how they do these things," Whitehall said. "I don't know why they have all civilian ground instructors here except me. A lot of people still think I'm a pilot trainee, but I'm not. I've never been up in a PT-17. You couldn't get me up in one. No office space."

"Just the same," Faulstick said, "the boys really respect you, and so do these combat-dodgers, these so-called Training Command check-riders. But you don't care about them; I don't; nobody does. The main thing is the boys. They're the ones who're going to have to do it."

"I'm happy to be of some use to them," Whitehall said. "Maybe I can keep some of them from getting killed." He paused. "But the one they really looked up to was this man's boy."

Cahill waited, thinking of what he might say. He was strongly alert, ready.

"He sure was," Faulstick said. "I was not in his flight; he flew mornings when I flew afternoons, and vice versa. But everything my flight did, he was brought into, in some kind of way. I remember my instructor quoting something I'm sure came from him. It had to do with the change in a person's mind when he is flying rather than walking around, or standing on something solid. It made a big impression on Ganz, my instructor, who was—is, I should say—practically illiterate, and has a hard time getting over very simple points; you have to carry him in some of his own talk, and interpret the instructions he's trying to give you, back to him. Anyway, he used this business about the airplane standing still and the earth moving under you, bringing things to you— rivers, mountains, towns, pilotage visuals—to every student in my group. It was the idea that you sat still up there and controlled what the earth under you was doing; that with your body you could make it give you what you want. It helped me a lot; I still fly that way. It makes a difference."

"I only saw him on the ground," Whitehall said, "but there were always a lot of other boys around him, asking him one thing and another. It was my impression that he didn't say a whole lot, but when he did, the rest of them would clam up, and I actually saw one or two of them take notes. I was only alone with him the one time, and I was very much flattered that he listened to me talk astronomy and navigation for a good fifteen minutes without saying a word. The expression on his face was like some child that was absolutely spellbound by what he was hearing. He sat there taking it in like a person being let in on some very great secret. It shook me a little; I had never considered myself all that much of a spellbinder, but that boy sat looking at me with those pale eyes, those light blue eyes, with his mouth just a little bit open—at least not quite closed—and never said a thing until I'd finished talking about triangulation: the solution of the spherical triangle. He took down some of the names of the stars, which seemed to fascinate him just for the sound. I read off maybe ten or twelve of them.

Cahill was surprised to find the upper part of his face contracting at the names, the syllables, the odd intonation of the voice that the words required; he wondered if the others had noticed he was frowning, and might give the appearance of being disturbed. What was it? He had heard only snatches of any foreign language, and had paid no attention, but this was different, the sound was unique; these were names and sounds that nobody could make up; they belonged to something totally other than anything he had experienced. He erased his frown with his fingers.

"Alioth . . . Alphecca . . . Enif . . . Hadar . . . Kochab . . . Mirfak . . . Nunki . . . Schedar . . . Suhail . . . Zubenelgenubi.

"You get to have favorites amongst them, you know. Some you are friendly with because they are easier to identify; you know where to find them at different times of the year, at different latitudes. Then other things come into it; Vega and those two other stars saved us on the Rabaul mission; those three and nothing else. But there's something more to it, you know. There is that fascination in the names, that mystery, at least to someone who's not an Arab or a Greek. Adhara . . . De-

219

nebola . . . Alnilam . . . Gienah
. . . Miaplacidus . . . Procyon
. . . Rasalhague."

You know, Cahill said to himself, this must be the first time in my life that I have ever been truly drunk, but I am. His head was insulated; there was a far sharpness to the other voices; the distances to them were greater than normal, although he had no trouble making them out. One man was answering the other; the one who had listed the stars was talking, but about something else.

"I don't have anything set, after the war," Whitehall said. "I don't think many people do. I'd like to go back to school, probably graduate school somewhere, and then maybe eventually teach, in some little college where there are not any great issues, but with a lot of grass and sun and some old lab buildings, and half-intelligent students that might produce a genius about every twenty years, when one of them found out his intelligence was meant to go more than halfway. I'd be looking for that one, and trying to help him. If I had my druthers, I think I would just teach in the math department somewhere. I've had all I want to do with applied mathematics. I don't want life and death hanging on numbers any more; I don't want anything crucial, but just the numbers themselves, and people interested in them not for what they can do, but for what they are. That'd be best for me, I think. I can even see getting old that way, until I started to look like the school. I've never seen a school like that, but there must be one. That's where I'm going, whether it's in Indiana or Texas or Vermont."

"How did we get off on this?" Faulstick said. "I had some vague connection with the lumber business, but I don't really care all that much about it. If I can get through this phase of flight training, I might be talked into applying for a permanent commission. But I'll have to get better; I ought to be better than these boys, but really I'm not. When I think airplanes, I think bombing, and it could be that's all I'll ever be good for. The bombsight has swallowed me up, and I'm trying to get out in a little toy plane that's like something you'd pay a quarter to ride in."

"Whiskey's gone," McLendon announced. "Ain't no more on the premises."

"Thank God," Cahill said, and meant it. "I'm right at my limit. Or I might be just past it, a little bit."

"It works out," McLendon said. "You've got somebody waiting for you, here. He's been out in the hall awhile."

"Who is it?" Cahill asked.

"One of the cadets," said McLendon. "Come on in, son," he said to Harbelis, who had been standing in the hall outside the doorless frame.

"Cahill stood up. "Is that you, Harbelis?" he asked, turning his head uncertainly. "Or who is it?"

"It's me," Harbelis said, coming in, trying not to let his clean conspicuous ODs make any difference.

"We're all through," McLendon said.

"I guess so," said Faulstick. "And," to Cahill, "I hope we were some help to you."

"I hope so too," said Captain Whitehall. "We just got to rambling on and on. You can't stop a man from talking, once he's been in a war. Do you think you know any more than when we started all this?"

"A little," Cahill said. "I sure appreciate your comin' in here, when you could'a been doin' something else."

"You're a good audience," Whitehall said. "A good audience for war stories. None of 'em are true, you know. Faulstick is a mess officer in a GI stockade, and I'm an accountant for the adjutant general."

"There's been many a time when I wished I was," Faulstick said.

"You will be yet, Claude. The prisoners are looking for a man like you."

"Good night," Cahill said, raising a hand.

"Good night, sir," said Whitehall, moving away. "We'll see you before you go. Come out Sunday and listen to the band. Nobody on the post can play; even the bugler can't blow retreat the same way every time. It ought to be a lot of fun for everybody."

"It's the way out of Peckover, anyway," Faulstick said.

"For you, maybe. I'm Permanent Party."

They left, Whitehall nodding at Harbelis, who was in one of his classes. Cahill motioned for someone, and Harbelis and McLendon both stepped closer.

"We can go along now, sir, if you like," Harbelis said. "It's not far; only a couple of blocks. We can walk."

"Just a minute, son," Cahill said. "Let me have a word with the hostman, here." Harbelis returned to his place in the hall. "Do you have any more sugar?" Cahill asked McLendon. "I'm not sure how all this drinking is going to sit with me. That first whiskey was awful sweet, and I'm not supposed to take on much real sugar, except when I overdose with the other stuff. I've still got those cubes you gave me before, but if I get to feeling bad, I may have to double up on the insulin. If I overbalance I want to have as much sugar as it takes. I don't want to be out somewhere, walkin' around or tryin' to get to some place, and not have what I need."

"Sure," McLendon said. "I'll get you some more; a whole handful. A double handful, if you like. I don't want anything to happen to you, either. The only dead man I ever wound up with before, here, was shot, and there wadn't no doubt about *him* being dead. I don't want you in here passed out from some chemicals in you that are messed up, and me not know what the hell's wrong with you, or what the hell to do. I'll keep you in sugar. I'll give you some more when you go out."

Cahill, the dog, and Harbelis worked down the hall and out into the café, Cahill counting steps patiently to himself. When they reached McLendon's voice, Cahill stopped and, instead of holding out his hand, held open his overcoat pocket. McLendon dumped half a dozen cubes into it.

"That ought to hold you," he said.

"Much obliged," Cahill said. "See you."

It was still snowing, harder than before. Harbelis walked on the outside of him, with Zack also to the outside as Cahill shuffled nightmarishly but solidly into the stinging fragments, the flocks, the bits of a sheet coming at him, many touching his lips with a darting of directness, of seeking out, and at the same time of glancing off; he went on, surrounded by air in particles of dodging helplessness, of small intense things meaning to be forthright, but dying; furled and hurtling. Cahill's mind spoke steadily to him in new images which he tried to assimilate, some of the hot whiskey still in his throat. The story of that bomb dropper: what had the fellow meant by it? Or was it even true? He looked for a moment at the sparks of his blindness passing in their terrific hurricane sideways sleet of light, and wondered if the shot from the enemy cannon which the bombardier Faulstick had described had been a part of these; a fragment, a spark like the sparks of these flakes of snow? Though he admired the other man, Whitehall, more—or felt he should admire him, maybe—he had been more strongly hit by the story of the cannon flame. But both stories were fading from around the image of his boy listening to the navigator. He had been real; he had existed. Cahill could not picture him, but someone's comment, he thought he remembered, had given Joel Cahill curly hair, and now Cahill gave him a lot of it, bushy and lively. The Navigator had said that his son had light blue eyes, and that he had been completely lost, carried away, listening.

"It's down this way," Harbelis said. "No more than half a block." He took Cahill's arm. "Come on, now. We've got to cross the street." A car went past, a loose chain thumping softly. They crossed, and were going toward voices: many, excited and vague—blocked off, heard through walls. Cahill imagined lighted windows. He kept his head down until Harbelis opened the door and the noise.

He let the last flakes swirl on him, and then stepped cautiously into the blare of people and music. Someone stepped back, away from him, and the sound died away as he slid his feet alternately into the room, feeling with a low hand for furniture, for anything that might be there. By now he was used to the temporary silence that occurred each time he appeared among people. It would pass, but it was always awkward at first.

"Hello," he said. "Keep doin' what you're doin'. We'll just stay a minute." A far conservation picked up, and then one not so far.

"Would you like some coffee, Mr. Cahill? How about a beer? You been drinking something stronger, prob'ly, and a beer would cool off your tongue."

"Okay," Cahill said, warm and feeling remarkably good with the combination of liquor and snow.

"Sit right here," Harbelis said. "I'll be back in no more than two seconds." Cahill backed by degrees into one end of a sofa, not in the middle of the room but out from the wall, so that the cadets and their few girls could circulate discreetly around it, looking at the blind man and the dog as though Cahill were holding court, greeting petitioners. The shape of the sofa agreed with him; the position of his back was good, and his last shot of insulin seemed to be in fortunate balance. He reached down to see how Zack was taking things, and the dog was calm and heavy, his head down. Who will come? Cahill thought. What the navigator had said out by the swimming pool was true: they're beginning to come to me. Who will it be?

Harbelis came back with a chill, handled glass, and Cahill put it on like brass knucks, then drifted deeply and gratifyingly.

"One more time," he said, holding the glass out. "Snow makes you thirsty."

He tuned to the situation, to the room. He was getting better at this, he was sure; what would

Some, perhaps a third, of them had seen him before, in the cadet mess or some place else at the

have been, a month ago, a blur of voices, a meaningless confusion of human sounds, now had a distinctiveness, a balance, a definite system of distances. Before much longer, he thought, I'll be able to listen in and out of conversations like nobody else in the world can do, because I'll work at it, and I'll know that I'm doing it. His interest in the moment increased as he now began actively to select words and phrases from all sides. Not a one of them knows what I'm doing, he assured himself; this is like being invisible. He decided to pick up the farthest voice, and then work back toward himself; to try for the most difficult first. To his left, barely within range, he made out a boy's harsh voice that said ". . . and that did it for me. I rolled it over, and Split-S'd out of it, and on down." A girl a little nearer said, ". . . it's all right except for the lint. It's not good to go around picking your nose, even if there's nothing in it."

"*Especially*, if there's nothing in it," a boy said.

"You let me know if I do it, now," the girl said. "I don't want to embarrass anybody." The nearest conversation was directly behind him, so close that he had had trouble tuning it out; now he accepted it, for one of the voices had an urgency that

base. The others were taking their first look at the blind man and his huge distrustful dog, and all of them took care not to come close; there was a constant turning of heads, but no movement forward. One cadet, talking to two girls, half raised his hand to point, then, shocked at what he was doing as impolite, dropped his gesture; realizing Cahill's condition once more, however, he raised his hand again. Harbelis and Cahill sat drinking beer; the drift of young people around them was tense and eager. To the cadets and mill girls, the three waitresses, the librarian, and the gym teacher, the presence of Cahill added an element of uncertainty to their temporary interlude, their enjoyment of themselves in a warm bright place. The room was full of gestures; a skinny boy turned his hand over and swung it downward past his side. A tiny darkish girl, lifting her head toward the face of a lumpish boy whose cheeks were the grainy red of a tubercular, plucked downward at her nose earnestly, explaining.

appealed to him. "I was just riding and rocking," the boy said. "I didn't think there was another airplane within ten miles of me. It was real clear up there, and bright. Things were calm and good. Visibility was good, and I was about out of time. I could see the base, and I was just fixing to start letting down. I had my head on a swivel too, like they tell us. And then, in just one eye blink—no, no: one half of an eye blink—the damned thing had come and gone, no more than thirty feet under me. It just whooshed by, and wasn't anywhere. I just caught that one little glimpse of it, under the port wing: a B-25 that looked like it was big as a freight train. If I had started that letdown a second sooner, it would've had my ass."

Two cadets behind Cahill's big solid head stood with bottles of beer, both tall, one listening with genuine interest, and the other speaking with a certain wonderment. He did not hesitate, but brought the words out of the situation he described, as though they were being given to him slowly by someone he was honor bound not to misrepresent.

Neither of them glanced at Cahill, near enough to touch, though the dog was hidden from their view, at Cahill's feet and half under the sofa. There was great ease and familiarity between them, as the taller went over his story again, unable to believe it and not willing to leave off.

Harbelis lifted his bottle to someone across the room, catching his eye. A slim, broad-shouldered cadet broke off courteously from a group of others and came to them.

"Here's somebody you may remember," Harbelis said to Cahill. "This is our cadet colonel, Malcolm Shears, from Oconomowoc, Wisconsin. He's got lots of power."

"All kinds," said Shears, smiling. "How are things with you, Mr. Cahill? Are they giving you the official tour?" He sat down beside Cahill, leaning forward like a football player getting ready to go into a game. Harbelis watched his handsome, intent face with approval.

"I've been talkin' to as many people as I can," Cahill said. "I think I'm beginnin' to get some kind of a picture. I really do thank all of you for takin' up your time. One more day will prob'ly do it for me, I reckon."

The expression on Harbelis's face changed anxiously. He shook his head, trying to make sure that Shears understood him. Shears held up an open palm, and turned full on to Cahill.

225

"I hope you can stay through Sunday, Mr. Cahill. If you're able to do that, it will be a great help to us."

"I don't quite understand what you mean," Cahill said, though he was moved in spite of himself. "How can I be any help to you? I think I'd more or less just be in the way."

"Believe me, you wouldn't, sir," Shears said. "A few of us want to talk to you, if you can make some time. There are some things that we can tell you that the others can't."

"We do want you to stay," Harbelis said. "We need you."

"You know, this is kind of hard for me to get used to," Cahill said. "Why in God's name, or anybody's name, you might need me all that much is somethin' that somebody's goin' to have to explain to me."

"We'll explain to you," Shears said, his eyes narrowing and intensifying their blue, and the incised cleft in his chin seeming to deepen, or so Harbelis believed. "We can't do it here, though. Some of the others are not in town tonight. There was no meeting called."

Cahill let this go, sensing the other's desire to pass on.

"I can reach the others tomorrow. How about late tomorrow, after retreat?"

"I'll try," said Cahill. "I don't know what they'll have me doin', though. McCaig wanted me to go over to where Joel crashed, and talk to the people who found him. I thought I might do that. It might run you late."

"All right," Shears said. "Tomorrow might be a little soon. But if you can stay through Sunday, we could get together with you on Friday, and I can make sure that everybody'll be there."

"All right," Cahill said, uncertainly. "If it's all that important to you, I can at least stay through Friday."

"That's good," said Shears. "That's very good. Don't be nervous, everything's falling right into place. I'll see you on Friday. Harbelis will probably be with you tomorrow, and he'll tell you where to meet with us."

"Good enough," Cahill said. "How did your football game go?"

"I saw you out there," Shears said, grinning. "I almost ran over you, you and Joel's crazy instructor."

"Sounded like a herd of buffaloes to me, that's all. McCaig said they were after you. Did the buffaloes get you?"

"They did on that play," Shears said. "Somebody tripped me up. But we won anyway. I hope all those feet—all those hooves—didn't scare you."

"No," Cahill said. "I just stood where I was at, hopin' somebody had some sense. There wadn't no other place I could go."

"We'll see you Friday," Shears said, getting up. "Our friend from the Acropolis will find us for you. Just follow the smell of goat cheese."

"Farewell, Commandante," Harbelis said. "Keep things straight."

"They're straight," Shears said, and walked away.

Harbelis turned to Cahill. "I just saw somebody come in, and I guess I better bring him over. I'll get us a couple more beers first, though. I don't think he'll stay long."

"Who is it?"

"Foy," Harbelis said. "Lieutenant Foy, one of the Army check-riders around here. Any of these civilians can fly better than he can. He comes around here all the time, because there's no officers club."

"I may already have done met him. I'm no good on names, but I think I met him. Sure, bring him over if you want to, or if you have to."

Harbelis left and, though he knew the seat beside him was empty, Cahill felt the space tentatively, since he did not want to make a mistake and talk to emptiness. As soon as he pulled his hand back, someone sat down. The body was light, very light; Cahill did not feel his own seat change in depth. It was either a child or a woman, and it was not likely to be a child.

"Hello," Cahill said. "My name is Frank Cahill. I'm from Atlanta. And this is my dog Zack, and he won't hurt you, so don't ask me how many people he's killed. He's still waitin' for the first one. The right one; it has to be the right one. It's not you, whoever you are."

A girl had been talking to a fat pale cadet, and when Harbelis rose she came directly and took his seat, leaning backward with her arm down the arm of the sofa but with her head thrust slightly forward, dry-lipped, her eyes large with unnatural heat. She too was pale, with no color except her eyes—dark gray—her savagely lipsticked mouth, and her clothes, a yellow wool sweater tucked into a plaid skirt, and a red patent-leather belt around a waist not much larger than Cahill's bicep. She wore sheer rayon stockings with a heavy seam, and flat shoes like those of a nurse or prison matron.

"I ain't afraid of him," the girl said. "I never had no trouble with dogs."

Cahill was unprepared for the voice, which was like that of some thin, urgent country spirit, aggressive, enthusiastic, and sullen.

Someone stood in front of him; maybe more than one.

"This is Lieutenant Foy," Harbelis's voice said. "He thought he'd come over and say hello."

"Fine," said Cahill. "Hello. How are you?"

He pushed down on the seat with both hands to get up, expecting the other to assure him that he needn't. There was nothing of this sort, however, and Cahill thrust out a hand and waited. After a second or two it was taken. Cahill felt for the short bones of the inner hand; fingers were around his with little conviction.

"I believe I met you over in the other place, didn't I? You was talkin' about flying in circles, somethin' I didn't quite get. Somethin' about circling over a road—roads, wind—some such." He continued to hold the lieutenant's hand.

The girl watched upward, concentrating on Cahill's broad face and blind shining forehead, his dark glasses catching the lights from the cheap chandelier into a held-in and flat forest green. She passed from them to Lieutenant Foy's pink face, his combed-across thinning hair, amongst the roots of which a light sweat was developing. Harbelis was also looking at the lieutenant, and nearly anyone who noted his expression would have seen satisfaction, a certain confirmation.

"Over on the flight line, you mean. I was trying to explain for the hundredth time a very simple maneuver to one of these hammer-headed clunks. He may make the quota, if it stays up. They must need pilots mighty bad, if they take him, or about half the others around here. If they tighten up the quotas that one will be in the

Cahill had a slow impulse to harden; a kind of trembling came into his fingers; it would have been impossible for the other not to feel it. Cahill fought with himself not to make use of what he had, to tense all-out and break something. Not even a quarter of his strength was going into his hand; there was plenty in reserve, quivering to concentrate.

As he let go he noticed that the room was dead quiet. With his calves against the seat he folded back and down onto the sofa.

first bunch on the way to radio school, or cooks and bakers.

"Really," Foy went on, like a man talking against time, with a little bluster, "it's not hard to do. Not hard at all. If you can control the airplane, you can fly an eight-pattern over a road. You just have to know where the wind is, to make it come out right. Where the wind is, and how much of it there is."

He peered intently at Cahill's glasses, with the chandelier pattern in them. He took a step back and passed the released palm across his forehead and back over his wet hair.

"Will you be around for a while, Lieutenant?" Harbelis asked pleasantly.

"I may," said Foy. "And I may not. I think I'll just have a beer and go sack out. Mr. Cahill's dog doesn't seem to like me."

"Get on with it, Zack," Cahill said to the dog, nudging him with a foot, kicking at Zack's front knee joints to make them fold and the dog lie down once more. "And shut up, too. Nobody's done nothin' to you." Zack subsided, though he continued to make a low boiling sound far back in his throat.

"I'm going along,"Lieutenant Foy said. "I believe I already said I'm sorry about what happened to your boy. A thing like that hurts us all."

"There's not anything anybody can do," Cahill said. "And you don't seem able to tell me much about him. I don't have nothin' more to ask about."

"Well," said the lieutenant, not willing to leave on what seemed a wrong note, "he was impressive. He impressed a lot of people, as I guess some of them told you. I never flew with him, though." He glanced at Harbelis, who was smiling guardedly. "You finding this funny, Cadet?"

"No, sir," Harbelis said. "I just got to thinking about something else, that's all. My head wandered off."

"You never made the figure eight over the road with my boy, you say?" Cahill cut in. "Never told him about the wind?"

"No, I never did," said Foy. "But from what we can tell, it was the wind that got him. He was flying over a fire, and under altitude, too. That's strictly off limits. There must have been a lot of turbulence. It would pitch that little Stearman around like . . . like . . ." He appealed with his eyes to Harbelis for a word, and then to the girl, who shook her head. ". . . like nothing. And it would've happened fast. It did happen fast. That's what we think."

"Wrong circles," Cahill said, surprising himself. "Wrong figure to fly, in the wrong place."

"I guess so," Lieutenant Foy replied. "If that's the way you want to put it."

"Thanks for coming up, Lieutenant," Cahill said. "I'm sorry if my dog bothered you."

"He didn't bother me," Foy said, putting his eyes briefly to Zack. "He's okay. Let me know what you need, Mr. Cahill. I'll try to oblige."

After Foy had left for the bar, Harbelis waited until he was out of sight.

"We got through that easy," he said. "Usually he'll talk on and on, all down. You know, down *to* you. I never heard him say anybody did anything right. I don't believe he'd certify a single one of us if he could help it."

"I don't like him," Cahill said matter-of-factly and truthfully. "You can tell when somebody wants to say somethin' mean, and is just holding himself back because he's afraid of somethin'. Maybe it was Zack."

"Maybe it was and maybe it wasn't," said Harbelis, giving way to his grin.

"It wadn't your dog," the girl said, with a tough jaw, but smiling also. "That's not all of it. He's scared to death of you, blind man."

"How much can you bench-press?" Harbelis asked without warning.

"Bench-press? You mean now? About three hundred, I reckon. I used to could do a little more. But I haven't worked out for a while. I may get back to it. Then I'll tell you what I can do."

"Well," Harbelis said, "that's all the excitement. Lieutenant Purcell Foy has just shaken hands with a man who can press three hundred pounds. That ought to give him something to think about."

"I don't know what," Cahill said. "Fuck him."

"*I* wouldn't fuck him, I can tell you," said the girl. "And I'm fairly generous."

"You're fairly good, Hannah," Harbelis said. "You've got more guts than a burglar." He touched Cahill's shoulder. "This here's Hannah Pelham, the wild mountain flower of the cotton mills."

"Why don't you tell him some more about my past life, Cadet Harbelis?"

"Because I don't know any more, Pelham. Why don't you tell him?"

"I'll tell him," she said. She turned to Cahill, narrowing her face. "You think we might get together, like, say, tomorrow night? I'll fix you something to eat."

"That might be just fine," said Cahill. "Me and my boy's instructor are going out in the country tomorrow, but if you'll drop by McLendon's about six or six-thirty, we can go on from there."

"I'll sure do it," she said. "Ain't you getting hot in that overcoat?"

"I am," he said, "damned if I ain't." He was sweating not so much from any exertion with Lieutenant Foy, but with the effort he had made to avoid putting more force—all his force—into his grip. Why didn't I? he wondered. Then, what good would it have done? Still, he wished he had borne down more. "What I'd really like, I think," he said, "is some air. Maybe we could go out on the street for a minute or two."

"We can do better than that," said Harbelis. "They've got a kind of garden place in back. When it's not so cold, people go out there. You like walled gardens?"

"Never been in one," Cahill said. "Let's give it a go."

Aside from his body heat, Cahill felt strong and well, and a little excited, as Harbelis guided him through the others and out the back door of the kitchen. They worked past a group of boys, two of whom were arguing loudly. Cadet Shears stood to one side, his arms folded, observing.

"Watch your step going down," Harbelis said. "There are three steps."

"I'll make it," Cahill said. "All hands off."

The coldness struck him immediately as what he wanted. After the stairs he moved forward a few feet, stopped, and turned slowly around. His sense of smell, which he thought had been leaving him for twenty years, and on which he did not much depend, seemed to have

Though the bricked roofless space they stood in was small, the size of a medium bedroom, it seemed too large for the three of them, for there was nothing else in it except a rack of empty clay flower pots on the far wall. Harbelis glanced up and out once, and saw that the square sky was clear-

revived. Zack, his head up, sniffed as Cahill was doing. He was not sure that he could remember how a rose smelled, or any other flower, but this was definitely something like what he would have imagined. He associated flowers with heat, with fields and spaces, with the roll of grass, and with someone else, such as his wife, remarking on how pleasant the warm air was, full of them. But, though this was sweet, it had nothing of warmth about it, though perhaps of space. If you could think of something like cold flowers—not many but a few strong ones —it would be like this, he reflected.

"Y'all smell that?" he asked. "What is it?"

"You don't smell somethin' sweet, something like flowers, maybe? Didn't you say there was supposed to be a garden here?"

ing; one star went by through what might have been the last cloud. Both he and the girl put their hands under their arms and watched Cahill turn and sniff, waiting for him to speak. Light from the cracked kitchen door lay in a blurred rod across the floor brick, and in and out of this Cahill moved, trying all directions. The dog, which had begun to circle Cahill in token obedience, now stood foursquare, absorbed in something else.

"I don't smell anything," Harbelis said, trying. "Maybe somebody took a leak out here. It wouldn't be the first time."

"I don't either," said Hannah. "This cold weather is freezin' up the inside of my nose, and that's good. I'm glad we came out. How long you want to stay?"

"They'd be dead flowers now," said Harbelis. "I think they have some plants out here in the summertime, but there's not anything but bare walls now."

232

With a tremendous explosive crash the rod at Cahill's feet blew wide open, flooding the garden with light. Through the door two boys, flailing with inaccurate and murderous force, struggled, fell over the stairs and each other, rolled on the brick, fought briefly on their knees, and then on their feet, smashed at each other as hard as was possible to them.

"Jesus," Harbelis said, thrusting Cahill back toward the far wall, where he brought up under the pots, instinctively feeling for Zack's collar. From the door several other cadets came down, and one of them made a half-hearted attempt to hold the smaller, more furious boy's arm.

"Spain! Spain! Listen to me! You know what this'll get you! It's not worth it." In answer, Spain landed a solid, sickening right fist straight into the nose of the larger pink-skinned, out-of-shape-looking cadet. The big boy stumbled backward into Cahill, and Spain was on him again.

He was not used to having anything hit him so unexpectedly, or with so much area. In an instant of contact, though, he knew the condition of the other body, which was helpless, out of control. On reflex he tried to hold the other body up, to keep it from falling away from him, but as he did this the shape he held was struck again, and again and again. A hard object hit Cahill in the nose; the other body took a punch that came through to his, then another one, harder, much harder. A great noise was around, many young voices yelling, a flood of curses from the frantic hammering cadet, and through these, the pleading and sobbing of the boy against him. "Here," Cahill heard himself saying, "get out there. Don't let

Cadets leaped down into the arena, but such was the fury of Cadet Spain that any resolution they might have had about restraining him was weak in comparison. The garden itself seemed, despite the open house door, to have become a place sealed off from the rest of the world for only this purpose: a room into which combatants are locked, and from which only one could emerge. Harbelis, attempting to protect Cahill, had no real way to do it. He stood helplessly, as the blind man kept the bleeding cadet from falling. Spain lashed into the boy's sides, and then lifted to the head, the punches coming fast and hard, one out of three now landing, the beaten boy calling out wordlessly. He half turned toward Cahill, into the bricks.

him do this to you." The body left him, and the noise increased. Cahill set his glasses back, and swept his arm around for whatever, whomever he could find. But before he reached Harbelis, the big cadet was flung back against him again, and this time fell to his knees. Cahill, reaching for the dog, found the boy's head, and jerking back when he understood what it was, pulled his fingers across the face. Straightening, he palped the fingertips quickly. They were greasy and wet; the taste was salt when he tongued.

"God damn it," he said loudly, "quit this!" He felt down for the boy again, who rose up and leaned into him. Almost immediately he was struck again, it must have been in the stomach, and moaned in a way past enduring. Cahill pushed him again, this time to the side, and smashed straight out with all he had, hoping to kill.

"God *damn* it!" he shouted hoarsely. "I said *quit* this."

The boy stumbled forward again into better light.

"Come on, Willis," a cadet said, outdone, excited and frightened. "Do something! *Do* something!"

"Kill him, Spain!" another screamed. "Kill the son-of-a-bitch!" Harbelis tried to take things in, to find something he could do. He was already tired of blood. No one in the arena wanted to edge into Spain's attack, or even to touch him; his rage was too pure for the rest of them. Harbelis tried to look past. Above the fight, at the top of the three steps, Malcolm Shears stood in the door, taking up half the light. He raised his palm peacefully to Harbelis, and shook his head enough for Harbelis to see. When the bleeding boy, Willis, stepped forward again into the full of Spain's onslaught, Shears disappeared into the house, and Harbelis was sure, afterward, that he had not seen Cahill let drive with his two hundred pounds, coming off the wall.

Going out from himself to his fist, out—it surprised him immediately as he felt it—from his right heel planted where the wall and floor came together with great authority, up through his calf, loins, back, and bunched, firing-out shoulder through his biceps and forearm, Cahill understood with superb elation that there had never been such a punch directed anywhere. Whether it hit anything or not did not matter. What the people around him thought was not important. Everything was in the undirected flail-out; it could not have been foolish; they could make whatever they wanted to of it.

He missed, but not by much. Cadet Spain stopped where he was, his hands up, his fighting saliva running thickly from one side of his uncut mouth, his hands up, his fury dead-ended. There was a shocked, superior quietness. Zack, who had been sitting propped up, rose to all legs. Spain turned from one side to the other, as the fat beaten boy, his hand to his nose, moved off, leaving Cahill drawing his arm back, getting his balance, facing the stocky cadet. Again Spain looked around; he dropped his arms, perhaps too suddenly. In one jump, silently, Zack laid open the boy's pants leg, and with a convulsion of beast-sound, went after the bared calf.

"Good God!" Harbelis cried. "Don't let him do it! Don't let him!" Cahill threw himself in the direction of the sound, and managed on his knees to grab the dog with both hands by the hair of his haunches and pull him back, snapping and thrashing. Twisted in his overcoat, he fought with the animal, pulling it to himself by whatever means he could find, backing for the wall. Once he had Zack by a foot, then by two, then by a foot and the tail, by the heavy scruff of his side with one hand, then both, and finally by the collar. His hat was off, and his glasses; he pulled backward with all his strength against the wall, until, little by little, it came to him that the dog was no longer fighting, and lay between his legs, the big head on Cahill's thigh. "Zack," he said into his lap. "Zack, are you all right? Did I do it to you?"

"No, sir, you didn't," Harbelis said. "You almost did, but you didn't. You better let up on that collar though. Give him some air."

The garden had filled with boys and a few girls, thronging around Cadet Spain. Shears came from them and spoke to Harbelis above Cahill and the vibrating dog, now rumbling deeply but not pulling.

Harbelis leaned down to Cahill. "Shears says why don't we just go on. No use staying around here."

Cahill pulled up a leg, and placed Zack's head on the bricks, where it lifted back toward the hand that had held it.

"Calm down, boy," Cahill said, though Zack was calm, and looked up at him as he sprawled with the skin of his head against the brick grit.

"Can you walk OK, sir?" Harbelis asked.

"Sure I can. Question is, can Zack walk?" He rattled the chain collar. "Get up, big boy," he said.

Zack stood uncertainly, and shook his head with tentative, then concentrated emphasis.

"That's right, Hog-head, flap them ears. I'm sorry I got rough with you, but you was after somebody you didn't have no business bein' after."

"After him, is right," said Hannah Pelham, who was there. "I never seen nothin' like it. That boy thought *he* was doing somethin' rough. He did, before they toted him out."

"Let's go on," said Harbelis, a little nervously. "We ain't lost nothing in this place."

"Did I break my glasses?" Cahill asked, painfully straightening, working his back up the rough wall.

"No, sir," said Hannah, "I've got 'em. Ain't nothin' been broke."

He turned toward her and reached for the glasses, but they were not put into his hand. She was staring at his eyes, and as she did so her mouth slowly opened. Human eyes, animal eyes, the eyes of fish and insects, the eyes of birds, are relatively steady, and as she remembered this, all the eyes of every kind she had ever seen fell away, and would take some time to come back, for the eyeballs of the big bald man in the twisted overcoat were jerking and shuttling in a way that filled her with such curious and unfair terror that she could not bring herself to make any movement toward him, no matter what. It was not that she had never seen such eyes, such behavior as this in a human face, but that she could never have imagined it. So rapid and so random was the movement, so capricious and possessed, that she could not tell, she did not want to tell, whether the movement of the eyes was coordinated, or if each eyeball were moving, slanting, leaping, rolling, trembling, staring in place, swiveling, jerking, independent of the other. There was no law. At first stopped, beyond will, she gave him the glasses quickly now, to cover himself.

"What'll we do?" Hannah asked.

"Not stand here," Harbelis said. "Let's get Mr. Cahill home."

Cahill had put his hat on, and was turning his head from one side to the other. He smelled his fingers and a sleeve of his coat.

"What is it?" Harbelis asked.

"The same thing," Cahill said. "I still smell the same thing as when I came out here. Cold flowers, I can make out just a little bit. Not dead, either. Cold but not dead. Grassy."

"Come on," Harbelis said, looking from the clay pots to the door. "Let's go ahead on."

Stooping, holding Zack by the collar and Harbelis by the elbow, following the wall, Cahill made it to the kitchen stairs, and out through the house. There was no more snow in the air, but the footing gave and slid. It was not until they were a block from the cadet club and had reached complete silence, and she spoke, that Cahill realized that the girl was with them still.

"I don't think you ought to worry about Zack gettin' after that boy," she said. "I think he was more scared than anything."

"I wouldn't be so sure about that," Harbelis said. "From what I could tell, your dog ripped up Spain's leg pretty good. There came to be some blood on them bricks, right fast. Somebody'll have to hose that place down."

"What's next?" Cahill asked. "I expect they'll get after me and Zack for cuttin' that boy."

"You might have to talk to the colonel in the morning; this is not part of the S.O.P. around here. Dog wounds; they'll have to look up what to do. I'll try to find out about Spain tomorrow," Harbelis concluded. "I'll let you know."

"To tell the truth," Cahill said, "I was more worried about the boy I was trying to hold up than I was about the one Zack got after. What was all that for, anyway? Does this happen all the time?"

"Spain is a good boy," Harbelis said. "A real hard knocker. He's right in there with Shears and the other high-up guys. He's right under Shears."

"In the cadets?" Cahill asked, straightening.

"No, not in cadets. In Alnilam."

"What?"

Harbelis went on. "He was fairly close to Joel. It's too bad he was the one that your dog bit. That's out of phase."

"How the hell is a damn dog supposed to know all this, Stathis?" the girl asked. "He just thought Frank Spain was comin' after Mr. Cahill, and he wadn't gonna let him. That's all."

"Well, it is too bad," Harbelis said. "Spain was one that Joel thought a lot of. I heard him tell Spain one time that he wouldn't mind if Spain flew his wing; more than that: he said he *wanted* him to do it. 'I want you on my wing, Frank,' is what he said. That's it just exactly."

"Maybe I could go see him tomorrow, or meet up with him some place. The other boy, too," Cahill offered.

"I wouldn't go see Willis. You don't need to have anything to do with him."

"Why not?" Cahill asked, still feeling the shocked, hurting weight of the boy against his chest. "Why not go see him?"

"He's not worth the time," Harbelis said, with conviction. "He's just a dung-heel."

"A what?"

"A shit-kicker, a dung-heel, a nothing. He tried to get in with us. Nobody wanted him."

"As near as I can tell," Cahill said, "he must have been gettin' beat up pretty bad."

"He was," Hannah said. "You should'a seen his face. Or maybe you shouldn't."

"He must've said something to Spain. It wouldn't've had to be much. Spain ought to hold back on himself more, though. Something like this, that's not the place for violence. No conservation possible. No gather. Nothing but a waste."

They turned a corner, moving into the main part of town, their steps felted, with a slight twisting skreak of dry snow.

"Zack is going along OK, now," Harbelis said. "Looks like he could carry rum around his neck in a little barrel, way off in the mountains. Rescue somebody. And make 'em feel better, too. Has he ever done anything like this before?"

"Not exactly," Cahill said. "He might'a been pretty close to it a couple of times. Once a bread truck almost hit me, backin' out of somebody's driveway, and Zack went after the tires. The guy explained everything, from his cab. He had a open-door van, and he stayed up there to do his apologizin'; he wouldn't come down. Zack don't like drivers of things. Tonight, though, he saw all that fightin'. Dogs get excited when other dogs fight, or when anything fights. It's just some-thin' in 'em. When I was holdin' up that fat boy, and then he went to one side and left me and the other boy with nobody in between us, Zack went after him. I guess the boy must'a made too quick of a move, or somethin'. When he's keyed up, Zack'll fire right out."

"Tell that to the colonel. He's got a good side, or in some ways he's got a good side. He'll probably just tell you to put a leash on the dog, or get some way to hold him, hold him back when he gets excited."

"I wouldn't mind that, I guess. Zack might."

"You just get squared away with the colonel, and maybe go see Spain in the infirmary. That'll make it all right. I'm sure it will."

"That seems fair," Cahill said. "I'm sorry the boy got hurt. Could'a been worse, though."

"I believe it."

"Shouldn't'a happened. This whole thing is my fault. I shouldn't'a hit out at that kid like that. I don't know why I did it. You get frustrated when you can't see. It must'a looked really stupid. Did I come anywhere near him?"

"You missed him by exactly about one inch," Hannah said. "If you'd'a connected there wouldn't'a been no use to take him to the hospital. His head would'a been all over them bricks. You don't fool around, mister. I don't mean to tell you what to do, Mr. Cahill, but if you can't see what you're doin', you getter watch out what it is."

"I'll take that, ma'am," Cahill said, "and I'll take it kindly. A blind fool is maybe a little bit more of a fool than you are. But he can put limits on himself, just like everybody else."

"I told you I'd fix you something to eat, didn't I?" Hannah said, after a moment.

"You do, and I'll eat it; I don't care what it is. What can you make?"

"Collard greens."

"I hate collard greens," Cahill said truthfully.

"You ain't tasted mine. They don't even taste like collard greens. A lot of pig fat is the answer. If you want to call it whistlin' pig, I'll know what you mean. I could fix that, and maybe some big hominy."

"OK," said Cahill, "you're on. Check in with me around six-thirty tomorrow night, and we'll go eat your pig and the whistle of it, too. And big hominy's not so bad."

"Probably Corporal Phillipson will come after you in the morning," Harbelis said. "He don't have much else to do."

"We're home, Mr. Cahill," Hannah said. "You can prob'ly smell it. McLendon's smells good if you're hungry, but bad if you ain't. Anyway, this here is it."

"You want me to go in with you?" Harbelis asked.

"No, I'm used to it now. I've got it figured."

"Are you coming to the base tomorrow?"

"I might in the afternoon. McCaig and I have got somewhere to go in the mornin'. If I come it'll be after lunch. I think the colonel's got a couple more people for me to talk to."

"I done told you 'bout supper, now," Hannah said. "I'll take care of your dog, too, if he'll eat scraps."

"He will," Cahill said. "What do you think he gets at home?"

"I'll be here to get you around six-thirty. We can walk; it's not far."

"That'd be better than good," Cahill said, his heavy body yearning upward toward the bed. He needed to drink fluid, and also to drain it off.

239

"Good night, Mr. Cahill," Harbelis said.

"Good night, sandrunner. Go cut a second off your time."

"I'll do it if you hold the watch," Harbelis said. "Maybe tomorrow."

He stayed, his hands on the door, listening for their steps to begin and go away, but when there were none he understood that they would not leave until he went in.

"All let go," he said.

"All gone," said Harbelis.

The door swung closed on its spring behind him; Cahill stepped warmthward and felt with his foot for the first stair.

At the counter, talking to a farmer about the possibility of winter wheat in North Carolina, McLendon saw him come in, and went to him. "Where you think you're goin', young fella?" he asked. "And where have you been? You don't look so good. We don't sleep in overcoats in Sullins County."

He was surprised, but also gratified that McLendon should be there so suddenly and amiably as this. He reached for the knob on the banister and it was in the world, perfectly to his timing and position. "I got into a fight," Cahill said.

"You're full of shit."

"No, I'm tellin' you the truth," Cahill said. "I didn't exactly get into a fight myself; I got caught in the middle of one. A couple of others'; a couple of boys."

"Did you try to break it up, or what?"

"No; it wadn't that, either. I didn't try to break it up, I tried to finish it. And I did finish it. Or Zack finished it; put one of the boys in the hospital."

McLendon peered into Cahill's glasses like a man reencountering a source of surprise and instruction that he could depend on. "You goin' right to bed?" he asked. "I've got some more whiskey, and it ain't Four Roses this time. It's good stuff, out of Kentucky. Even the bottle is good-lookin'. Just like a ornament; you could make a lamp out of it."

"I tell you what," Cahill said. "I've done got onto somethin' in this place. Somethin' very good for blind people; better than it is for people that can see. It's called a whiskey bath."

"Now wait a minute," McLendon said, hands on his hips like a coach on a practice field. "I ain't got enough for you to take a bath in. I just got this one bottle out of Kentucky, where I used to go huntin'. A buddy sent it over."

"Don't worry," Cahill said. "What you do is run a bath, hot as you can stand it and get in it and have yourself a couple of shots. You float, see, kind of, and all your blood vessels open up, especially the ones in your head. Your brain vitality cells open up. Makes you just like Einstein."

"I see what you mean," McLendon said. "Or I just might. Go on up to your place and start the water comin' at you."

Cahill grinned and pawed awkwardly for the other. "I will if you'll squeal like a eagle for me."

"It wadn't the eagle doin' the squealin'. It was what the eagle was after."

He waited, leaning against the banister, while McLendon went for the whiskey, then took the naked bottle, turned, and moved upward, counting.

Under the gray flat sky they were riding east, on a secondary state road, in McCaig's 1934 Ford. Zack lay behind them on the floor; there was no back seat. McCaig, used to flying as much as driving, glanced upward now and then at the cloud cover with an intensity inside of which there was another kind of intensity. Through a ceiling of perhaps eight thousand feet, smaller and lighter gray clouds were passing at an angle across the main color, which covered everything. McCaig had seen this cross-play many times before, and from the ground had stopped to watch it, but never with so much interest as now. The smaller scraps and formless tatters of cloud appeared to move transparently within the main darkness, with a sense of both purpose and escape, going northwest, rag after rag. Most of the snow had thawed from the fields, and, though a few of these had been plowed, most were in weeds, unfenced, the brown of sandy clay. McCaig glanced at Cahill, who sat with part of his back on the seat, his knees up, his window down, his arm and hand on the frame with the fingers open.

"Say, blind man," McCaig said. "What you thinkin' about, over there in the foolish cold part of the car? And why don't you put the window up?"

"I'm thinkin' what a goddamn fool I was to come up here, takin' up your time, and everybody else's. I can't see nothin', I can't find out nothin' about my boy, and even if I could, what difference would it make?"

"That ain't the way to talk," McCaig said, looking directly at Cahill for a moment, and then back front. "If you didn't do nothin' else, you would still have got me goin' on something I really wanted to do. You done give me an excuse to look into a few things around here. Don't none of this satisfy me."

"None of what?"

"None of the business about your boy. There was not enough of an investigation, for one thing. I never saw none of the accident reports, but there didn't seem to me to be enough attention paid to the whole thing. Except by the boys. Most of 'em, anyway. Some of 'em—Shears and Spain and that crew—especially. They want to know what I want to know."

"What is that, exactly?"

"I want to know what happened over here, and I want to know why it happened." McCaig resolved, and said, "I think Joel might have been fuckin' that little girl in Supply. You remember talkin' to her?"

"I do," Cahill said. "She was the one told me these goggles the colonel gave me were new when my boy got 'em. That's all I found out, in that place all packed up in the sheeps."

McCaig smiled. "I don't doubt that it might not be a bad place to bed down, in all that stuff. It'd be like fuckin' in a cloud, sort of. A hot cloud. Warm, anyway."

"I ain't never done it," Cahill said.

"Question is, did he do it? Your boy."

"Do you think he did?"

"I think he prob'ly did. If he wanted to, he would have. The fact that she was supposed to be the colonel's girl would prob'ly 'a been enough for him."

"What did he have against the colonel?"

"Well, nobody much likes him. I don't think he's had a whole lot of experience in runnin' a trainin' base. But then there's not many that have. There's a lot of bases now, though, and I expect if we could look around, and had a choice, we could find a good many that's better than he is."

"What's the matter with him?"

"He's not really a commandin' officer. He don't have the ramrod or the guts. He just goes by the rules; he does more or less a good job of followin' the book. But he's a little too much like somebody you'd find as the assistant principal in a high school; or somebody connected with a high school, a boy's school, but not the football coach. He's not a commander, and he don't connect up with the boys any too well; his distance from 'em is too much distance, and his friendliness, you might say, is not very friendly; it don't really work."

"What about Joel and him?"

"I know for a fact that Joel didn't like him. Joel would respect anybody he could learn somethin' from, like that captain that teaches navigation. You met him?"

"Yeah, I've met him. He can talk."

"He's the nearest thing we've got to a hero around here. He don't fly in our airplanes, but he's got a lot of medals from where the real flyin' goes on. He's not just talkin'."

"I had some whiskey with him last night. With him and another fellow that's been in the war. He was telling me about droppin' bombs, and gettin' shot at."

"That's Captain Faulstick, I think. I know him better than I do Whitehall. I rode with him once, and I don't think he's goin' to make it. He might be good enough on the bombsight, and he may have as many medals as Whitehall, but he's not much for handlin' an airplane."

"Why not?"

"He's uncoordinated, and what little he can do is just mechanical; he don't have no feel for the air. The plane is between it and him, like a wall: it's movin', but with him in it, it's just standing there, in between. That don't make a pilot. To fly good, the air has got to be natural for you. It's got to be your element, something you belong in. It's not enough to say you feel that way about it; you've got to know it without even thinkin' about it. Every move you make has got to be made by the air itself, and come into you, so that you fly like it flies. Faulstick don't have that. It'd be better for him to go back into heavies and drop bombs, or else get a ground job."

"I'm sorry to hear that," Cahill said.

"It ain't no great matter. He's not all that crazy about flyin'. If he was my student I'd wash him out. Be less dangerous for everybody, especially him."

"How're we doing on this here road, pilot?" Cahill asked, shifting his position.

"We're gettin' there," McCaig said. "We got to cross the river and angle off on this dirt road, and kind of double back toward the river. I ain't never been to this guy's house, but I think I can sort of circle in on it. Shouldn't be too much trouble. But we're doin' fine; your dog's doin' all right, too. Got him a right nice nest back there, where I carry my chickens."

"You sell chickens?"

"No, I fight chickens. Any time I get the chance."

"I thought that was supposed to be against the law."

"It is, in every state but Florida. That's why they have the international tournament there every year, at Orlando. I'm goin' down, one of these days, if I can get some money, and good enough chickens."

"Good luck."

"It takes that, and some other things. I'm tryin' to develop a new strain, myself, combination of a Traveler and a Shawl-neck. Should be a real pretty bird. Game, too. I don't breed no dung-heels."

"You say dung-heels," Cahill said, catching at something.

"That's what we call 'em when they won't fight; when they run; that's the kind of chicken that gets eat up; I don't mean by foxes or dogs or hawks, but by people. Only thing they're good for."

"Dung-heels, eh?"

"Yeah; a dung-heel is a chicken that *is* chicken. I've had a few of 'em. One of 'em lost me about all my money, in a derby down in South Carolina a couple of years ago. The son-of-a-bitch ran, and I was so mad at him I picked him up and kicked him like he was a football. Feathers all over the place. Some of 'em prob'ly still comin' down."

"I don't reckon it'd do no good for me to ask you why you torment them poor birds."

McCaig nodded for his own benefit. "It wouldn't do no good," McCaig said, "but I'll tell you anyway. It's because every man watchin' a chicken fight gets somethin' from the chickens, even the ones that lose, the ones that get rattled and killed."

"I get everything but 'rattled.' You mean confused?"

"No," McCaig went on, with eager patience. "When a chicken is rattled it means that he's been stuck, one time or more than one; that he's got loose blood in him. It sounds in the throat. As soon as you hear that, you know he's gonna start slingin' blood soon, out of his bill." Using what sounded like a very thin saliva, but loud enough to come through over the engine, McCaig forced from himself a desperate harsh defiant gurgling. "That don't mean he's been beat. I've seen many a cock fly right straight up into his own rattle, and kill the other chicken on the next shuffle, and the one that rattled him be dead before he hit the ground."

Cahill sighed and shook his head. "It is true," he said. "Blind people live on noises. They hear this, they listen for that. Time goes on, you get righter and righter; you don't think one thing is somethin' it ain't. But since I've been up here I can guarantee that I have come on some sounds I ain't never heard before. The other night a man screamed like a eagle—no, something the eagle had holt of—and now you rattle like a chicken, which is even worse. Supposed to be a death rattle—right? But they can still kill you, you say?"

"They can. But they got to do it fast. They lose much blood, they can't get high enough up in the shuffle, and the other cock gets on top of 'em." He paused. "A shuffle is when the two birds fly up off the ground together, fly into each other, wings doin' all they can on the outside, and the heels kickin' underneath. They hang up there for a second or two, doin' all the damage they can. It's something to see, I tell you." He broke off again. "I'm a short-heel man myself. I use a short drop gaff on my cocks. That's the way the truth of the thing comes out; which chicken's the best."

"You might as well explain that, too," Cahill said, slightly interested, trying to picture it.

"A gaff is like a steel version of the chicken's natural heel, his spur. We cut that off, and put gaffs on him. A short-heeled chicken can get more licks in, and he has to hit the other cock more times to kill him. You fight long heels, which are almost as long as your finger, and a bad rooster can kill a good one with one lucky lick. That's not what chicken fightin's about. Hell, in Mexico and Cuba they even fight what they call slashers."

"That sounds bloody."

"Bloody it is. A slasher is a heel that's sharpened on both sides, like a Gillette Blue Blade. Some Mexican fella showed some at a tournament I was at a couple of years back. A friend of mine was fool enough to put a chicken of his in there—long heels, too, with that Mexican shake—that means unlimited class, you know, like a heavyweight prize fighter. The slashers took his head right off, the first pittin.'"

"Took it off clean?"

"Well, not exactly. But you wouldn't have to use much extra knife to get it off. It was just disgustin'; there's no game that way, no guts, no sport to it. It's like dynamitin' a trout stream. If all you want is fish, you might as well use dynamite."

"Well," Cahill said, shifting position, "you ain't made a believer yet. You paint a pretty good picture, though. And I wouldn't be surprised if your rattle's not right up there with the best of 'em, just as good as a dyin' rooster's."

"I been in chicken fightin' most all my life," McCaig said. "It just appeals to me. When two good cocks shuffle, there's just that second when they're right up as high as they can get, just hangin' there, and so much is going on that you have to watch cockfights for years before you have any idea what's goin' on. To somebody who ain't never seen one, it just seems like two roosters fly at each other and come down, and they're either hung up together by the feet or one of 'em's dead when they hit the floor. Everything's a blur. But if you know what to watch for, you can see most of what happens; most but not all; a good chicken is real fast with his feet. He don't ask for nothin' but a little air under him, a little room, and another male chicken that's tryin' to kill him. At the top of the shuffle, that's the real concentration. Everything is just right there. Any man that watches a chicken fight wishes he could be in on somethin' like that: do it himself—somethin' that fast, that's over that quick, that he could stand up to and either win everything, and walk away from it, or lose, and it be over, and nothing sad about it."

"Nothin' sad," Cahill repeated.

"No; every one of my Shawl-necks is gonna fight like that, if I'm right about my bloodlines."

"Blood is all the same," Cahill said, wondering what he meant.

"The hell it is," McCaig said immediately. "It may look the same, whether it's yours or a cow's or a buzzard's or a chicken's, but it carries . . . what it carries. It carries that Shawl-neck strain, for one thing. How it does it, I don't know; there are some things you can control, but the main thing, the underneath thing, is in the blood itself. You can breed it different ways, but the blood is what you breed."

"Chickens, maybe. Horses, maybe. Dogs. With people you can't tell."

"Can damn well tell. It may not be the same kind of blood, but it's blood. It hands down; it improves or falls off; it gets better or worse; it thicks up or thins out. It carries the feathers. It carries the eyes: blue eyes, brown eyes, green eyes. They come on down."

Cahill drew in from the wind, turned, and dropped his arm over the back of the seat, passing his fingers back and forth until they ran over the tips of Zack's back-fur. He knew by the resistance of the hairs the direction of the head, and changed his position enough to find it. Lying pleasantly on a couple of croaker sacks stuck with feathers, Zack raised himself partially on his forepaws, and subsided.

"Zack is enjoyin' himself," Cahill said, his arm again on the sill and air going up his sleeve. "He likes to ride; all dogs do. If he could, he'd put his old grizzly head out in this wind and drink it for as long as you

246

could drive. I wonder what it feels like to a dog, smellin' things as fast as he would have to, going along here at forty, fifty miles an hour; however fast we're goin'?"

"I ain't given much thought to it," McCaig said, hunching and peering ahead. "But I've got a proposition for you. See if you can tell what's fixin' to happen to us."

Three months, Cahill thought, and I don't even remember what color my eyes are. But who would care? What importance could that have to anybody? He watched the powerful sleet of golden arrows go across. I believe they were light blue or gray —grayish, anyway. Though he didn't, he knew he could put the tips of his fingers on his eyelids and feel the odd movements of the balls. The girl back where the boys were fighting pulled back before she handed me my glasses; I must have been right where she could look at me, and there must have been some light. But that's on the outside. I shouldn't let people see it, though.

He reached back again, and this time pressed down through Zack's fur, and found the big bone at the top of the spine.

"All right," McCaig said. "Get ready now."

"What's the matter?" McCaig asked. "Your dog all right? You keep doin' that."

247

"He's all right," Cahill said. "This is just the way I feel the road. You said somethin' was comin' up. I want to see if I can outguess you." He adjusted— "fine-tuned," as he thought of it —to the feel of Zack's body, and the road coming through it. But he was not prepared, even so. There was a quick clank, as though they had run over a metal object that should not have been on the road; the tires changed their sound to a kind of hollow sizzle. Cahill smiled grimly. "It's a fuckin' bridge," he said. "We got air under us. I know it, even if Zack don't."

"You know somethin'," McCaig said with satisfaction, "you're right. It's a bridge, sure enough; long, high, and risin'. This is a big river; the biggest around here."

They lifted, the road smoother than the regular highway. It was colder; a ghostly cold. Cahill sensed that the car might have entered into a terrible vulnerability. They leveled off. The struts and spars and wires of the bridge beat at him as they went by. He was sure the bridge was swaying. He leaned a little way out of the window to bear down with his hearing into the complex snatching sound of the bridge structure. Long things were in it, he guessed, long and slender, bolted but not rigid; also an alternating edge-noise

This is a mighty old bridge, Mc-Caig thought. There used to be model bridges like this made out of erector sets, which kind of

248

that was like a successive cutting of grasses; there was nothing to stop it. He kept being plucked at and untouched, suspended and riding in his body, no longer in contact with the dog. "Roller coaster," he said, and with pleasure and excitement. "We must be way up." Then, "I used to skate a lot, you know. I used to skate all the time when I was little. All over Atlanta, looking for the big hills. The best one I ever found was on somebody's driveway. You could really get to flyin' down that thing, and I wouldn't be surprised if I hadn't'a closed my eyes once or twice going down, and down and down, you know, and *on* down. Hell, the thing was like a ski jump, runnin' down through a bunch of bushes. I believe I could still go down it, right now, at this minute. I believe I could, if somebody would get me there. And I'd keep my eyes open all the way; I wouldn't bat 'em. Not no more, I wouldn't."

stood up, stood up too high, and it seems like all the struts and wires are on too flimsy a foundation; that the thing is top-heavy, and put together by one person who had a fairly good idea for a bridge, though not the best, working with a bunch of others who didn't know exactly what they were doing. But Cahill's listening was a matter of interest; the near side of his upper lip was raised, and his face relaxed, the head cocked, intent.

"We're goin' down now," Mc-Caig said, pushing forward on the wheel as though it were a control column. "There's the rest of the runway right in front of us, all the way to the Atlantic Ocean. Runway's got a lot of curve in it, though. Somebody ought to do somethin' about that. Makes it hard to land when the runway's curvin', especially when there's any wind. Have to cross-control a lot." McCaig jiggled the wheel so that the car wavered. "Feel that? That's what you call yawin'; fishtailin'."

"You son-of-a-bitch," said Cahill pulling back from the window. "I can skate better than you can drive. Or fly either, I clue you."

"That's yawin', which is one of the things a airplane can do, mostly when you don't want it to. The other two are pitchin' and rollin', which you can do in a airplane but not in a car, unless you run off the road."

"You don't need to explain all that. Just don't make the car switch around no more, or whatever you're doin'. I don't need it."

"I don't need it either. I don't need it, and I won't do it. I'm sorry if it bothered you." McCaig glanced outward, and shook his head.

The fire had come to the edge of the river; even the plants on the steepish banks were burned away, and beyond them, the place the car was entering was as black and desolate as the heel of a shoe, and looked crushed, imprinted, not by many heels but by one huge one. Through Cahill's window came the smell of the frozen afterburn, a smell of dead smoke, dirt, and rusty nails. But as they moved deeper, McCaig could tell that the river bank had held only the outlying part of the fire, and that they were passing from what had been only a scrappy blackening into a sort of all-out desolation that McCaig felt imposed upon to have to accept. Like the beginning of nausea an involuntary shudder came into his stomach, and he realized with surprise and confusion that he was not sick, and that it was fear that had reached him. "We're goin' off," he said. "We're turnin' off onto a little road." Cautiously they edged off the highway onto a dirt road covered with ash and black limbs. My God, McCaig wondered, it's one thing to fly over something like this, but it's something else to be in it. And what in the name of God am I doing bringing a blind man out to a place like this? "We got to go slow through here, big man," he said. "We got to do what they call pick our way. This was a fire you wouldn't believe."

"I can smell smoke, still," Cahill said.

"Anything else?"

"I don't think so. They tell me your senses are supposed to get better when you go blind. I can hear better, and maybe touch better. But I can't smell no better, but just try harder at it. Why? Is there somethin' else I ought to be pickin' up?"

"Meat," McCaig said, and realized too late how merciless it must have sounded. "I done seen a dead rabbit, and what was prob'ly a dog. I'm just sittin' hopin' it wadn't a deer. I don't think it was a deer. The birds are the lucky ones, around here. Last week I'll bet there was many a one a-rising off the trees. Maybe they didn't have no easy time, either." Why don't I just shut up, McCaig said suddenly to himself. Everything I give out with is liable to be making this man feel worse. It was not the birds that came to McCaig's mind, but the image of a small aircraft in heavy smoke, in tremendous turbulence, and the figure in it fighting the bucking plane, and the loss of control that plunged the aircraft somewhere into a wild and ragged heat that would melt iron. But why don't I just go on and tell him what I think? Why don't I give him my version of the thing? That's what we're out here for; maybe not my version but some version. We might as well get started, right here.

"Mr. Cahill," he said, his voice so low and grave that he could hardly believe he was using it, "I'm not sure how big this fire was, but it was big, I'd say at least five hundred acres, maybe more. There's a whole lot of turbulence over a fire, especially a big open fire like this one. Those boys back at the base know that it's death and damnation to fly over any fire. Death it would likely be for some of 'em; it's dangerous. A lot of 'em would do it, just like kids want to fly under bridges and buzz girls' houses, but they won't do it because they want to get through this place and go on through Basic and Advanced and out to the war. They won't do it because it's against orders, off limits, and if they get caught it's an immediate washout; I mean it's automatic, and there's no way to get reinstated."

Cahill said nothing but turned his head and leant inward.

"I've flown over a few fires, myself, some in the line of duty, some not. But I've never been over one at minimum altitude, five hundred feet; I was pretty well above. The air knocked me around some, and once or twice the visibility was bad. But the worst part of it is that you feel like you've brought the aircraft into a place, a kind of situation, where it won't work, where it was not meant to work. You remember me telling you about the feel of the air that you've got to have before you can really do what you call flyin'? Fire destroys that; it does away with the connection of your body and the aircraft; the air goes back on you. For a young guy with less than, say, a hundred hours, it's suicide. Unless . . ."

"Unless what?"

"Unless it was him: Joel. Mr. Cahill, your boy could fly an airplane. I've been with him when he flew part of an inverted fallin' leaf, and that's something I can't do myself. I told you we never tried it, but we did."

"What is it, again?"

"It's one of the hardest things you can do. Have you ever seen a poker chip in a glass of water?"

"No, but I've seen dimes and quarters fallin' down through a swimmin' pool. Is that what it's like?"

"Yeah, it would be like that. It really is like a leaf comin' down from a tree. It goes this way, and then it kind of swings up on edge, you know, and then it swings under and down, and on up to the other edge, and all the time it's losin' altitude. It's a kind of a lazy-lookin' maneuver, and very pretty to watch. It takes a lot of precision and timin'. It takes coordination that the good Lord don't just give, give away to anybody. And he could do it upside down. He could make the leaf fall with his head looking at the ground and fillin' up with blood. Unnatural. That didn't bother him none. He didn't learn it from me, and he didn't learn it from anybody else around here. I asked him where he did learn it, and he said from a book. He said he just figured it out from a book, and as soon as he got out on solo he tried it."

"And you think that maybe . . . ?"

"I don't know what to think, Mr. Cahill. If I said that he was just the kind of boy to take on a challenge of some sort, especially if it had somethin' to do with flyin', that would maybe be sort of true, but I don't think that's what really happened. No sir, I don't."

"All right, take it right on through. I'm listening."

"Some of the boys won't let you forget that Colonel Hoccleve was up in his AT-6 when Joel went in. I say that that's almost sure to be just a coincidence, though."

"Almost?"

"Almost, is right. Spain and them either believe or want to believe that the colonel might'a forced Joel down, when he saw Joel was somewhere around the smoke, with bad visibility, and all. He might'a buzzed him or sheared off on him, and the plane might'a got away from Joel in the turbulence. He would just have needed to lose it for a second. That's all. Just one second, at minimum altitude. Then he'd be right into the fire. Into the ground."

"But what would my . . . what was Joel doin' flyin' over the fire, in the first place?"

"He could have just been lookin' it over, or flyin' around the edges of it, maybe, just to see what was what. That's what I want to ask these people out here about. Lieutenant Foy, who was on the accident board, told me that this farmer said he heard the engine, just before the plane hit. I want to ask him if he heard two engines. I'd like to know that."

"Are we gettin' close to where we're goin'?"

"I think so. This looks like it might be part of a firebreak we're just coming to. If we can find a house still around in here somewhere, a house that ain't been burned down, that'll have to be it. I don't see it yet, but somebody has mounded this ground up, it had to be in a big hurry, and pushed over a lot of trees, it looks like with a bulldozer. A few of the trees are not burned up."

The road turned toward the river, and they passed through a section of land not so blackened, though covered with whitish ash; a few pine trees were still standing, and a low fence of bushes, through which they also passed.

"This is it," said McCaig. "This must be it. The man's got a Caterpillar tractor and a Model A. He's got a barn and a well, and a low house with a high roof. No wonder he rammed up this land. You could cook yourself right well in that house, and right fast, if fire set to it. He beat it, though. He beat it, and here he comes. Here he comes, him and his wife too. I'll go talk to 'em just a minute, and then come back after you. Why don't you just get out and stretch a little, and let Zack get used to the place? That might take some doin'."

Slowly Cahill got out, listening and smelling. Zack followed him, brushed against the side of Between the house and the car, glancing and pointing as though guilty of something, McCaig did

253

his leg, and was gone. Cahill said nothing to him, but leaned back against the car and tried to interpret. There were human words at some distance from him, but at first he could not pick them up, although he could make out some of the intonation, the quiet country accents. "Hit was right over yonder. Hit was . . ." a woman's voice said. He left the car and moved toward it, but could make out no more. Without touching anything but the ground he was vaguely bothered, and raised his arms to their length and swung them around in an arc, and then again. Stepping on ash and ruin, he began to move in the direction of McCaig's voice, which was giving his name and McCaig's own. Putting one foot carefully before the other, always solid and ready, he came on, once passing a hand before his face, and then with the same hand settling his hat.

his best to explain why they had come. "It was this man's boy, you see," he said. "He's a blind man, and he's done come all the way up here from Atlanta to talk to people about his boy; find out what he can." The small strong farmer, bloodshot and proud-looking, nodded. His larger wife pointed with both hands.

"Hit was right over yonder. Hit was right out chere about three hundred yards," she said. The three of them looked at Cahill, standing in a black and gray patch of burn and ashes, swinging his arms like an object set there to do what it was doing, for reasons not known. Beyond him Zack ranged over the devastated earth, the fields on the windward side of the farmhouse. It was quiet, and in the space between words, as Zack moved over the field they could hear brittleness crackling, the crisped bark of burned trees breaking under his feet, and to McCaig the scene was filled with a strange horror of the air itself that stood above the fields, of things that were once solid now rendered weightless, and the sense of a vast floating of dead things around them.

They moved to him, and McCaig ceremoniously introduced. About the possible handshake the farmer was not sure, but McCaig lifted Cahill's hand gently by the sleeve of his overcoat, and the farmer took it and held it. Then he put out the other hand, and the woman grasped it. McCaig waited for Cahill to say something, but he did not. Neither did the man and his wife, but McCaig could tell that the man was deeply moved by their standing silent and together in this way. The wife looked questioningly at McCaig, and then back into Cahill's terrible glasses, catching now a little fire from the sun which had just come out with surprising light and even more surprising warmth.

"It's been right warm here," the farmer said. "Weather changed real fast. For a little, the snow made this place like it didn't look so bad; not as bad as it does now. I never been so happy to see it snow in my life. But it's all gone now, and we done gone back to black around here. All these ashes done dried out again."

"Your big old dog over yonder," the woman said, "he likes it around here. He's rollin' in the ashes."

"Damn if he ain't," said the farmer, Bledsoe. "Kin you get him back over here? If you want to, we kin all go in the house and talk. Might be better'n out here."

Cahill crooked his thumb and forefinger into his mouth and blew a high hard cutting whistle that was both penetrating and stunning. "My Jesus," the woman said, "that ought to git him." Zack lay in the ashes on his back, his feet in the air, wriggling in a way that was oddly snakelike. Ash dust rose from him and floated where it was. He got up at the whistle, shook more dust into the cloud, and came on. "He's done made another dog outta hisself, Mr. Cahill," the wife said.

"Yeah, Frank," McCaig said. "Zack is a ghost-dog now. Way off yonder, you can't hardly see him against the ashes."

Cahill whistled again, like a deep and hellish needle. "Come on here, idiot-head," he said. "We ain't got time to stand around here all day."

"I ain't never seen such a big one as that," said Bledsoe. "He's just the right one for this damn place, least like it is now. He's what oughtta be here. I believe he could'a done drove the fire off."

"Zack don't fight 'em," McCaig said, adopting half consciously the country intonation, with which he had grown up and partially still owned. "He joins up with 'em. He's a old gray ghost-dog now. He never had such a good time."

They moved toward the house, Cahill with his head down and his hands behind him, feeling with his feet and listening.

"We had a real dry winter here, and I was scared to death of fire," Bledsoe said.

"You ever had it before?" McCaig asked.

"Never have, but we got what you might call a steady wind out of the west around here, and it bothers me that the air base was over that way.

As it was, the wind come around from the other side, from the east, and blew the fire in on us, like it was comin' in from a-hind us, like I never would'a thought would'a happened in a million years. I was just as sure as I could be about the base, and fire comin' from over thataway, and maybe in a big wind blowin' all the way across the river."

"I don't believe I understand what you mean," McCaig said. "What's the matter with the base? What's the matter with the base bein' where it is?"

"I looked at it more or less like this here. There was bound to be a lot of fire in that place, all that gasoline, all that oil."

"That's in the airplanes," McCaig said, but not condescendingly.

"I know it's in the airplanes," Bledsoe said, smiling. "But ain't all of it in the airplanes. It's sittin' around in tanks, and in trucks, in whatever they keep that much gas in. And you just think about this. That whole base was made out of wood. I was thinkin' about maybe goin' over there and gettin' me a job buildin'. I ain't the best carpenter in the world, but I'm better than most of them people they got doin' all that hammerin' and bangin', missin' the nails half the time, sparks all over the place. I don't like it over there; it's dangerous. Gas . . . oil . . . And just think about all that *paper* they got to have, keepin' track of all them boys. Like I say, I don't like it."

"I don't neither," McCaig said. "I ain't gonna be there much longer."

"Now I tell you," Bledsoe said, "we can go on in the house, and I kin give you some water outta my well. I got the best well water in North Carolina. Or we kin walk on out if you like and I kin show you where your boy's plane come down, Mr. Cahill. I kin show you just where it hit the ground."

McCaig turned inquiringly to Cahill. "You want some water first, Frank? Could you use it?"

"No," Cahill said. "Let's go over, where the man says. We can drink water later on."

"You sure?" McCaig asked.

"I'm sure. Let's go there now. I got the feelin' for it."

"A-del kin go on back to the house," the farmer said. "We got some other things we might could show you."

Mrs. Bledsoe broke off from them as they turned at almost a right angle and started across the wide ground hazed with ash, the dust of it rising and going with them.

"On my land," the farmer went on, "like you can . . . like you can

256

tell . . ." He turned to McCaig, disturbed at what he was saying and how he was saying it, ". . . all around inside this here firebreak, the fire got in, but it never did git in big, you see. All the time I was out in the bushes, tearin' down trees and tryin' to build up this here kind of wall, tryin' to not give it anything to burn, leastways nothin' that'd let it git to the house, it would blow in anyway, and catch stuff. The main firebreak kept the big fire out, but it was so goddamn hot that I was afraid the house was gonna catch, just from the heat. It was just terrible. You never felt nothin' like it in your life. I don't want to go to hell; I done been there. I fought it with every damn thing I could think of. I made my stand here inside the break. I couldn't keep runnin' to get water, so whenever anything started burning inside the break, I went to it as best I could and tried to beat it out. I beat out a hunderd little fires with croaker sacks, until I just about give out. My wife and two boys and my little girl was inside, there; I wanted A-del in there with 'em, tryin' to keep the smoke outta the house; I didn't want 'em smothered, and they couldn't'a been much help, outside. I just kept beatin' down them flames, about dead from the smoke. One time the sack in my hands caught on fire. I just throwed it in the flames and started in with another one I had, beatin' on the same fire. I got it out, too, and then went on to another one. I don't know how long it took, how long I was doin' that, but there come to be wind; the smoke would blow by, it'd open up, and, as tired and hot as I was, I could kind of feel the main part of the fire swing, that's the only way I know how to put it. It kind of swung all around us, you see; it swung around the firebreak and the house, and, just a little while after it seemed like I could tell when it done that swingin', I could see the stuff on the other side of the firebreak burnin' a whole lot worse than it had been doin'. The main part of the fire, right when I was makin' my best fight, and I thought that nothin' I could do was a-gonna save us—the fire had done gone past us, on over toward the river: hit was a-goin' for the river. I stood up, thinkin' Hallelujah and great God Almighty, your man Luther Bledsoe and his people are gonna live. We done helt this ground. I straightened up with the wind blowin' the smoke, blowin' through the smoke, leavin' places over yonderways where you could see—and that's right when I heard it."

"God Almighty," McCaig said, closing his eyes on the gutted field.

"I ain't never liked to hear a engine sound like it was tryin' to do too much. I don't like to hear nobody gun a car engine with it sittin' still, but this was a lot worse'n that. It was like it was a-comin' right at me. I knowed it was a airplane; couldn'a been nothin' else. I didn't know what the hell to do. Then it changed, and it wadn't so bad, there just for a minute. It seemed like the engine had done been pulled back, not just a little but a lot. I looked on out and it was comin' right at me. But it wadn't comin' straight down like I thought it was, like it sounded like it was at first. It was comin' down shore enough, and there wadn't no way for it not to hit the ground, but—and this is as near as I can tell you—it looked to me, right when it hit, that it was just about leveled off, almost like it was tryin' to land. It was just a few feet off the ground, about a hunderd yards out thataway. And then the smoke filled in, and I heard it hit the ground, and I thought, what in the world can I do. The wind cut the smoke again and I saw where the airplane was back in the air, like it had just hit and bounced, and then it hit again, and just kind of sat down —sat down fast and hard. It had done broke off the wheels the first time it hit, and it—I want you to kind of see more or less what happened—if I can . . . if I can just . . ."

"Did it turn over?" McCaig asked, his throat very dry, not wanting to see how Cahill was taking this.

"No, sir, it didn't. The best I can tell you is that it skidded and slammed over, what you might call tilted and went up on one side, on one wing, and stopped."

"And you went and got him out, did you?" McCaig asked.

"I sure did, mister. I was over my firebreak before I even knowed what I was doin', and out in the patches of big fire. I got to him without even knowing if I was on fire myself, or not. I wadn't gonna let that boy burn up, or whoever it might'a been. I was the only one he had. I didn't think that then, but I do now. Or maybe I did think it then. Anyway, I got there fast. The smoke had got bad again, but I could see whoever was in there—the boy in there—was struggling, was doin' his best to git out. As I remember I climbed up on a little stump, or maybe it was a limb on the ground or somethin', and got a-holt of him by the shoulders and pulled him most of the way out. He had his helmet on, and them glasses over his eyes, and then he slid on out and we both fell down, down onto the ground, and I looked at him and got up on my knees and asked him if he could walk. I pulled off his helmet, and that boy's face was broke up bad. He was sittin' up, and he kept puttin' his hand up to his head and reachin' for something. I didn't have nothin' to give him but his own helmet, like, and I give it back to him, and that seemed like it was what he wanted. I believe the one arm was broke. His face and his mouth was bleedin' very bad, and he had some teeth knocked out. A whole lot of blood was comin' out his nose, and his mouth was full of blood. But he wadn't dead, and I knowed he would be all right. I knowed it right then. I told him. And they could'a done somethin' for that face, too. And his arm would'a been all right, if we could just'a got some kind of help for him. I got him up, and helt on to him. He helt on to me. The smoke was mighty bad, and it was lucky that we was in a little clearin'.''

"It's lucky the gas in that plane didn't catch," said McCaig. "Then you would'a seen some fire sure enough."

"I didn't even think about that," the farmer said. "Turns out, it did catch, and blew up. But we was outta there by that time. We was back inside the firebreak when it let go." He paused, and they had all stopped walking. "It was right here," the farmer said. "It was right here, right plumb on. You can see the tire marks, where they done hauled the plane off."

Cahill took off his hat, wondering why he did. It was very quiet. The sun was warm on the skin of his head. A little air stirred, and he had suddenly a sense of openness above and around him like the openness in the middle of the city of Atlanta, so many years ago, everything mysterious and meaningless, everything waiting. With the new sun there was a sense of the burning of the openness he was in. My boy hit the ground here, he tried to tell, he did tell himself. Here, and not any place else. Where does that leave me? What am I supposed to do? I can't cry. I can't say anything. Let them tell me.

McCaig kicked at a tire mark, the up-edge gouging of earth already blunting with weather. The bare-headed man in glasses stood almost as though this were a military occasion, or as though he were trying for the outward part of religious observation, but not really reaching it. Suddenly McCaig was aware of the loss of what should have been around them, the gone woods, the dry gaunt pines of North Carolina, the tangles of underbrush and twigs, the bushes and thorns, and thought of the flight of animals and birds, now many of them—animals, surely, and probably some birds too—flakes of ash, in an upward or suspended snowing, and many lying with the other ash.

"This here place, Frank, is . . ." McCaig could no longer keep the depression out of his voice; he could not imagine his own stupidity and foolishness in causing and being part of such a scene. The blind man

259

did not even seem to hear him; he was not shaking with grief, and did not appear to be breathing, or even to be alive, behind his glasses. McCaig made an effort to go on. "You might want to have some way . . . some way to remember this place, Frank. I may talk too much a lot of the time, but I don't know exactly what to say about this . . . this-here. We're in the middle of a great big field that's been burned out. The river I'd say is about a half a mile away from here." He broke off and consulted the farmer.

"A little more," Bledsoe said, "maybe three quarters."

"Three quarters of a mile, but you can't see it." McCaig picked up. "Everything around us is black and dead as hell. You can't tell anything about what kind of a place the plane made when it hit, because it's been dragged off with tractors or a dragline, or somethin'. The ground is tore up; there's nothin' here." He kicked the ashes and dirt.

"I wish we had somethin' left to give you, but there wadn't nothin'," Bledsoe said. "My boys come out here with me last week and watched them tote the plane off. They don't get to see nothin' like that, every day. It blowed up and burnt some, but I don't recollect that the plane was as bad tore up as I thought it was when I saw it in the smoke. I didn't look inside."

McCaig bent over and pulled something loose from the ground. "I don't know whether this is from Joel's plane," he said to Cahill, "but it might be." He passed Cahill a bent and black-dusted piece of wire about eight inches long. "It might be part of one of the brace wires. Off the struts." Cahill fingered it and put it into his overcoat pocket. Airplanes and wire, Cahill thought, in his mind an awkward twin-pusher model tensing with rubber bands. One minute in the air.

"Makes me think of bats," McCaig said, desperate to bring in another subject, the more irrelevant the better. "You remember me tellin' you, Frank, about that new kind of radio signal, over there in England? The one they got from the bats?"

"I think so," Cahill said. "What does that have to do with anything?"

"I don't know," McCaig went on, with some of the actual relief he needed, "I just think it's interestin', the way they test the bats, and make 'em fly around in a dark room full of wires. *Hundreds* of loops of wire, a whole *cloud* of wire. And they don't touch a one. They make this high-frequency holler, and it comes back on 'em. You can't hear it, but they pick it up, with them big bat ears."

"I wonder if any bats burned up out here?" Cahill said, with an

260

unexpected hard smile as he bent down and felt for Zack, panting beside his leg. "You found any bats, big boy?"

"Ghost-bats," McCaig said. "Zack is a ghost-dog, a old gray ghost-dog. First he was a airborne bridge-dog and now he's a ghost-dog."

"Bats, I don't know," Bledsoe said, "but if one of 'em caught on fire, he might just make a sound you could hear."

"I thought you said this was interestin'," Cahill said. "I ain't interested. We can go back now; go to Mr. Bledsoe's well."

"I'm sorry I gave down on you, Frank," McCaig said, starting toward the firebreak. "I told you what I could. You'll just have to remember from what I told you, if you still want to."

"You didn't bring a camera, or anything, did you?" Cahill asked.

"No, just me. Just remember that it's a black, black place. Your boy died," McCaig faltered as the farmer looked at him sharply, "your boy went down in a place that was on fire, and after he died it turned black. It'll be black for a long time. Ain't that so, Mr. Bledsoe?"

"Too long," said the farmer. "It'll take a while for things to grow back, after this. Right now, the bats have got it, and they can have it."

They trudged, going no faster toward the house and the well than they had toward the crash site. McCaig looked forward to cold water, to something from underground that had not been touched by fire.

"This is the way we come back, me and your boy, Mr. Cahill," Bledsoe said. "He was not as hard to hold up as you might think; I was as bad off as he was, nearly 'bout. He was chokin' on smoke and blood, but the main fire was on back of us, toward the river. There was still plenty of fire all over, all around, and the smoke was just as bad as it was when the fire blowed in on us the wrong way, from the coast."

McCaig had read of an aircraft—a B-17, he thought he remembered —that had missed a navigational checkpoint and run out of fuel in the Sahara Desert. The crew had tried to walk out, and were found in the sand, one by one. That must have been something like this, he imagined, but no worse than this. He looked at himself, and was both surprised and unsurprised to find himself covered with ash, as gray as Zack, who had been rolling in it. They were getting no nearer the house, and only kept plodding where they were, somewhere in the black barrens, the aftermath, the finished, and the unbegun. McCaig kept closing his eyes and touching Cahill's overcoat every few steps. The blind man's glasses no longer had the faintest tint of green, but were as gray as if coated with paint.

261

They were there, though; they had got there, and stood on the porch slapping at pants legs and knocking shoes on the floorboards.

"Let me git some of this-here stuff off of you, Mr. Cahill," Bledsoe said. "Might have to beat on you just a little bit; it's hard to git out. I kin beat good, though. Won't hurt you none."

Again, Cahill was sweating badly. He asked himself if he felt weak, if he . . . what was it the doctor had told him? If he overinjected, he would have a little time when he could tell, as the doctor had put it, that he "wasn't thinking just right." No, he concluded, I can think the same as ever; it's no different. But he dug for the sugar cubes anyway, and counted five of them, as he now was used to doing. If he needed the sugar quickly, would it be better to have them in the pocket with the goggles, or the one with the wire? They were with the goggles, and the sliver of one eye had not yet come loose; it was there, jagged and fragile. He would keep them where they were; he was not familiar, yet, with the wire, and wondered if it had really belonged to the plane, if it had ever been in the air. It was medium-sized, a little thicker than chicken wire. I'll bet it would sound like a hell of a thing if it was going fast enough, he thought; I'll bet it would sound like a knife.

Mrs. Bledsoe helped open the door. They went in, and the farmer guided Cahill, his overcoat off now, to a rocking chair. Almost in his face, Mrs. Bledsoe said, "Would you like some cornbread and honey, Mr. Cahill?"

"I sure would. And could I have some water? I would thank you a real whole lot for some water, now."

He rocked from the bones out, so tired he believed he could not possibly recover.

"Here 'tis," said Mrs. Bledsoe. "Here's your water."

The glass put into his hand was barrel-shaped, chilled, and covered with raised places, like bumps or pimples. He drank, and kept on.

There was no liquor in it; the taste was clear, clean. This is supposed to be healthy for you, he reminded himself. It's hard to get used to it. I'm glad to have a taste like this again though; this North Carolina is making a drunk out of me. Along with his tiredness, a strange amount of The woman beckoned, and McCaig sat with her, at the other end of a dark wine-colored sofa, old, but in good repair. Bledsoe brought a kitchen chair from beside the sink, which was in the same room, and sat on it, angled toward Cahill, crossing his legs. He had on khaki pants and a blue

interest in his surroundings and its people awakened. The man, the farmer, would have to be relatively young, and Cahill constructed him from a civics teacher he had had at Boys' High School in Atlanta, who had a thick cracker accent, and also, curiously, from Darrell Cochran, his lifeguard, who came not from any specific small town in Georgia, but from Union County, as he pointed out if you asked him.

Cahill felt for the sugar cubes, fingered them and thought it out. "I could have some, I guess. I've got the blood sugar, and I got to watch what I eat. Enough sugar'd kill me, my doctor back in Atlanta says. And so would enough of the other stuff I have to take. But right now everything's fine, and I'd appreciate your honey." Her clothes moved past him, it may have been in several layers. He drank again from the studded glass, and sighed as the chill clean water sank through him.

work shirt; he was a pale, strained brown, very strong in the jaws and mouth, with graying blond hair spread out just over his thick dark eyebrows. His eyes were blue and bloodshot; he rubbed a stiff finger across his upper lip, moved his head toward McCaig, who could think of no way to respond, and shrugged, hoping that something to say would come to Bledsoe. His wife, a stout pale woman with small brown eyes and very thin skin, beginning to crack into wrinkles in a difficult and unmistakable design, sat staring out from the sofa, as uncertain as the others. "Just let me know when you want some honey," she said quietly. "It's real good; I been savin' it. And I just made some fresh cornbread that you might like."

The room was long, unusually long for a farmhouse. McCaig guessed that there may be two others, but probably no inside plumbing. The space above them was shadowy, and at the end of the room McCaig could make out rafters which disappeared into the darkness above where they sat. At the far end, where there was a little window-light, and the sun shone directly on a heavy mass of something that looked like fabric, and McCaig understood that the rafters served as an attic, for whatever might be of shape to lie across them. A ladder stood in and out of the sunlight.

Something, a dish, probably, was put on his knee. He reached and took it, feeling for its contents. There was bread, and a substance on it. He bit and chewed, and his mouth filled with coarse warmth. He drank, and the well water cleared his taste of all but a light, airy sweetness. He savored this, rolled his shoulders, and stretched out, remembering picnics where food had been good, but never this good.

"What's that?" Cahill asked, biting off more. An impression of gentle sunlight was with him, and though he made an effort to imagine bees, he only saw the unthreatening brightness they were in, with dark green beneath it and light blue above.

"This here's from over at Mizzis Cornelia Crowder's place," Mrs. Bledsoe said. "She's got some hives, and gives me honey whenever she's got just a little more'n she wants. I mean," she went on, "I done *seen* them bees. They's a lot of 'em, over yonder. And you know what?"

"You can take and move them there hives. Move 'em just a few feet, and them bees can't find 'em. They come back'n commence to swarm in the place where their hive used to be, and they'll stay there, till somebody moves the hive back where it was."

"A-del kin read hands," said the farmer. "And she kin read eye skin."

"I notice ever hand I see," said Mrs. Bledsoe. "When Luther come in out of the smoke, when he come in here with your boy, both of 'em black as a coffeepot, first thing I noticed about your boy was how he was holdin' his arm. I thought his hand might be broke. It was broke; I'm might' near sure it was broke."

"We didn't know what to do, Mr. Cahill," said Bledsoe. "I still wadn't sure the fire didn't have us, and it wouldn't't'a taken much more for all of us to get burned up, your boy right along with A-del and my chilrun."

"I knowed that boy was hurt bad," Mrs. Bledsoe said. "I didn't have no idea where Luther found him, where Luther got him from, but blood

264

was all over him, comin' out of his face. And it 'us pourin' out, not just drippin'."

"We walked him on back into the bedroom," Bledsoe said, "and got him to lay down. My chilrun wanted to see, but we kept 'em out, and tried to get his coat—that big old wool coat he had on—off of him. But he didn't want to stay down. He kept sittin' up and tryin' to stand up, tried to push us away. We couldn't talk to him, and I don't think he could'a talked either, because in the mouth and . . . and the jaw, you know, that's where he was hurt the worst."

"I did see that some of his teeth was gone," Mrs. Bledsoe said. "All of his front teeth was knocked out. He kept chokin', and I thought maybe one of 'em had done been knocked down his throat, lodged in his windpipe, maybe. He kept tryin', you know, to sit, to git up."

"I went back and took a look out the door," said the farmer. "I knowed I had better git back out there and start back in with the fire again, start tryin' to do somethin'. I told A-del to try to clean him up, and see if she couldn't find him a rag or somethin' for his mouth. Then I went on back outside, because the wind had picked up, and more sparks and burnin' branches were comin' in from the East. I kept after the big patches that were burnin' inside the firebreak, and I just went on and on figurin' I'd go till I dropped down and couldn't move no more. I went from one to the other. I took a line fifteen feet from the house, and I told myself that if one spark got that close, got inside the line, or even got on me when I was standin' on the line, I'd go jump the firebreak and right into the fire; I'd swallow up all the smoke there was, and finish myself; I couldn'a stood seeing the house burn up, and my chilrun. But that didn't happen. Most of the fire, all the really big fire, had done gone around us, and was blowin' toward the river, over past where I pulled your son out of his airplane, Mr. Cahill. By that time I was just fightin' the last of it, the little stuff, but I kept on, going from one patch to the next one I see'd. All I had to do was to keep the little fires from blowin' onto the house. And that wadn't no easy job, neither. I just went on and on, till A-del come out and got me."

"When Luther went on back out in the yard," his wife said, "I done taken all the water in the house, hit was in that bucket right yonder, and I come back to the bed and that boy with his good arm over his face, turnin' this way and that way. I asked him could he take his arm up from off'n his face, so I could git at him with the water and try to make him feel a little bit better, but I couldn't do nothin' with him. I talked to him ever way I knowed, I told him we was not gonna let anything happen to him, that we was not gonna do nothin' to him but try to help him, but he wouldn't listen to me. I commenced to try to clean up his hands, or one of 'em, the one that was hurt, but he wouldn't even let me do that. I put his hand in the bucket, but that didn't do no good. I thought maybe if I went to the well and got some more water, it would be colder, and maybe it would help him. I went to the well, and drawed the pail up, poured it in another bucket, put the dipper in it, and went back, and he was just goin' out the door, headin' around the house on the other side from where Luther was."

Cahill pushed back, put a foot under the rocker, and leaned his head against the rest. He collected his saliva, added to it, and swallowed; he wanted no taste. "And you just let him go?" he said. "He just got up and walked out?"

"Mr. Cahill, I done all I could. I run out there after him, I grabbed him by the arm—it might'a even been the arm that 'us hurt—I tried to turn him around, I helt onto him, I tried to throw myself down on the ground, still a-holdin' onto him, I hollered as loud as I could for Luther, but I couldn't do nothin'; I couldn't do nothin' with him. He done left me on the ground. Two or three steps and he was done gone. I run after him again, but I couldn't find him in the smoke. My skirt caught on fire. I tore off the hem and come back to the house, and then went out on the other side and got Luther."

"We went back," said the farmer. "We went on back out through the firebreak, and on into the smoke. We couldn't even find the airplane. The wind just give us barely enough air to breathe, but even when we could breathe we was still breathin' smoke." He crouched directly in front of Cahill, who had folded his fingers in front of him. "We did everything we could, but it 'us all too much for us. Just too much."

"I know you did, sir," said Cahill, his mouth dry and still a little sweet with honey. "And after that, after you looked for him, and it cleared off, did you look for him some more?"

"We sure did," Bledsoe said. "Me and my whole family first, and then the people from the base. They stayed out here, goin' over my land, and all the land out toward the river, but they never found nothin'. They found some rabbits, one dog, I think it was, and a fawn deer, a baby. That's all. Everything else that might'a burned up either burned up and scattered, or was buried under the ashes."

McCaig said nothing about bones, but they were in his mind.

"One lieutenant said they was going to send some more people out when they had time, as many as they could spare, and do something they called a foot search."

"Foot by foot," McCaig said. "I ain't never been on one, but I've heard they do it. Whether anybody at the base knows *how* to do it, or even if they'll ever get around to doin' it, is something I doubt."

"Did they look in the river?" Cahill asked.

"I heard they did," said Bledsoe. "I heard they did drag, but I don't know how long they kept it up. I don't think he went in the river."

"What do you think happened to him?" Cahill asked. "Was there any chance he could have got through the fire?"

"Not much," Bledsoe said. "Specially not in the shape he was in. And it looks like if he did git through, and maybe made it to the river or the highway, somebody would shore have seen him, and, you know, done somethin' for him, got him on back to the base."

"So . . ." Cahill said, his mind black with the aftermath of all the fires he had ever seen, or could remember, ". . . so, as far as you know, he's out there on your land somewhere."

"He's out there on my land, or on the county's land. My land don't run out but about five hunderd yards. From there on over to the river belongs to the county. There was a fence, but it ain't there now; the posts all got burned up. If your boy got that far, the wire would prob'ly already be down; he could've gone on acrost."

"He didn't make it," McCaig said softly. "They'll find him. If they don't find him while you're here, they will later on. He couldn't just disappear."

"Do you reckon . . ." Cahill said, with a notion that had come to him, ". . . there's any chance that somebody might'a found him, and maybe . . . maybe for some reason or other . . ."

"What do you mean, Frank?" McCaig said, leaning forward intently. "What is it you're gettin' at?"

"I mean," Cahill said, trying to help words come, "is it impossible, is it really completely impossible, that he could'a met up with somebody, or somebody could'a been out there somewhere, some county person, maybe, maybe somebody from the Fire Department, or somebody fightin' the fire like you was doin', Mr. Bledsoe, and took him someplace? Could somethin' like that'a happened, maybe? There was all that smoke you was tellin' me about, and all." A thread of interpretation came to him; he followed it, surprised at his eagerness and ingenuity. "Remember, you didn't expect to see him, either, Mr. Bledsoe. He just come to you, out of the smoke and the fire. Now couldn't he just'a appeared, you might say, couldn't he just'a come to somebody else, over by the river, over on the county land? Couldn't he just'a come to somebody else, like he did to you?"

McCaig turned to the farmer, and could not keep himself from shaking his head. Mrs. Bledsoe put her hands over her face and rocked again, shaking silently.

"It'd be one chance in a million that somethin' like that could'a happened, Mr. Cahill," Bledsoe said, shaking his head also. "There wadn't nobody over there. There's not any road that goes in there, on that strip of land. There's nothin' for anybody to try to save. If they'd'a been anything the Fire Department could'a done, they'd'a been in there with me, doin' what they could for my place, my house, and all." More assertive, he said with final emphasis, "There wouldn't'a been nobody on that land. Even if there was somebody there, somebody who knew your boy was wanderin' around in the fire—even if somebody was out there, just *to* meet him, there wouldn't'a been no way, in that smoke, to find him, to get together with him."

Good Lord, McCaig wondered, what are these people trying to develop? What has this blind man got on his mind? A fear such as he had felt only a few times had a strong, sickening and exciting hold on him. He began to speak carefully.

"Frank, I know how you must feel. If there's any chance that your boy might'a got through this, through the fire and on out of it, I'd be the first to say let's go back out there and look, let's go talk to everybody around here we can find. If there was any possibility, any at all that your boy is still alive, is not . . . is not . . . wadn't lost out there in the fire, I'd go in with you on anything I could. I'd go over this ground one foot after the other, I'd talk to everybody in the county, and everybody at the base that come out here and looked for him. But that's all been done, Frank. We can't do what they couldn't do. Like I say, they'll come out again, maybe after you've gone on back to Atlanta, and they'll find him, and probably somewhere on Mr. Bledsoe's land, too." He turned his body to the farmer. "He prob'ly didn't get as far as the fence, did he?"

"It ain't likely. It ain't likely a-tall."

"All right," Cahill said, "you all can tell more about it than I can."

"And if he did meet up with somebody, Frank, what would'a happened then?"

"How would I know?" Cahill said, fully from his position, foursquare. "It was just a idea. I wanted to try out everything I could come up with, and see what you'all thought about it. But that's as much as I can think of. I'm satisfied."

McCaig was not; he could say more; he was anxious to say more. "Look, Frank," he went on, less frightened now, drawing strength from his logic, "you got a badly hurt boy. Say he gits out through the fire and somebody finds him. Now think about this for just a minute. Somebody finds a boy that's been in a airplane crash, who's got blood and soot all over him, who don't even know where he is. The first thing that anybody'd do would be to get him to a hospital. You can't get around that. Why would anybody want to do anything else?"

"All right," Cahill said, rising to his feet. "All right," he said, "you got me convinced."

Logic vanished for McCaig, and the fear came back. The base personnel had searched for a long time. What he had told Cahill was the truth; there would be another search before the incident was closed for good; the military does not like to leave bodies unaccounted for. Through the far window a square of the black farm stood, farther and farther out, and with a surge of terror that tightened and shook him, McCaig realized that he was quite certain that nothing would be found this time, either.

"Thank you for your time, Mr. Bledsoe," Cahill said, putting out his hand. "I appreciate this a lot, believe me. I appreciate you lookin' out after my boy. I appreciate everything you tried to do."

Bledsoe wiped his heavy hair from across his eyebrows. He bore down on Cahill's with his hard hand. "I wish I could'a done more'n I done," he said. "If he hadn't'a got up and gone off like that, we might could'a kept him till the fire went out, and then things would'a been different. If I hadn'a had to go back and beat on the fire with my sacks, I believe me and A-del could'a helt onto him. But she couldn't do it by herself. She just couldn't."

Mrs. Bledsoe pushed past her husband, past McCaig, and stood closer to Cahill than one human being usually stands to another, tilting her pale, porcelain-webbed face straight up at his.

"I want you to come on back here, back into the bedroom," she said. "I want to show you somethin'. You can feel it. I want to put it in your hands."

"Sure," Cahill said. "Mac, you want to come with us? Or would you like to stay here with Zack?"

McCaig glanced down at Zack still gray with soot, a nearby animal ghost. "I'll come," he said. "Will Zack stay here all right?"

"He will if I say so," Cahill said. Then, "Go on, ma'am, I'm with you."

He stopped and felt for Zack, who came to him, clicking on the planks. "Stay here, big boy. Stay right here." Zack sank down and positioned his head, then lifted it. McCaig looked upward with the dog. There were faint sounds above them, rustlings as though a great distance away, feathers, wings, leaves, substances rubbing on wood, somewhere among them a suggestion of a voice, voices. Under these, McCaig holding Cahill's elbow, they left the room.

He could tell when they came through the door into a smaller place; the boards underfoot gave back the sound of their feet more personally, as if closed in, and in some way rounded off. Cahill had no notion of what furniture might be there. Maybe McCaig was keeping him from touching any; it bothered him when he could not touch furniture. It was warm, and he believed, though he could feel no heat coming to him from any direction, that the sun might be shining through a window.

There's not much a blind man can do, most of the time, he said to himself. Just stand around and listen to what other people say. Or sit. It's better when you sit, because you can always find something to do with your hands; there's usually a table, and you can fool with whatever's on it.

It was very quiet now. If Zack had been with him he would probably have said something to him, but now he felt defenseless and uncertain. What the hell

The room was hot, close, and clean. There were no windows and no decorations, no rugs. The big bed, almost square, was in the middle, with the head not pushed against the unpainted wall but centered on the floor, so that one could walk around it, as though it were there for some kind of demonstration. A white quilt spread over it, toward the foot end of which was a sharp-edged fleur-de-lis of a crude deep blue. "That is some kind of pretty, Mrs. Bledsoe," McCaig said. "That is a pretty quilt. Where'd you get the design?"

"I got it out of a magazine," she said, "and scaled it up." Then, "I make all my quilts white. White and one other color, it don't matter which one."

"This blue'll do for right now," McCaig said. "I don't think you could beat it."

"A-del's all right," said the farmer, jogging her with an elbow.

"Some of the time," she said.

does she want? he thought irritably. What are we here for?

Something touched the front of his coat, and he understood he was to take it, or feel it. He took the light awkward load on both hands and with his forearms, not actually believing it was what it was. He found himself weighing, hefting the load, bulky but not heavy, smelling of smoke.

It was lifted from him; he shifted from one foot to the other and dropped his hands, turning his head to locate things. There was a human sound, a sharp suck, an intake. He stepped toward it, waiting for what would surely be said, struggling to find a matching emotion, ready with several. He knew he would have to react in some way to the quilt. From his brief holding of it he had been

She went to a corner of the room where a pipe projected along the wall; on this were hanging Bledsoe's clothes—overalls and work shirts and one dark suit—and her dresses, mostly cotton. On the corner floor, folded but not quite neatly, was another quilt. She picked it up and brought it to Cahill.

"This here's . . . this here's what he . . . what your boy was a-layin' on. I was goin' to wash it out, when we could get things together around here; you know, after the fire, and all. I ain't washed it yet. It's just like it was when he left."

"Why don't we . . . I'm not . . . maybe we could just . . . just spread it out on the bed, maybe . . . and we could . . ." Bledsoe came to Cahill. "If you could just let me have that for a minute, Mr. Cahill, we could lay it down here and you could . . . Mr. McKay, here, could . . ." He took the quilt from Cahill's still hands, opened it and spread it carefully over the other one.

McCaig gasped. On the soot-streaked white fabric the central design was that of a church, a cathedral window, made of dozens of small yellow squares in the center of each of which was a colored circle divided down the middle, so that the impression was that these would unfold, would open outward: as though the window were

271

able to tell nothing but that it had been light, bulky and folded, and this had brought an image of other quilts: the half-joking, half-apprehensive first afternoon, during the last weeks of his eyesight, when Ruíz and he had torn apart two old quilts and tied them with heavy string over Ruíz's forearms, and Cahill had watched the dog made savage in failing sad shadowy light, and deafening animal sounds of frustration and assault.

"What? What is it?" Cahill asked, moving closer.

Cahill nodded slowly. He straightened his arm over the bed, and then bent forward at the waist so that the hand went down to the quilt, at a place where there was heavy soot but no blood. He drew back his hand and rubbed his thumb over the fingers a few inches in front of

made of many little doors, all closed but ready to open to any hand. The upper part, where the window crossed the white material, was solid with blood. On both sides of the main concentration there was other blood, as though flung and spattered; there was more of this on one side than the other, and ended in a smaller splotch which might have been where the injured arm—the hand probably—had rested. It was possible to make out by the position of dried blood the form of an upper body; if I didn't already know that he was hurt in the head and one arm, McCaig realized sickeningly, I could tell by this. He backed off a half step, and touched the spread where there was no blood on it. What on earth can I say? he wondered wretchedly. How can you describe something like this? He looked back over his shoulder. Where Cahill came to stand in relation to himself was of great importance.

"Frank," he said, "this . . . this here quilt . . . has . . . has got some blood on it."

Bledsoe and his wife drew together; he put his arm around her. She lifted her hand to her mouth and put the palm over it; the fingers were trembling so strongly that she seemed to be patting herself.

his face, as though he were looking at them.

He put his flat hand again on the
bed, far in toward the center of
it, turned the hand over and
rubbed the knuckles on several
of the shapes, once more put the
palm down and traveled up the
quilt, sliding toward where he
imagined the head had lain.

The surface changed; it stiffened and matted; flakes came off.
"This it?" he asked. "This what
you're talking about?"

Cahill put one knee on the bed
and felt with both hands, tracing
with a finger the division between the matted area and the
soft soot, returning always to the
flaking blood, as though trying
to invent a form by means of it.
He drew back and stood up,
holding both hands in front of
him.

Cahill folded his arms across his
chest.

McCaig watched the blind man's
broad back as he rubbed his fingers together, first with the thumb
and then with the fingers and,
oddly, the inner wrist of the other
hand.
McCaig watched, arms down, almost in an attitude of standing at
attention. Though he felt that it
would not be right for him to do
more than glance at Bledsoe and
his wife, he did glance, and could
not break the contact. Mrs. Bledsoe now had both hands on her
face, over the cheeks.

"Yes," McCaig said. "That's
blood." Then, "There's . . .
there's a lot, a whole lot of it.
Right where you are now is . . .
is where his head was. There's
kind of a . . . kind of a splotch
. . . like a . . . a big blot, you
might could say."

McCaig felt himself go white as he
looked at Cahill's face through the
hands, which were, as nearly as he
could tell, holding an emptiness
that was the size of an actual head.

273

"Excuse me," McCaig heard himself saying. "You-all excuse me for a minute. I'll be back in just a little while." He turned and plunged into the other dark of the house, and out the door.

"You want to go back and . . . and sit in the rocker?" Mrs. Bledsoe asked. "I kin git you some more honey, if you'd like that."

"No, thank you," Cahill said. "Some more water, maybe. I could use some more water."

She pulled the quilt toward her, and out of habit shook it. Something small and hard, perhaps disturbed by Cahill's rubbing, fell from it and ticked on the floor.

Cahill heard the sound. "What was that?" he asked. "Was that somethin' I ought to know about?"

Bledsoe bent and picked up what had fallen. His wife shook her head intensely, her finger to her lips, but her husband paid no attention.

"It looks like . . ." he said, ". . . it looks like it might be . . . might be part of . . ."

"Part of what?" Cahill asked, his voice rising with irritation.

"Part of a tooth," said the farmer. "We never did notice it, before."

"Give it to me," Cahill said, holding out his hand.

It was a front tooth, because not thick enough for any other. Where it had broken off was jagged, and painful even to imagine in its breaking; the

Bledsoe placed the tooth, which was whole except for the root, in Cahill's palm, and watched closely, his arm around his wife

274

other end had the delicate saw-edge of young teeth. He felt with his tongue in his own mouth, but could find no similar edge. He turned the tooth loose into his pocket.

"That'll be fine," he said. He turned, found the door, and, helped by Bledsoe's touch, sat down, balancing. He took the knobby glass and drank gratefully.

"That so?" Cahill said.

"She read yours?"

"Can't tell about all that yet, I don't reckon," said Cahill, to have some words coming from him.

again, as Cahill felt the tooth with his other fingers, then closed his hand around it and put it in the pocket of his coat.

Mrs. Bledsoe put the quilt in the corner where it had been. "Come on out of here," she said to Cahill. "Let's go back in the other room, and you kin sit in your rockin' chair."

"A-del kin read hands."

"It is," Bledsoe said with satisfaction. "She's got her own way of doin' it. Nobody never showed her nothin' about it." He paused. "Shoot, she could tell any of them others about it. I ain't never seen her be wrong one single time."

"She done it when we first got married. She told me I was gonna live till I was seventy-five, and have eleven grandchilrun, and be arrested twice't, and that I would put in a strawberry patch and git stung by a swarm of bees."

"No," the farmer said. "But I did put in the strawberry patch, and it did all right till the fire got to it. But A-del, she goes and gets the honey, from that old woman. I don't go over yonder."

"You sure you don't want some more?" she asked Cahill.

"No, but here's my hand, if you want to look at it. You could do that, I guess."

"Come on," Bledsoe said. "Bring your chair on over here, A-del, while I go get Mr. Cahill some water."

The farm came around him again, but differently. When McCaig stepped from the door it was grayish, but as he passed through the firebreak, a cloud moved over the sun, and stayed, piling more on itself from the east, very high, and the land turned dead black. Though there was wind, the thought of the fire, its size, the unrestraint of it, made him sweat. He had no clear idea as to where he was going, or why he had left the house, but he felt that he had not done enough, in this place where someone had been killed and others nearly burned alive, and he knew he would not come back to it, after today. Except for the stir of air everything was still; the ash did not blow, but lay like weightless slag on the uneven ground. He passed a single wagon wheel—from something that had been animal-drawn, surely—and kicked at it, jarring himself on the smoked-over rim, then straightened and began to look once more for the place where the plane had been. There are two things I can do, he instructed himself, knowing that neither was likely to produce any-thing that might be of value to Cahill. I can figure out more or less how the plane must have come down, and after that I can go on out toward the river and see if I can find anything, anything at all.

Without much trouble he returned to the crash site, marked with several kinds of moveless turbulence, the most noticeable the slant grooves of tractor tires and the metal tread-slashes of road machinery. The only unmarked part of the ground was where the plane must have rested; it did not seem to have been dragged—they lifted it onto some-thing with a crane, he thought; probably put it on a flatbed. He stood in place between the slash marks and other gougings, faced west and started to pace, like a man measuring distance and trying conscien-tiously to make sure that every step was an exact three feet. The aircraft had slid for about thirty yards; he could see part of its passage, though there were markings over it. If I can find where it hit and broke off the landing gear, he said to himself out loud, I'll know . . . I'll know more than I did. I could probably make an educated guess as to whether he had his power cut back. McCaig did not know how much credit to give the farmer's story, though he did not discount it. I need to know one thing, he said; I need to know if Joel tried to put on power, just before he hit; whether he was trying to pull up and get out.

At a hundred and seventy-seven paces he found a shallow short trench, and twelve paces beyond that, another, deeper one; between these was a third, barely noticeable. He hit hard on one wheel, McCaig said to the black farm. That throwed him over on the other wheel real hard, and the tail wheel hit. His face went into the panel, and he may have fire-walled the engine. But by that time he had been hit that first lick—might even have been unconscious; he fell over on the stick and flew it back into the ground.

McCaig swallowed and stood, still facing west, and started out again. The landscape was overwhelming him with fatigue; his feet moved under him with terrifying reluctance and obstinancy, gray with ash, far from him. He could see neither fence nor river, but only the haggard, toneless dark over which—in which—he bore his body onward as savagely heartless as he could make himself, his eyes roaming everywhere immediately in front of each step, more indifferent and keener than they had ever been. Except for low mounds, which he avoided, there was nothing he passed over that was different from anywhere else. I would never make an explorer, he thought; they spend most of their lives walking like this, over the snow or somewhere in the jungle. Days on end, they do it.

In ten minutes he came among a few dead trees that looked sand-blasted as well as burned limbless. This is probably the county's land, he reasoned, so I've gone past the fence, and might be able to go back and figure out where it was. He turned back into the farm and began to scuff his feet through the ash and dirt, trying to feel wire. At last he did feel it, picked it up with the top of his foot, and held it between the barbs as though expecting electricity to come through it, some pain or other surprise. He pulled it up from the ash, a little at first, and then with a jerk he did not understand hauled on it and held it overhead, spinning unparticled gray dust around him. It was a bottom strand, he figured as he followed it, hand over hand down the black barbs, still pulling and holding high every few feet. It was fastened, under the ash, to a black stob, and as he lifted his eyes he could see, barely above the surface, another stob, and believed he could even make out the bulge of a third beyond it. He turned to the tree side again, letting the wire fall, and moved along the way in which he had followed the wire, the dust he had raised settling back. He had cleared what amounted to a small, meaningless path, and there was a projection into it that did not seem to be a root. He bent down and picked it up. It was a zipper, and even in its ruined, half-fused condition he could tell that it was not from a jacket, or from pants. This here's from a boot, he said, knowing that he was almost surely right, and, in the uncertainty of everything he was doing, assured by his voice. This is from a flying boot, and Joel Cahill is right around here someplace. Either that, or he went on through. He's either here, or between here and the river. Or he's in the river. But he was here. He was *right* here.

Between the three posts he made a large half circle, scuffing his feet as he had done when searching for the wire. He worked back and forth across this for half an hour, extended the area and crisscrossed the new part. There was nothing else. Filled now with excitement and dread, his heartlessness easily defeated, he slogged over his many trails, turned, and slogged through them again in the opposite direction. Behind the cloud the light was lessening, though it was near noon. He hugged himself, touching the black zipper in which there was no glint of metal. He squatted and felt in the cold dust of fire, but finally, the excitement dying with the light, but the fear concentrating in his lower chest, he stood and walked in amongst the gutted trunks, wanting to tell Cahill and the farmer that he had been all the way to the river.

He held his hand open on his knee, and kept waiting for her to touch him, but she did not.

"You got a very strong hand, Mr. Cahill. Right now I'm just lookin' over the whole thing, kind of like it was a map, you know. You used to could run fast. Ain't that right?"

"No," Cahill said, wondering at this, his mind filling with the buffalo-powerful boy from the high school track, with the slash-

ing gold up the side of his blue trunks. "I used to skate a lot. I could skate pretty fast. Maybe that's what you mean." He remembered the wind, the air of his own motion. "How long am I gonna live? Ain't that the main thing you try to figure out, from somebody's hand?"

"You're gonna live a long time. What other people call the line of life is not the real one. The line of life is not this-here long one down the middle of your hand, like everybody thinks it is. The line of life is this'n, right under your longest finger. This-here other one, where it crosses, is your wife, and this one other one is your boy. You don't have no more chilrun, and you won't have no more, neither."

She did touch him now, almost like a serious tickling of his palm, near the fingers.

"You sure about that long life? I've got a bad disease. It put out my eyes, and if it can do that it can do anything else it wants to."

"That don't matter," she said. "What's down here says what it says. You're gonna live a long time, and you're gonna do a lot of work. Do you use tools?"

"Yes I do," he said. "I was a carpenter before I went blind. I could make just about anything you wanted. I made a skatin' rink and a dance pavilion. I made two towers—two watchtowers—where you could look all over Atlanta from any one of 'em. I made a fun house where there was eight main rooms and four secret ones, and five trap doors and a long tunnel. I used to put a rubber rattlesnake in one of the rooms, and it'd scare the hell out of you. Sometimes I'd forget where I put him, and I'd be scared to go in there, myself."

"You don't believe none of this?" Cahill asked, thrown off. "Why should I make it up?"

"That's somethin' I can't tell about."

She touched him with more assurance at what must have been an inch below his forefinger; he felt the point of her nail.

"What's the line supposed to be for?" he asked, interested in spite of himself. "The one I ain't got?"

"What you say ain't all the time what you mean," she said unexpectedly.

"I mean you keep a lot to yourself. You don't like many people. People are always watchin' you, and don't know what to say."

"There's a lot of open places in your hand; I never seen so many. Even with all the work you must do, a whole lot of this is open. This-here . . ."

". . . this-here is the answer to you. There's somethin' that you can't control, right in here. You think you can, but you can't. It's right here, right in this wide-open place, where most other people have a line."

"It's got to do with what you

280

"That ain't so," Cahill said, closing his hand and pushing back in the rocker. "I made it through high school all right, and I used to could drive a nail with anybody around Atlanta. I could read a blueprint better than the people who draw 'em. I picked it up in no time a-tall. A friend of mine is a electrician, and he's gonna show me how to wire, and maybe I can do some of that. And I guarantee I'll get on to it fast, even like this, blind and all."

"I can already wire *some*," Cahill said. "I wired my fun house. I wired my towers, too. But it's different when you can't see. There ought to be a way to do it, though. I can prob'ly figure somethin' out, if I make up my mind."

"What is it?" Cahill asked. "What kind of thing you talkin' about?"

"What?"

know, with your education, like. It's gonna be hard for you to learn. It's already hard; it's been hard."

She rose, raised the chair by the back, set it against the wall, and went to her husband, who had been looking down on them with an expression of attentive pride. They glanced together overhead at some slight noise that the blind man did not seem to notice. After that they were quite still, and listened closely, believing what they heard.

"I can't do none of that," the farmer said. "We don't have to worry about no electricity."

"I got to do one more thing," the woman said, again unexpectedly.

"I don't mean have to," she said. "I mean it's somethin' I can do, if you want me to."

"I got a way that I can tell if what I been sayin' about your hand is true, or if I ain't read it right."

"How would you do that?"

"If you can . . . if you could . . ." She glanced at her husband.

"She means," Bledsoe said, "that if . . . that if you wouldn't . . . if you wouldn't mind, Mr. Cahill . . . wouldn't mind takin' off your glasses for just a minute, A-del could tell by . . . by what's right around your eyes—the skin, you know, like—she could tell you all this . . . all this for a fact."

"OK," Cahill said, unexpectedly himself, leaning his head against the chair back and taking off his glasses with one motion. "Go right on. Tell me what you see."

The woman crouched and peered, and an eagerness came into the whole position of her body as she passed her hand in front of Cahill's eyes as though part of a spell. "This is somethin' don't many know," she said. "I learnt it from a old woman was a friend of my great-aunt, a long time ago. It'll tell you a lot more than a hand; it'll tell you what a hand couldn't never tell you."

Cahill felt himself go very still; stiller and stiller, and waited for what he would see in his mind. Nothing came; then the flicker of a memory of a blueprint; a plan, a few lines: fragility, precision; then gone.

She dropped her arm, moved her eyes closer to Cahill, her head on one side, her lids almost closed. "You learn hard," she said. "And there's some things

"So?" Cahill said. "What would them be?"

"What else?"

"That everything?" Cahill asked, sitting up as in a dentist's chair with his mouth full of cleaning water. "That the whole thing?"

"I'll be watchin' out," Cahill said, relaxing and nodding a little. "I'll be watchin' out, on down the road."

you ain't never goin' to learn. It ain't in you."

"I can't say what they are," she said. "Them lines don't tell me that. But there's gonna be some thing you can't get at, and you might want to. That part might not be too good, for you."

"You're goin' to live a long time. Even longer than I thought. Eighty years; maybe more." She held back, peered again, and went on. "And one big thing you're gonna get, along in there somewhere. It might not be the right big thing for you to have, but it'll come to you. You got a crossin'-place that shows it, and what put it there knows, already. It's in front, maybe a couple of years, and after you come up to it, it'll go on; it'll go on with you, all the way till you die."

"It's all I got," she said, straightening.

Mrs. Bledsoe turned to her husband. "You gettin' tired?" she asked. "Just a little bit?"

"It's tough," the farmer said. "It's tough walkin' around in them ashes. We probably went over a mile, out yonder and back."

"I am too," Cahill said. "I am kind of tired. The longer I sit here, the heavier I get."

"Why don't you just tip back in the chair and go to sleep for a little while? You could go on back and lay down on our bed, if you want to."

"No, this is all right. Let me see if I can't drift off, just like this."

There was no dream, but he entered into reverie so deeply and with such fatigue that there was no difference. Except for his childhood skating and the walking he had done in the Atlanta parks, he had never been physically very active, but since his blindness had taken full hold he had enlarged the images in his memory so that the spaces he had sought out years before, such as Piedmont Park, now became much greater than they had been. He believed he stood in one now, and could not imagine the buildings of Atlanta on any side; there was, as far off as he could make out, only a grayish haze that seemed to curve upward, as though he were in an insubstantial globe. The grass underfoot was distinct, however, and also grayish. The sky was nothing, but as he noted this, and the cloudlessness over him, a sound—several sounds apparently related to each other—came from there. They could not have been anything but voices, thin, wordless, and excited; a single innocent, conspiratorial sound. It was the one element that had been missing from the spaces he remembered, from the tennis courts and baseball diamonds, and from the encounter with the studious boy and his twin-pusher model, which had been far too silent, which had lacked voices—perhaps these very voices—into which the plane should have ascended, as coming into its home territory, ghostly and necessary. He was then between the twin falls he remembered from the picnic with his wife. Then, there was only the hoarse pouring past both sides as he stood on the wet moss of the rock, a sound made of many thin sounds woven together, essentially delicate, mannerly even, but now in bulk, gone past control. It filled his ears, his mind, but inmixed with it, of it and yet above, was a small, quietly mysterious, secretly excited murmur, not like leaves or like birds but like creatures—people, children— who lived in the air, who spoke constantly in a way known only to them, and were always there, and never seen; who followed but did not threaten, who could not descend, who went with, and never slept. Now they concentrated as though in a kind of cone, and took on more urgency and more volume.

An engine was hanging where the light had been. Confusedly he knew he had never seen it; had been told of it, and from this the engine had constructed itself, in heavy chains hanging free and swinging a little for no reason, surrounded by the voices coming down around it.

"Your man's back," someone said to him.

"Thanks," Cahill said, shifting and setting his feet flat. "Did you find anything?"

"Maybe," McCaig said, blackened so that the whites of his eyes looked comical, the way Al Jolson's in blackface are supposed to do. "I was out to the fence, and I found this." He put the zipper on Cahill's big thigh. "I went on as far as the river, but this is all I came up with."

Cahill palmed the object, half limp, and ran his thumb down part of it. "What is it?"

"It's a zipper," McCaig said. "What it come off of I don't know right now, but I believe it's part of a flyin' boot."

"You sure about that?" Cahill asked.

"Are you sure?" Bledsoe repeated.

"Look at it," McCaig said to the farmer. "If that's not a zipper I'll eat it."

"You found this at the fence?" Cahill asked. "How did you find the fence?"

"If this is Joel's," Cahill said, "it means he got as far as the fence."

"He couldn'a got tangled up in the fence, could he? Or anything like that?"

"Give it here," Cahill said. "I'll keep it." He put it in the pocket with the piece of wire.

The overhead voices had come out of the dream with him, but they were still dreamlike; he suspected he would listen for them later, for they seemed quite ready to be a part of everything he did: to be present in every ceiling, over every water

Bledsoe took the zipper from Cahill and turned it over in the dim light. He walked across the room to the window, examined it, and came back. "It's a zipper, all right. That don't belong to nobody around here."

"I kicked it up," McCaig said. "I found the bob wire. This was right between the stobs, used to be the posts."

"Or through there, and on."

"This is all I found," McCaig said. "And I looked hard, all around there. There wadn't nothin' else."

"I guess we better get on back," McCaig said to Cahill. "The colonel wants you to come by. He's got an appointment set up for you; I think it's with the flight surgeon."

whether running or still, every wide space. "What's going on up there?" he asked, pointing upward and jogging his arm up and down without raising his face.

"Them's my chilrun," Bledsoe said. "They git up in them rafters, and you cain't git 'em to come down for nothin'. They's two boys and a girl. She's three; she's really too little to go up yonder and play with them two hardheaded boys, but you can't stop her from doin' it. She was born to climb."

"She did fall once," Mrs. Bledsoe said. "She sure did. Fell on the sofa though."

"Better watch out," Bledsoe said. "She might fall down on your head."

Cahill stood, this time turning his eyes upward, where the darkness roiled with his relentless barbaric explosions of heatless gold.

"Nah, I didn't mean it," the farmer said. "They're not really my chilrun. I mean, they used to be my chilrun. Now they just haunt the place."

He had taken his overcoat off this time, for it was warmer outside, and warmer in the office. He relaxed around the Krystal cheeseburger he had eaten with McCaig on the way back into town, and waited for the colonel's move.

Colonel Hoccleve sat forward over his desk, fingers touching a silver penholder, the other hand closed on the chair arm. "Are you getting along all right?" he asked. "Are you seeing the people you need to?"

"I'm gettin' along fine," Cahill said, meaning nothing. "You've got

287

some good boys here; they don't mind helpin' you. I don't have a single thing to complain about."

"They are good boys," the colonel said, "most of them. They try as hard as they can. They come from a lot of different kinds of backgrounds, and it's not easy for some of them to adjust."

Cahill waited still, holding his teeth set into each other. "It's not easy for you, either, I don't reckon," he said finally. "I mean for you and the other grown people around here."

"We don't want anything making it any harder," the colonel said, "that's for sure." He waited it out, then come to it. "It makes it especially hard when you get a situation nobody's expecting: something you really shouldn't have to deal with."

"You mean like what?" Cahill asked. "Like me and Zack, maybe?"

"Not you," the colonel said. "Not you at all. But I've got a cadet in the infirmary, Mr. Cahill, and he's going to have to have rabies shots. Costs five hundred dollars a series. That's some government money, and some government time, plus a lot of inconvenience, not to say anything about the pain. From what the flight surgeon tells me, the shots are worse than the bite."

"You can save the government some money, then," Cahill said, angered, but acting more angered than he was. "Zack ain't got nothin' like that. He don't hardly ever get out with no other dogs. Ain't that where you're supposed to get that kind of stuff?"

"I don't know where you're supposed to get it," the colonel said, exaggerating the "supposed" enough for Cahill to notice. "But a man can't pass a six-four without it, if he's been bitten; and if he can't pass a six-four he can't fly, and if he can't get all his time in, he can't go out with his class."

"Can't what?"

"Can't graduate on Sunday. We're going to have to hold Cadet Spain back a class, and he's one of the top cadets here. He'll have to repeat, at least the last phase, and our quota to Basic won't be full. All this is bad news. And completely unnecessary."

I'm coming up on something I don't like, Cahill told himself. I really don't like to apologize.

"I'm as sorry as I can be about that, Colonel," he said. "It seems like there was two boys fightin' over somethin', and Zack jumped in and got hold of one of 'em. There wadn't nothin' much I could do."

"What were you doing at the cadet club to begin with?" the colonel asked, on his own ground. "That's only for cadets and their dates. Nobody else."

"I went there with one of your boys," Cahill said. "I didn't just wander in, like. How the hell would I know where the place was?"

"I won't make an issue out of it," the colonel said. "But Cadet Spain did get hurt, and we can't let any more things like that happen. If you can't get a leash or some way to hold your dog back, we can't let you on the base anymore."

"I'll see what I can do," Cahill said grudgingly. "I don't know how Zack's gonna take to that, though; he ain't never had nobody holdin' him, not even me. I've got a friend in town that can maybe give me somethin' I can hold him with."

"How much longer do you think you might want to stay, Mr. Cahill?" the colonel asked, reaching for the pen to note down the answer.

"One, two more days," Cahill said. "The boys wanted me to stay through Sunday. That would'a been my . . . that would'a been Joel's graduation, too, like they say. It seems to mean a lot to 'em. If it's all right with you, I'd like to stay through Sunday."

"I expect we can manage," Colonel Hoccleve said, easing off. "I don't want you to think we're inhospitable, and God knows I don't want to interfere with your relationship with your dog. Just fix it where he can't jump on our poor cadets. That's all." He smiled, surprising himself, and certain that the blind man could tell, and would be reassured. "And we'd be happy for you to stay on through Sunday. We're going to have a parade; the whole graduating class will do a flyover. All the trainers on the base; at least all of them we can get in the air. Maybe . . . I think . . . I'm sure you'd enjoy it. All those engines, and everything. Makes quite a sound. Sounds like . . . sounds like one great big . . ."

Cahill had not really been listening, but thinking of what might happen to him in his next dream, when he could see. He had no particular favorites, though if he could skate again through the streets of North Atlanta, where there were hills and curves, it would be good time for him.

Then coming back to where he was, "Engine sounds," he said. "I know. I hear 'em every morning, all the way back in town. It's quite a way to wake up. They all sound like they're tryin' to kill each other. They sound like they won't never get off the ground a-tall, but just stand there and tune in to one another, as loud as they can get."

"We'll try to get 'em all up," said the colonel. "All but a couple ought to be in commission. Then you'll hear something sure enough, and not on the ground, either. You just come out, come Sunday."

"Right," said Cahill. "And I'll have Zack on a leash, or have a handle on him, some way. He won't bother nobody else, I guarantee."

"Now, if you want to, you can go visit with the flight surgeon; I told him you'd be over some time this afternoon. Joel was on sick call, a lot of the last two weeks he was here. Didn't keep him on the ground, though. If I remember from the report, he had something wrong with his feet. Major Iannone was treating him; whatever it was he did must've worked, because Joel was not on report when he was killed."

Cahill had felt the long marks in the ash with his feet; had felt them with his hands. He had done this. They were in ash that had been snowed on; the marks of aircraft wheels. They had hit, and lifted into the air, and hit again, where he had stood.

"I went out to where Joel's plane went down," Cahill said. "I been out there all mornin'."

The colonel glanced through the door into the outer office. A clerk-typist with a folder passed and disappeared.

"You did? Out past the river? Over where that farmer said he saw him come down?"

"That's right. I talked to him. Him and his wife. I don't have no reason to doubt what they said."

"Who took you over there? Did you go with any of the base personnel?"

"I went with Mr. McCaig, that I met in this office. He took me over, and stayed with me."

"Was it any satisfaction to you?"

"I don't come at you, Colonel," Cahill said, reborn for combat. "What kind of satisfaction am I supposed to get? That's where my boy went down. I went there, and I talked to the people who saw him go down; the ones that tried to do somethin' for him." He pulled back and clenched. "What did you do?"

"I went over, too," the colonel said evenly. "I took a good many Air Corps personnel from the base, and brought over some other investigators from Fayetteville. We did the best job we could."

"And you didn't find nothin'?"

"No," the colonel said, glancing again at the door, not sure of whether he should ask Cahill to lower his voice. "We found the aircraft, and we found where it had hit the ground and broke off the landing gear. We didn't find the body. If we had, you'd be the first to know, as designated next of kin."

"And you talked to Bledsoe? To that-there farmer, was with him?"

"We talked to him. *I* talked to him. He claimed he took your son into his house, and that Joel got away from him and his wife and went out into the fire."

"And you don't believe that?"

"I don't know," Colonel Hoccleve said, and then, determining, said, "No, in fact, I don't believe it. There's no real evidence. You just have to go on what they say. It doesn't seem likely that he would go with them, and then break loose and run off into what he must surely have known, even in a traumatized condition, he couldn't handle." The colonel leaned forward as though at a staff meeting, with officers who could see him, and understand his position of body sincerity. "Look, Mr. Cahill. Figure to yourself. You have this badly hurt boy: severe injuries to his head, and probably to his arm."

"His right arm," Cahill said.

"Understood. Injuries to his head and right arm. These people try to take care of him. What is he going to do? What would *you* do?"

"If I had a reason to get out, I'd get out. Nobody could stop me."

"That would have to be a hell of a reason, Mr. Cahill, if you'll pardon me. The easiest thing to assume is that he was temporarily out of it, out of his head. That is, if you believe the man's story."

"And his wife's. It's what they told me."

"We never got any further than that," the colonel said. "We spent most of our time out in the field. When we go back, we'll go over all the ground again, and we'll find—chances are, we'll find—the evidence." He paused. "The evidence we don't want to find, that nobody wants to find, but—I hope you'll forgive me, and the military mentality—the evidence that has got to be there."

"I went around there," Cahill said, his hands in his pockets. "I . . . we found a couple of things."

"Go ahead," said the colonel. "Go ahead, I'm with you. You don't think so, but I really am. This is hellacious all around. Training Command is having to explain, all over the place. What two things?"

"Did you go all the way to the fence?"

"What do you mean?"

"I mean exactly what I said. Did you go to the fence between Bledsoe's land and the county's?"

"We went from the impact site to the river, and back."

"That's not what I asked you. I want to know if you went to the fence, if you knew where it was. That's what I want to know. I also want to know if *you* went. You're supposed to be the head man around here. And you say your men didn't find anything. *Anything?* Anything but the airplane?"

"We didn't. And we laid down a very good search, too. If there'd been anything, we'd've found it." He agreed with himself that he could add nothing more. "We're going back, like I told you. I plan to do it after graduation, when we have a little more time. When the weather's better. We'll turn the whole place up with a plow, if we have to, but I don't think we'll find anything, but maybe . . . maybe some evidence of your boy."

The wire in his pocket pronged his fingertip, and his other hand pushed aside the spring grip to run its thumb along the coarseness of the zipper. He settled the items in new relations. The zipper, the spring grip, and the sugar cubes were on one side of him, and the bent wire and the goggles on the other. And the tooth; he made sure.

"Some of this we can talk about later," the colonel said, pressing himself upward. "I thought it would be best for you to go ahead and find out whatever there is to find, from the others; from the cadets and instructors, you know, before I put in my two cents' worth. But I'll do that before you go, I can promise you. If you want my opinion of Joel Cahill, I'll tell you, and I'll go over his records with you. Everything. You're his father, and the Air Corps understands how you must feel. I've got two sons of my own, and they both want to be pilots, God help 'em."

Cahill understood that the other man was on his feet now, facing him, probably across something; he believed the man's eyes were looking straight into his own. Every time he wished for there to be a battle of eyes, there was one, and there was no way for the opponent to win; no one could face down a blind man. "All right," he said, in motion, exploring tentatively toward the door with a hand. "Maybe I will want you to show me them records, later on."

"I'll be happy to go over them with you. I'll put a note on the pad." The colonel reached forward over the desk top, but, glancing toward Cahill and the dog, straightened once more and came to them. "Corporal Phillipson will take you over to the flight surgeon's. His name is Major Iannone: easy to talk to, has a lot of opinions."

"Lookin' forward to it," Cahill said, easing also; he would see the colonel only once more, if that; he had not backed off, not given down.

The colonel stepped to the door and beckoned to Corporal Phillipson, gesturing inward vigorously with four joined fingers. Stepping nearer Cahill, he said, touching the black overcoat shoulder, "And while you're there at the hospital," he said, "you might want to drop in and say hello to Cadet Spain. He's still there getting his shots."

"I'll do that," said Cahill. "I hope he's feelin' better. I know you don't want no mad-dog cadets runnin' around here."

"That's right," the colonel said, as Corporal Phillipson came in. "We want to keep those to a minimum." Then, "Come back tomorrow, if you want, and we'll get straight about the graduation."

On the porch it was warm, almost pleasant. Needing no excuse, he stuck his tongue out to take the heat and light, which lay on his taste buds, newly connected with him, like something almost substanceless, but meaningful; a wafer, perhaps, or fish food. Where had he tasted it before? He remembered: the one time he had been to a Catholic church, with his wife and a friend of hers from high school, and he had awkwardly, with many sideways glances for instruction, taken Communion. Fish food it was like, he was sure, tasteless and there. But why important?

"Tell you what I'll do," he said to Phillipson.

"What's that, sir?" Phillipson asked, maintaining an exact distance. "What do you have in mind?"

"We're going to the infirm'ry. That the place?"

"Yes, sir."

"If you'll tell me what it's near, I'll navigate us over there. That fair enough?"

"Yes, sir. Very fair. It's on the other side of the cadet club. I'll tell you what; if you and Zack can get us to the cadet club, I'll take us the rest of the way. It's not far."

"You know Zack's name is Zack," Cahill said, pleased. "Do you remember from before, or what?"

"I remember. But everybody around here knows Zack by now. Probably everybody on the base."

"All right, Buffalo-head," he said downward. "You heard that. Let's go. Don't make me look bad."

The main yard was sand again; the snow had melted, and Cahill moved confidently, having been across the open space the several times that he had. The games-voices reached him from behind and to the right; behind and to the left were the engines, two of them now, one near and the other farther beyond it, tuning together, still untuned.

Basing his angle on these, he lifted his chin and strode out like a man who could see, the warmth that would be afternoon sun on his left cheek. "This about right?" he asked.

"This's almost just about exactly right," Phillipson said, alive with game-interest. "Maybe two points to starboard, would put us right on the nail."

"Starboard?" Cahill questioned. "Don't that have somethin' to do with ships? Ain't that the Navy?"

"We use it here, too," the corporal said. "At least the cadets and instructors do. If you and me and Zack can ease over just a little to the right, we'd be in fine shape."

A high engine directly above them, standing for the moment, not moving on, made suddenly the abrupt blast-and-twist he had heard once before, and added to it a short intent zoom or swerve which subsided into an even tone, now truly passing beyond them, and on out of hearing.

"That was a snap roll, up there," Cahill said, pointing upward as though at a ceiling which anyone, without looking, would assume to be there: the overhead of a familiar room.

"It started out to be a snap roll," Phillipson said, "but he let it go on too long. It went around a half a time too many, and ended up on his back. Had to split-S out. It wasn't none too good."

"How come you not to get into flyin'?" Cahill asked. "Ain't you about the same age as these-here other boys?"

"You wouldn't get me up in one of those things for a million dollars, and promotion to full colonel. I like it where I am, just walking along."

"You don't want to be a cadet? Never did want to?"

"Never did," Phillipson said. "I like 'em, though. I like all these other guys. I don't want to see any of them get hurt, or even go off to combat. But there's not much I can do about it. I just work with the papers, and do what Colonel Hoccleve asks me to do. Sometimes it's not bad duty, and I'm permanent party. That makes it easier."

"But you're here with all these kids your age, and all this talk about flyin', and the noise of these airplanes all day and all night. And you never wanted to get into it?"

"I never did," Phillipson said. "I don't feel like I belong up there. That's for the others. That's for Shears and Spain and Adler and Thomasovich, and maybe Harbelis and Armistead and Rolader and Neilson. They'll all make it through, and go on."

"All but Joel," Cahill said. "I never asked you: did you know him?"

"No, sir, I didn't know him. I knew who he was, and I saw him around with the others, mainly Shears and Spain and Harbelis and Adler. That was his main bunch. They were always around, near him, or as near as they could get. The only contact I had with him was when he would walk tours, and I'd go out and check on his time; I was supposed to make sure he walked every minute he was supposed to."

"Tours? I heard it before. What's it mean?"

"Punishment tours, they're called. I think the name is supposed to be like a joke, probably. A tour is like a tour of duty; I mean that you're assigned to a time in that place. If a cadet gets ground demerits for inspection, or for something he does that's unmilitary, like being out of uniform, or signing in late from open post, he gets these tours that he has to walk off. One hour's walk—strictly in cadence time—for every demerit. Joel Cahill had a lot of those. Sometimes his buddies would walk with him. That happened a couple of times, and then the colonel made them stop. He used to have to walk back and forth in front of the Administration Building, where we just came from. He was out there a lot."

"Some war," said Cahill.

"You could say that, sir. But you needn't worry about him being mistreated, or anything. He took it all right."

"How do you know? Did he say anything to you about it?"

"Not much, but it didn't seem to tire him out. He said the Second Body did it."

"The what?"

"The Second Body did it. It was an idea he had. After he finished walking tours, he'd take off his uniform and go right out and play basketball. I'd ask him which body played ball, and he said mostly the first, but sometimes the second, when his team got behind. He was a good player, as good as has come through here, that were not from college teams. His outfit, with Rolader and Spain, won the intermurals when he was an underclassman. They had a big beer bash in town, and everybody got docked for signing in late."

"We're ninety-seven steps out now," Cahill said. "Ninety-seven steps from the stairs. How do the boys say that?"

"Into the mission," Phillipson said, catching on. "Ninety-seven steps into the mission."

"As I figure it," Cahill said, "we're going catty-cornered across this open place, which should put us somewhere over near the barracks."

"That's where we are, at the north end."

"Am I still on course?"

"Just about," Phillipson said, not quite truthfully. "If you'll bank back a little port, a little to the left, and then straighten out, that'll take us right between the swimming pool and the cadet club."

"Are those chairs, those big wooden ones, still sittin' out there?"

"They sure are," Phillipson said with genuine admiration. "Nobody's moved them."

"I sat in one the other day while somebody made a phone call. I wouldn't mind doing it again."

"Fine," Phillipson said. "I'll go in and get you a Coke. I'm not a cadet, but I'm Permanent Party."

"And that's good, you say?"

"It is as far as I'm concerned," the corporal said. "It means I'll be around."

He hunched in the chair like hovering, grateful to be almost boxed in boards he now found deeply gratifying to inhabit, the nails in the big slabs giving very little on both sides as he tested them, pressing hard. The suspension was almost complete, and he waited in warmth that he was sure was of a light gold; even as he sat, full of a vague excitement, he understood that the day was losing what it had had, the full sun that had begun in the farmer's house across the river, and stayed above him since, especially on the side of his face as he and Phillipson had walked across the assembly area. He listened as the aircraft came in, one after the other, trying to picture them as McCaig had said they appeared to be doing, settling into an unbroken forest.

The air to one side of him changed, and became music, several male voices singing again about a paper doll that, for reasons they made clear, they intended to get, and he realized that a door—the door to the cadet club, surely—had opened, and he supposed that it would be Corporal Phillipson.

Captain Faulstick and Cadet Billy Crider came out of the cadet club, saw Cahill and his dog, and came to them.

"Hello," Faulstick said. "How're you doin'?"

296

"Hello," Cahill said. "How are you? *Who* are you?"

"You remember me, I hope," Faulstick said. "We had dinner last night in town. I don't know about you, but I had a good time. That man's wild meat was good, and I never drank so much good whiskey in my life."

"You the man with the bombs?"

"I'm the man with all the bombs," Faulstick said. "I know where they go. But I did something else today. I passed my final Army check-ride. I just barely passed, though. I screwed up a slow roll, because I still can't do one to the left, but I did everything else about as well as I've ever done, and I got by. I rode with Lieutenant Guinyard, and he said he'd send me on to Basic next week. Me and Cadet Billy Crider, here, have just been celebrating with a couple of milk shakes. He passed, too, and he rode with Lieutenant Purcell Foy, the super-asshole of the base."

Trying to connect, he wondered if the plane which made the screwing sound and the zoom-out that he had heard earlier had been Faulstick's plane. But no; this was too soon after.

He decided that he wanted to keep the voice coming down to him, at least for a little while.

He also liked the second voice, full of happy insolence, very young and high.

"I can fly better than he can," said Crider, a small freckled boy with a thin turned-up nose and thick lips. "I wrung that thing out, sure enough. There wasn't nothing Foy could do but hang on."

"Why 'ont you'all sit down, till my man gets back?" Cahill asked.

"There's only one other chair," Faulstick said, "or we would."

"You sit in it, Captain," the cadet said. "I don't feel like sitting down anyway, except in an airplane. I wish we had something else to drink besides milk. This ain't the time for milk, no matter how they shake it."

"We'll get that later on," Faulstick said, sitting down in the vast clumsy chair and sliding to reach the back. "Maybe Mr. Cahill can join up with us in town, or somewhere. He can drink."

"That stuff's too good for me," Cahill said. "I feel like hell, to tell you the truth. I'm used to bad whiskey."

"We fought the whole war last night for Mr. Cahill, me in Europe and Lennox Whitehall in the Pacific."

"I learned a lot," Cahill said, realizing that this was true. "I'm glad the air didn't kill neither one of you."

"The air's all right, some of the time," Faulstick said. "We're all doing good in the air, especially Billy Crider."

"I thought Foy was gonna get on me. He didn't like Joel."

"I don't like him," Faulstick said assuredly. "I don't believe I could pass one of his rides."

"I didn't say a single word to him," Cadet Crider said, shaking his head to show totality. "Not one. He'd tell me to do something, and I'd do it. Slow roll to the left, eight-point slow roll to the right, Chandelle, lazy eight, stall it, spin it, snap-roll it. For the last fifteen minutes he just let me have it, and I cavorted around some. I was thinking about doing a falling leaf, but I decided I probably ought not to. I doubt if he would know what one was. I think he's scared of airplanes."

"I still am, a little bit," Faulstick said. "I don't like little airplanes in the same way I don't like big horses. I'm never sure whether I've really got control."

"They'll do what you say," Crider said. "They'll do what you think. And they'll do better than that: they'll do what you feel; what you dream, even. You can even use them to dowse; you know, find water."

"It's a good thing you didn't say anything to Foy," Faulstick said dryly. "He's not on that kind of wave length, or whichever way you're talking."

"One of these days I'm going to have to give you a free lesson, Captain. I really can show you some things, I think. I'd be glad to try."

"I don't think I could learn anything from any of you naturals," Faulstick said. "I have to do it by the book."

"I was not a natural when I started," Crider said. "I got natural, just about two weeks ago. And it was a good thing, too. If I hadn't, I'd be at

Lowry Field out in Denver being reclassified, or some damn thing. I sure wouldn't be going to Basic. I got natural, and I naturaled the hell out of Lieutenant Purcell Foy, who flies in an airplane like he was opening a can by the instructions."

"How'd you do all this?" Cahill asked, anticipating the answer with excitement and a little fear.

"Another cadet showed me," Crider said. "I just talked to him for a few minutes in the barracks. I sat on the side of one of the bunks, and in five minutes I knew everything."

"Who was it?" Cahill asked.

"You know who it was," Cadet Crider said.

"Well, *I* don't know who it was," Faulstick said. "I wished I'd known. Maybe I could use some of that kind of help, after all."

"Must'a been my boy," Cahill said. "Sounds like what people've been tellin' me."

"It was him," Crider said.

"What did he tell you?" Faulstick asked. "I'm interested."

"What he said gets you on the other side of words. Where you don't need any words."

"How do you do that?" Faulstick asked. "How does someone tell you a thing, using words, that gets you into some kind of place, some kind of situation, where you don't need them?"

"It gets you into the Second Body," Cadet Crider said. "The Second Body never speaks, and never thinks. But I won't say any more."

"I wish you would," Cahill said.

"I can't," Crider said, "or, anyway, I won't."

"Maybe in Basic," Captain Faulstick said. "If I get into trouble, or if an instructor like Foy gets ahold of me. Then you can tell me."

"I'll see about it," Crider said seriously. "I'll find out if I can. But I've got to tell you now, everybody's not cut out for it. Just a few. Some people don't have the other body, or they can't find it."

Corporal Phillipson came out of the building and set a paper cup on the arm of Cahill's chair. "Here you go," he said. "Here's your Coke."

"Where you been for so long?"

"The counter was jammed up," Phillipson said. "Everybody's time is in. Flying's over, for this class. Most of 'em, anyway. They're all in there congratulating each other, everybody but the ones who busted out; I don't know where they are. I don't reckon they'd want to be in there with all of them that made it. There won't be any of them flying over the base, come Sunday."

"It does seem too bad," Cadet Crider said. "I was just about in the same fix myself, like I told Mr. Cahill. But I don't feel too sorry for any of 'em. Washouts are dangerous; the Air Corps is not shittin' you about that. Some of those guys have had their lives saved. They're a whole lot better off on the ground."

"Well, we'll be in the air together, Billy boy," said Faulstick. "They're gonna let me fly in the graduation exercise with all the kids. That'll be something."

"It sure will," said Cadet Crider, an odd tone in his voice. "Don't miss it."

"I wouldn't for anything," Faulstick said. "I'm getting a bigger kick out of this than I would out of knocking out three marshaling yards from a Fort, or twenty rail junctions or a thousand trucks."

"Good luck," said Cahill, arming himself to his feet. "Me, I've got to get on with it. I'm supposed to see the flight surgeon."

"Hootnanny?"

"That what they call him?" Cahill asked.

"Yeah, but don't you."

"He's okay," Captain Faulstick said. "He gave me some good medicine for trench mouth. Just like the stuff you put on telephone poles. Imagine me, twenty-eight years old and a combat survivor, gettin' trench mouth up in the air. Don't make sense."

"Do this, Captain," Crider said. "It don't take teeth." He closed his eyes, held his arms straight out from his side, and brought his forefingers exactly together in front of him. Faulstick tried the same thing, more slowly, the fingers obviously feeling for each other, but could only achieve a shearing action as the tips missed.

"You're out," said Cadet Crider.

"No, I'm in," Faulstick said with satisfaction. "I'm with the golden boys, going out to the BT-14, the Vultee Vibrator, that's all rudder and don't fly like no other airplane. After that, who knows? I might get my own Fort, and be right back in it."

They moved away toward the classroom building, and were gone.

"You still navigating, sir?" asked Phillipson.

"I'll try," said Cahill, listening to what surrounded him. "Do we go starboard here?"

"No, sir," Phillipson answered. "Starboard is straight into the swimming pool. We go straightaway, and after about ten or twelve steps, a little port, through the bushes and right on in."

When the bushes closed around them for a few seconds, Cahill felt of the leaves, which were flat and slick as though painted. The infirmary had four steps.

For the last day or so Cahill had not paid much attention to his game of visualizing the people he met, but now he wanted to go back to it. The images that he invented for them were after all the human beings as they must exist for him, and this were important. He would never actually see any of them, but he believed he had very exact references for Colonel Hoccleve and Harbelis, and for McCaig, and, though he had not worked at them, his picturizations of the farmer, Bledsoe, and his wife were very strong, very individual for him, and brought with them a surge of liking, good will, and well-being. Gilbeau, brought nothing yet, but he sounded smallish, and very Yankeefied, probably from around New York, he judged.

Cahill stood where he was, waiting for whatever the new man might suggest.

Cahill stayed standing, and so did Phillipson, though Zack sank to his haunches and looked around, his tongue out as from running.

"This is Pfc. Parris Gilbeau," said Corporal Phillipson, as the door was opened to them by a blond, balding heavy young man with lead-colored cheeks and pale blue eyes. "He's our only medic. Major Iannone and him are the whole medical team for all this personnel. Plenty of forms. Idn't that right, Gil?"

"Sure is," said Gilbeau. "Looks like we can't keep 'em all well at once. We could use about ten more people and about five more rooms, or three little rooms and a big one."

Through Gilbeau's thin hair the curve of the part ran perfectly. His OD shirt was creased down each side as though with a ruler, and at the neckline, across the white T-shirt, the chain of his dogtags glinted as though polished. He wore frameless glasses, and the eyes, made slightly larger, did not quite match in color.

"I'll go see what the mighty major's doing," Gilbeau said. "Sit down, if you want to."

A heavy dark man returned with Pfc. Gilbeau and stopped in front

301

of Cahill as Gilbeau went back to his desk. He wore salmon-pink pants with a sharp crease, and a fir-green dress blouse on which the Air Corps wings—small twin golds on the lapels and dense single silver over the heart—stood forth rigidly, as did the gold leaves on his shoulders. "Welcome to the common fay-et in the winter hills of North Carolina, the playing fields of the air, and all that. If Wellington could win Waterloo on the cricket pitch at Eton, we can win this war in Peckover, Boondock County, North Carolina."

The other man sounded big—certainly he was trying to be hearty, as a lot of big Southerners do and some are, but from the position of his hand Cahill knew he was not tall.

"The common what?" Cahill asked, holding out his hand.

"The major is from Charleston," the medic said, looking up from a chart. "He just talks that way. He means 'fate.' Don't ask him anything that has to do with a boat, a date, or being late, or ask him to wait. Anything that ends with a vowel and a 't,' he can't say like other people."

The major raised both hands to eye level and brought the fingers and thumb of each hand vigorously and repeatedly together.

"Hear that?" he asked. "Know what it is?"

"Sounds like you're poppin' your fingers," Cahill said.

"In the low country, down on the salt as we say in Charleston, that's called the crawfish clap. We do it when we like something, or

302

"I hope not," Cahill said, working to be humorous. "I hear you can get some strange things in Charleston. Maybe that's why I ain't never been near there."

somebody. Not everybody gets the crawfish clap."

"Come on back to the office," the major said. "We can talk about some things."

"How long do you think you might be, sir?" asked Corporal Phillipson.

"I'm not sure," Cahill said. "Give us an hour. Would that be all right, Doctor?"

"We'll make it all ry-et," said Major Iannone. "My first name is Bruno, and this is my turf."

"First of all," said the major, "how did you lose your eyesight?"

"I went blind from diabetes three months ago. My doctor in Atlanta, my eye doctor, Dr. Ghil, his name is, told me it came on faster than it usually does in people my age. And I wadn't overweight, neither, at least not too much. He couldn't explain it."

"It's a very odd dis-eus," the major said, putting his hands behind his head, stretching and leaning back. "Nobody knows why it happens to certain people, but it does run in families."

"Not in mine," Cahill said. "I never heard of the damn disease before I got it."

"How much insulin do you use?" the major asked. "How many times a day do you inject?"

"Seventy units. Around that, I think. I usually stick myself twice a day. I don't like to do it unless I start feelin' bad."

The major made as if to whistle, but did not blow. "Do you have a candy bar with you?"

"No; I carry around some sugar cubes, you know, like you put in your coffee. Never had to use one."

"About this bad feeling, this discomfort you mentioned. What is that like?"

303

"I get sleepy," Cahill said. "I get sleepy and mean and thirsty. I have to drain out a lot, and my thinkin' fogs up some. Then I drill in on my leg or my gut, and pretty soon everything comes back normal."

"You're not using enough insulin, Mr. Cahill. Not for a man who's gone blind from the dis-eus. Seventy units is not nearly enough. A hundred would be more like it; ninety at lee-est. And you ought to be more regular about what you're doing. I can tell already that you're taking a cavalier attitude about the whole thing, but you shouldn't. Diabetes is nothing to fool around with. Regularity is the main thing about treatment. You've got to live by the clock, and you've got to be accurate about what you're doing, and not leave anything to chance, or to feeling. You probably need divided units, twice a day. Why don't you do something for me?"

"Do what?"

"Come in here tomorrow and let me give you a glucose tolerance test."

"I've already had that. I'd just as soon keep my blood."

"If I could test you I could pinpoint what you need. You'd be a lot better off. Don't you know what a chance you're taking, coming up here like this, with nothing but a dog? Don't you have any other children? A wife? Friends, maybe?"

"I'm not married," Cahill said. "And I don't have no other chilrun." He realized with an instantaneous shock that he had pronounced the word as Bledsoe had done that morning, with the voices overhead. "I don't need nobody but myself."

"You ought not to be running around loose," said the major, only half jokingly. "It's not that you are sure—you are *certain*—to get into real trouble this way; you're already in real trouble, just as you sit here; you're in trouble every time the clock ticks. On that chair, you are sitting way out over the black pit, and it's infinite. It's endless, and there's no way to come back from it."

"Thanks for your interest," Cahill said, "but you can save yourself from worryin' about me. I come here to talk about my boy."

The major shook his head, at first regretfully and then sharply, to snap himself out of one attitude into another. "Hold on," he said, "and I'll get his file."

Cahill held on, listening for the major's sounds; paper was picked up and rattled, as though pages were being overleafed.

"The official story, the medical story on your son is that he was basically very healthy except for two departures, one of them external and temporary and the other internal and unpredictable, a matter of enzymes, or enzyme deficiency, or so we think."

Cahill waited. "What was the first?" he asked.

"That was the easiest," the major said. "For once I knew what to do about feet. He had seed warts, ingrown warts in the soles of his feet; real bad ones, and deep. Plantar warts."

"What causes that?"

"Physical irritation of one kind or another that people who are on their feet a lot tend to get. It used to be a kind of floorwalkers' affliction, or something that bothered postmen. Now it's shifted to the infantry. I did some time with the infantry at Fort Benning, and I saw a lot of it. Your boy had the same thing, and I suspect it had something to do with all those punishment tours he was asked to walk. Seems like every time I went by the Administration Building, he was out there walking tours. And very military he looked, too; very precise; he was giving the Air Corps what they asked for; he was not trying to get away with anything. He was a fine-looking kid, even doing something ridiculous. I'm awfully sorry we lost him, Mr. Cahill."

"I know; I hear that from a lot of people."

"Anyway," the major said, glad to change back, "he had these deep seed warts on his feet. But he came to the right place, because I had not only dealt with infantry feet, but I have discovered a solution for that particular problem brought on by numerous forty-mile hikes. If you ever get seed warts, I'll tell you what to do." He got up, went to a white cabinet, took out a roll of material, peeled back a flap of it, and handed it to Cahill. "Feel that," he said. "Both sides."

"Can't tell much," Cahill said. "It's smooth on one side and sticky on the other. Feels like a pelt, except for the glue, or whatever it is. Might be some kind of animal skin."

"It is," said the major with satisfaction. "It's not really from an animal, but it's called moleskin. That's what I do my wart cure with."

"How?" Cahill asked, fingering the flap, and wondering how it would feel to walk on it, especially for a long way. "Is this stuff white?" he asked. "I'm guessin' white."

"It is at first," Iannone said. "This piece is as white as a cloud, but the idea is to leave it on for a long time. What you do," he went on, with enthusiasm becoming real, "is to scrape up a couple of regular aspirins into powder, and clot the wart with it; clog it up, you know. Then you cut yourself a piece of moleskin and plank it down over the wart, and let the aspirin work on the place without any air. Believe me, when it's really doing the work, it's not white. After about a week it rots the wart, including the root, and you can just take and core it out, root and all, just like you would core out an apple. It doesn't hurt at all, or bleed, and it heals right up. Joel's feet were in fine shape, the last time I saw him. I didn't expect him to come back in here, at least not for forty-mile warts."

"What was the other thing?"

"The other thing," the major said, "was a dermatological malfunction, a skin thing called psoriasis. It's about as mysterious as diabetes, and in some cases it's actually harder to treat, though it's not dangerous. Only bothersome, especially in the wintertime, when there's not much real sun."

"What kind of a thing is it?" Cahill asked. "Is it like athlete's foot, or jock itch? Some kind of itch?"

"No, it does itch, a little. But athlete's foot and other things like it are fungal infections, just local. Psoriasis is general, and it comes from some sort of malfunction that makes the body generate more skin than it needs. The regulatory system, or factor, or whatever you'd call it, breaks down and lets this happen, and the skin gets rough and blotchy, and it does itch a little. The nearest thing I can compare it to is dandruff. I don't know whether . . ."

"I don't remember," Cahill said, almost smiling.

"The skin flakes off," Iannone said. "It usually has to run its course, but we go through the motions of trying to treat it. Some doctors think it's caused by an enzyme deficiency, but they don't know which enzyme."

"What do you do for it?"

"Hardly more than mumbo-jumbo," the major said. "Up until recently exposure to sunlight was supposed to be good for it. Clutching at straws, we put Joel under a sunlamp, but it didn't make any difference either way. It's just as well, because a lot of doctors are now saying that the sun is not the thing for psoriasis; that it's actually harmful to it. The only other treatment that *I* know anything about is immersion in a creosote solution; you take a bath in tar-water. He did that, too."

"Seems like you Army doctors use tar a whole lot of ways," Cahill said. "I was talking to some fellow that said you put some on his teeth. Seems like you don't use nothin' *but* tar."

"Don't sell it short. It worked out pretty well for Joel. He was only in the black stuff a few times. Pfc. Gilbeau was in charge." He got up and called out the door. "Come on in here, Gil, and tell Mr. Cahill about the black magic of creosote on scaly skin."

"What skin?" Gilbeau said, standing in the door.

"Joel Cahill's skin," the major said. "It says here that we sunk him in the black pit four times, and we kind of made out like it did some good. Actually," he turned full to Cahill, as though expecting, because of his honesty, to be forgiven, "he just wore the scales out, I think. But we like to credit the stuff off the telephone poles, because it was our idea."

Gilbeau, still holding papers, leaned against the jamb. "Well, what can I tell you? We tried to keep him down about an hour each time. He'd talk, and we'd carry on for a while, and then I'd pour in more creosote solution. From everything I'd heard about him, I thought he'd be restless, but he wasn't. He was very relaxed, and easygoing. One time he still had the moleskin patches on his feet that the major put on him, but the last time he didn't have them, as I remember."

"I told you we don't fool around, didn't I? We get 'em back up in the blue."

"Anything more?" Cahill asked.

The major broke in. "You might like to know, Mr. Cahill, that I did say something to the colonel about Joel's feet. He was making what I thought was an unnecessary hardship on the boy, with all those tours he laid on him. I thought it was unnecessary. That many of them, anyway."

"What had he done?"

"Not much of anything, is my impression. Just petty stuff having to do with the little piss-ant inspections they have around here, not keeping his foot-locker straight, say, when Lieutenant Spigner, the tac officer, popped in. A little light insubordination, a little talking back, a little insolence. He could get you told, but you could never tell exactly what he meant. Did he strike you that way, Gilbeau?"

"Yes, he did, Major. I probably talked to him more than you did, and he was certainly an unusual young guy. I never saw such an intense expression on anybody's face as there was on his. He always seemed about to say just one word that would . . . would, I'm not sure, would resolve something, would get somebody to do something that had maybe been set up: like he was always ready to say something like 'Go. All right. Go on. Do it. Get on with it. *Now.*' He seemed always getting ready to say *now,* and if you knew what it was he wanted you to do, you would do it, and you wouldn't fool around."

"What did you talk about?" Cahill asked. "You had a lot of time to talk, with him layin' there like the tar baby."

"I was in and out of the bathroom," Gilbeau said. "I didn't stay there all the time; I had other things to do. I'd just go back when I could, and see if he needed anything; get him a Coke, or whatever he wanted. He liked Fig Newtons, and ate up a couple of packages, which I bought myself; they're not S.O.P. around here."

"And you just talked about skin?" Cahill asked. "Is that all?"

"No, I don't want to give you that impression. We talked about a lot of things, but just in snatches. He had sure read a lot, and he had just an amazing memory. Everything meant something it didn't, or didn't know it meant; everything stood for something else; there was a secret behind it. Some of what he talked about sounded like religion, and some of it like psychology."

"Did he talk about the stars any?" asked Cahill on sudden impulse.

"No, I don't believe so. He talked about the human body, though in the most unlikely way I ever heard. Here I am, supposed to be dealing with bodies and their well-being, and their trouble, and I might even end up being a doctor myself, if Major Iannone doesn't disillusion me with all his malpractices. I couldn't keep up with Cadet Cahill, though."

"You may make it, Gilbeau. Just listen to what you hear in this office and tell your patients to do the opposite, and you won't even need to go to medical school."

"What did he say about his body?" Cahill asked.

"It wasn't just his he was interested in, though he sure had a good one, as quick as a knife, and always moving, even in the water. He was an example, he said, black as the middle of a cave. The first thing he used to do was to tilt his head back under water and disappear in the tub, and then come up with his hair slicked back, blacker than Al Jolson, with those super-white teeth and those eyes just a little lighter blue than anything you'd call light blue. Somebody said rattlesnakes had light blue eyes; that'd be about right. He'd come up and sit there talking about Archimedes, and Hiero's crown."

"About what?"

"Hiero's crown was an experiment in physics having to do with the displacement of liquid by mass," Major Iannone said. "Does that mean anything to you? Did you take physics in school?"

"I did, but I don't remember that. I don't think we had any royalty where I went to school."

"The story is that some king named Hiero was given a crown, and he turned it over to Archimedes, this early scientist back in the Greek days, this philosopher, and told him that he would bust his ass if he didn't find out how much gold there was in the crown, as opposed to all the other shit that was probably in it. He figured it out from lying in his bath and watching the water rise up the side when he got in and go down when he got out. That's supposed to be what made him jump out buck naked and run around the streets hollerin' Eureka."

"I never heard of that either," Cahill said.

"It means I found the son-of-a-bitch," the major said, "and he had. Saved his ass, too."

"He said you can turn in water so easily," Gilbeau said, as though he had been speaking all along, "you have another dimension. He said it was strange, and good, that in water you can support a hundred-and-sixty-pound body with one finger; he used to lie there propped up on his two thumbs, smiling away, happy as he could be, as far as I could tell. You could see just his head and toes; the rest was out of sight. His slick clean head and his toes."

"Good enough, Gil," the major said, with a flicker of irritation he did not allow until Gilbeau had turned his back. "We'll just be a few more minutes." He got up and closed the door. "There really isn't anything else," he said, coming back and glancing down at the dog.

"What about him and the other boys?" Cahill asked, leaning toward the creak of the other chair. "Zack got aholt of one of his friends, and I thought I'd go by and see him, apologize to him, if that's all right with you. The colonel thought it would be a good idea, and I'd like to do it."

"Yes," the major said, tapping his grayish-pink knee. "Joel had a group of friends, something like a little club; they went around together. Cadet Frank Spain was one, and he did get dog-bit, and it was your dog and I'm trying to save Cadet Spain from going mad, and ain't you sorry about it all?"

"I am sorry, but your cadet ain't gonna go mad, because my dog is all right."

"How do you know he's all right?" Iannone asked. "Have you cut off his head and sent it to the lab?"

"No, but he's all right, anyway. Except for jumpin' on that boy that was fightin' with that other boy, and got him all confused and excited, he's just been like he's always been. He don't go around foamin' at the mouth, and all that. He's not out to hurt nobody. He's just for me; he takes me where I take him. That's all there is to it."

"You know," said Iannone, "you might not believe it, and I might not believe it, but I was a boy once myself. I can remember a little about being that age, what you do, the attitudes you take, the things you focus on."

"Is that somethin' you feel like you got to apologize for?"

"No, not exactly. But it takes some understanding, after you've grown out of it. I don't have any children, myself; I'm my own boy, and I'm losing him. I just barely remember, but I do remember."

"Remember what? Why was it so different?"

"I don't know why it is," the major said, "but it is. I'm not a psychiatrist, but in a sense every doctor has to deal with the way people act, and the way they act is based on what they think. Boys like to get together in groups, and be against. They like secrets. They like knowing things that nobody else knows. You'd think that young fellows in the Army, especially the Air Corps, and most especially the pilots and other air crew, and the air crew trainees, would think of themselves as being part of the most powerful and spectacular elite in the world. But some of them don't; a few of them don't. That's not what they want. They're against the others; the others that are not them."

"What do they want? Are you talkin' about Joel, and maybe this Spain? Is that it?"

"Mostly they want to be to themselves, they want to take things in their own way, and interpret them in a way that's like, well, like make-believe. And, yes, I am talking about Joel and his bunch. Spain was one of them, and he was hard hit when Joel was killed, I can tell you. He's better now, though: your dog's biting him might even have been therapeutic. I keep telling you, there's some things I don't know about the upkeep of people. I cure 'em with the stuff off telephone poles. That's my play. All the rest of this so-called therapy is just sugar water."

"There seems to be somethin' about the situation that you don't like, Doctor," Cahill said. "What could it be? Didn't you like my boy havin' his friends?"

"I didn't mind that; of course not," the major said. "I do like it. One of the main attitudes the Air Corps tries to promote is team pride, dependency, *esprit de corps*, and all that. If you have enough *esprit de corps*, and follow orders, the thing turns into what used to be called duty, and everybody gets satisfied, including your country. Question is, whose orders?" He went on. "We've started to get back a good many reports from overseas outfits; the first class that went through here is only a few months from being ready to cross over the ocean, either the east one or the west one. We read *Stars and Stripes*, and the other service newspapers, and you can't help noticing the tremendous pride in organizations there is: in wings and squadrons, and in crews. The smaller the outfit, the more spirit there is in it, the more it insists on its own identity. The names of the airplanes, themselves, is a case in point—*Memphis Belle, Franklin Freight.* The Americans who come in contact with the British end up by acting like them and talking like them. They don't do it among the British, but they do it among the other Americans, as a sign of their own uniqueness, their exclusiveness, their particular kind of group identity, their I've-got-something-you-haven't. There's a lot of cultism in the service, Mr. Cahill. A whole lot. It's one of the things that makes wars possible, armies possible, like football teams. If you're in a large group more or less against your will, a certain kind of man—most especially a certain kind of boy—will form his own group within that, and have his own say, his own secrets, his own friends, and his own rules."

Cahill shifted in his chair and took hold of the floor through his shoes, gripping hard. "How did you come to know all this?" he asked. "How much more do you know than you're tellin' me?"

"I don't know anything more, and I don't believe there is anything. I was just struck by the extraordinary hold your son had over some of these other boys. There wasn't anything sinister about it, but it was very marked, very obvious."

"Sinister?" Cahill said sharply, believing at once that the word would not have come into the conversation without good reason, without being a slip he could catch.

"I didn't say it was sinister," Iannone answered. "I'm saying cults can be sinister. They become sinister when they last, when they pick up influence." He hesitated, then said, "When they have a leader, especially of a certain type."

"What type?"

"Who doesn't question himself. Who knows beyond any proof that he can't be wrong."

Cahill was more disturbed than he had been since the first panic of total blindness. Talking to the flight surgeon, he had come to feel that the major was the first really adult person, the first with any usable judgment, any power of understanding and interpreting situations, that he had come across since he had left Atlanta, and he could think of no way to get from him any further information or opinion; he shifted again and plunged his hand into the pocket where the spring grip was. He found this and fastened on it, tightening his fist and his jaw muscles at the same time, again counting.

The major gazed intently at Cahill's face, and changed the subject. "It takes about seventy-five people on the ground to put one man in the air," he said. "All the ones on the ground, including the officers, are automatic slaves, inferiors. Technically I'm not one, but really I am. These wings on my chickenhearted chest are not real wings; they won't fly, and they sure God won't fight. The Air Corps is foolish to give me flying pay, but they do, and I take it, because I'd be just as foolish not to. All I do is get in my four hours a month with the colonel in his AT-6, but that's not really flying; that's sandbagging, deadheading. I no more belong in that vehicle than I do in the car of Apollo going across the sky, when something like a human creature was driving it, before it got smart and changed into the sun. Excuse me," he said parenthetically, "that's my literary education, and about all I remember. It's sort of like my American history education at Duke, when I was an undergraduate. All I can remember about American history is Fifty-four Forty or Fight, Don't Tread on Me, and the Whiskey Rebellion, although what whiskey ever did to be rebelled against, I never did figure out. I don't rebel against it, I do something else."

Cahill sat silent, believing that there was enough momentum in the major's line of talk to carry it past his lack of response.

"I dread that four hours every month," the major went on. "The airplane is so rigid, it is so entirely rigid around you. I don't know what else I expect it might be, but the rigidity is the first thing I noticed about being in an aircraft, and I still can't shake it off. It's not like the rigidity of a car, because when you're in the air you feel—or I feel—completely unsupported. I always ask the colonel to fly straight and level when I go up with him, because any maneuver, even a turn in the traffic pattern, is just about too much for me. I don't suppose you would want to try to understand this," he said, "but the idea of the whole earth tilting up like it does when you turn is so disturbing that, once you've seen it, once you've been in on it, you never come back to believing there's any stability in life. If that can happen in the air, it can happen anywhere. Your mind itself can turn like that; your mind is the last place you can be safe. I wish I had never been off the ground. My part of flying is a farce. I wish it wasn't, but it is."

Cahill rose, and Zack with him. "If you'll show me where the victim of the wild-dog attack is hidin' out," Cahill said, stamping his foot for circulation, "I'll go say hello to him. Me and Zack would like to apologize, and offer blood. We'll give him some of Zack's blood. Think he'd like that?"

312

"I'm sure he would," said the major. "It'll make him big and mean and hairy, instead of little and mean and hairy. Don't tell him I said that." He went to the door and signaled. "Front and center, Corpsman Gilbeau. Take this man back to look at exhibit A, animal crimes against sky-blue personnel."

Gilbeau snapped to an exaggerated military posture and saluted palm out, as though British.

"Good-bye, Major," Cahill said. "You've helped me a lot, more than anybody else."

"I didn't do much," said the major. "I just have to keep coming back to what I said before. It's hard to lose people. I was really shook by what happened; I still am. I can still see that boy in all that creosote, can still see his big thin feet, with new moleskin on them."

"No more," Cahill said. "No more. They tell me they'll find him, but I won't be here. This is all I want. Just through Sunday. I told Shears and Harbelis and some of the others I would stay. Maybe I'll run into you again. Are you comin' to the parade?"

"I have to," the major said, "otherwise I wouldn't. I'll look for you out there. That would be one good thing."

"We could go along now," Gilbeau said, at Cahill's side.

"Don't get back there and stand around, Gilbeau," the major said. "The Air Corps flies through this office on paper, and we've got to keep them pale little wings fluttering, on . . . on . . . and"—he made a loud raspberry noise with his tongue—"until they call the whole thing off."

Gilbeau opened a back door, and he and Cahill and the dog went through it into a long wooden tunnel lit by bare bulbs in wire cages. There was curious stirring of air that came back in their faces as they went along it, Gilbeau a half-step ahead, between solid banks of filing cabinets that extended almost out of sight. "We call this the wind tunnel," Gilbeau said. "The air in here is always moving, for some reason; nobody knows where it comes from. We keep all the records here, but we're either going to have to find some other place for them, or we're going to have to make the tunnel longer. Only a couple of classes, and all the space we've got is full of paper. So far we've been able to keep all of it in here, out of the weather, but we can't do it much longer. I keep trying to transfer out, because I have to spend most of my time in this goddamn tunnel, and it's about to drive me berserk. Here," he said, "feel this."

There was the sound of a metal drawer being pulled, and then he had hold of a stack of paper. The slight flow of air riffled the top sheet, and as he half listened to Gilbeau he set himself to sympathize with what the other was saying, but not with much attention, for he understood from the beginning that the situation would not, did not, have the same effect on him. He had learned that in order to discount an idea, a point of view, an attitude, he had at least to make a show of understanding it, and he did this now with the paper making its small flittering as he turned it slightly away from and toward the oncoming air. In it there was indeed a feeling of fragility, of something that could be crushed, but must not be, and he stood holding it, being careful despite himself, and now listening more fully, thinking a little of the other, who feared this vulnerable, almost bodiless shaking, and who was stuck with it day after day, life after life.

"Sometimes you have to hunt up things, hunt for the right page of somebody's file, but back here, with that little wind, the information on these guys is never really still. The air is always trying to turn the page on you," Gilbeau said. "It's uncanny, like the paper was trying to get loose from you, like it had some kind of life that it didn't have in the file case, that starts up just as soon as you open it. I'm where I can hardly get myself to put my hand inside one of those cabinets, like there was a snake in there, or something, because I know I'm going to have to bring it out and feel that paper rattle in my hand, until my hand is shaking worse than the paper. This might not bother anybody else, but it does me; these are people's lives, you know. The only thing I can do is to take the file back into the office, and then when the major's finished with it, bring it back, but that makes for so much extra legwork that we get further behind than we were before. I'm looking to get out, but I don't know if I ever will. The major can't see any reason for me to transfer, and this tunnel would not seem to the Air Corps much of a reason, either."

Gilbeau replaced the file, and they went on, the planks giving a little, Zack's paws ticking. Then a hand, Gilbeau's surely, held him gently but forcibly back. The tone of the voice was not exasperated, as a moment before, but low and sincere, and came with some urgency. "If you want," Gilbeau said, "and if you can make time, it may be possible for me to see you without the major. I can't talk in front of him."

"Talk now," Cahill said. "I wouldn't think anybody could hear you. Ain't nobody here but these records, from what you tell me. I don't hear nothin'; I don't feel nobody around. Zack don't either. Go ahead."

"Not enough time," Gilbeau said. "I don't need a lot, but this is not enough. I can't explain. I will later. There was some of Joel's talk you ought to know about."

"Okay," Cahill said, put out more than suited him. "I'll be on the base again tomorrow, and I'll get Harbelis or somebody to bring me by."

"No," Gilbeau said. "Town would be better. Tonight, maybe?"

"Not tonight," Cahill said. "I have to eat some big hominy and greens and some other stuff I can just barely put up with. I wish I could have got hold of you sooner. But I'll check in with you again."

They walked on and broke out, through a canvas curtain into the sunny sick bay, still, warm, and white.

There seemed to be better boards underfoot. Though Cahill tested them by walking slowly, and putting all his weight on each foot, they did not give. For the first time since he had been blind, however, he realized that what he feared was not coming upon an obstacle that he had no notion was there, or of stepping off the edge of something, but that the surface he stood or sat upon—or, more intensely, with him—that he walked upon, would give way, for any reason or for no reason, and he was for the first time acutely aware that this apprehension was not a result of his blindness; that he had always had it, though not to this extent. Perhaps this was what his boyhood skating had meant, had

"We'll have to go all the way down to the other end," said Gilbeau. "Spain is down there with a couple of his friends. Go right along; there's plenty of room. This is a big bay, and not many in it."

There were five boys in sight, grouped in low wide cots on either side. Two of them, both sitting on the same bed and facing toward the entrance, watched Cahill carefully as he and Gilbeau approached and passed them. Farther down, under a window just beneath the eave of the bay, the three cadets did not notice until Cahill was past the first two. Then the boy with the bandaged leg, lying on the GI spread, lifted his hand and pointed. The other two turned, and all three smiled with

included. This—one of his main memories, his most heartening resources of motion—came back to him once more as he paced down the ward with Gilbeau, feeling the streets of Atlanta fall away beneath him in long hills which he crouched down like a skier. But all the time under his rolling feet there was something that went with him, that matched his exact position and velocity; it was understood between him and whatever hurtled, buried, down Lindbergh Drive, whatever took the blind flat curves of Rivers Road with him, that it was his speed on the surface that kept the surface intact, that kept his pursuer barely contained by the fragile stiff pitted skin down which he fled. His spirits moved upward with the memory, but something about it was changed, and he tried to catch what it was. He should have been more apprehensive with blindness, now that he moved in such a considered way, almost in slow motion, without his body-speed to protect him, but this floor, here and now, not only felt solid to him but was indeed solid, with nothing haunting through, nothing underneath matching him step for step, and threatening.

Not underfoot. What had been with him was still there, or was a new thing, but with him, not silent anymore, and not buried. It the same slow smile. Gilbeau did not matter; slowly the blind man in his heavy coat, half-smashed hat and black-green glasses came on with his huge head-down dog. The two cadets who could stand faced him, relaxed though almost at positions of attention. They did not look at one another, but nodded and waited.

The blind man had stopped, or almost stopped. For the first time the cadets looked at each other, and the shorter of the two un-

316

might be able to make the sigh of the landing aircraft sinking into the forest, as McCaig had said it seemed to do, when seen from the highway. Or would that be it? His hair prickled at the lower edge of his baldness. Would it? From somewhere above him, maybe now, maybe at the next step, maybe before he could say anything to the boys he was approaching, might it, could it be possible that McLendon's rabbit scream would shudder, would split him wide open? Or would it be that he would scream like that, so that his pursuer could find him, fall to him? He was not sure, now, that he would be able to speak at all, even though he had to; despite all his will, he did not know that he would not scream. But was the sound, was the pursuit, was the air so entirely terrible? What place was this? Were there rafters here?

Cahill held the squarish hand, but did not imagine. "You'all are just like me," he said, mostly past his fear now. "You done

wounded ones started forward, but was restrained by the other. Cahill seemed to be listening to something they could not hear, and then, slowly and deliberately he turned his face upward and swung his head very carefully from side to side, no expression on his face, then lowered it, put one foot forward, placed the other before it, and came at them once more.

Gripping Malcolm Shears by the web belt, Cadet Spain swung his white leg over the side of the bed and sat between the other two.

"Welcome to the rear area," Shears said, with his arm around a short strong boy with blond hair so curly it looked as though it had been singed. "I want you to meet Cadet Ira Lew Adler, the Jewish eagle."

"Nearsighted," Cadet Adler said. "Nearsighted Jewish eagle."

come to see the boy that Zack got
after. Is he here, or have I ended
up in the wrong place again?"

"I'm right here, Mr. Cahill," Spain said, hitching himself around,
"and I ain't a damn bit afraid of your dog."

"No need," Cahill said. "He won't bother you. I'm real sorry about
this, son. It was just a accident. He was confused, you know, because he
was in a strange place, with all the noise, and all. I'm sorry you have to
take those shots."

"It's not all that bad," Spain said. "I get a long needle in the stomach,
when the clock says so. Not so bad; the needle's not square, like some of
them."

"I know what you mean," Cahill said. "I get a needle in the stomach,
too, but it's short. The clock's supposed to be in on it, but I don't always
come on time." He waited, searching for a transition. "The colonel,
over yonder, tells me that you're not gonna be able to graduate on
Sunday. I feel like it's my fault. Will you be out there?"

"Not flying," Spain answered, "but I'll be there." He paused and
grinned. "I'll come if you will."

"Bein' held back," Cahill said, wanting reassurance, "that don't seem
to bother you much, not going out with your class."

"It don't bother me a-tall," Spain said. "I'll catch up with the rest of
'em, somewhere else; maybe in Transition or RTU, in the States, maybe
overseas."

"And you don't think there's any chance you might bust out, wash
out, or whatever you'all call it?"

"Not any," Spain said. "You can rest easy. It's like the Japanese
weight lifter at the Olympics, who was going for the gold, and lifting for
the world's record. He looked at the weight down at his feet, and
somebody asked him why he seemed so confident. 'It's already lifted,'
he said. That's the way we do things, in Peckover and everywhere."

"And it is," said the cadet colonel. He turned to Gilbeau. "You can
head on back, Gil," he said. "We'll bring Mr. Cahill out with us."

When Gilbeau had disappeared through the curtain, Shears sat on
the bed beside Cadet Spain. "How much time can you give us?" he
asked matter-of-factly.

"How much do you want?"

"We need to see you Saturday, maybe Saturday night. And in town.
Anywhere there's a blank wall. This is important."

318

"Saturday night." Cahill thought. "Saturday night. I could do that. What do you mean about a wall? What wall?"

"Just a wall. We'll tell you. There'll be about fifteen of us. We need a blank wall and an electrical outlet. How about the place where you're staying?"

"I'll ask. The guy's got some rooms he don't use much, and he's got a shed outside, where he keeps his deer meat, and the hogs he's shot."

"That'll be all right," Shears said. "Should be fine."

"You'd better fill me in, son. You're way ahead of me."

"No, I'm not," Shears said. "And we'll tell you; don't worry about that. Can you, also, make us a little time tomorrow morning? This could be on the base. Classes are over, flying's over, mostly. Could you get together with us in the morning, about nine? In Second Barracks?"

"I guess I could," Cahill said.

"We'll meet you at the door, at nine o'clock."

"You sure will," Cahill said. "I think you're all crazy."

"Maybe," said Cadet Adler. "You be there, and we'll tell you about it."

Cahill made as if to look around the ward. "Where's the other boy that got hurt?" he asked. "The one was in the fight with you?"

"That asshole," Spain said, as though with commonplace knowledge. "His name is Willis, and he wasn't hurt bad enough to get put in here. If he was in here, I wouldn't be. He's just a dung-heel. If your dog hadn't grabbed me, I would've put him in here sure enough."

"He's lucky to be alive," Shears said with a conviction whose cold frankness Cahill struggled to assimilate.

"What on earth was wrong?" Cahill asked. "What were you fightin' about?"

"He wanted something we didn't want to give him. Nobody ever asked him to do a damn thing. We didn't even know he was alive."

"Well, I'm glad he didn't get hurt. I held him up for a while, there, you know."

"You were the only thing that did," Spain said. "I ain't very big, but I'm wound up tight. I was fixing to uncoil on him."

"It's over now," Shears said. "You don't ever have to think about Cadet Willis again, Mr. Cahill. He'll stay to himself."

"I guess I'd better get goin'," Cahill said. "I did more walkin' than I'm used to this morning. Me and Zack are tired out."

"Where were you?" Spain asked, leaning forward. "Were you where we think you were?"

319

"I was out where there was a big fire. McCaig took me; he said it was like a big black farm, black everywhere you could see."

"The plane's not still there, is it?" Adler asked.

"No," said Cahill. "We went where it had done been."

"They didn't bring it back here," Shears said. "We'd've seen it. Nobody will tell us where they took it."

"Maybe it don't matter," Cahill said. "Maybe it's not any of your business."

"They think it ain't," Spain said. "The colonel and them others."

"Did you and McCaig find anything?" Shears asked.

"McCaig found this," Cahill said, bringing out the fused zipper. "This was at the fence that runs between the farmer's land and the county's. It's farther—a lot farther—than anybody said Joel ought to be able to go. That's where this was, buried in the ashes."

Shears took the zipper, and the others crowded to him. Adler touched it. "I know what this is, if you don't," he said.

"It's what it is," Shears said with finality.

"Did Joel know anybody besides you? Besides the people at the base?" Cahill asked.

"He knew some others," said Shears, nodding his head seriously. "A few. There were a few civilians he trusted. He kept those separate, though. The main thrust was the military prong. It still is. We're essential, the guts of it."

"At the fence," Spain said. "All the way to the fence, through the fire. How far was it?"

"Half a mile," Cahill said. "And there was plenty of fire. Like to have burned the farmer and his wife and chilrun up. They were real lucky; the fire went around 'em, and on past to the river."

Reluctantly Shears handed the zipper back to Cahill, but instead of putting it away he continued to hold it, and went back to his pocket with the other hand. "This too," he said, bringing out the piece of wire. "McCaig says this might'a come off one of the wings, or was maybe in between the wings. See what you think."

Shears took the wire, and the cadets examined it and felt it. "Could be," said Adler. "Looks about right. Where was this?"

"Where the plane was," Cahill said. "Where they hauled it off from. I got this and the zipper out yonder, and I got this earlier. The colonel gave it to me. Joel left it in the farmer's house, and somebody from the base picked it up and brought it in." He held out the cracked goggles and strap.

Cahill waited in the heavy silence; he felt for Zack with his foot. "That's what I've got," he said. "That's all there is, that anybody has, from him and the plane he was in."

"You're carrying them all," Adler said. "Damned if you're not."

"That's right," Cahill said, with an energy that surprised him.

"We won't ask you for those," Shears said, handing back the goggles. "Bring them Saturday." He thought. "Bring them Saturday, and bring them tomorrow morning, too. I want some other people to see what we've just seen, and to hear what you and Double-Mac did out yonder; what it was like. You talked to the farmer, did you? And you can tell these others what he said?"

"I can tell 'em," Cahill said speaking with as much formality as he could command. "I'll tell whoever you want, but right now I got to go along." He put out his hand.

"This is the way we do it," Shears said. "This is for public occasions, when just about anybody could be around."

His hand was taken firmly, but strangeness quickly became part of the contact when he felt a finger encircling the lower joints of his thumb, and another finger splitting between his ring and little fingers. Before he could summon his own grip, he was withdrawn from.

"And this is for private use. This is when everybody understands what's going on."

His hand was raised by another to shoulder level; his thumb was encircled by a whole hand, and in order to respond he had to encircle the other thumb. He stood with Shears for a moment

Facing into the dark of Cahill's glasses, Shears stood firm, smiling, as in a friendly contest. Adler brought his feet together and unfolded his arms, and Spain clasped his hands together and

321

in a silence different from any others, with a sensation like a terrified singing suddenly a part of him, a singing at once solid and disembodied, and composed both of an essential part of himself and that part connected outside with something that took him in. He made no effort to free himself, but when the pressure lessened he let his hand down as the other disengaged. "All right," he said. "I'll see you Saturday."

"I've heard it," Cahill said. "I'll be there."

shook them softly as though at the conclusion of a bargain with himself.

"No," Shears said. "Don't forget. Tomorrow. At Second Barracks, where the long glass shakes in the wind."

Corporal Phillipson was waiting for him in Major Iannone's office. Cadet Adler, who had come back with him through the unequal air of the corridor, left him, and he and Phillipson and the lagging dog started through the heavy trees toward the motor pool.

As he walked it struck Cahill that he would have been bluffing if he had told Phillipson that he considered himself now, after three days on the base, on more or less familiar ground. It was true that he had been over this particular part of the base before, going one way or the other in perhaps these exact steps, but he knew also—had learned—that a blind man's feet can never become that well educated; there is always something in front of him he could not know about, could not remember with any exactness, that has grown there unbeknownst to him, or been put there. He had not done so much walking in the three months of his blindness as he had in the last three days, and now fatigue, and the enormous weight—the inertia that blindness puts on the blind, the inevitable and apprehensive physical effort—of the future, of all the distances he would have to try to negotiate, lay on him like a just manageable vast heaviness filled with sleeplike and hopeless depression. The full barren precariousness of his existence with Zack came over him. There is no doubt, he said silently to himself, that I will get to the motor pool; that this patient boy whose face I will never succeed in seeing will make sure that I make it, and he will also drive me and my dog back to town, where I will, trying to keep from being helped by anybody but myself, get down from the vehicle and go in, where I will maybe run into McLendon, and maybe go up to my room and inject myself with insulin. In three days I will leave, will get on the bus and go back to Atlanta. What then? To his surprise, both cutting through his depression and increasing his sense of the uncertainty of the rest of his life, he realized that in a sense he was being taken care of by the personnel on the base: by the officers, by the enlisted men and the civilian instructors, by the cadets and the medical personnel: that he was living, for these few days, under what amounted to privileged conditions. It was true; he acknowledged it: his time at Peckover was a period he would never repeat. Everything after this, everything else may be nothing, he thought, with a rise—a slight form of it—of the interest he had come to depend on since his blindness, as part of an agreement with himself that he understood the structure of events pertaining to him: that his presence at the base was the center of a block of experience fraught with special meanings and significances, implicit with disclosures, but this brief lift was buried again in desolation, as he realized that whatever was to be revealed to him would have to come from someone else, someone who revealed it of his own will, and for his own purposes. Again he concentrated on his steps, one before the other; they were all familiar, and all unfamiliar, all the same, but he took no confidence or comfort from his belief that the man alongside him would not allow him to step off the edge of what was underfoot, or an obstacle be placed directly in his path, or a new tree grow.

They cleared the trees and came out in the sandy circle of the motor pool, where a line of jeeps, an ambulance, four weapons carriers, two six-by-sixes, and a yellow Deere tractor sat in lines opposing the large vehicles to the small. Several civilian cars were parked haphazardly, out of the way of the military transport, and from one, a '34 Ford, McCaig turned, straightened, smiled at Phillipson as though he could not believe what he saw coming out of the woods, and met them at the edge of the raked sand, where the pine needles ended.

"What say?" McCaig said, believing, hoping that Cahill would recognize his voice.

"Doin' good," Cahill said. "Did you get the ashes off?"

"I did," McCaig said. "I beat 'em all off. You look okay, too. And Zack done left his ghost out yonder where we was; he looks just like he always did." He glanced at the sun, and then at his watch. "You goin' home now?"

"What else?" Cahill said. "I'm walked out."

"You want to come over to the Link Trainer with me for a minute or two? Won't take long. I'll drive you on back."

"The what?"

"I need to see the guy that runs the Link Trainer, over in the back hangar. I have to clear the base when this class leaves, and I need to have some Link time certified, so I can go up to Canada, and get in with them long-eared creatures that hear what they can't see. I'm bound and determined to fly on the night side—the bat side—of this war, and the best way to get into it is with a lot of instrument time, which you can't get at a Primary Training Base, except on the Link Trainer."

"I don't know if I can, Mac," Cahill said. "I'd prob'ly just be in your way."

"Naw, you wouldn't," said McCaig good-naturedly, really wanting him to come. "It's not far from here; eighty steps, maybe ninety. And you can sit down while I talk to the guy for just a little minute, and then we'll run back to town and have a beer."

"All right," Cahill said reluctantly. "I can't get too much tireder. Remember, I've got to go out to that girl's tonight."

"What girl?" McCaig asked. "Joel's girlfriend? Everybody's girl?"

"Her name is Hannah somethin'," Cahill said defensively. "She seems all right."

"Sure," McCaig said, finding satisfaction. "She's a good girl. She's rougher'n a night in jail in south Georgia. But there's nothin' wrong with south Georgia, the parts I been in."

"Anyway," Cahill said, "that's where I'm goin', so leave me some energy. It's gettin' cold again. I lose energy that way; blind people shrivel up when it gets cold."

"Take off, Phillipson," McCaig said, and touched Cahill's arm with more forthrightness than he had at any time before. "Come on," he said. "It's warm in yonder, and dark as hell. Maybe there's some more cadets in there you can talk to, while I get my forms all stamped and straightened out."

Persuading himself that he was dazed with fatigue, but actually finding something like a second wind, Cahill trudged over the pebbles until McCaig opened what sounded like a heavy door; there was a skreak of metal in it, and a pounding when it closed.

The silence around him, a very whole silence, was electrical, and was not quite silence. His grammar school civics class had once taken a tour to the Atlanta waterworks, where the enormous green turbines, bolted into the cement floor, had run on and on, and he had stood among the other children, not listening to the foreman's or his teacher's explanation, but to the strange hum from the machines that surrounded him, and touched the back of the throat of his closed mouth as though that part of his body responded, and was perhaps itself giving back an equal vibration, a signal it had kept for this. The sound here was like that, but more closed, and as he listened it lessened and increased, still authoritative but with a suggestion of tilting, or suspension, hanging: something very large.

In the small, insulated room, an oblong of heavy cement floor and acoustic-paneled walls, the darkness was almost complete, except for what could be shown by the one red bare bulb in the wall, under which sat Cadet Stathis Harbelis, his grommetless hat on the back of his head and the ring of steel grommet in his hand like a tambourine. The bulb showed also, ending out of sight, a desk with a clipboard of forms, a filing cabinet, and part of a fastidious metal table on which a mechanical pen traced slowly over a map. A wide-faced, narrow-shouldered three-stripe sergeant straightened from the table, pushed one foam-rubber earphone forward from his ear, and looked at McCaig questioningly.

"This is Mr. Frank Cahill from Atlanta," McCaig said, suiting his voice to the sound, and hearing it come out gravely, as though he were in a hospital. "Joel Cahill's father."

Sergeant Garber did not hold out a hand when Cahill didn't, but pushed the other earphone back and swallowed. "I'm sorry," he said.

"Everybody's sorry," Cahill said, tired of official expressions of what were supposed to be human feelings. Impatient enough to do so, he nearly said something to this effect, already framing the words "it won't do." But what would be better? What did he expect?

When no one offered him a chair, or indicated where there was one, he usually leaned, and he did so now, finding the wall easily and concentrating not on the voices spaced dimly beyond him, but on the profound humming, inclining his head in the ways in which he thought the tilts went, might be going.

"Who is it?" Cahill asked, nudging Zack, who was beginning to seem disturbed, with his foot, and reaching down for him with his hand.

"I didn't know him," Sergeant Garber said. "I hardly ever get out of the dark, out of the Peckover red-light district: one red light and no whores."

"I wouldn't say that," said Mc-Caig, winking with the light red eyelid the room gave him. "You been grazin' with the sheep yet, over in Three Hangar? They tell me you can bury yourself in all kinds of wool, in there."

"That's the colonel's business," Garber said. "You better stay out of his woolpack." Settling the earphones back in place, he went back to the table, watched the slow, definite needle, and made a note on a clipboarded form.

"Frank," McCaig said loudly. "Here's a friend of yours from the outside world. He don't want to bother what it is you're thinkin' about, over there by the switch panel."

"It's me," Harbelis said. "Swift-footed Achilles, the Greek streak. I just got out of the Link, and I'm waiting to see how much better I

The humming died, and at the same time the room came level, or the object that had tilted came level with it. A door somewhere a little above his head opened, and another person apparently descended to the floor.

Even when he had been eager to assimilate, or to give the impression that he was, when he first came to the base, when he had talked to the two combat captains over the wild meat, Cahill had not been able to keep his attention from drifting. He was by now thoroughly tired of talk about flying, of having its special terms explained to him. Only a few images remained with him: McCaig's described aircraft sighing into the forest, Faulstick's headless gunner overhead and the orange blink that had killed him, and Joel's aircraft, close to the ground in heavy smoke: a

did than this other guy."

Sergeant Garber, who had just spoken into a hand mike and pushed back his earphones in time to hear, said, "A whole lot better. And he's not bad, either." He spoke into the microphone again.

"Too many people in here," Sergeant Garber said. "It's all right when one's in the Link, but when everybody stands around it's crowded with five."

"You know I tore up your problem," the cadet just out of the Trainer said, picking up his stiff hat from the dark part of the table.

"Not all that good," Sergeant Garber said. "Most of your flight was pretty accurate. Your climb was good, and your descent was just about the same. But you messed up on your procedure turn. Look right here." The cadet, straightening his cap, bent over the table and followed Garber's finger. "You didn't meet yourself coming back. This line ought to run right back over this other line. You not only didn't come right out on a hundred and eighty degrees, you actually set up a diverging angle. You've got to be able to fly an accurate reciprocal. If you can't do that, you're going to fuck yourself."

"I passed, though?" the cadet

327

body with two wings and wheels which, even as he called them to mind, hit the black ground and broke off.

With the machine off, Cahill found himself unpleasantly open to the discord between the two young voices. Without wanting to, he sided with Bobo, who had not, he felt, provoked Harbelis's tone, or his attitude. He had persuaded himself that it would be easier for a blind man to keep things uncomplicated, to promote simplicity on the part of others in his presence, to cow them into it, but it was not so. It was harder, a lot harder; this, too.

Cahill asked his usual question, understanding that the other was uncomfortable. "Did

asked. "I thought that was my best ride in the Link."

"It was your best ride," Garber said, looking at his board. "And you did pass, but you better true 'em up in Basic. If you can't make a procedure turn by the time you finish Basic, you'll go right out through the machine, the Messerschmitt Maytag."

"Good, Bobo," Harbelis said, swinging his feet. "You might make it in the heavies. Or maybe ATC."

"Hold back, boys," McCaig said. "Bobo, I got somebody I want you to meet."

"I know who you are, sir," Cadet Bobo said. "I didn't know your son very well, but I'm sorry what happened, happened. I'm sorry he did what he did."

"Bobo, you know what Joel said about you?" Harbelis said.

"No," Bobo said, "and maybe you better not tell me. Not in here, anyway."

"He said that you could fly an airplane better if you just spent all your time up there playing switch-finger."

"Take it slow, silver-heels," McCaig said. "Take it slow."

"I'll explain later," Harbelis said to Cahill. "Bobo knows what I'm talking about."

you know my boy, here?" he asked. "I mean, at all?"

Cadet Bobo looked questioningly at Sergeant Garber, and then at Harbelis, who had folded his arms and was swinging only one foot. "I knew who he was," he said.

"That all?" Cahill said, forcing.

"I did; I did know who he was." He paused and drew breath. "I stayed away from him. I was not like Harbelis and Spain and Blazek and them. I was not in his flight, or his section. I just saw him go by, every now and then. I saw him walking tours, out in front of the Administration Building. He was there a lot of the time."

"Stayed away from him?" Cahill asked, certain that he was closing in on something. "A lot of 'em around here, they didn't stay away from him."

"That's their business," Bobo said. "Harbelis and Shears can tell you about that part of it." He looked at Sergeant Garber with the red shadow of the light around him, but not at Harbelis, who now had both feet down. "I didn't need him," Bobo said. "I can fly all right by myself."

"Switch-finger," said Harbelis, from under his visor pulled down low.

"Fuck off, Harbelis," Bobo said. "Close down. Leave me alone."

"You'all can do that some other time," Cahill said. "This ain't givin' me nothin'. You're just goin' back and forth. Save it for after I leave."

"Time to go, Bobo," Harbelis said. "Time's up. Basic's waiting for you, the Vultee Vibrator. An all-rudder airplane. Watch your torque on takeoff. Hold rudder, like they tell you: full right, but not quite. Trouble you won't have, and fly you will not."

"We'll see," Bobo said, putting on his rigid cap. "We'll see how we all do."

The temperature changed, and the air, one puff of it from another place, and then changed back; Cahill understood that Bobo had gone.

"And that's all of that," said Harbelis. "I'll let him get clear, and then I'll take off myself."

"What did you get on him for?" Cahill asked. "He do something to you?"

"No," Harbelis said, "he never did anything to me. He's just exactly what the Air Corps wants. But he ain't what we want; he ain't what I want."

"He's okay," said Sergeant Garber, a little irritated. "I wish all of 'em would try to do what you tell 'em to do, and try as hard as he does."

"That's his trouble," Harbelis said. "He's a perfect system-slave; they've got him on all sides. He's in the institutional lock, if you know what I mean."

"I don't know what you mean, but he flies a pretty fair Link mission."

"Wait till he gets into the real stuff. There's a line between the ones that fly like monkeys that men teach how to fly, and the way monkeys would fly if they had their own airplanes. I mean airplanes that they made, themselves."

"That'll be the day," Sergeant Garber said, turning to McCaig. "I've got to dig around a little for your records, Mac. Talk a minute, and excuse me while I hunt."

"You know what a gibbon is?" Harbelis asked Sergeant Garber as he bent toward one of the filing cabinets. "You ever been to the zoo?"

"Don't know what you mean," said Garber, pulling out a dim drawer.

"Gibbons are black monkeys with long arms. Very long arms, Sergeant, and big hands."

"Times I've been to the zoo," Sergeant Garber said, still stooping and peering, thumbing folders, "I didn't like what I saw the monkeys doing with their big hands."

"Watch them do something else, next time," Harbelis said. "Gibbons have an enormous leverage on their bodies. They also have a great loose rhythm. Next time, stand there and watch them swing, and something will break in on you."

"Uh-huh," said Garber, from the low darkness.

"Whatever the gibbon has got hold of is already something else; it's the next thing he's going to have hold of. The present thing is not *being* replaced by the next thing he's going to catch; it already *is* the next thing, and the next thing after that is already coming into place, coming at him, coming to him. There's no way that it can't come, or that he would miss it. His catching it is not only built into his body and his rhythm, but it's built into the branch or the limb or the part of a wall that he takes into the rhythm. His whole environment gives itself to him in the rhythm, it flows around him, everything is linked, everything is together for him, and is part of his motion, it's all flow and it's all him, as long as he keeps it up. You better watch, Sergeant Garber, or else you'll be missing part of your life, something that could have been."

Bothered by an approach to the body other than his own, and remembering Ruíz swimming in his T-shirt, passing through the wool-green of the underwater lights like a shadow, Cahill said, outward and down toward Garber, "You never did tell me whether you knew my boy, Sergeant."

Garber stood up, not holding a folder. McCaig shifted so that Garber's head was held in the bulb's subtle, conspiratorial light; this is the closest I'll ever come to making movies, he thought.

"I never laid eyes on him but once," Garber said. "He came in here and argued with me about his time on the Link."

"I didn't know that," McCaig said. "I thought he had all his time in—all kind of time—except for maybe two or three hours' flyin'."

"He didn't have it," Sergeant Garber said. "He was only in the Trainer one time."

"How did he do?" Harbelis asked.

331

"He did fair," Garber said. "About like Bobo, or maybe a little better. He didn't seem to have much interest in it. He wanted to get out and argue about his time."

"What about his time?"

"He said that he'd arranged to get it all in at once, before graduation, and I told him I couldn't do it that way. All the slots where he was supposed to come in here and fly these Link missions are blank. I never did hear any more from him. I let the colonel know, and he never said anything to me either."

"What's your explanation?" McCaig asked.

"I don't have any," Garber said. "When he left, he told me he didn't trust the Link, and I told him he'd better." He stooped again to the file, and said, over his shoulder, "This may take a while, Double-Mac. The other sergeant must have shifted some of this stuff around."

"The Trainer's just sittin' there," McCaig said. "You got anybody scheduled?"

"No; interior flight's all over for the day. The Link's closed down."

"Cost you anything to run it?"

"Nope; not a thing. The government runs it."

"I've got a proposition for you," McCaig said.

"The answer's already no," said Garber. "Don't ask me for any favors."

"Why don't you let Mr. Cahill fly your mock-up, here?"

"I told you; it's government property. No civilians are supposed to fool with it."

"I'm a civilian, and I fool with it."

"You're attached to the base, though. That's the difference. You've got some business with it."

"Mr. Cahill has got some business with it," McCaig said decisively, wanting for reasons not entirely clear to him to bring this about.

"That's all right," Cahill said. "I wouldn't know what to do with the damn thing. It don't matter. Let's go back to town."

"No," Harbelis said, quickly and urgently. "Let him do it, Garber. Who's gonna tell anybody? I won't, McCaig won't, Mr. Cahill won't, the dog won't. Let him get up there and fly this thing, Sergeant Garber. Talk him through the mission. It might even be like he was fillin' out some of Joel's Link time. Think about it that way."

Garber straightened again, still with no file; the side of his face to the light showed crimson teeth. "Now wouldn't *that* be something."

"That would be what?" Cahill said.

"That's right," McCaig said. "What would it be?"

"Come on, Garber," Harbelis urged. "You don't get this kind of blind flyin' every day."

"Well," Cahill said, fixing on the novelty, no matter how slight, that offers a few minutes of preoccupation to the blind, "do we or don't we?"

Garber went to the shed door, unsealed it, and looked around. He ducked his head back in. "Just like Buster Keaton in *The Navigator*," he said, "looking to see if everything is clear."

"Is it?" McCaig asked, the situation entered, and now closed around them.

"It is," said Sergeant Garber. He stepped directly to Cahill, and, in a low, rapid parody of what he usually said, of what he had said to dozens of cadet trainees, went through his prepared instructions.

"This device is called a Link Trainer. It is devised to give the student a simulation of the controls and the flight patterns of an actual aircraft. Except for acrobatics, the Link Trainer gives the student an approximation of the different attitudes—climb and descent, turns, rate of climb, rate of descent and angle of turn—to be found in actual aircraft. You will find," he glanced from his crimson shadow into Cahill's black eyes, "when you get into the Link Trainer that your feet will naturally come to rest on the two pedals that control the rudder, and, in its natural position, the stick that controls the elevators and the ailerons will be found, when you have your feet on the pedals, between your legs. Pushing the stick forward causes the nose of the airplane to drop. As you know from your experience in the air, this is because the elevators are deflected down against the airstream."

"He can do it without all this," Harbelis said. "Let's just see how he does, without officials. You've got your needles and your scribbles. Let's see what happens."

"Sure," McCaig said. "Just talk him through the mission, and let's see what your scribbler over there scribbles."

"I don't know," Garber said. "I'm supposed to go through all this, before I let anybody in the Link."

"All right," McCaig said. "Go through the rest of it, but let's get the man in the blue."

Garber returned with relief to his explanation, saying, "When you push the stick forward, you deflect the elevator down against the airstream. Now don't get fascinated with this, and fly the thing into the

333

ground. Some of them do it." He regathered, and went on. "Pull the stick back, and you deflect the elevator upward, and you cause the nose of the aircraft to rise. If you push the stick right or left, the ailerons are deflected in opposite directions, causing the airplane to roll about the longitudinal axis in the direction the stick is moved."

"What does that mean?" Harbelis asked, grinning. "Do you know what that means, Garber? All that lingo?"

"I know," Garber said, "but I don't need to go into it any further."

"You've got the back of the airplane, the rudder, with your feet . . ."

"Now you're talking," Harbelis said, and Cahill picked up.

". . . and the wings, and the up-and-down in your hand."

"See," Harbelis said, with sudden seriousness, "the airplane is already disappearing. There's not anything but you."

"You think you understand now?" Sergeant Garber said, touching Cahill on the side of the shoulder as though he were sending him into a football game with instructions.

Cahill had a chill of possibility, of danger, but let himself be guided to the Trainer by the sergeant. "Beware of the dog," he said.

He took off his overcoat, with an impulse to transfer some of the things—a thing—from the pockets into his pants, but did not. Instructed, he heaved himself up one step from the floor, a live, trembling step, onto something made of long, slender metal, he was sure, and came down, carefully arranged by Sergeant Garber, into a seat. There was a grated object in his right hand something like a bicycle handlebar, and his feet settled on two places of rest he found he could move. His left hand was placed by another hand on a knob. "This here's the throttle," Garber's voice explained. "Forward is faster, and backward is slower. Just listen, and I'll tell you what to do, I'll tell you what I want."

"Am I supposed to be able to talk to you?" Cahill said as earphones were being placed on his head.

"No," Garber said. "Just listen to me, and try to do what I tell you. But if you feel like you *have* to talk, push *this* button. I'll put a throat-mike on you, so you can get to me."

He heard the slender metal creak and seem to vibrate, and a thing closed over him from above. He sat, completely ready, braced and alert.

Where he sat, everything around him, everything in dream and reality, in memory, in sunlight and nightmare, began to hum. Without gravitational sense, he felt himself lifted and suspended in a vast, timeless aliveness centering on himself. He could do anything. He held the stick in a quivering movelessness; his fingers on the ball-shaped throttle

334

were, he felt with a shooting rise of affirmation, sensitive enough to solve delicate combinations of numbers, crack any safe on earth.

"You are now at nine thousand feet," a voice said in both ears, clearly and with authority, secret and final. "Ease the stick backward very slightly, and advance the throttle."

He pulled back toward himself, and tilted, pushing his left hand forward.

"Too much," the voice said, a little excited. "You're going to stall. Push forward, but not too much. Pull back the throttle. Pull it back."

He did, and came level; he was sure he was level. What was underneath him?

"You are now at nine thousand, three hundred feet, flying a course of two-niner-four degrees. You are straight and level, and your air speed is one seven five knots, your ground speed, one six eight knots. Continue straight and level."

He waited, re-alerting, resensitizing himself, determined not to overcontrol. He was sweating heavily, but young and strong.

He had never been in an aircraft before, and never imagined what it would be like: what the land under him would show, and the way in which it would be shown, but now, with his hands and feet placed with powerful sensitivity on the controls, his mind began, beyond his will, to spread beneath him an enormous landscape in which, little by little and then in cutting, hard-edged detail, objects, masses, different strikings of light, appeared, intensified, and stayed. To see beneath him he did not have to look to his left or right, to peer around the cockpit, the wing, the engine, going as he was levelly forward over an enormous terrain, and he began to give himself completely to a condition better than any dream he had ever had. It was afternoon, and to his left, as he moved steadily over the dark green, the sun, an exactly round and vibrating red-orange ball, was going down. Not shifting his attention from the front, he could look directly at it, into the core of it, from the side of his eye; he could penetrate it as he wished, without blinking. There was no engine where he flew; his look was through no propeller; the small harmless horizon was as clear to him as a string held up before him in the position he asked of it. To his right was a river in long turns and loops, aimless and unchanging; he hung above it for a long time before it disappeared into the green which did not darken but held the same color as when it first unrolled beneath him. At one place and another there were houses, all of them white, many two-storied, their windows

335

sharp black grains, but he could make out, and looked for, no cities, no railroad tracks, no roads.

His head very silent, he tilted himself gently with his hands and feet, letting the landscape in his imagination fail, the earth fail beneath him, and little by little drew back the stick. A very distinct soft voice said to him, "More throttle. Advance the throttle, Mr. Cahill; don't stall it out." Cahill pushed forward on his left hand, inclining backward, being lifted, rising in himself. Where was he? Where could he imagine? He tried for the landscape again, which had come of itself in the beginning, but there was no green beneath him in his mind, only, everywhere he looked or imagined, the crossing sparks he carried with him, the streaked and streaking web of gold that had begun in the wooden tunnel he had nailed together in Atlanta. Yet, commanding such power as hung in the machine where he sat, and concentrating, he reencountered the hurtling self-gold of his eyes as a tissue, now, that he might break through, might break out of, might in some way ride above and possess differently. He eased the stick back farther, and without prompting advanced the throttle.

"Your rate of climb is critical," said his earphones. "Let the nose down and ease off on the throttle."

Cahill was reluctant to do this, and he hesitated, rising still toward the shooting gold he held. "How high do you want to go?" asked Sergeant Garber's voice. "You're at ten thousand feet now, and a Stearman won't go any higher. You're hanging on the prop."

Cahill sat waiting. "All right," he said, pressing down on the button Garber had indicated, and speaking into the throat-mike that rested exactly on the pulses of his neck.

"Come straight and level. I'll bring you down in a long spiral."

Let me see how level I can get this thing, he said to himself, and, moving the controls, tried to bring his sense of balance right. After some experimentation he believed that his equilibrium had come true. "How's that?" he said to the throat-mike.

"That's just about exactly right," said Garber's voice, and broke off as if to speak to someone else.

Ten thousand feet, he thought. You must be able to see a long way from that high up. Or maybe there are clouds. What about them? What would that be like?

He was in clouds, now, in whiteness so dazzling that he was in awe of it. There was no sense of speed, and he realized that speed had never been a part of it; the things that mattered were the being lifted, the

336

rising-toward, the possible breaking out, and now the being-in. The color in which he sat was so weightless and absolute, and his hiddenness and control so powerful, personal, and remote, that it was hard for him to acknowledge that someone was speaking to him, giving instructions, making demands.

"I want you to come back on the throttle just a tad, Mr. Cahill. Are you right-handed or left-handed?" Then, after a moment, "I'll assume right-handed."

"Right-handed," Cahill said. "My right hand's got all kinds of powers."

"Push the stick a little to the right," Sergeant Garber said, "and a little forward, and come in with a little right rudder."

Cahill eased into the new positions, his mind changing.

"That's good," Garber said. "Now come off the rudder, and hold the rest of what you've got, until I tell you."

A new voice came in, younger and more definite, with an excited clarity to it. "What's it like up there, Mr. Cahill? How are things at the upper limit?"

"Good," Cahill said. "I was in the clouds."

"You better watch out," Harbelis said. "You can't tell about clouds."

"Do you know Captain Whitehall?" Cahill asked.

"Yeah, I know him," Harbelis said. "He was in New Guinea."

"Right," Cahill said, "and he told me that if you see a cloud in New Guinea there's bound to be a mountain inside it. Maybe I'll hit one."

"There's no mountains in the Link," Harbelis said, enjoying the situation. "The only thing you have to worry about running into is the ground."

In a long tilting curve he was floating voiceless now, all interior vision gone, nothing of the will involved. He could not be touched or even known; the voices of Sergeant Garber and Harbelis were of a startling unreality, but were not so unreal as the answers he gave not from his mouth but from his clamped throat. The main sensation was that of coming to a point, of penetrating, as if flowing upon some river without a bed that cut through a substance that yielded to it as by consent: at the same time penetrating and leaving the track of his trajectory behind him, enigmatic and fulfilled; he thought briefly of Sergeant Garber watching the needle move over the piece of paper he had been told about, the map with its lines, but this was not the record he was leaving. He felt his balance absolutely perfect, as acute and sensitive, quivering with correct position, as the moon in the carpenter's bubble back in his

337

wooden tower in Atlanta. Collision—Whitehall's mountain in the cloud —hovered always just in front of his infinitely piercing movement downward, but could not bring itself to touch him, and lent only the exhilaration of danger, a sense of vulnerability and abandon almost sexual, to the amplitude of his incisive enormous sweep. He found himself saying, without touching the mike button, "A minute. A whole minute in the air." He could have cut through stone, but he was not in stone, but only somewhere within a great openness upon which he left a mark.

"Okay," Sergeant Garber said. "That's good. I'll talk you through a landing. Come back straight and level now, and I'll line you up with the runway. Just neutralize your hands and feet. Back on the throttle a little more. I had you in a power descent. Now we need to cut back some."

Cahill rode level; he found himself smiling.

"That's it," Sergeant Garber said. "A little port, now; a little to the left. Now back starboard."

Cahill complied. "Beware of the dog," he said.

"Concentrate on what you're doing," Garber said a little sharply. "Don't bust your ass. Cut your power back slow."

Cahill did so, with no feeling of difference.

"Now cut it all the way. Pull the stick slowly back."

Cahill waited out the silence.

"Okay, now all the way back in your lap. Keep your feet straight, and you're right on a dime."

He sat still in this latest position as the humming died out. The roof over him opened, and someone patted him on the shoulder. "That's it," Sergeant Garber said. "You done made the ride."

No longer tired at all, he climbed down the steps with Harbelis's help. McCaig, who had watched silently, came to him. "It's too bad you can't see your mission," he said to Cahill. "You done good. Remarkable, brother."

"I wouldn't say remarkable, exactly," said Sergeant Garber, "but I would say damn good, all right. I don't see exactly how you could do it without being able to see the instruments."

"He don't need no instruments," Harbelis said. "The people on the ground never will understand that." He turned to Garber. "You ever been up, Sergeant Garber?"

"Which way is that?" Garber said. "I just run the trainer. And I can certify, just among us, that we had a good first mission out of the man with the dog."

"Well," said Cahill, feeling the kind of confidence that comes from the revelation of some resource never suspected, "I just did what you told me. And I kind of balanced it out. Like a bubble, you know."

"What bubble?" McCaig asked. "That's one of the instruments."

"I've got my own," Cahill said, pleased at fitting things together. "I true-up the moon and the bubble."

"We'll leave you with that one, Garber," McCaig said.

"Best you do," said the sergeant. "And don't say anything about this to anybody. It's not something I do every day, and there's no way I could ever explain it."

"Thank the Lord," McCaig said. He helped Cahill with his coat. "You won't have to explain anything to anybody. Just say we came by and talked a little bit, like Mr. Cahill's been doin' with the others."

"Come back," Sergeant Garber said. "This is a lonesome place between classes, sitting around looking at the kind of thing that's supposed to be flying but don't."

"I doubt we'll be back by," Cahill said. "But I do thank you. It's all an illusion, anyway. This and everything else. That's a big word for me, but I know what it means."

"Take care," said Garber, as the four of them went out into the cold, which was almost black dark, and closed the door.

"What did you think of that?" Harbelis asked, very boyishly, Cahill thought.

"It was all right," Cahill said. "Why do you reckon Joel didn't like it? I'd think that any kid his age would think it was fun, maybe like a ride at the fair, which is the nearest thing to it that I ever did."

"He never said. I think it was . . . maybe it was because . . ." Harbelis struggled to make clear, make out what he meant, ". . . I mean like, there's no feel of the air in one of those things. It's like you're not really *in* anything. He used to talk about the air, and the huge way that it was . . . that it's . . . that it's alive all around you. You'd have to go up in an airplane to understand what he meant. But as soon as you understand what that feeling is all about, what your body has to do with it, this being, well, lifted up on this enormous *body* that's sensitive from hundreds of miles up, and down to the smallest, the very smallest grass blade, and you're *in* it, don't you see, and you understand how you relate to it, and what you can do not against it but with it, not what it'll do to you but what it'll do for you, that's when you can fly. You don't get any of that in the Link Trainer. That's just a machine, and what it's in is not alive; the lift is not a real lift, and there's no way you can fall. Falling is one of the most beautiful things there is, in an airplane. It's always right with you; it's nothing to be afraid of."

They walked on, with Cahill's fatigue returning. Without talk it was stronger.

"I went by to see Cadet Spain today. And I talked to the flight surgeon."

"How's Spain doing? Was there anybody over there with him?"

"Cadet Shears was there, and some new fellow, some Jewish cadet who said he was a eagle."

"You met Cadet Adler, did you? How'd you like him?"

"Seems okay," Cahill said.

"He's moved up to number two, and he's good; should be there. The fight was bad for Spain. He doesn't understand the distance we need to keep."

"Adler seems to be having some kind of trouble with his eyes," Cahill said. "He's come to the right place for sympathy, you might say."

"Joel found him at the Classification Center at Nashville. He had all these high scores, higher than anybody else around. His eyes are not the best, and with his math and his test scores it looked like he would go on to navigation, where they'll give you a little leeway on vision. But Joel thought he should be a pilot, and he came in with us. He squeezed by on the eyes, and it may be that he fudged a little; I think Joel helped him memorize some stuff; he's got a memory like a bear trap with a thousand teeth. He's a very good man, he's the brains amongst us, and now he's right up there with Shears."

"You mean in the cadets?" Cahill asked trying to remember when he had gone through the same bafflement.

"No," Harbelis said. "Tomorrow. Shears says tomorrow. Then we'll tell you. You've been here long enough, now."

"I'll wait, if you say so. I sure want to hear all this explainin'."

"Adler is going to work out," Harbelis said. "He's nearly out of the mechanical phase; he's almost through the machine, and will leave it behind him before we get out of Basic."

"What is it you're after?" Cahill asked. "What do you and Joel and the others want? What is it you want to try to do?"

"To fly without the airplane," Harbelis said.

"So," said McLendon, "where you been? What have you been doin'?"

Cahill, propped against the big bottom dowel of the staircase again as a place he could count on, took off his glasses, closed his eyes and rubbed them. "I was up in a airplane that didn't go nowhere. I went up to ten thousand feet, and saw all over hell. Then I came down, just like the man said."

"How's that?"

"It was a trainer," Cahill said. "The sergeant said I did all right. It's a kind of a thing that sort of tilts around. When you tilt back you're supposed to be going up, and when you lean forward you're comin' down. They let me fly it, you know," Cahill concluded, holding position. "They're not supposed to, but they did. I did the whole thing without any instruments."

"What else did you do? You in the trainer all day, or what?"

"Joel's instructor, McCaig, and I did some other things," Cahill said, not wanting to talk about the black farm, or have to explain what McCaig had picked up there, or the bedspread with the partial shape of blood, or the cornbread, or the well water and honey. "I'll go back tomorrow, and talk to some of the same boys. That and Sunday should be about it."

"Here comes your girlfriend," McLendon said. "She's got on a coat down to her feet with buttons as big as pie plates."

"I heard that, Boysie," she said, undoing the top button. "This was my old man's coat, and these are my old man's boots. But this here blouse is mine, though; it lights up everything that sees it, just like I light 'em up."

"I *have* seen purple in my time," McLendon said, "but you're right; this is a new color, that ain't nowhere else to be found. Why 'ont y'all stay here and eat? I'll eat with you, or not with you. And you can have a beer; for nothin', too."

"It's too hot in here," Hannah said. "Who but you could stand it so hot? Look at Mr. Cahill's dog. His tongue is hanging out like he was runnin' a rabbit."

"Have a beer, anyway."

"We'll do that," she said. "You want to take advantage of him, Mr. Cahill?"

"Sure," Cahill said. "I feel all right; I could do it."

They sat, Hannah and McLendon facing Cahill, in a rigid booth whose backrests were so erect that the natural position of the sitters was to lean forward, and eventually to rest elbows and forearms on the table. The boy, Raymond, brought three bottles of beer and uncapped them.

"You should stay around here tonight," McLendon said, "hot or not. We might even could have a good time."

"No thanks, Boyd McLendon," she said. "I got stuff cooking at home. Greens and big hominy."

"Could you use a ride?" McLendon asked.

"We don't need it," she said. "It's just three blocks over and four down. I ain't afraid of the dark. Are you, Mr. Cahill?"

"Not a bit," Cahill said, oddly tasting the roughness of cornbread as he drank the beer as though it were cold water.

"We'll leave you," Hannah said, and got up.

"Look for me when you see me," Cahill said. "I'll be back after while."

"I won't worry," McLendon said. "Shake hands one more time. I like what you do when you do it."

Cahill came near smiling as he took the other hand.

"My God," McLendon said, freeing himself. "Don't get after me with that thing; don't grab me."

"I won't do it," Cahill said. "Don't put no fear in your mind."

"It's better for me to be on the inside," Cahill said, "next to the buildin's. I'll walk there, and Zack next to me, and you just come along and tell me which way to go."

"What do you do?" Hannah asked, looking up at him toughly with her broad sharp-nosed face. "Do you kind of run your hand along the buildin's?"

She watched with undisguised and strong interest the way in which he undertook to move through the town, seeming to settle into the actions that were right for him, the making of deliberate progress, a slow drive forward.

"No," Cahill said. "I don't need that much. I touch one of 'em every now and then, and sort of knee out for Zack on the other side.

"The trouble is," he said, "that I just got two choices. If I take off my glove so that I can touch out for stuff, my fingers get numb, and if I keep my glove on I can't feel what it is."

342

"That would be a problem," she said. "Do you really have to know what it is?"

She watched as he reached out, and with a heavy awkward delicacy put his forefinger on the glass of a dry-goods-store window, tracing, as he walked, an almost straight line as nearly as she could tell. The store ended, the finger moved onto brick, the hand clenched, the finger touched the building tentatively again, and withdrew, as they reached the end of the block.

"No," he said, with an unexpected rise of confidence and involvement at her attempt to understand his situation. "I just need to know that somethin's there. When it's warm, though, it's a little better if I can, you know, tell whether I'm walkin' alongside of glass, or wood, or granite, or marble, or whatever it might be. Warm weather is better; you learn not to get splinters from the wood. But I wouldn't do that anyway; I used to be a carpenter, and I understand about wood. You can trust it some, if you know just how much."

He felt in the air beyond the building, and then with his foot for the curb. "This where we turn? Turn right? Starboard?"

"No," she said narrowing one eye and peering at him intently under the streetlight. "Why would you think that? We got to go another block this way."

"I thought I remembered the cadet club bein' this way somewhere," he said. "I was just guessin'."

"I'll tell you where we go," she said. "You don't even need to ask. It ain't far."

He pulled his glove off and they started again, first across the street and then with a new building, this one of rough stone, under his hand. There was glass in it, very smooth and cold. A space appeared—a short gap —for a door. Stone followed, and then a ripple of metal, more glass, and another break into full air.

"You live by yourself?" he asked. "Have you got a whole house?"

"Went on? Went where?" He turned outward from the building into the emptiness where she moved beside him.

"How about your mother?" Cahill asked, moving over the sidewalk now with his hands in his pockets.

"This is where we turn," she said. "Now we're gonna have to leave most of the lights."

"I do live by myself, and I have got a whole house. It ain't much, but it's mine. My father left it to me when he went on from here five years ago."

"He went to whatever reward you get when you have a stroke. He had the high blood, and he wouldn't keep from eatin' and runnin' around. He could drink more beer than Boyd McLendon could sell in a year, in his place. My old man could do that in a weekend."

"She died when I was little, and me and Pop lived in this same house, and both worked in the same mill."

344

"A cotton mill? Some kind of textiles?"

"No, artificial silk. It's made out of chemicals. They're making parachutes over there now, but it'll be a colder day than this 'un before I'd go back."

"Don't tell me about it," Cahill said.

"It wouldn't do no good," she said, glancing at him again in the near dark between streets. "And I ain't fixin' to tell you about it."

With his toe he found the down-step from the curb.

"This here's a wide street, for this town. When we get on the other side, there's not no need for you to feel around for a buildin' or nothin', because there's just a big vacant lot. When we get on beyondst it, we turn one more time, and go on down to the house."

"Zack," he said, feeling downward, "this is where you do your stuff." A little startled, he drew back, and then felt again. The dog had stopped; his head was down, his neck hair bristling; a low vibration had come into him and was mounting into sound.

"Uh-oh," she said, "we got company."

"What is it?" Cahill asked, half crouching and holding to Zack's collar.

"This here's a right big dog," she said, "big and square-headed. He's coming acrost the lot."

345

"Let's try to go on," Cahill said, taking tighter hold. He went forward across the street, deeply bent, the dog pulling hard, reached the far curb, and stumbled, still holding.

The new dog, high-eared and deep-chested, came to Zack, snarling openly. Making no attempt to help Cahill straighten, or hold the dog, the girl moved to him and stood in the one light shining partway into the field. "We better stay right here," she said. "He's gonna follow us, no matter what. And here comes two more. No, three. Four more. Let's just stand right here, and hold what we got."

"How far is it to your house?" Cahill said, rearing back against Zack's force, now going desperate and nearing the limit of what Cahill could hold.

"They're all around us," she said. "I ain't sure what to do. Can you hold him?"

"I'm tryin'," said Cahill. They were on all sides of him now, sounds of anger and harsh breath; even though he was on cement he could feel the intensity of movement where he stood, the leaps, the turns, the quick shifts of bodies. The side of his right leg was hit. Believing he could catch his balance, he tried to get his leg set again under him, groping. Zack tore loose, and Cahill understood

"If we could get this here big 'un to run, we wouldn't have no trouble with none of them others. There's one that's got some kind of collar on but the others, they're just feist." The big dog bent low and faked as if to lunge at Zack, then lunged. Zack moved, and the dog went against Cahill's leg with a hard brush. At the split second after contact the scene exploded. Cahill was on the ground, Zack

346

that he was pitching head foremost into a solid mass of raging dogs, but, in the midst of a fury of sound such as he had never heard, he came to the concrete cleanly; only one body passed across the backs of his legs, and lightly.

He turned over, and tried to interpret, tried to picture what was going on around him, even if he was wrong, tried to find Zack somewhere in the growling, yelping, whining, intolerable mixture of furious racket made up of what seemed to him, rushing at him and then stopped, one after another release of frustration and hatred that burst at him out of an impulse that the other creature, after a lifetime, could no longer stand to withhold. But Zack's deep voice was not amongst the others; Cahill had never heard him raise it, or even bark. Whine, yes, when he was hungry, or when he wanted Cahill to take notice of him, but not bark or yelp. His sound of fury, of uncertainty, of hostility, was low, a vibration from some absolute and frightening place that would shake the ground he stood on, even if it was cement. But, though the roaring, the bawling, the dog-screaming, came toward him, retreated and returned, he could not make out where Zack was; there was nothing from him at all. Cahill sat up wondering, hands around his

had the high-eared dog by the shoulder, and the other dogs leaped in and out at Zack's sides and flanks with terrible daring and cowardice, all in a sound of animal fury impossible to bear, except that it was there to be borne.

From the time the first dog had moved to them—she had glimpsed him in the light across the field, before he disappeared into the central darkness between —she had been apprehensive, even frightened, when the dog was invisible, and even more so when he materialized into the near heavy-shadowing streetlight, having come directly across the lot from where she had first seen him, but now that the attack had been made, Cahill's dog freed of the man's hold and fighting as he wished, she was not afraid but interested and excited. There were five dogs with Zack in the middle of them, concentrating on the deep-chested dog, almost as big as he was, but pouring blood from his throat and lower lip. With a terrible effort he pulled away, and Zack fastened instantaneously on a front leg, which he shook, clamped to it, moving his head in powerful tearing spasms. The dog fell, and Zack was at his throat again, the other dogs leaping in and out yelping and frenzily snapping. A long low dog bit hard on a rear leg, and more quickly than she could have imagined, was on its back, twisting and grotesque,

knees, knowing that he could do nothing, able to hear what the girl said to him only one or two words at a time. He readjusted his glasses, which were hanging from one ear, and felt around him, expecting either teeth to grab his hand or the hard ground to be empty. Something was in the way, that should not have been there, upright and wrapped.

He went back to sitting, pulling up his knees and putting his heels to his genitals. He no longer needed to listen for Zack; he should have known from the beginning that this was not necessary. Zack was where the other dogs were; where the anger was, where the fear and the desperation were, where the screams of pain were, at Cahill's back—he did not turn—on both sides, and coming at him, straight into his face, but never touching. It was as though Zack's protection were being woven around him everywhere, and so strong was Cahill's new sense of calm that he believed that nothing could get at him from above, either; that he was covered by a net of fury that he controlled, and that nothing could break. He rolled and came to one knee, like a fighter waiting out the count.

pouring with blood, its collar glinting once, then twice, then no more as Zack turned on one of the others and had him. She looked at the man at her feet, sitting as though at the center of a circle, hunched up on himself, seemingly resigned, not worried. She was not sorry for him, putting the ear flange of his glasses back in place, and now feeling along the ground where he could.

"Turn loose," she said. "You got me. I ain't goin' nowhere. You got me by the foot. Turn loose."

Three dogs were down, and the noise lessened. The big dog was weakly trying to get to its three feet, the crushed foreleg dangling, shaking its head and showering blood, the spotted dog still, completely still a few feet away, and the small low dog scrabbling its rear feet weakly, the body trying to make a circle around the almost severed head. Zack turned and crouched as Hannah had never seen a dog do—more like a wildcat or mountain lion, she thought—and out of the crouch sprang in a whipping unstoppable curve on a black dog half his size; his wide mouth, all teeth that caught the overhead light in a flash more final and terrible than a die-stamper in a mill, bit through the other dog's neck and left him thrashing, the legs kicking as if they might get hold of something in the air to run on. At her feet the man moved also, rising.

A scream, so high and terrible as to penetrate into solid rock, so despairing that it might have come from a human being raised by pain past the ability to make words, went through Cahill's bones, more the bones of his breast than his head. He got the rest of the way to his feet in a silence somewhere in which he discovered, far off, a soft gasping moan, and something that sounded like eating.

"They gone?" he said, more weakly than he wanted. "They all gone?"

"Where's Zack? What was that last thing I heard? Did you see what it was?"

"What happened?" Cahill asked, the scream still quivering in his breastbone.

"No," the girl said. "Stay down. Don't do nothin'. It's just about over. One's runnin', and the other one's tryin' to."

She knew she had had enough, and she turned away from the large dog, now fallen to its side, as Zack, still crouching, completely soundless, went toward him, purposefully, head dropping. She raised her forearm over her eyes as against excessive light, but then lowered it and stared across the sleeve.

"They're gone," she said. "They're dead and they're gone. All of 'em."

"It was that first big dog that came over here botherin' your'n. It was him. He was hurt too bad to get away. He should'a got away when Zack was fightin' with them others. It's too bad for him, is what I'd say. He should'a taken off when he could."

"Zack finished with them others and went back, went back after him."

349

"And he ran him off?" Cahill asked, knowing that this was not the case, and despite himself fascinated by the details.

"He's done ripped out his whole guts," Hannah said. "He knocked him down, cut his throat, and tore him open from asshole to appetite. His guts are all over this here yard, and your dog's eating 'em."

"See if you can get him to come over here."

"You crazy? He's your dog. If you seen what he done to them others, you'd leave him alone, right now. If he wants to come over here, he'll come when he gets through."

"It went on a long time," he said. "All that. Seemed like a long time."

"Not so long. But there was plenty goin' on. This town ain't ever seen so much blood in one place since Wilbert Lightsey killed his grandmother and his two aunts with a shotgun."

"Let's get everything together," Cahill said, feeling in his pockets. "You see my hat around anywhere?"

"Your hat's out in the middle of the street, when they 'us fightin' over that way. I can get it."

"I'd appreciate that," Cahill said, making exaggerated and useless motions to dust himself off at the knees and seat.

He stood listening to the field

She drew off, out from the light, picked up the hat and looked back, where the figures were caught very darkly against the

and beyond, hoping to pick up some indication of normalcy, an automobile or truck going through town two blocks away, or an aircraft. He turned his face upward.

There had never been such a quiet street. The girl's footsteps were gone from him; the quiet was more disturbing than the fight had been, more unsettling than anything but the last scream. He could not hear Zack's jaws in the field any longer. "Zack," he said, there being no aircraft, either; the first engines would begin after he had slept. "Come on here, Zack," he said, louder now. "Come back over here and let me see about you."

He did not hear the breath or the nail tick until the dog had reached the sidewalk, and when they came they were right beside him. He bent down, and the head, first the muzzle and then the square skull, was under his hand. Cahill crouched and felt the matted head hair and then down both sides at the same time; they were rising and falling evenly. He fingered the legs, each carefully from the body to the ground, turned the big weight of the dog and felt down his backbone to the tail, out to the end. "Well," he said, "all that, and they didn't break your tail. Old Anvil-head; they

glow. The man rose off the ground, his clothes loose on him, and stood in what could either have been resignation or bewilderment. His bald head shone; about this there was nothing odd, but as she started toward him he turned his face upward, and for the first time she saw on it an expression she could recognize; it was eager and expectant; she could not remember having seen anything like it on the face of anyone his age, or even on a child. Why a blind man should have it she could not think. He bent to the dog, and she stood with the hat as they blended into one black mass, his hands going here and there along the dog. Though she had not heard what he said, he had begun by talking, but now she understood that he would not say anything more to the dog while he felt of him, and she had no wish to break in. His hands, coming back along the dog's upper sides against the grain of the hairs, lifted patches of soaked hair and, without haste, smoothed them down again as they would lie. He smoothed the long tail; its end hairs were as fragile as a feather's in the light nearest the ground.

couldn't even break your tail. They didn't do nothin' to your tail."

He put the hat on, adjusted it, and swung his shoulders this way and that, all sides quiet to any turn he made. "How's my dog look?" he asked. "He don't seem to be hurt none, far as I can tell."

"All of 'em dead?" Cahill asked uneasily, but still feeding on details; they strengthened his imagination of a scene he was sure he would keep; the fury in it was energy; he could feel the strength of it in his forearms and jaw muscles; he was sure that his grip would increase in strength every time he thought of it, and he entered into the different ways in which he would be able to imagine it.

He found himself listening as though to an account of some sports event that he had already seen, whose outcome he knew

"Here's your hat," the girl said. "No holes in it, except the one for your head."

"I don't think he's hurt. He could fight right on; fight some more. He's got blood all over him, but that belongs to them others. They're layin' out there, three of 'em in the field, and one in the road, right near where your hat was."

"There was five of 'em, all at once. The big one come across the field, and two what looked like feist. Then there was another one that might have had some bird dog in him; he'us black-and-white spotted. Then there was one little dog, one of them little old long dogs looked like somebody's pet, maybe; looked like he might'a belonged to some lady. One of the feist got away; he run off when your dog got hold of that-there bird dog, and was finishin' him off when the others was yappin' at

and enjoyed because he had been on the right side either emotionally, because of identification with a participant or a team, or, even better, because he had bet money.

him. Soon as he killed that one, he turned around and caught that little bitty one, and took his head right off, just bam, like that, with one snap. That's when that one feist got away; he really didn't want to fight. The little one, he just got caught. If it hadn'a been for his collar, Zack would'a taken his head clean off."

"Let's go on," he said. "Let's go wherever we're goin'."

"I don't reckon it'd be any use to try to find out whose dog he was," Cahill said.

"I don't see none. He's still dyin', but there ain't nothin' we can do for him. I sure can't, the poor little thing."

Cahill looked at her accusingly. "What the hell can I do for it? Don't make me feel bad. Them dogs might'a got after me. What am I supposed to do?"

"Nothin'," she said. "Ain't nothin', ain't nobody in this town ready for you, Mr. Cahill. Ain't nobody ever brought a timber wolf to Peckover."

"He's thirsty," Cahill said. "I'd think that blood would make you thirsty."

"It does," she said. "I don't know about somebody else's, but your own makes you thirsty."

"Let's go get some water, cold water. Maybe beer. I could use it."

"No," she said, "we'll have to go with water, but it's cold."

Leaving the field and the street with the motionless dogs they went slowly to the next street and turned. As they did so, the girl looked back at the four shapes, each isolated in different strengths of electric light, and saw that the small dog had finished all the movements of his legs.

"This is it," she said, after some slow walking, "right chere. To the left and on up. Screen door and one other one. I'll get 'em."

He worked up uneven stone or concrete, one step bowed down in the middle and the next bowed up, changed to wood, and crossed a porch in two steps, heavily creaking. He stubbed a toe deliberately where he believed the main front door was, and was right. The door closed behind him.

"Let me take your coat," the girl said.

"I'll be damned if I will," Cahill said. "It's as cold in here as it is outside. Don't you have no kind of heat? This place would freeze . . ."

". . . would freeze the balls off a brass monkey," she said.

"I hope he's brass," Cahill said. "Maybe he wouldn't feel as much. How come you to keep it so cold in here? This ain't no way to do people."

"The people that come here don't mind it all that much," she said. "I like it this way. Does something for me."

"I won't ask what," he said sitting down in a kitchen chair, the only other one in the room besides a bristling lounge chair and a purplish-brown sofa with one arm rubbed white.

"I'll get your dog some water," she said.

"Break the ice on it," Cahill said, turning up his collar.

Without much interest he listened to the kitchen, glass clinks and light metal clashes. It was a long time since he had sat, distanced, and heard them, but they brought nothing back that was good. Liquid poured; there was a sloshing, and an object, being slid, grated on sand or dirt. Zack was drinking there, thick eager slopping. "Water," Cahill said. "Water for me too. I'm right over here."

She brought him a glass, thin, very thin when he had expected a mug, something with a handle. He drank. "How many of these glasses have you broke?" he asked. "This-here's about as thin as a fingernail. Ain't nothin' to it. Caruso could'a broke it on his worst day, when he had the hiccups."

"Who's that?"

"He's some singer, used to break glasses with all that opera-hollerin'."

"Don't holler, then."

"Caruso pinched my aunt in the ass one time."

"Why'd he do that?"

"She'us at a party, and was goin' through a door, and she felt this-here twinge back there, you know, and there was this little Eyetalian. She used to say he thought she liked it."

"Well," she said, and sighed, "I can't say. You don't know about other people. I've knowed a lot of people, some of 'em with Eyetalian names, but I never did know any real Eyetalians."

Measuring through the words were the pad-weights of his dog. He listened for the drinking sounds he had temporarily lost, and could not find them. Zack was between the kitchen and him, or he was nowhere.

"Your dog's back in here," she said.

"I know he is. He's OK. He's tired, I reckon. Too much exercise."

"Exercise, my ass," she said. "Are you sure we're gonna be safe, with that thing in this house?"

"You better not try to leave him outside," Cahill said, nodding his head and turning down the corners of his mouth with satisfaction. "He don't like that. He'd try to tear this house up. He couldn't blow it down, like the Wolf, but he could level down on it. That screen door wouldn't stand up for very long."

"It won't, anyway. He don't need to get after it. He can sleep where he wants to."

"It ain't just the screen porch," Cahill said. "This whole house feels rickety. Either your nails ain't long enough, or the wood's too soft, or the house has been here too long. It's leanin' to one side."

"How would you know? You're sittin' straight."

"I'm sittin' straight, but the whole house is leanin' thisaway." He pointed off.

She turned to the blank wall toward which his hand went out.

"You have to pull back against it." He settled and leaned inward. "It's liable to flop on you; the nails are already about half out."

"Well," she said, sitting on the sofa and putting her elbow on the white place, "That's too bad. Maybe I could paint it. Paint the inside."

"That's more like a woman talkin' than any woman I've been talkin' to. Paint is not gonna hold nothin' together." He reflected. "You don't believe that, anyway. You got good sense. Why'd you say it?"

"I want to get you to go on," she said. "Just go on."

"I told you I used to be a carpenter, didn't I? I told you, out yonder on the street, up by McLendon's place. Ain't that right?"

"You told me," she said. "Now what? What you got?"

"I build floors and walls specially good," said Cahill, unsettling from the spines of the chair and settling again forward, thrusting from the hips and getting square. "I can build cabinets, tables, chairs, racks, rooms, halls, tunnels, just about anything. I build the best shelves in the business. Unless the boards warp, there won't be the variation of a sixteenth of an inch in a twelve-foot shelf I put in, if I support it from underneath." He took off his hat and threw it somewhere. Zack, on the floor at his side, raised his head.

"I built a dance pavilion and a little roller rink. You know"—he broke off, flooded-at by a memory of motion—"skatin' used to be my thing. I could go all over hell, all over Atlanta. But I didn't even like skatin' on my own rink; it's always to the left, leanin' one way, and it's just round and round. I like to go somewhere. I like to go right at somethin'."

"You're gonna have to tell me. That ain't what we do, up around here."

"Well," he said, "I built it anyway, but I let them have it; them others; whoever wanted it. I built a couple of watchtowers. Two of 'em, and about half of two more. I could see all over Atlanta. You know why I built them towers?"

"I don't have no idea."

"Because I like nails. I built them towers, and before I went blind I was buildin' a kind of fun house that—you know—you kin get lost in. It'll also scare your ass off. I built the part that'll scare you, first. First of all. It's still there. It's got a rattlesnake in it. He'll jump right out at you."

"Nails. What about nails?"

"I just like nails, whole barrels of 'em, all sizes, the shape of every one of 'em, and what they do. You can do a lot with nails. With my towers, I nailed up. You know," he pointed, "up and up, you know, and you climb on your own nails and . . . and you go as far as you can trust what you do. I built up into my towers, and they was as solid as Stone Mountain. I built up with 'em, you know, and with my fun house, I built *on*, flat-like; I built on forward, and I went in, I built *in*. Nobody knew where I was, and neither did I, till I went back to the blueprints. When I got down in the wood, though, I wadn't always sure the thing was goin' to come out like the blueprint. You ever seen blueprints?"

"No. I mean, I have seen 'em, but I never paid no partic'lar attention. I never had to build nothin' with 'em."

"Well," he said, "the next time you get a chance to look at blueprints, you ought'a look. If I could see, that'd be the first thing I would want to look at. The whole layout is blue, see," he said, both elbows now on his knees. "It's this kind of machine blue, you know, and through that, just like . . . just like . . . I don't know, but just like somethin' had done come through it from the wrong side and was just exactly right without knowin' it; there're these kind of pale lines, and they can't be wrong. They can *not* be wrong." He settled all the way back into the chair, against the uncomfortable fanned spines. "I used to build my own divin' boards," he said lacing his blunt fingers. "Nine-ply spruce, bevel and sand down to specifications. You lay the boards side-on and bind 'em with epoxy. The ones I made would throw them boys right up there." He shot his arms up, flat-handed. "Scare the shit out of 'em, first time. They didn't know what hit 'em; they didn't know what they come out of, way up there where them other boards never put 'em. They had time to do all kind of stuff, but they felt lucky to get back in the water. I've got a real deep divin' tank; two foot deeper than the Olympics. When some of them boys got used to my boards, they could really get up there and twist around. They had all day in the air. All afternoon, anyway."

"That sounds real interestin'," she said. "I couldn't build a shithouse. Neither could my old man. He didn't know nothin', outside of that one corner of Denaway Mills. They carried him out of there. They really did. He died, right yonder at the end of Loom Four."

"Hellacious," Cahill said. "I couldn't do it. I need the sun. I used to like to feel the air move. Still do."

"You always plan everything you build?"

"Most of it," he said, "because, you know, I like blueprints, like I told you. When I made my skatin' rink, I laid the print, and then I worked it out in tongue-and-groove, and it come out just exactly right, all the way 'round, the banks on the turns and everything. I wadn't out a quarter of an inch, wherever the fit was. God couldn'a done no better."

"You must miss all that."

"I do miss it," he said, "but I'll get back to doin' it, or some of it, anyway. I got a guy who helps me, a young Mexican guy. He don't know nothing about carpenterin', but he can hand me stuff, and measure. With just that much, I can get by; I can do the rest myself."

"Everything you do's outdoors?"

"Well, in a way it is. The only other thing was this here playhouse, this fun house I was tellin' you about. That was all in the dark. It's real funny, all the last stuff I did, all the last job I give myself, was in the dark, under a big canvas tent that liked to 'a broiled me like a lobster. I worked in nothin' but my own steam, and I never had such a good time in my life. No plans, neither. I wanted the whole thing to be a secret, see, even from myself. I've got a big lot there, plenty of space, seventeen acres, and I can go any way I want, go every which way, thisaway up in the sun, or thataway down in the dark, like a mole."

"You was buildin' a tunnel? I mean like under the ground?" she asked, crossing her feet the other way. "You dug down?"

"No, it was like a bunch of wooden halls, all fittin' together and branchin' off this way some of the time and then this other way, and they was little rooms they come into, and steps where they went up to other rooms, and around and about, and all."

"I would think that would take a whole lot of plans, a whole lot of plannin'."

"No," he said, "that's not the way I did it. I brought in a big bunch of lumber, stacked up twelve or fifteen feet high. I built the platform for the first room, which was . . . which is like a kind of . . . kind of like a lobby, see, and all the halls go out of that, wherever they're goin'. You could take off any way you wanted, but where you went, what you got, you had to deal with it."

"I don't think I'd like that," the girl said. "I ain't never been in no such of a place."

"You might get to like it," Cahill said. "I ain't never been in no such of a place like it, neither. The house of mirrors out at Lakewood Park ain't in it with my pinewood Honeycomb. I don't need no mirrors to scare the ass off anybody that goes in there."

"No plans? None of them blueprints?"

"Well," Cahill said, "I guess I must'a had some kind of a plan when I started out, but it kept changin' around, you see. I didn't draw no plans, because I didn't want to be locked into 'em." He thought, and then smiled, and it felt very welcome and real on his face. "Or, nailed into 'em, you might say." He paused again. "So I just started out, when they got the tent up. I laid the floors down as I went. When I felt like I'd got far enough in one direction, I'd just put the protracter down and take off at another angle, and go wherever it went. If I was gonna build a crazy house, I thought it ought to be part of the bargain that I 'us crazy when I built it. That seems fair, don't it?"

"Sure does," she said, putting one arm over the back of her chair. "Sure does seem to be."

"It's not finished yet," he said, "but I'll get back to it. I've got some ideas, some more ideas, but I'll probably change *them* around too. When I get used to this goddamn life of a blind man, and get back to sawin' and hammerin' some, I won't even need to take my Mexican in there with me. I'll just get down in there with the moles, and do everything by feel, by feelin' of it, feelin' for it. I'm doin' that mostly now, anyway. Smell never did me much good; maybe that'll come along, later on. I can feel better than I can hear, right now. But I can hear pretty good, too."

He had forgotten the cold; the memory of the heat of his body, the suffused sun under the canvas, the fading of the hand-carried bulb he shoved along before him down the wooden tunnel, and the pink-edged spark traveling across his eyes for the first time, had been strong enough to replace the iron cold of the room, but now it returned, except for the back of his right hand.

"You're about as cold as I am," she said, "but the difference is, you ain't used to it." She left her small blunt hand printed on his for a moment, and then said, "Let's go on out in the kitchen, where it's warmer than it is in here. We can eat. I got all that stuff I said I had."

He stood up and stretched; the cold, fatigue, and his weight combined, and the renewed thought of his blindness added to these brought a deep bone-shock of depression through him.

"Come on this way," she said. "Zack's already out yonder again."

He went forward, toward a drinking-and-scraping sound, feeling for door jambs separating rooms.

"Here you go," she said, guiding him into a stout brown chair. The room was a dim white, with cracks in the paint, and the enameled table was the same color, with a black chip at the corner where Cahill sat.

A little less cold in the new place, he sat, pulling his overcoat from around his neck and propping his forearms on what was in front of him. Something was set between them, and he understood by small clashes that a knife and fork, surely, and probably a spoon had been put down also.

There were two pots and an open dish the girl had taken from the black stove. "This is cold by now," she said. "If you could give me time I could heat it up some."

"No," he said, "don't bother with that. I'm not all that hungry. In a cold kitchen, you oughta eat cold food."

"There's part of a chicken, and big hominy and collard greens. I'll get you some bread. What do you want to drink? I've got milk. Buttermilk, anyway. You can use buttermilk for other things besides drinkin' it, you know."

"That'd be good," he said, finding the fork and prodding into the greens with it. He ate, chewing slowly. "What things?" he asked, feeling for the milk, if she had set it down yet.

"Your skin," she said, pouring the milk and putting it near his free hand. "Buttermilk is real good for your skin. And it's good for bites, anything from a mosquito to a bee or a hornet or a wast'. Buttermilk will draw out just about anything, any kind of poison; draw it right on out."

"This is good," Cahill said decisively, forking in more greens. "How do you get it to taste so good when it's so bitter?"

She smiled, tore off a piece of the end of the loaf, the nubbin, and put it in her mouth. "A lot of fat," she said. "I use about twice't as much strickaleen as anybody else."

"You use what?" Cahill asked, lifting his face toward her. "Strick-aleen? Ain't that some kind of poison? Don't they poison dogs with that stuff? Don't give Zack none of it."

"It ain't poison," she said. "It's white bacon, mostly all fat. I chop it up and put it in there with the greens. Whenever I make bacon, any kind of bacon, I save the grease, and I just pour it on in, into the greens."

"Well, this is some kind of good, no matter what you do," he said, grudgingly and admiringly. "This other puffy stuff is good, too. Needs more salt, though. Can I have some more?"

"Sure," she said, "all you want." She served him again, and sat watching.

"Ain't you eatin' nothin'?" he asked. "Don't let me take it all."

"I don't eat much," she said. "When I'm not workin', I don't get real hungry. I've got a couple of things wrong with me. That's why the house is so cold."

Cahill lifted toward her again, greens still on his fork. "What do you mean?"

"The colder it is, the better it is for what ails me. It's good for my nose. I eat bread and drink whiskey, and some orange juice. When I was workin', I could eat anything, and when I was in jail I could eat any-thing. I could do a lot more than I can now."

"Jail, shit," Cahill said slowly chasing the big grains of hominy around his plate. "You ain't never been in jail in your life, woman, and you know it."

"I been in jail," she said with satisfaction. "I been under the jail. I'll tell you about it later on." She frowned slightly. "Don't you want the rest of that chicken?"

"No," he said, "give it to Zack. This other stuff is so good, and I'm damn if I understand why."

"You was prob'ly hungrier than you thought."

"No, that ain't it. The taste you done put on these greens, it's like— it's rich and bitter." He hesitated and then came back with conviction. "It's rich and bitter. How you gonna think of that? It is, though. Rich and bitter; damn if it ain't."

"If you say so. Just a lot of bacon grease. Maybe I'll put in more next time, more than you got there."

"That ought to be somethin' else," he said, finishing. "Joel ever eat with you?" he asked, wiping his hands on each other. "He ever eat this stuff?"

"He did," she answered. "It's the best thing I fix, but he didn't like it like you do."

"What did he like?"

"He kept after me to get him carrots. He said they didn't hardly ever have 'em at the base, and he needed 'em."

"Carrots?" Cahill asked. "What about carrots?"

"He had the idea that they could make him see better at night, that with enough carrots he would be able to see at night, like a cat. Or a owl, maybe."

"What are you givin' me?" Cahill said, lifting and pushing back from the table. "These boys don't even fly at night. They ain't even got no radio, or nothin' like that. What are you talking about, seein' at night? You made that up."

"No I didn't make it up," she said. "I used to scrounge all the carrots I could find, and I would buy whatever ones the grocery store had, and he would eat carrots and drink carrots, every time he came over here."

"*Drink* 'em?"

"Yeah; I'd squeeze the juice out of 'em. I've got a meat press for gravy, and I used to use that. That was one thing he liked. He said that if he could eat enough carrots and drink enough carrot juice, he'd have a big advantage when he flew at night. He said that he could see the other planes, you know, like the Japs, and they couldn't see him. He said it would be like he was invisible, like the man in that movie that un-wrapped all them bandages from round his head, and there wadn't no head there; there wadn't no man there. Joel thought that drinkin' carrot juice would make him invisible; that he would be just like a ghost."

"Like I tell you, these planes don't fly at night. Had he ever even been up at night?"

"I don't know. But these ain't the only planes. This ain't where the war is."

He thought, and came on something to ask. "What else did he eat?"

"He used to like rice, cooked real soft. He liked gravy a lot, and we got up something that was the best, for him."

Cahill waited.

"I told you about my press. I used to get hold of stew meat and cook it, and then press the juice out of it and put it on the rice. He could eat a blueing-tub of that."

"That's one I ain't never tried."

361

"Well," she said, "it's just blood, you know, cooked a little bit. It's so salty you don't need no salt on the rice."

"You got any?"

"Sure," she said, moving her plate so that it pushed his aside. "Try some of mine. If you like it I can get you some more."

He prodded the empty part of the plate, then found the rice. He scooped it, backed the rice against a finger of his other hand, and ate. He chewed and thought. "Damn," he said. "This ain't bad. You got a name for it? Your own name?"

"I just call it beef juice and rice. That's what it is, and that's all it is."

"You just squeeze the blood out, and put it on the rice?"

"That's what I do. It's cooked blood, you know," she added, "it ain't raw."

"I don't believe it'd be much different," he said, cornering more on his fork. "It's good either way. It's just damn good, I'm tellin' you. You got yourself another customer, on this stuff."

He stood up. "I guess I better be gettin' on back," he said, pulling up the collar of his coat, "but thanks a lot. This is the best meal I ever had in a igloo."

"I'm glad you liked it."

"Let's head out," he said turning away from the table and shoving the chair farther back with his knee.

"Let's don't head out."

"What?" he asked bending his ear toward her rather than his face.

"Stay here. Come on upstairs. I'll tell you about my time in the North Carolina Reformatory for Girls at Lazear, where some of the girls under eighteen are over thirty. Don't you want to hear about that?"

"Now why in the hell would I want to hear about it?"

"Joel liked to hear about it. That's the only thing that'd make him put down his ruler. Then he'd pick it back up."

"His ruler? What ruler?"

"One of them rulers that's got a middle piece that slides up and down. He was always foolin' with that."

"You mean, like a slide rule?"

"That sounds right. It'd slide, anyway."

"What was he doin' with it?" Cahill asked, baffled and intent.

"He was working out puzzles, kind of. Messages, you know, like when you say somethin' that means somethin' else, and somebody else knows what it means, can figure it out. Somebody can; not everybody."

"You mean like a code? Some kind of a code?"

"I guess so. Anyway, he had a lot of 'em, a whole book full of 'em. All of 'em was nothin' but numbers."

"Have you got the book?" Cahill asked, understanding belatedly that he had pronged his finger on a piece of wire in his pocket.

"No," she said, "Shears has got it. Cadet Shears; he come and took it. It wadn't no use to me. I couldn't understand none of it. All that business was somethin' that Shears and Blazek and them was in on. I don't know nothin' about it." She rose, and rocked back on one leg. "Come on upstairs and I'll tell you what I do know about."

"No shit?" he said, pulling on his coat. "I got to hear about North Carolina's jails full of women?"

"Yes, and I'll tell you about a big fire I was in, a roadhouse fire in a firetrap. I'll tell you about some boys I used to know, before all these cadets come here. They was not as good-a boys, but we had a good time. We used to gun around these back roads, all the time at night. My skinny redheaded man could drive like a bat. He got killed in the fire."

Cahill hesitated, and as he did so fatigue increased as though coming on his body from every long labor men had done since the beginning of time. "You'd help me get back if I felt like I had to go, wouldn't you?" he asked.

"Sure I would," she said. "You think I'd turn you loose out yonder by yourself, just you and Zack? Some of them other dogs might come back. You better stay here."

"You got another room? Another bed? Maybe I could sleep on the sofa."

"I got another room, but there ain't no bed in it. And don't sleep on the sofa, neither. It ain't big enough. You come on upstairs with me, and we'll get warm. I'll tell you about the fire, and about how they used to get after us girls in the reformatory. Some of us hadn't done nothin', neither."

He still hesitated, almost certain that there would have to be some kind of decision about sex. His period of blindness had been a case of survival, and he had had no time to think of anything except his own way of adapting to his new situation in which the world threatened him at every moment of the day and night, where he could take nothing for granted that he could not hear or feel, and was more often than not in doubt about those things as well. He did not know what he might do about sex, but the idea of going back on the night streets of the town, even with the girl, of feeling for curbs with his feet, of reaching for the sides of buildings so that something—anything—would be there, unsettled him badly; without showing it he shuddered at the thought of touching another chill pane of storefront glass. "Okay," he said, "I'll stay here. McLendon and them can do without me for a while. But you got to get me back to the station by nine tomorrow. I've got a meetin' out at the field. This one they tell me I can't miss."

"I'll get you there," she said. "It'll be a lot easier. And we don't have to go back by that field where them dogs was botherin' your'n."

"No," he said looking down toward where Zack had last been heard scraping his metal bowl of water along the floor. "We can go back that way. You can tell me what you see."

"Right now," she said, "let's go up, up the stairs, up over your head."

"Good enough," Cahill said. "Like these boys around here say, let's get 'em. Let's get 'em in the blue."

There were always stairs, and he was always counting them. Sometimes the numbers remained, so could make a decent try at coming down them when it was time. The girl in front of him, very quiet except for her footsteps he could hear, some in time with his own, others between them, might make it possible for him to remember the number of these particular ones in the morning. Sixteen, seventeen, he said, and came out flat-footed, with no barrier, nothing upright no matter which way he nudged. "Now what?" he asked.

There was a bare bulb on the upper landing, and she lifted them toward that, not saying anything and not looking at Cahill. His feet were heavy and deliberate; things which she felt might possibly break through. In the stairwell she was most conscious of his breath, as deep as the sound of a seashell she had once heard, and like the breathing of someone with half a cold. When she came to the landing she moved to one side to give him room under the light.

"Thisaway," she said pushing on his right shoulder blade. "Come on, now. Just on through the door. The bed's over yonder against the far wall, under the window. Just go toward where the air's comin' in."

He started forward toward a stir he could already feel in the hallway. When he passed the jamb—he was sure he had passed it—wind took the lower part of his coat, shuddering it around one leg. "Good God. Ain't you goin' to close that window?"

"I can't," she said. "I done told you already. It's got to be cold where I sleep. My head's got to be cold."

"I don't ask no questions to idiots," he said. "Can I sleep in my overcoat? How 'bout my shoes? My feet are freezin'."

"You don't need your overcoat," she said, undoing the top button of it. And you don't need your shoes. I got plenty of quilts. I bank 'em up and get under 'em. You come on now. Get them shoes off, and let's you and me pile in."

He crouched and untied his shoes, rose and kicked them off, listening for one to hit the other; it did not happen. "Did Zack come up here?" he asked, pulling off his overcoat and feeling it taken. "Zack," he said, "you here? Where are you, big boy?"

"He's here. He's over in the corner. You don't need to bother him. He had all he wanted to drink, and he had that leather chicken."

She sat on a plain bench at the foot of the bed and took off her boots, setting them on the floor

He felt the stairs under him yet, and was sorry he was not still climbing them, going up and up.

365

His feet in socks on the unequal boards had the sense of the house descending from them, falling slowly from him under his efforts. He took off his overcoat and then his jacket as though fighting, which he was doing, struggling against the panic that was never far from him; this was helplessness, and a vulnerability he could do nothing about. "Turn down that bed," he said, "if you ain't already done it. Pile them quilts up." He opened his shirt from the throat down, took it off and stood bare-armed. "How come you askin' me to do this?" he asked, his shoulders gone colder than his arms or hands. "There really ain't no reason for it. I don't let people feel sorry for me. You better know that."

"What is it, then? You ain't nothin' to me but a voice. That's all anybody is. What reason you got, gettin' me up here like this?"

with their high tops leaning against each other. She reached behind her neck and undid the top button of her dress, leaned forward, her hair falling almost to the floor, and ran the zipper down.

She twined her fingers and put them under her chin, elbows on her knees, to watch the huge man in the hall light battle with his clothes. The one-sided glow fell on an extreme paleness, button by button as it appeared. Beneath the up-matted hair at his throat he was as white as a coal miner. As big as he was, his forearms were out of proportion with the rest of him; they're like sacks of salt, she thought; they're like Popeye's.

"Feel sorry for you?" she said. "That ain't never been in my mind. It'd be a colder night than this'n before I'd feel sorry for you, or anybody like you."

"You got somethin' I might want. First, I wanted to meet you because you was Joel Cahill's daddy; anybody he came out of, I would like to know; I would like to know who is back of somebody like him. A lot of people would like to know that."

"You see what you see," he said, stripping his undershirt over his head and unbuckling his belt. He let his pants fall and stood in them to the ankles. "This is what I've got. That's all there is."

"No it ain't, blind man. You got more, a lot more. I saw the way you killed them dogs out yonder."

"*I* killed 'em? What the hell did I have to do with it? Zack killed 'em. Maybe he shouldn'a, but he did it. You was there."

"No, you did it. That dog wouldn't be like he is without you. I don't know how you done it, but you was the one that made him that way. And you was the one that made Joel like he was, too. Must'a been."

"You're wrong, twice't."

"Come on," she said, pulling her dress over her head. "Shuck them panties and pile in. I'll tell you stories."

He did as she said, and moved toward the freshest cold, where the air stirred, toward his hope for the location of the bed. "I got some things to tell you, too, little buddy," he said. "I got my own things."

He sat, and swung his legs around. As far as he could tell the bed was all sheet, and he lay back, his head sinking into a pillow. Then from over him, from around him, covers breathed and settled; on top of them, more weight—light weight, but weight—was laid or pulled. His arms relaxed, and then his feet, and then his back. Of the good things he had had since going blind, he knew almost immediately that this was the best; better than the whiskey with McLendon and the two captains, better than his brief sensation of absolute control in the Link Trainer, and what he believed was the very real admiration of the operator, Garber; better even than the honey and well water at the farm where his son had lain on a quilt in the next room. It was the Link Trainer that came back most strongly to him now, not mainly, as he had thought earlier, in the ways in which he had been able to change the angles of his body with his hands and feet, though he would like to have had more of that, more of the belief that he was making himself rise or come down, but even more what his imagination had done while he was riding. When Sergeant Garber had said "You're at nine thousand feet now" he was sure that there would be clouds there; he would be either in them or above them, and he had pictured—he pictured now—that he was just above them. The clouds flowing beneath the Trainer merged with and became clouds he had seen; these were the main clouds now, the only clouds. Walking the great spaces of Piedmont Park, the wide, unclosed city field, he believed he remembered clouds best, and this was from the time when he had helped the boy wind up the rubber bands of his twin-pusher model, and had watched the aircraft climb against the drift of gray that was darkening with twilight, but showed the outline of the plane, delicate, purposeful and disappearing, until only the cloud was left. This is like that, he thought, not thinking of the Link now but of the clouds, big, solid, and shapeless. Solid, he thought strongly; those things look solid; I can't believe they won't hold you up. I'd be willing to bet that everybody thinks that; nobody can look at them and not think that. He relaxed more, and lay more deeply, warming.

"I dropped all my money, takin' off my pants," he said. "I was too anxious to get warm."

She raised her head and looked past him. "We'll get 'em in the mornin'. The moon's shinin' in, and I can see 'em all, most them, anyway, except maybe the pennies. They ain't goin' nowhere."

He turned sideways, toward the killing freshness, and sent out a hand, but not far. "Whereabouts are you?" he said. "You hidin'?"

"I'm right here," she said. "I waitin' for whatever's gonna be."

"What do you want?"

"We'll see," she said. "I won't fight you."

He reached her this time, not with his hand but with a foot. "We got to get them feet warm," he said, "then we can figure out what we want. I ain't interested in fightin', neither. Like you say, Zack does my fightin' for me." In a short silence he was sure that the dog had heard its name.

"Come here," he said softly. "Come on over, Zack. Say good night to us." The dog's nails clicked on the floor unhurriedly; Cahill was sure the boards gave a little; they would have to give. His arm hung down from the bed, cold, almost numbed out. Halfway up his forearm, the hairs stirred and were warm, nearing life. He reached toward the breath with the same arm, and the hand came down on Zack's body, somewhere not the head. He found the head, and the ears. "Don't you go stealin' my money, you big jackass," he said. "You can have the pennies, but them dimes and quarters, I need." He gave the dog a slight push. "You can go on back now, back over where you was. We're all gonna sail off somewhere, and freeze to death." Zack left him slowly, his paws ticking and shuffling, his breath gone from Cahill's arm, its sound disappearing. Cahill lay back without the girl, without thinking of her or even imagining that she could exist. This was every room, every bed he had slept in since he had been blind, and there was nothing he could say to himself or think about that would make it any other way, make the soft force against his back that held him up any other but that bed, although it was in a colder place than any of the others. His worst fear came to him fully as he tried to imagine the room around him, and make it be. What a lost place this is, he thought. How lost this street is, and the town; I am absolutely and utterly alone, stone blind, and in a kind of center wherever I go or wherever I lie down, but it is the center of nothing, of the dark that will never change.

"I was a weaver," she said, "I was a metal-loom weaver, and I was a textile weaver. I made chain-link fences and I made percale. And I made some chenille, but I don't like to do that, because that belongs to the real people, back up in the hills. That and quiltin'. Chenille don't belong in them mills, with all that noise. Screw that." She said nothing for a moment, and Cahill, still listening for Zack to breathe, breathed himself, and switched his hearing nearer, and opposite. "I can weave on a wood loom, too," she said. "I used to do that at a friend of mine's house, my best girlfriend. She had a wood loom, and I could do it, feet and all, almost right from the first time I ever tried it. I could spin the thread right on out, and make whatever I wanted. There's supposed to be a cat in the room when you weave, and my girl friend had a old cat, and I would sit there and weave, and then pull it all out, and weave it again, because we didn't have all that much thread. That was about eight or nine years ago."

"Too bad," Cahill said, not knowing what else to say. "Maybe you could go back to it, later on."

"I could do it," she said. "And that ain't all I can do. Wait till I get my overcoat on, and I'll play you some stuff."

She went off the bed, apparently over him without touching him, her feet on the floor beyond him, then coming back, but not reaching the bed. He pulled the covers up over where she had been. A chair scraped on the floor.

"Now what?" he said. "Get back in here. I was gettin' warm; I was fixin' to sail on out."

A whinging sound almost musical, and then musical in a sense beyond or different from any kind of music he had ever heard, was thinly in the room. It was strings of some sort, shy, brushed-across, containing several thin nasal tones, like a beating of high, harmonious broomstraws, a ghostly swishing where the differences in pitch were not abrupt but changed without change from one to the other. "What is that?" he asked, huddling toward the inner bed, where the gravity of his weight pulled to place him.

"It's a dulcimore. My friend give it to me. It was broke, and I fixed it up. It's strung with banjo strings and catgut I got in a music store in Fayetteville. You play it with a popsicle stick and a goose feather. My goose is gettin' kinda wore down, but it was a real goose it come from."

She swept out the music, without singing, the straw-sound high and melancholy. For some reason this brought back into his mouth the aftertaste of the greens he had eaten; his gums held the flavor as he licked them, and he lay quietly, continuing to taste and to listen.

"That's all I remember of that one," she said, the strings humming themselves out. "I learnt it when I went down one summer to work in Ellijay, Georgia. And I worked in Dalton, Georgia, which is supposed to be the chenille capital of the world, but I didn't like it there, like I said, and I stayed in Ellijay, where they was some girls that could sing, and play this kind of stuff."

"That's good," he said sincerely. "That's real good. What else can you do? What else can you play?"

"I can play some more on this thing. If I had a French harp I could play the Fox-hunt for you, where I'm the fox and the dogs and the man singin', all at the same time. The way I sing it, they don't never catch the fox. He gets away, but I can keep him runnin' for a long time, till I get just about as much out of breath as the fox does; he don't have to play the harp at the same time."

"I'll wait on that," Cahill said. "Come on back in here, and let's settle down."

"You don't want to hear about the fox?" she asked.

"You can tell me about it back over here," he said. "You don't have to sit way out yonder, wherever you are."

Again she passed over him, not touching him and seeming almost not to touch the bed either; Cahill did not believe that a person who depended on his eyes, and had closed his eyes, would have known when she went across. The covers rearranged themselves by something he had not done. " 'And the fox he ran, and the dogs they ran, / And the hunters headlong after, / And loud they shouted man to man, / Filling the woods with laughter. / And when the sun was on the rim / Of the hills like a staring eye, / With a fierce black hound by the side of him / A man came running by. / And Orey Duval came suddenly / On the man in the autumn wood, / Leaning against a black gum tree / In a black and terrible mood. / And the man said, "Run as the fox has run / In the blue and bitter air!" / And he snatched forth Duval's horn and gun, / And he leaped on Duval's mare.' "

"Is that all?" he asked, settling again.

"No, there's a lot more. It goes on and on. It's a kind of a ghost story. The fox is the ghost, and the dogs and the men, they keep after him. They don't never find out who the stranger is, that jumped on Duval's mare. 'And still they say the strange man rides / Hard on his stolen mare, / And the black hound stirs the cold hillsides / With his yelps in the frosty air. / And any man who will go alone / When the day has come to a hush / Can hear the hoofs on the clattering stone, / And the foxes break from the brush!' "

He did not try to picture it, but relaxed in great comfort. He understood, now, that the girl was no more a stranger to him than anyone else he might meet. They were all strangers, voices, people who came near him and said what they wanted to say for whatever reasons they said it. Shears, Harbelis, McCaig, Major Iannone, the colonel, even Ruíz back in Atlanta were equally near and equally far. They had to embody themselves by means of their voices, and there was really no difference in them, in spite of pitch, intensity, or meaning. In his head a large sure thing revolved, and clicked deeply into place, a kind of acceptance based on the situation in which he lay, his warmth and comfort building. Whatever comes is all right, he thought. When you're blind and it comes in to you, you go with it as best you can. This town, this room, this bed with this girl in it, don't happen to no ordinary people. When you're blind, what happens just kind of folds in around you; it can come in, it has to come in from anywhere. He sighed, and trued up what he felt.

"I feel like I'm takin' up too much of this bed," he said. "You can come on over a little, if you want to. I ain't goin' to do nothin'."

Her foot hit him in the ankle, almost like a kick. "Don't you go to sleep now, while I'm talkin' to you."

"Talk on," he said. "If I ain't snorin' I ain't sleepin'."

"I'll tell you about some things that are hot. One of 'em was a fire I was in, and the other was my ass, about six or seven years ago."

"You're gonna have to explain that one to me."

"You got to come up with something hot first," she said matter-of-factly.

"Well, wadn't I tellin' you about workin' under that big tent, building them tunnels for my fun house? Didn't I tell you how hard it is to build something like a slidin' trap door in the dark? Or almost in the dark, anyway? I can tell you, it was hot in them tunnels I was makin'. I don't even know why I was doin' it, but I ended up with a house that there's not another one like it in the world, I guarantee that. It's not quite finished yet, but when I put a shingle roof over the whole thing, it's gonna be somethin' else, I tell you. I'm just as liable to get lost in there as anybody."

"I know what you mean about them wooden tunnels," she said. "That was where I was in that-there fire that killed them people. It was in a roadhouse, between here and Albemarle. A man in the lumber business in Albemarle owned it. It was one-story, real spread out. You went in there, you could go any whichever way. The waitress'd find you sooner or later; I don't know how she would. Them was old waitresses, as I remember; it'd take a long time to learn your way around in that place."

"What were you doin' in there?"

"I was usually there with the same people, the ones I used to run around with."

"Prob'ly a bad crowd, huh?" he said, intending to be contradicted.

To his surprise she came back immediately, and with enthusiasm. "They was bad," she said. "Not the worst, not what you would call mean, but just sorry. They never killed nobody, or hurt nobody. But they would steal, you know; they liked it. Especially cars. I don't think that's so bad, do you?"

"Not all that bad," he said. "I never had one, myself. I used to like to walk. When I was young, I used to skate a lot; I liked to do the movin' on my own; you know, move everything myself."

"The judge said that we was somethin' he called a ring, like me and them others was all organized, and stole cars and sold 'em all over everywhere, and made money out of it." She paused. "But, shoot, there wadn't nothin' to that. We stole three cars, one in Rockfish and another one up yonder in Sanford, and I was only with 'em when they taken the last two. We come down out of Sanford in a thirty-seven Packard, and ended up in that roadhouse with the tunnels. We didn't even know what we was goin' to do with it."

"You was already in trouble, no matter what you done with it."

"We knew that, we should'a knowed it, but we was havin' too good a time to worry about it. We used to come down to that one roadhouse, and wherever we was comin' from, we used to do it on all back roads. Those are great at night; greatest you ever saw. Sometimes you'll see a possum, and I never was on a trip with 'em that I didn't see at least one deer, either on the road or right near it. Once I saw a fox, and it wadn't no ghost-fox, neither. He was just trottin' along, comin' right to us; his eye'us just like diamonds in the car lights. Brighter."

"Them? Who is 'them?' "

"Them three boys I used to know. They was a good lot of fun, drinkin' and cuttin' up."

"That all you did? Ride around with 'em and look at possums?"

"Well, no," she said. "I was fuckin' 'em all, to tell the truth."

"I'll bet."

"I was fuckin' 'em all," she said with more satisfaction, "and I liked 'em all. One of 'em more than the others. He was the one was lookin' to do me in, but I didn't find out about it till we got back to the roadhouse and got to drinkin'."

"What do you mean, do you in? You mean he was fixin' to kill you?"

"No. He was gonna run off with somebody else. He might'a even been goin' to get married. I wadn't havin' none of that."

"What could you do about it?"

"I didn't know right then, but I'd'a done somethin'."

He waited, for there was no way that she could fail to continue from where she was.

"See," she said, "I have bad revenge problems. I don't like nobody doin' nothin' against me."

"I don't neither," Cahill said, not knowing what he meant, but meaning it.

"We parked that Packard, and went way on back into the roadhouse with a pitcher of beer. We was windin' on and on, till we dead-ended in a little booth which was all carved up with people's names. There was a man's head carved on the table, looked like a monkey; I can still see it. He ain't comin' back." She was silent again. "That's when they told me."

"About the other girl?"

"About her, and about something else they did, with her, and with another car."

"What?"

"They went over in Sampson County, them three and that-there girl, and picked up a car in Clinton and was drivin' back in the early mornin'. She was drivin', I know damn well she was, and they run into the back of a school bus. The sign was up, too, come to find out later on. The chilrun was comin' around the front of the bus, crossin' the highway, and she banked off the side of the bus and run over two of 'em and killed 'em. Two little girls. If I'd'a knowed they done that I wouldn'a never gone out with 'em again. I wouldn'a never seen Roland Albright again. I won't see him again, anyway. He's still in the fire. Ain't nothin' left of him."

"What did happen? Was he the only one that was killed?"

"What happened was that a fire got started, somewhere off in the other part of the roadhouse, maybe in the kitchen, or in the trash, or somewhere like that. And there was five other people burned up besides Roland. They was over in the other part. Roland was the only one in our part that didn't get out. I was in the ladies' room when it must'a started, and I had just got back to Roland and them when I smelt the smoke. We always did call that place a firetrap, and now we was liable to be trapped in it, you might say. We didn't even know exactly where we was, in all them board tunnels. When they got to fillin' up with smoke we was really bad off." She paused, and touched his shoulder. "How 'bout when you was doin' it?"

"Doin' what?"

"When you was buildin' that place you was tellin' me about? Didn't you never think about that thing catchin' on fire, and you trapped up in there?"

He had honestly not thought of it, but it could have happened; he felt the possibility with shocking force, and thought of fire driving him into walls he had nailed up around himself, walls from which he had not made a way to escape. "You're great," he said sourly. "Now I'll be scared to go back in there. I never did think about it catching fire before, though. I was hot enough as it was." Then, "There wadn't no place for a fire to start."

"Nobody ever knows where it starts. They don't know where, and they don't know how, and they don't know why. Usually there ain't no why to it, far as you can tell."

"There's somethin' you ain't bringin' out, about all this. It might be I could be puttin' some things together."

"You don't have to; you'd find out anyway, so I may as well tell you."

"You did it," he said. "You killed them people. Talk about me and my dog, and them other dogs. You set fire to that honky-tonk, didn't you?"

"No, I didn't, neither. They said I did it, but I didn't; they said I did it with Roland's cigarette lighter, which I did have on me. But if I'd'a done that, I sure wouldn'a gone back in there where they was; I'd'a got out of there, and got in that Packard and took off; I had the keys to it. I went back in there with Roland and them. But they said I done it, anyway. The others, the other two said it."

"You better tell me. You said you had a revenge problem. Is that what it was?"

"No, that ain't what it was. I swear it wadn't. I do get real mad at people, but I just think about what I might could do to 'em. But I don't never really do nothin'. I never hurt nobody in my life."

"When you first smelled the smoke, what did you do?"

"I had just got back to Haddon and that other boy, Tommy Gaffin, his name was, and Roland was comin' behind me, just turnin' in from the other alley where the bar was, carryin' a pitcher of beer. Just as soon as I turned around the smoke come in behind him, and before Haddon and Tommy could even get up out of the booth, the fire showed at the corner, and then was comin' right to us; the smoke was just boilin'."

"How did you get out?" he asked.

"We broke out. Haddon Truitt rammed out through the side of the booth. Tore his arm open on a nail. He went out, and then Tommy, and then me. I turned around to look for Roland, but the fire had done come up through the floor, and was between him and me. I got just one little look at him. When Haddon busted out through the wall I saw Roland in the fire. He was tryin' to say something, but so much was goin' on I never did hear it. The flames was just blastin' all around him. He didn't have his hands over his face, or anything, it didn't seem like; they was up in the air. There wadn't nothin' I could do. The fire was behind him, and in front of him; I think he was already on fire himself.

The way it was, he was just exactly like a shadow, a shadow with fire coming out of it, all along the arms, and maybe his hair, too. I couldn't help him. Nobody could'a helped him. He was gone, him and his shadow; his shadow burned up with him. They never did find his body."

"My God," Cahill said. "That was worse than a lot of things."

"The Fire Department got there toreckly. The whole roadhouse was on fire by that time; we went on out, tryin' to get away from the smoke, and sort of stumbled around in the parkin' lot. We couldn't get to the Packard; it was too hot where we had done left it. All the Fire Department men did was stand around in their fireman hats and looked at the fire, talkin' about what a hell of a fire it was, what a hell of a sight it was. They finally turned on one hose, and just piddled around with it. Finally the police come along, and we talked to 'em for a while. We couldn't leave, and we stayed there in the parkin' lot with the police, and with the others that had got out, until the whole thing had done burned down to the ground. There wadn't nothin' but some cars left; we stayed back from 'em because we thought they might blow up. After most all of the fire burnt out, the policemen went around with their flashlights, looking at the cars, and you could see where most of the paint had been blistered off of 'em. They looked like somebody had been after 'em with a blowtorch. After they checked the license plates, a couple of 'em went to a patrol car and made a call, and then come back and talked to us some more; not to anybody but us. Tommy Gaffin was cryin'; he loved Roland; he'd follow him around anywhere. He give them policemen the idea that I done the whole thing, and Haddon, he was standin' there and lettin' the policeman wrap his arm up, and he didn't say nothin'; he didn't say I did or I didn't. Later on, he said I did. He said I asked Roland for his lighter, and he told 'em I was mad at Roland on account of this other thing, this other girl. And I *was* mad at him, but I don't think I showed it. I didn't show it that much, anyway. I didn't burn him and them other people up. They can say what they want to, they can think what they want to. I didn't do it."

"What did you need the lighter for?"

"I used to borry it from Roland all the time. I wadn't really used to smokin' nowhere but in the bathroom, like in the mill. I went in there and smoked part of a Lucky Strike, and then came right on back."

"What then? Did they arrest you? Did they book you for the car?"

"They did book us. My father got me out on bail the next day, but they made a case against us. Tommy Gaffin and I got three years in the reformatory, and Haddon went to the state work farm at Blakeney, because he was over twenty-one, and him and Roland had done been caught a couple of times before. Right up to the last I thought they was goin' to let me off, because I never had been in no kind of trouble before, but the business about the fire was somethin' they couldn't forget about, after Tommy told 'em. They never could prove nothin', but they helt it against me, and I went up to the State Girls' Reformatory at Lazear. That was a rough-ass place, I can tell you."

"Did you do the whole three years?"

"I did every blessèd minute of 'em. I never tried so hard in my life to do what people wanted me to do, but just as soon as I got in there, seems like, they'us after me for bein' a troublemaker. Everything that happened in that place was my fault. If the laundry quota wadn't up, it was because of me. If some girl stuck a sewing needle in some other one, it had somethin' to do with me. No, I didn't get no time off for good behavior, because they wouldn't give me credit for none. I was there the whole time, every day and every night."

"That must change things around for you," Cahill said.

"Well, you got to learn to live a different way in there, that's all. There was some real good girls; a lot of 'em just had bad luck, but there was some girls in there that'd just as soon kill you as look at you; some of 'em had ruther. You was in there with all kinds."

"I reckon you learn right quick which ones to stay away from."

"You couldn't stay away from 'em, though," she said. "They'd come after you. Some of 'em you couldn't tell from a man. Three or four of them kind took some poor little new girl off back in a dressmakin' shop and laid her on a cuttin' table and did all kind of stuff to her all one afternoon. Scissors was part of it, maybe. You could hear her hollerin' all the way into C-Block, where I was, way off in the other corner of the damn place. I don't know what they was doin' to her, and I don't want to know. The matrons didn't do nothin', and there was plenty of 'em around; there was about as many of them as there was of us."

"Was that the worst?"

"It might'a been the worst for her, but it wadn't the worst for me, or for some pretty good friends of mine."

"I ought not to want to hear about all this," Cahill said. "But go ahead. You might as well."

"You got to hear about it," she said, and Cahill thought that there might even be indignation in the way she spoke. "I'm comin' up on my big scene."

The bed shifted; her leg was against his, but he did not change position. "Go on," he said. "And it better be good."

"I ain't quite there yet," she said. "You got to know more about the place, about what it was like in there, before you can really understand what I'm talkin' about."

"I'm still here."

"The one thing on my side was that I had two good cellmates. We had three real beds, and not, you know, bunk beds. That was good. And we could fix the room up a little bit. One of 'em, Brenda Lee Tinsley from Wilson, who was in there for gettin' caught shopliftin' about ninety times, could cut some interestin' things out of paper, and she made us some nice decorations for the walls. She wadn't afraid of nothin'; she come in there after I did, and she said that them matrons would have it to do if they fooled with her. But they did fool with her, and she put up with it after they took her down to the warden's office and liked to have beat the ass off her. But she was tough, and a good friend; real good. The other girl, Arlene Cothran, was a real quiet black-headed little skinny thing from Avery County, over by Linville. She was a real hillbilly; she was the one taught me that song about the fox hunt. She kilt her mother and one of her aunts with a shotgun when she was fourteen years old; she never would say why. She was real religious; and didn't read nothin' but the Bible and them little pages she got from the chaplain; she was devotional, that's the word, and didn't make no trouble for nobody. She could sew up a storm; she worked in the dress shop, and would even sew when she came back to C-Block; sit there and sew. I can see her now."

"It's good to have friends," Cahill said lamely, shifting away, but not completely clear of her thin leg.

"It was us against the matrons. They didn't have no cause to hate us, but they did hate us. And we had plenty of cause to hate them, I can tell you. Seems like they liked to work us over, sometimes for nothin', just to have somethin' to do. I know damn well they liked it. We had to take it, though; there wadn't nothin' else we could do. They didn't care how bad they hurt you; I'm surprised they didn't kill somebody. About every two weeks the whole place got beat, whether anybody did anything or not."

"That's tough," Cahill said. "I'd think that'd make a bad situation."

"It was plenty bad. What's the sense of tryin' to keep yourself in line, and do what they told you to do, if they was gonna get after you anyway?

When one of us did somethin', or them matrons thought she did, we'd all get it, either one at a time or all at once."

"I'm not followin' you," Cahill said, nothing cold now but his nose, his hands moist under the covers, his thigh uncomfortable with the girl's heat.

"Let me tell you somethin'," she said, now talking more rapidly and urgently. "About five girls from A-Block got in the bakery, and the warden and them couldn't get 'em out for two days. They put the furniture against the door, and damned if they was goin' to come out; they was holed up in there good. They wanted to make a deal, and make a situation where we could tell people some of the things we thought was wrong, where we could *make* 'em treat us better than they was doin'; where we could, you know, fool around amongst ourselves if we wanted to, but not them fool with us, or gang up on us and make us do things. We was all pullin' for 'em to hold out."

"What happened?"

"They sent a note to the warden and she said she would talk to 'em, treat 'em fair, if they'd come out; she said she was willing to work with 'em. Mrs. Durfoss was her name. I never had even seen her before. I never did see her until that next day."

"Did things get better?"

"You crazy? Soon as them girls took that furniture off the door, the guards went in and got 'em. We didn't hear no more about it until the next day. Little Arlene cried all night long, and prayed so much and so loud that Brenda Lee and me couldn't get no sleep."

"I can't either," Cahill said, stirring with an unfamiliar excitement. "How long is this gonna take?"

"As long as it takes," she said. "Now you just listen to what I tell you. There wadn't no work call the next morning. We just sat there in the cell waitin' for them to come after us. About ten o'clock they did. They took everybody on C-Block out across the main yard and into the mess hall. They got the girls in the other blocks later on. Why they started with us, I never will know. But there we was, lined up in the mess hall, and it looked like every matron in the place was in there with us. Some of 'em I never had even seen before. They locked the doors at both ends. A lot of the girls was already cryin'."

"Did you just stand there?" he said, feeling her hand on his side.

"Not for long. The warden come in, come out in front of us, and stood up on the bench of the table that run down all that part of the room; about a hundred foot of table, or right near to it. She was a dumpy big old woman, wide as a ax handle, and had on these kind of glasses that don't have no rim around 'em. She told us we was all responsible for them girls holin' up in the bakery; shit, I didn't even know which ones they was. She said that after that morning, wouldn't no more of that be happenin'. We just stood there shakin', while about half of the matrons—more'n half, I expect—went around the table and lined up on the other side. One of the girls started screamin' and broke out of line, but two of the matrons went and got her and dragged her over the table. Two matrons on the other side taken hold of her arms and pulled her down flat on the table, with her legs under the seat, which was like a long bench, and was bolted into the table, don't you see. She was the first one they taken over there, and then they come and done the same thing to the rest of us. Some of us they had to drag, and I saw 'em pick up and carry one big fat girl that was fightin' like a heifer. Me, I just kind of walked on over and sat down. I knew it wadn't no use to do anything else. If they didn't kill me, I could stand it. I didn't like it, but I could stand it."

"I hope you're not talkin' about what I'm thinkin'," Cahill said, breaking sweat with a terrifying warmth. "They wouldn't do that," he said. "They got laws in those places, same as everywhere else. They wouldn't beat you. People on the outside would hear about it."

"The hell they wouldn't beat us, and if anybody on the outside heard it, they would be hearin' us out through the walls. There was a whole lot of noise."

Something deadly and breathless was rising in him; more deadly and breathless than he had ever felt. "Go on," he said, his arm falling around her close body, though she did not need to be pulled in to him.

"I just sat there, across a table from Miss MacNichols and Miss Fayerweather, who didn't have no use for me. 'Put out your hands,' Miss Fayerweather said. 'Both of 'em.' I did, and they took holt of 'em and pulled me down acrost the table. Miss Garrett was behind me, and it was her pinned the back of my dress up between my shoulders. Down to one side of me I heard a strap smack, and some girl hollered like her throat had done been cut. Then one on the other side of me started in, and then they was a whole lot of 'em carryin' on, and that's when I felt my pants go down."

Cahill swallowed, and wiped his eyes. The pinked-edged sparks were shooting across with an intensity they had not had since he had first seen them hurtle in the days just before his final blindness, and he had sat watching in fascination. His loins came up with a grim unstoppable solidity, and he had no power to push her hand away. She was saying to him "You got to *see* it, you got to *see* it." He listened with shocking involvement. "Right yonder in front of me was old Mrs. McNichols, her false teeth clamped down till she sweat', holdin' one of my hands, and right next to her was Miss Fayerweather, her hair pulled on back around her ugly head, and her glasses set right straight across her big white nose, holdin' the other one. I was pulled down flat, and my legs was under the seat. I couldn't see behind me, but I knew damn well it was Mrs. Garrett, who had done beat up on me three or four times, and had been looking for a chance to do it right, all she wanted. All up and down the table the matrons had started in, and the hollerin' from all them girls was like to have drove the table through the wall."

Cahill's stomach turned over, looking for escape, but an escape which could not take place, but which would go deeper and higher into what was happening to him.

"Then it come down acrost me, like a flash that wanted to cut me in two, acrost my bare ass. I jumped and squealed and bellowed like a wild hog. Then it went acrost me again, and I started in kickin' and cryin' with the rest of 'em full time. Before they was through I like to have kicked that seat down into match-wood."

She stopped the movement of her hand, and there was a light rasping above him where her face might have been. She took hold of him again, in a new smoother dimension of rhythmic intensity. Then she stopped, and he heard her say with no-nonsense authority, as the covers went from him, "Sit up, now, and turn around. Put your feet on the floor." He heard Zack snarl, but did not hear his feet. Something was placed unexpectedly in his hand. It was flat, metal or wood—if wood, slick with paint—like part of a small heavy lath or split shingle or a paling.

"All right," she said, "now you *do* it." Her light body came with sudden and planted warmth across his knees.

"Do what?" he asked, holding her weight, now still, across his lap, and the flat object in his right hand.

"Go on, now," she said, down and away from him. "Smack it good."

"I can't do that," he said. "I wouldn't want to hurt . . . I mean why . . . ? Who . . . ?"

"You know who," she said. "Now come down on me with that thing. Give it to me. I like it. I'm gonna cut up some, like I didn't like it, but I do. Get after me now. Whip me like a bad girl."

"This is a mistake," he said. "This is a bad mistake," he held her and said, sparring for a purchase, a hold on his own words, too far gone in a new kind of event to know what it was he was trying to tell her. "Let's get on back in bed, little girl," he said. "That's enough of this. I ain't gonna hit you with this thing, or with anything else."

"The hell you're not," she said, evidently turning her face part way around to him. "This is just us, right here and right now. You're gonna do something I done learned and learned to like, and I'm gonna make you like it. You hold me good, and you give it to me good. Don't tell me you don't like it. You got all your blood right where it belongs, standin' up and wantin' in. Hold on, now, and do like I tell you."

What do I have? he thought, knowing that now he must deal with the situation, no matter what; there was nowhere he could go. "My God, little girl," he said, his voice coming out low. "Damn if you ain't skinny as a sparrow."

"I'm waitin'," she said.

He took hold of her around the ribs, and raised her partially, shifting her from contact with his organ. "Now if I give you just a little of what you want," he said, "you gonna be good and get back in bed and go to sleep?"

"I ain't promisin'," she said again turning back to him. "You do it, and we'll see."

He brought the object in his hand down where he thought her buttocks probably were, and then again. "More," she said. "I want more, a lot more."

Slowly, at first not using any real force but increasing the force in spite of himself, he was drawn into the overpowering emotion of her reaction. Abruptly, as he was beginning to be aware that real injury might be possible, might be very close, she stood up from him and pushed him backward to the bed, grasping his feet and turning him. "Lay back," she said, and was astride him. He no longer cared what he had done or where he was, who he was with, or who he was. The bed beneath him, astonishingly deep and unlayered, dropping away to a distance beyond conception, sustained him, lifted him into a demonic and rhythmic heat that burned his maleness away and restored it in a place, a region, a secret access wild with uncontrollable power, stroked with all-side parallels of justified sensation; gathering from his most essential body, somewhere hidden and waiting lifelong among all his organs, his being drove with all it could command, and more, with a helpless, once-usable, and unified violence, straight up from cloud, hung, burst, renewed, burst again, and was withdrawn, softening back through him and disappearing beneath.

"Good," she said intently. "Real good," but almost at once, just after she spoke, or as she was speaking, the heat had changed position, but not changed. A hot splashing scalding struck his right eyelid, and then the bridge of his nose; there was a white-hot point at his throat like the end of a wire, and then several more across his chest and shoulder as her main heat, the heat that had pinned him, left, and from a position somewhere else in the room she said, coughing and sneezing, leaving over his arm a delicate spray of warmth, "Let me get a towel right quick." He heard water running, and raised his fingers to feel his eyelids and between them, palping the moisture. She came back as he was tasting his forefinger. Her voice was nasal as it had not been. "I'm real sorry," she said. And then, "Can you hear me all right?"

"I can hear you," he said. "What's the matter?"

"I got toilet paper stuck up my nose," she said. "These nosebleeds just come on me, and I can't help it. That's why I keep it so cold in here. But I guess we got too hot, maybe. Anyway, I'm sorry. Let me clean you up. I done bled all over everything, all over the floor. But I can get it off you; I can do that, anyway." She passed a warm rough cloth over his face and throat. "It gets thin in there, you know; it thins out, your nose thins out inside, like it was milk, skim milk. You can feel it runnin', but not like somethin' you want to blow out. You want to keep it, you sniff it back, you suck it in, but it still runs; you feel it thin out and run, just when you don't want it to, and it comes out blood."

"You been to the doctor about this?" he said, still tense.

"Not in a long time. The one I went to, it looked like he didn't really know what was wrong with me. Sometimes I do feel right weak, and my nose bleeds, and it might be that I've got somethin' really wrong with me, but if it don't get no worse than this I ain't gonna worry about it."

"That's OK," he said, pushing her hand back. "That's good enough. I'll be all right. Now come on back. And really do let's go to sleep, this time."

She came over him again, passed, and settled between him and the window. When she was still she said, "You know, you're all right, blind man. In the dark, you're as good as any of 'em. You are some man, sure enough. You don't need to make no apologies."

"I don't apologize; that's something I don't do." Then, "What was that I was hittin' you with?"

"That was your boy's ruler," she said. "The one that slides back and forth. You know, the one with all the numbers on it. He put enough numbers on my butt with that thing to build a highway bridge."

Cahill let this pass, for he had no way to deal with it. "I didn't really hurt you, did I?"

"No," she said, "not really *hurt* hurt, like you was trying to injure me, or somethin' like that. It was just one of those things that Joel and I did. He liked to imagine all this stuff, make it up, and I had been in jail where they really done it, or somethin' like it, and we just happened to get together, and found out that was what we wanted to do; we was just lucky, you could say. You know when it's right, like it was just now, when you do what you really want to do, what you been thinkin' about; when you get on down in there with it, where don't nothin' else matter."

"I guess you and him was up here a lot," Cahill said. "Is that so?"

"Not all that much," she said. "Before he met up with me, Joel used to be fuckin' that girl that works in Supply, the one the colonel fools around with, Lucille her name is, but when he started comin' out here, he didn't go back in amongst them dead sheeps no more. He used to tell me about all that wool, and the dead feelin' about it. But we got down to where it really is; him and me, we had live animals. Everything was off of us but that."

They were still, and the dog got up, stood among the bright coins, put his head down and lapped here and there at the floor. The moon shone in halved and utter radiance, picking out what coins the floor held for it within the laid frame of the window.

They slowed, and rolled motionless; the enclosed jeep held its air around them as Corporal Phillipson killed the engine and still cold set in. Cahill felt for the door handle, opened the door, and let himself down and out, his farther foot squeaking when it hit. It had snowed again; the level was up past his shoe sole. Zack scrambled down and brushed strongly and quickly past him as he closed the door, leaned against it and turned his head this way and that.

There was no snow in the air,

Corporal Phillipson got out and went around the back of the jeep. The ground fog had become so thick, especially after he had turned in from the highway, that he was a little frightened. There had not been anything like this since he had been at the Base: such a solid surround of dark but intense quiet; there were no boys' voices, though he knew by now that he stood at the edge of the PT area, which stretched out from the motor pool, away from the Administration Building and along the backs of the hangars, and he was used to the sound of their games.

No voice, but a quick bursting-in of engine-sound, both reluctant and assertive, hoarse and thick-throated, which rose to include a suggestion of mechanical flapping or beating. Cahill listened, for the sound was there, and not quite as he had heard it before. The beating, though emphatic, was not sharply defined; it was more like a battering of quilts. All of it fell, then, coughed twice, and ended. Cahill took off a glove and passed his hand back and forth through the air, then rubbed the fingers with his thumb.

"Socked in," he said. "You don't have to tell me."

Cahill automatically put out his hand; the other's handshake was quick, decisive, and small. The whiteness he had never been in; he felt lucky to have been able to find the motor pool through the pine grove, especially the way the track wound around; with the road now the same color as the air.

At the level of Phillipson's own head another head materialized, and came close, red-faced under a pulled-down ski cap that might have been another tone from the whiteout; gray, maybe. The head, which at first had seemed, not as an illusion but to be, quite actually, detached, was now close enough for its dim body, dressed in a wool warm-up suit, to be there. Toward the engine-sound the man went into the fighting antics of Donald Duck—one fist straight out, the other pump-handling rigidly up and down beside it; Phillipson had seen him do this before. He turned to Phillipson, bobbing and weaving. Jack Dempsey now. Then he straightened, his hands on his hips, and looked quietly and with real interest at Cahill, readjusting the white towel, almost luminous, around his neck and tucking it into his sweater.

"This is Captain Claymore," Phillipson said, "the PT instructor for the Post."

"Socked in it is," Claymore said. "The birds ain't walking today; they're on their knees, they're crawling on their belly like

voice was Southern-country but educated; not a cracker voice; probably small town, with relatives in the country somewhere maybe not far off.

a copperhead trying to get in under the chicken wire. It's a good thing flying's over, almost all of it, anyway. Most of the boys have got their time in."

"There's a few more hours that need to be got," said Phillipson. "Make-up flights. Maybe it'll clear off."

"Well, that ain't really our concern, is it Phil? We just keep the records."

Claymore, from behind himself, where it had been held to his back by the waistband of his warm-ups, produced a clipboard, also almost invisible.

"What do you do?" Cahill asked. "Coach these kids, or somethin'?" He was tiring, now, of trying to assess people by what he could feel and hear of them; this had become a distinct effort, with so many, one after the other.

"I do more testing than coaching," Claymore said. "I run 'em, I sit 'em up, I push 'em up, I chin 'em. I've got notes on everybody, statistics, the works. They all go on the 1-A."

"Must be interestin'," Cahill said without interest.

"It's not so bad as you might think," Claymore said. "This new one is only the third class, and I still keep coming up on little things that keep the job from getting dull. It may get dull later, if the war goes on. I can see how it might."

"Joel was out here doin' this stuff, was he?" Cahill asked, settling, only half there, into his routine question. Claymore looked closely at Cahill, disturbed, like the others, by the lack of expression.

"He sure was," Claymore said. "The first part of each period we spend on calisthenics, where everybody does pretty much the same. The last part I turn 'em loose, and they do whatever they like."

"What do they like?"

"Mostly football and basketball. As you can . . . well, we've got a football field that's almost two hundred yards long, or it can be, if the boys want it to be. Makes it almost a different sport from what you see on a regulation field; opens up the game a lot. And it's a good deal rougher too, because with more people playing—around here, it's re-

ally true that any number can play—and more room for 'em to acceler-
ate; the blocking gets a mite enthusiastic sometimes. It's just touch
football, but the blocking is just like regular ball. I spend a lot of my
time trying to keep 'em from getting hurt. Major Iannone, the doc
around here, has got real good at bloody noses."

"Joel play football?"

"No," Captain Claymore said, "I never did see him on that big field.
He could have played, though. He was pretty fast, as I remember. But
he always played basketball. We've got more or less regulation courts,
and we try to keep the sand and gravel rolled down so the ball will
bounce, or at least bounce some. He used to be out there with his team,
every period. Shears, his big buddy, used to take care of the football."

"Yeah," Cahill said, "he liked to have run over me the other day."

"I prowl, you know," Claymore said, picking an end of his towel out
of the sweater and wiping his eyes. "I never heard the word 'monitor'
until I was in OTC in Miami. I'm supposed to monitor these games, and
sometimes referee, especially the football games, and sometimes I do
the passing for both sides. The team I pass for the most loses usually,
and I feel OK about going back to monitoring. I watch the basketball on
these four courts, where there's not quite so much bashing, although
there is some; a few of these boys played basketball in college, and they
throw elbows; they'll muscle you out, under the basket. All that, I've got
charge of, or so it says in the TO."

"Table of organization," Phillipson supplied.

"Joel played basketball, on your gravel courts?"

"Well," Claymore said, smiling, "not *all* gravel. Yeah, he played out
here, with his bunch, Harbelis, Blazek, Crider, and a little weasel named
Mewshaw, who could steal a ball out of a monkey's jockstrap. He
brought the ball down court, him and Crider. Cahill played forward on
the right side, usually. He had excellent depth perception, and told me
once that he didn't need the backboard to shoot; said he'd rather not
have it."

"Tell me about all this," Cahill said, oddly remembering Harbelis's
request when he had first come to the base, and the intake-of-breath
sound when he had finally dropped the ball through.

"Well," Claymore said, "Cahill was not one of these goons. The cadet
height limit is six feet three, and I'd say he was about two or three
inches under that. He was quick more than he was fast, but he was not as
fast as somebody like Harbelis. We've got a Greek boy here who can run

a ten-flat in tennis shoes. Ten-flat is fast. Almost nobody who says he can do it can really do it."

Cahill held his fire for a moment, and then sprang what he had. "I know," he said, "I've timed him. I got ten-eight."

"No shit," said Claymore, puzzled but impressed. "He can do that any time. But basketball, uh-uh. Harbelis was just average. I don't think he'd ever played much before. He was just out there with Joel."

"And what happened?" Cahill asked. "What would happen?"

Claymore thought, his eyes down, and then raised them honestly. "Well, the best I can tell you is that he was a very good what you would call floor man, whether your floor is hardwood or gravel. He seemed to know where everybody was, all the time. Both teams."

"How could he do that? Ain't they all runnin' around, back and forth, and everything?"

"Some people can do it, and they're the valuable ones. I tell you, Mr. Cahill," Claymore went on, saying whatever he could think of to put the situation in the best light it could take, "*I'd*'ve recruited him, I can tell you. He could set up a play before an ordinary person could even think of it, and do it on the dead run. His people—Harbelis and Mewshaw and them—all knew where to be. He'd just flick a finger or glance somewhere on the court, and they'd be there. He could blindside pass like you couldn't believe. I heard Mewshaw say, when they first started playing together, that the ball just seemed to come out of nowhere. I remember him saying 'Joel's got it, and then if I'm open I've got it, and going up for the shot.' "

"And he would shoot, too?" Cahill asked, still remembering the ball leaving his own hand into the usual dark, and the fact that he had hit, finally, what he aimed at.

"Not so much as you might think. Usually one of the guards controls the game, the speed of it, the rhythm of it, but for some reason Joel liked to run things from that right-hand corner; you know, work it in from there. He told me he used to play guard, but that now he was doing guard duty in a forward area. It was very seldom that he would pass back out, though he would do that, once in a while. They had a tall boy named Francis Cook in the middle, and he did most of the scoring, and Mewshaw did some, coming in fast. Joel would feed these guys in the strangest ways; he was very unselfish about the ball, and about shooting. He would take the right shot and was better than average when he did, but mostly he'd pass off. I told him to shoot more, and he said he'd rather somebody else would do that."

388

"That don't sound exactly like . . . I mean . . ."

"I know it doesn't," Claymore said. "He told me he didn't claim to do everything." He hesitated. "He did say that, you know."

"You couldn't prove that by some of these other cadets," Phillipson said. "If he didn't claim it, they'd claim it for him."

"There was one thing, though," Claymore said, hesitating and looking from Cahill to Phillipson, and then going on as the memory took him. "None of his boys seemed to be in very good shape. I mean, that they might have been when they came out of Pre-Flight, but they didn't stay that way. Joel and everybody that had anything to do with him were underweight, and you could almost say they were run-down. They didn't have any wind, and they were not strong, either. Their scores fell off, a little at first, and then a lot, and at the end they were bad, real bad. It was the damnedest thing. Not a one of 'em was sick; nobody went on sick call, except Joel, and there was something else wrong with him that didn't have anything to do with his wind, or the push-ups he could do; it was his feet, as I recollect."

"Yeah," Cahill said. "He had warts on his feet; seed warts, ingrown, like. They got 'em out with moleskin and aspirin."

"He didn't miss any of my tests, though," Claymore said, tapping the clipboard. "He could run all right, but not very far. We have 'em do three hundred yards, on a shuttle basis; you know, back and forth. He didn't seem to want to look like he was dogging it—he'd just stride up and down the fifty we laid out, not gutting himself—but I could tell he was really trying, anyway; he just didn't have any poop, any stamina. Harbelis, Blazek, Rolader, and Spain, they were all the same way. Shears too. I kept telling Shears that he was supposed to set an example, but he couldn't do any better either; they'd all just wind down on the last fifty. They didn't give up, they gave out. Damned if I can understand it. The rest of the boys did fine; some of 'em even improved. But not Adler and Rolader, and not Cahill and Spain."

"What was wrong, do you reckon?" Cahill asked.

"I don't know. Major Iannone don't know. My records know what, but they don't know why. None of 'em were sick."

"It's not your fault, sir," said Phillipson.

"Well," said Claymore, "I used to think it might be. I used to get on 'em a lot, especially Harbelis, who was physically, you know, the best athlete amongst 'em. I used to say, 'Listen, you dumb sponge-diver: if you ever want to do anything in the two-twenty, or run the relay when you get back in school, you're gonna have to get hold of some wind somewhere, or you'll feel like you've done put on one of them divin' suits somewhere in the last seventy-five yards, helmet and all.' But it didn't do any good; he was struggling at the end, just like the others."

"They'll all be gone after Sunday," Corporal Phillipson said, glancing belatedly at Cahill, who was propped with strange nonchalance against the car, his hands in his overcoat pockets. "Then you can start in with another class where maybe that won't happen."

His back was resting well, and the air in his nostrils, at the same time cutting and thick with moisture, was unusual, and something he could stand for a while; his hands fingered things that he had become used to, careful not to be cut.

Zack bumped his leg, and was making a grim preliminary noise. Cahill pulled a hand free and reached down to calm him, his face chin up, listening and trying to smell through the cold wall he was breathing.

"Who is it now?" he asked; there had been no new steps. Or had there? Zack's sounds did not increase, but went on.

Corporal Phillipson waited as patiently as he could, looking into the whiteout past Captain Claymore, who, even at close range, was still indistinct, with a voice unusually loud for a man not entirely present. Beside him—a little behind him, surely—a short black line formed in the air at about the level of Phillipson's nose, and Cadet Frank Spain's high-boned face began to focus around the dark unbroken eyebrows. The eyes were light gray, no different from the air, and Phillipson was surprised he could not see clearly into the other's head.

The head descended, as Spain went, with a little effort, to the deep-knee position.

"How about you, Zack?" he said, close to the dog. "Here I am again. Don't get after me no more; I'm a friendly."

"Who is it?" Cahill asked, pushing off from the car.

"Cadet Spain, sir," Phillipson said.

"Good God," Cahill said. "Be still, Zack. Don't bite him again."

"Can I pet him?" Spain asked, ground-level fog stirring with his shifts.

"I guess," Cahill said. "Do everything real slow."

Smoothed between his ears, Zack sank again to his haunches, watching guardedly; his sound backed into him and was gone.

"See," the cadet said, "I didn't draw back a nub." He stood up and flexed a leg. "It's great to be out."

"How did you know we were at the motor pool?" Corporal Phillipson asked. "I couldn't hardly see to drive in here."

"We were looking," Spain said. "We knew where you were, and about when you'd get here."

"Well," Phillipson said, "if you know that you also know Mr. Cahill has a meeting with the colonel this morning, as soon as we can get over there. Anything else'll have to wait."

"We know it," Spain said, "and we can wait. I just came out here to stretch my leg a little, and to remind Mr. Cahill to come by Second Barracks after he's through with the colonel."

A cautious low-gear engine moved toward them from the direction of the forest; a car came to rest a few feet from theirs, and quieted. In a moment Captain Faulstick was with them, turning up the collar of his salmon pink overcoat, thinking of something to say.

"All finished?" Spain asked. "Your Form Five all locked up?"

"I'm done," Captain Faulstick said, looking around and seeing nothing but the others. "Manetta passed me. I needed one more check-ride, just for them to be sure, and Manetta said I did OK."

"That's good," Spain said, without real approval. "He can be tough, they tell me."

"I was able to do everything I was supposed to do. The slow roll to the left was not the best, but the Immelmann came out all right, and I did pretty well on emergency procedure. Anyway, I'm glad it's over. A little more ground school and the parade, and we can all pack up and leave this cold woolly place."

"We're just busting up," Spain said. "Everybody's due somewhere."

"Stay a little," Faulstick said, looking around again. "My car is warm. Come in and sit down. Relax; take it easy."

Spain turned. "That'd be OK," he said. "And thanks for the hospitality, in advance." And then, turning, "Phillipson, you can peel off, and tell the colonel Mr. Cahill will be along in a minute or two."

"I've got to look busy, too," Captain Claymore said. "Come on, Phil; I'll walk back over with you."

His hand on Spain's shoulder, leaving Zack, Cahill crossed to Faulstick's car and got in. His door closed and two others. Everything was very still and hot. Sweat started and itched in the middle of Cahill's chest; in his pockets the palms moistened, still uninjured.

"It's good to be just this still," Faulstick said. "Feel how solid this thing sits, on what it's sitting on. If we were even one foot—if we were just six inches off the ground, this white stuff would be dangerous; it'd be deadly."

"That depends," Spain said from behind them. "It doesn't have to be."

Cahill was disturbed by the captain's tone, which carried a pleading uncertainty, an anxiousness that Cahill had not heard in a human voice since he had been blind.

"You're a combat veteran," Spain said evenly. "This ought not to bother you too much."

"Well, it does bother me," Faulstick said. "I was not flying the airplane then. I had another kind of job, Mr. Spain, as you may know. I left the rest of it to the boys with the thousand-hour crush in their hats."

"You may get a thousand hours yourself, one of these days," Spain said. "I mean as a pilot. You just may. Who knows?"

"I'm still glad I'm not up in this stuff," Faulstick said, and then plunged on. "I've been dreaming about something I heard, when I first came into the Training Command. Something that happened at Gardner Field, California. Basic. I checked it out, and it did happen. Only a few months ago. It happened, and they relieved the commanding officer. They could have court-martialed him, too. Maybe they should have."

Oddly, Spain said nothing. After he had waited a moment, and still expecting the cadet to speak, Cahill asked "What happened out yonder?"

"They had a situation where the weather was bad, and they couldn't get the flights up. The CO was a new guy, had just made colonel, and this was one of his first classes; it might even have been the first. Anyway, they had this situation where the area was socked in all during the last part of the class's tour, and they were having all kinds of trouble getting time in. There was a possibility that they were going to have to hold the class back, and that wouldn't look good on anybody's record, especially the CO's. Then the weather broke, and they got some flying time, almost enough but not quite."

Cahill waited for something disastrous to happen. Faulstick's voice seemed to be drawn forward into whatever it might be, and was more and more painful with it.

"They start night flying in Basic, Mr. Cahill," Faulstick went on. "But all on visuals; there was no radio in those particular BTs. At least I don't think there was."

"You're gonna like that night stuff a lot, I'll bet," Spain said. "It's coming up next, you know; in about six or seven weeks. Shaw Field, Sumter, South Carolina, is where we're all gonna be buzzing around like lightning bugs. You too, Captain."

"Go on," Cahill said, hoping his willed interest would help. "It got bad again, but they had to fly anyway. I can see it comin'."

"That's right," Spain said. "A cadet in D-barracks, the class before us, got a letter from his brother, who was in the first section that flew that mission. It was a long letter. I never did read it, but we all knew about it, and what we didn't actually know, we could imagine. It was a real bad-news night, out yonder."

"Well," Cahill said, "*I* can't imagine it. You'll have to tell me."

Spain leaned forward, and Captain Faulstick looked back over his shoulder at him, and kept his face side on as the cadet talked.

"The way I heard it," Spain said, "the boys were just sittin' around the ready room, waiting for the mission to be scrubbed. When it got dark, there wasn't much ground fog, but everybody believed there would be more. That's the way it was two or three nights before this one; some ground fog, and then a lot of other stuff coming in behind it from the west. They scrubbed those missions, so why wouldn't they scrub this one? Everybody was writing letters or reading books; nobody thought they'd let the flight stay in. But they did. The guy in the letter's supposed to have said that when he walked out to the BT the fog was around his feet, but he could still see 'em. But he wasn't any too happy about losing the ground. Nobody in the first flight was, and you could imagine how the others were taking it, who had to wait till the first echelon brought the planes back to fly the mission. By that time everything would be blinded out sure enough; even the worms would be uneasy, and they had contact. Without it, and with no radio, you'd be in some trouble. That kind of air will kill you dead. When it turns white, Captain." Spain paused until Faulstick looked around, which he did, then made an enclosing gesture. "Like this."

"Why was it all that important?" asked Cahill, bothered by the odd tension of the seat against his back and wondering what kind of position Captain Faulstick might be in to cause it.

"It had to be on the Form Five," Spain said. "You know, the record. It's got to be on there that you made one solo night mission. There's a beacon about fifty miles north of Gardner, and you were just supposed to take off, fly up there, mainly on instruments, make a hundred-and-eighty-degree procedure turn around the position of the beacon, and come on back down to base and land. With visual contact, it wasn't supposed to be too hard, because if you were on course, or even anywhere near it, you couldn't miss the beacon. But if you couldn't see it, you were fucked. You might be able to guess the position of the beacon by time-rate DR, and you could make the turn—or *a* turn—but if you couldn't see base when you got back you were double-fucked. You were dead, and some of 'em were."

"I can't believe that," Faulstick said, shifting again and looking almost directly at Spain. "It seems to me that the operations officer . . . I mean that's not what I . . ."

"The operations officer is not the base commander," Spain said. "To him it was a matter of getting the time in. He was willing to take a chance. He gambled with the weather, and lost. Or the cadets lost, if you wanted to put it that way."

"What was the end of it?" Faulstick asked. "How did it come out?"

"All kinds of ways," Spain said. "Seven or eight cadets went in, stayed with the aircraft until they ran out of gas, probably up there circling and climbing, and coming down, and not finding anything except more white all around 'em. The instruments'll tell you just so much, but they can't see the ground for you; they can't tell you where the mountains are. One kid went all the way over into the Arizona mountains before he pranged in. A couple of 'em just ran into the ground, one of 'em not far from the field."

"Nobody got out?" Faulstick asked. "Nobody got back?"

"Nobody got back to Gardner. One cadet landed over in the desert east of there, and didn't even hurt the airplane. He found a place where he could see enough to let down, and landed it on the hardpan; had hundreds of miles of runway, all directions. And two or three bailed out, and made it, all right; they lived. And that's maybe the end of the story."

"Maybe?" Captain Faulstick said sharply. "What do you mean, maybe?"

"Well," Spain said, "there was an investigation, and the base commander was relieved. They should have shot the son-of-a-bitch, or at least sent him to Leavenworth. Could be they did, come to think of it; I don't know what happened to him."

"And that *is* all," Faulstick said, and turned forward once again.

"Well, like I say," Spain said, leaning back and sighing, "maybe. There was one other thing about it, though, that is right strange. It really happened, too. It was in the papers."

"You mean there was something about this business that wasn't a fuck-up?" Cahill asked.

"No," Spain said, "I didn't say that. I would never say that. This was maybe the worst fuck-up of all, but it's kind of funny, no matter what."

"Well then," Cahill asked, "what?"

"Here was this one kid, must have been real nervous, one of the last on the second echelon; when he walked out to the aircraft he probably *couldn't* see his feet. So he gets in, and he starts the engine. He looks around him. He can barely make out the parking area, and he can't see the taxiway, much less the runway. So he sits there watching the fog roll in. About that time, it had probably got to be just about like this is now, Captain. The real fog had come in, and was sitting on top of the ground fog. Rolled in off the ocean, probably, and this poor son-of-a-bitch is sitting there in the whiteout with the engine roaring back at him, and everything just fine in the cockpit check. He goes through it once; everything's all right. He goes through it again; it's all right again; better than all right. He can't just sit there. He's got to go. So he goes."

"Just how in the hell do you know all this, Spain?" Faulstick asked.

"I don't *know* it," Spain said evenly, "but I can imagine it. I can be in that cockpit with him." He paused, and Cahill himself turned, feeling the warm air intensify. "Can you do it? Try to do it, Captain. You've got all the same conditions. This fog is probably just exactly like that fog."

"But I don't have to take off in it," Faulstick said. "I wouldn't, either."

"That's right, Captain," Spain said. "You wouldn't, but he did. He went on, he managed to get on to the taxiway, he made it to the runway, and did the best he could to get himself lined up. Then he advanced the throttle—you know, Captain, that's what you're supposed to do when you take off—and he gets the thing rolling. He rolls and rolls. The tail wheel comes off. He must still be on the runway, 'cause he hadn't hit anything yet. He goes on and on; he's still alive. He's right where he is, he doesn't think forward for even one second. And then it happens."

"He hits an oil truck. He hits the barracks. He runs off into the mesquite," Faulstick said, with ironic impatience.

"No," Spain said. "Worse. Much worse, Captain Faulstick. He panics."

Cahill waited for Faulstick to respond; the seat had tensed again; the closed heat of the car was dying.

"He panicked, Captain. He lost it; he lost it all. He really didn't know where he was, and it wasn't just the fog that did it to him, either. Somehow or other he thought wrong; he cut back the engine, opened the canopy and got out on the wing, to leave that fucked-up bird, and let it die, let it go on in and smash into the ground, or whatever would be where it hit.''

"And what happened then?'' Cahill asked, nearly in the situation, but not entirely sure he understood it.

"The aircraft rolled to a stop,'' Spain said, settling back again. "The wheels had never left the ground. He stood there, taking it all in, finally understanding the situation—he thought—and then he jumped. He bailed out. About eighteen inches. The ground was there, and he was on it. Somebody came back later and got the aircraft; the engine was still running. They tell me that kid washed himself out; he never wanted to go near another airplane as long as he lived. And he shouldn't, either. He didn't, and he shouldn't. That's what you call a happy ending. For him, anyway.''

"What do you think of all this, Mr. Cahill?'' Faulstick asked, against Spain. "Do you see any point in going over it? Something that didn't even happen here?''

"It didn't happen here,'' Spain said and eased forward, "but it could. Your reactions are the things that matter, bombardier. They've got to be trained so that they just happen when they need to. And then, in a way that nobody will ever be able to explain, you go beyond the training. That cadet never even got the results of his training down into his motor circuits. The first thing he should have done was to look at his altimeter; that's just basic. But he panicked, and just wanted to get back into some kind of contact with the ground, with what he thought he'd lost in the big white fuck-all. The aircraft represented something to him that was taking him away from it. Or so he thought; the animal went the wrong way. It can do that, you know, Captain. Panic is the strongest force in the world. If you're not on the other side of it, if it hasn't turned into the greatest calm in the world, where you don't even have to think, it will do you in every time. That cadet was just damn lucky the plane was not about fifty feet up, or a hundred.''

"Well,'' Faulstick said uncertainly, "it wasn't. It came out all right.'' He settled his shoulders, and opened the door of the car. "And I reckon that's all there is to it, Mr. Spain.''

Spain said nothing, as Cahill somehow knew he would not.

"I think I'll stumble on over to ground school,'' Faulstick said. "I have a dim recollection that there's a class going on.''

The door closed.

"Don't you want to go over there with him?" Spain asked. "Every-thing's right in the same area, you know."

"No," Cahill said, passing his hand back and forth over the empty driver's seat. "Let him go. We're not in any big hurry."

No one spoke as the engine heat died. After a time Cahill felt for the door handle, opened the body of the car, and stood up outside. Spain followed, and they started off across the skreaking field. The whiteout was going, and they walked at almost the speed of a normal man, Cahill quiet, arranging things in his mind, getting ready to believe that he would know when they entered the assembly area between the Admin-istration Building and the barracks, would know when buildings closed around him. Zack bumped his leg and was gone again.

It was partly this that had caused him to miscalculate, he was sure, when, with no inkling of walls and glass coming to him, he heard Spain say, "OK; here we are. Here's the Administration Building. Watch the steps."

Cahill swung this way and that, listening, turning the angle of his hearing from side to side, but he did no better. Fear rose a little; he was at the center of nothingness again; he could not tell.

"We'll all be in the barracks, Mr. Cahill," Cadet Spain said. "Come on over, whenever you want to."

"Right," Cahill answered. "Just hold on. I don't think this will take very long."

With objects to touch, like the handrail of the stairs and the handle of the door, he felt better, and with some confidence he went inside, found the colonel's office, and knocked on the solid jamb, for the door was open.

"Come in," said Colonel Hoccleve. "Come in and sit down. The chair's just over to your left, where it was before."

The colonel watched the blind man as he moved for the chair, reached for it, had it, and sat down, half facing him. He looked down at his desk and examined a sheet of paper, picked up some others, placed them over the first, thumbed through them, glancing briefly, and then brought the original one to the top again.

For the first time since Cahill had been in Peckover, there was a quality of silence that bothered him. Sound was a texture, solid or thin, continuous or broken, interspersed, always, with a number of inexplica-ble variations and intrusions. But when he expected to hear a voice and did not he was thrown off, for it had always been difficult for him to open a conversation, and now it was almost impossible, unless he felt he had the right to do so by asking for information.

With what might have been some effort Colonel Hoccleve raised his eyes from his papers to Cahill's black figure and broad pale expressionless face. "We've got troubles, Mr. Cahill," he said.

"Who has?"

"Well, you have," the colonel said. "You and your dog. Some rumors have come in from town. I want to take a day and check them out properly. Then I'll talk to you again."

The colonel leaned forward, both elbows on the table and his forearms folded. It was disconcerting to talk to a man from whom you could draw no response by your attitude or posture. He waited, lining up his points and his displays of reasonable authority, one behind the other.

"Meantime I'll have to ask you again to use some form of restraint on your dog. Just keep him where you or somebody else can hold him back. Remember, I requested you to do this after he bit Cadet Spain. And now the civilians are getting into it, and we don't want to give them anything to complain about if we can help it. We try to keep relations with the people around here as calm and friendly as we can, but some of them don't like us, and that makes things harder. They don't need to be harder."

Cahill stood up slowly and turned inch by inch toward where he believed the door was; he was right.

Over his shoulder, he said, surprising himself and strangely excited, "I'll hold on to Zack, and I'll hold off on some other things too, if you don't push me."

"What do you mean?" Colonel Hoccleve said, looking up sharply.

"Things," he said. "Some things. Just some things I've found out since I've been here. I don't think they amount to much, but they don't suit me."

"Come back in and sit down," the colonel said. "If something doesn't suit you, get it out in the open. Nobody's hiding anything from you. Give me some idea what you're talking about."

"Blind people are just naturally suspicious, Commander," he said. "When you go blind, it don't take long to find that out. People think they can hide anything in the world from you, and you'll never know where it is, or what it is. They even think they can talk to you about it; because you can't see they feel like they can sort of diddle with you, and you'll never find out what they don't want you to know."

"What do you want to know, Mr. Cahill? There's no place you've

398

wanted to go you haven't been, and no member of personnel we haven't made available to answer your questions and to tell you what he could. What else could you want?"

"Maybe not much," Cahill said, "and maybe a lot. But I've found out from my time in the military here, you might say—which I can tell you will be the last I ever have anything to do with it—I've learned one thing: that if you hear a rumor long enough, there's somethin' to it." In himself he fell back: he would hold what he had. Probably he would not need it. Certainly he didn't need it now. Later, if the colonel made a move, he would make his own.

The colonel frowned, and when Cahill remained standing, the frown tightened, though he said easily, "There are always rumors, Mr. Cahill; lots of them. The service is made of them. Just which ones are bothering you?"

Not changing his position, Cahill said, "There's not anything I'd want to talk about right now. I may tell you before I leave."

"When will that be, Mr. Cahill? What are your plans? We'll try to accommodate you."

"I'll stay through Sunday. You asked me to do that, if I remember."

"Well," the colonel said, "I didn't ask you, exactly, but you can stay through Sunday if you like, just as long as you see to it that your dog doesn't cause any more trouble."

"I'll leave when my son would'a left," Cahill said, turning away and straightening, struck by a double reaction as he realized that he had only one notion of where his son would have gone when he left Peckover: into the air, somewhere into the air of the world, the air of the war, a place he could not follow. He tried to bring feeling into his forearms, reassurance, tensing his fists in his pockets, the knuckles of one of them grazing broken glass.

Colonel Hoccleve got up and moved around his desk, careful not to touch it. Signaling primly, he motioned past Cahill to a pfc. clerk-typist to show him the outer door.

When someone touched his arm, Cahill thought it was the colonel, and shook off the touch angrily, but when he heard a neutral voice he held back his own, changed it in his mind, and asked civilly, "Is Phillipson around?"

"Yes, sir," said the typist. "He's back in Records."

"See if you can get him to take me over to the barracks."

When Corporal Phillipson was brought to him, they moved into the cold once more, down the slick steps and out across the sand, the rags of snow.

Another door opened, and at both sides there was a rattle of what was probably, what had to be, glass. Warmth came to him as he stepped forward. He halted: there was someone in front of him.

"This is Lieutenant Spigner, Mr. Cahill," Phillipson said. "He is the tactical officer for the Base, and has charge of these barracks. I'll leave you with him."

"Thanks, son," Cahill said. "Shears and them are supposed to be over here, and I'll just take up with them." The door closed behind him, and another voice began. He put out his hand as a matter of course, and it was taken by one smaller.

"I suppose you want to know . . ." began Spigner, a small dark officer in salmon-pink trousers and a dark green shirt against which the gold bar and Air Corps wings of the collar would have seemed too bright to anyone but an inspection team; there were no wings on the chest.

"Whatever you can tell me," Cahill said. "Like the others."

"There really isn't very much, Mr. Cahill," the lieutenant said. "The main concern of all these boys is flying, and what they do on the ground is strictly secondary, almost off limits, at least to them. I don't fly, as you may know, and my business with them is on the ground, their conduct as potential officers, how they keep themselves, their equipment, their personal effects, and so on. I hold an inspection every other day, and on the weekend I do a more thorough one, and go over the whole barracks and its condition as well as the footlockers and the cadets' appearance and deportment."

"So?" Cahill said. "How did my boy stack up? Did he give you any trouble?"

"Not real trouble," Spigner said. "He ended up with a lot of demerits, but just for minor infractions. I had to give those, because he was in some ways very unmilitary, very unofficerlike. And, as far as my part of things is concerned, I kept a pretty close eye on him, and sent him out walking punishment tours, because—I hate to say this, but it's true—he was something of a bad influence on the others, or at least some of the others."

"How was that?"

"Well," Spigner said, "regulations. He never paid any particular attention to the letter of the law, although he would go through the motions if I sat on him hard enough, or there was something he wanted to do in town—I think there was some little mill girl he used to go around with—and he wanted open post. Two or three times I asked him to make a real effort to straighten up, to keep the display in his footlocker consistent with regulations, to shave every day—as I remember, he had a real heavy beard that was kind of darkish, and grew fast, even though he had blond hair—to shine his shoes every now and then. If I had been able to get him to do these things, the others would have been more likely to do them, and everything would have been a lot better. One of the troubles is that Primary Flight Training is a relaxation for these boys after Pre-Flight, which is real military, almost like OCS, where I come from." He smiled self-deprecatingly. "They think pilots act like this; I mean, act like the military part of the Air Corps is more or less of a joke. We try to convince them that there may be a little good in our part of things; maybe not a whole lot, but some. I wish he could have seen that a little more clearly."

"I'm sorry if he gave you a bad time," Cahill said. "It's over now."

"I wouldn't like to leave it at that, Mr. Cahill," Spigner said, almost putting out his hand again, but thinking better of it. "I liked Joel. I used to look forward to seeing him here, even when I had to get on him about some little nit-shit thing that he didn't even notice. He was so full of some strange kind of enthusiasm, some kind of energy . . . it used to make me feel old and out of it, though I don't guess I'm more than five or six years older than he was. Whenever I'd see Joel, I felt like what I was doing was more or less beside the point, that I had missed something, that I was just ticking off a bunch of dead rules; that that was all I did, and all I could do, but that somewhere along in there, maybe when I was younger, about like these kids, there could have been something else. I felt like I didn't ask as much as he did, that I didn't look for enough, or some damn thing." He hesitated. "But like you say, it's over now. I'm sorry. I'm as sorry as anybody here, and you can believe that."

"I believe it," Cahill said, and stepping to what he believed to be one side of the lieutenant, walked slowly forward.

There was space around him and he believed there were no stairs anywhere. He stamped his foot for the sound, and the space was large. I'll just keep walking on, he said to himself: There will be somebody there.

At the far end of the open-bay barracks Malcolm Shears, cadets Adler, Blazek, Harbelis, and several others stood waiting, and remained still, until Lieutenant Spigner had gone out the door.

A step, then another, matched his. He stopped; the other came on; only one man. His right arm was taken by the sleeve, and he let it move with the grasp, let it rise until a hand took his at shoulder level. Spain, in the hospital, had done this. Cahill needed little force to hold his arm in place; only enough to maintain the sense of life in it.

"That other fellow gone?" Cahill asked. "That inspector?"

"Good," said Shears. "We're all here. Just a little ways along, straight ahead of you."

"He's gone. That was Lieutenant Spigner. He has to come around when they tell him. Nobody pays any attention to him." He let Cahill's hand down, released it, and stepped back.

Cahill put the hand in his pocket. "We can get on with it," he said, and moved to pass Shears, or go through him.

Whatever area he had entered filled with bodies; though he was reasonably sure that these were making an effort to be still, he could hear what they could not: a foot-scrape, a rubbing of material—cloths—and stopped before Shears or anyone else could prompt him. He reached down for Zack, already gone solid enough to be on his haunches.

"We're down here at the end of Cadet Second Barracks," Shears said softly and clearly. "If you'll turn a little to your right you'll be facing Joel's and my bunk." He

402

Should I do that? he wondered. Should I turn? What would it matter? He turned, and was facing differently. Two boys were here, he forced himself to believe, one lying above the other. This would have been at night, in the dark. They were in this place to fly, and they were both probably thinking about flying; about the planes, the engines, about the air. He could do that, himself. The air was the air, dark or not, and he had heard the engines, as they had lain here and done; must have.

"What?" Cahill asked. "What do you mean? What are you talkin' about? Are you talkin' to me?"

"I'm sorry, Mr. Shears," Cahill said, "but you're not gettin' over to me, at all. I can't follow anything you're sayin'."

Not trying to make sense of what he was hearing, Cahill simply listened, believing that some kind of explanation would surely have to come, whenever Shears thought it was due. Within the listening he became slowly

peered, but not narrowly, as though he wished to see if Cahill would reach to touch the bunk, and when this did not happen, went on. "Joel had the bottom bunk, which was all right with me, because you don't have so much a sense of confinement up topside." Again he waited, expectantly enough to make Cadet Blazek shift uncertainly.

" 'The rocks are cloven,' " said Shears.

" 'The rocks are cloven,' " Shears repeated. " 'I see cars drawn which trample the dim winds.' "

" 'A wild-eyed' . . ." he paused, breaking off and turning to Harbelis. "What's the next word, right in there?"
"I think it's 'charioteer,' " Harbelis supplied. "I'm almost sure that's what it says."
" 'I see cars drawn which trample the dim winds,' " Shears went on. " 'A wild-eyed charioteer urging their flight.' "

403

aware that other voices were saying the same words as Shears, a tone of assent developing through them.

Shears's voice was lost within the others, and Cahill found himself imagining vividly; there were many young faces, and much wind, the faces almost childish, flushed and clear, and all the hair was curly, blond and blond-gold. Pale blue was the color behind them.

There was a strong, full sigh, and then silence. Cahill felt a lift of inexplicable confidence, understanding that it was up to him, now, to speak.

" 'I see no shapes but the keen stars.' "

" 'Others, with burning eyes, lean forth, and drink
With eager lips the wind of their own speed . . .
. . . their bright locks
Stream like a comet's flashing hair: they all
'Sweep onward.' "

"Now what?" Cahill asked. "I won't ask you what all that was about, unless you want to tell me." He thought briefly. "Is that somethin' Joel said, maybe? Did he write that?"

"No," Shears said. "He copied it out from something in this book. I think he got the book from Grevey College, where, you know, he went to school for a while."

"Let me see," Cahill asked, and a large book was put into both the hands he held out; it was open. Cahill passed his fingers over the pages, the break in the middle, and then underneath, palping the back and the dented and thready spine. "Feels like its fallin' apart," he said. "This is maybe a used book, you reckon?"

"I don't think so," Harbelis broke in. "He read in it a lot, and wrote in it. And then we took care of the rest. He'd let us see it every now and then, what he'd been thinking."

Shears was suddenly formal. Cahill stood, holding the open book, determined to respond to the information the cadet was slowly giving him, with something of the conviction of a lawyer outlining his points to a jury.

404

"This is our group, right here, Mr. Cahill. These are the key people. You know Cadet Harbelis."

"I do," said Cahill. "I been knowin' him."

"These others you've met, but you may not remember all the names."

"Who've you got?"

"Cadets Adler . . ."

"Welcome, sir," said Adler. We already owe you a lot."

Shears went on. "Cadets Blazek . . . Crider . . . Mahoney . . . Followill . . . Brosnan . . . Sorbo . . . Neilson . . . Rolader. Those were all the first ones, in at the beginning of the whole thing." He paused. "Now we've also got Cadets Youngblood, Byers, Richie, Ingwersen, Hultgren, Klienheinz, Baldwin, and Kalb. There'll be no more from this base. We have five other Air Corps training bases involved, and have three men—good ones—in Infantry Basic in Georgia and South Carolina. This is what we're going from, come Sunday. They'll all know.

"How about Spain?" Cahill asked.

"I almost forgot," Shears said. "I thought you already knew about him. Spain's right here."

"Don't forget Spain," Cahill said, half smiling. "He's somebody *I* owe somethin' to. Me and Zack. I wish there was some way I could make up for it."

"You don't need to worry about that," Spain said. Everything's ready to go. We've got the big team in."

"So," Cahill began again "what is this . . . this thing you've got? All you-all? Is it like a club, sort of? A kind of group of buddies? Friends of Joel, like?"

"No, Mr. Cahill," Shears said quietly. "It's more than that. Much more."

"What, then?" Cahill asked. "Tell me what you want me to know. I'm here."

"Joel will tell you," Shears said. "We'll let him do it."

Cahill waited, and as he did the book was taken from him.

"Some of these things are underlined," Shears explained. "But most of what he wanted to say he wrote wherever there was any room, inside the covers and out on the sides of the pages."

"Well, what is it he said?"

" 'It is not our wish to be everything, but to participate in existence in a new way.' We can start there, Mr. Cahill. That's behind everything else."

"What 'new way' is this, he's talkin' about?"

"The basis of what Joel was on to, and what we think we're on to, is the air itself, and the way we take it, and the way we fly in it, and the organization we've arrived at, based on this kind of understanding that we have."

"You've got to come down to it more," Cahill said. "I don't follow you, because it don't seem to me that there's very much to follow. What about the air? Do you know somethin' about it that nobody else does? Or you think you do?"

"We think we do," Shears said. "We believe that flying is like the deepest sleep you could ever get down into—or up into. Joel says, right here, that 'it's like a sleep that is all movement and repose at the same time. If God had intended for men to fly, He would have given them wings. That's true. He did not give men wings; men gave them to themselves, but they are still not intended to fly. There is the sense of a constant transgression, like the swivel-thrill of orgasm.' That's what we're after. There's not a man in this room that has not felt it."

In the low murmur around him, in which he was sure there were heads being nodded, Cahill could think of nothing to say except "Keep on." He said this.

"Muscle and machine parts are not dissimilar," Shears read, moving his finger on the page. "One is based on the other, in fact. The principles of leverage are the same. What matters is what is between the acting unit and what puts it in motion, and directs it. The purpose for either is unknown."

"That means," Harbelis stepped closer and said, "that an aircraft is like any other machine in some ways, and some it's not. You get into an airplane and it lifts you up, it supports you and carries you in what you actually are breathing. The air is not like water, or like the ground. The body has got to take it another way. The dimensions you're in are different; you have to give to the machine, at the same time you're controlling it. In one place Joel says—I never have forgotten it—'you must learn to dream by means of the lungs; to move the body and its carrier from the lungs.' "

"And he says," Cadet Blazek broke in, "that 'whoever masters the air masters the breath of every creature living, every other man, and masters him from the inside.' "

"You heard us do those lines about . . . about the charioteers, just now, Mr. Cahill," Shears said, a little more excited. "We use that and things like it as a kind of spell. It's right here: 'through incantation, each thinks he has summoned the words from some deep place in himself that only he knows. Thus the many enter into a gigantic reflex, which is like a touched muscle belonging to them all. Yet each feels it as his own.' " He paused, and Cahill could hear him draw breath.

" 'This notion can be extended,' " Shears went on. " 'The rag-tag of a military institution, like this air base, can be . . . can be molded into something that nobody here would ever believe was possible. This is kind of what the Army is trying to do, anyway, but only unsuccessfully. Nothing reaches the true being of any man here. But the true being exists, and it can be reached. And there are many men. Alnilam, if it begins strongly here, will spread; it is inevitable.' This is on page two seventy-eight. I believe it. Every day you can see the possibilities."

"What is this idea, this notion you've got? This Al-ni-lám? Cahill turned, facing Shears's last voice, knowing that either the other would have to back off now and hedge, or bring out what they all stood there to bring.

"The name," Shears said, marking the syllables in the air, "is just a name. It's something we use to give some notion of what holds it all together. Al-nilám is the name of the middle star in the belt of Orion, which is the main thing in the night sky, this time of year. Orion is the Hunter, up there with his dog Sirius, the Dog Star. Alnilam is the center of him, the center of the hunter, as well as the center of the hunt. Without Alnilam there wouldn't *be* any center."

He stood, his back to his own arena, the fires of blindness shooting.

"All this," Cahill said. "You got stars, you got airplanes, you got the air. You got a bunch of boys. What else you got?"

Shears, nodding slightly and smiling, readied his next disclosure, his lips moving slightly as he framed it.

His mind went without control, the orange flares racing through it, to his conception of the boys facing him. Again, with this cold their faces must be flushed. Some were taller than others, surely, but as they were there for him, they were the same size. He saw pinkness and neatly combed hair, and when he fixed on eyes they were blue, and without veins. In his pocket he touched a fragment of hardness. A rock? No; part was ragged. A tooth; a thing he had. He drew back.

"Where? What is—like you say—'beyond the engine'?"

"Electricity?" Cahill said, fighting off helplessness; this was out of his range.

Wiring: blueprints and wiring diagrams; it occurred to him that he had never worked on a church.

"Steel," he said. "Aluminum, iron, copper. Anything metal. We want that, for ourselves. We want to get rid of all of the usual human characteristics, the things that slow you down, that get in the way, like too much sympathy, too much analysis, too much mind-complication." He watched Cahill carefully. "Precision steel, Mr. Cahill, that's what the Alnilam men are made out of. And what we practice is precision mysticism. We not only make the engine, but we *are* the engine, and beyond the engine."

"A huge field, where there's nothing—well, there are two fields, actually: a field of electricity and a field of flowers. One visible, and the other invisible, and both of them right there, together."

"Electricity, you bet," Shears said conclusively. "Something that's essentially spiritual. What is sacred is dangerous; it has sanctity."

"Don't think that's funny," Harbelis said. "One cadet said a notion like that is like using Jesus Christ as a pfc.: Private First Christ. He was out quick; in fact, he was never in; that's as far as he got."

"He had some of it, himself,"

Cahill forced a smile which, after he had begun it, he realized was partly genuine. Shears had nothing, really. He should try to put in real electrical wiring; then he'd have some notion of what he was talking about. All this was only words.

"And where's all this gonna be?"

Tuned to that voice and what it seemed to be trying to develop, Cahill was not prepared for another he did not remember having heard. He shuffled and leaned his ear differently.

Shears said, "Joel did. Nobody touched him. Or only a few did."

"I did," said Cadet Crider.

"I did," said Spain, differently.

"I did, too," Blazek said. "Or, I think I did."

"When we have what we want," Shears continued, "that'll be our only power plant. Electricity. It'll run everything. It's the only mystery, you know. The first and the last. Einstein says so." Shears stiffened slightly at Cahill's change of expression. He glanced at the cadet closest to him—Adler—and then went on. "When we get where we're going, we will be just coming out of a war, this war, called a World War, into the real one, that has never been fought, or even imagined. It is one that we have initiated. There is only one victory, and the main thing about it is that when we get it we'll throw it away, and live in a world of nihilism and music. We'll be weightless, in the Second Body, the Old Brain, but still control the ground under our feet."

"Partly in the mind, partly outside. We'll make the outside come to us; it has certain things we need. The rest we'll bring. Nobody else has ever had it."

Cadet Crider, a small bleached-looking boy, broke in shrilly, with a strong mountain accent.

409

A colored dream . . . ? Green, he remembered. Where was this? Where had it been? It was in some way or another connected with his hands and feet.

Comes back. What is coming back now? What if I put my hand over my mouth, Cahill thought, and just imagined, and just let come? What would be there? Why should I not? I will be giving them nothing.

The boys vanished, all one size, vulnerable and pink. The curly hair faded; the blue of all the eyes, of one eye, of no eyes, was left, enormous.

What was it he had thought of in the trainer? The trainer for flying blind? There was some green, there were houses—here and there was one, another, then

"It's the real country you see when you're flyin'," Crider said. "That's where we're goin'. The first time I seen it I knowed I wanted to go there, when I was in the in-doc-trination flight with my instructor. It's like a colored dream; you know that when you get back down there it's not goin' to be any different from what it was before you took off, but you want it to be. God, you really do want it to be. If you could really come down from flyin', and you'd be in a place that's exactly like it looks from the air, you'd be in the best place there is. It'd be better than Heaven. There's no dirt there."

Shears came back, his finger in the book once more. "A great blue field, the color of the most direct and softest eye, and an extension of water that does not move, but that is glittering with initials. That can change the world. For that field, Orion was put in the sky, and Alnilam put into the middle of it. No one who stays with me, and is not killed, will fail to see that field. And some will enter it. Then we will see what there is for us. No one will be there who does not understand, and the long music will start."

For a moment there were no voices, and then Crider said, "The first time I was off the ground, I wanted to go there. I knew I could never do it, except maybe in a

to the right: houses with eyes like pinpoints, dead black and with a pressureless vitality. These were his. Not live there, never live there, but own. Be over, and if he were to come down and walk in . . .

"And then what? What's there?"

What could be like that? Cahill asked himself. What did he remember about distances? About a place impossible to get to, that won't leave your mind alone? That gets into sleep, where your vision is clear, and you can see anything that comes to you, for whatever reason it has to be there? That kind of distance to him was gray, gray with smoke and city-haze, and he let it come to him where he had stood in the great open city-space of Piedmont Park in Atlanta. Toward the dimmest and farthest gray, a pair of wings rose out of someone's hands.

He realized that he was drawing breath too quickly, and that

dream, or somethin'. Joel Cahill was the one who said it was there, it'd always been there; that it was up to us to get to it, and that we could get to it. He showed me how to fly over it, showed how the airplane led to it and then dropped off; showed me how I could go on around the dream, by myself, and then with the others, and get there."

Shears took up again. "The purple country," he said. "The one you see from the air. It's like something that's always at a distance, and it has all the qualities of distance, except you're right in it, this time. All the frustrations, all the longing to be there and not being able to get there—all that'll be part of it. We won't lose that, but we won't be far from the place —the feeling—any more, or up above it. We'll be in it, where we want to be. We'll have things our way, and everybody'll see that that's the way the whole thing was meant to be, from the start. It's the original soft country. Just before melting. Staying like that. Just before melting, but not.

"You have to imagine, Mr. Cahill," Shears went on, "a place, a kind of place where human beings have got on through to the other side of the machine. The aircraft engine is what we use. We have become the machine, like a kind of

his mouth was partly open. He closed it, and began to try to think of a reasonable question. "And when you get to this . . . this place, what are you goin' to do? How will you live? What will you eat? You gonna live in houses, or just wander around in the purple fields, thinkin' about what a great place you've done got yourself to? What are you gonna do? How're you gonna live?"

I can feel the weevil start to get into my brain, Cahill thought. How can these kids possibly believe this stuff? Even Boy Scouts were not so ridiculous. He was sure he could blow away this whole web of foolishness with one comment, one question. He turned it over in his mind as though in his mouth, as Shears talked on.

He was ready. "Now just," he said, putting a series of soft emphatic slashes into the air with his forefinger, "now just where is your electricity gonna come from? You've got this nice purple country, and all this what you call distance-magic, and you're in it, and electricity is your good buddy. *Now* what? You've got to

ghost, and gone on out through to the other side, to a place where no machine can ever touch us again. We can leave it. We will be human full time and all the time. Only human, but completely. That's what we want. That's all we want, and it's everything. We won't lose it, once we have it."

Shears leaned against the post of the bunk, smiling with quiet confidence, his arms folded.

"As far as mechanical force," Shears said, "we admit only one. Electricity. It has its laws, and we respect them and can use them, because underneath the laws is a mystery that no one can solve, not even Newton or Einstein, or anybody. The mystery is built in; no understanding can ever reach it. We like that; electricity is a friend of ours: what loads we want moved, what little simple things we want made, electricity will do it for us. Not one of us will ever have to eat the crap that comes out of cans. All that doctored-up pulp." He spat.

Shears remained relaxed, not looking around, his eyes on Cahill's glasses. He was surprised, turning with a certain irritation, when a voice behind him and to one side, answered the blind man.

eat. You've got to have somethin' to do. Where're you gonna get your electricity, anyway?"

Falling water; falling past on both sides like arms. Endless arms; white, full of air. Ground was soft green, with life in it like a breath held on and on.

"It will, will it?" Cahill said, feeling belligerency rise like well-being, a return of health. "And all this hazy stuff, like you say things look from the air. What about that?"

The talk was going past him again now; he clung to what he had got together in his head, brought one word out of Shears's flow, and went with it.

"Everything soft, eh?" Cahill said. "Shit, you'd be as bad off as I am. Why would you not want to see things good? How would you read?" His own thought pierced him: read: read what?

"Water," Cadet Hultgren said, from his wide fleshy and ugly mouth. "There's plenty of it. It'll give us all the current we want."

"Well," Shears said, picking up, "it'll just be that way. Everything will be soft and kind of indistinct; you won't need to see things like they were real sharp. It's better the other way. All the colors will be kind of giving to one another, if you know what I mean. No hard edges. Hard edges are what we have to kill, and we'll do that by mastering them, by being more hard-edged than they are, more like a machine than a machine is. Then we'll throw it away. Throw it away for good. There'll never be any more hard edges; no more propellers, no more cylinder-heads."

413

"In airplanes, you told me," Cahill said. "In machinery. Machinery that makes everything purple, and where you can't see nothin'."

"What is it you want?" Cahill asked. He took a half step backward, and then held.

The tone of the words was, to Cahill, partly enthusiastic and partly somewhere between impatience and fear. It made him uneasy, and he was prepared not to like what he was evidently going to be asked to do. He flexed his toes downward, one foot and then the other.

"What do you mean? How?"

"When we needed to, we would read. We'd still have glasses, when we wanted them."

Shears straightened. "First we have to get there."

Shears stepped closer, but did not touch. "Would you allow us to show you something, Mr. Cahill? It'll explain a lot."

"Won't hurt," Shears said, smiling and showing no teeth. "This is the way we keep the boys in the blue. Keep 'em out of the machine. The washing machine, that is. Death's baby machine, we call it. The gears you get caught in when they're trying to route you out of here, and send you to Cooks and Bakers School. Joel never lost a man to Cooks and Bakers School, or to the Signal Corps, or to Radio School, or even to Aerial Gunnery. If Joel wanted to keep anybody in this program, he kept him."

"We'll show you how," Shears said, "if Cadet Ingwersen or somebody'll just bring me a chair and a broomstick."

"Here you go," said Cadet Crider, shoving a canvas-seated

414

chair with one hand and holding out a broom with the other. "Here's the same chair I done learned on. The same chair and the same broom."

Something touched him in the back of his legs at the bend, and his arm was taken; he sat slowly. In his right hand was placed a hard roundness that could be moved. He sat holding it still.

Shears saw Cahill seated, guiding him down without condescension; Crider placed the broom in his hand, its straws cocked on the floor broadside to Cahill's feet.

"All right now," Shears said. "You've got it."

"I've got it, maybe," Cahill said, "and now what'm I goin' to do with it?" A smile entered his face from some game he had never played. "How high am I?"

Shears smiled also, this time with his teeth. "It doesn't matter how high you are," he said. "High enough to see purple. High enough for the colors to be giving to one another."

"Good enough," Cahill said. "I've got it. I see everything. I can't get to it, but I know it's there." And then, spoken out of some part of him that he had never used or known about, he said, "I'm with you. Let's go."

Shears bent forward, his hands on his knees like an alert, gentle halfback before the shift.

"Remember now," he said, "and then forget. Remember that you've got this aircraft, and it'll do anything you say. Remember that your whole body, and the whole body of the aircraft, is in your hands and feet. Don't think about coordinating the throttle. Just think about both feet and your

Cahill hung motionless, tightening and relaxing his hand on the stick, breathing as the tension in his fingers came and went. He realized with strong exhilaration that he was afraid, that he was beginning to sweat; that under his feet was great space, and a country that no one else knew about.

He could not move.

He lifted his chin. He could do nothing with his right hand; he could not remember it. He was certain that the floor, or whatever was under him, had changed, was changing.

With a strange and excited sense of accomplishment, of acting with terrible secret and exact

right hand. Think like you were dreaming it all, and you didn't have any weight, and wherever you wished, whatever direction you wished in, you could go, because things are set up that way." He paused, and repeated slowly, a little louder and with greater emphasis, "Things are set up that way. They have been from the beginning."

"All right, now," said Shears, leaning forward, with his palms turned up and held between himself and Cahill, fingers together. "Up, now. Your body wants up, wants to rise. There's not any aircraft with you. Only you, in your feet and right hand. Lean back and rise. Rise, pilot. Rise like the sun; inevitable."

"Rise," Shears commanded. "Right hand. Right hand rising. Look up a little. Lean back. Remember: right hand rising. Then forget."

A long, low sound came from the cadets, leaning forward as in a huddle listening to the quarterback; someone popped his hands together: a light unfleshly sound.

"Level now," said Shears. "You want to be level, straight and level. You want to be level, level as a bubble. The plane doesn't know

rightness, Cahill brought his chin down and eased his upper body little by little forward, until all distances over and beneath him and on all sides equaled out, became each other. There was a riding satisfaction now, a racing and raiding peace, a stay as at the center of a fabulous hurtling, a floating on-go, precarious, momentary, prolonging.

He rode and did not breathe, maintaining steadily.

What will this one be like? he wondered. Can I let the level go? Can I turn loose of the bubble?

Deep in him, in a hidden location near or the same as the most hidden of his sexuality, something shifted, and it might have been that at the same time a kept heaviness, the water in his bladder, swung one way. All of balance shifted; he swam in curvature, in a lengthening bent soaring, a sustained, sustaining portion of a necessary round.

you. Nobody knows you. Nobody else knows what 'level' is. Nobody knows. Nobody knows. You don't know level; you *are* level. Level. Level."

"You've got it," Shears said quietly. "You've got it, quicker than anybody I ever saw. You've got it. You're in there."

"Come right, now," Shears urged. "Don't do anything but think it. Right. A long, round right. Think of leaning. Think and forget. Think. Think right and forget. The slant will come over you. Don't lean; think the lean. Then don't."

"A long rangy right, just like a big sleepy smile that nobody sees. You want to dissolve to the right. Your body wants to disappear to the right; disappear through your right foot and hand. Then they'll disappear too. Think right, and forget everything. You can't fall. Level will come back when you want it. This one is right. A long, slow right."

Shears watched, narrowing his eyes. "That's a beauty," he said. "That's what you hope for, in the

417

With some dim notion of towers rising to the same height as each other, he trued once more; the dreaminess of the curve left him, the exhilaration of stability returned, and the sense of destination, of leaping forward from himself, all-out into the concentrated and directional force.

He rode; he was riding. The direction was absolute.

Finding it difficult, Cahill relaxed, and eased his lower back; the chair creaked like a chair.

"Am I not gonna get to land this thing?" he asked, hoping that this would certify his involvement.

"What floor?" Cahill asked. "I been up yonder, at any altitude I wanted. You said so yourself. And the next time I get a broomstick on my hand I'm liable to take off again." He paused, resisting a little as the stick was taken from him. "And I bet I *could* land it, too."

dream of a curve: that you're in it; that you're inventing it." He caught himself up sharply, deliberately not looking behind him or to any side.

"All right, level it out again, now. Dream level. Dream the bubble. You've been there before. You know where it is. The air doesn't know it, but you know it. Let the bubble come around you."

"Good," said Shears. "That's it. That's all you need to do. It's our main approach." He straightened and folded his arms again. The half-circle group of boys undid a little, and two or three of them nodded to one another.

"Like I say, no need," Shears said. "You've got our message. You could go up now, and you'd do just as well airborne as you did on this floor."

"I don't doubt it," Shears said, looking at his watch. Not a bit do I doubt it. But this part of things has to be over, now. We've got to move on."

He stood up, listening again, not acting. It was easier to do something, to respond to instructions, even if they only involved a broom and a chair, than to try to follow Shears through an explanation that seemed to explain nothing. What did the meaning of the world have to do with imagining he was making a long curve in the air, or that he conceived of an endless unrolling of purple underneath him, or with a body—his own—balanced like a bubble in a situation that trued it up, and at the same time seemed to have entire possession of a direction, like a fast ruler line across a blueprint? What was the boy talking about now?

He girded himself, wary again, angling for time. "This-here, now," he said. "This's something else of my boy's . . . of Joel's? Right?"

"What does he mean?"

Shears said formally, "The idea that the world is given to men as an enigma to resolve is not ours. The enigma must remain an enigma, and the resolution, if there is one, is to increase the enigmatic quality, so that the mystery is deepened beyond the hope of even provisional solutions. This accounts for our interest in codes. These can be solved, leaving men the notion that they have come to terms with something, when the real point is that all they have done is to resolve problems into which they themselves have built the solutions. So the real mystery is left intact."

"Right," Shears replied. "It's one of the things written out to the side, in the book we just sh . . . in the book you just had hold of."

"All of what he means, we don't know. We'll be a long time catching up with that. But the code we can show you about." He turned to the group. "Somebody let me have an E-6B, right quick." Harbelis handed him the object, and he extended it to Cahill. "Harbelis tells me you've already

419

He felt in the air before him, and took the flat studded shape. Holding it in one hand, he ran the fingers of the other over the surface. Experimentally he slid the leaf through the round metal.

"I remember," he said. "We were out in the middle of the snow. This is some sort of instrument, that's got somethin' to do with . . ."

"Why is it so important that you've got to give me the thing twice?" Cahill asked. "I didn't understand it the first time. What's so important about it?" He grated with laughter that sounded a little meaner than he intended. "Hell, I'm a pilot, not a navigator. I just got my wings. Ain't that so?"

been introduced to this thing. Do you remember it?"

". . . with navigation," Shears said. "It's called an E-6B calculator, and it'll tell you where you are, if you know how to use it. It can tell you your course, where the wind is and what it's doing, how much fuel you have, how much you need, and most of the things you have to know to get where you're going. Everybody has one; all air-crew trainees; it's issue."

Several of the cadets had also produced calculators, and stood sliding or turning them; one had a piece of paper he also glanced at.

"Navigation is the purpose of the calculator," Shears said. "That is, it's the public purpose. The manuals tell you how to use it; the instructors tell you how to use it. Captain Whitehall is a whiz with the thing; *he'll* get you home!" He waited, and tapped his cheekbone at the thinnest skin. "We can do all that with it. But we can also do something else." He reached over and put a small emphatic wagging into the computer Cahill held. "What you've got in your hand, here, Mr. Cahill, is not just a lot of numbers and directions. It's also a language. Our language. First Joel's and now ours. It's the language of Alnilam: the group here, and the others in the other places."

Cold still, it was. By now he knew that there was a thing that slid and a thing that turned. The desolation of being totally closed out trembled near him; he must get away from where he was, or understand it. "What does it say?" he asked.

"It says what we want it to say," Shears answered. "What you need to know first, though, is how it says it; what we've done with it, and what we use it for."

"All right. Like I said, I'm with you. Or as far as I can follow you, anyway."

"The computer is something that you solve problems with: problems of course and course correction, problems of fuel consumption; time, speed, and distance problems, and so on. Everything having to do with flying. It's got all the answers; wind; everything. What *we* do, though, is to code the computer by number, by matchup; code it our own way."

"Go ahead," Cahill said, resisting the impulse to shake the computer in his hand, make it speak.

"What we do is this. When a problem is set up on the computer, certain numbers coincide: that is, they'll come out opposite each other. This is true on either side of the computer: on the dial side with time-speed-distance problems and fuel consumption, altimeter settings and so on, and on the other side, with wind drift and other problems having to do with course: vector problems. We've got both sides to work with. We can code-in problems that will make any set of numbers come out to be opposite. The second number, the one that corresponds not to the

421

problem but to the message, is part of the Alnilam Code, which is the language I was telling you about."

I must try to stay with this, Cahill forced himself to acknowledge, trying desperately for codes in his memory. He had a brief flash of recollection from somewhere in school—high school? grammar school?—but got nothing from it he could use: only something written on a beetle's back, or having to do with a beetle in some way: yes, the beetle was dropped through the eye of a skull; there was money, a treasure involved, and a code, for which he had not even been able to understand the explanation.

"Cadets are always being asked to solve problems," Shears went on. "We work out with these computers like fighters do on the speed bag or the skip rope. The more we do it the better the instructors like it. It means they're earning their money. We're in their camp, we're doing their business, and they like that. The fact that getting good on these things may save lives is just gravy, strictly incidental. But the main thing is that they like to see us doing it; they can't get enough of it. And that's where they play right into our hands; that's where we've got *them*."

Cahill turned the computer over once more; there were two circles that rotated, not one. He listened, and spinning the ring that was empty in the middle, he thought numbers, and tried to find some way into the possible mind that brought them to rest against each other, according to some pattern.

Shears took a piece of paper from Cadet Hultgren. "Now, sir, follow me real close."

Cahill nodded, holding the computer by the ends of its central flange.

"Suppose we set this problem. Your fuel rate is thirteen gallons an hour. You've run for an hour and thirty minutes. That's ninety minutes. Right? We set the speed—or gallons-per-hour—needle on thirteen, and then read above ninety on the inside dial—the one that moves—nineteen and a half, for the total fuel used, in gallons. You with me so far?" He glanced up, holding Hultgren's paper behind his own computer.

"Yeah," Cahill said, "I guess. If you say so."

"That's just the solution to the problem, one of the easiest kinds. Anybody and everybody can do it. But that's not what we want out of the matchup."

"Nineteen and a half. I got it."

"From the gallons-per-hour needle, we read to the right, clockwise, every numeral of ten, and decode to the numbers on the outside dial. That gives you, for seventy, fifteen point two, for eighty, fifteen point four, for ninety, fifteen point five, until we reach the end of the message. We don't use the fractions on the outer dial, the decimal fractions, but just the nearest whole number. Fifteen point two is fifteen, seventeen point four is seventeen. In the case of an exact half, like the nineteen and a half, we use the next highest whole number, so it'd be twenty."

"I can more or less follow that," Cahill said. "But why should it mean any more to you than it does to anybody else? I mean to any cadet, navigator, or anybody who knew how to work the thing?"

"Because it decodes into a private language. One that only we know. A code that uses a private language is almost impossible to break. You have to have a referent. And if you keep changing the words of the language, they can't ever catch up with you."

With the computer in one hand and Hultgren's paper in the other, he continued. "For fifteen the word is 'relle.' For seventeen it is 'liades.' For twenty it is 'yakat.' Every two weeks we change words, and send out the new list to our people. This is the current one. After Sunday, we'll change it."

"But what does it mean? What do them partic'lar words mean?"

"Reading clockwise, and on around, it says . . ." he broke off. "Do you want the code words? Maybe you would like to have them. We could copy them out for you."

"No," Cahill said, angry with suspense. "I don't want the damned code words. What does the thing *say?*"

Speaking slowly and gravely, as though coming over from a foreign tongue, Shears read: *Alnilam will destroy all aircraft Peckover, twenty-four January. Inform personnel. Instructions later.*

Shears watched him keenly; the other cadets leaned toward him again.

"I'm gonna have to let that pass, for a minute," he said. "We can come back to it."

Shears took up: "We have a word list that goes out every two weeks, or we will have; this is just the first set, since Joel has only been . . . since it hasn't been two weeks since Joel made this one up. We bury the words in regular letters, to the people on other bases that we want to have them. The words are in one letter; the personnel who get them know what to look for."

"How do they?" Cahill asked, drawn past big issues by the details of small ones, and by the natural persuasion of intrigue.

"We have to use some ingenuity about that. Joel was good at this part of it; he felt that a kind of joking mood would fit, and the words in the Alnilam language were, well, like private sex words, mainly, and they referred, well. to doings with girls and women that we at this end and the people at the other bases all remember, you know, from back in Basic Training or Classification or Pre-Flight or somewhere else. Words about what we did, or would like to do. All the girls were imaginary, but that doesn't make any difference."

"Buried in letters, huh?" Cahill said, as an idea dawned, and became half-humorous. "Girls buried in letters, none of 'em real, all screwin' everybody. That's some way to fool people. Believe me, *I'd'*a never thought of it."

Shears smiled, and was, for an instant and even to the other cadets, very boyish; or not boyish, but a boy.

"Don't fool with my . . ."

"Don't fool with my yakat," Blazek said, bright-eyed and round as a porcupine.

"Better not," Harbelis said. "Means 'destroy.'"

"You said somethin' about one letter. There's a follow-up to this first one, like?" Cahill asked, in line, logically, as far as he could tell.

"Yes," said Shears, picking up formally. "We can send the second letter as a follow-up, or we can send them both at the same time. It's probably better to have a day or two in between."

"What's in the other one?"

"The problem."

"Like . . . ?"

"Like the problem you're holding in your hands, there. That's the solution to the problem and the decoding device, at the same time."

"So what you do . . ."

"So what we do is to send E6B problems—*an* E6B problem—through the mail, like people playing chess. It can be a fuel-consumption problem, a time-speed-distance problem, an altimeter problem, a course problem, or drift, something off the wind-face. We can use either side of the computer; whatever we decide. In the first letter we also bury a number, either one or two; one is for the slide-rule side, two is for the wind-face. It's that simple."

"Simple," Cahill repeated, suddenly not knowing what the word meant.

"It works," Shears said with satisfaction. "There's no way it can miss. We want somebody to know something, we can see to it that he knows it.

There's no way that a censor, or anybody in the military or anywhere else can get on to us. Not unless we tell him."

"What's your . . . I mean how many . . . ?"

"We have units at several bases, all over the South. Most personnel have been recruited at Basic Training, Classification, and Pre-Flight, where Joel was very active off duty." Shears turned to the nearest cadets. "He picked me at a bowling alley in Birmingham. When we got up here I asked him why he did. I had been a flight leader, down in Alabama, and I asked him if he liked the way my sword used to flash in the sun, on the parade ground. I was kidding, but only half. He said no; that it was because I could roll a very hard ball with only two steps on the approach. He said he'd never seen me until that night."

"I used to bowl some," Cahill said, "Back in Atlanta in the old days. I wasn't too bad, to tell you the truth." He swept his arm in a low arc.

"Pow," said Cadet Kalb. "Swerved it in!"

Cahill hesitated, wondering if he recalled what he said he did. "And they say there're some blind bowlers, round and about. That's somethin' I might want to get back into." He could tell that this did not register with them, and dropped it; he was not really interested, either.

"Everybody on the Alnilam Project is on our alert. All contacts have been made and acknowledged. When they see what we do here—what we do here on Sunday—they will understand what they're in on; they'll do what we say; they'll be eager to do it. As soon as this action takes place, and maybe one more somewhere else, everyone who's been notified can be implicated—conspiracy, destroying government property, abetting the enemy, God knows what; even treason. But there won't be any leaks. Joel picked the right people; they're all with us. After Sunday there won't be any doubt."

He returned to his pockets: should he show these other boys what he had? No; no; he should not. The emotion around him was rising until he felt it almost as solid. He unclasped his fingers from a bent prong, from around broken glass.

Shears put down the computer and the paper and took up the book again. He read: "Electrical power, and the simplest moving parts." He hesitated, as if to make sure that this had sunk as deep as it would go. "Electricity, because its unknowability is equal to its power. It will serve, but cannot be understood."

"Joel said this? He believed this?" Cahill asked, despising himself for his helplessness. "And he made up . . . he got up your code, and all?"

"He did everything," Shears said, nodding. "He picked us all. He sketched out the plot, and filled it in. He taught every one of us how to fly, here, in the barracks. Most of us probably would have washed out, if it hadn't been for him; we all had troubles. Blazek was going down the well on airsickness."

"Boy, was I ever," Blazek said. "I was airsick on the ground. Every time I thought about my instructor."

"Kalb had a coordination problem, Klienheinz and Billy Crider didn't show enough progress, Neilson couldn't do anything with acrobatics, and I"—Shears shook his head, wondering over something that had passed—"I just couldn't catch on to what they wanted me to do. Get this: me the cadet colonel: they told me I couldn't interpret instructions correctly: that I couldn't follow orders. I can't speak for the others —only sort of—but when Joel got us together and started talking to us, there was some doubt about what he was trying to get across. He told us that all that would be taken care of, as soon as we got back into the air: back into the air from this barracks. As soon as *he* got into the air, word got around fast, not only from the boys but from the instructors. The more he flew, the more we believed him; the more pressure his flying put on the instructors, the more they talked him up, the more behind him we were. The more tours he walked, according to Lieutenant Spigner's orders and the colonel's, the more we went with *his* orders."

"The colonel was airborne when Joel went in," someone blurted out.

"I heard that," said Cahill. "I don't know what to make of it."

"Joel was fooling around with the colonel's girl," Cadet Adler said. "Lucille. Works in Supply."

"I heard that, too," said Cahill. "Why do you feel like you need to tell me now?"

"I think you ought to know," said Adler. "She's some kind of bad news."

"Why didn't you tell *him?*" Cahill asked.

"Who was I to tell Joel Cahill anything?" Adler said, shaking his head and drawing breath. "Somebody who'd memorize the eye charts for me . . . what the hell. His sex life was not any of my business."

"You been in Supply, Mr. Cahill?" a cadet named Brenner asked.

"I been in there," Cahill answered. "I talked to the young lady for a minute."

"We call her place the Sheep Shack," Harbelis said. "Jackets, pants, boots, all heavy-lined. Hundreds of sheep in there, all dead. Smells like it, too."

"Become a sheep and you will see the wolf," Cadet Kalb said. "Come Sunday."

"Maybe I'll get back, before I leave," Cahill said. "She may want to tell me somethin'. Somethin' she didn't remember the first time."

There was a general shifting of cloth. Either something was coming from them or they were getting ready to break up, Cahill guessed.

Shears read: " 'First the steel phase, the rigidity of metal, truly entered, truly participated in. We will break through the machine without breaking it, without disturbing one rotation of it.'

" 'Every form of machinery must deal with, must acknowledge the primacy of the human trance.'

" 'Out of metal, one terrifying moment of sleep, trance, ceremony, and then on. On and in . . .' "

Cahill could find no way to fill the long pause.

" 'The construction of a god out of high-speed metals, and the abandonment of the god,' " continued Shears.

" 'Wandering. Much wandering,' " Harbelis said. "I know that one without the book."

There was no need, now, to distinguish one voice from any other.

" 'Do not cut the heart,' " said Adler. "I know that one."

Gasoline . . . Gasoline . . . Was not this in some way related to gasoline? Where had he heard it? Why gasoline?

"The infinite music, the initialed water, and the unknowable name on it," Youngblood said.

"No one will evade," said Harbelis. " 'There will be nothing to evade, for everything will be desirable and endless.' "

Shears read: " 'Part of the air will tear open, and there will be a descent, and much confusion.' "

Neilson said, reading over Shears's shoulder: " 'A spirit more dangerous than reason, more solid than bread, will be dismembered, will lose the blood of its mouth.' "

Where was Zack? He had forgotten him, and felt for him with his feet. The rising of emotion around him was like a well; the stones held it, the underground water poured into it; there was no other way. Too much of this and there was no telling what Zack might do; excitement and confusion were things he had not learned to deal with.

" 'The flight of an aircraft is the image of an endless rail. The end is where we leave it, and descend,' " continued Neilson.

Several voices: " 'Our indoctrination is simple, but crucial. We ought to be able to tell—I can tell—who will do and who will not. It is a simple test of the eyes, as the fingers are touched. You would have to be blind to evade the answer.' "

Shears again, joined by Harbelis: " 'The other test is the ability to respond without question to a situation that could not have been known beforehand. The Alnilam candidate must handle the unknown thing. If he asks why, he will not be allowed the attempt; the problem will not be presented.' "

It was time; Cahill had had enough. If he was contributing to this, to the pressure, the thickening tension, the buildup that seemed nearly out of hand, he should not just stand there and let it go on.

"All right," he said suddenly. "This is as far as I can go. It's not only that I can't take in any more, but I can't *take* any more. Just answer me one question."

Shears looked around the other cadets. Not all of them nodded, but most of them did.

"We know the question," Shears said, now watching Cahill steadily and raising the book.

"Tell me, then."

"Joel will tell you," Shears said.

There was much silence now, and Cahill could find no way to break it, or, as seemed to him more accurate, to break into it.

Shears turned some pages. His lips moved silently as he read to himself. Then he said slowly, again looking straight at Cahill's glasses: " 'When the father comes, Orion will leap free.' "

His pockets were not full; all things were past interpretation. He held to the objects that were there, turned them loose, closed on them again.

"You can't be . . . I mean, if you mean what I think you mean . . . what I think you *might* mean . . ."

"I told you we knew the question," Shears said. "That's the answer. Joel knew you would come. And here you are: here: right here."

"But . . . Lord . . ." Cahill fumbled. "He couldn't have . . . I mean this was only . . . this happened . . ."

"He knew weeks ago," Shears said strongly. "And maybe before that. He knew you would come when we needed you. Everything he said has been right in line."

"And all this business . . . like . . . I mean about out yonder in the snow . . . Harbelis runnin' . . . and . . . and the basketball and . . . I mean that was all . . . was that all . . . ?"

"The basketball shot was the unknown thing," Harbelis said. "That was left up to me to come up with. Shears left it up to me. The running was my own thing. I had to have some excuse to be out there."

Cahill went back to the cold of his first day at the base, and the round air of the basketball in his hands. Now, he needed some relief from the direction they had set him in; some diversion, some side issue.

"Did I really hit that thing?" he asked.

"You did really," Harbelis said. "It took you a couple of times, but you finally hit it. You hit the hole that stays up there in the air, with a net around it. You hit the middle, where there's nothing, where there can't be anything, ever."

"You're tellin' me the truth?"

"I wouldn't tell you anything else. You wouldn't be here if you hadn't hit it. That, and the fact that you didn't ask me what it was all about. That figured, just like the book says. I was scared to death you were gonna ask why I asked you to fool around with a damn basketball, when there wasn't any reason for it that you could see—that you could possibly see—but you didn't. Everything went right. You didn't ask any questions, and I didn't, either. We just went on from there."

"Well," Cahill reflected, a little calmer, with a vague but growing sense of confidence returning, "I'm here, sure enough. I'll be at the graduation Sunday, God willin'. Is that what you want?"

"That's part of what we want," Shears said. "That's an absolute must. For the boys, here, to know that you *are* there: that the predictions are right; that everything is running true."

"I'll be there, then," he said. "If Zack don't give down on me. I'll be there even if he does."

"The main thing you need to do for us—and for Joel—you've already done, which is to come here. The rest you can leave to us. After we wrap this thing up Sunday, we'll keep in touch with you, with the code and by other ways. You're in the thing. There'll be lots happening."

"What about Sunday, now?" Cahill asked. "I don't have much of a picture, yet."

"Just a little rumpus in the parking area, is all, Mr. Cahill. A little bump and brush-by. Just something to get around the bases, and let them know we mean business, that we'll do what we say we'll do. Nobody'll get hurt. A little preliminary confusion before the real stuff later on. That's all."

"Well now, listen . . ." Cahill began. "I don't want to . . . I mean, I don't want to be . . ."

"You're not going to have to do anything. You and Zack just be over

429

in the stands, or whatever they have fixed up for civilians. We'll see you. I think there's going to be a band. Wait it out. Then you'll hear a lot of engines."

"I've heard 'em," Cahill said. "I can hear 'em all the way into town. I wake up hearin' 'em."

"This will be a little different," said Shears. "But don't move from where you are. Don't move. Nothing's going to happen to you. Just stay where you are; hold on to what you've got."

"Yeah, now, but listen," Cahill said, wanting to be sure and knowing he could not. "You said 'destroy.' Didn't you say 'destroy'? 'Destroy the aircraft'?"

"That was our message. But there may be some exaggeration in that; it shouldn't worry you. We may not destroy 'em, but we'll bang some of 'em up a bit. They'll know they've been in a fracas. And that'll catch the rabbit, like they say. Remember: this is just a preliminary show of force; just a start."

Shears was winding down; Cahill was sure of it. No more, he brain-begged; don't give me any more.

"It's only a start, Mr. Cahill, but it's important that we have all the elements. So you make sure you and Zack are over there by the band somewhere, and stay there. Our start-engine time is right around fifteen thirty, which is three-thirty. Anyway, you won't have any trouble telling when we start. All you have to do is hold. Hold; hold on."

" 'Show of force.' What does that mean?"

"Show of force, show of power . . . You'll find out what it means."

Under both coats his arms changed, beginning with shoulders. There was a good thing in his head, now, that made his arms from the shoulders of a different kind of strength from the strength of Karl Kesmodl and the other lifters and bodybuilders of Willow Plunge. Again it had come to him: the picture in his head was a vivid green, and contained a solitude full of both still and rushing vitality, of elation and falling, when from the picnic with his wife Florence,

To the cadets, Cahill seemed to stand without strain, in something that looked a little like a military stance, almost the position of parade rest. They kept glancing at him, waiting for what he would say, might say, but he stood quietly, his hands in his pockets. Shears turned and handed the book to Harbelis, who looked at it

430

full of cold, delicious food, he had walked off into the woods and followed the creek out over the high rock that split it, and then went down the little path that led down and back and under and then out again between the two falling streams—endless falling, white, weightless and yet falling, falling past, not changing. It was his arms that were changing not then but now. Endless arms, endless power, rain in them, all water, and the whitest color on earth. Endless arms.

Cahill was not caught out this time, or only a little; he had heard Shears do this before, and hadn't understood why, the first time. There was no need to ask questions now. Shears was either reading or speaking from memory; either way, he was bound to do it.

That's the coincidence of all time, he thought, tuning in to the bright heatless thrusts across the black of his vision: javelins, spears; that's what they're like. Not knives, or anything little. They're long, and they go far, and they keep coming; there's a throw to them.

The imaged fire was cut through by his other fire; his fires, the sideways sleet.

intently and then gave it to Adler, who sent it on. The book passed through the semicircle of boys and came back to Shears. They stayed as they were, as the book reached him.

" 'As I came through the desert thus it was,' " Shears said.

" 'As I came through the desert: Meteors ran /
And crossed their javelins on the black sky-span . . .' "
The cadets bent toward Cahill, the lips of some of them moving with Shears's; they were alert and relaxed, like runners called to the line.

" 'The zenith opened to a gulf of flame . . .

431

" 'The dreadful thunderbolts
jarred earth's thick frame;
The air all heaved in waves of fire
    that surged
And weltered round me sole there
    unsubmerged;
Yet I rode on austere;
No hope could have no fear.' "

He stayed on the last thought;
with the lengthening silence he
was sure that Shears meant for
him to be in.

Shears left off his intoning voice
and began to talk plainly, almost
in classroom terms; the break in
his address was so abrupt as to be
both startling and in a way expected, as when it is understood
that the speaker is on a stage.

"To us, the air is a desert, Mr.
Cahill. That's a very fruitful con-
cept, and lets you know a lot of
things about the air that nobody
else does. It lets you live, it helps
you live, but the main fact about it
is the emptiness, the nothing of it;
you experience the whole air as a
nothing. A huge desert that is everywhere the earth is."

"No sand, but a desert anyway," Cahill said, something like
a runner's second wind coming
to his mind. There were some
ways in which he could deal with
this.

"Yes, that's right," Shears continued. "It's a desert you can see
through in every direction; in any
direction. If weather doesn't get
in the way—clouds, fogs, and so

I wonder if they think, he asked himself, that I'm absolutely fascinated by all this, all these notions and theories that Joel is supposed to have had? He was not; he had already listened to more than enough of them, and, beginning to be downright bored, he did not find it odd that he was now more certain than not that there was a side of his boy that he would not have liked.

"Now wait a minute," Cahill said. "That's all you need to do. I've got the picture."

on—it won't oppose your seeing whatever you want to see; whatever's there. It's a sensitive desert, all around you. You breathe this emptiness—this essential emptiness—you live in it, sometimes you die for the lack of it. You're not on it, like you are on the land, say, of a desert: you're *in* it. You're breathing it, and in an airplane you're riding in it. It holds you up, but you're giving away too much to it if you don't understand that it's a desert, first, last, and always. You make a mistake to be happy in it, or to be unhappy in it, or to be afraid. We don't want to forget—we *don't* forget—that our main weapon is indifference. Indifference and austerity: to let nothing give us an emotion. That's the basis of Alnilam. Or of this phase of it, anyway: the steel phase, the metal phase. The sleep phase."

Shears began again, in his public voice. " 'As I came through the desert thus it was,
As I came through the desert: I was twain,
Two selves distinct that cannot join again . . .' "

"We're just about finished," Shears said, having trouble keeping the impatience out of his voice. He waited until he was satisfied that Cahill would not break in again.

433

" 'One stood apart and knew but could not stir . . .' "

It was important not to allow himself to be silenced. "All right. Amen. So be it. Here ends the lesson. Whatever you want to say. Let's get on down the road."

" 'Yet I rode on austere.
No hope could have no fear.' "

"Where's my dog?" Cahill asked, swinging his arms vigorously in front of him as if to get the circulation back.

"You see," Shears said, now almost apologetic, "incantation is valuable to us." He thumbed through the book and read from it, holding it at a curious slant. "Through incantation, each thinks he has summoned the words from some deep place in himself that only he knows. The more familiar with the words he is, even if he memorized them from some other place at the beginning, the more sure of this he is; the more he thinks the words belong to him; that they come from him. Thus the many enter into a gigantic reflex, which is like a touched muscle belonging to them all. Yet each feels it as his own."

He had always despised singing, especially in places like church, where people did it together. He could think of no embarrassment worse than being included in a hymn; than being in it with the kind of people who would be singing.

He leaned forward and touched the sleeve of Cahill's overcoat at the forearm.

No, he said to himself. The boy is wrong; the words would never belong to me. "I've heard all that," he said. "This is where I came in."

"Try it with us this time. Will you? Just the last two lines; they're the main ones."

"And that'll be the end, will it?"

Shears nodded with satisfaction. "That'll be the end of the end." He paused. "The end of the end, the end of the beginning."

"All right," Cahill said resignedly. "How does it go, now?"

"It just goes," Shears said, "Yet I rode on austere. No hope could have no fear.' "

"Actually," he added, "Joel changed one word. It was originally 'I *strode* on austere,' but the other way fits us better."

"Crank it up, then."

" 'As I came through the desert thus it was,
As I came through the desert: On the left
The sun arose and crowned a broad crag-cleft;
There stopped and burned out black, except a rim,
A bleeding eyeless socket, red and dim;
Whereon the moon fell suddenly southwest,
And stood above the right-hand cliffs at rest; . . .
Still I rode on austere . . .
No hope could have no fear.' "

He waited for the words he had been given, reluctantly holding them ready.

What the hell kind of boys are these? he thought indignantly, brought up short by the images put before him. Didn't they know better than to talk to a blind man about bleeding eyes, and all such as that?

Yet when the words Shears had given him came up, he said them, and the loudness, with his voice in it, was a new and terrible human sound, and strong. Solemn, low, terrible with conviction, ground out, unstoppable, it carried him, and in it he was carrying himself.

The cadets stood like choirboys, their eyes bright and focused, looking out somewhere beyond what was there for them to see: beyond the bunks on the other side of the barracks, beyond

435

If I had hope, what would it be for? he wondered as he said the words. But fear; no, I won't have that, austere or not; I've got my own ways to keep that out. the small windows opposite the large one, beyond the footlockers and the open closets, beyond the shelves and the painted wood.

"That winds it up," Shears said. "Now you know everything we know, or just about. We hope you can stay, Mr. Cahill. Just stay through Sunday. Whether we see you or no, I expect we'll know whether you're there. It would mean a great deal for us to know that."

"I plan to be there," Cahill said evenly. "I don't see how anybody could keep me out." Feeling he should say something else, something more conventional and fitting for someone in his fifties to say to boys, he added, "But for God's sake, don't let anybody get hurt."

"You don't have to worry," Harbelis said. "Joel didn't want that, either."

Shears read, for the last time, from the book. "It is better for our purposes to be inhuman than superhuman. It is also harder, for our actions must contain as little cruelty as possible."

"Well, see that you keep it that way," Cahill said lamely. "Do that and I'll be there."

Some of the cadets started for the door; others sat on the lower bunks, or turned to the lockers and shelves. One boy, moving for the latrine, said, "What we will, God does," and was gone; the other sounds, those of conventional young men, took over the air.

"Spain," Cahill said, in his own nearly normal voice. "Cadet Spain. Spain-with-a-first-name-like-mine. Are you around anywhere?"

"Right here, sir," Cadet Spain said, from a bunk he was smoothing. "Front and center, I am. What's your pleasure, sir?"

"You have a few minutes?"

"I do, sir. A few, and a few more. I have to fly in a couple of hours, with the rest of the stragglers. I've been cleared, and the colonel's going to let me get in the rest of my time. But I don't have anything to do until around two-thirty, when the bus leaves."

"You want to have a Coke with me? I'll buy you one. Maybe two."

"Sure," Spain said. "I'll sure enough take one of 'em, anyway. We can go over to the cadet club."

Cahill prodded Zack with his foot, where he had come to rest, inching along the floor as Shears and the others had been speaking. "Come on,

Anvil-head," Cahill said to him. "I thought you was prob'ly asleep somewhere around here. All this don't mean nothin' to you, does it?"

"We can go along," Spain said. "There's nothing to hold us."

"How's your leg?" Cahill asked as they reached the door.

"Not so bad," Spain said. "The stitches are pulling a little. The shots were worse than anything Zack did. I hope I didn't poison Zack."

"That's a mighty big attitude, son," Cahill said in genuine admiration. "Zack sure ain't come to no harm. He just gets a little bit confused when there's a lot of noise, when there's some other kind of confusion goin' on."

"Would he like something to eat?" Spain asked politely, as they moved over the crisp ground.

"Prob'ly would," Cahill said. "He likes the mayonnaise at your club, here. He's done already told me that. He likes blood and mayonnaise, though I don't believe he's ever had 'em at the same time. Blood: you know, cooked blood, like the kind you put on rice. He likes that."

Spain had stopped, and Cahill had gone on a step or two before he realized it; he was disgruntled and apprehensive as he frequently was, now, because a situation had come about when he was talking only to himself, believing someone else was there who was not: who had left him, who had never been sufficiently there; who had never been there.

"Spain," he said. "What is it? Where have you got to?"

Spain came up. "It's not anything," he said. "Not anything but Captain Lennox Whitehall leaning up against a pine tree, with a box of mirrors in his hand, trying to look like he's doing something with the sun. The sun, or something else up there."

"All cadets, shut your ignorant heads up," said Whitehall, from the patch of sun on the tree he leaned against. "You damned near made me miss it." He looked at his watch. "But you didn't. Lucky for you."

"What is it you're doing?" Spain asked. "You're supposed to do that at night, with the stars. Don't you know that?"

"The sun is better," the captain replied. "It's better than any; better than everything else up there. The sun at noon, wherever you are: that's the real locational magic."

"How come you never showed us any of that stuff?" Spain asked, with actual interest.

"You're too dumb," Whitehall said. "You're truck drivers and taxi drivers. Navigation is for the aristocrats, the smart people, the intellectuals of the wild blue yonder. If you'd'a had the sense, if you'd'a qualified, you'd be in navigation; right now you'd be maybe on the beach in

California or Florida, flying in offices in nice warm AT-9s, instead of in this dump in the pine barrens, freezing your ass off in an open cockpit. Too bad for you."

"You done left me out again," Cahill said, shuffling his feet in the stiff grass blades. "It's cold. Let's find the inside of somethin'. Come on with us, Captain. I like your stories."

"Just a little minute," Whitehall said. "I ought to take one more sight, just to make sure."

He brought up the rubber eyepiece and settled against the tree. Cahill faced between him and the intently watching Spain; the stillness belonged to the other two as well, guaranteeing Whitehall's, his right hand holding the sextant, his left adjusting its small wheel. His lips were parted slightly; he was not breathing.

"Got it. Got you that time," he said, looking quickly at his watch. "Seventeen twenty-three oh eight. That should catch the rabbit; the celestial rabbit, right by the balls."

"You still should have showed us, Captain Whitehall," Spain said. "Might have saved somebody."

"No, it wouldn't," Whitehall answered with conviction. "You have to have a whole setup in the airplane to do celestial. You have to have a big airplane, that doesn't jump around as much as these others. You have to have a pure glass astrodome. Plexiglas is no good; too much distortion. You have to have a little library of tables, and you have to have a place where you can spread out your charts and mark out your courses. Try all that in a P-40 or an A-20. Celestial'd be a waste of time. You learn pilotage and Dead Reckoning real well; they'll be all you're gonna need. And if I didn't get them over to you, I've been wasting *my* time; you've been wasting my time, if you don't know the E-6B like you know your mama's nipples."

"Can I have a feel of that thing you've got there?" Cahill asked, **realizing too late how this sounded. "And don't tell me not to drop it, because I won't." He pulled off his gloves and Spain took them.**

"I been getting me," Cahill said, as he passed his fingers over the mirrors and lenses, **"a** "Why, sure," Whitehall replied, startled and not sure how to transfer the sextant. When Cahill put

438

whole new country of feels." He nodded gravely. "You bet. Since I've been up here I've got myself a whole lot of stuff I didn't have before." He spoke outward more, toward where he believed Captain Whitehall to be standing. "I'm a carpenter, you know, Captain. I plan to keep on with it. And the better my feelin' gets, the better I'm goin' to be able to do. Now," he said slowly, holding up the sextant before his face, "I already know your other thing, your E6B you was talkin' about; I'd know it if you'us to put one in my hand. I know it and I know what it does. This one . . . this one . . ." he said with gravity and respect, "this one is more complicated. A lot more complicated," he went on, passing his left ring-finger over the index mirror. "This here's glass," he said.

The surfaces were a number of built-in slants; Cahill sensed parallels, an order of lines against no surface.

out both hands, he placed the instrument in them, released it, and stood ready to catch it in case it fell, as if it were not so much fragile as dangerous, perhaps explosive.

Watching the blind man talk to the tree beside him, Whitehall slowly lowered his hands as Cahill turned the sextant over, touching various parts of it with a delicacy so extreme that the captain could almost believe that he loved it. Whitehall had some interest in music, and had once tried to build a harpsichord; as blunt and brutal as Cahill's fingers were, there was something about them that definitely suggested musicianship; Whitehall was strangely moved.

"Right," the Navigator said. "That's a mirror." He went briefly to his classroom manner, which he liked to think was—and actually was—a combination of relaxed banter and exact definition. "You see, sir," he said, "no matter how high the aircraft is off the ground, it's still too high for you to use the earth horizon, like you do on ships. Besides, from an aircraft you can't see the horizon well, from up there; even when you can see it you can't make out exactly

"Bubbles," Cahill said. "That's all I need. This flyin' . . . damn; the whole damn thing is bubbles. You get in a bubble when you're trying to fly the thing level, you got a bubble in a box with a lot of mirrors that's supposed to tell you . . ."

where it is. So . . . you have to have a bubble."

"You get bubbles in your fuel line and you're in some kind of trouble, too. Don't worry; I won't make it rhyme," Spain said, speaking as an equal, in repartee at least.

"I never thought of that," Whitehall said, his eyes on the sextant that the blind man seemed to have no notion of giving back. "But I calibrate my sextant two or three times a week. I know where Peckover, North Carolina, is, and I can tell you the maps of this area are a little off. We're at least half a mile east of where the charts say we are. If we were on a mission, that would cost us."

"You come out here and do this every two or three days?" Cahill asked. "You ain't got nothing better to do?"

"I sure don't have anything better, and I probably never will have. I'm the only one around here that really knows where he is. *Really* knows, I mean, according to the way things are set up."

The last was a phrase that had stuck with him enough for him

440

to remember it. Before he could bring up any more words, or think of what they might be, Whitehall was talking again.

"I figure I owe it to the whole discipline. I plan to do this every clear day—and when I can, at night—for the rest of my life. I owe it a lot. I owe the stars a lot, like I told you the other night, in town. I owe the stars a lot, especially three of them." He stopped, for the blind man, outlining the viewfinder with his fingers, was lifting the sextant to his face, to his eye. Spain looked questioningly at the Navigator, who raised his shoulders, turned his palms up and the corners of his mouth down.

Cahill stayed in his position, holding the sextant almost correctly. With his left hand he reached, found the tracking wheel, and turned it slowly. "I hope I'm not messin' up your numbers," he said, absently, as one obligated to say something from an important activity in which he is engaged.

"Oh no, not at all," Whitehall said. "The angle of the sun at its highest point, and the time, that's all I need. I've already got it."

"The sun's in this box, is it?" Cahill asked.

"It sure is. It's in there, and the way it moves, and the answer to the sun, and its exact relation to you. The sun and the secret of the

He turned the tiny wheel, half waiting for there to be some change in the black field he carried with him, and the long-shooting paths of heatless fire. There was not, but what there had been: no substance, but endless motion. He would have it for the rest of his time; would have it in the same sense that he had life. In a way it stood for life; it was part of his perception; what center it had, he was. Holding the dead sextant, he watched the tracks go across.

sun, and the key; they're all in there."

"It's not really all, though," Spain said. "It's just what can be figured."

"That's where you and I part company, Mr. Spain," Whitehall said. "Those are things you might feel, but they don't really do any good; don't do anybody any good. They're just for books. I don't read those kind of books."

"There are books and books," Cadet Spain said. "How do you know what's in the books you say you don't read?"

"We won't go into that now," Whitehall said good-naturedly, adjusting his gray trench coat. "We might could talk about it some time; some time before your class ships out."

"That would be good," Spain said. "You taught me a lot. To tell you the truth, you taught Joel Cahill a lot."

"That's quite an admission," said Whitehall, "coming from one of you fellows. I'd like to believe you."

"You can," Spain said. "He told me."

"He and I talked some," Whitehall said, his face going back to Cahill's, still motionless behind the sextant.

"He was always talking about what was beyond: what was beyond this and what was beyond that; what was underneath this surface, what was hidden by this,

442

He lowered the sextant, realizing that he was coming back into information about his son. I must pay attention, he said almost aloud; this is what I came up here for. Here I am, looking through mirrors into nothing but the same thing, and people are trying to give me what I asked for, and maybe more than that, and here I don't have any idea about what the man's been talking about, right at me, right in my face.

The sun was available to the instrument he held. There was in his hands a give-and-take fragility, a balancement of objects seen, a relation between them that could be controlled: controlled by the eye, the fingers, and the slants and angles of glasses: mirrors: lenses. He longed for whatever revelations

that, or the other thing. Air was not really air, water was not really water. An engine was doing some other thing than it was supposed to be doing; than what it thought it was doing. Navigation was really a form of poetry. So was mathematics in general. You would think"—he focused sharply on Cahill—"you would think, a kid like him . . . would . . . would have all this stuff come tumbling out, just kind of pell-mell; you'd think that he would talk real fast. But he didn't. Everything he said came out very slow, like he'd been thinking about it for a long time. The riddles he used to bring out were like riddles that he'd had a hard time getting hold of, but that he was sure of, once he had a lock on them."

Spain said nothing, and Whitehall took this as a kind of answer to which he felt justified in responding, in refuting.

"It's just that I don't hold with notions that don't seem to go anywhere. Joel Cahill seemed to believe that there's some kind of freedom that's beyond all discipline, beyond all skill: that there's a supermathematics beyond mathematics, that isn't mathematics, a superphysics that isn't physics. That's a little rarefied for me. That's making mystery into a kind of principle that . . . that's not a principle." He shook his head and settled the shoulders of his coat

he might be holding to his forehead: for the sun, for something in the sky, or beyond the sky, to appear there, among the long heartless flashes of his blindness. Behind the dark, he thought, his neck muscles stiffening against his collar: beyond it: beyond.

His yearning broke; he brought the rubber eyepiece from his face.

"Fire," Cahill said, and then paused, with his free hands. "But I had that already."

once more. "No; I think that the discipline *is* the freedom. Mathematics, trig, navigation: they're what they are. A numerical system, it's what it is; there's not anything beyond."

"It's the way you come at it," Spain said.

"And I'll tell you another thing," Whitehall said. "The working out of the numbers is the mystery, because nobody knows why it's set up to be that way. That's enough mystery for me. Give me something that works out. Give me a real plan. I'll learn it, and I'll get home with it. Everything is in that; to have something in your hand that'll get you home."

He took the sextant from Cahill, and he could not keep ceremoniousness out, nor, though he knew he should be biting his tongue while doing it, could he help asking a question, he was sure, that few ever got to ask.

"What were your ideas, Mr. Cahill? You were standing there with my sextant a good while. What was in there for you? Something you remembered?" Whitehall could not help himself. "What did you see?"

"Come on with us," Spain said to Whitehall. "We're going over to the club and get us a Coke or something."

"Sure," said Whitehall. "Let me throw my instrument back in the box."

They skirted the swimming pool, with its low dregs of ice.

"Edge over a little to your left, Mr. Cahill," Spain said. "We're going around the corner of the pool."

Cahill swept his arm at waist level. "Where's my chair?" he asked. "Wadn't I sittin' out here the other day?"

"You sure were," said Captain Whitehall. "And I was sitting with you. It was not a bad exchange, either. You're the first blind man I ever talked to. Seems like a person can get along with them."

"You're the only one I ever talked to about the stars," Cahill said. "I don't expect there'll be any others." He ranged his hand some more. "But where the hell's my chair? I thought I had the thing spotted."

"They moved it," Spain said. "I don't know why, or where, but they did."

"Shit," said Cahill, "when you move somethin' from where a blind man thought it was, you might as well be movin' it out of the world."

"Sorry," Whitehall said. "I liked to sit out here, too, cold or not. It beats all that body heat inside, and all that noise."

"Well, you take something away," Spain said, "and you ought to put something back. There's not anything here in this corner that's much good, any more. There's one frozen leaf, down there in the ice, that's kind of pretty. A green leaf, too; all the others are brown. It looks like it's still falling. But that don't matter."

Inside they shoved into a booth, with Cahill on the end, pulling Zack down beside his feet. When Cahill lifted his hat off by the crown, someone took it. Whitehall went to the counter.

"Here comes Captain Faulstick, the mad bomber," Spain said to Cahill. "Can you put up with him?"

"Sure can," Cahill said. "I know his whole story. Tell him to come over and sit down."

Spain got up and returned with Faulstick, whose cruelly close shave made him seem paler.

"Ready for the big doings Sunday?" Spain asked.

"I guess," Captain Faulstick said. "I wish the god-damned thing was over. I'm supposed to be flying Crider's wing, with Neilson on the other side. That right?"

"If you say so," Spain said evenly. "If that's the way it is in the mock-up."

"That's what they told me," Faulstick said. "We're supposed to fly in echelons of three, and our three is supposed to assemble at eight hundred and fifty feet. Then we turn on course two-six-oh, make another turn over Fredonia, and come back over the field. When we get to the reservoir on course eight-oh we disassemble. Crider breaks starboard and I break port; Neilson flies straight ahead. We keep looking around and around and around . . ." Faulstick lolled his head in a circle, almost touching his shoulders, his eyeballs turned up, and then rotated it exaggeratedly and mechanically, left and right and front. "Then we all come in and land."

"Better watch out all the time," Spain said. "Look all around, *really.* It's not all that much of a joke, when somebody prangs you."

"I know that, Mr. Spain," Faulstick said. "But for the Lord's sake wouldn't you think that they'd've given us a little more experience? We haven't had even a single dry run on this."

"You're supposed to know what you're doing by now. You're through Primary; you've got all your time in. You've passed your check-rides. You made it. That's what the book says."

"The book can say what it wants to," Faulstick said, watching the bubbles in his paper cup. "But formation . . . Jesus. I had one little formation flight solo, over to Tazewell and back. I was on Crider's wing, lolling in and out, closing up and then falling back. The damn flyover is not going to look like much with me in it, I can tell you. These civilians around here they're trying to impress are going to believe that none of us belongs up there in the damn air."

"You can do it," Spain said. "We can do it. Just because there's no provision for formation in Primary is not to say we can't do it if we have to. You just get your throttle synchronized with Crider's and Neilson's, and keep with 'em, but keep out of their way. You'll be all right."

"Shit, I don't know," said Faulstick, leaning back and letting the air out of himself. "I'll never make it through Basic, if this is what you have to do. I've got a good mind to quit while I can."

"Can't quit now, Captain. Your country needs you, and all. You made it through this place. You beat the machine. You didn't go down in flames in the Maytag."

"Let's don't bring in the horseshit, Spain," Faulstick said. "Let's be clear. They don't want to wash out combat veterans, if they don't absolutely have to. It's bad for morale, it's bad publicity, it's bad all round. But I know it, whether my instructor knows it or not; and I don't see how you could *not* know it: I can't really do what you fellows can do, Spain. Or what Billy Crider can do, or any of them. I'm not fooling myself. My one slow roll, the check-rider did most of it. I would no more start one to the left than I would eat the engine-block, so I started one to the right. I got the aircraft inverted, and the instructor eased it on around. It came out on a point, and I didn't argue, but I didn't start another one, either. When we got down, he asked me, 'Did you understand that all right, Captain? Do you think you can do it OK, now?' I told him I thought so, and he passed me. I told him I thought so, but I can't. Upside down confuses me; I get my directions mixed up; I really *don't* know left from right."

"Straight and level on Sunday, Captain," said Spain. "That's all you're gonna need. That, and a lot of looking around."

"I don't think . . . they wouldn't really carry you all that much, would they?" Cahill asked. "I'll bet you can do better than you say."

"Not so," Faulstick said. "I'm not modest; believe me, it's not that."

"Just get up there with them other boys," Cahill said, surprised at his advice, and the authority with which he gave it. "The Air Corps is not doin' you any favors. You're up there because you can fly."

"Thanks for your good words, Mr. Cahill," Faulstick said. "Don't think I don't appreciate them. But there are things that you don't know, and that everybody else does. This, for just one instance." He leaned forward and took a long sip from his creased cup. "About a year and a half ago, when I was just starting bombardier school, there was a famous All-American football player. I won't tell you his name." Faulstick smiled half conspiratorially, half shyly. "Actually, his name was Ron Nicholson. You know, Knocker Nicholson, the Scourge from Syracuse."

"What about him?" Spain asked. "He was good. Is he in the Air Corps?"

"He is," Faulstick said. "He's one of us. I'm surprised you didn't know; there was so much publicity about it, about him going through Cadets, getting his wings, and all that."

"He went through?"

"He went through, but they tell me he had his troubles. Anyway, they got him through, when maybe they shouldn't have. They gave him a B-25, and he got into trouble in North Africa. The great bulldozing fullback, the idol of American youth, promptly bailed out on his crew; he was the only survivor."

"That all?" asked Spain. "That's a bad thing to do, sure enough."

"Bad, but there's worse. The Air Corps still felt like it couldn't show him up, at least not publicly. Enlistment might suffer. So they took him out of medium bombers and put him in fighters, where he couldn't hurt anybody but himself. Seemed like a good idea at the time."

"How did that work out?" Spain asked, gazing watchfully out between Faulstick and Cahill. "One to an airplane. Seems fair enough, for somebody who'd bail out on his crew. Not too easy to hurt other people. But I guess it can be done."

"It can be done. They sent him to China, and sure enough, he went down again. I don't know what happened to him or his aircraft; I don't think he was shot down, but down he went. He was fairly far inland, so I heard, and he silked out into the rice paddies, and came down all right; he wasn't hurt."

"So he got back?"

"He did. The Chinese partisans got him out, passing him from village to village, keeping him away from the Japanese. It took them a while; I should think they'd have to do most of their traveling at night. But they got him out; he was returned to the living, and to the Air Corps. He's right with us."

"That the end of the story?" Cahill asked. He had tried to picture none of this. China was too far away, and he had never heard of the ex-football player.

"Not quite," Faulstick said, finishing his Coke. "Naturally the press wanted to know all about it, about his daring escape—escapes, maybe—his courage, his resourcefulness, and all those good things. It's my impression that the Air Corps might even got a little more mileage out of him so far as incentive was concerned. Knocker Nicholson was very happy to comply. He gave dates, he gave geographical locations, he gave names, he gave organizations, he gave the names of villages, all to the press. I read some of the stuff myself. The thought of security didn't cross my mind, or if it did, it crossed real fast."

"Security?" Spain asked. "What about security?"

"I said it didn't cross my mind at the time," Faulstick said. "And it apparently didn't cross Nicholson's either, as it turns out. He spilled his heroic guts to the press, and as a result, thanks to his pinpointing of everybody and every village that tried to help him, the Japs went in and wiped them out, some one at a time, some at the same time, the same day or night. Killed hundreds of people. Whole families, women, children, everybody they could find who even might have had anything to do with the Syracuse powerhouse. Shot them, burned them alive, God knows what else they did to them. It's one of the worst stories the military has ever hushed up."

"What track are we on now?" Cahill asked, held by the story, now that it was over. "What point did we get off of?"

"We're still on the point, Mr. Cahill," Faulstick said, reaching for his hat. "The point is that the Air Corps will draw back from washing out people that they ought not to let go through. Knocker Nicholson was one of them, and maybe I'm another one. I don't have flying in my bones. I'm lucky to have my bones. No; listen. Knocker Nicholson is the answer to what we were talking about. I haven't been to Africa or China, but I've been to Europe. I've been over France, Belgium, and the Netherlands. I've flown a tour of duty in the ETO, Eighth Air Force. I have fifty missions. Seven hundred and seventy-five hours of combat. It would embarrass the Air Corps to bust me out. I have the Air Medal with two oak-leaf clusters. I have the DFC. The Distinguished Flying Cross. Get that. My flying is not distinguished. It is only distinguished by the fact that I am not a flyer. I am a rider, a long-down-distance marksman, a sharpshooter with heavy weapons, cross-hairs, and gravity. That's where the medals come from. The point is that they did come." He put his hand on them where they spread in neat rows over the left side of his chest. "No, the Air Corps is not going to wash me out. Not in Primary, anyway. That would be ridiculous. It would be bad news; other officer trainees might not come into the program, and they need 'em. They need everybody they can get. Even you, Spain. You and me against the Krauts and Nips. How do you like that?"

"Come on, now, Captain," Spain said. "Where's your combat blood? You've had fifty missions; more than anybody that's been through this place; been through up to now, anyway."

"My combat blood is going to get my real blood spilled in the Training Command," Faulstick said. "But I've made it this far, and I'll go as far as I can." He stood and looked down at Cahill with a strange expression of wonderment and sadness, longing, bafflement, and resignation. "I'm no Joel Cahill," he said, dropping a hand softly on Cahill's black shoulder. "That ain't the kind of blood I've got."

"Keep your eyes open, Captain," Spain said, narrowing his own eyes. "Don't do what the cadet did just before graduation at Bennetsville, South Carolina, two months ago."

"What'd he do?" Faulstick asked, turning in his step.

"They were on the taxiway. He thought another cadet was going to

449

run into him. He saw this other plane coming, with the throttle fire-walled, and he made a bad mistake. He tried to get out of the cockpit, and the other guy ran right over him. Pinned him against his own plane. Cut off his arm and split his head right down the middle; it's a good thing you couldn't hear the sound. It must have been a mess. They found one of his eyes about ten yards off. His teeth were scattered around, his tongue was cut loose from him. A propeller can do a lot of damage."

"What's the moral?" Faulstick asked, bringing his olive-drab muffler around his neck, making some of the moves of tying it but failing to reach whatever knot he had in mind.

"Well, I don't know," Spain said. "I don't know if there is one. If it was me I'd've gunned the ship and got the hell out of the way."

"Yeah," said Faulstick. "He could've maybe done that."

"Sure he could," Spain said. "When he heard that other engine open up, and saw the guy coming, that's when he should have gunned his: let off the brakes and jumped it; got out of there."

"Out of there, out of here. Out. Out is a big word with the military. Everybody wants it."

From behind Faulstick the square bulk of the flight surgeon thrust affably, between two cadets flying with their hands. "Here I am," he said. "Anybody looking for me? Everybody looking for me?"

"Nobody's looking for you," Spain said. "I've done got out of your krankenhaus."

"You feeling all right, Mr. Spain?" Iannone asked, edging toward his duties.

"Sure," Spain said. "I'm finishing my time this afternoon, over at the auxiliary. Things should be all right."

Iannone turned to Cahill. "Mr. Cahill, how's your level?"

"Fine," Cahill said. "I feel all right."

"Let me know if you need any more insulin," the Major said. "And lay off the Cokes and liquor, unless you want to see me when you don't want to see me."

"You'll be the first to know," Cahill said. "And I can take you or leave you."

"You want to go back to town now, or what?" Spain asked, as they stood in the pool corner again.

"Not just yet," Cahill said. "I heard somethin' I need to go see about in there. I heard somethin' I heard before. It keeps comin' at me."

"What they say," Spain said, relaxing away from his hurt leg, "is that, in the Army, if you hear a rumor enough times, there's bound to be something in it."

The boy, thin, fine-boned, almost chicken-boned, beardless, with sunken eyes and pale convalescent skin that was still not sickly, waited, as the slanting ground wind came past, as the blind man swung his head, tuning, setting his foot this way and that, picking up what he could. But there was no aircraft there, no noise from above them. The pinewoods of the base were giving off only their main sound, their essential sound, an uninsistent varying whisper; there were no engines sighing, sinking among them, or meeting their sound.

"Can I ask you to do somethin' for me?" Cahill asked.

"You can ask me, and I'm damned if I won't do it," Spain said. "What's your pleasure?"

"Would you consider," Cahill said, with strong slowness, "takin' me back to the place where I was talkin' to the girl? The place that's over near where they work on the airplanes?"

"You mean Supply?" Spain asked. "Where Lucille deals out the sheepskins? That where you want to go?"

"It is," Cahill said. "The place where it's the stillest. You can just take me and leave me."

"Nothing easier," Spain said. "Turn a bit to your left. We'll take us a fix, and go right on over there."

"This here's the place," he heard Spain say, after a time. "It's where all the little sheep go to heaven."

"I been here," Cahill said, "but I didn't know what I was doin' here."

"You want me to go in with you?" Spain asked. "Me and Lucille don't have too much in common. Or I could wait out here for you, if you want."

"No, there ain't no need for that," Cahill said. "I try to get around by myself as much as I can. I have to keep practicin' a whole bunch of new things. I take it on myself, like. There's a lot I ain't got on to yet."

"If you say so," Spain said. "This is a pretty big base. I wouldn't like to think anything'd happened to you, because of me."

Toward the place in the dark that he thought was Spain he directed his face, and pushed at the air with his hand flat. "I'll be all right, son. It's a help for you to bring me over here, because I'm really not sure I could find the buildin', and I might'a, you know, gone on out past it, out where the planes are carryin' on, if somebody hadn'a stopped me. But on back the other way, I can make that all right. Where the colonel is, and the school, and all, I can find that. I done been the same road back, a couple of times, and Zack has, too. We can make it."

He heard no movement of the foot, and he popped his fingers at his ear. "I don't hear nothing movin', on this here ground," he said. "Get on, on your way. Don't let me catch you standin' around."

"I'll be over in the squadron area," Spain said. "And when I get there I'm afraid I'm going to have to disobey your orders, because I'm going to stand around over there until you come back."

"Suit yourself," Cahill said. "Stand where you like, but don't be here."

Now the only other person he could reach was moving; he was somewhere among his steps, leaving slowly, skreak by skreak; there were a few silent intervals, where the snow must have thawed; then the skreaks took up again, fainter, determined, being set off. Cahill turned to the door, and found the heavy, uncertainly set knob in one pass. The door swung away from him, and he moved into a closed warmth, edging into it, and doing what he could to keep the heat; fumbling a little, he pulled the door to.

"Ma'am," he said to the stillness. "You that I was talkin' to the other day. You still around? You in here somewhere?"

"I'm here," the female voice said, country, high in the nose and not welcoming. Country, the more words there were; bad country. "I'm over here behind the counter, where I always am. What do you want?"

Not sure how to start, he fell back on his own silence, unwilling to acknowledge the encounter until he was ready. This was a terrible place to try to communicate with somebody; but he was used to feeling that way; every place was the same; it was either cold or warm or comfortable, and either large or small. But where he now groped in his pocket for the goggles that were supposed to be the beginning of what he had to say, wanted to say, was sure he had a right to say, the sense of unnatural suspension made his voice hesitate; it did not want to come out: out into the echoless space that the woman apparently stood in, the wadded silence, the area in front of him which, as nearly as he could tell, did nothing but absorb. How can you say anything when your head is packed? he thought. How can anybody hear you? How can you even get your voice out, clear of your tongue? Whatever's in here is not supposed to be so crowded, he thought. Spain and the others talked about sheep, about sheepskins, but that did him no good. Was everything in boxes, or were the jackets, boots and other things just piled up on one

452

another? He could not deal with being in an echoless room where he could get no return for his voice; no sense of space was with him.

He fumbled up the goggles and laid them outward on his palm.

"Remember when I was in here before . . ." he began, thrusting the goggles forward. "Remember I asked you about these?"

"Yeah, and I told you they was new issue, brand-new. And I told you I didn't know nothin' about what he wrote on the strap, or why he did it, or nothin'."

"OK. OK," he said, putting the goggles away. "I hadn' found out nothin' either."

"Well, if you do find out, don't tell me. It don't have no interest for me. Keep it to yourself."

"How about this-here?" he asked, drawing up the caked zipper; whatever was on it—smoke, fire, ash—was coming off on his palm; he was sure his hand was black with it.

"You got to come over here," she said. "You're standin' out yonder in the dark."

He stepped forward, feeling with his free hand. At the counter he put the zipper down, with one finger still on it; when it moved he flinched before he could catch himself.

"What is it?" she asked irritably. "I can't see it like that. Turn loose." It slipped from under; Cahill ran his fingertips over the counter, waiting.

The quality of the silence came over him again, with its layers. "Is that anything you ever seen before?" he asked. "Does that look like anything you got around here?"

"No," she said. "I don't think I ever seen it. What is it? Somethin' that come out of a trash can? A burnin'-barrel, or somethin'?"

"And you ain't ever seen nothin' like this before?" Cahill asked. "Nothin' a-tall?"

"I told you. I never did."

"I'm callin' you a god-damned liar," Cahill said, his voice hardening with no effort, and surprising him with the release given by the return of its usual sound. "If this didn't come off of one of your damned sheep boots, I'll eat it."

In his defensive position, getting an attack, a counterattack ready, he was surprised again. Her voice changed, was gentler, and even carried some concern, or what could have been her version of it. "Why don't you let me look at it a minute? Let me go see if it's about as long as the ones in these boots."

453

Cahill reached down for Zack, found him, straightened.

"You know, that might be what it is," she said. "It's all twisted up and burned up, but it's a zipper if it's anything. And if it's a zipper about that size, it come off a boot, if it come off anything we got in here."

He heard the counter scrape, and reached and had back the locked teeth.

"Well, thanks," he said, standing holding them.

"Did them come off . . . ?" she said. "Was your boy . . . ? I mean did he . . . ?"

"I believe so," Cahill said. "The other ones think so. McCaig, his instructor, and all. There couldn'a been nobody else out in the field where we . . . where this was at."

"You mean this was . . . ?"

"Yeah," Cahill said. "It was in a big field, one that was burned out. It was right where there was part of a fence. The poles was all burned down. There wadn't nothin' but some of the bob wire left; that and this-here."

"But how did you . . . ? I mean . . . ?"

"It wadn't me. Joel's instructor—Mac, McCaig—he went out and picked this up. He might'a just stumbled, like, you know, stumbled over it. I don't know. But I don't believe there was any other kind of boots could'a been out yonder. It's got to be off one of these, like them that's in here."

Here. A dead place he was in; no place could be deader; not dead like an ordinary room with the windows closed, where even though the only air that moves is the air that shifts as your own body shifts, and there is always some suggestion of life, some in the furniture, settling, spraining, warping, or twisting you can hear if you tune to it, some give in the wood, the floor, the walls wherever you touched them. None of that was around him. Even McLendon's shed, in his memory, was a shaped emptiness, a cave hollow in which the two dead animals hung, not so far from life as anything that had ever been where he now stood; he could not move this air; nothing he could do would move it. Not his voice or the woman's; these least of all. Joel was supposed to have been here. He might have been behind the counter, might have lain in the sheepskins, been smothered in them, risen out of them alive. The boys believed it; McCaig believed it. He shook his head, refusing to accept, yet not wanting to turn loose of the idea; it was all he had. My God, he thought, what would sex in such a place be like? It must be like fucking after you

454

were dead; where you couldn't get your breath; where there was no breath to get, no air; none; everything packed down and forgotten.

The voice existed, in nothing but itself; there were no other tones of it that the room gave, or could give.

"What?" he asked, gathering for a second shot at meaning.

"I said I'm sorry. I wish there was something somebody could do."

"Well, there ain't," Cahill said, fury rising in him. "It's all been done."

"Was he . . . wadn't he . . . wadn't he a boy with real blond hair? Blond and curly? Real bright hair? And blue eyes?"

Everybody said blue eyes. Blue. The bluest you ever saw. Cahill mumbled something he could not understand, nodding formlessly.

"I've got to make out these-here papers," she said. "New class comin' in."

He could speak, with great forcing. "What you . . ." He seized his leg through both coats and his pants. "What you been doin' back there?"

"What're you talkin' about, mister?" she said. "What do you mean, what am I doin'? I work in Supply. I'm a civilian, and right now I'm makin' out requisition forms, if it's any of your business." In the silence in which he struggled, she said, "Right now I think it'd be better if you'us to get on out of here. That'd be the best."

"I hear," he said, locking into his idea, forcing himself along with it, "I hear you and my boy . . . I hear my boy used to come in here. I hear he used to come in here with you."

"What do you mean, 'in here'?" she said, her voice stronger and more country.

"I mean he done come around this-here counter," Cahill said, tapping with the heel of his hand. "I mean in there rollin' around with you and the sheeps."

"Listen here, mister," she said evenly, "you got to listen to me, and listen just as good as you can."

He waited, resting his hand on the heel-bone.

"I don't . . . I mean I don't give a shit what they say. What the boys say, what the instructors say, or what you say. That don't make no difference to me."

"I ain't askin' about nothin' but my boy. You and the colonel, and all that . . . I don't . . ."

"Me and the *colonel?*" she said, and he was sure she leaned toward him. "I don't know no more about him than anybody else does."

"Just my boy," Cahill said. "That's all I'm talkin' about."

"I don't remember nothin' about him, mister . . ." she tailed off, and Cahill filled in, taking advantage.

"Cahill," he said. "Frank Cahill. And my boy was Joel."

"Just blue eyes and curly hair," she said. "If that wadn't him I don't have no recollection of him."

He was aware of the motionless warmth of a heater at the level of his shins. He stamped to shake it off, and moved away.

"Them . . ." she said, her voice changing again, gone lower and less strong, more felt. She would not speak like this very much, he thought. "Them boys . . . all of 'em, him and the rest of 'em . . . they're just little boys, come to play. Come in here to play with all the stuff we got in here. Go up yonder in the air to play. That's all it is; that's all they're doin'." She changed again, this time abruptly, and to outrightness. "Blind man, what do you mean, comin' in here like this? Ain't you got nothin' better to do? Ain't there nobody else around here you'd ruther see?"

"Not right now," Cahill said. "I need to know some things."

Was she leaning toward him? He felt with the skin of his face for her breath, but the air did not move. His hand with the goggles in it came to rest on the knuckles, on the solid cold of the counter.

Not on his face, but over the back of his hand something went, or could have gone: some quick passing, a fanning, gone and gone. Her sleeve? Her arm? Her fingers?

"The colonel . . . Has he been back there?"

"I can tell you, sonny boy," she said. "Not one time has he been back here. Anybody who tells you that Colonel Hoccleve has ever been around this counter is goin' to have to tell me just when it was. He's gonna have to show me."

His hand receptive and excited, he held the goggles, feeling the splinters with his thumb, as he was used to doing. Would the same air come back? If it did he would lift his arm, and surprise what was there: meet in the air whatever human flesh was passing over him.

It came again, a whiff, almost a flicker, something waved, something traveling, but he did not raise a hand.

"Lock the door," he said. "Come on and lock the door."

"What do you want, blind man?" she said. "You know I ain't goin' to lock no door."

"Come on," he said. "I want to see what's back there."

"You're crazy," she said. "I ain't comin' around." She paused, but he

456

knew she would say more. "What you goin' to do if I don't? Sic your dog on me?"

"If I 'us to tell this dog to get back there," he said, "them dead sheep'd come up runnin'."

"Do you really want me to come around there, blind man?" she said, dead-leveling with him. "What would you do if I did?"

"You can't tell," he said, remembering, with confidence and fear, the girl's nose bleeding on him, hot in drops, and then with one searing stripe across his face as she left him, quickly drawn there, her weight all gone. "I might just show you something these little boys ain't got."

"You want what you think your boy got?"

From him, nothing.

"It ain't gonna be," she said. And then, "Don't do nothin'. Don't do nothin' but leave."

His sexual assertion, at best only a strong wavering, collapsed. He pushed back his hat and grinned. "You ain't comin'," he said. "And I ain't comin'. You're right. I don't have nothin' for you."

"Save it, whatever you got," she said. He had heard many sluts, all ages, talk like this.

"I will," he said. And then, "My God, ain't there no decent women in this town?"

"Some of them old ones, maybe. Maybe one or two of them might like what you got. Go see 'em. Take your dog."

"I'm goin'," he said. "I won't bother you no more."

"You ain't botherin' me none," she said. "Don't nothin' bother me. I'm just fine."

"I'll be out of here in a couple of days," he said. "When my boy's class graduates, I'm gone."

"That'll be Sunday," she said. "You comin' out for the big doin's?"

"Yeah," he said. "I'll be around somewhere. I told the boys I would."

"Maybe I'll see you there."

"You do that," he said, turning. He bent, feeling for Zack with his goggled hand. "Come on, big 'un. We're goin'."

"Tell the colonel hello for me," he said, his hand sliding down the door for the handle.

"You tell him," she said. "You'll see him before I do."

He went out, his legs hot, his hat tilted back like that of a newspaper reporter he had once seen in a movie, talking about a scoop to a tough-

457

looking blonde. The reporter had had a good line, full of sex and fun, but he could not remember what it was.

An engine was behind him in a long sigh: he set his feet away from it, and started back.

Without the game-cries, the field-voices Cahill usually kept to his right to guide him, the voice spoke directly, from some distance.

"You made it," Spain said, standing with Harbelis and Corporal Phillipson at the foot of the stairs to the Administration Building. "We were fixing to come after you."

"Best you didn't," Cahill said. "I told you I'd make it back without no trouble."

"How'd you and Lucille get along?" Spain asked. "She treat you all right?"

Spain was not speaking just to him, or for him, he could tell. "Who's with you?" Cahill asked.

"Harbelis and Corporal Phillipson. If you want something to eat, you can come with Stathis and me. If you want to go back to town, Phil's here to take you."

"I want to go back to town," Cahill said. "I might even could get some sleep." As he spoke he was immediately aware of how much he wanted to lie down, not talk, not try to understand anything, but let the real blackness come in behind the other blackness.

"She tell you anything about Joel?" Spain asked, against Harbelis's lifted finger and shaken frowning head.

"We don't know about Joel," Spain went on, ignoring Harbelis. "He never said much about those sort of things. We never knew whether he laid down with the lamb or not. Some of the others did, or claimed they did. The colonel, now that's different. Everybody pretty much knows about that." He reflected, and grinned like a child at the ways of grown people. "He's married, too. Got two kids." He clicked his tongue, Tk, Tk, shaking his head.

Cahill was too relieved by the openness of the air to pay much attention. There would never be any reason to go back into the space he had just been in, where the walls did nothing but be where they were: had nothing for the ear, nothing for anyone who wanted to move either toward them or away. He had been there, he had asked questions, he had drawn either answers or evasions from the woman who was there, and now he was out.

"Let's go, Corporal Phil," he said. "Let's go where the town's at. I need to get off my feet."

He and Phillipson crunched—prisoner-crunched, as Cahill now thought it—around the building and across the corner of the playing field, now quiet; to their right and rear an aircraft engine ran up with brutal inconsequence, then failed back into ordinary sound.

"Get on in there, Zack," Cahill said. "You know where to go."

He hauled on Zack's collar, but only a little, for the dog was already scrambling for the back of the jeep; he was in; his claw-sound died, and Cahill stooped and groped, to do his part of things. He pulled the door to him, against his side, and he was complete, enclosed in military metal again, familiar and full of prongs, though it always bothered him, in these things, that the part of the vehicle overhead was not steady, was insubstantial and flopping; that there was too much air in the riding; too much outside, too much cold.

Phillipson, busy with the jeep, was for the moment involved in the mechanics of what he was doing, and glanced at the blind man only as a preliminary to the apology he felt he should be ready to give in case the engine did not start. But when the choke worked, the engine dredged from itself the sound of protesting confident assertion, he turned his head foursquare and looked directly at his passenger. The blind man sat with his arms folded over himself, becoming more and more one thing, an object, black stone, Phillipson thought: a shape that nothing could move, blocked out in itself so solidly that the engine-shaking of the jeep seemed not to touch it at all; the metal shook, but the blind man was still. Impenetrable. That is what he must want, Phillipson thought.

The other body settled itself; there was a pulling, as of scraping wires, and, near Cahill's feet, stamped and adjusted. The engine caught. With this cold, Cahill thought, there must be a lot of smoke, a lot of steam and heat coming out of the back of us. So what? It was winter.

They were winding, going from one side to the other more than he had been doing in any car he remembered with pleasure, pitched gently but unexpectedly from right to left, then back again, kept there a moment, then swayed irritatingly the other way. He reached down and backward for Zack, as much for the road beneath them as for reassurance of the dog's existence.

"We just about to the highway now?" he asked. "How much farther is it?"

"We're pretty near to it," Phillipson said. "This-here part of the base is through some trees. Snow's all over 'em."

"I know that," Cahill said sullenly. "I been out here."

"They're real pretty," Phillipson said without conviction, then brightened as another car came toward them.

"Look-a here," he said. "It's Mr. McCaig. His head's out the window and he's wavin' away like he knows somethin' good. Maybe the war's over."

Tires—underneath sounds—merged, then stopped. Phillipson reached across him and cranked; the air was freshened at his side.

"Hey, I got it, Frank Cahill," McCaig said, holding up a paper for Phillipson to see, as if for Cahill also. "I'm goin' to Canada. I'm goin' to Canada, and then I'm goin' to England. I'm 'on get in there amongst the bats."

"Come one more time," Cahill said. "You better backtrack some."

"Aw, come on, now," McCaig said, still enthusiastic, but slowed by the loss of something he believed could have been remembered; should, surely, have been. "Don't you know, I told you they was doin' some things over in England with bats, makin' 'em fly through cages full of wires, and all? Findin' out why the bats don't hit the wires, and then puttin' all that stuff in the airplanes? Them's the planes I'm gonna be in: the ones full of bat brains. I told you a couple of days ago."

"A couple of days." Cahill thought it over. "I've been here for three or four years. Maybe more." When nothing came back to him, he added, "But I'm glad you got what you wanted."

"You can do better than that," McCaig said, his arm and upper body out the window. "Why 'ont you ride on over to the auxil'ry field on the bus with me? We might do some good over there."

"No thanks," Cahill said, leaning toward Phillipson. "I'll see you before you go."

"I might have a surprise for you," McCaig said. "I just might."

"Bat-shit," said Cahill.

"No, no bat-shit," McCaig said. "That comes later. This is somethin' else."

"Well, maybe I wouldn't mind," Cahill said hesitantly. "I don't have nothin' else to do."

"Good," McCaig said. "Come on, then. Get yo' lazy ass out of there, and let's get on the bus."

"What about Zack?"

"We got time to take him back to town. McLendon can look after him. Don't he like it around there?"

"No," Cahill said. "I got a better idea. We can leave him with that little old girl."

"You talkin' about Hannah?" McCaig asked with some surprise. "You sure about that?"

"You're fuckin'-A," Cahill said. "And that's my military talk. You understand what I mean?"

"You're fuckin'-A," McCaig said. "Now come on, we got time, but not all that much."

"OK," Cahill said, feeling for the door handle with one hand and reaching to pat Phillipson's arm with the other. "But no more talkin' about bats. This is the airfield we're at, right now, bat-brains, not England."

He bullied Zack gently into the other car, brushing the coop wood and chicken wire, and settled once more beside McCaig, who then threshed the gears, turning the car around.

"I got to tell you just one more thing," McCaig said, his face ruddy with the future.

"No," said Cahill socking sideways for the driver's arm, and finding it. "I said no. You're gettin' to be a fanatic."

"Come on now, Frank," McCaig said, looking at him. "This is important. Don't you care nothin' about what's gonna happen to me?"

"Not all that much," Cahill said. "But some, maybe. Go ahead."

What would this be like? he wondered. What would be shown? The whole business is death: to kill somebody, to shoot down another airplane; but would there be something else before? What would it be like to pick another man's life out of the total darkness, and then shoot

"Now listen," McCaig said, "they're makin' a plywood airplane to put the bat brains in. And me in there with 'em. And we go up and hunt, see? We hunt 'em at night, when nobody can see but us. We're gonna have a new way of seein' 'em. One that nobody ever had, before. I want a part of that."

Again he glanced at the blind man, as he had got used to doing; he had seen others doing it as well; he was sure that this had become, this checking the blind man's reactions, part of the last

461

him? What would you know be-
fore that? When you first saw
him? Before you shot? When
you picked him up, when you
separated him from the white
dark? When you found him?

few days of nearly everyone's life at the base. In every conversation in which Cahill figured, McCaig now found himself watching the others, as he now watched himself.

"A plywood airplane," he repeated. "You ever hear of anything like that? They say it'll run off and leave you sittin' up there somewhere on your chute; run out from under you. You got to put the throttle up slow, they say."

Cahill did not answer; his mind was not with flight, or on it.

"Now look here," McCaig said. "You're sure you know what you're doin'? You're sure you want your dog over at Hannah's?"

"I'm sure," Cahill said. "Why not?"

"Well, I just asked," McCaig said. "Do you know where she lives? Can you get me to it?"

"I think so," Cahill said. "If you start out from McLendon's. I can count the streets, the blocks, and maybe even the houses."

"OK," said McCaig, rounding onto the highway. "You tell me, when we get in range."

"Roger," Cahill said. "Roger Wilco."

"And she can feed him, huh?"

"Yeah. She can make do. Blood and rice. And mayonnaise. That's what it takes."

In the solidity of this kind of movement, different not only from the jerkiness and upward bombardment of the base jeep, but also from the left-leaning and equally rough treatment that McCaig's chicken-feathered car gave him, Cahill got low and solid in his coat; the nearest thing to this, since he had been blind, was probably the other bus, the bus that had brought him to Peckover, but whatever comparison there might have been was not important. He got low, lower in his coat, and waited it out. Inadvertently he dropped his hand past his side, and down past the side of the seat, and it was then that he realized that most of his sense of motion, or at least motion in something in which he was carried, had become dependent on his picking up the vibrations of the

462

road, of the land, of the world, through Zack's body, through the thick-haired spine and the heavy sides, the breath of the animal incidental to the feel of the road. Not knowing what to do without this, he folded his hands over his chest, and made a blank of the landscape.

There were voices around him, in front of him and behind him; they were still the voices of boys. He thought to jog McCaig with his elbow, but he did not want to hear McCaig talk about bats any more, or about seeing at night, or about the advantages of new equipment, of new speed, of airplanes made out of wood. All this part of things was over; he doubted if he would remember much of it. The whole trip to Peck-over was probably a mistake. What had come of it? Still, he thought, he had done it. He had taken it on, and back in the other dark of Atlanta, back with Ruíz, the swimming pool and what went with it, he would know; he had taken it on, and would get back.

"Is it all right if we sing?" a boy's voice said, and in it there was leaning, a leaning-toward, surely. "Is it all right if we sing, sir?"

"Sure," Cahill said, nodding as much as he ever did. "Go ahead. Sing. Sing on."

But there was no singing, though he listened for the voices to get together out of their talk, to change, to become some sort of intended music. Nothing happened, and he turned his face toward McCaig. Then it came.

> "Many's the night I've spent with Minnie the Mermaid
> Down at the bottom of the sea . . ."

What about this? he thought. Mermaids? But he listened onward; there was nothing else to do. These were the voices that were, no matter what.

> "I lost my morals, down among the corals,
> Gee but she was awful good to me—"

Low voices, now: "Boom, boom, BOOM"

Low voices, and then a general return, with even excitement, prom-ise, what else there was no easy way to tell.

> "Many's the night, with the pale moon shining
> Down on her bungalow . . ."

All right, that's enough, Cahill thought. My God, who are they trying to fool? All they're thinking about is fucking, but why go get it up like that? Did Joel sing like this? Why should he? Did he sing with the other boys? Did he sing this particular thing about mermaids and fucking?

He lurched. He was prepared to lurch—he was always prepared—but not this much. His hand caught up on the floor, and not the fingers but the flat. "Jesus," he said. "What the fuck?"

The highway was off them, out from under them. There was the back-and-forth and side-to-side-to-side shift of a dirt road—dirt, sand, snow. But not pavement: Zack would have started to come up; would have had to be calmed.

> ". . . ashes to ashes, dust to dust,
> Two twin beds and only one of them mussed . . ."

They stopped; the brake was hearable; the engine quit, but the voices did not. There was an ending, and it was necessary to reach it.

> "She was just a sweet kid, she never knew what she did—
> She's just a *personal* friend of mine . . ."

Cahill leg-muscled himself up and stood swaying angrily.

> ". . . you can *believe* it . . ." said the unison.
> "She's just a personal *friend* of mine."

Where was the next bath? The next bed? The next bus? He stood in line, shaking McCaig off, and went forward with the other feet, on one after the other of his own.

The boards of his chair slanted backward, much like those of the chair beside the swimming pool, the one that had been moved; the arms were the same, the nails good. The field, the sound of engines, was in front of him; the wind that came from their direction made them vary only a little; the change in their intensity was, he was more or less sure, from their turning one way or the other, holding toward him or swinging away, still on the ground. He sat, both hands lev-

The field was of grass, and the blades moved slightly in the air that baffled the windsock into showing northeast currents. It was a curious sight, this auxiliary field which looked as though intended for sheep, cattle, or rabbits, and

464

eled on the chair arms, and listened out into the field. As far as he knew there were no other chairs on the porch, and the only other sound was the young murmur of voices behind him, talking about flight, the terms of which—at least a few—he understood better now than before. A light might have been cut on in the building, for there was a small warming of his neck above his coat collar.

was now filled clumsily with two-winged aircraft, some still but most moving loudly and carefully, snaking past each other, crawling through S-curves as though feeling with antennae, none coming close to another.

The old building, especially the long porch, creaked with the day-change. A light was cut on in it.

There was a touch on his shoulder, and then, almost simultaneously, one on the other side.

"Who is it?" Cahill asked, swiveling undecidedly. "Which one first?"

"Frank Spain here," Spain said, straightening. "Just checking in before I leave this place. I probably won't see you again, until maybe tomorrow night."

"Well, take it easy," Cahill said. "My dog's waitin' to take the last bite out of you. He's waitin' for your other leg."

"He'll have to catch me first," Spain said, leaving. "If he can get up to around four thousand feet, he can have me right now."

Cahill turned the other way. "Who's this one over here?" he asked. "That you, McCaig?"

"It's me," McCaig said. "And it's always gonna be me." He paused. "I've been tellin' you about-this here surprise I'm gonna hit you with in about forty-five minutes."

"What is it?"

"I've got an idea that'll rack up all the ideas since Napoleon shot the nose off the Sphinx."

"All right. What am I supposed to do?"

"I don't want you to take the bus back to the base."

"Why not? What in hell am I supposed to do to get back to the hotel? Fly?"

"You got it."

"I've got *what?*"

"I'm 'on take you back to the main field, when this-here cow pasture gets down to the last plane. That's when we'll go. That'll be our'n."

465

Cahill thought, the Link Trainer crowding around him, and the memory of controls. McCaig went on; Cahill propped into another position.

"I'm 'on take you back to the base. And some other places. Some by land, and some by sea, you know. That's what they say. And some by air. We'll just wait till everybody else leaves."

"What about the others I came over with?"

"Don't worry about some of these jokers askin' questions about why you ain't on the bus. I'll take care of all that. The boys will; Spain'll take care of it. He's already done done it."

Cahill raised his face. "Did you tell me that my boy was killed somewhere around here?"

"I don't know if I told you, but he was. He went down about twenty miles to the east. I know right where it is."

"Is it part of your idea to go flyin' over in there?"

"It might be. It is if you want it to be." He broke off, then picked up again, bearing down. "You listen to me, Frank Cahill. You come up here wantin' to know the people who knew your boy. You want to know the things he did here. All right. I'm 'on show you what he did, what he could do: what it feels like, what it sounds like. You and me're gonna fly on over to that place; fly over it. Somethin' might happen. I told you; I believe in them kind of things."

"I ain't never been called a nut, McCaig," Cahill said. "I'd just as soon get back on the bus."

"No, man," McCaig said. "You can't do that. You got to go on up there with me."

"The hell I do," Cahill said, arming himself to his feet. "The *hell* I do."

"The bus is gone," McCaig said quietly. "Do you hear anybody? Do you hear any engines?"

Cahill listened outward, and far. "Yeah. I do. One. It's in the air."

"That's Frank Spain," McCaig said. "He's the last, and he's long gone."

"God damn," Cahill said, standing with nothing to do. "You've got me in a fuckin' box."

"I'm tryin' to get you in a fuckin' airplane. You want to find out what the score is, up here. This is part of the score. The air is where it is."

"I've never been off the damned ground in my life," Cahill said, the Link Trainer melting from around him, his hands and feet with no more authority, no more place.

"That don't make no never-mind," McCaig said. "We gon' do it."

"What business have I got in a god-damned airplane, you fuckin' idiot?"

"What business has anybody got? If God had'a wanted men to fly he would'a given 'em wings! Ain't that what they tell you?"

"I've heard it," Cahill said. "I don't know that I don't believe it, neither."

"Except for one thing. We found out how to do it. So now let's go do some of it. You told me ain't nobody ever taken you for a nut. I ain't never heard nobody say you'd back off from anything, neither. Come on. Let's go down, and on, out and up."

"Well, all right," Cahill said hesitantly. "I ain't got no damned choice."

"Thisaway," McCaig said, turning him, an arm around Cahill's shoulders. "Right on over here."

"OK," Cahill replied, sighing savagely. "Just show me what to do. Just tell me."

"You fuckin'-A I'll tell you. I sure will. You and me're gonna get 'em in the blue. Or the gray. Gray now, black later. Clear stars and froze bones."

They moved toward the porch steps and down them, and the midwinter dark advanced from the building, solidified in the face-wind and crept against it forward into the grasses surrounding the frail single aircraft. Even at this distance they could hear the wind split apart and hiss with a low intent tone on the guy wires of the biplane; there were musical notes in the sound—there seemed to be some kind of four- or five-tone scale involved, including a temporary lulled silence—but the main listening was to a low merciless and endless imploring, an uncaring beseechment, a wheedling of knives.

"We're about on the ground now," McCaig said. "Watch your step; everything's fixin' to level out."

"Twenty-three steps," Cahill said, his foot on grass. "If you'd'a told me, you wouldn'a had to touch me. Or, you didn't have to tell me, even. I could'a made it."

"Good God A-mighty. You're as crazy as your boy was."

"That better be a compliment."

"It sure is," McCaig said. "There wadn't but one of him."

They moved together, reaching the aircraft slowly. "Turn loose," Cahill said. "I don't need none of that."

"OK," McCaig said, separating. "The plane's around thirty yards off."

"Shit," Cahill said, isolated and feeling with his feet. "I don't want to hurt your feelin's. I wouldn't do that. But if I was to depend on people leadin' me around, pretty soon I'd get where I couldn't do without 'em. I might even start feeling sorry for myself, and then everything would go. And that just ain't gonna be. Zack's the only one I'd ever depend on. Dogs, maybe; humans, no."

"We're about there," McCaig said. "All crews at the ready. We're set to scramble."

"Good," Cahill said. "Now I've got you."

"What you got?"

"Got you at a disadvantage."

"How so?" asked McCaig, interested.

For a moment Cahill stood watching the golden streaks traveling across his eyes. He had only to concentrate on them for their beauty to increase; the familiarity he had now come to feel for them made them more precious day by day. There they floated and drove and ran, always from right to left across both eyes. There never seemed to be any sense of discontinuity, of gap-jumping, although he was quite certain that each glowing vector was unique. A middle ground between them did not exist; there were only the soft-fired lines moving through, and on to another place, and others beginning.

"Tell me about my disadvantage."

"Comes with the dark, the big dark. And I'll tell you a story, too. A story my doctor told me when he was encouragin' me to go blind."

"I'm listenin'."

"I've never been there, but my doctor has. Old pink-headed Dr. Ghil, he's been there."

"Where?"

"London. London, England. You heard about them fogs they have over there?"

"Sure have. Bird-walking fogs. And I better know somethin' about 'em, because that's where I'm fixin' to go."

"Well, they tell me, when all that wool comes up out of the river, whatever the name of it is, people get trapped in the streets. And they get trapped in the buildin's. And, like everybody, some of 'em need to be somewhere else. Some of *them* are doctors, I reckon. But the river's got 'em all; it's done put their eyes out. None of 'em can see."

"That's tough shit. What do they do? Go out and get dogs?"

"No," Cahill said, waiting out and timing his point. "They couldn't see, either. But there's an answer. There's one way out."

468

"What is it?"

"Blind people. The blind beggars in the streets. You try to find yourself one; you get out there and hope you're lucky enough to come up on one. And when you find him you'd kill anybody who tried to take him away from you. Fog don't mean nothin' to a blind man. He can beat it. He can beat the river, and he can take you with him. Wherever you want to go, so long as you can walk there."

"All right," McCaig said admiringly. "When I get to London I'll tell the first blind man I see hello. I'll tell him you sent me."

"Don't do it," Cahill said abruptly, beyond his mind, beyond where he intended to be. "You don't need to go over there. You could maybe do more good here. Could be these boys need you. You get 'em started right, ain't that the truth? You said so yourself, a while back. You could maybe keep some of 'em from . . . you know . . ."

"Well I'll be fucked," McCaig said, staring at him. "Since when did you care about any of that?"

"I ain't all that patriotic," Cahill said, back with his thought again, controlling it. "But this ain't no game, Mac. They tell me it's a war."

"It's both," McCaig said. "You should have asked your boy. He'd'a set you straight."

"From what some of these other kids tell me, I may get a chance to ask him, yet." Cahill paused as the wind slanted off them. "It could be he ain't dead," he said. "And maybe some of the boys don't think he is."

There was a long silence, and into it the wheedling of wires came louder, and then fell off and the quiet was now something like breath, breath held an unbearably long time, as though under ground or under water, about to be exhaled deeply into ordinary air. Cahill listened with all his muscles for the word that would come with it. The word, the words were there, hidden and ready. He knew it.

"I don't either," McCaig said. "I don't. I truly don't."

"Well . . ." Cahill said, wanting more words.

"Listen," McCaig said. "Listen, Frank. He was hurt pretty bad. God knows, nobody would know that better than you and me. Prob'ly somethin' broken, his arm and maybe his head. He might'a died somewhere up in the woods, bled to death and burned up. He might'a stumbled on down, and off into the river." The wire-hum came back, and lifted a tone, hanging and sawing. "And he might not'a."

Cahill heeled the grass for the noise, so that the wires and wind would not have it all.

"Here it is," McCaig said, wrenching a change out of himself. "We're

469

right on top of it. Put your hand out; the wing's right in front of you."
As Cahill felt in the air, he went on, "This is almost the same aircraft the
fighter pilots flew in World War I. It's a slow old bird, but they were all
slow then. Maybe the Spads and the Nieuports and Fokkers had a few
more miles an hour, but not many. This is more or less the same plane
the Red Baron flew. People think he flew the Fokker triplane, because
it's crazy-looking, and kids like to build models of it. But mainly
Richthofen flew the regular Fokker biplane. Less drag."

"The only air name I know from that war is Rickenbacker. He got
hurt in a air crash near Atlanta, and there was a lot in the paper about
it."

"Yeah, he flew somethin' like this. Twenty-six kills. So did Mickey
Mannock, who was a Limey, or a Irishman, or somethin'. He was the top
ace on our side I *think*, but I may be wrong about that. Anyway, he had
around seventy-five or -six downs, before he bought it." McCaig smiled
to himself, smiled broadly, as though straight at Cahill, who might have
his own way of picking it up. "Mannock was a one-eyed guy, you know.
He was halfway to the place you're in, and look what *he* did! If he got
seventy-six Fritzes with one eye, think what he might'a done if he didn't
have any! Let's see—a hundred and fifty-two. That'd be your score,
Cahill. No German ace, even, ever got that many."

"Somethin' tells me it's not gonna be," Cahill said, but without
bitterness; he found that he liked this direction of talk. "I guess I'm too
old to learn blind flyin'."

"Not tonight, you ain't," McCaig said decisively. "Cram your hat in
your coat pocket, take your glasses off, and put this on."

Cahill balled up his soft hat with both hands and thrust it into his
coat, along with his dark glasses.

"This-here's what you might call a helmet. Goes on your head."

Out of the wind, molded leather came down and closed off part of his
hearing. He touched his new forehead, and found there twin smooth
chill curves; instinctively he felt for cracks.

"When we get upstairs, pull those down."

"What the hell for?"

"Keep your eyes from waterin'."

"No. Take 'em offa here. I've got my own."

"All right," McCaig said resignedly. "You're the man." He unsnapped the guides for the straps and took the goggles off. Cahill
reached into his other pocket and brought up the pair Colonel Hoccleve had given him on the first day.

"Ever see these?" he asked.

"No," McCaig said. "But I know whose they are."

"What're these things?" Cahill asked, adjusting the splintered goggles on his forehead and fingering two bent metals over his ears.

"Them's devil-horns," McCaig said. "That's the way the devil speaks to pilots from his control tower down under the ground, always on fire."

"Does he sing, down under there?" Cahill asked. "Does he sing like a Mexican?"

"He might. He tells the pilots where the fire is, up on the top of the ground. Or where it is in the air, or on the water. He tells 'em where to find it, where to drop it, and where to make it."

"That your way of talkin'?"

"No, it ain't."

"It don't seem to mean anything. You're just chippin' your teeth."

"You get to understand it," McCaig said, "and things open up. They get a lot more interestin'."

"How dark is it now?" Cahill asked, his hand on the fabric of the wing. "You sure you can still get us back?"

"I'm as sure as a cow shits a circle. It's the last part of the low light." He broke off, and peered into Cahill's listening, close but also far off; very far, maybe. "What you listening to? How about the moon? You listenin' to the moon? It's just comin' up. Is that it?"

"No," Cahill said, smiling, but not at McCaig. "It don't have no wires, and no wind. I hear the same thing as you."

"Now listen here," McCaig said. "Draw in your damn ears. You feel them horny things on your head? Them's where your gosport tubes go. The main tube splits, so you got two ears. Here; feel."

Cahill pinched the rubber tubing. "What're you figurin' to do? Give me a enema in the ears?"

"How'd you guess it? I do get to runnin' off too much, I guess."

"I don't mind. Blind men make a lot of bad jokes. That's about one of the only things they've got."

"Up yonder now," McCaig said, as though to a cadet, "I can talk to you, but you can't talk back. If you want to say anything, just beat on the plane and holler as loud as you can. I'll throttle back."

"Would it make a lot of difference if I asked you to wait a minute?"

"Shorely not," McCaig said. "What's on your mind?"

"I've got a notion I want to make my own shape out of this thing."

"Go right ahead. Have yourself a good feel."

He left the wing, and stepped toward what he was sure must be the propeller, the blades of air. There was no way he could not be close to them, moving on his cautious legs, centering the cry of wires, equalizing them on both sides, so that he would be exactly between them. When the shrill-soughing whistle surrounded him most, he stopped and reached forward. Nothing; only more wing. He had been wrong, but he took a new interest in the wing-skin, soft, slightly grainy and tense. Underneath were ribs, slanting downward a little as the open palm slid to the right, and upward now as it broadened, moving along incurved ribs to the left. The palm was best for feeling, he knew; the middle part was protected, sunk away from the worst calluses.

McCaig looked around. Now the forest across the field was not even the wall, the far black force it had been only a few minutes before. Second by second each blade of grass wove its shadow into the dark of all the others; all swayed and came forward. He glanced up as a small cloud stopped over the moon, and low over the blank far earth the supine outline of a stupendous sketch of stars began to lift its blue-white nailheads. That thing could be whatever you made it, McCaig thought. It could represent anything you wanted it to; it could mean anything.

McCaig kept on watching, now, as Cahill, using both hands, took hold of as much of the body of the aircraft as he could, high and low, and worked back along it toward the tail, and then, perhaps because the fuselage was narrowing, began to return in the other direction in a queer half-stooped position from which he rose as his arms widened. The rear cockpit appeared to interest him, for he reached up and then down into it as far as he could from his position. Finally he inched forward again until his leg touched the lower wing. McCaig shifted to his other foot with what was for him uneasiness, for he now realized fully that he was going to have to fly back to the main field at night in an aircraft with no lights and no radio, and to a field with no runway lights, but only a dim glow from the hangars, which, judging as well as he could, probably did not come out even through the parking area, much less reach the strip. But he was also aware of an excitement he had not known before. He had never been in the least afraid of anything in the air, but he was also sure that no pilot had ever flown under these particular conditions. His mind filled with images of what might happen, and then with words, as Cahill's shadow touched the wing. McCaig could not tell exactly why, but the shape of Cahill's body suggested that of a man fingering something rather than rubbing it or running his hand over it. The notion of music came in, and for a moment McCaig could not keep it off, or want to, particularly when it occurred to him that the tones of wind in the stretched wires were responding, were being made, by the hands on the aircraft, and that these would increase in strangeness and importance as long as Cahill stayed.

But he did not, and now he had left the wing: without asking he had put his foot on it, lifted himself, and was leaning into the front cockpit.

One hand was in a cold pit surrounded by a curving of rubber or leather. The hole in an aircraft could be bottomless, he thought; there was a seat, but to the left of it everything fell away. A man—a man or boy—was supposed to sit here and fly, and control what carried him, from the emptiness where he was groping.

The sounds varied and were the same, as McCaig stood with nothing to lean on. The dark shapeless figure hung to the side of the aircraft, carrying on some business inside the cockpit that was impossible to guess, all done to the riled whine of wire: the tones, especially the low ones, were like those made by a comb with a piece of paper over it, and like a human-made humming into tissued teeth rather than of blowing.

The dark mass of the other man dropped from the wing, turned one way and another, seemed to sway, and then, steadying itself on the wing, began to feel of it.

He straightened, felt with his foot—a long way—and reached the ground. His hand on the wing, as it had been on the glass storefronts of the town, as it had on the posts of the burnt-out farmer's bed, as it slid along tabletops and furniture everywhere, he worked toward the end of the wing, his overcoat with its syringe, sugar cubes and

473

other objects slathered around his legs. Surprisingly he was able, before he turned the round corner, to wobble part of the wing, but as he went on could not repeat this. At the front of the wing again, he fingered a slope of strung thread cold beyond the cold of death, the cold of space, and, with this in his hand, the sound changed once more, gone throaty with what it said.

Here it is, Cahill thought; the wing's given out to the inside, and I'm right back at the body of the thing, at the front of it. The engine should be right over me, and the propeller ought to be where I can feel it.

He was right. When he wanted, when he reached, the blade, incurved and still, was with him, and could not leave.

The widest spread of the fingers could touch the edges. This was called a blade, but it was not at all sharp. The hollow space between the edges was gritty, and was likely oil or grease from the engine mixed with dirt. Or maybe it had been caught out of the air; maybe it was the air's own dirt. He traced in the substance with his forefinger, going for the naked metal, but soon

McCaig watched sharply and silently as the blind man paused briefly at the aileron, not quite secure in its wooden clip, tested it, turned the corner and tried the same thing on the leading edge, paused, groped again, and came to hold the slant of the guy wire.

Now Cahill had let go, and come by slow cramped stages to the propeller, and the indignant throned engine. McCaig felt that perhaps he should say something or go to Cahill as he entered under the blades, for to have a human body so entirely in the zone of their power and danger was frightening to him, and to realize that this was a blind man doing this, helpless beyond all others, drew him without his will toward the plane, but quietly.

He stopped again, really not much nearer, remembering the belief among pilots that an engine would kick over, now and then, without there being any reason for it. Just one jump of a cylinder would kill Cahill exactly where he stood, moving his whole arm back and forth along the canted lower blade. He leaned and passed his hand over the coolant vanes of one of the cylinders, and it seemed to McCaig that he held

gave up, reached farther, inward, and ran the other hand over more metal, grimed slots, stubbornly thick-set and suggesting a willful and odd kind of honeycomb. That was all there was for him, there. He did not like the place where he stood, with its cocked and air-filthy blades, dull blades, its thickets of slots, nearly so much as he had the wing. Maybe the tail would be better, when he got there; he would go all the way down the far side.

the aircraft as he might have the head of an animal. But the metal whine of the Stearman, its wheedling of knives, was not that of a beast; it was musical still, or something that dodged in and out, that swayed back and forth near real music, and up and down, and was now not held by anyone, or changed, except by itself.

McCaig must have been thinking of something else, some other place, for when he turned Cahill was lounging, or looked to be, at the base of the rudder. He walked over to the half-horned form.

"What do you think?" McCaig asked.

"What do you mean, what do I think? It feels right clumsy to me. But then what the hell do I know about it? Will this thing really fly?"

"Sure, but so will a rock, if you throw it hard enough. That's where the engine comes in: to throw it hard enough. How'd you like the engine? Does it suit you?"

"Felt like a knifed-up anvil."

"Continental's prize present to heaven, to the wild blue. Two hundred and twenty little ponies with wings. Not a bad engine, though. Specially for kids."

"That right?"

"It's a good stunt ship. Slow and steady. Stable. It's a real forgivin' airplane. You can't find a better crop duster. Great for them that's after weevils; great for wing-walkers. One time I saw a guy on a Stearman do it blindfolded. You want to try it? I'll hold it straight and level."

"Maybe the next time. I don't feel like I'm ready for it yet."

"Why not?"

"Well, you know how it is; 'specially at night, and all."

After a short silence with no feeling of compression in it, Cahill said, "Don't you think we ought to be gettin' on with whatever we're gon' do?"

"No hurry," McCaig said. "Let the moon come in on us. I've got a little old piece of a flashlight for the panel, a little old piece of a airplane . . ."

". . . and a little old piece of a blind man," Cahill said. "This ought to win the war."

"It just might. It ain't been tried."

"Well, what's your plan?"

"My plan is this," said McCaig, as though at a mock briefing. "I'm goin' to do some cutups in this thing. We'll do some of that. Then I'll ease us on home." He paused, and bent his neck to look more closely at the splintered moon in Cahill's goggles, above the lit blank eyes. "You're the man with all the extra senses, Cahill. I want you to *feel* this airplane: feel it with your hands and feet, first. But that ain't all there is to it. I want you to feel it with your face and ears, too, and everything you've got, and the things that I ain't got."

"All right," Cahill said. "This is goin' to be my one time, I reckon. I might as well do all I can."

"Just follow through on the controls. Make out like you're helpin' me do what I'm doin'. You might not be able to hear me all the time through the gosport, but just follow me through on the rudder—with your feet—and the stick with your right hand. You needn't pay no attention to the throttle, if you don't want to, but if you do want to have a-holt of the whole thing, like we do, the throttle'll be just up to your left, right in front of your shoulder, more or less."

"Good enough. I'll prob'ly try to do it that way, then."

"Anything you feel me do, go right along with it. Don't try to make the ship do *more* than I'm doin', but just exactly the same. While we're goin' through this stuff, try to get some idea of what's happenin' to us. Get your own notions from where you are, in it; from where you are in the whole thing, the whole air. I'd want to know all that, if I was in your situation."

"I'm with you," Cahill said, pulling his goggles to see how they moved. "I'll try to remember."

"You'll prob'ly be able to tell when we level off, when I get the altitude I want. I'll pull the throttle back, and the engine'll slow down. Things'll get quiet for a little; it'll be kind of like we're floatin'. After that I'll start out with some simple stuff, and then work up to the kind of thing that Joel and I used to sneak off and try to do, way on out past the practice area. I'll try us a fallin' leaf." He paused; there might have been a response. "Yeah, I just may make a leaf out of us, rockin' on down."

"Is there any one move you're afraid to make?" Cahill asked suddenly.

"There's one the *plane* might be afraid to make. An outside loop, is what I mean."

"Try it. Go ahead. I'm layin' it to you."

"All right. I guess so. Yeah, I'll try. If your eyeballs are game."

"All my balls are game," Cahill said.

"Just your eyeballs, I'm talkin' about," McCaig said, smiling as broadly as he liked.

"They're game enough," Cahill said. "Have been so far."

He could not imagine the plane any longer without consulting the memory of what his fingers and palms had told him of it. The thin rigid ribs and frail skin of the wings, the stolid chopped form of the cylinders, were part of the vision where the aircraft was propped like a dragonfly in the traversing yellow sparks of his eyelids. From his touch on them, his mind made the wings transparent, letting through them the moonlight that was supposed to be there, to fall on the grass he felt blowing against his shoes, and perhaps some of the stars let through as well. He still did not like the slashed rigidity of the engine, and the fact that it was half metal and half air; neither the silver shimmer of wings nor the hacked stone of the cylinder-heads was entirely real, but they were what he had, or half had.

The only difference being made now was that made by the moon, and by what was said or withheld, or guessed. McCaig watched with great involvement as Cahill tested one of the guy wires, running it up and down inside his fist, an arm-moving shouldered intensification of the dark, in an attitude of placeless investigation. What he had said about Cahill's "extra senses" began to bother and excite McCaig. He did not want to bring the engine into sound, to make the silence cough and shuttle-roar, or get into the ordinary routines and procedures of flying, the mechanics of it he went through every day. Flight was one thing, and real enough, but this approach to it was another, and might have things in it you couldn't see.

**All that he understood himself to
possess were the wires, wherever
he could find them. It was hard
to turn loose, once he had hold.**

"Plenty of tension in them wires," McCaig said.

"Yeah," Cahill said. "You bet."

"There's not anything to worry about. This baby is stressed for negative strain; that's one of the things that make it a good stunt ship. It'd be the best of 'em, if it had a little more poop. A little more than two hundred and twenty horses. If this thing had a few more ponies you could fly it to hell and gone, in any attitude you wanted."

"Upside down, you mean?" Cahill asked. "You can do that?"

"Sure. You can do that on the horses we already done got. At least for a little while you can, before gravity gets a-holt of the gas. You can do all kinds of stuff with it. I even used to do skywritin' in one just like this. I could write anything you like. I could put 'Fuck the world' up there, if I took a notion, and everybody'd see it. That was a hell of a lot of fun. Best kind of advertising there is, except that it don't stay around very long. Some real funny things happened, too. When you didn't like a guy, or you wanted to play a kind of joke on one of your buddies, you could take off and go put his telephone number up in the big blue. One pilot got married because of the number I put up there on that great big billboard. Some gal called him, and they got together. Seven kids now, he's got. Just come to him out of the blue, you might say."

"Let's go."

"No hurry, now, damn it. It's not goin' to get much colder. And the moon's real big; it'll be just as bright as we want."

"I'll take your word for it."

"Canada," McCaig said unexpectedly and emphatically.

"Canada? What about Canada?"

"I'm goin', I tell you," McCaig said. "This is my last U.S. flight."

"Well, OK," Cahill said. "I believe you when you say."

"I don't have no doubt that as soon as I get through that RCAF trainin' I'll get sent on over there."

"You might wash out," Cahill said, and he, too, smiled.

"Shit," McCaig said. "The plane could blow up and I wouldn't wash out. I guarantee I've got more time than any of instructors. There's a lot I can do, can't none of them do. I'll guarantee you that, into the bargain."

"OK," Cahill said. "Go get 'em."

"I want to be right in the middle of whatever they got over there. England needs me; I'm a son-of-a-bitch if they don't. I want to be right in the middle of it. The middle. And at night."

"Why at night?"

"Two or three reasons, I guess," McCaig said, settling into his new track, remembering and inventing. "I've always liked to hunt. I was raised on a farm, and whenever I wadn't out crawling around in the soybeans and sloppin' the hogs, I'd be huntin'. There's just somethin' about it. I've killed a good many deer in my time, and with a twenty-two single-shot rifle, too, which ain't easy. I'd wait for 'em at the edge of a cornfield, or walk up real slow along a power line, where there's good forage, and they can ease out from the woods and get back in just one or two jumps. The best time for me was just about like it is now. Most hunters like the first light or the late light, where they can still see some. But for me it was the early part of the moon, and an open place on a deer track where I could set up in the bushes and get 'em crossin' the moon. Just that silhouette, you know, as they 'us headin' back up to the high ground, out of the fields. There's that split-second feeling, when you think there might be somethin' there, and then, by damn, it *is* there, comin' on by you like it was its own shadow goin' across that big white thing in the sky, and on a good night—a lucky night—you could even see the rack of the buck, if there was one. The biggest buck I ever shot did that; he did just exactly like I'm tellin' you: when he got right to the main part of the light, the dead middle of the moon, he stopped and just stood there, and I hung the sight on him, held it for a second, and pulled the trigger."

"Then what?"

"Then," McCaig said, with some surprise, "that's all there was to it. He was mine. But I'm talkin' about the feelin' at that one second, when the deer froze solid in my brain, right before I turned loose on him. And the moon like this 'un, like on a night . . . well, a night that had more in it, that had more to it than a real night. You know what I mean?"

Cahill found himself trying to know.

"That's what I want," McCaig went on. "That's what I want in England, or out over France, or wherever they send me. I want to stalk, up there at twenty-five thousand. I want to still-hunt. I want to catch that other airplane over against the moon, horns or no horns."

Deer, Cahill thought, why not? I can have one; I can have any one I want. In place of the aircraft he touched, he positioned a deer and a great calendar moon behind it, so that the tines of the buck's horns were fixed as sharply in cold, blowing light as if they had been set in tile. The sight needed something that only he could supply, and he stiffened with the strain of trying to pull the red flight-sparks of blindness around the image, and make it his. But the lines entangled themselves with another color, a new red-and-silver fury, and the deer dissolved without fleeing. Before it went from him he thought he made out a slight movement in the antlers, as of wind in cold-burning grass, as the animal lost its way from him, stormed out of sight by the amazing shuttle of fresh silver.

No change in the peaceful, sloping anticipation of the aircraft, and no change in the changing sound of wind through the flight-honed earthless grounded wires.

The blind man seemed to McCaig to be battling with himself, rocking back and forth, and McCaig waited for him to speak, to say what was on his mind. He wondered if he had said something wrong. Could he have put something in Cahill's mind that would have this much of an effect on him? Or had another thing come in? You can't know anybody else, McCaig thought. What's in their head changes too fast. Nobody knows what will come through there. Yourself, you don't know what will come to you, either, or when.

"If things go like I want," said McCaig, "I'm gonna hunt with bats. I'm gonna learn how the Canadian bats fly, and then do my fightin' with the Limey bats against the Kraut bats. God knows what's gonna happen then."

"You're bats yourself," Cahill said, stamping a foot. "I don't know what the hell you're talkin' about; I never did. But if we don't get goin' pretty soon, I'm gonna start walkin' back, myself."

"Oh no you're not," McCaig said. "You gotta have me. You gotta have me and this airplane. Just how you think you'd walk back?"

"You don't think I'd try it?"

"You just might. You might learn how to call yourself a fool, but I don't believe that would stop you for one fuckin' second." He moved, not toward the aircraft but toward Cahill. "What would you do? Tell me. No shit. What would you do, if you started out?"

"Just go one way or the other till I found a fence or a tree. Then I'd move from one tree to the next one until I heard cars. Anybody'd pick up a blind man. They sure would. Take him anywhere he wanted to go."

"Maybe."

"Come on, you asshole. Let's get in your contraption. You don't have nothin' to worry about. I ain't gonna walk."

"Just hold on here. Just a minute, and we'll go on. I got one more thing I need to talk to you about."

"This is just one shit-hole of a place to talk, don't you think?" Cahill said. "Let's do this some other time."

"How long did you tell me you been blind?" McCaig asked suddenly.

"Around three and a half months."

"Has your hearin' changed any?"

"I can't really tell, but it must have. I believe I could say that it's got better."

"Can you make out how far away you are from somethin', or it is from you?"

"Yeah," Cahill said. "Some. Sometimes. Not always. But I'm gettin' better. I have to." He moved his head, to be placing his right ear in a different relation to McCaig. "If it was you, now, I could tell where you was because your voice would be loud if you was near to me, or not as loud if you wadn't. I believe I could hear you farther off, now, than I could'a done when I could see."

"Suppose it wadn't me? Or anything else makin' a noise? Suppose it was a wall, like. Wouldn't you have to make some kind of noise, yourself, before you could tell there was a wall there? Or tell how far off it was?"

"Yeah," Cahill said, interested in McCaig's interest. "I got my own little set of noises, that I make when I think I might need 'em."

"I reckon you can hear more than you think you do, already."

"I keep listenin'."

"Do that. When you get where you can do it pretty well, I'll put you in the bat patrol. In a room made out of air and copper. In a cloud of wire."

"There you go again, McCaig. There ain't no stoppin' you. Get on to Canada."

"You got your hand on the guy wire now, Cahill," McCaig said, closing his hand over Cahill's. "Imagine you was in a room, and fill it full of wires like that one. Or real thin ones, if you want to, like piano wire. It don't make no difference which way you string 'em. You can have 'em strung up in patterns—any kind of design you want to make— you can curl 'em all around each other, you can have as many as you want. Any loops, any knots. Any air, any copper."

Cahill strove to establish a cunning order of wires, one that would confuse and trap anything, but the sparks across his lids were better for that than anything he could think of, and he owned them already.

McCaig held Cahill's hand and the taut string, and then left them. "Now," McCaig said, "we turn loose the bats, and close the door."

"What happens?"

"They fly."

"Is that all?"

"They fly, just like they would'a been doin' if there wadn't no wires, and wadn't no closed-up room. They fly just like they would'a done, with all the room in the world."

"So . . . they fly. But . . . like I say, what then?"

"They may be lookin' for gnats in there, so somebody might throw in a bucketful of gnats for 'em, so they'll have somethin' to go after, have somethin' to do. But mostly they fly, and don't hit nothin'. That's the whole idea. They don't hit nothin'. Not a thing. Not each other, not a wire. The wires don't even move, they don't even quiver, when them bats go by 'em. They know right where they are every second, every split second, and they know where everything is that's around 'em, and they just keep on goin'; they don't even think about it. They've got the dark beat."

"They do?" Cahill said. "That'll be the day."

"They do, though," McCaig said assuredly. "And that's why England's goin' to win, over there. In the air. In the dark. With the bats and the wires tellin' 'em all about it. Gnats and bats. They're the ones; they're the ones we're askin'."

"They got some kind of signal they send out, or somethin'?" Cahill said, with little interest. Getting into the air, as cold as it was, was one thing; all this talk was another. He wondered why McCaig kept talking.

"They do have. The Limeys have got some new no-name gadget that works the same way; you can tell where the other man—the other airplane—is, and he don't know where you are. You can tell where he is, and you can knock his ass off."

"The Germans don't have the same thing? Somethin' like it, maybe?"

"If you 'us to ask me, I think they prob'ly do, but we just have to hope we got a better bat than they do."

"Yeah. I reckon you'll know, once you get over there."

"It'll all prove out, one way or the other. And right soon."

"Keep in touch, as long as you can. I'd like to know, myself."

"I sure will, Frank," McCaig said, and knew immediately that he would write those letters, would say whatever came to him to say, and send it to the big clumsy moonlit form in front of him. "Now we'll go."

"I'm with you."

"Don't worry about nothin', now," McCaig said. "We got a field full of real good moonlight, fresh moonlight, and I've been flyin' this area for a long time. Light shines on water . . ."

"It does," Cahill said. "It does do it."

". . . and it'll be blazin' like hell on the reservoir. The field is due west of the dam, and it won't be a whole lot of trouble to line up on the nit-shit runway by the row of lights on the hangars. Accordin' to the rest of it, I don't need nothin' but feel, the altimeter, this flashlight, and the seat of my pants."

"I hope they're not filled up with shit, by the time we get there."

"Not a chance." He changed tones. "We got one parachute. You take it, and get on into the back cockpit. Follow me through real gentle on the controls. That's all."

"What am I supposed to do if I have to *use* the parachute?"

"You won't. But if you do—and don't do *nothin'* unless I tell you— knock the buckle on your seat belt open, throw off your shoulder straps. Get clear of the ship any way you can."

"And then what?" Cahill asked, his feet solid.

"Fall a while. Relax. Just fall a little, then put your right hand over your heart."

"Oh, yeah," Cahill said. "I can just see it. What do I do now that I got my hand on my heart?"

"You pull the handle that'll be there."

"How?"

"You pull it; you try to throw the handle away across your chest and off your right side. Then wait and hope. That's all any of us can do. When the whole air hits us, without the ship. Hope and float; float and hope. When you hit the ground, and you don't break nothin' doin' it, get yourself out of the chute and forget it. That's when you can start lookin' for them trees you was talkin' about. That's when you can start lookin' for that first tree, that one tree. Find that highway, and them

483

good sympathetic patriotic people in cars and trucks. And all the time listen. Listen like a bat."

"You think I could do all that?" Cahill asked. "You really do?"

"I could say I think you could do it, and not mean it, but I say I think you could, and I do mean it. You would give it a damn try. I know that much."

"Well, let's don't do it that way."

"You're not goin' to have to; I give you my word on it. We're just gonna go up and wring this thing out a little bit, in all this moonlight. That'll be all there is to it."

Cahill moved backward, and turned, touching for the aircraft.

"Now listen," McCaig said. "When we get back, I'll park out of sight of them lights, and we'll skirt on around back of the PT field. Then I'll leave you and go get the car. I'll have to cross the assembly area in front of the Administration Building, and I'd better do that by myself; I can explain me bein' there, but I can't explain you. So wait where I put you, till I come by. Just stand pat. There might be a couple of cadets on guard duty, but most likely they'll be Joel's boys. Even if they're not, even if they're MPs, I'll handle 'em; I do a lot of work over here at night; everybody's used to me. Everything'll be fine."

"I'm goin'," Cahill said, both hands on the plane.

"Right now," McCaig said, "we're just gonna have ourselves a hell of a ride."

"All right. Climb up," McCaig's voice said, with another accent. "Put your foot right here"—he placed Cahill's foot uncompromisingly on something higher than the ground—"and reach up and grab a-holt of the edge of the cockpit."

Cahill obeyed, and the aircraft bent toward him with his weight.

"Take it slow, and climb on in."

With many small-movement adjustments and mistakes, Cahill got his feet and legs into the narrow pit, surrounding himself with metal, and thrust them forward until his feet stopped. Without a sound McCaig was beside him, buckling straps and making abrupt gentle fittings at the sides of his head.

"Your feet are gonna control the rudder, and this stick here works the ailerons and the elevators. Sideways with anything means you're gonna be helping yourself curve off to the right or left, and backwards and forwards with your hand means up and down. There's not no use for me to explain any more than that right now; it'd take too long. Hold on to the stick with your right hand, and follow me through. Catch a-holt of the throttle—right here—with your left. We'll crack the throttle a little, and I'll go wind us up."

"Tell me. Keep tellin' me."

"You'll hear this whine, see. This whine, like, and it'll keep gettin' higher and higher. That'll be me and my little crank, persuadin' the engine. When the noise gets about as high as you can stand to hear it, turn this-here thing till the engine catches. We might have to try a couple of times, so don't worry. But it ain't really hard. All you have to do is listen for that high whine; the highest; it'd run Zack crazy, I guarantee you. Here, I'll shove this flap of your helmet out of the way so you can hear better. Pull your goggles down, because there's gonna be a mighty wind a-comin'."

He drew the goggles down, and passed his glove over them.

"As soon as you turn that switch, them Continental ponies are gonna quit whinin' and start chargin'. All two hundred and twenty of 'em. You ready, now?"

"I'm ready."

Bound down in his strange hole, Cahill sat leaning his head one way and the other. In his open ear a low grinding moan began. Slowly, as with great effort, an effort with a whole body in it, a rounding, a hanging and hanging-on, the sound mounted; though desperate and imploring, there was nothing human in it. When it had reached a level from which he was certain it could not rise, it could never rise, when a sense of balance came into it, a whistling and tottering, he turned the switch. The aircraft shook once, twice, as if the ground of the hole he was in were fighting for a last-ditch breath, for a brutal first heartbeat. His open trap shocked and shuddered as the propeller whacked at the air, the engine popped loudly and defeatedly twice, and all sound died for the field wind to take up its place in the wires once more.

"No," McCaig said, appearing almost immediately in his ear. "We need a little more squealin'. You ain't workin' me hard enough yet. This time, you just keep lettin' that noise go on up. Let it go up past where you think you can't stand it no more. Let it go to where you can't hardly hear it: so high there wouldn't be nothin' but that big dog of your'n could hear it. That's when we'll be able to get this piece of bat-shit in the air."

"All right. Roger." The sound began again, spiraling, straining up. Surely the inertia starter—or whatever it was—must take a great deal of energy and strength on the part of the man who cranked it. Cahill was more and more aware of the quality of hanging in the ground-out hoarseness, and it occurred to him that this might have been caused by the crank—the engine—pulling McCaig to his toes, or even off his feet. From this sullen, gritting catarrh of a bad pulley, the sound moved upward, and the hang periods came closer together. As the inertia built and thinned in sound, a sense of inevitability, of a force that, once begun, could not be stopped, began to be part of the aircraft: something like a seized breath of mechanical hysteria, of an ungovernable impetus, and Cahill could now envision McCaig dancing in the air at the top of his crank-arc like a hanged man, his feet jigging and flailing in the shrieking wheeze of the process he had begun. Cahill waited, determined to hold out, one hand on the ignition switch and the other absorbing the vibrations of the whirling starter through the throttle. The pitch rose beyond what it had been before at its highest. Still Cahill did not move. Then, into the engine's scream as though fed into it rather than made by it, came a warbling unearthly and unmusical, like the teeth of a small-bladed saw being planed off. Cahill waited for even this to go up yet one more tone, and turned the switch.

The engine kicked and caught, and this time there was no doubt about its determination. Holding the ignition switch full on, and on, Cahill pushed the throttle forward; the thrashing fury in front of him bracketed into a purposeful, throaty held-back blasting, a steady uproar. With very small movements Cahill willed and changed with one hand his idea of power, smoothing the boom and blossoming of the engine, the shudder of the aircraft, tempering the great wind full-face at him. Under the goggles his eyes were warm; the mindless eagerness of the aircraft and the familiar sparks of his eyes combined. What was there? What he wished? No. What did he wish? Nothing, but what had come? What was there? The first blindness; the first of it. A naked one-legged girl, then coins falling, light-spread, another girl with a hurt toe, a coil of blood in green water, and over everything a great sun being taken apart piece by piece.

His toes leaned back to the limits they could reach with his heels remaining where they were, his left hand inched forward, the engine built confidently, and the plane began to move. In the first few feet of difference there was a ground-shudder of anticipation and daring. He pulled back on the throttle, heard the engine lower its voice a fraction, and then, as his hand moved, this time without his having anything to do with it, rise again. They were picking up speed, weaving and trundling. Cahill's feet moved again in involuntary response, the aircraft stopped and stood, the throttle and the engine advanced until the plane shook with insane balked fury. There was a brief intermittency of sound, but almost at once the full murderous violating enthusiasm of the engine reinstalled itself. He pulled down the one earflap against it, but there was no need, for the sound had fallen off once more. A thin country voice blew itself into life in his ears. "We're ready to roll."

Cahill nodded invisibly. They started forward again, this time in a straight line, the rear of the plane at first seeming to swing left and right. His feet were asked to work, to follow some manner of adjustment, and then to hold themselves and the plane steady, but with the right foot for some reason forward of the left. For the first time the stick moved: away from him. He pitched into his straps and rose almost off the seat. The front part of the plane still trundled, though with lightening thumps that changed to mere touches of the ground. The stick now came back to him, and the last contact of earth failed gently; his body rose, with everything he had ever had; in his right hand he held a whole new form of being borne; there was no doubt that he had done what he had done; that he had lifted himself.

Both he and the air now existed as extensions of a position: a crouch; his crouch. The minute tremors of the flow passing over his packed form were of a marvelous and unending fertility of unexpected invention. Among these were placed, like dangerous, benign and thrilling obstacles, larger encounters, blocs, step-downs and recoveries, at first in his nerves as quick and vivid as the smash of a highway wreck but immediately passed, surpassed: the small flutterings of the ridden flow were as they had been, but now with the taste of righteous victory in them, as he opened his mouth to take them in, for no reason but that he did it, and was continuously restored.

Again his hand helped to pull the engine back into what seemed to be its best, hoped-for smoothness. There was now almost no sense of disturbance—he was already used to the engine—and the airflow past him had nothing to do with motion. His position at the heart of it was a place at which all things battered without injury; he inhaled what was surely level flight. It was possible; there was such a place, such a condition; he trusted where he was, and what he was doing; he strode, strolled, wallowed and sang, forming with hands, feet, mouth and wild-volleying eyes actions not possible before; he could not have thought them.

In the midst of this his legs changed; his stick-hand took a new position in the void. Where he sat, taking not one of his nerves from the nerves of the aircraft, or from McCaig's, he began to slide with the

487

whole posture he was in; the entirety of darkness tilted, and he was leaning, was in a longing slope to the left: not a plunge but rather a kind of off-falling. Then, as if they had reached the bottom of a certain part of the air, his legs reformulated themselves, his primed fist moved inexorably toward the right rear corner of his enclosure. Though his guts tried as they could to keep on in the original direction of the slant, they stayed with him and were lifted in a sucking curve that went up toward another darkness and stayed there. When the levelness of peace returned as though he were in an automobile that had barely made it to the top of a hill, his throttle-hand and the engine subsided, and a voice like a shouted whisper said something like "Candle." He waited; the engine did not resume its urgency; they were sustained, part of a long sigh as expectant as it was unhurried.

"Straight," his ears said, or he thought they did. He crouched for sound below the rim of the cockpit, where the air made only a sifted murmur, and pushed in hard on his head, on the gosport horns.

"Straight loop. Down up and down around. Follow me."

The nose edged over and down once more; the uprushing blackness tore at his face. He parted his lips; the night entered his mouth like a whole thing; one cheek and then the other ballooned outward from his teeth. At the same time his left hand turned loose the throttle and approached his genitals, confidently, as though making for some known source of power. The engine sound rose; he pressed down into the seat and hung upward, more and more, and more and more slowly. All invisibility inverted. He sagged as he should have been doing if pulled upward, but his face was gorged with blood. He and the stick kept drawing against his middle. The aircraft shaped the top of the circle and swung down; blood swarmed from Cahill's face and reached its right proportions. The plane and he throttled back.

"Now you try one," McCaig said distinctly.

"No," Cahill bellowed into the desolation. "Hell no. You son-of-a-bitch."

"Take it," McCaig said. "I'm turnin' loose."

The stick came away to him at the far side of everything he had ever held. The aircraft was loose and furious, and entirely his, and in the blankness of his grasp his arm muscles hardened and re-

McCaig rode the new wallowing in strong peace, hunkered down in the cockpit with a blind man behind him, his feet off the pedals and his arms folded. As the craft jinked and yawed he smiled, a

joiced, and, underneath and forward of him, the tendons of his ankles, ready for anything. The strange element snared and rushed into him with another purpose as he moved the plane left and right with his feet, commanding and questioning at once, the answer coming to him from the childish behavior of the aircraft shifting from side to side as though thrusting its shoulders. His left hand made itself more fast to the numbed throttle. He held the stick as though it were a link to the new beginning that his life of blindness had brought him. At first he had been afraid to let go of things. As soon as full sightlessness had come he had found himself in the worst of the terror, not so much of being lost but of losing whatever it was he had been able to find. This was the panic of dropping a fork to the floor and having it disappear from existence, of being sure that it had fallen out of the world, of groping for it, even so, trying for it this way and that, learning the weave of a carpet or curtain, the joinings of cold wood nailed into a floor, never *quite* hammered in truly or flush —he had taken to feeling floors with his hands, and kept doing it —but not the fork: never the fork on his own terms. Until his distance-hearing—or instinct, sixth sense, or something else—devel-

grave and friendly night-smile at what he imagined Cahill might be thinking. Below on all sides were single lights and a few that were grouped in splintery assortments, haphazard as jackstraws, and to his right the river burned in the cold, shining in meaningless half knots; even after it coiled into the lake it was still not quite invisible, at least not in the moonlight of this night; where the stream-silver entered it the reservoir had a suggestion of movement, of life, of unrest under the brightness. Just over the top cylinders McCaig meandered with his eyes and the serene engine, and on into the great insliding bed of the reservoir, floating his look along the invented current. Despite the number of hours he had spent in the air he had not thought before about how pleasant flying was without attention to its technical details; it was another state entirely, and brought abnormal and confident ideas. Blind flying; it's best for the ones that can see, he thought, as the leading edge of the lower starboard wing cut into the mercury-shade fire of the reservoir.

oped further or was discovered, he had no real *direction* anywhere: this was the thing he sought. But here in the air he needed none, and memories, objects, people, events and imaginings pressed to him, hurtled face-on, as driven through his head by the wind.

What lake? Was it land, now, coming under him, coming to him, as the aircraft slanted his blood to the right? Was there any difference of weight, of thought, as he passed from water to land? No; what could there have been? Maybe more solidity of the main darkness that gained something every way he turned: or it could have been that a thread broke in the imagination as the idea of a lake, watched from high up and carrying blank light, gave way, gave up on flight; he had never seen it.

Again the engine fell off, sighed backward.

"East of here," McCaig said as distinctly and matter-of-factly as he could, breaking the lake from him with an effort. "We got to go east: over east of the lake."

"This is pretty near where it was," McCaig said. "We can't be more than half a mile off. We're right over them black fields." Then, louder, "Here: you want the plane back? I'll give it to you. Do what you want."

The sustainment was purer, now, almost hushed without the engine burning. The aircraft wavered, comically drunk, unmuscled and brainless. Cahill made no move, but sat again trying to image. What did McCaig expect him to do? What was he supposed to make happen at this time and place? At this point in the air? In the dark McCaig could not even imagine? At this altitude, this height of the moon, this crossroads? Over the black fields he had walked on? In this air-knot over a dead brush fire in which there might in some way be a presence, a sign waiting to be released by will and location, kinship and invisibility? Curly hair, Joel had. He was, he had been, tall and thin, maybe even skinny. His eyes had been bluish like his own, or it could have been more like his mother's color of blue. What color was that?

To try what would be, he willed his hand forward, with the stick in it, and brought it back. The ship, with him in it, nodded; straightened. A left-right move came, spontaneous, almost humorous, and his head as well moved; the aircraft rocked.

Cautiously he pushed the throttle; from behind an undeniable and gentle solidity pressed him forward. He drew back on the handle, and the engine

Out of the situation, out of the strong moon, the unequal air, out of the conversion of the aircraft from something he controlled to something that carried him through the moonlight and the fresh stars, from the blinding lake and the blind man, the invisible hands and feet behind him, out of the desperation of trying to remember everything he could about the man's son, to bring back more than arrogance and blue eyes, a notion, an idea of something he might do with what he had, built itself with positive and unquestioning force. McCaig tapped his gloves together, his mind made up. He waited.

This is not a cadet, McCaig said, and repeated, out loud to himself: watch out what you're doing; watch out what you're letting happen. Yet he could not be nervous, though he had to steel his body to keep it away from the controls.

found, soft and clear in its roaring work, a sigh which it had rather have, and could have given more to. The pressure on his back returned as he inched the throttle forward again. I've got this thing now, he thought; I sure have; I can't feel McCaig, or anybody, on it anywhere; no: not on it and not in it. The whole thing is mine; it's all mine.

He charged his feet and hands with energy, and, not asking himself what to do, moved everything forward and down, and leaned decisively, overwhelmingly to the right. And why not?

The air rush over him rounded until it was nearly side on, held like a violence-trembling wall against his right cheek. His organs changed; his heart moved to the left and up. He came slowly center with the stick; the air squared off head-on. His heart had not re-placed itself, his seat in the aircraft was as light as it had become; he was still going down. The hill he had been on years ago was suddenly the whole of his mind; a backpouring and flicker on both sides brought the color green to such life that he felt it had welled up from his whole existence, and was velocity itself, hurtling down under control; barely under control. He crouched as on skates, the pedals under his feet like a road that tried to reel, tried to

That done, though, the reassertion of needing to control and instruct beaten back, he realized that he had never been so relaxed in an aircraft before. It's like being flown by a ghost, he thought. And, less satisfactorily, maybe a ghost would be better than a blind man. But he did not believe it.

Like I tell you, boy, McCaig said to himself as the nose lurched, drew the dim horizon over it and firmed up downward: like I tell you: don't let him have too much. He kicked lightly at the rudder pedals and understood that he could have them back if he wished; the pressure, the presence on them was not decisive. The stick, though more positively held, could also be moved; there was play in it; some. He glanced at the altimeter; they had a little over eight thousand feet. The plane must have been mushing; how, exactly, did we get this high? he wondered. It could have been that long chandelle I did, he thought; that was one hell of a chandelle.

throw him off it to one side, to any side but was held to its smeared streaming power by muscle and balance. There was that driveway, he recognized, open-mouthed; it was there, between those bushes, and this is the way I went down it. This is exactly it.

He was easing the stick back; his spine bent with new weight. The exhilaration of skating, his memory of the long driveway and its rushing shrubs went from him, but there was still, somewhere in his eyeballs or his mind, a suspicion of green, as he pulled back the throttle and quieted the aircraft so that he could shout up to McCaig.

"Candle," he screamed.

"Go ahead. You got it now."

As though shoved by a foot in his back, Cahill leaned like the unstoppable beginning of a fall on his face. He came back to his original position almost immediately. McCaig was opening the throttle, but something else was happening that came from more than speed. His chin lifted; the back of his head met his spine; his mouth jammed open. His

McCaig watched the altimeter needles go around backward. At six thousand feet he reached for the stick, but it moved of itself; the plane was already leveling. McCaig took hold of it.

"Good," McCaig hollered back. Damn good. Good on you. We're here; you got us here.

"Well, all right," McCaig yelled. "Now I'll try somethin' of my own. Check your straps. Hold on to yourself."

eyeballs hurt from behind, as though pushing for their freedom: freedom to burst forth, burst from, beyond, more and more, or just burst, as the aircraft strove with everything it had to pass beneath a vast, chosen unnecessary shape, face-out: to round the under-air of a mountain. As far as he knew he was upside down, straps keeping him but not wanting to. The pain in his eyeballs increased beyond what he thought might ever be possible; certainly beyond what was possible to stand. Another kind of redness was beginning to fill them: a sick and violent color, outrageous, deepening: in front of a solid fire made of small flames—all-new flames—a color beyond all color darted and renewed. Centering on his eyes, the whole of his head was more and more one out-thrust of bright agony, a fire in which something lived. He screamed with violation and helplessness and pounded on his goggles, holding the glass down to keep his eyeballs from being pulled out of his face, out of the aircraft and lost in the crimson darkness. As the flames gained inward on each other and came together the redness went from them and his eyes were sheer light, a simple, single brightness there was nothing that could have been said about: a sincere diamond

The stick had only a little more forward that it could go. McCaig pushed for it; the dive stage passed; they were into the bottom round-out, inverted and roaring. Relentlessly McCaig shoved on the stick, growing superhuman with pain in his harness, drawn toward the instrument panel and the dark beyond it. He firewalled the throttle; his eyes started with a terrible pressure that the usual world could not have wished. He could try for the rest of the loop— the hardest and most painful part —or roll free and dive out of it.

A blazing scarlet tinge, like that of sourceless anger, filled McCaig's vision. He tried to open the throttle all out, but it was already there, braced and helpless with light without the diamond, light that made itself out of nothing, to be nothing but light. In there, where nothing could live, a figure materialized in and out in pieces: first a short-horned head, then an arm and a hand with still fingers, two unrelated leaping legs, a torso settling itself between them and quivering out of relation, then all of these together, then none, then almost all again, dancing ironically, not hurting, beyond Cahill's pain, pitiless, homeless, imperious.

Cahill started for the fire, calling. The face there came at him like the sun, like a thorn-haired devil, like a pile of nails in the sand. Cahill climbed and screamed toward it with tremendous muscular strength, and unguessed human energy, a vision worth the pain.

The flame took on its red again, and tired; the forced cannoning of the engine brought out its sigh; they floated. Cahill might have been sitting on top of a great wind-sensitive hill, a ball-shaped part of nature, a wave that had crested with him, by means of him.

limit. He pressed harder on the stick, forcing, forcing, rounded on the other side of the bottom-out, and clawed, raging, into the climb.

With the engine surpassing itself, the plane fought upward until it was in a vertical slowdown, an inching, almost a hang, a stall. A little more, a little more, McCaig urged, crooning; the nose is wanting to come through. The plane wavered from wing to wing, a coming stall spreading over it, breaking back and forth across it like a wave. They were close; they were very close.

"We made it, crazy man," McCaig yelled through the one ear of the gosport Cahill still had. "We made it. Outside loop. We made it

495

all the way around, red-out and all."

Red-out and all, Cahill thought. And all.

"Open your eyes," McCaig said backward. "Go on. Open 'em."

With Ruíz at his side and Zack behind him, he was holding to an iron spike of the fence that went around his apartment building. He had never touched the fence when he could see, but had often been bothered, late in the afternoon, by the nowhere-racketing of sticks that invisible children ran along it under his window. Standing there sightless, in the first of the dark that would never leave him, still and dependent, he had tried to take charge of the scene in a different way from the passing-by and irritable overlooking of his former life. Here, in an aircraft, in cold, sensitive, powerful half-controlled air, he remembered this, and frowned into the roar of the inescapable propeller as into the beginning of the darkness, the playground attached to the place he lived in. He tightened his grip on the stick as he had on cemented steel, remembering also that a child had been killed by such metal, by lightning and a home fence, somewhere in the newspaper; it had been holding a toy golf club against the railing when lightning struck. The gaze through Cahill's mind became more careful; his grasp on the playground—the stick, the spike, the toy club—was firmer, had more assurance; it mattered now that there were child-reds only in winter, on the swings, slides and monkey-bars. Yes, winter; winter. He had last seen them fully the winter before this one. After that, things must have begun to haze, even before the sparks had started to shoot across whatever he looked at. Last winter was the last clear time. The ground was gray dirt and trampled brown grass; there was a ragged softball diamond to his left; to the right was the formless ground of dodgeball, where girls drew into a ganged circle, and in it chose the one to bombard. Where that happened, more than anywhere else on the playground, space was splendid, and the gaze good anywhere. As he watched on three levels—from memory, from the first imagination of his blindness, and from the aircraft—it seemed to him that every track his feet had ever made on the world, every instant his sole had touched the earth, had been wiped out: the world was clean of him; no other human being, no animal could have guessed or smelled where he was. The girls in the ring, various sizes of small, were given to him in a fresh way he could never have expected; the threads that had tied him to his existence—passion, will, hunger—were broken, and in this triple gaze, his sight faceted like a fly's, he entered into the liberty of himself, surpassing all laws, especially those he had created, becoming an invisible onlooker into the circle of a game beyond all the freedoms of sunlight. To the extent that he kept himself from action, from wishing or willing, his power grew. His sense of invisibility was mixed with that of a criminal: one who knows he will not and cannot be caught. He felt the yard-spike sharpen in his hand, its point at the level of his eyes.

"Turn loose, Frank," Ruíz said. "Go on and let go, and go on to the next one. Turn loose the fence, and turn loose of Zack."

But he could not; there were still a few girls in the ring. The ball struck one child between the shoulder blades; she fell crying to the ground. Cahill could not move, for there were now only two girls in the circle. Immediately, in a tremendous shedding of sparks, she was hit in the face, and was gone. The last child turned, turned . . .

"God damn you," Cahill screamed into the whole wind, "Go on. Get out of here. This is the same god-damn thing. I almost . . . there was . . ." And then, "This ain't nothin' but the same thing. It ain't good enough." He seized the spike with another grip, to tear it from the fence, to force it out of the world. "I ain't goin' with this no more."

He took the wrist of his right hand in the fingers of his left and pushed the stick with holding-energy forward, as one goes down a steep slope still braking upward and against. Quickly, then, he disengaged his left hand and shoved open the throttle. With an astonished blurred roar the engine answered; the plane overtopped and rammed downward, Cahill now with his double grip again.

Before he could move for the controls, his arms still folded, his eyes still on the clean wide minting of the reservoir, McCaig saw

497

the situation he had put himself in. The aircraft had hold of itself from behind; the stick was locked forward like that of a plane whose control cables had been soldered to the airframe in the death position. "Turn loose, you goddamned fool," McCaig screamed into the gosport, the reservoir dilating in his face like a farm of last-minute light, given, given, given for nothing. McCaig banged himself on the top of the head with his palm, showing Takeover: showing I've got it: I want it: showing I've got to have it, as he got nothing, as the night horizon disappeared into the world-consuming silver of the lake.

Many a death-dive must have started like this, Cahill thought; if we're not going straight down and wide open, I ain't found out the way to make us do it.

The gosport echo, never anything more than faint, was now only the thinnest stretch of a voice, saying, whispering over and over, Fool . . . fool . . . fool . . .

Clearheaded as he had never been, Cahill stood hard on the rudder with his right foot, and jerked back without reason on the stick. And yet the engine slowed. Slowed more, and he realized that McCaig had hold of it. He reached again for the throttle, thought better of it, and grabbed the stick again with

McCaig pulled the throttle back and held it back, in a flash of thanks for the movement he could make.

both hands, full back against his belly.

There had never been a spinning of the brain like this, the body thrown leaning against the left straps, the head cramped face up, the stick in his lap banging at him, trying one thing and another, quivering pitifully, his right foot down and unbroken. I'm giving the devil this airplane, he said; he may just already have it.

—Where?

In the fire and the writing in voices. In the angle through the ring. In the sound of matching numbers. In the coins and the dark hairs. In musical wood. In the book and the margin. In the stars moving the numbers. In the self-destruction hidden in the cylinder. In the foot that leaves the ground. In the winding of rubber. In something like a vein you can follow. Follow. In the minute in the air.

—What shape is it?

Round. All round. In the speeding up of the circle. In the rink. In the city square.

—When?

Which girl is still in the circle where all the others are gone? Which face outlasted the death ball? She came at him as through the eye of a lock. His chest was the sound of a coring-drill; in his belly, it massed with the unbroken sullenness of organ music.

The lake wheeled on its vastness as though its own hanging moon-force turned on its heel around them, easily and naturally at first and then with an insane and righteous will to spin faster and faster, holding them paralyzed, until something or everything gave way.

McCaig raged and screamed at Cahill and into the engine, trying everything he could to break out of what he was in, to bring the plane back to itself, trying with hands, feet, head, voice: trying whatever he had taught, whatever he had learned, whatever he had dreamed of in the imagery of spell-breaking and domination, whatever of rescue and reasoning, whatever of survival and immortality, of impulse, of life at the end of life, of his muscles yanking and sobbing over the dazed growing water-granite, the slab, the drunk white blank whirling up to smash him truly dead.

McCaig fought on. There was nothing he could do about the stick. It was wedged back, then sideways, then in one position after another, all somewhere inside a huge block of paleness made of the whole air. He turned, calling on the savage panic the lake gave him, and battled with his shoes, driving them into the rudder pedals, squirming and scrambling to

—I have been blind for three months, and all the time I could see—every minute of fifty years—I never really saw anything or anybody that mattered. I can't even remember my wife's face. I don't have much left of my father and mother, and of my brother only his face through a window, and the bright lights he told me he was fighting under. Skates and bicycles Hammering nails into boards and the grain of wood, the pale scratches of blueprints, the greased stupid bodies of the weight lifters at my pool. Four-walled singing, the boom of Spanish from underground, Ruíz's dark form, a human shadow, a dream-shadow riding the wool green under-lights of the water.

But that was not everything, either. He had been wrong; there must be more, for things had happened to him; he had been places and lived through minutes and people that nobody else had. He had been where they were.

Sex: fragility and bright colors, and the wish to protect them, or whoever had them, or was near them. How could he ever have said this? How could he believe it now? It was true, though.

There had been flowers, a snake that had been meant as

get both feet on the left pedal, and bring the entire force of his life—the faces and feet of his wife Jo-anne and his children Ham and Letta—into it. There was no way for him to tell whether the lake was closer than it had been, except that it was, except that it was brighter—a lot brighter—and its wheel was nearly all over him. Then slowly, calmly, he sat back and let it have what it wanted.

I can't do it, McCaig felt his throat say again, but not his lips; I'm already tired of trying. It's over; there's no way I can break it. Something has got me. Some stranger wants me to die in this lake, and all I wanted to do was to show off to a blind man. I liked his boy, what I knew of him, and maybe I even wanted to help a little. That's all; that's all I want to say.

Three hundred feet were gone. Is this when I said I'd do it?

One more thing. Why not?

500

something a snake was not supposed to mean, there had been the dark moving boy in the pool, muscled water around him, and a one-leggèd girl in the last sun. There was still, there in its nails and grains, in its trapdoors and mirrors, the house of lostness he had started. And now there was his boy, who existed only in descriptions, only in what other people had said about him, but the being of whose face he could not feel, could not image, or know what shape his knees and ankles and backbone were; had been. Joel was three times gone: once before he was born, when Florence had left, then by the years he had lived in the world without an image Cahill could draw on with his eyes, and last by his disappearance at a place somewhere over which, in the grip of himself, his father was now spiraling down.

His mind like a strange ball revolved opposite to the direction in which his body was moving, being moved; he held the fence hard against him, with the spike; he thought he did.

The fence sprang sickeningly from him, away from his belly, and at the same time the engine indrew a long, primed breath. The left rudder pedal shot forward under his foot, and at once the aircraft was breathless—they were all breathless—and revolv-

So this:

The back cockpit's got to know I've done give it up. He's got to *know* it, not think it. That means I've got to wait some more. Then, just one, two, three moves, fast, so fast they seem like they're all happening at once. I can wait now; I can still wait; I still have some time to wait: wait while he thinks he's already killed me: wait with the altimeter blurring down. I can wait for a hundred more feet. I can do it or not do it. I can do it, or I can just watch. It don't really matter.

It still did not matter. He touched nothing, his feet free, his hands again under his arms.

It mattered. With a leap coming up from his tailbone, McCaig shoved at the stick and felt it tear through Cahill's hands. He socked the stick head from him all the way, and while Cahill tried to recover it pulled back the throttle to the stop and ground the left rud-

ing more and more slowly, a feather, a vertical leaf whose whirlpool was dying.

Resting now in a brimming equilibrium, Cahill wondered what it had all been about. He had not really wanted to die—though the notion had surely been with him, gone through him—and if control of the plane had meant so much to him, why had he made every move he could to destroy it? Why had he done this, when McCaig had only wanted him to feel and control the ship? It was just that I wanted the plane without him, Cahill said, his face still; that's as near as I can come. I wanted it, no matter what I did with it. It's just that I wanted the thing without him or anybody else touching it, he reasoned in the understanding flutter-bumps of corrected air. I wanted the whole business, and for a little while I had it; I had it in my hands.

Cahill stripped off a glove and felt his face, not surprised to find that he was sweating, and that

der pedal to the floorboard; and at once McCaig was demonstrating, as he did every day, the recovery of a spinning aircraft. He neutralized his feet and the stick and brought the plane into a leveling, almost soundless, calm. Fifty feet above the reservoir they breathed, they were breathing one altitude, floating.

Habit filling his senses so that they called for nothing else, McCaig followed his eyes over the stilled instruments, pausing on the charmed altimeter, which appeared to point absolutely not

the sweat was drying cold in the wind. He passed his fingers over the cracked goggles and then pushed them up; tears crossed his face straight back into the helmet. He drew the goggles back over the old flashes, then his eyelids to confirm those fires, and slid his legs forward, his head settling lower than the rim of the cockpit, freeing himself of any further mysteries or decisions, of any straining to do or be anything.

Was he? What to say?

An arm went up from him over his head and bucked as the sleeve of his overcoat flirred against it. He let this happen until the plane balanced his true

only to his courage and skill but to the events of his life leading up to the needle's position: the endless hours of instructing, the hundreds of questions, answers, and conclusions fed back and forth through the taut metal of control wires to the hands and feet, the muscles and minds of dozens of boys, the air-talk through hoses, and most importantly, the various distances from the ground at which he had been, and had caused others to be. The long altimeter needle dwelt now on that inevitable *fifty*, and McCaig knew that from then on he would bet money, if he had it, on anything that arrived at or gave back fifty. With the assurance of the needle, with the phosphorescence of the reservoir in his voice, he whooshed into the gosport tube. "You all right?"

"If you're all right, hold up your hand."

McCaig twisted as well as he could in his seat, but could not make out any sign from the rear cockpit. Gently he shaded the aircraft into a slow swing. The moon rode around part of a circle until it was behind them. Again McCaig torsioned his upper body and craned.

Cahill's grotesque arm, wavering in the slipstream, was unmistakably up, hilarious, cowboylike, impaling the shape of full light be-

503

weight once more, and then pulled back, hulking, below the wind.

In a tilt that pulled from a ponderous, leisurely direction, they broke, they faded through another turn and settled. Was this enough? What had he expected? The stranger—himself—with his strong frozen hands, being passed in his body along the unforced ripples that should lie overhead forever, over the solid upbearing of the earth he now remembered as having an extra dimension, the sound of the self he had abandoned underfoot, the crunching of gravel and sand, the squeal of snow, the night-stalking reassurance of cement, Zack beside him, somewhere in the past, watchful in his fur, came to him from great distances, maybe from beyond life, beyond death, beyond anything that was supposed to be.

There was no use bothering about any of that. He wondered, but wondered not really caring, how McCaig kept enough feeling in his hands and feet to get through to the wings and tail, to the god-damned airplane, whatever it was he wanted it to do. Gloves, maybe, but he had those, himself. Heavy boots, McCaig had, like those in that woman's place—what was her name?— that still place, that nothing place where she . . . where he

fore McCaig turned back to the business of flying.

McCaig bucked pleasantly in the sheepskin of his feet and torso, in clothes that would, with light, be dirty again. The stick, the throttle he touched now and then but did not change, the slowly revolving altimeter, going the right way this time, placed his life back in the hand, the palm whose lines he knew; it would not close on him or drop him. The unevennesses of the air themselves were reassuring, and he was astonished, more than he had been before, that they made some cadets uncomfortable and inefficient at first, even when he told class after class that the jolts and drops were normal, and would even be fun when they got used to them. When you walk, you don't notice the ground jamming back at you, do you? You don't bother about every little bump or crack in the sidewalk. Damn right you don't; you just walk. Same thing here; if the air drops you a little, there's some other air, good air, right there under it to pick you up.

might've . . . Boots, shoes; on the trembling pedals, the footsteps that turned you. Cahill huddled in his overcoat like any drunk in a February city, near no thinkable warmth, and in undying wind coming into him from ice-covered surfaces: lakes, fields, streets. There was no change in the old rays hurtling under his goggles; they were double-caged.

From the imagined sheepskins on McCaig's feet, on the feet of boys, his mind moved to sheep, themselves, in the pasture of some sort; a color plate in a grade-school geography book. When they began to move and browse in the picture he left them and went to Zack, to his brown eyes, to the sliding of his pelt along Cahill's leg, the complex tick of his claws on a hard floor (louder on linoleum than on naked wood; linoleum carried a slight extra sound, maybe even an echo, in it: a threat, a chill, pursuit). Zack was with Hannah—McCaig had taken care of it—and Cahill did not question; it had been his idea. Soon, with luck, he would be closed with both of them in a building, a room somewhere, and the bumps and tussles of air would be overhead again where they belonged, reached only by chilled human bodies in clumsy machines. As for him, what?

As they passed westward from the reservoir, McCaig began to imagine patterns into the land lights advancing toward where they hung. There was not yet much need for that, though, and he opened his concentration and swung his eyes back and forth through the propeller and along the side of the aircraft over the unassorted fractions of light placed where they were for no reason to be known by him, as they slid under. From among these the farm-woman, Mrs. Bledsoe, came to him, and was there in connection with the still lines of his own palm, intent with their meaning, puzzling over the short lifeline in one hand and the long one in the other; she held both wrists, working along the routes in the skin, and the aircraft rode carefully there, and on dim stipples of light, on dark like a flattened cliff—every pressure, height, and weight of dark—on crushed farms and sparse highways and the broken parts of towns. Thus thinking, thus watching, thus carried, he had less and less interest in why Cahill had wanted to kill him, to kill himself, to take hold of the aircraft, or to leave the controls alone after McCaig had got them back. Had Cahill forced the spin on impulse—people who didn't

What would land be like? How could anyone know, how could he explain that he would come through Hannah's leaning door carrying, among other things, a horned fire demon in his frozen headache: a creature which had lived somewhere within, in a redness pulled forward out of the brain like the heavy suck-gathered mucus in a doctor's sinus machine, at the time he had first seen the still sheep, the moving sheep, in the geography picture? Then, he had been told to count for as long as he could stand it, and the numbers up to ten snarled and snorted in building agony in the bent glass tube in his nostril. Increasing, increasing, they held out in the stem for the last of themselves, and Cahill knew that somewhere close, closer, somewhere in the double figures, he would faint. That was how his eyes had felt in the ring, the loop, in the game McCaig had put them in, back there. The shaking of the stall across the wings had made no difference; to reach the number nine was all that mattered: that was salvation; that was when it had quit: at nine. This time, at a one-count the figure had appeared in some of its pieces. At two three and four his hurt had been clearer, quivering with everything it had to come together; at six and

know better, and had hold of aircraft controls are more liable to give in to impulse than others; like wanting to jump off a building when you're on top of one. Or had he done it because of his blindness, his son, or for some other reason? There was no telling, and McCaig guessed that Cahill would not tell him if he asked; though he would ask. Or maybe on his own, later on, Cahill would tell him.

Flying; riding.

506

seven it was almost one thing, and began to scream through Cahill's mouth. At nine it was the nearest it could get to the flame-shape of pure being, cocked and crazed like a one-legged girl in the homemade house of the lost when a glass fell open, a shutter flew back, a rattlesnake crackled at her ankle in a sudden blinding focus of sun, and she stumbled backward onto the skeleton that had locked the door behind her, one foot gripping the floor for two, for the balance taken and hidden. That was nine. At ten the shutter closed; the snake's buzz, like the flattened tongue of a human mouth trying to make the noise of an engine, lessened, the form in the outstriving eyeballs dissolved, all but the horns, and then they, and survival-peace came over, drew back, drew into the familiar cross-rain of Cahill's sockets.

Cahill raised his hand.

Now in the blue-freckled unrolling, the hard small glows nailed into the dark, he could make out the position of the field: the hangars would have to be the longest connected form of light he would be able to see. They gave off a dull ghost-yellow, in a badly congealed rectangle; the dirt strip would be to the left of them. More than once he had shown a cadet that he could land a Stearman blindfolded, once he had the runway lined up, and it was true that, by counting and by the sound of the engine at different times within the count, he could come close enough to doing it to impress the student with the need to learn what he had to teach. The cadet could see, of course, and could true the ship up if McCaig happened to be off in his count and his tunings. But this was a good deal different. He cut the throttle evenly, according to an idea.

"Follow me through," he said. "Catch a-holt." There was no answer from the stick. He shunted it from side to side. The aircraft shook, but the stick was still only McCaig's. He turned again and yelled into the gosport. "Can you hear me? If you can, hold your hand up."

"Now put it back on the stick, and ride right with me. Get into it.

507

"What?" Cahill screamed. "Get into *what?*"

Get into the tree. We're gonna leave it."

His gone feet groped for pedals; he took hold of the stick. What had it at the same time was McCaig, but it might also not be completely McCaig, it might be something else, it might be himself but not only himself, himself and another part of himself, a part that lived up here, and knew what to do, could think, could unthink, could move, could be what to do.

"Follow on."

It was to the left, as with a soft voice; a sinking, a delicate midmotion with the hand; and then the left side rose. Cahill felt that he was intended to straighten in the seat; he did not, but stayed at the full of the slant until it stopped high and hung without strain; it started down the other way, in a side-slide, Cahill and whatever else, controlling. A deep repose of swooping came under them; they flattened, with no pull on the blood, and started up to the right. It was like the end of the best drunk you had ever been on, when you find the bed; the drinking, the party, the fucking is all over, and you lie down for good. That is when the slant comes out of the bed; it gives its side-rise to you, its slope; it understands the wall;

McCaig flew as if leading an orchestra; the motion was waltzlike, and the lilting descent ordered and grave and yet at the same time humorous, excessive. The controls responded beautifully, and yet McCaig was aware that he alone was not holding them. In some way he was being matched, and even anticipated; he would have liked to have had a cadet who showed so much coordination, so much feeling for the aircraft and the air, so little nervousness and hesitation as this.

508

the wall is with it and part of it; you go up sideways as high as it wants to go; the ceiling does not matter; it is not there. You do not change the position of your body or even try to hold on to the bed, but let it all be done.

They started down again, into the swoop; they flattened; they rose again on the left wing; high; higher.

He got used to it; the space he was in seemed better doing this than anything else he knew about, moving up a tilt and sinking back on a long slide, to lift into the opposite, as though falling through a climb, settling downward through what should have been a rise, but which some great fatherlike intuitive power —a power which was part of the movement—knew it was not; in this, going and coming back, was a single moment of rapturous executional delight which combined with a sense of being between bodily states, into a condition better, more creative and more natural, than either land or air: of having mortal weight grow secretive and more living, then withdraw, and, from another direction, come back again.

The lights to one side swung up and stood, swept, swept back and under, and others, or others yet the same, came to rest in a counterbalancing, overjoying equilibrium, then went under as before, to sustain, to hold the rhythm as it desired to be held, and which could go on, for it had the hands and feet, the wings and lights for it.

"Good, good; that's the way to do it," McCaig said, pulling the low engine back even more, until the wind was louder than it.

"We're just about right in the pattern," McCaig said, though they were not. "Keep a-holt. We're gonna grease this thing."

They were at five hundred feet again, and McCaig could make out —or intuit with the off-slant of his peripheral vision—the nearest row of Stearmans but not the second. That was enough, though; they should touch down on the first third of the runway if he were correct in assuming that the plane he saw as parked farthest from the hangars did not have, outside of it in the row, one or more others, not there until they killed you.

He turned from the base leg to the final approach, and McCaig could tell, now, that there were no ghost ships in line with the track he would lay down; the beaten strip was clear in the moonlight, and toward it he placed them. Easily, they were on.

Land now, Cahill said, and could not help bracing himself. We've got to get this thing back on to the land. What will I do? What will I do then?

The engine drew in its breath until it could not be heard; the sensitivity of the aircraft was ultra-quiet and poised; poising.

They were on; the riding had changed; what came to them from underneath was solid; the jolts were set in something; there were no more falls and recoveries, no more suspension, but an upthrust. They trundled and turned—turned around, he judged—and waddled for a time with the engine gunning quietly and retiring, then wheeled once more. The engine balked, chuckered briefly, and died with a final tremor of the whole plane. In his granite seat, his overcoat on him

When the speed was what he wanted, the body weight entirely his own, he turned, jockeyed the aircraft into line on the outer position of the last row, and killed the engine. The cold, not all in his face, or alive with flow and force, came back on all sides, and was

510

in still-whirling folds, Cahill lost his hands in coarse webs and found buckles, but had no success with them. Suddenly he wanted to be free, to stand, to move without handles.

Though padded and distant, the voice came to him from the real world. He knocked the gosport pipes loose from the helmet and took it off and sat in the windless freeze holding it in his lap, getting used to the idea that power and noise were not holding him up. Slowly he unsnapped the strap guides on the helmet, pulled the goggles loose and put them in his pocket. With his ears clear, he found that he wanted to hear McCaig speak again, from wherever he was. McCaig was beside him, though, touching the top of his shoulder, then his chest. Body metal ground and snapped loose. He stood up where he was.

He got out of the cockpit, live with dead nerves, and stood on the wing. It was the wings of all

colder. For a moment he listened to Cahill fumbling in the back seat.

"Just a minute," McCaig said. "Let me fake the Form One."

"What I needed to do," McCaig explained, reasonably and instructorlike, "was to write up an engine malfunction, like, you know, I had to fly it around a little bit to get a notion why it might be runnin' rough, or some damn thing. That'll give 'em somethin' to think about. For a while, anyway. Some greaseball'll brag that he was the one that fixed it."

511

these planes, he thought; it was, it might have been like what he saw in his head when he first woke up in this place, the day after he got off the bus: a wing that went on and on: one long wing of nothing but snow, as far as you could see, not a mark on it.

He leaned forward; his forearms were taken.

"Hop," McCaig said. "About three feet, and all straight down. It's that long first step you hear about, only this one won't kill you."

"What was that you did?" Cahill asked, not wanting to go in any direction, but to stand and talk, to listen to a voice he could hear without trouble.

"What is *what* I did?" McCaig asked. "I did two things, one hard and one easy. Which one you talkin' about?"

"Not just before we come down. I mean that other thing, on back yonder."

"That was a outside loop. Pull your balls up through your eyeballs. Put 'em right on your goggles." He peered intently at Cahill's naked lit head. "Did you see red, you murderin' blind bugger?"

"Damned if I didn't," Cahill said. "I saw plenty of that."

"That all you saw?" McCaig said, leaning forward. "What else? Did you see anything else? We was right . . ."

"I saw . . ." Cahill began, then began again. "I saw . . . I thought maybe . . . I saw somethin' like . . ."

"Somethin' like what?"

"Somethin' like . . . well, it was a lot of things . . . they were all squirmin' around . . . I don't know . . . It was like they was tryin' . . ."

McCaig could not even shift to the other foot. He wished the wind would blow; he could not say what he wanted to, either. And yet he knew he would make some kind of try. This time must not go past.

"Well, there was things . . . it's like there was . . . there were some pieces of things that, right there when it was like my head was . . . that it would . . . that it was like to 'a blowed wide open . . . that's when the thing just about . . . it just about got . . ."

"What was it? What did it look like? What did it look like, Frank?"

"I couldn't get it," Cahill said. "I never did have it. It never did come, all the way. Somethin' looked like it had horns. I swear it did. There's nothin' in the worst dream you ever had, could'a looked like it. It had horns, though; I swear it did. They was orange. They was orange, and you couldn't see nothin' else."

McCaig took a step to go, and then turned, like a man turning on someone, on something; turned on Cahill.

"What on earth would'a caused you to do somethin' like you done?"

"Like what?" Cahill said, far off from the voice that came at him.

"You know damned well what. You took a-holt of the airplane and wouldn't turn loose. I thought we was goin' straight into the lake. I didn't know what the hell had a-holt of you. What was it? What the hell did you think *you* was doin'?"

"To see if I could, maybe. That's all I can tell you. Just to see if I could."

"No," said McCaig.

" 'No'? No? No, what?"

"I mean, no that ain't it. That ain't why you grabbed the stick."

"All right, then," Cahill said, facing him. "You tell me. What was it?"

"Your god-damned meanness, Frank, is what it is; that's what done it; it liked to 'uv taken us away from here. It's the meanness of your god-damned will power. It's when you get a-holt of somethin'. Then you think you got it; you think you got it all."

"Well, we're all right. Nothin' happened. We're right here."

"It's your god-damned will power," McCaig repeated.

"What else have I got?"

There was no answer possible and McCaig changed to something he could say. "You know how much altitude you left us with?"

"How would I know?"

"No more'n about fifty feet. The lake was all over us. The lake was right in our hair."

"Yours, maybe," Cahill said, and smiled, a clear moonlit smile. "I bet you couldn 'a drove a needle up your asshole with a sledge hammer."

"Naw," McCaig said, pawing a noise from the ground. "You didn't scare me none. I figured you didn't want to die, either."

"We just goin' to stand here?"

"No, come on around the end of the hangars and wait for me, till I get the car. I'll have to drive in acrost the basketball courts. I can explain me walkin' acrost under the lights, over by the barracks, but I can't explain you. When we get there, just hold on to the hangar till I get back. Don't go off nowhere."

After some stiff bushes, when they had got where he was told to stand, Cahill stood, stood easily with his palm prickling on the corrugated ripples of the hangar, until he heard the cautious crunch of a car. The engine idled; he went toward it until McCaig's hand led him in, into heat; great heat.

"How's it feel in here?" McCaig asked. "Pretty good, huh?"

"What was that other thing?"

"Oh. You mean that last thing I done in the airplane? That's what you call a fallin' leaf. One side to the other side, losin' altitude all the time. That's the way me and Joel used to come down; used to come down into the pattern. I thought you'd appreciate that."

"Sure enough."

"I thought you would," McCaig said, beginning to inch the car, in low, out on to the basketball courts. "Now listen here, young feller. Listen here, you old fucker. Don't you never try to kill none of us no more. That ain't the way we gon' do."

"You'll get home."

"You ain't listened enough. That thing, that fallin' leaf, that was for you. I done that for you to make my peace." He shifted into second. "I done it to tell you I ain't gonna get after you, for what you done. I said I ain't, and I ain't. I don't blame you none. A airplane's got a crazy way of takin' a-holt of you, once you got a-holt of it. When you first get the notion that it'll do anything you want it to. More than one man's died from that feelin'. But I'll tell you one more thing, too. You ain't no buddy of mine."

"Yes I am," Cahill said, as they moved out, under the weak nets.

He had shaved and injected, and, though he still had a slight headache, the pain was a clear one, and was already leaving. He eased his lower back in the colonel's chair, collar comfortable around his neck, Zack at his right foot.

"Well, how are you this morning?" the colonel asked, more or less pleasantly.

"I'm fine," Cahill said. "I got some pretty good sleep last night, and the sun's out, it feels like. Two more days, and I'm gone."

"I'm afraid you're not going to get them, Mr. Cahill."

Cahill said nothing, and was careful not to change his position; he relaxed every muscle, and sat quietly with the morning sun in his face, warm on the skin around his glasses. He would not speak until something else was said to him. He knew he was good at silence, and especially good at that part of conversations, where the effort to communication was forced on the other person.

"I assume you heard me, Mr. Cahill," the colonel said.

"I heard you."

"It won't be possible for you to spend any more time on this base. I hope you know whatever you came to find out, for the base is off limits to you from now on."

"What's the trouble? What you got on your mind? What's your main trouble, Colonel?"

"This is not personal, Mr. Cahill, but a bill of very serious particulars has been run up against you since you've been in the area. Some of these are your business, and your dog's. But some of them are the Air Corps's business, the government's business, and therefore they're *my* business."

Again Cahill did not respond, but sat with the sun in circles around both eyes. He was listening for the colonel to shift in his seat. He did, and Cahill knew he would try for a point he considered important; he must have been leaning forward.

"I'm curious," the colonel said, his voice a little lower, pedantic but intent. "Hasn't anyone ever pointed out to you, hasn't anyone ever *told* you how dangerous that animal is? Is he . . . have you had him . . . has he gone through the authorized training for what he does? Is he qualified?"

"He's as qualified as he needs to be. He's as qualified as he's gonna get."

"Do you have papers on him?"

"I don't need no papers. Neither does he."

"I'd say you're in for some trouble with the law, sooner or later."

"I'll wait."

"You're responsible for what he does, though. Like what happened in town Thursday night. You remember that, I imagine."

"You mean them other dogs that was messin' with him? They ought to 'a knowed better than that."

"They were dogs, Mr. Cahill. That's all. Just other dogs."

Cahill shifted, himself, despite everything. "Zack ain't never killed nothin' before," he said. "Least, not while I've had him, he ain't."

"You might try telling that to five or six dogs lying on the pavement of

Harmon Square, back in town. They'd like to hear it, and so would the people they belonged to."

"They was botherin' him. They shouldn'a been runnin' around loose, anyway."

"That's not for you to say, Mr. Cahill. It's up to you to take care of your own dog."

"They was botherin' him. They should'a knowed better than to mess with him. Zack don't fool around."

"Neither does the Air Corps fool around, Mr. Cahill. I want you to get yourself and your dog off this base and stay off it. Go back to town. Go back to Atlanta. You don't have any need to be here any longer," the colonel said, and sat back. "If you ever did."

"I ain't askin' you for nothin'. Not a damned thing."

"I want you to leave us, and leave us alone."

"You're fuckin' right I'll leave you alone."

"I want you off this base," the colonel repeated. "Now. As of *right* now."

"That supposed to be an order?"

"You can call it whatever you like. You're a civilian. I'm not authorized to give you any orders. But I can give this base orders, and those are to keep you off it. Now and from now on."

"Fuck your base. You can have it," Cahill said evenly and distinctly.

"Furthermore," the colonel went on, "base personnel are not allowed to speak to you on any occasion. Neither on base or off base."

"I ain't comin' on your base no more," Cahill said. "I've had enough of it. And as far as who I talk to, that's my business, and their business. You ain't God, and I ain't one of these kids around here." He thought briefly. "And as far as that matter goes, you act worse than any of 'em yourself. My Lord A-mighty"—he threw up one hand—"is that all you got against me? That a dog run off some other dogs that was fixin' to get after a blind man in the middle of the night? That what you call fightin' a war?"

"The war has nothing to do with it, Mr. Cahill. And, no, that's not all I've got against you."

"What else you got, Mr. Colonel?"

"You were in the Link Trainer Building, which is off limits to any but base personnel. And further than that, you were in the Link Trainer; you caused it to function; you manipulated it."

"I sat in it, if that's what you're talkin' about. What's wrong with that? How does that hurt anything?"

"It's government property, and it's classified. Your sitting in it, as you say, was unauthorized."

"So what? Is it against the law?"

"In a manner of speaking, it is. There are witnesses. You could be prosecuted, and you could serve time. I'd advise you to leave this area as soon as you can. If it were not for your son's accident, I would throw the book at you. Or some of the book, anyway."

"If it wadn't for my boy's accident I wouldn't be here, no way," Cahill said. "And you wouldn't be tryin' to get me out of here before I find out more than I already know."

"And just what do you know, Mr. Cahill? I'd be most interested to hear. It'd give me a good rundown on the rumors that're current; every military establishment has them."

"The boys tell me that if you hear a rumor long enough, there's somethin' to it. Not most of the time but all the time."

"I won't debate that," the colonel said, "but just bring up one or two more matters with you before you go. These also concern Mr. McCaig, with whom I think you're acquainted: one of our civilian instructors who has also just left us. I'll have him come in for a minute or two."

The colonel stepped past him and spoke through the door. He returned, and McCaig came in and stood behind Cahill's chair.

"McCaig," said the colonel, "you have managed to cut up a good deal in the past few days; you and this gentleman. What do you have to say? What's been going on?"

"Seems like you already know," McCaig said. "Tell me what you don't like, Colonel. Me and Frank wouldn't be in here if you liked everything. Or even if you liked anything; anything that has to do with us, I mean."

"First of all, it has been brought to my attention that you and Mr. Cahill saw occasion to visit the accident site, the property of a Mr. . . . I believe a Mr. Bledsoe, and that you spent some time on the property, and some time with Mr. Bledsoe and with his wife and children."

"His chilrun live up in the roof, Colonel," Cahill said, and he was quite sure that McCaig was smiling at this. "Up in the air. They never did come down to the ground. We never said a word to 'em."

"You were there," the colonel persisted. "You visited the location of the accident, and you brought away with you some things, some articles you happened to come on. Does either of you still happen to have those articles?"

"What articles you talkin' about, Colonel? Can you put a name to what you think we got?" McCaig asked.

"You were seen to have picked up something from the ground on or near where Cadet Cahill's aircraft came to rest."

"So?" McCaig said. "What might that'a been?"

"That's for you to tell me, Mr. McCaig. And, incidentally, I blame you for all this more than I do Mr. Cahill. You should know better. You belong to this place."

"The hell I do," McCaig said. "Not if you have anything to do with it."

The colonel heightened his color, and lifted his face past Cahill directly toward McCaig's. "While Mr. Cahill was inside Mr. Bledsoe's house, you took it on yourself to make some kind of search over various areas of the property. You took some time doing this, accompanied by Mr. Cahill's dog. And you, too, seemed to have found something, though not at the impact site, or adjacent to it. What is this?"

"Why don't you ask Zack?" McCaig asked. "He was there, too. You said so yourself."

"This-here's what it was," Cahill said, half rising and dredging his pocket. He held up the fused zipper. "It come out of one of your sheep boots, near as we can tell. That's what your lady-friend done told me. She said it was his'n. Joel's; my boy's."

"Might I have it?" the colonel asked.

"Sure," Cahill said. "Come on over here and get it." Holding the zipper up, he reached down to the dog's head with the other hand. "Like you say, Colonel, it belongs to the government. You can have it any time you want it."

The colonel rose and came to the side of his desk, placing the dog on the far side of Cahill. "You're not thinking of making this some kind of threat, are you, Mr. Cahill?" he asked, with his eyes on both Cahill and Zack. "I wouldn't do that if I were you."

"Who said anything about a threat?" Cahill said. "If you're afraid of my dog . . ." He lifted his head straight back toward McCaig, and said to him, "Here, Mac, give him these. He wants 'em; give 'em to him."

Cahill found the bent piece of wire, and McCaig took it and the zipper and put them at the center of the colonel's desk, on the arranged papers there.

"Here you go, sir," he said. "Here's just what you want. I hope you got some use for 'em. I hope you get a lot of pleasure out of 'em."

"Here's one more thing," Cahill said, bringing up the goggles. "You gave 'em to me the other day. If you want that piece of wire and that zipper, you might could find some way to use these, too."

McCaig put the goggles on the desk.

"But you might want to watch out for one thing," Cahill said, and this time did not wait out the colonel's reply. "I done had those on, so that might'a fucked 'em up. I had 'em on my head, you know, like. And if you don't mind, I was up in the air with 'em on. Whether you know it or not, that was what I was doin' with 'em. Maybe you think the whole air is your'n, but it ain't. I was up in it with them goggles on. Maybe you don't know about it, but that's where I was, and there ain't nothin' you can do about it."

"It would be far from anything I'd want to do," the colonel said, "to call a middle-aged blind man childish, but if you want to consider that as my opinion, you're welcome to it."

"Thank you, sir," Cahill said, as near as he could come to irony, and getting ready to leave on that note. "I sure do thank you for everything."

"I'm not quite done yet, however," the colonel said. "As a matter of record, I am quite cognizant of the fact that you were in one of our aircraft last night, though I must say I didn't know you wore the goggles. That you were a passenger in a PT-17-type aircraft attached to the U.S. Army Air Corps at Peckover is a matter of the gravest consequence, however. It is not only against regulations; it is against the law. The degree to which I hold you and McCaig responsible will be determined by the amount of your cooperation in what I request."

"And just what do you re-quest?" McCaig asked.

"I'll come to that," the colonel answered, putting both hands on the desk on their palms. "But first I want to be sure you know what you've done."

"We know what we done," McCaig said. "Don't we, Frank?"

"We were shore God up there," Cahill said, and nodded. "We were shore God up there somewhere."

"Both of you are civilians," the colonel went on. "McCaig is a civilian instructor, in our employ. Or he was, until today. Who occupies the aircraft when Mr. McCaig is at the controls, who rides in the other cockpit, is a matter of regulations, and not merely a matter of policy. The passengers must be military personnel, or duly authorized civilian instructors, or such parties as may be designated by myself or other members of the Air Corps staff here."

"The devil's got me, Colonel," Cahill said, taken with an assertiveness that he could not and did not want to control. "I wadn't just a passenger, up yonder."

McCaig leaned quickly toward Cahill, and, seeing there was nothing he could do, straightened again.

"You were . . . you were not . . ." the colonel began, surely not ready for this. "You don't mean to tell me that you actually took . . . that you . . ."

"I had a-holt of it, for a while, there, Colonel," Cahill said, nodding his head with what he hoped the colonel would see as self-satisfaction. "I flew it all over the fuckin' place. There wadn't nothin' in the air I didn't do with it. Ain't that right, Mac? Didn't I fly that thing all over hell?"

For the first time McCaig backed off. "I did . . . I did . . . Colonel . . . well, I did let him feel the controls, kind of. Just to give him some kind of notion . . . just some kind of . . . it really . . . I mean it wadn't like he was . . . it . . . he wadn't really . . ."

The colonel sat back, and let his hands fall into his lap with exaggerated weight. "I could sure rack you up over this, McCaig. I could have you taken out of here in handcuffs. You'd never see Canada, or England, or another airplane. You'd never see anything but a lot of steel bars, out in Leavenworth, Kansas, or wherever they'd wind up putting you. This is provable stuff, all the way down to your signature on the Form One, which incidentally, was a false report in itself; there was nothing wrong with the aircraft."

"Well, fire away, Colonel," McCaig said resignedly. "We done what we done. No harm come of it, though. You might, but I can't see none."

"Harm? Harm?" the colonel said, as though he had never heard the word before. "Anything is harm that's outside the rules that're set down. What would this base be if we didn't hold the line on every rule, every regulation we have? I'll tell you what it'd be, McCaig. It would be a wilderness. It would be a slum of boys. You understand that? A slum."

"What is it now?" McCaig asked.

"It's no slum. We will graduate our quota, Mr. McCaig. To use a phrase of yours and Mr. Cahill's, whether you like it or not."

"All of my kids made it," McCaig said. "All except one."

"We can't do anything about that," the colonel said. "We can't do anything we haven't already done."

No one spoke; McCaig was as still as the blind man.

Finally the colonel said, "I'm not going to make an example of you, McCaig, because we don't need an example. The other instructors are very cooperative; they want to see these boys learn to fly. And, although they are civilians, they want to see them become good officers. That's minimum. They don't want to see them get killed through incompetence, lack of discipline, or anything else. That's maximum. That they live. Or, if they don't, that their death is not on anybody's hands."

"That's real interestin'," McCaig said.

"Does it interest you equally, Mr. Cahill?"

"Sure," Cahill said. "Maybe in another way." He thought. "Or maybe in the same way."

"So, where does that leave us, Colonel?" McCaig asked, now with some politeness.

"A little forward from where we were," the colonel said. "As far as where it leaves *you*, it's in the clear, more or less, though if anybody asks me I won't give you a recommendation. It leaves you out of here, and on your way to Canada, or England, or wherever else you want to go." He bent forward, and rose a little from the desk. "I can even wish you luck."

"Can I refuse that, Colonel?"

The colonel looked at the offered hand, his own, in the air in front of him with nothing to do. "Yes," he said. "You can do that."

McCaig touched Cahill, who craned backward and up to hear him. "I'll wait for you outside," he said. "Take your time." At the door he turned, considered, and said, "I'll be lookin' for your AT-6 over there, Colonel. They tell me they've got new equipment that can pick up a signal on anything, even stuff that ain't liable to see combat."

The colonel went around Cahill, again on the far side of the dog, and closed the door. He walked to a corner of the room and stood feeling his chin. "We've got one last subject to talk about, Mr. Cahill. If it hadn't been so unpleasant this morning, if it hadn't been for McCaig's deliberate insolence—and yours—I would have been inclined to let it go. Now I want to press you a little. I want to ask you some questions you may not like, and ask you to give me some personal information that you may dislike giving me even more."

"Come on," Cahill said, shifting toward the colonel's voice. "Come on with it."

"How close to your son, Cadet Joel Cahill, were you during his life?"

"Well, I was . . ." Cahill began. "Well, I'm his father. I'm his next of kin. It's right there on your records, ain't it? Ain't that so?"

"No one is intimating that you are not his father. He did designate you next of kin. And, yes, it is on our records." He said nothing else for a moment, and Cahill felt the cruelty of silence, which there was now no way for him to use. "But that's not what I asked you." The silence was on Cahill again, and worse. "How well did you know Cadet Cahill? What was he like? What did you think of him?"

"Well, I just came up here, that's all. That's all there is to it. He wanted me to come, and I did. Me and my dog, we came up here."

The colonel took a step into the room. "Mr. Cahill," he said, "there's not any sense in fooling around about this. You know as well as I do— you know better than I do—that you never laid eyes on your son in your life. If it were possible, I could show you a picture of him, with other boys, and you wouldn't be able to pick him out. Now just suppose you tell me why you've come here. You've been nothing but trouble, needless trouble. And over what?"

"Over the fact that my boy got killed in one of your airplanes," Cahill said, shifting not himself but his whole chair, trying for a way to get back on the offensive. "You want to face up to things, you want me to face up to things; you face up to that."

"You never laid eyes on him," the colonel repeated.

"How do you know?" Cahill asked. "What business is it of yours?"

"Cadet Cahill was in my command. It is my responsibility to deal with him: with his military personality, with his flight progress, with all the circumstances that bear on him, and that he bears on. When he went down I immediately called his mother, though his request was that you be designated next of kin. I used Joel's own address in Memphis."

"How did she take it?"

"How would you imagine?"

"I'm askin' you."

"She was very distressed, and wanted to know if she should come to Peckover. I told her that we had not recovered the body."

"Are you still lookin'?"

"We are, Mr. Cahill, but we don't seem to be having much success."

"Is that why Florence didn't show up?"

"It is my impression that it isn't the reason, at least not the whole reason."

"Well, what is, then?"

"I told her that Joel had given you as next of kin."

"How did she take *that?*"

"She appeared not to be able to understand it; at first she refused to believe it."

"And then what?"

"She said that she preferred not to come if you were to be here."

"That figures," Cahill said. "I'd just as soon she wadn't around. She wouldn't understand none of this."

"Have you communicated with her?"

"No; I don't, usually. We don't have nothin' to say. She lives in Memphis."

"I have her number," the colonel said. "Would you like it?"

"I reckon," Cahill said, not seeing how he could refuse.

The colonel came and pushed a slip of paper between Cahill's hand and the arm of the chair. Slowly Cahill drew it into his palm.

"She might like to hear from you now," the colonel said. "I think you might find some things to say, even if you don't the rest of the time."

Cahill shook his head, like a fighter who has taken a hard punch; without anger he was lost. "I'd appreciate you leavin' my family out of this," he said. "You got no claim to tell us what to do."

"I have no intention of interfering with your 'family,' Mr. Cahill," the colonel said. "What advice I give is human advice, not military advice. If I've offended you, I'm sorry."

"Not as sorry as you're gonna be," Cahill said, and with the words felt his naturalness rise and be with him. "I know some things—them human things you was talkin' about, and not military things, either—that's gonna make some mighty fine listenin' to some people."

"Mr. Cahill, I think it's about time you left. You bluffed your way in here because your son was killed; a son you had given not the slightest damn about for twenty years. Your whole attitude, and I daresay your whole existence, is bluff. You've lied, you've given people to assume and believe what was in no way the truth, and on the basis of these things you've caused a good deal of trouble where none need have been. I'm looking for an explanation for all this, but I have a pretty good idea I won't get one, because you don't know yourself. I don't think you had the least notion as to why you came to Peckover. You don't belong here. You said something about claims a little while ago; said I had no claim on your family. You're right; I don't. But neither do you have any claim on this base, or on the Air Corps, or on me or any of the personnel here. Your son had an accident, and because of some personality trait—trait, defect, whimsey, whatever you want to call it— named you as next of kin and not the mother who raised him and took care of him when you deserted them both, and that placed a temporary responsibility on us, here, to deal with you, to explain things to you as best we could, and to try to take care of the unfortunate matter in a way acceptable to both you and to the service of which your son was a member. We have tried to do this, and I have even overstepped my limits a bit to accommodate you, to introduce you to the people and places that were part of Joel's world, here, and, although I knew from your wife what your situation regarding your son was, I went along with your presentation of yourself because I believed it might involve some kind of search, something that was important for you. And in your condition, I felt that you could use this kind of help." He paused, now able, he was sure, to deal with Cahill's silences. "Now I see that I didn't handle the situation as well as I might have done; but then there was no precedent: we've never had a fatal accident here, as you may know. I might have done things differently, but again I'm not sure. My mistake was to go along with your game, your bluff. I don't think you feel the slightest grief, loss, or even interest in the death of your only son. It will bother me for the rest of my days that I can't figure out why you came here, unless you tell me. And from what I've seen of you, you would be the last person on earth to know."

"That's somethin' you don't know nothin' about," Cahill said. His attack stilled down, and had in it a place where there was no breath at all. "You better get to thinkin' about your own family, before you start tellin' somebody else how to run his."

"This is all the time I have, Mr. Cahill," the colonel said. "Corporal Phillipson will drive you back to town. Or you can ride with McCaig. But this is all there is. I'll tell you what I told McCaig: good luck, and get on with it."

I ought to be glad to get off this easy, Cahill thought, but I'm not; I'm not going out of here like this. "I ain't talkin' about your family direckly," he said, "but I am, about somethin' they might be interested in, especially your wife would, if she don't already know."

"I said good-bye, Mr. Cahill. If you don't leave I'll either have you thrown out or restrained."

"I'm talkin' about the sheeps," Cahill said, "and the one that looks after 'em. I'm talkin' about that place where there ain't no air, and that-there counter it ain't too hard to get around. I'm talkin' about the sheeps, Colonel, and I'm talkin' about your airplane, that AT, or UT, or fuck-T, or whatever the hell the name of it is. You know damn well what I'm talkin' about: the one you was up in when my boy got killed: the one you done run him down into the fire with, because he was gettin' back in there amongst the sheeps, where you been spendin' most of your time, instead of out there fightin' the war, like that bomb man and that navigator, that Whitehall, was doin'." He stooped, almost out of breath; the thought of Lucille and her room took the rest of what he had.

"I have warned you once, and this is the last time I'm going to do it," the colonel said, and then, realizing the gesture would not be noted, sat back. "The episode is closed."

"Go get her," Cahill kept on. "Go get your woman out of that hot room."

"If you mean Miss Lucille Wick from Supply, I have no intention of sending for her," the colonel said. "Or for anyone else you specify. The next person I call will be an MP."

"She told me a lot, Colonel, and what she didn't tell me, the boys did; them and some others." When the Colonel said nothing, he went on. "And don't tell me Joel wadn't back there gettin' some wool. Wool. Wool, Mr. Colonel. There's plenty of it in yonder. Enough for everybody. Not just for you."

The colonel reached for the phone, but Cahill shifted himself deeper into the chair, as though preparing to stay for a while.

"Now you was up in your airplane when my boy went down into the fire. You gonna say you wadn't?"

"Mr. Cahill," the colonel said, outdone, but with some actual tiredness, "for the last time: I am not accountable to you."

"The shit you're not."

Picking up the phone, the colonel said into it distinctly, "Could you send Sergeant Shellnut to my office right away? Sergeant Shellnut and two men?" He hung up, and turned to his papers. "Your escort will be here in a few minutes," he said to Cahill. "If you please, you may wait outside."

Cahill stood up; Zack came to the sitting position.

"Zack," he said. "Get ready. Get ready, big boy. "There's gonna be some people comin' after us."

"Now, really," said the colonel. "This is just a little more melodrama than we need."

"He'll do it, if I say so," Cahill told him in a low voice, almost a whisper. "He don't ask no questions. He never asked a question in his life."

"Stay right where you are," said the colonel, "and go out slowly. If you don't, the MPs will shoot him."

"They might," Cahill said, "after they get here."

The colonel forced himself to look at the dog, which was now on all feet, crouching a little on the hind ones, his neck-fur, where Cahill had

525

his hand, bristling, his back raised in the middle, his teeth parting, and a low continuous impatient sound—it was not like any sound the colonel associated with dogs—coming not so much from him as from around him, as from a whole atmosphere of concentrated threat that had a black animal center.

"He comes fast when he comes, Colonel," Cahill said, in a voice almost as low as the dog's. "Real fast, and there ain't nothin' you can do. He broke a man's arm through three coats and a raincoat, and he was just playin'; I was trainin' him." He spoke down to Zack. "Wait. Wait just a minute, Anvil-head. Let him just look at you." He turned again to the colonel, his green eyes on fire with the morning sun. "Colonel, you done the same thing as them dogs back in town. You done made him mad."

"Take it easy, Mr. Cahill. I'm telling you to take it easy. You don't know what you're doing. You don't know what kind of trouble you're letting yourself in for."

"Yes I do, Colonel," Cahill said. "I know it all. We done got it down to one word. It's either go or no-go. He'll come after you if I say so. It ain't your word, Colonel. It's *my* word."

They hung there. Cahill was aware that the moment could not last for long, that things were as he said—do it or don't do it—but he was not bothered; the balance was his, the solidity of his feet, Zack's fur under his hand, the sunlight on his face, the cool of his eyelids under the glasses. "If I say it, he'll come at you," he spoke into the room where the colonel was. "If I say it, he's gone, from me to you, and there ain't nothin' mortal can help you. If I turn loose I don't think I could get him to come back."

For a little he held on, and listened with penetration, with a depth of field he had never had, for any sound the colonel might make; the shift of a foot, the slide of paper; he listened for the movement of a hand in the air.

Outside, behind him through the door, and then behind him in the room, there were steps and fabrics far too loud to be important; they did not belong.

They did not, but they were there. Cahill felt for the dog's head. "Get on down, boy," he said. "It's all right. You don't have to do nothin'."

"You called us, Colonel?" a Northern voice to his left rear said past him. "What's the trouble?"

"Nothing . . . no . . . there's nothing wrong, Sergeant. I just wanted to make sure that Mr. Cahill, here, gets a proper escort off base, and is . . . and is more or less taken care of."

He had held on too long, Cahill figured; talked too much; let the colonel talk.

"We'll take care of it for you, Colonel," said the sergeant, glancing briefly at the two MP privates with him, and then at the dog. "We got all morning."

"Go ahead and wait outside," the colonel said to the MPs, his confidence and habit of command returning, and he riding with them. "I want to make sure I haven't forgotten anything."

"You ain't forgotten nothin', Colonel," Cahill said, turning out of the space he had held as though it had been molded around him. "Not a thing." He waited, understanding that he had a good last shot, and timing it. "And neither have I."

Before Cahill reached the door, the colonel said, "I don't think you would have done it."

"I can't say, about that," Cahill answered, again pleased that he was ready with something. "I don't know about me. But Zack might'a."

"Those little things . . . those little affairs . . ." the colonel said, not able to leave off.

"Good-bye, Colonel," Cahill said, facing out the door and moving away. "Good-bye. I'm gone."

"Those little mystiques, those pseudo-mystiques, like you and Mc-Caig play with, those in-group camaraderies. I've seen all that, Cahill. I see it every day."

"No shit," Cahill answered, still moving, but less. Don't give anything away, he told himself. Don't tell him a damn thing about Shears and the others; not a thing about the boys. Let's let them go ahead.

"I'm sorry about your son," the colonel said. "I told you, and I want you to go out of here remembering it."

"Yeah, you told me," Cahill said, in what must have been profile, and then, surprisingly, perhaps to play on what he was sure was fear, "He's out there somewhere."

"Little mystiques," the colonel repeated. "You and McCaig, and the rest of them. Everybody that goes in for them. Some people must need them, I suppose. Otherwise you wouldn't do what you do."

"Sure, Colonel," Cahill said, beginning to move again. "You got it right."

"Just makes trouble for the rest of us, who have a job to do." The colonel readied his final word, and then delivered it. "A big job."

"Gone," Cahill said. "I'm gone. Can you say that, Colonel? It ain't military, but can you say it?"

"Gone," said the colonel, and then, "No, God damn it, there *is* one more thing."

Cahill smiled, actually grinned. "One more, after all the other one mores?"

"I'd appreciate it if you wouldn't bother Miss Wick again. Even if you see her in town."

"I ain't goin' to 'bother' her, soldier boy. And I sure ain't gonna see her."

"And this little mill girl—Pelham, I think her name is . . ."

"What about her?" Cahill asked, almost turning back into the room. "I don't want you botherin' *her*."

"Believe me, I won't," the colonel said. "But for your own good I thought you might like to know that she's infected about half the personnel of this base with gonorrhea. I'll leave you with that last bit of information."

Jesus, Cahill thought, is that what I've got to look forward to?

"How about these other soldiers?" Cahill asked, on another tack.

"Oh," the colonel said, and thought; decided. "You won't need them. Send Sergeant Shellnut back in here, and you and McCaig go."

At the door to the building the MPs were waiting for him.

"The colonel says he wants to see you," Cahill said to all three of them. "He'll tell you; you don't need to do nothin' for me."

"We'll check with him," said the sergeant. "You're the one whose boy got killed out there in that fire, ain't you? We 'us all sorry to hear about that."

"Yeah," Cahill said. "Everybody was. Everybody tells me."

"You been gettin' around some," the sergeant said.

"As much as I could," Cahill said. "But that's all over. I'm leavin' out of here."

"I heard you don't take nothin' from nobody."

"Not if I can help it," Cahill said, wondering how the man had heard this.

"We could use you in my outfit," the sergeant said. "We need some that are tougher than the ones we got."

"The next war, maybe," Cahill said. "The next war, the next life, the next somethin'."

The door closed behind him, and he was alone with the cold, getting ready in his mind for the steps down. There did not seem to be anyone else on the landing with him: he felt for the railing.

"How did it go?" a voice asked before Cahill's foot found the edge. "What else did that shit-head have to say?"

He looks smaller, McCaig thought; smaller and tighter and tireder; he can't take much more.

"He told me you'd be out here," Cahill said toward the voice and the building. "But I didn't think you would be."

"Why wouldn't I?" said McCaig. "You done said me and you was buddies. Let's go back to McLendon's and have a beer. Fuck all this out here."

Cahill had the count he had started, and he held on to it, and followed it and the railing down. There were rocks under his shoes; the snow must be gone; yes, there's no squeak down there anywhere; it's gone.

McCaig moved them slowly out of the squadron area and into the pine wood where the road to the motor pool wound. "Can you hear them trees?" he asked, though there was no wind.

"Yeah, I more or less can," Cahill said. "A lot of the time, I just think I hear things, but if I keep thinkin' it, damn if that ain't what's happenin' right where I am, right along."

"Well," McCaig said, "it's real pretty through here. These trees are almost as big around as a man. If it wadn't for this road bein' so sandy you'd think you was off up in Alaska, somewhere."

"Yeah," Cahill said, slowing. "I was walkin' out here the other day with a boy; with one of these boys."

"Harbelis, wadn't it?"

"It was him. They got some good boys here. Real good. I hope they'll all . . . I hope . . . well, shit: there's not anything I can do."

It came up again, and he leaned his ear up toward it, noticing the aircraft above him for the first time: the down-sound, and the quick wrenching, the wringing in it, the swirl, as of engine-noise twisted suddenly out of a cave.

McCaig looked up as the aircraft straightened. "There it is, Frank. That's your good-bye, your salute. It's what you might call the last snap roll."

Cahill kept listening, but there were no more sudden twists of the air; only a lessening of the sound of what must have been the same aircraft, until he could not hear it.

McCaig watched the blind man closely, as he had done from the beginning; now, alone with him here among these heavy trees and little sun, he was comfortable in keeping his eyes on Cahill for as long as he liked. At last, when Cahill dropped the angle of his glasses from the tops of the firs and swung toward him, McCaig picked up where he had left off, but stopped almost as soon as he started.

Cahill walked again, until he felt McCaig's hand. He shook at it angrily, at first not paying attention to the voice.

"We got a friend of yours aboard," McCaig said, as Lieutenant Purcell Foy appeared, his blouse the same green as the trees, his salmon-pink pants odd but not unpleasantly contrasting with the gray road. "Lieutenant Foy, Instructor, Army Check Rider, United States Army Air Corps, is dead ahead and closing, on collision course."

"I think I remember him," Cahill said. "Walk on by."

This is outside, Cahill reminded himself. This is not where he had that poor boy hemmed up in a room that was so full of steam the sweat jumped. He was talking about something the airplane was supposed to do with the road; supposed to do to the road. That and the wind. The wind blew you back and forth across the road, and you were supposed to do something about it.

"I don't know," Cahill said. "Prob'ly not. The colonel just told me he don't like me."

But Foy stood in front of them, his hands not in his pockets despite the cold.

"What're you doin' out in the woods, Lieutenant?" McCaig asked. "All your little birds nestin' in the trees?"

"All of them that are going to Basic," said Foy. "The others are on their way to Cooks and Bakers, or MPs, or Radio School. We got the quota, though. This class did more or less OK." He turned to Cahill.

"You going to be with us through Sunday?"

"That's too bad," said the lieutenant. "I won't ask you why this is the case. Believe me, lads, I won't ask."

"Then don't," said McCaig. "The word now is 'Pass, friend.'

We've got business on the other side of you."

Foy moved aside, narrowing his eyes. He said to McCaig, "I understand things're going to be a little different for you from now on. You're going military, at last."

"Yeah," McCaig said. "Another kind of military, where they fight."

"Your kingdom's gone, Mr. Mc-Caig. All these kids that hang

He listened, his lips filling with blood, growing, not tight together but not parted.

around you and listen to your stories. Dusting the crops in the depression days, and walking the wings for the farmers. Writing on the sky, telephone numbers of your buddies, jokes in the clouds, unauthorized acrobatics. You're going to have to come up to the chalk, now. There's not going to be any more disciples for you."

"Where are yours?" McCaig asked quietly.

"There's not going to be any more of that, for you," Foy went on, not moving aside any farther. "No more; no more like this man's sky-blue son. No more of the antidiscipline boys; no more stallions."

"You ain't said nothin' to me," Cahill said, standing where he was. "Don't talk about my boy in front of me without talkin' to me. I'm right here."

"I don't have anything to say to you," the lieutenant said, shaking his head without looking face to face. "Your boy was misguided

He flexed the spring grip in his right-hand pocket; the metal tension flowed up, settled in his shoulder, and hardened.

and paid for it. Maybe he had the wrong instructor; he should have had one who would stick with the ways, the procedures that produce good pilots."

"There's plenty of good pilots that're dead, Lieutenant," McCaig said, pushing his hair back. "But there ain't a damned one of 'em that was a chicken-shit."

"I'll let that pass, McCaig," Foy said. "I shouldn't, but I will."

"Just let *us* pass," McCaig said. "We're gon' do it anyway. So just move it off the road, Lieutenant. We need it for other things."

"Yeah," Cahill said. "The bus is fixin' to leave, in a couple of hours. I got to see some people; say good-bye. You know."

"Your son's girlfriend, is that one of them? That little mill mouse, lives in a hog wallow over on Brockett Street?"

"That ain't exactly the way I'd put it, if it was me," Cahill said. "But, yeah, we might be talkin' about somebody we both of us know. I been to her house. You been there?"

"I know where it is," said the lieutenant.

"You ever hear her play what she plays?"

"*Play?* Play what, except play-for-pay?"

"Play what she plays," Cahill repeated, stepping toward him. "Play the broom."

"Screw this," Foy said, outdone, brushing aside the air between him and Cahill. "Strike it; get on with it." He stepped to one side of Cahill's solid position. "Stay out of the air," he glanced at McCaig, "both of you."

"I said the broom," Cahill said. "If a broom could make any kind of music, that's what it would sound like. She can do that, and she can feed you on blood. She can make blood taste like you don't never want nothin' else. That's the livin' truth."

"OK," Foy said, moving past him. "Go get some of it. Drink a lot."

"Aw shit," Cahill said, changing, his hand loose in the pocket, his shoulder tight. "Don't go off like that, Lieutenant." His hand cleared the coat, and he put it out. "I been here. You belong here. We got together for a little while. I can't help it if you ain't never heard a broom playin'. Maybe you got that to look forward to, after I leave."

Foy hesitated. "Drink a lot," he said again, his hand rising slowly.

Cahill had forgotten, already, which way the talk had been going. "Sure," he murmured. "I'll drink a lot. Whatever I can get."

"Blood," Foy said. "You and that loom-bunny. Drink a lot."

"I already have," Cahill said, his hand in the air in a definite place. Then, "Say good-bye to my son."

533

McCaig looked on, his eyes paining him, trying with everything he could to think of the right thing to do. The cold gave him no answer, as the two men came together in the space between them, the blind man's close-shaven jaw the same as it always was, his glasses black more than green, the lieutenant's face a flooded healthy but uneven pink. "Your son," Foy picked up and gave back. "You want *me* to say good-bye?"

"I do," said Cahill. "Everybody that knew him."

"But *me?* From what I hear, he used to go around telling people . . ."

"Everybody," Cahill said. "We're finishin' up. I don't want to leave nobody out."

A bird sounded in a tree close to them. It must have been in a tree; it was overhead, and it did not go by, did not move. Ah-*Ah,* the sound was.

"Say, listen," McCaig said, not helpfully. "That's a fishin' crow; that's some kind of a fishin' crow. I ain't ever heard one before, this far from the ocean."

"Good-bye," Foy said, making a definite offer with his hand. "Good-bye to Joel Cahill. And I'll say what I think."

"Say it," Cahill murmured, almost whispered, at the first touch.

"Good-bye, Cadet Cahill," Foy said. "They say you had talent.

534

He stood holding.

He felt the bones running up to the little finger, and the tendons over them.

One more and I'm coming down, Cahill told himself, although he knew that he would come down anyway.

When it happens it happens, Cahill thought, beginning to exist in his hand more than in the rest of him; he would do it until there was no other place for him, at all.

His grasp came together more solidly, out and down from the shoulders, up from the feet; the bones of the other hand came together in his. He could have

But I don't know. I never rode with you."

"You're fuckin'-A, you didn't," McCaig said. "You're fuckin'-A."

Foy made as though to pay no mind, though he nodded his head briefly in McCaig's direction.

"You took it the wrong way, Cadet," he said, "and you ended up where you ended up." His hand more or less comfortably in Cahill's, he went on.

"You won't be flying my wing," he said. "And that's something. I'm glad of that. I sure am."

"What wing you got, check-rider?" McCaig burst out. "You fucked up in Transition, they tell me. That's why you ended up in a God-damned primary training school, with the other crows."

"And that's my good-bye," the lieutenant said, loosening his token grip to pull away. "That's my last word on everything."

"That's OK," Foy said, pulling. "That should do it. Let's . . . Jesus . . . listen. God *damn* it . . ."

McCaig saw the color go from

535

rolled the knuckles, like a boy in school; he remembered that kind of pain, which was great, but the deliberateness of such cruelty was not what he wanted. He did not go beyond where he stood with his power growing, centered and beyond reach, grounded and lifted at the same time. All his strength was bonded into something he could do, and, though he understood that McCaig was screaming at him, was clawing at him, he was not ready to give it up. I have more I can put into it; a little more; a little more than is there now, he was sure, and it came to him; then something beyond the little more, a pulsation he had no idea was with him, or could come from anywhere he could imagine. He felt the bone go; bone somewhere.

"You heard about grovelin'," Cahill said. "I ain't ever seen it. Is he grovelin', Mac? Is this'n grovelin'?"

the lieutenant's face more quickly than seemed possible, almost in a blink, a stroke, a pass of white. Cahill stood planted, his hat firmly on his head, his eyes flat black, his left hand in the pocket of his overcoat.

"Frank," McCaig said, then called; yelled. "Frank! Watch out what the hell you're doin'! Turn loose! Turn loose of him, Frank! That's enough!" He grabbed Cahill's arm, but it was not human. Lieutenant Foy was halfway to one knee; no, both knees. "O Jesus, God," he said terribly. "You son-of-a-bitch . . . I'll . . . God damn damn damn you . . . when I . . ."

There was a dull snap—McCaig was sure there was splintering in it, and Foy was down on his knees all the way, hissing and flinging his head; his cap came off and lay pale side up. He beat weakly at Cahill's still legs with his free hand.

"Frank, God damn you," McCaig said, angry enough now to speak clearly. "You let the lieutenant go. You done enough. Turn

536

"He's grovelin', ain't he?"

Little by little, reluctantly, he gave his fingers back into their ordinary condition; his forearm; his shoulder; dropped his arm to his side. "That ought to hold you," he said. "That's what me and my boy've got to say to you. Tell the little boys in your steam room what we done said."

"Zack didn't say a damn thing," Cahill said. "He didn't make a damn sound. That son-of-a-bitch could'a been killin' me."

He released his feet from their stand. "You're right," he said. "I got to get out of town." He started forward, around the noise of sobbing at his feet. "Zack didn't do this. I did it. I don't know what got . . . I mean, I was just . . ."

loose, now. This ain't gettin' us nowhere."

"All right, Frank. He's grovelin'. If that's what you want."

"Come on, now, Frank," McCaig said, hauling on him. "Leave him be. We got to clear this place." He thought. "We got to get you out of here. Let's go before they close off the damn base."

"Come on, come on, God damn it. We got to hustle. We got to get on down the road, right fast."

"You did it sure enough, buddy-boy," McCaig said, as they stumbled together toward the motor

He held, without Zack, without any other way to go forward, a hard exhilaration in his legs. On. This one, that one. No stairs. No other feet. Nothing to trip on. He held to what was, and went with it, his mind empty and very clear.

pool, powerfully, as though ramming.

"I wish you'd'a wrung his neck." McCaig looked back as they turned the next curve, and glimpsed Lieutenant Foy as he now was, the pink restored to his profile, the silver on his near shoulder glinting, his hand under the other arm of his fir-green blouse. "I wish you'd'a wrung it, or that we'd'a just gone right on by."

"Mr. Boysie," he said. "I'd like to ask you to do a little somethin' for me. I'd like to ask you, Boyd McLendon."

"What is it?" McLendon asked. "I'll do anything I kin, that's in my limits somewheres."

"This may not be in your limits," Cahill said. "But I'm gonna ask you to do it anyway."

"Put it out here, and I'll see," McLendon answered. "And why don't you take off your coat and hat, every now and then? It ain't cold in here."

"I want you to hide me out," Cahill said, leaning forward in the chair to put his weight on all four legs. "I want to move my stuff somewhere else. This afternoon. I want to get out of your room, and out of the buildin'. Anywhere you can think of. I want tonight and most of tomorrow, and then I'll be gone, I promise you. I want just that much time, and nobody but a couple of people to know I'm still around here. That's all."

"Go slow, big man," McLendon said, pulling up a chair and sitting to face Cahill directly, leaning with his elbows on his thighs. "What's your situation? You tell me whatever 'tis I need to know, about all this."

"There ain't nothin' special you need to know," Cahill said. "I'd just like to be here through Sunday, like I was asked to do from the beginnin'. That ain't too much, is it? It was Colonel Hoccleve's notion, to begin with. He was the one done had the idea."

"That ain't all there is to it, Frank," McLendon said. "You ain't levelin' with me, and if you can't do that I can't do nothin' for you."

"What do you want to know?"

"I want to know why you started off talkin', just now, about hidin' out. That sure ain't normal. There ain't nothin' normal about it. You must'a done somethin'. Or maybe Zack done somethin'. Somethin' else beside killin' them town dogs."

"Well," Cahill said consideredly, "I got into it with the colonel, a little bit. He said some things I didn't like, and I might'a . . . I might'a got after him some. Anyway, he don't want me to come back on the base."

"You ain't got to go back out there. Ain't you had enough of it?"

"You're fuckin'-A I've had enough of it. But I got to stay one more day."

"How come?"

"I told the boys I would. I told some of 'em. I told Malcolm Shears and that Greek boy, and a couple of others. And I ain't gonna go back on 'em. That's all there is to it."

"That all you done? Just argue with that shit-head?"

Cahill ran a finger inside his collar and moved it back and forth. "No, that ain't all. That ain't exactly all."

"What you done, Frank? You can tell me, right on the nail. I ain't gonna do nothin' but listen."

"I grabbed one son-of-a-bitch out there. I grabbed him when me and the other Mac was walkin' in the woods, and he come up to me and said somethin' I didn't like. I taken a-holt of him, and . . . and I might'a hurt his hand a little, just to show him, you know, just to show him about it."

"Who was it?"

"One of the instructors. One of the guys in the Army. Double-Mac says he's nothin'; he's no good."

"You're in some trouble, buddy," McLendon said, leaning back. "If you hurt one of them Army people, they're gonna be comin' after you. There ain't nothin' I can do about it."

"Yes there is, McLendon," Cahill said, pushing his hat back off the yellow sweat-light of his forehead. "You can help me move my stuff before they get here. You can tell 'em I took the bus; you can tell 'em I'm gone."

"All this ain't gonna do any good, Frank," McLendon said sympathetically. "They know where you are. They can come after you whenever they want to. They can get the sheriff, they can get the civilian police after you. There ain't many of 'em, and they ain't any too smart, but they know where this place is."

"Where can I go, Mac? You and McCaig's the only friends I got here, 'cept that one girl, and the boys. The boys can't do nothin' for me." He took his hat off all the way, finally. "One more day, Mac. One more day and one more night. That's all I'm askin'."

"Why is it all this important? The colonel don't want you on his base, so don't go on it. Go on back to Atlanta, where you got some business to be."

"My business is right here," Cahill said, his arms strengthening again. "It's right here, until Sunday evenin'." He sat still; stiller than before. "I told 'em I 'us gonna be here, and I am. As long as I can find me a way, I'm gonna be out there on Sunday."

"The boys you're talkin' about—that Shears and them—they ain't even gonna know you're there, Frank."

"That's right," Cahill said. "But I'll know it. This is gonna be the one thing I ever did for my boy. He started all this, and I'm gonna finish it."

"You ain't doin' it for your boy, Frank. That's bullshit. You ain't doin' it for him, and you ain't doin' it for the other boys, either. You're doin' it for yourself, just like always. You're doin' it because the colonel throwed you out."

"No," Cahill said doggedly. "That ain't it."

"It is, Frank. Slack off some. Come on in with the rest of us. Other people ain't so bad, when you get used to 'em. There's some that ain't, anyway."

"You can say what you want to," Cahill said, strong and tired. "You help me, you son-of-a-bitch, or I swear Zack will lay you low."

"You poor fucker," McLendon said. "All I have to do is walk in the next room and get a rifle, and I could have Zack out there hangin' in the shed with the buck and that-there hog. Anyhow, Zack ain't even around here. Now how the hell's he gonna get me, huh?"

"I left him over with Hannah again, just in case you wouldn't give me no place to hole up. But I believe you will. I do believe it." He broke his blank expression. "And you wouldn't shoot him if he was here. It's me that wants to go out in your shed, yonder. You can fix that up, if you want to. You can get me a couple of blankets, maybe a mattress. That'll be enough. Just so long as I got a place to go."

"All right," McLendon said, moving toward Cahill, almost touching him. "I ain't goin' back on you. I don't believe you done anything all that wrong. If they come after you, all I did was move you out to the shed. I can tell 'em I have to have the room. Clean it up, put somebody else in it; some damn thing."

"Good," Cahill said, nodding. "That's good. I won't be there long."

"You damn well won't, I'll clue you," McLendon said. "It'll freeze the turds in your guts, out there. How come you think I keep them wild animules hangin' in there? It's better than a freezer; better than a food locker."

"Get me a mattress and some blankets, and let's go on."

"OK. I got a old iron bed stacked up in pieces, in my garage. I'll see if I can't put it together."

"Do that," Cahill said. "That'd be real good. If you could get me the pieces, and some screws, and all, I could prob'ly put it together by myself. Anyway, I can try it, if you'll go on over to the girl's house and bring Zack back here with you. See can you do that."

"I'll try," McLendon said. "Will he come with me?"

Cahill thought. "Bring her with you. He likes her all right. Both you'all come on back, and we'll see what's what."

"Good enough," McLendon said. "But if the MPs or the sheriff or the colonel or Hitler or anybody else comes after you, don't say I didn't tell you they would."

"They won't, if you don't tell 'em," Cahill said. "They won't look out there where your meat is. Later on they might, but I'll be gone by then."

"OK," McLendon said resignedly. "I'll go get your dog and your mean-faced little old girl for you. Far as you're concerned, you can start matchin' up your screws."

Cahill stood, swinging this way and that for sound, ready to move when he had solved it.

"You want somethin' to drink, before you go out yonder and hang yourself on a hook?"

"What you got?"

"Gin. That's a lot easier to come by than that soft stuff we was into the other night, with them captains."

"OK."

"I'll fix you something that'll be good for you. I'm the only man in the world that likes it. Maybe you can be number two." He cracked the cap from a bottle, poured, and mixed in gin from a flask. "That'll get to you, if it don't kill you. If you like it, you ain't ever gonna die."

Cahill tasted, and put the glass back out into the air. "I'm gonna die," he said. "You can have all that stuff you can drink. How in the God-damned hell can you keep it down? What the shit is it, anyway?"

"Clam juice and gin," McLendon said, drinking off what he had given Cahill. "I can't get enough of it." He drank more. "What's the matter? Don't you like seafood? It's good for you. I'm the onliest one that can drink it, though. You ain't no big help to me, in my crusade for the best. I'm disappointed. I thought my clam-a-diddle might have one more customer."

"Diddle you," Cahill said. "I'm 'on have a hard time gettin' rid of that taste. Just give me the gin, by itself."

"No more," said McLendon. "Not till after you get set up in the shed. If you can last out there on through supper, and if our own elected sheriff don't come get you, I might give you some more. If you can put that bed together by yourself, I'll give you some. And that's the onliest way I'll play it."

In the shed Cahill stood buttoned up while McLendon clanked and hauled at metal, throwing what sounded like hollow bars down near Cahill's feet.

"If the boys come lookin' for me, tell 'em where I am. Will you do that?"

"Any of 'em?" McLendon asked, looking up.

"No. Just Shears and Harbelis. Maybe Spain. Yeah; I would see him. Just them, though, and nobody else."

"Let's see," McLendon said, counting on his fingers, ironic for himself. "That's three cadets and me and the girl. And that's all. That's five people who're already gonna know where your hideout is. You sure there ain't no more?"

"No more," Cahill said. "Ain't that enough?"

"What you want, Raymond?" McLendon asked the boy who had just showed up in the door. "You want to thaw out some meat? We can't eat no more. We just got to find us a place to bury them things, now."

"No, sir," the boy said. "There's somebody here to see Mr. Cahill. He's up in the restaurant."

"Uh-oh," McLendon said. "See what I done told you. The man's done come." He clanked the iron bed-bars. "They gonna chain you up, Mr. Frank. They're gonna put you in the stockade or the hoosegow."

"Stockade, my ass," Cahill said, resisting the reflex to feel for Zack. "Him and who else?"

"No," Raymond said. "It's not the MPs. It's a cadet."

"No shit," Cahill said, pulling back. "Just one of 'em?"

"Just one. He asked me to see if I could find you."

"OK," Cahill said. "I'll come in."

Inside, in the air that was already too warm after the cold, he shook hands with Malcolm Shears. "I'd like to talk to you for a minute," the cadet colonel said. "It won't take long. I just have to catch you up on some things."

"You can go on back in there where we was talkin' with the captains," McLendon said. "I'll show you where it is."

In the dark hot oak-walled room they sat at the table where Cahill and the others had eaten. Raymond closed the door on them.

"We've got it set up," Shears said. "Everything's ready."

"You better tell me what you got in mind to do," Cahill said. "The colonel's tryin' to make things a little hard on me. I better know somethin'."

"Not yet," Shears said. "It's got to spring. It'll come when it comes. Joel was sure. We're sure. All we want you to do is be there. Just be there somewhere when it starts; be there while it goes on. Just tell us—tell me—you'll be there, and we'll do the rest. We're gonna take this baby and run with it."

"I still don't know nothin'. You ain't told me nothin'."

Shears leaned forward, his arms wide and fists clenched. "We're talking about panic, Mr. Cahill. Panic and the control of it. You can bring anybody down if you can cause his panic, and direct it. We put the fear in the other people; it goes from us to them. Surprise and that gut-panic; on the other side, no one has any control. It will happen too fast, and there'll be no leader, no communication. Joel said so. And tomorrow we'll clear the road. The people who need to know, know; they'll be watching us. When we lay the wood to the other side, we'll have with us the ones we want; there'll be lots more we can pick from." He unclenched his hands and clenched them again. "This is the first real action of Alnilam, and we won't miss. What we say we will do, we will do." He touched Cahill's knee. "Just be with us, whether we know where you are, or not."

"I might not could get there," Cahill said, truly not knowing what to say, or what he was going to do. "They won't let me in the gate."

"The base is big," Shears said. "There's only one guard on the whole other side."

"Well . . ."

"Listen, Mr. Cahill," Shears said, and could not have been lying. "The others—Spain and Harbelis and Adler and the others in it with us —think you came up here without knowing why you did. I think that, too. We think that Joel had his own way of getting to you."

"Well . . . God . . . I don't know what to say . . ." Cahill said, fumbling as best he could. "It is true in a way, maybe. I mean, I didn't really have any . . . I mean it was sure a . . . it was a surprise to me, and I . . . well, I just thought I ought to . . . I mean in my whole life there was not any . . ."

"Mr. Cahill," Shears said quietly. "We know what a shock it must have been for you, when you heard."

"Listen, Shears," Cahill said, and he could not keep the desperation out of his voice. "I got to tell you somethin'."

"We already know it," Shears said. "You didn't know Joel. You didn't know him at all." He waited. "And it doesn't matter. You're his father. And that does matter. The two things that matter are that you gave Joel his blood, and that you came up here not because of a telegram from the military, but in response to that. He didn't know you any better than you knew him. But here you are. Whether you answered him, or whether you answered something in yourself, or what, the facts are just what they are. Alnilam is ready, and you're right here with us. It's exactly what Joel wanted, what he said would happen: 'When the father comes, Orion will leap free.' The situation is exactly right for Alnilam; it was made for us. No communication on the other side, and no leader; nobody to give orders, to say what to do, only the ordinary military. Sunday will answer everything. The whole plan is together, exactly like Joel said. The situation is right there for us; we can't miss, and we can't back out, once the thing's in motion. But nobody wants to back out. We are the ones who are up there; we're in the overlook."

"You talk a lot, Mr. Shears," Cahill said, shifting, doing what he could to establish ground. "You're maybe a little too sure. You may have got some things wrong."

"We've got no real problem with tomorrow," Shears went on, shaking his head. "Tonight we do, maybe. Could be you could help us out."

"What can I do?" Cahill asked. "I can't come on the base, and I'll be lucky if the colonel don't have me arrested. That's what McLendon says, anyway. I can't help you none. It'll be all I can do to get out yonder tomorrow, if I can do even that."

"We're off duty until twelve tonight. Open post for everybody, not just the graduating class. We want a place to get our people together, and not on the base. We need someplace where there's electricity, an outlet or generator."

"For what?"

"We want to show some film. There's a little bit of it that's important to show, and most of our members haven't seen it yet. I've seen it, and I think Spain said he saw it, but the others haven't. It's important that they see it. Special Services has charge of the film, but we can get hold of it, and a projector. All we need is a place to show it."

"I can't offer nothin'. I'm gonna have to be hidin' out, myself. Maybe you could ask McLendon."

"Will you say it's all right? Can I tell Mr. McLendon that you approve?"

"Tell him what you want," Cahill said. "I've done learnt not to try to figure anything out, around here. Go on and ask him. It don't make no never-mind to me."

He sat with one hand feeling out the other, his mind sad and blank, but Shears came back quickly.

"He says it's all right," Shears said. "We can use a shed he's got. He can rig up a generator."

"The *shed?*" Cahill said, astonished. "That's where *I'm* gonna be. My God, ain't I ever gonna get no privacy, even when I'm hangin' up with dead hogs?"

"It'll be an all-right place," Shears said confidently. "We'd be foolish to use the cadet club, and we don't want to be in any of Mr. McLendon's rooms, or inside any place that's got other people around. The shed'll be just fine. There won't be anybody but us. We'll show the film. Then I'll tell the others a few things, say a few things, and we'll be out of your way."

"When's this gonna be?"

"When it gets dark."

"When's that? How long?"

"About three hours. Be there. We need you. Remember this: Alnilam is Orion: the center, the dead center of him. Everything has to have a center. Alnilam is our name, and the center of us, too; Joel said it was his. It's all together, Alnilam and Joel Cahill's father, just coming out of the blue. But we knew you would be here; everybody knew it. It all comes; it comes right together."

"Go ahead, now," Cahill said, tired again, and more than he had been. "I can't take no more. I'm gonna sit out in the shed and wait for my dog. Then I'll sit and wait for you. Only don't talk so much, when you get back. Don't talk quite so much. I can't take it all in."

"Just a few things, Mr. Cahill. Few but important. Few," Shears concluded, "but crucial."

"Crucial," Cahill repeated. "You never did tell me what's crucial, Mr. Shears."

545

"You'll see tomorrow," Shears said. "Everything is beginning." He rubbed his hand over the back of Cahill's. "I'll be back in three hours."

"I don't know what it is you're gonna try to get away with," Cahill said, feeling suddenly that he still did not know enough; that he did not know anything at all. "Don't get yourself into any trouble. And don't hurt nobody."

"We won't. We don't think we will. Joel didn't want that."

"What did he want?"

"Just some actions, some events that nobody can look away from, that nobody can set aside. Some actions, to make some points, to establish certain things."

"You go raisin' hell out there at that base and they'll nail you, right off. The first place they'd look would be you. They'd come right to you, you and your bunch."

"They will?" Shears said, turning back to Cahill. "Suppose they do? What will they find? They'll find that a bunch of cadets panicked when one of them did. There's not much chance they'll know which one did; nobody's going to know where it started. Even if they did, and found out which one gunned his engine, so what? We're real inexperienced personnel, Mr. Cahill. Not one of us has had over a hundred and twenty hours. An airplane is still a strange thing to us: a beast, a monster, a mystery. In this kind of situation, anybody can make a mistake. Advancing the throttle at the wrong time, what is that? We're all going to be just sitting there, ready to go, ready to follow orders. The colonel's orders, supposedly. So somebody guns up too soon; a little previous, like they say. Somebody else sees him coming, hears him coming, feels like he's got to get out of the way, and then it all follows. The whole thing shouldn't take more than five minutes. It'll never go ten."

"I don't like it," Cahill said uncertainly. "Or, maybe, I don't like it enough."

"Remember, Mr. Cahill," Shears said, so that his voice would come from farther off. "Remember the colonel's AT-6. It was up there somewhere when Joel went down. Every one of us believes it was up over that fire, and in all that smoke and turbulence . . ."

"I don't want to help wreck a lot of airplanes because of some story that don't nobody really know is true, or not."

"You're not going to have to wreck anything, Mr. Cahill. How could you do that? No; all we want is to know that you're around somewhere, for us, and for Joel. That's all. That's really all. Then you can go. Go back to Atlanta; go home."

"The more I hear about this the less I like it," Cahill said, but he did not know whether he meant it or not. "I can't promise you anything. I might try to find a way to get out there, but nothin' ain't come to me yet."

"The other side of the base," Shears said. "There's just a wire fence running through some woods. There's not more than a hundred yards between the runway and the woods. Nobody's going to be looking for anybody in the woods. You can stand in there, in the trees, and . . . and hear it all." He brightened; Cahill could tell. "I'll let the others know that's where you'll be."

"Woods," Cahill said. "It's been a long time since I been in any woods. What the hell would I be doin' in woods?"

"Listening," Shears said. "You'll be listening. I'll guarantee you'll be hearing something you'll hear only once in your life. It's going to be one of those times."

"All I'm tellin' you," Cahill said stubbornly, "is that you can have the shed, for a little while tonight, if McLendon says so. About tomorrow, we'll have to see. I'll try, but I don't know right now what it is I'm gonna try."

"I'm going now. I'll be back in a little while, with the others."

"Three hours? I'll try to get a readin', somebody to tell me."

"Two and a half, now. Hold on."

He sat for a time, a short time with a long feel to it, and then got up and ran his hand over the first wall he came to. He had done this everywhere he had been since his first blindness, and could tell, now, which way the grain ran, even through a layer of varnish, though paint stopped him. Raw wood he could identify almost every time, he was sure, but there had not been that much of it on this trip; he would have to wait until he got back to Atlanta; he had a sudden image of himself sitting in a chair by a pile of lumber, going over the planks with his fingertips, with his palms. The grain he now slid along, following its direction upward and then back down, was dense, under the thin coating—varnish, maybe; lacquer—and the boards were stiff; probably thick, oddly thick for a room in a country bus station; there was no bend, no splay, no warp in them anywhere. He tried several, and after the last, the door stood, a hollowness behind itself. He opened it and started to push his hand through, but his fingers did not trust the space, and drew back from it. "McLendon," he yelled into the opening, into the hall, the still building. "Where the hell are you? Don't you know I've got to get out of here?"

He turned back and found the chair again. Heavy-headed he sat there, his body going from him piece by piece, beginning at the knee joints. He tried to hold on to his hands, but they were going too.

"Frank," McLendon said, shaking his arm gently. "Frank. Wake up. We're back. Your dog's here."

Cahill stirred, and rousted his shoulders. "OK. OK. I'm comin'," he said, struggling more, rocking himself a little. "Give me just a second."

"Take your time," McLendon said. "Everybody's right here. I got Miss Hannah Pelham with me, like you done said."

"Zack," Cahill said. "Come on, boy. Give me that big head. Give me that-there long mouth."

The dog came under his hand, and Cahill ran his fingers down the muzzle. "You been fuckin' up?" Cahill asked. "What you been doin', Horse-head?"

"He's been real good," Hannah said. "He sure ain't no trouble to me."

"Did he eat somethin'?"

"He ate what I ate. Strickaleen and rice, and some more greens."

"He don't eat greens," Cahill said. "Don't give me that shit."

"He eat these greens. He did eat 'em, whether you like it or not."

"Let's go get your stuff," McLendon said. "If you really want to go out yonder in the shed, we prob'ly ought to get you on over there."

"All right," Cahill said. "I don't have a whole lot. Just one suitcase. That's all I brought with me."

In Cahill's room they opened the suitcase onto the bed. "What you want in here first, Frank?" McLendon asked.

"Who made up the bed?"

"I did. I come up here and did it, when you was out to the base."

Cahill swung toward him. "Well . . ." he began. "That's OK. That's all right. But that ain't somethin' . . . well, shit, it don't matter."

"What goes first in your suitcase?" McLendon asked again. "What do you want on the bottom?"

"I tell you," Cahill said. "Just hand me the stuff that's in the dresser, just . . . like . . . one thing at a time, and I'll put everything in. I got my own way of doin' it."

Slowly they packed, the articles passing through Cahill's hands: one suit, a pair of work pants, two sleeveless undershirts, drawers, three pairs of socks, a worn hairbrush. "There's stuff in the bathroom," Cahill said. "Bring that, and we'll put it in last."

McLendon brought the razor, blades, the toothbrush, and the kit with the syringe and insulin bottle, clear liquid in clear glass. Before McLendon handed the kit to Cahill, the girl put her finger to her mouth, and signaled with the other hand. McLendon gave her the kit, and she stood looking down at it, and up at Cahill. She turned to McLendon, on her face an expression he would never have expected to be there; that he had never seen on anybody: helplessness, incomprehension, frustration, anger; what else? Something else; he would have liked to believe there was something else, though he could not have named it; or wanted to. He took the kit and handed it to Cahill, who stowed it on top of the underwear and the one necktie, and closed the case.

At the bottom of the stairs, close to the rattling of the restaurant, McLendon drew up. "You want an afternoon beer, 'fore you go out yonder with the hangin' zoo?"

"No thanks."

"How about a clam-a-diddle?"

"No clams."

"Gin maybe, later? When you get the bed together?"

"Yeah, maybe. Right now, just a glass of water. I wouldn't mind that, a-tall."

McLendon got the water from the counter. "Here's somebody," he said.

"Who is it?" Cahill asked, dropping his hand for Zack.

"Captain Whitehall," McLendon said, "from the other night."

"How are you?" Cahill said, lifting the same hand, but not near Whitehall. The captain came to him and took it.

"You're not leaving?" he said. "I thought you were going to be here through tomorrow, for the colonel's big party."

"Can't make it," Cahill said. "I got throwed off the base."

"I can't say I didn't hear about Foy," Whitehall said. "I thought maybe the colonel would do something about it. I wouldn't, but I thought he might."

"He did do somethin' about it," Cahill said. "He's keepin' me off the base, like I told you."

"I don't think you'll be missing anything much," Whitehall said. "The colonel's party at seven hundred feet. I might look up at it once, because of the noise. But I won't be in it. I don't fly airplanes. I ride in 'em; I tell the pilots where to fly 'em. I either do that, or I look up at 'em."

"I want to thank you for your story," Cahill said suddenly. "I want to, and I do. I do thank you."

Whitehall glanced at McLendon, and then smiled with half his mouth.

"You're welcome," said the captain. "That's the story I've got. The epic of Vunakanau Strip, and the new boys from Mareeba, and how the Falling Buzzard came up at the right time. I'm pleased that you remember. I'm very pleased."

"And I also want to thank you, Mr. . . . ."

"Captain," McLendon said gently. "Captain Whitehall."

"And I also want to thank you, Captain Whitehall," Cahill said like a schoolboy reciting, "for lettin' me . . . for lettin' me hold that thing you . . . you remember, out yonder by the tree . . . ? Out yonder the other day by the tree . . . ?"

"Why, goodness, Mr. Cahill," Whitehall said. "That's sure all right. I was glad to do it. You can hold my sextant any time."

"What was the name of that place, that airfield you went bombin' to . . . ?"

"Rabaul," Whitehall said. "Vunakanau Airstrip, Rabaul, New Britain. It was the first big raid there, and we let 'em hold a bunch of powder."

"Well," Cahill said. "It was a good story. I couldn't understand it all, you know, about the parts of the airplane, but I won't forget it. You was real good to tell me all that, you and the other fellow."

"Oh, Faulstick, you mean," Whitehall said, relieved, and yet not. "Now, you know, he *will* be up there tomorrow. Flying formation with cadets. First formation. I'm glad I don't have to do it."

"Tell him good-bye for me. Tell him I liked what he said, too."

"I will," Whitehall said. "I sure will."

Cahill put down his suitcase; he opened his hand toward Whitehall. "Good luck to you," he said. "I don't reckon I'll see no more of you." His lips changed, and the smile broke pretty well, he thought. "Don't go up in the air, tomorrow."

"I won't," Whitehall said. "Like I told you, I don't get off the ground in anything without an office. You couldn't get me up there with those half-ass kids. I might give 'em one or two looks, if I happen to think about it, and crack another beer."

"Yeah," Cahill said. "Maybe you could watch 'em through your telescope; your sun-thing."

"I might," Whitehall said. "It ain't been tried."

Cahill let go, listened to Whitehall's steps as he went, and stooped for his suitcase. Before he reached it, though, he straightened. "McLendon," he said. "You still around here?"

"I am," said McLendon, taking his eyes from Whitehall's back. "What you want?"

"I want to make a phone call. Long distance. I'll pay for it."

"Yeah," McLendon said. "We can fix you up. There's a phone in the hall, where it's fairly quiet. Or you can come on back in my place, where it's quiet enough to wake the dead."

"The hall will be all right," Cahill said. "Will you get the number for me?"

"Sure, if you'll tell me what it is. You goin' to call Atlanta?"

"No; Memphis." He handed McLendon the piece of paper the colonel had given him.

"Who is it?"

"My wife. My ex-wife, I mean. She lives there, and works in a flower shop, but I don't know whether she works on Saturday."

"We could try, anyway," McLendon said. "Is she married again?"

"Not as far as I know," Cahill said. "Just see if there's a Miz Frank Cahill, or maybe just Florence Cahill. Her name was Acree when I married her, but I don't think she ever went back to it."

"Stay here," McLendon said. "I'll go see what I can do."

He stood near the counter of the restaurant, one leg against his suitcase and the other against Zack, doing what he could to identify the smells that came from the kitchen when somebody opened the door. Bacon, he was almost sure he could tell by now. Cooking meat was the first smell he had felt confident about since the dark; when he could tell one kind from the other, and not have to think about it, he would have more than he had before. Bacon; bacon? Why bacon at this time of day?

"She's there," McLendon said.

"How does she sound?" Cahill asked, wondering, now, what he was going to say, why he was calling.

"Go find out, yourself," McLendon said, taking Cahill by the arm without fear. "As far as you're concerned, big man, she's back here in this-here alcove. You can't miss it, 'specially when I show you where it is. It's the only alcove I got; it's the only alcove in Peckover."

He sat cautiously, took off his hat, and put it on his foot.

"Hello," he said. "Hello, Florence."

At first he thought she had left the phone, but there was no buzz of a disconnection.

"What you doin', callin' me, Frank?"

"I just thought I would. You know, just to check in with you. Somethin' like that, maybe."

"What you doin', callin' me? Is it about Joel?"

"Well, yes . . . yeah it is, Florence. It . . . I'm up here in North Carolina, where he was in flyin' school, and . . . and I been here talkin' to some people, and . . . you know . . . askin' 'em about things . . . about what happened, and all." He hesitated. "They told you, did they? Who called you?"

"They told me, when they got around to it. Somebody in the Army, some colonel or somethin', he called me. He said Joel was killed in a fire. He didn't . . . he wadn't . . . I mean he wadn't burned . . . burned up . . . I mean it wadn't like he was . . . ?"

"Don't do that," Cahill heard himself saying. "Don't carry on, now. There ain't nothin' anybody can do. They ain't found him yet. They're still lookin' for him. But I can tell you . . ." He waited for his information to gather force, so that he could give it the importance it should have. ". . . I can tell you he wadn't burned up. He didn't have no . . . he didn't have no burn injuries. He got out of the plane, all right. And . . . and he got out of the fire. He got through the fire, you know. All the way through it. Through it and out of it, and there was some people right near there, that took him in with 'em, into their home, and tried to take care of him, look out after him. I think he might'a broke his arm, and he was . . . he was banged up some. But he got through the fire. The fire didn't hurt him none. The people told me that." He waited again. "I was out there, and that's what they told me."

"You say they can't tell . . . they don't even know where . . . ?"

"When they wadn't lookin', he got up and left. The man was gone, and the lady there with the house, the house and the chilrun, she couldn't do nothin' with him. Nobody could stop him. He got up and went on. Went on back out."

"Then how do you know he wadn't . . . ?"

"I just don't believe he was, that's all. They never found nothin', in the fire. They never found a thing, where the fire was at."

"You say you was out there? Out there where his airplane . . . ?"

"Yeah. I was. He went down where there was a big fire; it was a big brush fire, like. A lot of fields were burnin' up at the same time, they tell me. I went out when somebody told me where it was. I went with another man, had been Joel's instructor, his teacher, is what he was; I went on over yonder, it's acrost this-here river, with him and . . . and my dog."

"Your what? Your *dog?*"

He thought that most likely she would know; that she would have

552

been told, would have found out. But he also knew that he did not want her to repeat the question. He drew a long breath and waited, anyway. She must have been waiting, as well. "I'm blind, Florence," he said finally.

"Frank, you don't mean that." When he did not answer, she went on, and the concern in her voice was stronger than he would have expected; even when it turned sarcastic he understood that it was to bring in another interpretation than the truth. "Now, you don't mean *blind*, Frank. I know you. What you mean is blind drunk."

"No, I don't."

"You're tellin' me that you done *gone* blind? That you can't see nothin'?"

"I'm not blind drunk; I'm *blind*, blind. And you're right, I can't see nothin'. I can't, and I won't never be able to. All the lights are done gone out."

"Well, I don't understand," she said, recovering, speaking almost matter-of-factly. "I don't know why this 'us to happen to you. You was always a strong 'un. You was strong as a elephant."

"I can still do all right," he said. "I'm just blind, Florence. I ain't dead."

There was another long silence, until she asked, "What happened to you? Some kind of machinery, maybe? A band-saw blade break off and hit you? Somethin' like that?"

"No, I found out I had the sugar diabetes. It come on me real fast; doctor told me he never had seen it hit anybody so hard, so quick. I could'a maybe saved my eyes if I'd'a knowed about it sooner, but I didn't think it was anything. I just used to get real thirsty, and my weight fell off some. And I used to get . . ." He broke off. "But you don't really want to hear all this. Prob'ly put you to sleep."

"No," she said without hesitation. "Go ahead. What was it? What happened then?"

"I got to where I was seein' these things; red things movin' acrost in front of me, and all, and I used to get this feelin' . . . it was a kind of feelin', like . . . like I wadn't thinkin' right . . . that it wadn't the way I'd . . . that I would usually . . ." He gave up, changed, and tried to end. "Anyway, I lucked up on a good doctor, and he got me straightened out. I'm fine, now. I'm takin' my medicine, and I got myself a great dog. His name is Zack, and you'd like him pretty good. I know you would. Him and me get along better than anything you ever saw."

"That's fine, Frank. That's real good. It's nice to hear from you, and find out you're doin' well, that you ain't wantin' for anything. That you're just like you used to be. I do think about you, sometimes. It wadn't too bad, a long time ago. It could'a been a lot worse. We could'a give one another a lot worse time than we did."

"I don't know . . ." He began another way. "I don't know, Florence. I don't know why the colonel up here, he . . . I don't know why Joel . . ."

"I don't neither, Frank. I been askin' myself. I don't know nobody else to ask."

"Well, yeah," Cahill said, "I know what you mean. There's a lot I can't get a-holt of. I got the telegram last week, though, and I come on up here, like . . . like I was asked to do. I come up here, and I went out to where the fire was, like I said. I been doin' everything I can. I think I might stay one more day. Just that one day, when Joel would'a finished up. Some of 'em . . . some of his buddies want me to stay."

"How come?" she said, and her voice rose and hardened. "How come, Frank? You ain't never in your life paid the slightest bit of attention to Joel. Not a damn bit; not any, a-tall. Now he gets killed in a fire, and you turn up in North Carolina, a blind man with a dog. How come? How come you to do this?"

"Florence, for shit's sake, I don't know. My boy wanted me to come up here, and I did. What's so hard to understand about that?"

"Your boy, my foot. They must'a made a mistake on his records, or somethin'."

"There ain't no mistake," Cahill said slowly. "You can put that out of your head." He began to think about hanging up, but he was not ready. "You could'a come, too," he said. "There's buses in Memphis. You could'a come on over here, when you found out."

"What would I do? I don't see what good I could do. You tell me they ain't even found him, yet." She broke, but came back fast, with hardly any change in her sound. "Jesus God; they don't even know where my boy is. Maybe there ain't nothin' left of him. Nothin', a-tall. Maybe nothin'."

"Yes there is," Cahill said, and used all his will to cut himself off.

"Why did he do what he did?" she asked all at once.

"Well . . . you mean . . . there was that fire . . . that fire and a lot of smoke . . . his instructor, McCaig, he says . . ."

"No; no. That ain't what I'm talkin' about, Frank, and you know it. Will you tell me why he asked for you? Why he asked for you to come up there, and not me? Asked for you after he was dead? Will you tell me that?"

"I don't know no more than you do."

"I raised him. I looked after him. You never did nothin' with him, or nothin' about him. You never knew whether he was sick or well, or how he was doin' in school." She broke off with what she had just thought, and then brought it out. "Do you have any pictures of Joel, Frank? Do you know what he looked like? Do you know the color of his hair? How about his eyes, Frank? How about the color of your son's eyes?"

"Blue eyes," Cahill said, trying to remember who had told him. "He had blue eyes and curly hair. Curly blond hair. And . . . and he was a good basketball player. Captain . . . Captain . . . the captain told me he was."

"You still ain't told me, Frank. Why was it he put you down? Why was it you? He didn't owe you nothin'. He wouldn'a knowed you from nobody."

"This is . . . is just the way it turned out, Florence. That's all I can say."

"Well, he must'a wanted you. You and not me. Why he did I don't know, but he did."

"I don't know, either," Cahill broke in, suddenly having something to say. "But when I got here I found out some things that might . . . that might have something to do with . . . well, some things from the other boys. Some reasons he might'a wanted me to come."

"When you figure it out, be sure to let me know, Frank. Don't wait another nineteen and a half years to call me."

Relieved, he began to talk faster than usual, understanding that an end was possible; that he could put down the phone and never have to hold it and talk on the subject again. "I will tell you," he said. "Soon as I know anything, I'll get right to you. If I'm the first to know, you're gonna be the second."

"Good-bye, Frank. Let's let be."

He made the one move, but she caught him just short of finishing it.

"And, listen, Frank, if they . . . if they find Joel . . . if . . . if it looks like there's goin' to need to be a funeral, then . . ."

"We'll work it out," Cahill said. "We'll work it out all right, Florence. I promise you. He can be buried in Memphis, if that would be what you want. We can do it any way you want."

"That's . . . that's good, Frank. That's real good of you. I'll think about it."

"And listen," he said unnaturally, and startled to hear himself, "no matter how all this turns out, I might just come over there and see you, one of these days. Shit, you can't never tell."

"I won't hold my breath."

"You don't have to do that. You don't have to do nothin' special. Me and Zack, we might just show up. I can travel all over hell, you know. Bein' blind, that don't stop me. Didn't stop me from comin' up here, and it wouldn't stop me from comin' to Memphis, neither."

"Be careful, Frank. Be careful what you're doin'."

Now, he thought: now can I get off? But he could not.

"Is that all?" she asked. She rattled the phone. "You still there? Is that all, Frank?"

He could not hang up, and he did not know what he wanted to say, or if he could say anything. All at once, in a change of thought like a swerve in wind, he was no longer glad that he would never have to talk this way again, but was afraid he would not get a chance to.

"If I was . . ." he started. "If I was to come over that way, Florence, could you . . . would you fix me a cold egg?"

"Would I *what?*"

"Would you fix some eggs for me, you know, like you used to do, when we'd go off in the field, or maybe into Piedmont Park, and have us a picnic? That wadn't too bad, was it?"

"No; it wadn't. I remember some of it. I remember you told me you went out and found a waterfall, that was real pretty."

"I did. I did that."

"No you didn't, Frank. That was a bunch of lies."

"I did, God damn it. I went off back yonder, where there was a waterfall. I can still see it."

"You never done it. You went off back in the woods, and you might'a walked around a while and come back when you wanted another bottle of beer, but there wadn't no waterfall in them woods. That's just somethin' you made up."

"All right, now," he said, and could not remember any talk between them ever being this good-natured. "If you'll make me some cold eggs, I'll show you the waterfall. I know just where it is. If you'll take me and Zack where you and me was sittin', I'll show you the waterfall, next time. I can go right to it."

"I reckon I'll have to take your word for it. But I don't."

"I'm tellin' you, Florence," he said, remembering vividly. "That waterfall was right there. And there was more than one; more than one of

556

'em. There was a big rock that split one of 'em off from the other one, and you could get out on it. You could get right out there on it, and the water would fall on down past you; fall on down on both sides, just like nothin'. It was great. I ain't never had no feelin' like it. You could swear you was flyin'; that you was lifted up. That you was risin' straight on up. If you closed your eyes you'd know that you was just standin' on a rock, but if you opened 'em, and all that white water was fallin' by you on both sides, you felt like you was flyin'. It's the real flyin'; it's better than real flyin'."

"You ain't been flyin', Frank. That's another one of your lies."

"The hell I ain't. I was up with Joel's instructor, a couple of days ago. We flew all over hell."

"You? A blind man? Up in a airplane? I don't believe that for one minute."

"It's true, though," he said doggedly, but with conviction and excitement. "I don't give a damn whether you believe it or not. I was up there. Shit, I even had a-holt of the controls. I was flyin' the thing, myself. Joel's instructor said I did great."

"I got to get on off the phone," she said, and Cahill could tell that her interest, which had not really been strong, had all but gone completely. He held to the place where her voice was, though; he was not finished.

"Did he ever say anything about me?" he asked abruptly.

"Who?" she asked, but it was the suddenness that startled her rather than the question.

"Joel. Did he ever say anything about me? Ask about me? Where I was? What was I like?" He touched his face with his free hand. "Did he ever ask you why I wadn't around?"

He stayed in the silence, ready to wait, however long it took.

"Once in a while, he would," she said slowly. "He would ask me where you were, where you lived, and all."

"What'd you tell him?"

"I told him what I knew, which wadn't much. I told him that as far as I knew you were still livin' in Atlanta." Again she paused, and said in a different voice, "I told him what I knew, not what I thought."

"He never asked you what I did?"

"What do you mean, 'what you did'? You didn't do nothin', Frank. That was your trouble. Not where your family was concerned, you didn't."

"I mean, what I did to make a livin'?"

"I did. I did tell him that."

"Told him what?"

"I told him you 'us a good carpenter. I told him about all the things you could make. I told him about your planks, and all the different kinds of things you used to be able to do with 'em. I told him about the nails."

"The blueprints. You tell him about 'em?"

"Yes I did, Frank," she said, but he was not sure whether she really remembered this. "I told him about your blueprints, and about your nails. I told him about your barrels of nails, and how you used to say you liked to watch the shine off of 'em."

"They're like jackstraws," he said. "They're like jackstraws, out yonder in the sun. They really crisscross. You can build anything you want with 'em. Anything, any kind of way."

"You could do it, Frank," she said. "You won't got no argument out of me."

"How did you . . . how did you get on with him? Was he hard to . . . did he have any kind of . . . ?"

"Well, he was sort of hard to get along with, part of the time. Specially after he got on up into high school. He stayed to himself a lot."

"He played basketball, didn't he? He played up here. The captain that knew him said he did; said he was as good as he ever saw."

"Yes, he played on the high school team, and he was pretty good, from what they said. He was real quick; the other boys seemed to like him, and looked up to him. I think you'd'a been proud of him."

"Proud of him," Cahill repeated, and could not find a way to go on. "And, you say . . . you tell me . . ."

"Mostly, these-here last few years, he'd just read. He'd get off by himself and read."

"Books, eh? He kept a lot of books around? Library books, maybe? Schoolbooks? There's a book of his up here, that . . ."

"Some, but most of 'em was magazines. Cheap magazines. Some of 'em was awful-lookin'. It'd scare you to look at 'em, the front of 'em." She hesitated. "I could go get one, if you want me to. There're still some around, in his room. He never would throw any of 'em away."

"Well, I'll be damned," Cahill said. "You really could do that, couldn't you?" He smiled and relaxed in the chair. "Sure," he said. "Go get one, and tell me about it. I'll be right here. I ain't goin' nowhere."

He held on, in the expectant silence, listening to what he could hear of the inside of the distant house. Her footsteps returned, there was a rustling, a tap on the mouthpiece, and she said, "You asked for it, Frank. Here's the first one I picked up."

558

"Good," he said. "Roger. Go ahead."

"I don't know Roger, but this here's called *Terror Tales,* and it's for this same month, two years ago. On the front of it, it's got . . . let me see, here, how to put it . . . it's got a picture of a woman, and she's . . . she's in what's left of her underwear, and she's tied up, and it looks like there's these two big muscled-up men with black masks, and it looks like they're fixin' to put her in a furnace, or some kind of thing that's got fire in it; a furnace or like a pit, maybe, a hole."

"I've seen them things in drugstores," he said. "I ain't never read one. How's this-here gal takin' it?"

"She looks like she's hollerin' and carryin' on. My Lord help us, wouldn't you be?"

"What else is in there? Any other pictures?"

"Yeah. It looks like just about every story has one, but ain't none of the others in colors."

"What do they look like?"

"Well, the first one is named 'The Bride of the Thing in the Box,' and it's by somebody named Arthur Leo Zagat."

"My foot," Cahill said. "What about the picture?"

"There's this big box, right up in front. Sort of like a casket, near as I can tell. There's some men dressed up in tuxedoes, and they've got on these little bitty masks, not like them other ones, that go all over their whole head, but, you know, just over their eyes, and they're holdin' this woman, or more like a girl, to tell the truth, and she don't have on nothin' at all, except just a veil. But you can't really tell what's she's got on, because she's over behind the box."

"What's in the box?"

"You can just see a tiny little bit of what it is, lookin' through a hole, but it's some kind of snake-thing; it's got a long head, and a little eye, so little you can't hardly make it out, and they're draggin' this girl to where that thing is. Makes you wonder, don't it?"

"Wonder about what?"

"About what kind of people make these things up."

"Yeah, I guess so," Cahill said. "There any others?"

"Here's one that's called 'The Web of Pain,' and *it's* got this place supposed to look like a haunted house, and some old women, witches, maybe, have got a-holt of another girl, and they're pullin' her clothes off behind this big enormous spider web. She don't have nothin' on but rags; you can see her rear end through what's left of her dress." Paper rattled. "Is that gonna do you, Frank?"

559

"That'll do me," he said. "How about sendin' me one or two of 'em, when I get back to Atlanta? You know, just so I'll have 'em."

"I'll send you all of 'em I can find. This ain't the part of Joel I want to keep. You can have every one of these things."

"Just send 'em to me at Willow Plunge Park, Cumberland Highway, Atlanta. That'll get right to me."

"I'll do it, sure enough. But right now I've got to go."

"Good luck with your flowers. That's your name, come to think of it. 'Florence.' Don't that have somethin' to do with flowers?"

"My flowers'll be all right," she said, in a concluding voice. "I'm fixin' to buy into the shop. We're doin' real good. Wartime is good for flowers, like it is for anything else that makes money. Ain't that so?"

"It is," he said. "I got more to do in Atlanta than I can handle. Come on down next summer and I'll give you a free swim."

"I ain't lost nothin' in Atlanta," she said. "I tried it once, and I ain't anxious to go back."

"Good luck with your Memphis flowers, anyway," he said, loosening the phone from his ear. "Like I told you."

"You don't need to worry, Frank Cahill," she said. "I've done got to be one of the best around."

"I knew your eggs was good. The colder the better."

"My flowers are better than my eggs," she said. "You won't believe this, but I won second prize in the state, this year. Should'a won the whole thing, everybody tells me."

"That so? Good on you, they say around here."

"It was for a funeral wreath. The only reason I didn't win was that I put too many carnations in. The judge said they wadn't the right amount, because too many of 'em cut down on the profit. But I thought it looked better the way it was. So did the people that used it, for their little girl. Everything came out all right."

"Good-bye, Florence. It was good to talk to you."

"Good-bye, Frank. I'll send you these-here magazines."

"Thanks. I'd like it if you would."

"Give me another call, whenever you feel like it. I might be around for another twenty years. Who knows?"

"Let's both try to make it," he said, and hung up slowly, working back along the wire to the cradle.

"Come on, Zack," he said to the dog, whose breathing he could now distinguish at his feet. "We got to find us the shed, and get set up." He rose, his overcoat a strong relentless weight all over him. "We'll go down the counter and through the back," he said out loud, learning step by step that the overcoat was a load he could still carry. He turned into the diner, as he reckoned, and went slowly along the row of seats, giving no sign when a chair had someone in it, though he knew.

Two farmers, a trucker, a bus driver and a pfc. from the base watched him come toward and along them, and turned their heads one by one as he went past. At the end of the counter a boy in olive drab got up and pushed the loose hair from his eyes.

"Mr. Cahill," he said.

"What is it?" Cahill asked. "Who are you and what do you want?"

"I'm Cadet Willis," the boy said, heavy and ruddy. "I was the one fighting with Cadet Spain the other night at the cadet club, when your dog bit Spain on the leg."

"Oh?" Cahill said. He expected to meet Spain again before he left, but not this boy, whom he had more or less forgotten.

"Mr. McLendon said to tell you that he had your things out back; that he'll wait on you out there."

"That's fine, son," Cahill said, moving away. "Thanks for tellin' me. And good luck to you. Don't get in no more fights. You might not have Zack and me around."

"I won't," Willis said. "But I want to thank you for stepping in when you did. You took quite a lick, yourself. You didn't have to do that."

"It's all in the war," Cahill said. "All in the day's work. From now on, get up in the air to do your fightin'. Don't stay on the ground, tanglin' with your buddies."

"With Joel Cahill's buddies," Willis said. "Spain's the one that wants the most to be like Joel Cahill, but I've got news for him. He's not gonna make it."

"Did you make it, son? Seems to me, if I remember right, that you 'us gettin' the shit kicked out of you, last time I run up on you."

"No, sir," Willis said, coloring nearly to purple. "I tried, but Joel didn't want me; didn't want me in. I think that's the only mistake he made. For him to take Frank Spain and not me is . . . is not right."

I just need to get out of here, and on out to the bed, Cahill thought, through the hot words surrounding him. Just that; that's all, and it's not too much to ask. Just let me get something in my hands that I can do.

"Joel didn't know how I feel," Willis continued. "He didn't know what I'd do. I'd do more than Frank Spain could even think about doing." He gathered, consolidated, and went on. "Look," he said. "Let me explain it to you."

Cahill stopped, but made no attempt to face Willis; the position of his body still headed for the door.

"I've never been even anywhere near washing out," Willis said. "I never had to repeat a lesson. I passed every check-ride with minimum comment. I was the first in my class to solo, right after Joel Cahill"—he paused—"right after Joel Cahill and Blazek and Neilson. I soloed before Malcolm Shears did."

"That so?"

"Yes, sir, it is. I can prove everything I say. When this . . . when all this was starting I went to Joel Cahill and asked him if . . ."

"Asked him what, son?"

". . . asked him if . . . if I could do anything. Asked him what I needed to do."

"What'd he tell you?"

"He just told me not to ask questions, and more or less not to bother him and the others: him and Harbelis and Neilson and Shears. All those. He wasn't mean about it; he wasn't superior. But he wouldn't do it. He didn't want me, and I won't figure it out till my dying day. I would'a been the best right hand he ever had. I would then, and I still would."

"Well, I can't do anything about that," Cahill said, turning his face in the direction of his body. "You'll just have to do the best you can now, I reckon." He moved off; the back door must have been no more than five steps. After that McLendon would find him.

His arm was caught. It was not held; he jerked it loose. "What the hell, Willis?" he said angrily. "Is that you? What the hell do you want now?"

With a look that combined desperation and hope, Cadet Willis had leaned forward and taken hold of Cahill's turning sleeve, then drawn back at the abrupt savagery of the blind man's reaction.

"Please, sir, just let me . . . let me just . . ."

Again Cahill stood, silent and hostile.

"Let me just tell you the only thing I ever heard him say, in the way . . . in the way he used to talk to Harbelis and them."

Cahill nodded slowly.

"I wasn't supposed to hear this. I was just passing by, going out to fly. I was the section marcher, and Joel Cahill and his echelon were just coming off the line, not in formation. They went by, and I happened to hear him."

"But what did he *say?*" Cahill asked irritably. "What the shit did he say?"

Willis cleared his throat. "He said, 'You have to fly as though you were the last man to do it. Not the first man, but the last. Then everything that's familiar will be new.' That's what he said, word for word."

"You're sure?"

"Yes, it is," Willis said, nodding vigorously. "I would have done what he said, Mr. Cahill. Anything. I was ready. I still am."

"It's too late now. Go ahead and fly like . . . however you can fly. My boy's gone."

"No he isn't," Willis said passionately. "Why would I remember that? Why would I still think about it all the time, if he was gone?"

Cahill did not feel himself as stock-still anymore, or was he set to move, as he had been. He hesitated; he strove not to hesitate.

"Listen to me, Mr. Cahill. This'll be the last time I'll ever get to talk to you. Listen."

Cahill nodded once more, held by the sincerity and urgency of the boy's voice, despite himself.

"Even if he was burned up, even if he was drownded, it wouldn't make any difference." The boy shrugged, trembling with conviction and helplessness. "Only . . . only there wasn't time. There wasn't time to . . ."

"Time?" Cahill echoed, as if he had never heard the word before. "What time?"

"Time to let him know. Time to let him know that there were some others. If I could tell him, I would tell him now. I'd let him know that he's as much with me as he is with the others, with Shears and Adler and them. He should'a known that." His face cleared, and he stepped back and said, "Joel Cahill should know that. He should know it right now. That's why I'm telling you. It's the best I can do, now. It's just the best I can do. You're his father."

"I can't do nothin' about that, neither," Cahill said, not knowing what he meant. "The whole thing's done gone past me. I shouldn'a come up here."

"Don't say that, Mr. Cahill. Don't even think it. It matters a whole lot, that you came. There's not a cadet that's not glad you came. Shit," he said, borrowing the word from Cahill, "every one of 'em thinks you ought to be the commanding officer."

"That'd be the day," Cahill said, keeping his quick pleasure down. "That's all they need around here. A blind man the head of things."

"Everybody knows how you stood up to the colonel for us," Willis said. "Everybody knows how you backed him down."

"Well," Cahill said, more or less willing to take credit; why not? "If it was anybody, it was Zack, backed him down."

"And we heard about Lieutenant Foy's hand. Serves him right. Permanent Party KP would be too good for him."

"You boys take care of all that. I'm on my way." He truly set himself to go this time, and stepped off. Again he was caught, and let go quickly, before he could wrench.

"Tell me, sir," Willis said, not more than whispering, but with a hoarse urgency. "Are the others . . . are Shears and his . . . are Shears and his group going to . . . are you going to get together with them?"

I can't stall on this, he thought, as a sudden panic-convulsion hit him, out of uncertainty. I've got to say, one way or the other. Then resolving: just let it come, whichever way it wants to.

"No," he said. "What they do, what Shears and Spain and them others do, that's their business. I don't have no more to do with any of it."

"Are you sure?" asked Willis. "I had an idea you might . . ." He made his true appeal. "I mean, it would be a kind of last chance for me. They wouldn't regret it, I can tell you. Joel Cahill wouldn't regret it. If they would just let me come . . . if I could see the book, and find out . . . you know, all the stuff he said, and the rest of . . ."

"Good-bye, Mr. Willis," Cahill said. "And . . ." Again he hesitated, and again let it come as it would. "And watch out for . . . for other airplanes."

"We all do that, sir. We keep our head on a swivel."

"Watch out, now, son," Cahill repeated. "You watch out for them other airplanes."

He went through the door, Zack wedging past him into the coldness.

"Everything's out in the shed," McLendon said, gesturing. Hannah, standing next to him, turned with his hand, and then back. "Your bed's out there, and some screws, and I reckon whatever else it takes. The stuff from your room's in there."

"You didn't have to do that," Cahill said. "But thanks."

"It's all there," McLendon said, "but the gin. The gin is the payoff on the bet. You remember?"

"I remember, and you're gonna lose. If them screws'll fit, I'll put your bed together."

"There ain't no time limit," McLendon said. "Just let me know when you do it." He winked at Hannah. "Or when you don't."

"I'll get on it," Cahill said; then, "Some boys'll be here after while. When it gets dark. They'll know where I am. The ones that need to know, they'll know. Don't tell nobody else."

"I won't. You handle all that."

"One thing, 'fore I forget. You got a light out there, I believe you done told me."

"Yeah, I do. There's that one socket, and that one bulb. Runs off a generator."

"Do you have a double socket, maybe? The boys might want to hook somethin' up."

"Sure; I've got one. I'll bring it on out."

The air failed to move. They were inside, and Cahill closed the door. "This must be a hell of a place," he said. "There's a bunch of dead animals hangin' up. Or there used to be."

"They're still here," Hannah said. "Can we turn on the light?"

"Sure."

"I can't reach it," she said. "I can't quite get up there, and there ain't nothin' to stand on."

"Show me where it is, and kind of . . . kind of put my hand up, where I can feel around for it."

His arm was taken. He moved toward where it was pulled, and it was raised. He groped and found the bulb; turned it.

"God," she said, looking around. "God A-mighty. You gonna sleep in this place?"

"Sure. Why not? What's wrong with it?"

"It looks like a slaughterhouse. It's a good thing you can't see nothin'."

"Wouldn't bother me, no way," he said.

"Don't it bother Zack?" Narrowing her eyes she looked at the boar and the deer, half of each body in unreal light and the other half made of shadow, and the deep raw slashes where the meat had been cut from the thighs, the stopped blood on the lower sides of them.

"No. He likes it. He's used to it. He's been eatin' on these-here ani-mules. So have I. It ain't bad meat. Wild meat. It's got a green taste to it, you know. Some people call it gamy, but green is what it is. McLendon's just got 'em hangin' up till he can find some place to bury 'em. Shouldn't eat meat that's been thawed out and froze back."

Without shuddering, but shaking her head and pressing her lips together, she glanced around, had enough of it, and came back to Cahill.

"Where you gonna put your bed? You thought about that?"

"No, I ain't thought about it," he said. "You got any ideas?"

"Where you got the most room, I guess. Where you don't bump into them . . . them things hangin' up. You don't want to put yourself over by the wall, do you?"

"No," he said. "The middle's all right." He stood uncertainly. "Where're them rails, and the other stuff?"

She sized up the situation. "They're just a little to your right, and about ten feet from you, over against the wall."

He moved as she told him, his hand out to avoid the animals, and with almost no trouble found the metal bed rails where they were leaned against the rippling tin. He pulled one out from the rest and ran his hand along it, locating the holes. "This ain't gonna be hard," he said. "Shoot; ain't nothin' to it."

"You mind if I sit down?"

"No," he said. "If you got somethin' to sit on." He held up a finger. " 'Fore you do, hand me whatever they got in the way of screws around here."

"This must be them," she said, handing him a heavy lidless cardboard box.

He took it, and, picking a screw, felt it with a finger and ran his thumbnail along the groove. "Shit," he said, holding the screw up, head and point between finger and thumb.

"What's wrong?" she asked, fixing on the lit part of the screw.

"This-here's a number 9-B wood screw," he said. "What the shit's this doin' in there? Who does McLendon think he's talkin' to?" He felt of the screw again. "He don't know so much." He picked another. "This 'un ain't so bad. It might do. Now if I can find me some other ones."

She watched him go through the box, putting the screws he selected in his pocket.

"I got enough, I think," he said. "I got enough to start with."

"This-here's what I'm gonna do," he said, tapping the dirt floor with his foot. "I'm gonna put this thing together by the wall, over here, so I can lean these rails on it, and know right where they are. Then, when I get what I want, we can pull it on over into the middle; wherever looks good to you."

"That's fine," she said, sitting on the ground near the hanging boar and hugging her knees. "You sure you don't want me to help you?"

"No," he said. "Just keep me company." His hand on the long rail almost as though he were posing, perhaps with a spear, he found the direction of her voice, and spoke down to it. "This too cold in here for you?"

"No," she said. "It's all right. My nose sure won't bleed."

"That's one thing," he said. "You got to look on the good side. And," he went on with the idea, "we got plenty of room in here." He paused and grinned, more than she had seen him do. "All cold."

"Sure," she said. "We can do a whole lot with that. I don't know what, but whatever it is, we got room to do it."

He went to work, laying the rails, long and short, down on the dirt and kneeling on one knee in the midst of them. He examined everything he touched very slowly, finding the holes, pulling the screws from his pocket, and carefully, with very little groping most of the time, fitting the nuts on and turning them decisively; once he even flicked the nut and spun it down before he tightened it with his fingers. "I ought to have some pliers and a screwdriver," he said. "Maybe we can get 'em later. This bed's liable to be kind of wobbly this way, come whatever I might could do."

Finally there were no more holes in the rails, though most of the box was still filled with nuts, bolts, nails, brass hinges, tacks, and brads. The bed lay in the dirt, its legs up. Cahill stooped and turned it over, under the light. He tested it with his hand, then turned his back to it and sat cautiously. "That'll hold, just like it is," he said. "If I can get some pliers and a screwdriver and maybe a wrench, I might go over it again and tighten it up, but it oughtta keep me off the dirt, anyway. If it does, it does; if it don't, it don't."

"It's kind of a little bed, for you," she said, from the floor, her breath steaming and disappearing, like his.

"I don't need nothin' no bigger than this."

"You sure?"

"Yeah, I'm sure. Where would I get it, anyway?"

"I could sleep in that thing with you, just like it is."

"What?" he said, truly astonished. "You mean to tell me you'd come out here and sleep in this fuckin' rickety bed, in this place that ain't even got no floor in it? With these . . . with this dead deer? With this-here hog hangin' up?"

"I'd do it," she said. And then, defensively, "I would."

"I ain't goin' to ask you why," he said, "but I am gonna tell you no."

"All right, no," she said, pulling her feet up more. "I just thought I'd tell you."

"Now look here, little girl," he said, far from any area he was used to, "it ain't that I don't like you, or what you might think. I like you fine. You been real good about takin' care of Zack, and all. It's just that . . . it's just that some of the boys are gonna come over tonight, and . . . and, uh . . . and we're gonna need this place here, for . . . for some . . . well, for some things they're gonna want to do."

"Maybe I could come back after they leave. I could wait till they went back to the base."

"No," he said. "Couldn't do that. I don't have no idea how long they're gonna be here, or nothin'. You don't need to be waitin' around all that time. I don't want to be worried about that. This is my last night, and I need to . . . I need . . . well, I need to be with these kids, and you know . . . just be with 'em, and see what I might be able to do."

"All right," she said. "If that's what you want."

He changed the subject as soon as he could think of another, gratified at how quickly it came to him. "I won the gin," he said, patting himself on the leg. "We can go get it from McLendon any time. And I got a witness, too. You didn't put a single nut to a bolt. Would you swear to that?"

"I would do it."

"You want to have a drink with me? Maybe we can sneak into the other place, if there ain't no MPs around."

"Sure. A little one, maybe."

But he did not get up. He swung back and forth testing the legs of the bed, bouncing with gingerly weight on the metal laths the bed had instead of springs. "It'll hold me till I leave," he said. "Then McLendon can do whatever he wants to do with it."

"I got to hand it to you, mister," she said. "I didn't think you could do it; I wouldn'a believed it unless I seen it. I don't see how in the world you got all them little screws and things in the right places. I couldn't do that in a million years. I wouldn'a missed it, I can tell you."

"Like I told you 'fore I started," he said, settling his buttocks, "I know what I can do and what I can't do. This wadn't no real big thing. Somethin' that's already sized up for you, something that already has got parts to it, so that all you got to do is to put the parts together in the way they was supposed to be put together . . . shoot, there ain't nothin' to that. Puttin' something together is easy, because somebody else has already done done it for you. All you got to do is follow what some other man's done laid down. You'd feel bad if you fucked it up. I mean, you could get to feel real bad about that, because it would show that you was dumb. That's right," he said before she could answer. "That'd show how dumb you was, because you couldn't even do somethin' that somebody had already done done for you. You can't get no satisfaction out of that, if you do it, but you can feel bad about yourself if you can't. But it ain't the real thing to be doin', anyway. Somebody's got to do it, I reckon, for the dumb people. But it ain't what I like, and it ain't what I'm gonna be doin', when I get back."

"Are you gonna get somebody else to do everything for you? You got somebody like that? Are you rich?"

"What difference does that make?" he asked, flaring. "That ain't even what I'm talkin' about." He leaned forward, his own steam warming his face. "Listen here. You can put together, or you can make, yourself. There's a big difference, little girl. There's a whole lot of difference."

"I ain't with you," she said. "You got to tell me what you're talkin' about." She peered up at him. "I ain't dumb, though. I ain't all that dumb."

"Nobody said you was dumb," he said grudgingly, but meaning it. "You do all right. It's just that you ain't got no real call to know nothin' about this kind of stuff. That's all. You could learn about it, if you wanted to. If you put yourself to it, you could. It just takes some doin'."

She hitched forward. "What is it you say is better?" she asked. "Better 'n puttin' that bed together like that?"

"Well, makin' somethin' yourself, is better. You can make the plans, too, if you want to. That way you can have it . . . have it any way that suits you. Any way that's . . . that's right."

She had hold of a notion, of a kind that did not usually come to her. "But when you make . . . when you build whatever it is you're buildin', and you got the plans for it, even if you made the plans too, and then you build the thing, ain't that puttin' it together, just like you put that bed together? Ain't that doin' what you said you don't like? That you said ain't as good?"

"Well," he said, shaking his head, "you might have a point, but it ain't the right point." He rocked, getting his back muscles into it, rallying, to be sure enough. "No," he said hesitantly. "You see . . . blueprints are fine. I used to be real good with blueprints; I could draw 'em better than any engineer. You draw 'em, and then you run 'em through this . . . this special kind of machine, on this paper you got, and it's just beautiful; that's all I can say. It's pale, like . . . pale blue . . . like . . . well, like it was . . . there just is not no other color quite like a blueprint. The closest thing *I* ever seen is bluin', like in a washtub, you know; just a little of it, and not a whole lot of water; not deep." He caught himself, and wondered what he must look like as a blind man when he talked like this; how he must look to the girl, in whatever light there was.

"I've seen plenty of bluin'," she said, "in jail and out of jail."

He went on, a little dazed by the memory of color, half drunk on pale blue. "Now that I think about it," he said, "there's another thing that's like a blueprint, sometimes about the same color. You prob'ly seen some of these, too, in the country, and in town, in . . . in a town like this." When she did not answer, he continued. "I mean somebody's overhauls, like these farmers wear to work in. Overhauls that've been out in the weather a lot, out in the rain and the sun, and that've been sweated-up and washed a lot."

"Some of 'em in bluin'," she said.

"There you go," he said, pleased. "Overhauls can get the same color of a blueprint, every now and then. They sure can. The threads get to be almost just exactly like the lines you draw. They got that strange kind of white to 'em, like a . . . a ghost line, whatever that is. Like a line that a ghost might'a drawed. That's right," he said, caught up and going with it. "Like a ghost done drawed it, just right, comin' at it from the wrong side."

"That means a whole lot to you, don't it, Mr. Cahill? Them things you're bringin' on back?"

"They do," he said, feeling no weakness, no exposure. "Sure they do. I don't say much about 'em. But I got 'em. You know . . ." He was not sure how he would say this, or if he wanted to, but he went on. "If they 'us one thing I could go back and do . . . I mean, you know, go back and see . . . if I could see anything again, anything I wanted to, it would be that. It would just be that color, that light blue. It wouldn't have to be in a blueprint, or in a washtub, or in somethin' somebody was wearin', or was hangin' up. It could be the sky, like. It could be the whole sky, just for a minute. I wouldn't ask for nothin' but that."

"I hope that'll come back to you," she said. "If there was any kind of a way."

"There ain't one, yet," he said. "Maybe later on they'll think of somethin'. Right now I got to hang on to what I got."

"There's a whole lot to you, Mr. Cahill. I don't believe I ever seen so much."

"My boy, he had plenty to him, now," Cahill said. "Don't nobody around here know what to make of him."

He did not know what to expect, but he found that he expected something; he had no way to go on from where he was. "You knew him . . . in . . . in a way, so you tell me. You knew him about as well as anybody did, except maybe McCaig."

"I know a lot about him that McCaig don't know."

Again he waited. He did not want to be left with only this, and could not for the life of him figure out how to get more. "I won't ask you nothin' about how . . . about how you and him . . ."

"You already know most of that," she said matter-of-factly. He was startled when he heard what could not have been anything but a laugh, low and with complicity in it. Intimacy? "You and him done been there. Only you like music better than he did." She paused. "He heard it, though. Same music, same songs; everything."

"Too bad he didn't like it more." Collecting, remembering, he said, "We done heard the same broom. That's good, ma'am. We done heard the same broom singin'. I don't fight that, a-tall."

"He really wadn't much like you, Mr. Cahill. I gotta tell you. There was maybe some ways I didn't see, but I couldn'a told you had the same blood as him. Maybe in a few ways, but it'd be hard for anybody to make 'em out."

"You don't have to go into all that, little girl," he said. "I've done asked about all the questions I want to. One of these days somebody'll find out what happened. But I can't do it. It's more than I can get on to. They can have it. The colonel and them, they can have it. The Air Corps, the war, all of it. Me and Zack are gonna be here one more day, and that's all that's gonna be."

"Back to Atlanta," she said, more slowly. "Back down there, where you say the best is at?"

He was caught out, and he realized that he had not been following his own earlier talk closely enough. "What? The *what* is?"

"The best. Whatever's better than just puttin' things together."

"Yeah," he said, recovering. "That's right. I'll get back to buildin' on my park."

"How're you gonna do that, without bein' able to see no blueprints?"

"I'll find some way to get around that part of it," he said. "Besides, sometimes you don't need none. What you're makin', you just go with it, go along with it, wherever it wants to go—this way, that way, up, down, acrost. I like to build goin' up. That's *really* the best; that's the best that the best has got. That's where you can stand on what you're makin'. See all over hell."

"You could bust your ass."

He paid no attention. "I like to build up, but I like to build out, too. And build around. And I like to build in. In, where don't nobody but you know what the hell's goin' on."

"You must not be much of a carpenter, if you don't even know what you're doin' when you're doin' it."

"You ain't got the picture," he said. "You ain't got no idea what I'm talkin' about."

"No, I ain't."

"Look here, now. Say you got yourself some room. You got some planks, and some nails. You got tools, and you got a idea—just a idea— of what you might want to make. Then you start out. You start doin' it; you start goin' somewhere."

"Where? Where do you go?"

"It don't make no difference. Not at first, it don't. Now see," he said, flattening his hand on the air and sliding it edge-on, "suppose you was just startin' to lay yourself down a floor. Well, you can put one plank down alongside another one, can't you? You can lay one off the end of the last one, can't you?"

"I might could," she said. "But it ain't none too likely that I'll be doin' it, any time soon."

"But you *could* do it, God damn it," he said. "Anybody could get somethin' started. Right up to then, you're just goin' along . . . just goin' along, you see . . ."

"And you keep on?"

"Then," he said, clenching the hand as it stopped its slide, "then somethin' comes to you, right while you're workin'. What you've already done made tells you what to do. But that ain't all. Right in there, right when you're not thinkin' about what to do—you might even be makin' a point not to think about it—it comes to you: somethin' that you ain't never . . . than you never would'a thought of in a hundred years.

Not if you already done used a thousand boards. Somethin' you wouldn't think of in a million nails."

"Keep on," she said intently; he was sure that intentness was in the sounds.

"Then you go on, with whatever it tells you to do. It may be a turn—just a turn in the floor, at a . . . at a angle. It might be a window. A door, maybe. A trapdoor, up or down. It might be a mirror, in a certain place. And if you ain't got it with you, whatever it takes to do that thing, you go and get it right quick. You got to go with it. You don't get a idea like that every day; you got to go where it says." He stopped, tired and excited and confused. "I never thought about it, but that's what happens to you: the notion comes out of you, and . . . and you follow it on." He plucked at his chest with both hands. "Maybe, later on, you could come down and see some of this stuff, see my park. I'm buildin' the craziest house you ever saw, in the world."

He sat back, and found himself smiling; very cold and his lips wide, his teeth against the air and paining, between the still outside and his breath. "Let's take off," he said all at once. "I'm all finished up in here."

"What you got?"

"You mean in Atlanta? I told you, I . . ."

"I mean, what you got everywhere? What you got in the world? What you got in your head, blind man? Tell me. Tell me about it."

"Shit," he said, and realized immediately that he was stalling. "Tell you? What you want me to tell you?"

"What you got. What you done. What you're keepin' with you, when you can't see nothin'."

"What good'd that do?"

"Some, maybe. Wouldn't hurt nothin'."

"Where you want me to start?"

"Wherever the start is. Just like you said: whatever comes to you, first."

"Well," he said, almost counting, then counting on his fingers, "my father worked for Merita Bread Company. He 'us a baker. My mother was from Jonesboro . . ."

"That ain't what I'm talkin' about. You ain't lettin' it come."

What the hell is this? he thought.

"Come at me," she said boldly. "Come at me, blind man, right here and right now."

"All right, then," he said. "I used to skate a lot. And I had a brother

573

named Perrin, and he was a prize fighter. His fightin' name was Kid Tanazian. Does all that have some kind of interest for you?"

"It does have. But that ain't all. There's things more important than them."

"I'll just go along, then," he said, "if that's what you want."

"Tell me what you see. Tell me what you're lookin' at right now. All the things. Tell me just as fast as you can."

"Let's see . . ."

"Don't hold up. Talk, and keep on doin' it."

"Well, there was these-here other deer horns, was in a dream I had when I could see. There was all different parts of a devil I seen the other night, when I 'us up in a airplane with McCaig; I saw 'em just as sure as I ever saw anything before I went blind."

"Keep on."

"I saw that, and I saw . . . I saw a kind of long string of blood in my swimmin' pool, where there was a little girl had done pulled off her toenail on the ladder in the deep end; it kind of went round, it kind of spooled up on itself in that green water, you know, and was right there, just like that, for a second, and then it went on and faded out."

"But you kept a-holt of it."

"I did; that's one of the things."

"What else?"

"Well, there's my towers I done built. I used to climb up in one of 'em at night, climbed up it just like I was buildin' it all over again, you know, goin' up on every slat, every rung I nailed it, and . . . and I'd just sit up there, and listen to the dogs bark, in them yards that was down below and off to one side, and I could hear the cars and trucks on the highway, and all. Sometimes I'd have my level with me, up there, and I'd watch the bubble, and it and the moon'd balance out. That's how good my railin' was. Everything that was around trued up, and couldn't do no other way."

"There's somethin' to you. I done told you, now. There's more'n you think you got."

"When I'm back in my park, thinkin' about it, there's . . . there's just a lot of stuff. I got this Mexican boy, name is Ruíz Alonso, and you'd like him—anyway, he can swim like . . . just like some kind of a animal, at night, you know, and he's in that light green water; he's just like a shadow, and he goes along in them lights, them lights shining from under the water. And he can sing, too. I used to sit and listen to him when he 'us cleaning out the pool, that had done been drained, and you couldn't see him down there, and you could hear him singin' them Mexican songs, down in them walls, and it was like it was comin' out of . . . like it was comin' from somewhere that . . . that maybe wadn't really anywhere, anywhere at all, but you could hear it anyway, you was supposed to hear it, and me and my lifeguard, Darrell Cochran, he's a freckle-faced boy works for me in the summertime, we'd look over yonder toward the pool, and Darrell would put down one of them cheap magazines he was a-readin', this-here was about airplanes, too, where there was a red airplane with three wings and a skeleton was the pilot of it, supposed to be a German, and . . ."

"That's good, Mr. Cahill. I could listen to a whole lot of that."

"I ain't about to run out, now you got me started," he said. "What time is it, though? I want to be in here by myself when the boys get here." He grinned again, nearly as openly as before. "And I want to go collect that gin. It's mine." He got up. "It's mine, now, and McLendon's carryin' it around. We can't let him do that no longer, can we? He might take up with it."

He was up. With his getting to his feet he expected his overcoat, and his body with it, to increase in weight, to pull on him, to tell him how tired he was and how useless everything was that he had been doing for the last week. But it was not so. With his rising from the unsteady bed something else lifted also, and he stood squarely and full of power, his darkness creative and eager, ready for development and battle.

"One more time," she said. "Go on, right where you are. One more time."

"We got the shadow in the pool, swimmin' on out over the green lights, we got the blood spoolin' up on itself in that same water, in the daytime, we got the sun hittin' off the dimes and quarters."

"Back up. I didn't get that part."

"That's a little game I play with the people at the pool on Sunday. I throw up a bunch of dimes and quarters, and a few half-dollars and silver dollars, and anybody that wants to can go in after 'em, and keep what they can bring up. I don't care who gets what. It's when them silvers scatter out before they hit the water, that's pretty. And then . . . and then . . ."

She said nothing, did not encourage him, but the atmosphere was as it had been made, and he went on.

"I got a snake I made out of a real snakeskin—a rattlesnake skin I bought—a snakeskin and a buzzer and a bunch of springs, his name is Buster, and I got a waterfall I remember, that you could stand in amongst, with it goin' down, on down past you, and that my wife Florence don't even believe was there; she told me she didn't this afternoon, but it is, it is there, and it's better than flyin', a lot better, and the next best flyin' I ever saw was when there was this kid in Piedmont Park with a airplane that went backwards but it would really fly, stayed in the air a whole minute, went out of sight, over crost the lake, there, and when I first come up here, and I heard the airplanes out yonder on the base, heard 'em all the way back here in town, and they was just gettin' 'em started, early in the mornin', warmin' 'em up, you know, I just had this notion of this one wing, this one great big wing, you see"— he spread his arms, and then spread them wider—"and it's got snow on it. It went just as far as you could see; it went out of sight, but it was still a airplane wing, just one, that went on and on. That's what the engines done, the first mornin' I was up here. I was standin' at the window, and as soon as one of 'em cranked, that wing come into my head, and just stood there, all the way out to the trees. On out, too, maybe through the trees, and on." He tilted his head toward her. "They got trees around here—I mean, way on out from town, don't they? Way on out, like I'm talkin' about, far out?"

"Yeah," she said. "They got 'em. This place used to be all trees; the town, the base, the mills, the farms, and all. You can have your trees. They're out yonder, where they don't do nobody no good."

"That's all I got," he said, tiredness seeping back in, but not as deadly as it had been. "That's all for now, anyway. We got to get along."

"You stay here," she said, and meant for him to. "You stay here with Zack. And don't stand in the door. Don't let nobody see you. I'll go get McLendon."

"All right," he said, stretching his legs and feeling around him with his hand. "I'll be here."

He waited near the door, so that he could be near moving air. There was no wind, but the space just beyond him was not dead. Something had hold of the wall, there was more air, and McLendon spoke to him.

"Let me see that bed," McLendon said. "Let me feel that bed. Let me sit on that bed."

"You better not do nothin' else on that bed," Cahill said. "You're liable to be sorry."

"Let me bounce on that bed," McLendon said, " 'fore I give up this-here gin."

Metal squealed, and quit. "Here's your gin," McLendon said. "You earned it. And I'll even give you some pliers to tighten up your bunk, if you want 'em."

"It'll be all right, like that," Cahill said, finding the bottle where McLendon held it. "I'm tired of screwin' with them screws." He turned back into the shed.

"Some people was lookin' for you, Frank."

"What people? MPs?"

"One of 'em was a MP. The other one was from the sheriff's office. A fellow I went to high school with; Odell Hinson, his name is. He was basketball manager."

"What'd they want?"

"Wanted to know where you was."

"What'd you tell 'em?"

"I told 'em, Frank," McLendon said, his tone going easy, "that you was on down the road."

"I will be, soon enough," Cahill said. "I'll be on down in through them mountains, and on home. You won't have to worry about lyin' for me, 'cept this one time."

"This puts me in it with you, Frank," McLendon said, more seriously. "I hope you know what you're doin'. Trouble is what I don't need."

"Won't be none. I'd just like to ask you for a couple more things."

"If I got 'em."

"I'd like it if you 'us to drive me on out to the base tomorrow, right before they start the parade, and whatever else they're fixin' to do."

"Sure. I'll go out there with you."

"I want to go way around to the other side of the base. There ain't but one gate over there. One gate and one guard. The fence must be a couple of miles long, and we can . . . and you can prob'ly find me some way to get in there; me and Zack. Then, after the thing's over, you can pick me up. I'll make it so I won't be hard to find, when the boys get through."

"I don't know if I can do what you want," McLendon said. "But I'll go out there with you, and look around. We'll see what we can come up with. What was the other thing, now?"

"I need some more sugar. Can you give me some?"

"Yeah," McLendon said. "I guess so. What happened to them other cubes I give you? You eat 'em?"

"No, I didn't need 'em, a-tall. But I lost 'em, some way. I must'a left 'em up in that other room, where I was. They may still be up there, prob'ly in the bathroom."

577

"I'll get you some others, come tomorrow, if you think you can get along all right till then."

"I'll be fine," Cahill said. "I feel good; I feel as good as I have since I've been up here. But do give me some cubes in the mornin'; I'm supposed to keep 'em around."

"I'll remind you. Just don't fuck up with your needle between now and then."

"Can you look all around for me, right now?"

"I'm lookin'. What am I lookin' for?"

"That MP and the other fellow."

"They're gone on; I don't see 'em."

"Let's see if you and me and . . . Miss Hannah, here, see if we can't sneak on back into your parlor, and knock on this gin a little. You know, in that place where we 'us eatin' with the captains, where you got the good wood."

He waited on the bed against the wall, breathing slowly and deeply of the cold. The light in the double socket was warm; it was on. A small deal table was under the light, the two hanging animals, and one split-bottom chair. His hat on and down low, he waited, moving his feet occasionally in the dirt.

After a while Zack was not restless, though he did not move at first; Cahill heard him sniffing one of the animals. He wondered how much difference the cold, the frozenness of the meat, changed the smell, when the blood was hard. There must be much less to pick up; he could get nothing himself, though he tried, when he heard the dog. At last, though, Zack came back to him and settled against the side of his leg.

The shed rang. It was not the door; not a wood-sound, but one that hit far back in the head, involving the throat. He got up, and feeling something brush his knee, maybe the deer antler, went to the door, feeling from metal to wood.

"Who is it?" he asked.

"Harbelis. Cadet Harbelis."

"Come on in," Cahill said, moving back.

His hand was taken. Harbelis spoke in a low voice, though not a whisper. Low, though; something like a church voice. No; not something like; more or less exactly. "The others'll be here," he said. "They're right behind me."

"I ain't got much to offer you," Cahill said. "From what they tell me, this must be one hell of a place to meet. Full of critters. Must be like a upside-down zoo, or somethin'."

"It's good enough," said Harbelis. "As long as it's got electricity. That's all we need. It won't take long."

Another knock, this time on wood. Harbelis opened the door, enough. Cadet Adler came in, straight to Cahill, and took his hand in a strange strong grip. "Thank God," he said. "We've got the whole thing, now. We've got it. We can't thank you enough for staying, Mr. Cahill. We just can't thank you enough. This is the honor of my life."

"Well, come on in," Cahill said, holding to the hand and drawing on it. "Welcome to everything we got."

"What God does, we will," said Adler, taking a half step toward Cahill.

"What? Come again."

" 'What God does, we will,' " Adler repeated. " 'Will' is a verb in itself," he explained, "and not part of another verb. It means that what God does, we're already making happen, because we want it that way. At least that's what I think it means; it's the best thing it could mean. Especially right now, it is."

"This somethin' of Joel's?"

"Yes," Adler said. "One of the short things. Most of them are longer than that."

Another person was in the room; one whom Cahill had not heard come in. Adler let go his hand and another took it almost at once; there was hardly any emptiness between hands. But it was Adler's voice that spoke. "Here's Blazek, Mr. Cahill. He can quote you every one of 'em."

Cahill did not insist; he had not found any new way to indicate that he understood, when he did not.

" 'When the rock splits,' " Adler began.

"That ain't it," the voice now directly in front of him said. "You got that confused with 'the rocks are cloven': that other thing. That ain't what you mean."

"What do I mean, Mr. Blazek?"

"You say the first, again, and I'll bring in the other thing, and show you where you're wrong," Blazek said quietly, with a resonance unlike anything a young boy would have, or use.

" 'The rocks are cloven,' " Adler said, just as quietly.

" 'When the air splits, and closes again behind,' " Blazek said.

"All right," Adler said.

579

"All *right*," Blazek repeated, bearing down on the last sound with a satisfaction in which there was, at once, something very young.

"Crider's here," another voice said, which might have been Harbelis's. "Come on in, Billy. You're the man. You're gonna be the man. The man with the plan."

"It ain't my plan," said a country voice. "But I'm the man. I'm the one gonna do the thing. You know, the *thing*."

He shook with Cahill, very small-handed and cold. " 'When the father arrives, Orion will leap free,' " he said, pronouncing "arrives" as "ay-rives."

"Seems like I've heard that one before," Cahill said. "That one, I do know."

"Spain and Shears and Neilson and them ought to be here pretty soon," Harbelis said; Cahill could tell, now, that it was Harbelis, from his long walk with him in the snow. "Give us a couple more, Vaughan, while we're standin' around."

Someone cleared his throat, but the silence did not break. Before it had really gathered, however, Blazek said, reciting, slowly and with confidence, "The propeller is the face-on image of an endless rail."

"You're fuckin'-A," someone else said.

Blazek went on. "The end is where we leave it, and descend into the infinite field where there is nothing but nihilism and music; nothing but us."

"Nothing but us," two voices gave back.

From the door, more bodies; the chill pressed from there; warmed, even. A new voice said, "The construction of a god out of high-speed metals." Another followed immediately: "We break through the machine without breaking it, without disturbing one rotation of it." Yet another: "To be carried on what you breathe; is that not miracle enough? To ride on what is inside you, and is, literally, more vast than the world."

"Speakin' of the machine, we've got it," said a new voice, precise and not Southern. "Let's pull this table over, back a little ways."

"Where're you gonna show the thing?" another Northern voice asked. "We ain't got a sheet, or nothin'."

"We'll show it on the wall," the exact voice said. "It's got some ripples in it, but you ought to be able to make out when he comes on. If you can't tell, I'll tell you. I'll stop the film. I know just where he is, in it."

A long-boned hand took hold of Cahill's. "Malcolm Shears," the owner said. "We're all here now. The big team is in."

"All right," Cahill said. "Now what? What's on your mind?"

"You'll see," he said, and then immediately, "I'll tell you about it, while it's going on. Just stand right here, by the table, and I'll cue you."

"I'll hold what I got."

"While Spain sets this damned Special Services projector on your home table, here, we might get our own Cadet Blazek to give us a few more short words, if he don't mind." Then the same voice said quickly, before Blazek could start, "But first I've got one, to set the balance straight. Just to make sure the people who are not with us get their oar in. Joel said this, too. He believed in the balance, before you go past the balance."

"All right, Shears," a voice behind Cahill said; a voice as tall as he; taller. "Let's have it from the other side."

"If they call this a pipe dream, they're right. If they call it a schoolboy fantasy, they're right." He broke off. "Since you ask, what's the rest of it, Neilson?"

"But what schoolboy has ever tried?" the tall voice said.

"We got it," Shears said. "They'll say what I said, and we'll say what you said." He paused again. "And we'll do what we do."

"Amen," said Blazek. "We got time for one more?"

"One more's about it," Shears said. "Put it out there."

Once more Blazek intoned, low, rich, with each syllable distinct, as though over radio, from one aircraft to another: "When we move for full control we will be emerging from the war, called a World War, into the real one: the one that has never been fought, or even imagined. There is only one victory, and the main thing about it for Alnilam is that when we have it we will throw it away, and live in the silence and space and music where it has brought us. We shall be weightless, but still control the ground under our feet."

"It's all there, gentlemen," Shears said. "It's all there, beginning tomorrow. The big field. The purple that you see. The purple that's as far as you can see, right at the limit."

The low voice came in slowly, even more exact, as though giving numbers, headings that must be understood, frequencies, map coordinates: "A great field with no flowers, and an extension of clear water within the city, glittering with our initials. For that field Orion was put into the sky, and Alnilam put into the center of it. No one who stays with me"—a shudder came through the room, and took Cahill with it as well

—"and is not killed, will fail to see that field. And some will enter it. Then we will see what is there for us, and the long music will start."

"All set," said Spain's high forcing voice, almost a woman's. "We're all connected."

"Shoot it," Shears said, in the same tone as when Cahill had first heard him over the public address system. "Hit the lights."

Silence, of the sort where the sounds of the human throat, of the human tongue and teeth, fall off, though there are certain clickings, and the sounds of clothes take their place; of socks rubbing together, of shoes, of shoelaces, even the snick of lace tabs against each other. Cahill sat in this, and listened also to what was among them, between them, certain and uneven; a run as of continuous shedding, of crackling or peeling. Shears was close at his ear, not touching but quietly insistent, unhesitant, trying to give him images, one after the other.

On the table, braced now with a cadet on each side, the old projector, a Pathé EK-119 eight millimeter, spread its light forward. On the rippled side of the shed, blurred in a rectangle of impure light, the hangar of an airfield took place in what looked as though it might be hard sunlight, but here was rainy with streaks and shadow, intermittences of darkness that slotted and failed from the machine itself, but rallied, but came back to throw on the unsweating metal the hangar again, and two planes—no; there were more; there was a suggestion of many that were not shown, that could not be shown, but that were there; above the closest already were two flags, one of the United States and the other a round wind sock fluffed with soundless air.

He now heard Shears, truly heard him, where he had not before, caught in the click of shoelaces.

"Could you show that over?" he asked. "And tell me about it? I missed the start, some way."

"Crank it back," Shears said. "Start the whole thing over. We got to go round another time."

"All right, now," Shears said after a moment. "We're moving again."

"What's there, now?" Cahill asked, listening to the film peel and crackle, the teeth in the spools waver and pull.

"It's the front of the main hangar," Shears said. "You got the hangar, and you can see two, you can see two and a half planes, and the flags, and all. And now . . . and now . . . we got another shot, and there we are: there we are, the graduating class and the senior class, the rising class, you know, and the incoming class. There we all are. You can see the whole bunch, right now, you can see us, but you can't see anybody, you know, see anybody in particular."

Cahill understood that he was part of the breath around him in the dark; he was in the same rhythm; it felt right to him: he wanted to be there. The other bodies had done away with the cold, except for that cold just inside his nostrils, which was like a twin blade that turned not in pain but excitement, crisp, necessary, vital and creative. He inhaled, sucking-in his nose on the sharpness, leaning forward again; leaning more.

He sat among boys, imagining a line of them, set before him but moving toward him along his look, one fresh face after an-

"All right, now, here it comes," Shears said to the room, and then, to Cahill, "The long shot's gone, and we're just at the end of the line: we're just at the end of the line, Mr. Cahill. The colonel's got the incoming class first. There's Norcross, you might have met him; he almost got in here. There's Cate, who never did even

583

other, one silent, straightforward stand, and maybe—if the wind was blowing the flags, if it really was—clothes, even a piece of hair at the side of somebody's head as the camera moved, as the wind moved, quivering where you could see it; stirring, standing alive where it was, falling back, picked up again, not still.

More quiet; deeper, as the film peeled. But the quiet was different now; there was more breathing in it. Cahill held his position exactly, waiting for Shears to go on, but within the aura of the others he felt his own heartbeat increase, and he was on the point of reaching for Shears, to pull his voice from him, get him to go on describing, when Shears spoke without this.

Shears's calm voice rose and quickened, until it approached the sound of a sports announcer's, like—Cahill thought —like the man who announced the Joe Louis fights.

"God damn," a hushed voice behind him said. "Look. Look at that." Another, near Cahill's face, let out a long air with a sound in it, and control leaving.

solo. There's shit-head Willis, that you . . . that you were trying to help out the other night . . . at the club. And on down; we're going on down. There's Whitlock . . . there's Tyree. There's Minton Bell, who might make it; Joel liked him, what he saw of him . . ."

"Here's our class now. There I am a month ago. There Neilson is . . . now we're going . . . now we're going along slowly, Mr. Cahill, right down the line . . ."

"Here it comes. At first there's just a flicker . . . you can see . . . he's right behind Adler, there . . . now right between Adler and . . . what's that other cadet's name . . . now he's . . . Now."

584

Cahill gave all of himself forward, and put out the most absolute effort of his will, and beyond it, to create the screen. His imagination was strong enough for the line of boys, and he filled them in with the faces of boys he had known, and with those of some of the cadets as he had come to imagine them; he put in the pfc. from the bus with the cut hand; he put Ruíz into uniform, and any young face he could remember; his brother Perrin the welterweight, and the bull-boy from track practice, his blue trunks, his gold stripes slashing, but he could not reach what the boys around him were, within their presences; what one of them, far off in the room, was crying, was sobbing about as he looked, as another pounded his fist into some other flesh, most likely his own.

Against himself, and yet not, Cahill stood up, at first hesitantly and then fully. For a moment he stood in the room facing the invisible boy on the screen, with no description as part of it; with Shears silent. Then he sat down, leaning forward as before.

"And that's Joel Cahill," Shears said. "There's your son, right there, right there in the middle of the light." He spoke urgently to Spain. "Stop it right there," he said. "Back it up and stop it right on him. Give everybody a chance to get a good look. And I want to tell Mr. Cahill . . . tell him whatever I can."

With deadly excitement, Shears leaned to Cahill. "We've got him centered now. He's standing at attention, with the rest of our class. He's just standing there like everybody else."

"Can you see . . . can you see if he's . . . can you see what he's . . . ?"

"We're fairly close in on him now," Shears said.

"What is it, sir?" Shears asked. "What can I tell you?"

"I want to know if his hair is . . . is kind of . . ."

"You can't see that," Shears said. "He's got his hat on. Just one little piece, one lock, that looks like the wind might'a caught it. It didn't get to Adler's or Harbelis's. Just his."

"What else? What else about him?"

"I didn't notice it before, but his eyes are not straight forward, like, say Adler's are. He's looking just a little to one side. You can hardly notice it, but if you look real close you can see it. His face is not real serious, either. He's got an expression that . . . that some officer might tell him to wipe off his face."

"That'll be the day," Cahill heard somebody to his left come out with. "That'll be the day," another said. "It sure will."

"Ah, shit, shit," Neilson said helplessly. Shears turned around, but with understanding. "That's him, all right," Neilson said. "You remember what you remember, but when you see a thing, a thing like this, you know there's always something you didn't . . . you didn't quite . . ." he broke off.

Cahill believed he had the piece of hair, the one lock, the stir of wind on a head. That was all, but he had it, he was certain; his version of it.

Cahill closed his eyes, and did what he could to imagine what eyes on a movie screen looked like. He could not remember ever having tried to notice, and wondered if anyone had. Everything on the screen was either gray or black. Blue eyes would probably be light gray, and brown would be black. In front of him in the cold space where Cahill sat, the boy in the stopped picture must be standing there with light-colored eyes, light blue—maybe even gray-blue— looking to one side of center, amused at something that could not be known. They were blind now, Cahill felt with a hideous shock entirely new to him. They were blind, the body where no one could find it.

The new voice was deliberately calmed-down, not in what Cahill would have guessed its natural way of going, which must have been assertive, full of rapid reasons. Now it was slow, picking its way from point to point.

"But God A-mighty, that's him. Everything. Everything." Then, "Keep it on for a minute, Malcolm. Keep it on just like that."

"His eyes, now," Shears said, concentrating as much on memory as on the screen. "You can't tell from this, but . . ."

"They could'a been any color, Malcolm," Blazek said. "They were blue, but . . ."

"No; they were blue-green," Harbelis said quietly. "They were blue-green, and you could not see any veins in the white part; you could not see one red vein."

"Blue-green, blue; that don't matter all that much," Blazek said. "It was what was comin' through 'em, out of him. You could look straight at 'em, if he wanted you to, if he didn't mind, but if he did mind, you couldn't. They would tighten down, and light up. That was when you were comin' in to where he was. That was when you knew you could do anything. You didn't need to look at him any more."

"Let me tell you," said Adler, getting up and walking through the others, the lamp-twilight, to Cahill, and half squatting until their heads were level. "He's there looking off to his right. What might be there for him to see is just some woods, over across the runway. There's a long patch of trees that runs between

Cahill felt a fuller presentation than Shears had given him.

There was a little of the classroom in the atmosphere, now, as Adler talked; mathematics, maybe; and an instructor who knew the subject so well that he could afford to be friendly. And yet his sound was not matter-of-fact, but meditative, considered, with resignation in it somewhere, even bafflement.

The gear-grind started again, and inside it, with it, the stiff-paper crackling of film. The picture was moving off his son. Had it left him yet? Was there something else there now? Someone? Some other boy? Who? Was he gone?

"How about . . . how about the . . . the expression on his face?" Cahill asked, trying to keep desperation down. "Is that . . . is that like it was, the last . . . the last you . . . ?"

the field and the fence, and that's all you can see. He's either looking at that, or he's got his mind on something else.

"He's standing straight, but he's relaxed; he's a lot more relaxed than the rest of us." Adler leaned to Shears without taking his eyes off the screen. "Could we go on?" he asked. "I want to see if there's any kind of movement; anything he does that we can't see this way."

Shears nodded. "Everybody got this?"

No one said anything; a boy coughed into a handkerchief, making himself farther off, hidden.

"Go ahead, Spain," Shears said. "Pick it up."

"There's nothing else," Adler said.

"No, there isn't," Shears reiterated. "He didn't move a muscle."

"No," Adler said, considering, and then considering again. "His expression didn't change. When the projector . . . when the projector put the life back into him . . . you know, if you don't mind me putting . . ."

"I don't mind," Cahill said. "Tell me what you started out to tell me."

"When the camera moved on by him, the expression was just the same, like I told you, and Malcolm told you. Just before the camera went off him, and on down the line, his expression was like it was. The wind might'a caught in his hair one more time, but his expression didn't change at all. When the picture moved it didn't change him, but just made him more . . . more . . . more the same, I guess you could say."

"That all of it?" Cahill asked, feeling for the chair-back with his side, shifting for comfort.

"That's all that means anything," Shears said. "The rest is the graduating class."

"Fuck them," Billy Crider said.

"Right," Shears said. "Fuck them. They don't matter. They got here too early."

"I'm much obliged to you boys," Cahill said. "That's as close as I've done come to Joel. I ain't liable to come no closer." He stretched, and revolved his shoulders. "I'm much beholden to you, Mr. Shears, for everything you told me. And you too, Mr. Adler; you been a real big help. I thank all of you," he said, sweeping an arm to include the others. "I sure do."

"We're glad you could find us a place," Shears said. "I wanted everybody to see this, before tomorrow. To have you here, Mr. Cahill, and this . . . this shed, this building, like it is . . . I don't think anybody's going to forget it."

"Glad you could come," Cahill said, getting up. "And I'll do my best to be out there tomorrow. Now, I reckon we all ought to try to get us some sleep."

"We're not quite finished, Mr. Cahill," Shears said. "I want to say a few things, and we want to close out this . . . this session, like we used to do. We have some things we do together.

On his feet, Cahill listened, though he understood right away that Shears was addressing him only secondarily. There would be a time, before they left, that they would have to come back to him.

"We all know what to expect tomorrow," Shears said cleanly and strongly. "The weather will be good, maximum visibility and cold. No snow, no overcast, no mist; everybody can see. As soon as Billy makes his move, you're on your own." He stopped, and then repeated, more strongly. "All of us are on our own."

He stood and listened. The conviction in the boy's voice was nearly frightening, but the force of it was so great that it was impossible not to wait with full attention for the next words. Ca-

"It'll all be over in just a few minutes: three minutes; no more than five; I don't see how it could possibly go over five."

hill went with them, powerful in the cold, sweating, the breath from his mouth steaming his face.

Cahill knew that, no matter what, he would be across the field from them. What they could do, he could do; they would not have to go into the situation without him.

This was a new emotion for Cahill, and he would not deny it, either for their sake or for his. But what was it? How had it come over him, stronger than any longing, stronger than sex, stronger than strength, than his own arms and back?

Torrentially flight swept over Cahill, his time in the air, the lifting of his body from the ground in the irresistible and unstoppable noise, the near-solid rush past his head and up his sleeves, the dandled tilt of his position, the sense of precariousness and climb, the turning, as a thing that would happen in a dream, if it

"That won't matter," Neilson said. "Time will be gone."

"Anybody have any questions?" Shears asked. "Anybody have anything to say?"

"No," Blazek said. "We'll say it all tomorrow."

"Now remember," Shears said with finality. "Remember who you are. Remember what you're there for. Remember, right now, that the whole of Alnilam—all of it—is in this room right now. This is the middle of the Hunter. And the whole of Alnilam—everything we've got of it—will be out there on that field, in that parking area, in front of those hangars, tomorrow. This is where we start. This is where we go from."

"Don't talk it to death, Shears," Harbelis said. "Let Joel Cahill do the talking."

"I will, in just a minute," Shears said, holding his place. "Just tell yourselves, though, what you already can do, how you function, what you know that the others don't. Nothing mechanical, nothing man-made can go against you; no machines can fail you, because they can't survive mastery and contempt; they can't survive indifference. We reach through them to the purple field, but we leave them behind. We leave them behind in *this* field."

"Let it ride, Malcolm," Adler said. "We're all the same."

were wished for; if one arm were dropped and the other raised.

He was back; the cold around him was not flowing. He did not believe that his eyes would be pulled from his head in midair enough to bring back his sight. He was solid, cold, strong, and blind again; he knew where he was, and the room. The sweat was drying, and he was sleepy; he had had enough.

He caught himself back into the words. Know? Know what? What did anybody here know, that he could be sure about? Irritation brought back energy, which he wished had not come.

"Well now, wait," Cahill said. "I didn't tell you . . ."

"Go with your reflexes," Shears told them. "When you see, *do*. Do, at the same time. The only thing that'll kill you is hesitation. Don't let that happen. The only thing that'll kill you is a thought.

"And remember one more thing," Shears said. "We've got nothing against the military. Nothing against the Army Air Corps. They're just giving us what we need for a demonstration. We don't want anybody to get hurt, surely not deliberately. What happens, happens; who can tell? This is only to show what we can show. What it means, we'll bring out later; the right people will know, when it's time for them to know. To the rest, it'll just be something they can't explain; it'll be one of those unsolved things: a mystery. And that's all right, too."

Shears changed off, not exhorting now but explaining matter-of-factly.

"As far as we know," he said, "as far as we *know* . . .

. . . the only thing done against any of us by the military has been done against Mr. Cahill."

"Mr. Cahill had some things that belonged to us. They belonged to him, and they belonged to us. Colonel Hoccleve took them. He has them now, if he hasn't destroyed them."

He held himself; he would let Shears finish.

"Two days ago," Shears said slowly, "Colonel Vernon Hoccleve demanded that Mr. Cahill turn over to him a certain length of wire, part of a guy wire from the wing-strut assemblage of a PT-17 Type aircraft that was demolished as the result of a training accident."

"How do you know this, Malcolm?" a cadet named Thomasovich broke in.

Shears turned on him scornfully. "You think I don't know what goes on in the Administration Building? Do you think Alnilam does not have information sources in the orderly room? At the flight line? Do you think I don't know everything that goes on at this base?"

"What else?" Thomasovich asked.

Would he know the other things? Cahill puzzled, his hands turning on themselves in his pockets, the nails holding to the palm flesh. How would he know this? Who told him?

Shears itemized. "He took also a pair of goggles, with the letters

593

The protesting human throat-sounds around him were not like anything before; there was a compression in the cold that seemed to take on mass, and through it, over it, ran a sighing that was like the play of rumor over nerves themselves, in the open, nothing between.

Sound increased. Cahill wanted to rise, to get up, but he was already there.

"One more thing," Cahill said, breathing deep of pure cold, of unlimited purity. He reached into his right-hand pocket, as deep as he could go.

Very carefully he took out the piece of toilet paper and unwrapped it, put his thumb inside, and almost over it again. "Mr. Shears told you that the people here, the colonel and all, took away some of . . . some of what I come up here to get. He told

B.V. on them, retrieved not at the accident site by Peckover personnel but by a civilian party in the vicinity. These goggles had been presented to Mr. Cahill *by* the colonel on his arrival at the Peckover facility, and were reclaimed by him under threat of arrest and imprisonment.

"We could have with us tonight —but we don't—the zipper from a flight boot, found in a field burned over by forest fire, fused together but recognizable . . . and retrieved *by* Mr. Cahill and the civilian flight instructor McClintock McCaig *four hundred yards* from the accident site."

"Yes, sir," Shears said quietly and politely. The projector beam was still on, and in it Cahill swayed. On the wall, where the film picture had been, his shadow was alive between the deer's and boar's. The cadets watched him closely, most with narrowed eyes, as he brought up his hand.

you about the piece of wire, that was from . . . from the wing of my boy's airplane. His instructor, McCaig and me, we found it out in the field, there." He paused, and blew his nose without wiping it.

"The colonel, he took that. Said he needed it. I don't know what the hell he needed it for, but he took it.

The cadets stirred; one or two muttered and shifted.

"And . . . and we found . . . McCaig went out and found . . . him and my dog, they found part of a shoe, a boot, like, was way off from where . . . where the wreck was, from the place that they had done dragged it off from. McCaig found it out where there was part of a fence, he told me. It was a zipper, and you could feel where it was all burned together." He listened for the sound that he was sure would come from them, and it came. "I taken it in to your . . . your Supply lady, and she . . . she told me it come off'n one of your flyin' boots, and McCaig said it did, too. I carried it with me, carried it around in my pocket, before the colonel found out I had it. I told him I did. I wadn't hidin' nothin'. Anyway, he wanted that, too, and I gave it to him.

Some of the eyes widened, particularly those of Harbelis and Crider. Shears watched with his arms folded. Adler closed his jaw more firmly, inhaling deeply through his nose.

"And there was . . . there was some . . . there was a pair of goggles. They was Joel's. A lot

595

of the glass was broke out of 'em
. . ." He listened for the cadets,
the noise of restlessness, anger,
and then went on, when the
sound of uniform material rubbing against itself died off.
"There was some letterin' on the
band of 'em. The colonel didn't
know what it meant. There was
just them two initials, just the
B.V., on 'em."

"He took 'em back. He took
'em back when just the other day
he had done *give* 'em to me.
Handed 'em right to me. And I
believed he meant what he said.
Well," Cahill paused, "I ain't got
'em now. God knows where they
are."

Again the uniforms rustled;
they filled the space around him,
with the low voices.

Now, Cahill told himself,
working his hand. The time for it
is now; now. "But there's one
thing he didn't get," he said, as
clearly as Adler. He undid his
hand, and thrust it out where he
hoped the light was. "There's
one thing that don't belong to
the U-nited States Army Air
Corps." He opened the hand
from around the paper, where
his thumb had told him the
tooth, broken off jaggedly above

" 'As I came through the desert,' " Blazek said.

" 'As I came through the desert,
thus it was,' " Neilson took up.

"No hope could have no fear,"
Adler said clearly and honestly.

Warily the cadets came in
around the blind man, one or two
looking at Shears or at each other,

596

the root line, lay where they could see it. "Come look," he said, not loudly. "Come around and look, up close. This here's my boy's front tooth, was knocked out in the wreck."

He felt them pressing toward him. No one touched him, or the tooth, or the paper under it, but their in-closing created a kind of hover around his hand, and for him added to the light he hoped was there. "There it is," he said. "That's all I got."

They had seen enough, he figured, and began to close his hand.

but the main press was not hesitant as they came at first loosely and then tightened around and over the hand in the dim glow, the crumpled frail paper with the stained tooth giving back no light, but with the reality it had.

Cahill reopened his hand, and very steadily held it where it was.

"No," Shears said urgently. "Don't do that. Leave it out there. Leave it out there for just a little, Mr. Cahill. Hold it just like that. This'll be the only time . . . this'll be the only time we'll have a chance. Just hold on." His voice picked up confidence. "We'll remember this. And not only we will. History will remember it. History damn well will."

A single voice. It was Shears.

" 'He who makes the world alive is full of delight,' " Shears said, his eyes on Cahill's hand.

"Yes," Blazek said. Another, in darkness, said, "Yes."

" 'The flowers of the shield are opening their petals: glory spreads, it revolves about the earth.

There was no sound of engines, which for some reason Cahill believed he would hear now; should hear.

Cahill wondered with a quick shot of memory if he and Mc-Caig had flown through any clouds. He held stiller.

" 'Here is intoxication of death in the midst of the plain. Clouds are rising . . .

. . . He who gives life to the world is setting in the spring season.' "

Shears went on; someone else was with him, in a whisper.

" 'There the Eagle Tiger is fresh and in flower.' "

"Yeah," Thomasovich breathed. "Yeah," he said. "Go on. Don't stop."

" 'There the chieftain's fire . . .

Cahill heard the "Ah" come from one of them, and then spread through.

. . . There the chieftain's fire opens like a flower.' "

Quiet set in.

Will there be more? Cahill asked. More, or something different?

"All right," Shears said. "Here we go."

He started again, and this time all the other voices except Cahill's were his.

" 'Let us take pleasure, O friends,' " Shears said, intoning now, and not ashamed of it.

" 'Rejoice again, O princes.' "

A terrible exhilaration, worth more than anything in life, went through Cahill like a spasm of some outside power he would not have believed possible. These were ordinary boys, but here they were not ordinary. He stood with them, in the middle of them, in what they were doing, in what Shears and the others were making into one voice.

The farm that was supposed to be black, the dust of ashes, the ash-smell come off Zack's fur, he had returned to him, now. The farm had given up what it could. All but one thing, maybe.

The voices, the one voice, dropped.

Cahill kept to his position, arm out, in the resonance of the last words. It seemed the end, but he did not say anything. He would not, until somebody else did.

"It ain't all that much of a last time," Cahill said, folding the tissue and putting it back in his

" 'Rejoice again, O princes,' " Shears repeated. " 'One there is who shall come again . . .

. . . who shall come again to live in the midst of the plain.' "

" 'Only on loan we possess Shield-flowers and ardor of war.' "

"Thank you, Mr. Cahill," Shears said, like a man who has come down from something over his head. "We all thank you." He pulled at his tie. "And now we've got to hit for the base. This will be the last time we'll be able to get together with you, and we want you to know . . ."

pocket. "I told you I'd be out yonder tomorrow somewhere, and I will. I don't say I'm gonna do somethin' I don't do. You won't need to look for me. Wouldn't do you no good. But the reason you can be sure I'll be out there," he pulled up his neck muscle, his trapezius, "is that I'm tellin' you right here, before you go. If there's some way you can feel me bein' there, that's what we'll do. See if you can do it, when the time comes."

"We'll pick you up," Adler said, "from wherever you are."

"Good night, boys," Cahill said.

"Good night, sir," Shears said, reaching down for Cahill's hand and pressing it. "We won't give down."

"Neither will I," Cahill said. "Let them, let them others give down."

They came past him, one breath after the other, most of them level with his face, some lower, one, or maybe two, higher. "Good night, sir," said the first one after Shears, "Melvin Thomasovich, Alnilam. Good night and good luck."

"Good luck to you, son," Cahill said. "Look out for yourself. Get through the war, and have a good life, afterwards."

"We're not looking that far ahead," Thomasovich said. "Tomorrow's the thing, right now."

One held his hand longer than the others, and Cahill guessed that it might be Spain, but it was not. "I'll never forget you coming up here, sir," Harbelis said. "And out on the ball field. You caught me with the rightest time that anybody ever did catch. I've run a lot of hundreds, but that is my exact average time, right on the money. How the hell you did it, I'll never know."

600

"Just a matter of luck, prob'ly," Cahill said. "It was only just that one time."

"It's the time to end all times," Harbelis said. "At least for me it is."

More came by, identifying themselves. When little Crider touched him he put out his other hand and found the boy's delicate shoulder beneath him. "Be careful, son," he said. "Looks like they done put you on the spot."

"I been there before," Crider said. "They got the right man for it. I know what I'm doin'." Then "Do not speak of secret matters in a field full of little hills."

"I won't," Cahill said. "That I can promise you."

He kept putting his hand out, and was used to them without knowing it; was used to the pressure, then the withdrawing, the temporary return of the cold, and then another hand. But the space around him was beginning to turn desolate, and the cold had less and less against it, until he put his hand out, sure that there was still one more boy, but there was not. The door closed discreetly, and he pulled back his hand, into which no other had come. He felt for the bed with the back of his knees, could not find it, explored the air with his hand, and made it to the wall where the bed stood. He sat on it slowly, testing the looseness of the screws. "That's about it," he said to Zack. "I can't do no more. I don't even want a screwdriver. I'll go with it like it is; I'll go with what I done."

"There must not be many things," he said to Zack, "worse than bein' cold as hell and dirty as hell at the same time. I feel like the time I had to shit, when we 'us in that boarding house, or whatever it was, when the bus broke down. People, they don't understand the trouble a blind man's got." He rubbed Zack's head and felt for his teeth, which was one of the contacts they had. "But we got out and got back in, didn't we, boy? We left 'em somethin' out in the field." The dog chewed his finger, trembling with concern. "Easy, big boy," Cahill said, though he did not need to. "Save that for them others."

He stretched out on the bed and wobbled it. "This must be a hell of a place," he said. "But we'll be out of here tomorrow. We ought to get home late tomorrow night, and I'll buy us a big steak." He put his hat on the floor, and picked up the two big blankets McLendon had given him. "Feel like horse blankets," he said, palping them, and beginning to settle. A wind had come without his noticing it, and the shed-metal made it drone.

601

"You all right?" asked a voice, McLendon's. "The boys left the light on."

"I'm fine," Cahill said, waking slowly and twice as tired.

"Can I do anything for you?"

"No," Cahill said, and then thought. "You ever run your finger over a propeller blade, McLendon?"

"No," McLendon said. "Why would I do that?"

"It's got dirt on it. It's covered with dirt, and it feels like the dirtiest dirt there is. It's grimy; it's gritty; it's got oil in it. That thing must pick up everything in the air that the air don't want."

"That's interestin'," McLendon said, "but what has it got to do with anything? I mean, what're you gettin' at, Frank?"

"I'm gettin' at the fact that I feel like I've got the fuckin' stuff all over me, and I wouldn't mind gettin' some of it off. Now you tell me: just how am I gonna do that, out here in this godforsaken meat-house?"

"I'll tell you, since you ask me," McLendon said. "You can go up to your old room and take a bath. And you can stay there, too, if you want to."

"You mean there ain't been nobody lookin' for me?"

"Not since some of the cadets."

Cahill pondered this. "I might take you up on that," he said. "And on the way I might let you have a drink of this gin I done won off of you."

"I could have one nip, I guess," McLendon said. "But you keep the rest. You won it."

"OK," Cahill said, elbowing himself up to sit. "Let's go."

"How come you to know about them propellers?" McLendon asked, as they went out the door. "Do them others go around feelin' of 'em?"

"It'd take me too long to tell you," Cahill said, though he could have done so. He paced slowly to the house at McLendon's side, with the difference in his mind that it made when he remembered the auxiliary field with McCaig before they took off, the open field blowing around him, the smell of grass and snow that with the strange grit from the aircraft in his hand made one thing that he did not want to have to explain.

It was warmer here. Even though he was naked, he felt more comfortable and confident; he touched the walls, or two of them, affirming the space. He uncapped the bottle of gin and shook it. Nearly full, as far as he could tell; the liquid weight-shift was heavy. He drank, a little at first, a familiar burning but not as sharp as some, and then kept tilting and

602

swallowing until his mouth began truly to hurt. One more; one more swallow, he told himself to take, and took, until his eyes blazed. He put the bottle down on the head-side of the tub, stooped, searched out the plug and put it where it went, cut the water on and with the handles mixed it, tuning for the heat he wanted. Air hit the window hard, backed off and came at it again. Water poured as though it would go past him; he sat on the rim and put his feet in it, and took another drink, and it was as though his scalding feet and ankles rose into him, liked him, and made a good feeling for his chest and eyes, and traveled out along his arms.

The wind at the window glass battled with it, and now was on the house in more than that one place. All the wood to the side of him creaked, and Cahill would have sworn he heard nails pull. Behind him, next to the tub, Zack whined and scratched the floor; in a lull between gusts Cahill heard his tail brushing back and forth over the linoleum. He reached behind him. "Calm down, Buffalo-head," he said. "There ain't nothing out there to get after. There ain't nothin' for you to get a-holt of. It's just the wind. It's just the air, big boy. It does this sometimes."

He took another drink, and with it and the water rising up his legs he welcomed the plans that came to him. He would learn to swim. He would; he would learn to swim in his own pools, back in Atlanta. He might even learn to dive. With a powerful gladness he slid down, and in. His breath went out before he knew it did, and sweat popped on his face and all over his head. He grabbed the tub rim and reared up and half out, then sank back, able to stand it now. He took his breath back, deeper than before, and wiped his wet forehead with other wet. "God," he said. "There are good things in this world. Good things can happen."

He put his fists down and raised himself on his thumbs, suspended, touching nothing but his back and the floor of the tub, and listened to the air and the cold try to get at him. He had never heard such wind. Even at the roadhouse, on his way here, it had not been so strong, so unreasonable and so persistent. The last time he had been in this tub it had been snowing, but there were no particles now, nothing fluttering, no peltering, no sense of objects, rocks, gravel, or sheets that come face-on one piece at a time; no, but only sheer force, and a kind of rage that had nothing behind it, and was nothing but what the rage did. For some reason Zack seemed to be moving. Cahill reached outside the tub for him. He was not there. He had not gone out of the room; nothing had happened on the door side. He must be somewhere beyond the foot of the tub. Yes, he was at the wall maybe; under the window. A blast of wind hit the side of the house, almost hurricanelike, the kind of burst in which something has to fall, be forced back; in which something was intended to give way.

"Dad," was said. Cahill opened his eyes to the limits. Could he have really heard what it sounded like? He dropped his body from his thumbs and lay quietly, everything listening. The wind came and pulled back, not so hard this time, but not entirely off the house either.

"Dad," was said again, and he could hear it. He brought his hands from the water, and to his ears.

"Dad, I wanted . . . I want to . . ."

Cahill got to one knee like a fighter. "Who is it?" he said, but with no power. "Who is it? What do you want?"

"Listen," the other voice said. "Listen. I'm not . . ." and then, though the air it came from was too mixed with it for Cahill to be sure, said what might have been "Why did you . . ." or "Why didn't you . . . ?"

In the room Zack had hold of something, or was trying to get hold; the sounds from him were pure dog-fury, as though he were fighting with another dog, or more than one, or many from all sides, bashing from one wall to the other like an animal, or man, trying to break out of a cage by rage, by panic alone. "What?" Cahill heard himself say, then scream "What? What is it? Where are you? What do you . . . ?" He held out both arms, on his feet now, coughing with steam.

"Dad, please . . ." the voice said, "please don't . . . *please* . . ." It was the terror in the sound, the high, the highest note of panic possible, that went through him and cut off his own words before he could think. "What . . . ? Who . . . ?" was all he could say, repeating, keeping on. The wind fell, the voice could not be made out, but was still trying; through Zack's scrabbling and fighting Cahill heard, distantly and distinctly, an aircraft engine break: fire, cough; catch. "Please, *please,*" said the voice, "Dad, don't let them . . . don't let them take . . ."

Zack went by him, by the tub with a high-speed lurch to shake it, and went through the door into the bedroom, where he must have hit the wall, or the outer door, for there was an all-out impact, a scramble, a whine, lessening as Cahill slid back into the tub, into the only place.

*   *   *   *

604

"How do you feel?" McLendon asked as they rode.

"Not the best," Cahill said, his hand to the back of his neck.

"Son-of-a-bitch if I didn't think you was dead, in there. If your head had'a been under the water, had'a done gone under, drunk as you was, that'd'a been the end of it."

"I guess so. But it didn't, and it ain't," Cahill said, shifting uncomfortably. "How much farther we got to go?"

"Not far; a couple of miles, maybe three," McLendon said. "But I ain't gonna let you off from last night. I tell you I thought you was dead, when I come in there this mornin', and there you was sittin' in that ice-cold water. You looked dead; you did, I tell you." He laughed sympathetically, and with admiration. "You wadn't dead; you 'us dead drunk. You're lucky that water didn't freeze up around you. And there you was; you couldn't do nothin'. The room was in as bad a shape as you was. Zack had done shit all over everything. The chair and the settee was tore up, and so was the bed. Looked like your dog had done had a fit, or something. I ought to charge you for all that . . . what do they call it? . . . I ought to charge you for all that vandalism, you and your dog. All the gin was gone, too. I thought you 'us gonna give me some."

"That'll be all the gin you're gonna get," Cahill said, feeling better. "There ain't no more of that partic'lar gin." He pulled at his coat shoulders. "And don't be runnin' my dog down, neither. He's worth ten of you, and everybody else in this fuckin' town."

"What the hell would you do without that damn dog?" McLendon asked, glancing over the back seat, where Zack lay on the floor, listening to the highway. "What would you do? Get yourself another one?"

"There ain't no other one," Cahill said, feeling backward over the seat. "This here's the dog of peace."

"That's one I ain't heard," McLendon said. "You oughta take a look at that room."

"Next time," Cahill said, not offended.

"I'm sorry, Frank," McLendon said. "I said it wrong."

"The dog of peace, is what I'm talkin' about," Cahill said.

"How about them other dogs he killed, back in town?"

"That's just what I mean. You don't see 'em makin' no more trouble, do you? What kind of peace do you want?"

"That's one way of lookin' at it," McLendon said. "Them others'd do better to leave him alone."

"He's got a good heart to him, though," Cahill said. "He's just like a puppy, some of the time." He ran his palm over all of Zack's fur that he could reach. "He's got such a good heavy coat on him. He could'a been a sled dog, up in them snow places; up in Alaska, maybe, where they 'us after the gold, and had them dogs pullin' 'em around, and all; Zack could'a done that. He could'a made somebody rich."

"I'd bet on that," McLendon said. "The snow don't seem to bother him."

"Don't nothin' bother him," Cahill said, pulling gently on fur. "I've brushed the snow off of this-here fur, I've dried the rain off of him, and . . ." he waited for the other thing to come back, as fully as it would. "I've brushed the ashes off of him . . . a whole lot of ashes. Don't nothin' bother him."

"When was that?"

"When me and McCaig was out in the field, out yonder where my boy went down. McCaig said he was . . . said he had ashes from the fire all over him; said he was so black he was gray."

They rode for a while on the level two-lane highway, the sun bright and clear in McLendon's eyes, and precisely shaped on Cahill's glasses, intense yellow on the black green.

"You never did tell me," McLendon said.

"Tell you what?"

"What on earth went on, last night? You know," McLendon said, trouble-free and friendly, "this ain't something that happens in my place just every day. "A bunch of people showin' movies in my meat-house . . ."

"How do you know what we were doin'?" Cahill asked, facing him. "What business you got out there?"

"I just peeped in for a second, Frank," McLendon said apologetically. "I wanted to see if you 'us all right. I didn't see nothin'; I just saw there was a picture up on the wall."

"Yeah," Cahill said. "That's right. Joel was in it. They was tellin' me about it; what he looked like, and all."

"And you," McLendon said, carried past where he meant to be, "I didn't know where you was, at first. And then I seen you sittin' way down in that chair, with all them kids around you; all them serious kids was just froze there, in yonder all around you. Didn't a damn one of 'em ever know I was there. You looked like some kind of big Injun, like Sittin' Bull or somebody, was fixin' to have them boys come out of there hog-wild." He glanced at Cahill. "You did; you did, Frank. You looked like you had yourself a damn tribe in there, or somethin'."

"Well, they came, and they was there for a while, and showed . . .

and showed the movie. And then they went off. But there is . . ." he caught the idea as it flickered. "There is maybe somethin' you could . . . you could tell me about."

"What might it be?"

"Did you happen to notice . . . I mean after they left, and I went on back up to my room . . . did you happen to notice any of the boys that was . . . that stayed around for a while?"

"I did see some of 'em goin' on up the street, to wait for the bus," McLendon said. "Some of 'em might'a stayed in town. I think they let a few of 'em do that; the married ones, and all. But there wadn't none of 'em at my place. That I would know, sure enough."

"You didn't see nobody?"

"Nobody. I went outside and looked around, too. Not for none of them; I was afraid the wind would tear somethin' loose. There was plenty of it; the most I can remember around here. Knocked some things around; store signs; like that. The hardware-store sign was still out in the middle of the street, when you and me took off, a little while ago. It 'us still out there; people was drivin' around it."

"Nobody could'a come in, and you not hear him, in all that noise?"

"Nobody last night, but there was somebody this mornin', while you 'us gettin' yourself together, I about forgot."

"Who was it? A cadet?"

"No; some other fellow; somebody else from the base."

"One of them captains? The doctor, maybe?"

"No, but he's one of 'em that works with the doctor."

"There ain't but one of them."

"There sure ain't. You can have them kind, and all the rest of 'em like him."

"I know who you mean. He's the medic they got there; keeps the records, and gives shots, and stuff like that. He ain't all that bad a boy. What'd he want?"

"I never could figure out what he wanted," McLendon said, "to tell the truth. After I told him you 'us gone, he still wouldn't leave. I didn't have no time to stand around listenin' to him. He don't belong around where I am."

"Well, you could'a talked to him," Cahill said. "It took me a little while to get my stuff together, give myself a shot—a good 'un too; I feel strong as hell, if it wadn't for this headache—and it wouldn'a hurt you none to be more or less nice to the boy."

McLendon looked from the highway to Cahill longer than he ordinarily would have done. "Are you sure you and me're talkin' about the same man?"

"Yeah. I know him."

"He's the one that works with the doctors, out yonder? He ain't got no color to him; he's losin' his hair real bad; looks like it might hurt him?"

"I don't know about that," Cahill said. "But he knew my boy. He gave him a bath, one time."

"He *what?*"

"Wadn't long before Joel had his accident. The doctor told me he had some kind of skin thing, where they have to put tar all over you; you know, creosote, I think he said. That's supposed to do some good. I don't know whether it ever did with him, or not."

"Creosote? You mean the stuff that's on telephone poles?"

"Far as I know."

"What good does that do?"

"How the fuck would I know? I ain't the doctor."

"I can tell you one thing, Frank. I wouldn't take my clothes off with that guy around. I sure wouldn't get in no bathtub with him."

"Nobody's gonna ask you. Let's just get on out to the base. That's all we need to be doin'."

"Shit, Frank, I don't mean to . . . I mean, now look . . . if he's a friend of yours . . ."

"Look, yourself," Cahill said, his patience wearing, "I don't hardly know him. I talked to him once; he went and found some of Joel's records for me. That's all."

"He don't feel right to me," McLendon said, with assurance but not vindictively. "He just ain't my kind of folks. Havin' him turn up was one of them bad things you don't count on, that don't set right with you, like when you finished takin' a shit and your finger goes through the toilet paper."

"How long did he stay? You said he wouldn't leave. What'd he say? You never did tell me what he wanted."

"He was talkin' quiet and strange. Didn't make sense but not loud. And I will say one thing: he looked like he meant what he was sayin'. If you'd'a heard him you'd'a knowed he was off his course. But he meant it. He believed it; he was sweatin' like somebody hoein' a patch."

"What about? What was it he 'us talkin' about?"

"There's a tunnel, somewhere," McLendon said, his forehead drawing with effort. "It's somewhere around the hospital, out there; somewhere near where he works."

"I know where it is," Cahill said. "I been in there."

"He didn't talk about that at first, but it was the main part of what he talked about."

"What was first?" Cahill asked, taken suddenly with the need to know what he could; and all of it.

"He . . . he talked about your boy, and he kept sayin' stuff about his black . . . his black body . . . his black body and his blue eyes . . . and . . ."

"That'd be the bath in the tar, I guess, the stuff off of the telephone poles. He told me that already. That ain't nothin' new."

"I didn't have the slightest idea that was what he was talkin' about," McLendon said. "He just kept sayin' black, black . . . and blue eyes, blue eyes. He said your boy had a bad mouth; a ugly mouth, was twisted up to one side."

"Well, fuck him," Cahill said.

"If you ask me, I think he was lookin' for somebody to fuck him," McLendon said. "Your boy must'a turned him down, maybe."

"That's all?"

"No; then he got off on the other thing."

"Go on. Go ahead on."

"After he took the trouble to tell me that your boy was the devil, or was like the devil, that he was bad, that he was evil, that he had done been put into the world to do nothin' but what'd . . . what'd be opposite to . . . to the good things . . . what'd do nothin' but . . . what'd make people do . . . you know, would bring out the bad in 'em . . . he told me your boy was from the pit. From the pit, is what he said. He said he was a demon from the pit. I wouldn'a remembered it, if he wouldn've said it so much. The pit; what pit would that be, Frank?"

"The tar pit, maybe," Cahill said, with defensive sarcasm. "And then what?"

"He said he was in the tunnel, where the air is . . . is movin', he said . . . where there's always wind, some wind, there."

"I know," Cahill said. "I told you I done been there. He's right; that's the way it is."

"And he said . . . he said he heard your boy."

Slowly Cahill iced over. "When?" he asked.

"Yesterday afternoon. He said he heard him real plain. And that's when he took the notion to come after you."

"What was . . . what was my boy supposed to be sayin' to him?"

"A bunch of riddles, sounded like to me. I'll see if I can remember."

"Yeah; do that. I'd appreciate it," Cahill said, uneasiness now part of him.

"He said . . . he said something like"—McLendon's voice became too formal for him, mock-oratorical and not working—"like 'In turbulence I died, and out of turbulence I am born again.' "

"He made that up," Cahill said, pushing his voice out. "That queer made that up."

"He said, 'Tell my father I am waiting for him. Tell him he will know, wherever he is.' "

Good God, Cahill thought but did not say. "He did?" he finally got out. "He said that?"

"He did, Frank. He did; that's what he told me."

"That all? You seem to be rememberin' a whole lot, for a man who says he don't remember nothin'."

"Maybe I been tryin' to forget," McLendon said. "But you got me started, and maybe it's better for you to hear all this. It really wadn't my idea to tell you, though. Like I say, I thought it'd be better for me to forget it."

"Go on," Cahill said. "All you got."

"He said one more thing, he said your boy told him. He said 'Tell my father to look for me when Orion leaps.' Now that's *exact*, Frank. That's exactly what he said."

"And then he left? Just went on?"

"No; that's when the real sweatin' started. He taken hold of my arm, and I couldn't shake loose of him."

"Come on with it."

"He told me . . . he told me that if I knew where you was, that I . . . that I had better tell him. He told me he felt like . . . he told me he was *convinced* that your boy was goin' to try . . . to . . . to get rid of you. Kill you, some way. Or, like he said, destroy you. He said you needed him. That bald-headed queer boy told me you needed him."

"I don't need him," Cahill said, returning. "I don't need nobody; and I sure don't need him, that one."

"He said you did, though, Frank. He said you needed him, that he was the only one that could save you; that he was the only one that knew."

"Let it lay," Cahill said. "I know what I'm doin'."

"It's gone," McLendon said with relief. "That light-footed boy's done gone back to the doctor's office."

"We about there, now?"

"Just about got it. All we need to do is turn off this-here highway and go on down the dirt road that runs along by the fence. I used to know all this place back here since a long time before they built the base."

"When we got there I'll tell you what I want you to do."

"OK," McLendon said. "I'll be listenin' at you." He frowned and then smiled. "After this, Frank, what're you goin' to be doin'? When you go back to Atlanta, what then?"

"I got my place to look after, my swimmin' pools, my skatin' rink, the other stuff."

"How's your money situation, if you don't mind me askin'?"

"That ain't no problem. I got more'n I need. A lot more, to tell you the truth."

"How about time?"

"All I want. We ain't open except in the summer."

"Why 'ont you do some other things, then? I know what I'd do, if I was you."

"What would you do?"

"Eat, sleep, drink, fuck. And travel. I'd do me some travelin'; go all over hell, all over the world."

"There're fightin' a war all over the world, gourd-head. Ain't you got around to that, yet?"

"There's a lot of places you could still go in this country," McLendon asserted stoutly. "Grand Canyon, Niagara Falls. Lot's of sightseein' you could do."

"Now what exactly am I goin' to look at, McLendon?"

"You could take somebody with you, maybe. Like them boys was describin' that movie to you, last night. You could do that."

"No," Cahill said. "I got better things to do. There's somethin' better."

"What?"

"Work. Work is better. You got somethin' left when you finish."

"You mean, somethin' you made?"

"Yeah, more or less. Somethin' you made. Somethin' you thought up. Somethin' you found out the way to do, or made up the way to do."

"You still gonna be buildin' things?"

"You're fuckin'-A," Cahill said. "And that ain't all I'm gonna do."

"What else?"

"I thought I might learn wirin'. I really don't know enough about it; not as much as I want to. It couldn't be too hard. Anything with my hands I can do, just about; I don't have to look. I might even learn how to play some kind of music. Can you play anything? Didn't I come up on a piano in your place?"

"I got one, but can't nobody play it. Music I like all right, but it ain't in my line."

"How do you know it ain't?" Cahill asked. "I bet you ain't touched the damn thing."

"Ain't nobody touched it. My wife wanted to learn to play, but she never did. The thing just sits there."

"That's too bad," Cahill said. "But you ain't dead yet."

"Right," McLendon said. "We ain't dead today." He turned the wheel, leaning away from Cahill. "Hold on, now," he said. "We're comin' on to the dirt."

"What you do now," Cahill said, leaning forward and concentrating, "what I want you to do now is to find me some way to get in. Are we to the fence yet?"

"Just comin' to it. I'll go on down kind of slow, and see what we can find. I don't want to go far enough to get to the gate; they ain't no point in lettin' 'em see us. I don't want nobody to knew we was ever back here."

"How far is it to the gate?"

"I don't know. That's the trouble; I ain't been here since the fence 'us put up. I would reckon it'd be about a mile along, but I ain't plannin' to go that far. We ought to could find us somethin' before that."

They moved forward slowly, rising and falling rather than being jolted. McLendon watched the fence along the bottom, from time to time lifting his eyes to the end of the road, which stayed straight and disappeared between heavy pines. "Don't see nothin' yet," he said. "But it ain't too good of a fence. Anybody could get in, that wanted to cut the wire."

"Don't do that, if you can help it."

"I ain't about to do it. I don't want to damage none of the government's property. They're bad about gettin' on you, for that."

"So they tell me," Cahill said.

"I'm looking for some places that some other dogs might'a got in," McLendon said. "There's lots of rabbits around here, and the trees on the other side of the fence will hide 'em just as well as they will out here. Better, prob'ly; there's more of 'em. And dogs'd know that, and get in there after 'em."

"An air base must have to be real big," Cahill said. "All them planes goin' and comin'."

"Yeah," McLendon said. "There's a lot of land back in there. All kinds of animals. I bet you that the huntin' is just as good in there right now as it ever was before they put the fence up."

"When I get back home," Cahill said, "you might want to . . . I mean some time when you don't have nothin' else . . ."

"Hold on, Frank," McLendon said. "I think we got us somethin'." He pulled the car over and sat with the engine running. "They tell me that on some of these other army bases they let the hunters in, there's so much game. In the fall, they let 'em in. The colonel here, he don't do that. Us rabbit hunters's got to get in any way we can." He winked, and thought that Cahill might have got it. "Us and the dogs." He cut the engine off and opened the door. "Hold on," he said. "I'll be right back. Won't take a minute."

Cahill waited, listening through the open door. Band music there surely was; it was out there; in and out. There was a band far off, very far; he could not get enough to form a tune, but the horns were saying something, as from a football game across all the parking lots you had to walk through before you could get there. A night game; it was like the sound from a football stadium just before a night game; it was something you could get to, but it would take a while.

"If you don't mind scrunchin' down," McLendon said, rubbing red sandy dirt off his hands, "you can make it through, here. Won't be no trouble for Zack. Looks like it was somethin' damn near as big as he is, done made the hole."

"Let's go, then," Cahill said, opening his door and getting out. "Come on here, boy." As soon as he felt the dog he turned outward, to McLendon, to the music.

"Listen to me," he said.

McLendon glanced through the fence, and then back. "I don't know about this, Frank," he said. "I hope you got some idea about what you're doin'."

"Listen," Cahill said again.

"You mean to you, or to somethin' else?"

"You hear that music?"

McLendon tried the air, in the direction that went through the fence, first with one ear and then the other, then with his hands cupping both. "No," he said finally. "I don't; I don't hear nothin' but you and me."

"There's a band playin' over yonder," Cahill said, his heart rate rising. "You mean to tell me you can't hear it?"

"No," McLendon said. "Not a thing." He turned from the fence. "What else, now?"

"As soon as I get in, go on off. Come back in about a hour. Just cruise by a couple of times, till you see me. I don't think it'll take very long. I just want to stand out there till the planes . . . till the planes take off. Then I'll be on back out here at the fence. You ought not to have no trouble findin' me. Just cruise back and forth till I show up."

"I hate to leave you here by yourself, Frank."

"I been by myself before," Cahill said. "This is somethin' I got to do without nobody else." He walked past McLendon until the fence stopped him. "I got Zack; he ain't gonna let the rabbits get me."

McLendon pulled the sprung wire from the ground and Cahill scrambled through on his back. He stood up. "How's that?" he asked.

"Good," McLendon said, " 'cept you got your coat dirty. I'd brush you off, but I can't get at you through the fence."

"That ain't one of my big worries," Cahill said. "But you can do somethin' else for me, if you want to."

"I'll do it if I can," McLendon said, both hands crooked in the wire. "What is it?"

"Call down that thing out of the air," Cahill said. "Call the eagle for you, like you said you done."

"Shit," McLendon said. "I think you done gone crazy in the bathtub."

"Go on," Cahill said. "Do it."

"Somebody might come. Shit, the guard down yonder at the gate might hear me."

"What if he did? Even if he was to hear it, a mile off, he couldn't leave from where he is. Now go on. Make that noise. I been waitin' for this."

McLendon looked up the road and down, through the fence and back the other way, into the free woods. "All right," he said. "But I can't guarantee nothin'. It ain't just the critters in the air that hear this, you know. If a fox comes in, or a weasel, it ain't my fault."

Cahill swung slowly to face the woods, then halfway back in McLendon's direction, bringing something up from his clothes.

McLendon hesitated, his hands at the sides of his face. "What you fixin' to do?"

"Give myself a booster," Cahill said. "I feel OK, but I'm liable to need some more energy. Bound to be a lot of extra motion —waste motion, like—out yonder, 'fore I get back to you. I don't want to have to fuck around with needles, when I get where I'm goin'. I feel pretty strong, now. I aim to feel stronger, and stay that way awhile." He lifted the front of his shirt and freed the stomach hairs.

"Call that thing," Cahill said. "Call the eagle. Call the eagle, now, like you said you done."

Cahill held the needle, his thumb on the plunger, his glasses facing McLendon. "Go on. I dare your ass," he said, drawing the needle out with little attention to it.

McLendon put his hands to his mouth. The sound started, at once high-pitched but not loud. Cahill could feel the terror in it from the instant it began. As it rose, into high desperation, into a drawn frenzy of pain, hopeless appeal, of absolute desolation and abandonment, he sat on his heels beside Zack, calming him, as though looking past the trees.

McLendon let down the volume, and then quit. He put his fingers back in the wire and stood looking in through it as Cahill got up. "There ain't nothin' in the bushes," he said.

"How about in the air?" Cahill asked.

McLendon waited, scanning through the needles. "Not a thing," he said.

"Do it again," Cahill said. "Give it time."

"I'll be damned if I will," McLendon said, moving toward the car. "I can't do it no more. Makes me feel too sorry for the rabbit."

"Start your car," he hollered at McLendon. "Do like I tell you. Get on out of here." He heard the car start, and let go the fence.

"Now," he said to Zack, turning carefully to face the other way. "Now we're gonna go. We're gonna go there, big boy. Stay right with me, and don't run me into no ditches."

Slowly, one foot following the other, a hand in front of him, he moved forward toward the music, which blew in and out of hearing, and then came more strongly, little by little. At knee level there was a bush that stopped him, and he felt for the air around it, where there were none of the sharp small limbs that caught at him surprisingly, one prodding through his pants leg as though on purpose. "Where are the fuckin' trees?" he asked Zack. "Where are all them trees, supposed to be here?"

He hit one with his shoulder; his hand, fending off whatever might be there, must have gone past it. He stopped and felt the bark, and prized loose a piece, thin and brittle. "It's a damn pine tree," he said. "That means all the rest of 'em'll be pine trees, and won't be real close together." He patted the tree, worked around it with his hand on the trunk, making the shape, and went on from the other side.

He worked forward that way, from tree to tree, untangling his legs from the low growth, making mistakes he could not help, but moving toward the music that grew until the changes of air were not able to keep any of it from him.

But there were other things than the trees and bushes, and, because he knew, now, that he would not lose the music, he listened to the air for the echo of McLendon's rabbit cry which had been so piercing that it should still be there in some way. Had anything else heard it beside himself? Had the sound reached anything that would answer it? Foxes and weasels, threading through the brush where he moved cautiously, were nothing to worry about, or even to think about, while he had Zack with him. But above him, what was there? What might be there? What might be coming? He found himself listening for wings. Between the trees, when he had nothing to get hold of, when his only contact with anything solid was through his feet, he listened hardest. McLendon had said you never heard the wings until that one beat, right at your head, that seemed like it took the air apart. One; just that one. An eagle, hawk, whatever might be there, that might be coming to him, especially when he was in the open; when he was supposed not to know that anything

616

was near him: then it would come, if it had heard the scream. The scream had been made, had gone out, was up there above him, and around him. Whatever might answer, level with him, at his feet or above him, had been spoken to. He tried not to feel the explosion of feathers, the one split of air, the claws locking into his head. In the silence between trees his fear and anticipation, his excitement, became astounding.

But the music was closer, and he came back to it. He could make out, now, the shunting blat of trombones, oddly funny, forthright and devious at the same time, and two kinds of drums, one steady and dependable and the other nervous, higher, small and aggressive. The drums, the larger drums, took over more and more; it was impossible for Cahill not to adjust his body to them in some way; not to move in time with them. "Shit," he said. "You'd think I was marchin' in a parade, out here, bustin' my ass on these goddamn trees." But that was not all there was to it. He thought of lines of boys: those that were somewhere in front of him, and others besides them, wherever they might be doing the same thing, or something like it. He would be there soon, he was sure, across from the ones that were in the same place as he would be.

"You can't expect the damn trees to do what you want," he told himself, moving where there were none, and in the full open sound of the band. "You might'a run out of trees," he said. "And you're gonna fuck yourself if you go past 'em, and end up out where everybody and his brother can see you. Don't do that. Don't do that, Cahill. Go back a little. Find what you done left, and stay there." He turned carefully once more, and worked forward with the music at his back. A trunk came to his hand—the knuckles of his fist, actually—and when he groped to one side of it there was another. He put himself between them, propped, and settled his back. "I ain't lost," he said. "I ain't lost." He leaned a little out into the music-filled space that the backs of his hands, while he had been there, had told him was sunny; there must be sun everywhere you could look.

There was still the music, steady and forthright; the instruments making the tune were loud enough, near enough to cut, even to hurt a little, the drums were striding with them. He wondered if the cadets were Directly in front of the closed main hangar, on either side of the

in line, maybe marching. Or were they standing still? He had only Shears's description of the movie, the other graduation, to make up what he could of this one. He worked his mind to make the picture stronger. He had his version of the other one, and it had more power now, given by the time since he had been in the shed with the cadets; it had colors, very bright reds and blues, sharp-cut, like the ones in a flag. Maybe this formation was like the one he had, the one he was watching as the real music, the music of this one, played. Yes, maybe this was like the other one; maybe it was not something like it, but exactly. Why not? Exactly; it must be exactly, as it was there, beyond the curving violent gold, the slashing shots of his disease.

He ran his finger under his collar. It could not possibly be hot out here, but the inner cloth was wet. Between his legs was wet, as if he hadn't had a bath in a week. He tried to concentrate again.

Why was he tilting his head back? He was through with his neck; no, he could still feel it: his neck was still with . . . still part . . . it was wet, his shirt was wet, his face was unbreathable. There is something in this tree. There is. We . . . I . . . somebody told it to . . . Right over me. It

small sturdy band, the cadets were grouped. In platoon formation, two lines one behind the other, the two classes were drawn up; the undergraduate class, in olive drab, had its guidon-bearer almost against the corner of the mess hall; the boy could have touched it. On the other side of the band, under a large clean American flag, was the graduating class, in cracked and oiled leather flying gear, helmets and raised goggles, the sheepskin lining of their collars clean, but still not all the same color. There was a reviewing stand of fresh lumber, but not enough room between the hangar and the parked aircraft for a parade. A small group of civilians, mainly middle-aged or older, stood awkwardly bunched, past where the ranks of helmeted boys gave out.

Colonel Hoccleve stepped onto the stand, erectly climbing the

has come it is there something out of the air something from a long way off . . . feet . . . claws . . . it will shit on me . . . out of the air you can't tell it is there until . . . until it is . . . like I say until it is out . . . out of the air . . . everything is wet the inside of my mouth is filling up what is making . . . why is there so much spit I don't need it what is it for . . . Good God, what have I done to myself what do I have what don't I have what do I need . . . I need . . . it's not what I need but what I've got . . . the dark form swimming . . . the music from underground not this music maybe this music in the light green light . . . the gold light from the sides . . . shading the side of . . . shading green . . . the sides of . . . of under . . . the sides of under . . . Now . . . now what was it? No music: there were some words . . . somewhere . . . somebody was saying something . . . coming to him . . . coming out of . . . not far . . . not far away . . . not about the air . . . were they . . . were they for him . . . were they anywhere . . . were they everywhere? The fox? Dark body . . . green light . . . the moon balancing? The bubble in his hands? The eagle? Nails? One minute . . . one minute

three steps, and faced outward to the aircraft. He tapped the microphone. It squealed electrically as someone tuned, the sound very high and then fading off.

"I hope you can all hear me," he said, and motioned to the technician to turn the volume up. It came up; too much. "Welcome to the graduation exercises . . ." the colonel roared, then signaled again impatiently. "Welcome," he said again in a steady, carrying voice, "to the graduation exercises of the second class to be certified by Latham Field, the Peckover facility of the Air Corps; of the United States Army Air Corps.

"This should be a good occasion," the colonel went on, friendly and respectable, the loudspeaker giving out his voice without variation, "a good occasion for all of us. We've got a nice day for flying, and we're going to do something that I'm sure you good people have never seen before, in this area . . . or anywhere else, for that matter." The speaker system did what it could to convey his humor; some of the civilians responded and relaxed. "The grad-

now . . . one minute in the air I think we can get it . . . over the lake . . . water . . . coins scattering . . . and words: words now. They were loud, but what were they? What language was it? He should know . . . he should be able to tell: he was not in a foreign country . . . a country a fence girls hitting another girl with a ball . . . a girl in the middle . . . a girl with one leg . . . a mirror and a rattlesnake: he was in another . . . he was . . . he was where? He was not lost . . . not lost. Music from underground. No more. No more. Underground . . . singing from . . . come from . . . sent . . . coming to him from . . . from green . . . from under . . . No more. No more. Cahill slapped himself, trying to hit it and stop it, to strike down his running mind. He pulled his muscles up desperately, all over him. I stuck myself, he said. I must've done too much . . . too deep . . . too much of that stuff: too much in me. With all his strength he went into his pockets, overcoat pocket, jacket, pants. Good God Almighty, Jesus Christ in hell, he said, the images in his mind radiant with terror as they showed and fled. I got no sugar. I forgot to get it, God *damn* I forgot it McLendon forgot it I don't have

uating class is going to do a full-scale flyover for you. Every operational plane we've got will be up. Up and over. Over the field, and over you. That's the main course, you might say. Later, though, I'll do some aerobatics, and you can get some idea of what the planes that these cadets will eventually be flying, in the last part of their training careers, will be able to do." The colonel took a half step backward, and then returned to the mike, speaking more slowly. "These boys," he said, "these cadets in formation here, are like the boys you *were,* and like the boys that some of you, perhaps, have known, *do* know, as their parents; as their grandparents and cousins and friends. The fact that they are in uniform, the fact that they are learning to fly aircraft in preparation for wartime service, does not make them any different from the boys you know: those who farm, who go to school, who play on your football team here . . ." He broke his line of thought and raised both hands . . .

". . . and now, while I'm at it, how '*bout* them Rattlers! I saw every home game, I'll have you know!

none I'm going . . . I'm going to die I can't help it: no sugar I can't help it can't get it where will I get it. And then, showing almost clearly to his mind among the night swimming pool and its black figure, the swirl of blood in the pale sunny water, the one-leggèd girl, the new flag-colors that were part of every-thing, the moon and the carpen-ter's bubble, he saw the airbase as Shears had described it to him from the film, the rows of stand-ing boys, the planes parked next to the mess hall. "Zack," he said, down from himself. "Zack. Come on, big boy. We can't stay here . . . we got . . . we might could . . ."

He stumbled forward toward the words, whichever ones were there . . . wetness from his head . . . his mouth maybe . . . stringing from him. He knocked it away, ropes of it away, with his hand, slashing in front of him, going through it.

The ground is . . . the ground is mixing . . . my sweat has all this power, now . . . no airplanes in their sounds . . . no long one wing with snow all

"So, I want you to think about these boys that're going to be over your heads in just a few minutes: I want you to think about them as" —he paused and the drama was real; the civilians knew it—"as though they came from here, from your schools and your farms, from your stores and filling stations, from your mills and churches." He paused again. "It's your boys who are going to be up there." The colonel got ready to step back.

"Remember, now," he said,

621

the way out of sight . . . no window where the snow . . . where the sound . . . where the engine . . . the wing . . . the long wing all the way . . . out . . . out of . . . "Come on, Zack," he said. "Come on big boy . . . get your head out of your . . . get out of . . . get out of town they don't . . . get out . . . come on boy, let's get out, you and me . . . they can't . . . them others can't . . . soft ground. Now . . . now hard. Why? Hard now under . . . different."

He held himself; stamped his feet on the hardness. His mind focused for an instant. Under the racing strikes of self-flame through his eyes he saw the field again; the still aircraft, the mess hall next to them, seeming to be part of their line. He raised his arm and struck a vector through the air. "We've got it, Zack," he said, and then again, nearly screaming. "We got it, Hoghead; we're gonna get it. Right yonder it is; it's just right over yonder." He started forward again, in the direction of his arm, trying to stumble as he had been doing, but now there was nothing to stumble over except his feet, and he started to do his best to keep them apart.

"that what you will see is part of a war: a total war, a world war, and remember that we're in it together. Some of these boys you see here will die." He hesitated, then pulled up and surged. "But not today. Today they're going to show you what the Japanese and the Germans are up against; they're going to show you what Hitler is up against." He stepped back, and some of his words, the important ones, were lost, though he said them. "You and me and these boys, these cadets of the United States Army Air Corps. Here they go."

Stathis Harbelis, in the rear cockpit of his aircraft, raised as on a porch, concentrated on his instruments, his preflight proce-

He was on bad ground again he was on soft . . . he was on dirt he must have been wrong . . . he should go to his left no he should not . . . right he must go back he must get more to his right he might be going around . . . just around he had not lifted his arm . . . he had not lifted his arm in the right . . . his right arm . . . go back . . . there is not any way back . . . what was in the trees now what might be over his head had the bird . . . had the eagle the hawk come . . . had the owl . . . the bird come out of the night . . . come forward from the next night? . . . and now . . . and now it was not mixed . . . his feet . . . his feet were one thing again . . . on one thing: hard. Hard. He could go on: just keep the thing hard . . . keep his feet hard . . . keep going he was going . . . keep going . . . he must he would . . . "I will," he said, "I'm going to . . . I'll . . ."

There is this whine made by the fire . . . by my head . . . by the . . . the fire . . . by flying . . . by eyes . . . by fire fly-

dures. He went over everything again; he cracked the throttle a hair with his left hand; with his right on the ignition switch he waited for the underclassman—some new boy, a fat kid—to wind the inertia crank up to a pitch where the engine would take it. He listened outside also, for the others, but there was only the concentration of the other crank-whines centering on his, discordant, mechanical, more and more a sound that could not be stopped, that could not stop or lower of itself, but must be broken off, broken into by something more violent, with more strength and purpose, more authority.

Though he did not want to be the first, though he did not want to be the one to break the concentration of high desolate sound, Harbelis turned the switch; his own sound was already tuned; the fat boy's weight hit the ground and he wrung the switch more, ready with the throttle when the engine bucked. It did, and caught, and almost simultaneously another, and then several, and then a whole eruption of machinery in

ing . . . by underground . . . by . . .

A blast, a roar took him, an explosion in one ear, and others behind it, backing it, joining.

He stopped, and swung his head, centering the new sound nearly taking him off his feet, brought it face on, and stood holding it there, as he could. "We can't go that way," he said, he hollered above the roar to Zack. "We got to go . . . we can't go there we can't go straight at it . . . whatever . . . wherever it is . . . we got to go . . . we got to go to one side." Again he lifted his right arm, and pointed, he was sure, to one side of the noise. That was it. That was the way. It must be the way. With his hand out, but not a fist, he started. The dog brushed his leg. He felt and had the fur somewhere. He nudged again with his leg side for the body, and to the side . . . along the deafening side of it he was right he was dead right, he moved again.

He was not farther from the sound it was worse . . . there was a central mass of it clashing . . . a whicker and sizzle over it and through it . . . something touched . . . something a whiff or flick something else at his side at his leg pressed against him it was gone another whiff at his arm another at his neck he both ears, before and behind and all around.

The engine—his engine—was set in his hands; the brakes were in his feet. But he was afraid—a fear that found him easily—to look outside, where control was . . . where there would be no con . . .

Inside the brain-shaking roar of his and the other engines, a blasting impact, an impact that had begun as a tearing, a pull-through or shearing rip he thought was part of the one-sound of machinery, struck in from his right, and close: closer than any engine, he was sure, just after its searing scream and BLAM hit him not through the ear but through the shoulder. The aircraft to his right was tail on to him; it shook and stood: from around it came another, and with wounded and hysterical power, its whole left side gutted, Harbelis saw in a shot of sight as it turned and came straight at him, engine to engine. He gasped without hearing himself, but flooding with air, breath, he kicked loose the brakes, stood on the left pedal by reflex, and gunned the engine. His body leaped—what he was in leaped—having nothing to do with him but carrying him, and the oncoming engine slanted it would not come would not meet his, would not: he jarred, the other engine hit . . . had hit, caught his wingtip, turned, he turned—was turned—he had the thing though, grabbed his collar and tore it loose the rest of the way and was hit not hard but glancing a hard lick but he had been hit harder he would not go down stumbling trying to go forward . . . went . . . to one knee went he was down he must get up Zack he called in the roar Zack come here come on boy I need you . . . where . . . everything came over . . . he was crawling where his open hand flat hand was under . . . crushing . . . crushing itself . . . weight is off it . . . weight off pain . . . bad . . . very bad . . . he rolled the sound and what was in it rolled him over he spun he tried to spin on his back find his . . . tried to reach his knees found them in air that was . . . in air whirling straight into his face . . . he could not he would not let . . . on his knees on one knee now getting up . . . on his legs full of strength he stood there and now he had he had his fists with him they had to come to him God damn you, he screamed into the roar, God damn you, you mother-fucker, come to me, God damn you into the wild whickering and blasting, Come to *me* God damn you let me get at you let me get *at* you.

it it would turn with him, he could move it with his hands . . . his feet would move it everything he had would move it. The slam and shear of metal and fabric changed in every direction: at one side of his front view one aircraft turned over another and seemed to want to squat on it, the propeller beating back light. His cool heart pounding, Harbelis maneuvered around it. From the other side another plane bore down. Harbelis slewed, changed where he was going and was at the edge, looking in, his brakes on, engine cut back. Nothing came to him, nothing came at him from the locking, stammering yard, the unfocused deafening clutter of metal moving into itself, trapped and assaulting.

He looked out, where he could easily go: onto the athletic field, where a single plane chased a running figure, bowled it over, went past it. Harbelis turned back into the other planes, and charged.

In: he was back in: *in* it, here: he slewed and gunned toward what would be, would go across him, head toward. Swerving, he slung his tail section into the wing of another plane, staggered, whirled in place, gunned again almost to full power—going for enough to take off—and rolled toward another aircraft waddling slowly, quartering away, already slatted and gilled with rips, helpless with escape; Harbelis closed on it, sight-

He was there; he was still standing. He could scream anything he wanted, and keep on: he could scream louder, a little louder; maybe more than that.

He would not fall, no matter . . . he would not. He flooded through himself, and fell.

He got up.

An enormous wind was in his face. He would not fall, would not go down again, they could not make him.

He would not fall it was closer, great with air, almost solid he had better . . . he had better fall. He went down. Unfair but down. Unfair Zack he said, come here come here Zack where . . . ? He got up, groping right and left around him, trying to feel in a circle around his knees. He had it but not still it was not still it was going something went from him past . . . away from him for good past him and gone. Zack, God damn it, he screamed, Zack come on don't . . . don't do it you can't . . .

ing through his prop, centering on the rudder wagging with indecision, had it, smashed into it with the gray circle of his prop, scraps blowing past him now like sparks, chewed into the other craft until it almost stopped him, took almost all his forward motion, pulled free with power and one brake, and rammed the throttle forward again; full forward. He hunkered, then sprang . . . into . . . into a space forward of him where he could . . . No: something else: a figure: someone not in an airplane . . . out of . . . not in . . . somebody had got out . . . was trying . . . was in front of . . . a black shape . . . head and body down . . . went down . . . gone and another, lower form he could barely see . . . see for an instant just under him, came to him with a speed great as his, and could have been on him, a fury past anything human, teeth set in other black: in a stamp-print of vision there and gone. Harbelis screamed; jerked back the throttle: a slash of red across the windscreen and over him went as he ducked into the cockpit to awaken but could not as another body hit his, behind him and he fought to get clear, swiveled the ship to get out; this time truly out.

I won't go down *this* time I
won't. Again he was touched he
was hit he was down he rolled
over and was on a knee again
. . . the same knee, feeling for
the low air around him for Zack
he said he screamed now: Zack
he yelled in the clashing and
ramming noise, feeling for the
dog head.

Ground, cement, and gravel.
One place like another. Around
himself this way . . . that way
around himself . . . nothing . . .
cement . . . little rocks . . .
sand. Now

. . . he had . . . he had Zack by the . . . by the lips, had him by the
teeth, the teeth even and long his head was sideways in his hand . . .
his hands but it was Zack the long teeth locked come on big boy, he said
I got you now they can't they can't do he pulled the head to him and felt
for the fur the thick fur of the back let's get on up from here he said,
let's get up, Anvil-head, you big fuckin' Hog-head, let's get on out of
here gravel and sand wet this way not over here back to where the wet
was found it and trailing backward strung from the head there was
something, wet the head on his chest in his arm was wet he was wet his
chest was wet his pants were wet he got up with the head the head with
him he got and stumbled on himself he lurched he was going the noise
was to one side of where he was . . . one side that's right it should be
right it should still be right . . . going . . . going with it . . . come
on big boy I got you we're going with one hand I got you I ain't goin' to
turn loose of you I'm right with you we're gonna get there I know where
. . . we're gonna . . . come on I'm with you.

His hand hit something solid. Board. Board. Board, Zack, he gasped:
the thing's standin' up. With his free hand he found a corner, the corner
of a building it could not be anything else. He had it, he could go
around it he had done it before he could do it: his hand on it, he had it,
and followed, followed.

627

Colonel Vernon Hoccleve, in his silver AT-6 with the canopy open, watched from the place where he had just seen two aircraft that had seemed to fight over a man's prone body kicking on the ground, the propellers a weave of blades over him, and had seen the man get to his knees and then to his feet, cradling something, and lurch clear, while one of the aircraft that had stood over him, its engine wide open, made what looked like an attempt to guide the man . . . the figure . . . away from the mass of conflict, the berserk wilderness of aircraft, herded him, nudged him at least once with a wingtip, and was now sitting beside him at the prescribed forty-five-degree angle to the runway for preliminary warm-up, his PT-17 streaming with fabric, part of which was under its wheels. He and the cadet glanced once at each other, and not again. Neither raised a hand above cockpit level; neither showed a hand to the other.

Inside the mess hall, Pfc. Robert Sorbo, Permanent Party, permanent KP, from behind his GI bucket, still holding his mop, went to the door that was pounding and shaking, and the screaming that was there, saying over and over, sugar, sugar, you son-of-a-bitch. Sugar, I done come for it. Sorbo pulled the lock. The door burst in on him and a man covered with blood, his legs wet as if he had been wading in a creek, his eyes rolling crazily, carrying the head of a dog with a long blood vessel twined halfway around him, as he took one more step and went down said Sugar again, pleadingly, almost apologetically, as Sorbo turned loose the mop and caught him.

*   *   *   *

"What's your stay-ut?" the voice above him said. "Or as they say in the military, what's your stay-utus?"

"I don't know what my status is," Cahill said. "But I know what yours is, which is bein' from Charleston and talkin' like a geechee, that can't no white man understand, except another one from Charleston."

"True," Major Iannone said. "But I ought not to be asking you anyway. You don't even know where the hell you are."

"I must be still on the god-damned base," Cahill said. "I reckon I'm in your hospital. You gonna drown me in the tar?"

"No," said the major. "That ain't your problem. Your problem is your sugar." He turned serious. "How do you feel?"

"I feel all right," Cahill said, running a hand over himself under the covers. "I got some bruises on me, but as near as I can tell I'm not no different from what I was before."

"You overdosed yourself out there somewhere. Where'd you do it? In the woods, or where?"

"Both. Before, and then in the woods again."

"How much did you give yourself?"

"I got my own way of measurin' it out; I just do it by feel. I came up a little past my line, this time. I thought I might need the energy. I thought I ought to have more juice, because I'd be walkin' around, and all."

"You got a hell of a lot too much juice," the flight surgeon said. "I got some blood out of you last night. You had almost half again more insulin that you should have had."

"That so?"

"That's so. And to do that, and then get yourself trapped out somewhere where you can't get to any sweets—sugar, candy, even fruit— well, doin' that way, you didn't need them prop-blades to get you. If you hadn't made it to the mess hall you'd'a died anyway. When they brought you in here you were just a shade short of real coma, and when you go into that, most of the time you don't come out. Even if we could have kept you alive, you'd've been a vegetable."

"I don't like 'em," Cahill said. "I like meat. Me and Zack." He pulled his hand from under the cover, but he did not reach down. "Them propellers," he said. "They missed me, some way, but they must'a got him. I remember I felt . . . I picked up . . . it's not real clear, but didn't I . . . I mean, when . . ."

"That's as clear as you need to be," the doctor said quietly. "And you're right. Your dog was killed. A couple of the boys said he was trying to . . . well, he went right into . . ."

"That's him," Cahill said, his voice equally low. "That'd'a been him."

"And now," the major said, glad to have a subject to change to, "we need to get back to what's bothering you. You say you feel all right?"

"I do."

"I want you to listen to me."

"When did I ever do anything else? I ain't heard much I like."

"That true?" the major said; as a physician he was good at banter; it was one of the parts of the profession he most enjoyed. "I ain't ever given you no bad time. We always got along, seems to me."

"Right," Cahill said. "You're one I don't feel quite so much like actin' like a shit around. What do you want to tell me?"

"Nothing I haven't already told you. You've got to quit being so cavalier about your shots. Your shots and your diet, but most especially your shots."

"Well, you tell me about it, and I'll try to stay with you." And then, defensively, "I got another doctor in Atlanta, you know. Him and you might not agree."

"I don't know him, but no doctor in the world would advise you—or permit you, if he could help it—to handle the thing like you do. That's insanity. I'm surprised you've lived as long as you have."

"I did what I did. And I'm still here."

"I want to keep you here," Iannone said, and meant it. He touched the back of Cahill's hand. "Can you take this I-V a little longer?" he asked, tugging gently at the rubber tube in Cahill's other hand, so that the bottle in the wire rack trembled.

"I guess so. I don't like it, but if that's what it takes . . ." he shrugged, as he could. "I'll stay with it."

The major patted him. "Private Gilbeau will look after you, bring you what you need. I want to get some more blood. And I'll leave you something to pee in, which I'll also need. Gilbeau'll give you all the rumors. There're plenty of them around."

"One thing," Cahill said, as the weight left the edge of the bed. "I really ain't supposed to be in here, am I? I mean, ain't this place for the boys? For the Army, and them that's in it?"

"It is," the major said. "And it is true that we're not supposed to be treating you. But I'm a doctor before I am whatever it is I am in the Air Corps. I took what they call an oath. They bring you up in front of a stick with two snakes twisted around it and looking at each other. You can't go back on the snakes. That's the one thing you can't do. The snakes're what it's all about. That's why you're here. The snakes said I had to take care of you. But I would've done it anyway. They're just the best backup I had. They're the best, anywhere."

"I don't know about you-all from Charleston," Cahill said, lying back. "You got somethin' called crawfish clap, and you play with snakes."

"That's all we do," the major said. "Takes all our time." He looked at his watch. "You get me these samples, and I'll work up a complete report on you. We'll get you squared away."

"You sure I can stay here?"

"I'll make sure. It's true, there was some talk about having you transferred to the civilian hospital at Fayetteville, but that'd just be a lot of extra trouble. I'll take responsibility for you. If you do what I say, I can have you out of here in a couple of days."

"What then?"

"As far as I'm concerned, you can go back to Atlanta. But you know"—he shrugged and opened his fingers—"something like this happens, they've got to have an investigation. They'll have to have a board. The Air Corps is big on boards. Probably you'll come into it, in some way. You can talk to the colonel about it when you feel better."

"You see the colonel, tell him I'm ready to talk to him any time he can get around to it."

"I'll tell him," Iannone said. "And I'll be back later, myself. I'll give you a full report. Me and Pfc. Gilbeau, we're the medical board. All the rest of 'em ought to do it like we do."

*   *   *   *

He had slept again, not thinking of anything and not having any dreams come to him. Dreams were his place of color, and since he had been blind he had welcomed them, looked forward to their drama and the strange naturalness they gave the events and objects he remembered, and to those he had never seen. Not now; he was glad to be awake. The room was quiet, very quiet, as he felt his eyes open, knew that they were open. Had there been a sound?

Pfc. Parris Gilbeau and Colonel Hoccleve stood at the door, which Gilbeau held not by the knob but by the sharp wood, watching the blind man as he stirred, twisted his heavy head on the pillow, lifted his lids and stared straight up, then turned one way and the other; his eyes swept over them.

"Mr. Cahill," Gilbeau said. "Colonel Hoccleve is here. He'd like to talk to you."

"All right," Cahill said, coming out of it. "Come in and have a seat, if there is one." He half raised himself and put out his free hand.

The colonel came close to the bed, looking not at Cahill's hand but his face.

"I don't know if I better take that hand," he said. "You've already grounded one of my pilots. You've got more power than I've got."

"That may be," Cahill said, holding pleasure down but keeping the confidence this gave. "But you ought to grab it anyway. There ain't nothin' in it that'll hurt you. You got it if you want it."

631

The colonel took the hand, with pressure enough to be firm, to register as sincere.

"Captain Faulstick was killed," said the colonel quietly. "Did you know that? He left his aircraft, in the midst of all that . . . all that chaos. Somebody's propeller got him."

"This'n didn't have to happen," Cahill said, through his new terror and frustration. "Not a damn bit, it didn't. It was my boy's doin'. In some kind of way it was. I'm sorry. If it means anything for me to say it, I am."

"I want to explain some things to you," the colonel said. "To the best of my ability, I do. Then maybe, later on, if you want to, you can explain some things to me, and to the others who'll be wanting to know, to try to prevent this kind of thing from happening again, ever."

"I hope you can do that. I don't want nobody else out there amongst them propellers."

Colonel Hoccleve made as if to sit on the side of the bed, glanced at the door, from which Pfc. Gilbeau had disappeared, and stayed on his feet; his face relaxed, and was rueful and boyish. "How did you do it?" he asked. "How on earth did you do it? How did you get through all that?"

The engine sounds, all of them out of tune with each other but murderous with volume, came back, and the fanning of air in his face. I must fall, one side of him said; I must get up, said the other.

"I'll be fucked if I know," he said. "My poor dog didn't make it. For me, it was just a matter of luck, I guess. I kept fallin' down and gettin' up, gettin' up, and goin' on. Finally I fetched up against the boards, and went on in. That's all I remember. They tell me I had Zack's head with me. I pity the poor bastard that saw me come in like that. I wonder what the hell he thought, right then?"

"You don't have to tell me any more, now," the colonel said. "There'll be time for that later on. But I want you to know that I saw you out there. I never felt so helpless in my life. The thing was just beyond anybody's control. But you looked like you knew what you were doing. I wouldn't be telling the truth if I said that wasn't what you looked like. You'd go down, you'd disappear, then you'd get up somewhere else, just come right out of the ground where nobody could possibly believe you could be. You'd get up again, fighting mad; you looked like you could've torn any of those planes apart with your bare hands; rip the propellers right out of them."

"Well, I couldn'a," Cahill said. "It was just that luck I was tellin' you about. If it happened again, I couldn't go two feet."

"I don't believe a man who could see could have gone through it. The behavior of the aircraft was just too erratic; it was a complete chaos; for four or five minutes there was nothing, not one thing, not one aircraft or one person, that knew what it was going to do, or what *he* was going to do. Everything was completely unpredictable; you couldn't know. It was the worst bad dream anybody ever had. No nightmare was ever as terrible as that was."

"You won't get no argument out of me," Cahill said. "Let's just charge it off, and go on."

"We will," said the colonel. "A little at a time. But I do want you to know that everybody's got his version of you out there in that tornado of propeller blades. Nobody's got the truth, but everybody's got his own slant. But the truth, no. Nobody has it."

"I sure ain't got it," Cahill said. "You'll have to put together what you can find out from them that was where they could see."

"Little by little," the colonel said. "We'll try; we'll do our best, with what we have."

Cahill stretched his shoulders. "I wouldn't mind restin' up a couple of days," he said, "if it's all right. If it ain't, I'll leave out of here."

"You don't need to be in all that much of a hurry," the colonel said. "Just get yourself together; let Major Iannone take care of you. We'll be seeing you later on."

"What's that mean?"

"We have to investigate this . . . this situation. You might not see how—believe me, I don't see how, either—but you can see why. When we get things set up, we'd like to call you back in. You may be able to help us."

"I'll do what I can," Cahill said. "Just let me know when."

"We will. As for me, I don't have any doubt that I'll lose out, as a result of all this. I'll be replaced, and I may even have to stand court-martial. Neglect, misjudgment, some charge. But right now I've got to try to follow some sort of logic through this mess, try to get a cause-and-effect pattern to come out of it."

"Supposin' there ain't one?"

"We want to look, first. That's where you'll come in, when you come back. That'll be your time. Right now is my time."

"I can't follow you, unless you tell me more than you're doin'."

The bed moved. Cahill hitched himself to one side, but no pressure formed, or changed the way the bed held him. "What kind of time you talkin' about?"

"Some things I want you to know. Here, where there's nobody around. I want to cut through the rumors and make sure you understand what the truth is."

Cahill kept waiting, and finally had to say, "Go ahead," as he listened to the colonel's breath above him draw in, stop, and return with no sound but itself.

"Rumors," Cahill said. "You want to cut through the rumors."

"As best I can. Do away with them. Finish them off."

"From what I know around here, that ain't possible."

"No," the colonel said, and smiled slightly, but not so much like a boy, "it probably isn't. But it's tryable. I mean to try. I want you to know"—he slowed down, and spoke with careful plainness—"that I didn't have anything to do with your son's going down. I was not anywhere near that brush fire, or near his aircraft."

"You wadn't up there when he was?"

"I was airborne," the colonel said, even more slowly. "But I was not near the fire. I could see the smoke, plenty of it, and I can remember hoping that none of the cadets would be foolish enough to disobey orders and fly over it. Fire turbulence is very bad; very strong."

"So they tell me. What did you do?"

"I looked around. I put my head on the swivel, like we tell the boys to do."

"And then?"

"I told you. I didn't see anything. I saw no other aircraft in the area."

"Would you swear to that? You're here, talkin' about an investigation, a board, or whatever it is, and they're gonna ask you some questions, too, just like they are to me and the rest of 'em. Would you swear that you didn't see no other airplane up where you was, over by the fire? You never saw nobody go into the smoke? Would you swear that?" Cahill leaned and turned, as though to get up from the bed. "Would you?"

"I would swear it. I intend to swear it. There was no one there. So help me God and country."

"Well, the boys . . ." Cahill answered, hesitantly.

"Mr. Cahill," the colonel said patiently, beaming the words, "we can't lose sight of the fact that these *are* boys. They don't like authority. They're *against.* You were that way, I was that way. They'll get up anything they can against an older person. We in the military have to find ways to channel that aggression, so that when they get into positions of authority themselves, positions of responsibility, they'll know what to do. They'll know what they have to contend with, because they'll know what they've left behind."

Cahill lay still, as his body filled with resistance to what was being said. Reasoning on the part of another person always did this to him, but now particularly. Dislike and suspicion rose through him to eye level, and stayed there, though he could not think of anything to say.

"Don't worry, Colonel," he finally got out. "I can tell what the situation must be like. It ain't no easy time for you."

"And another thing, Mr. Cahill," the colonel said. "I didn't have— and I don't have—anything to do with Miss Wick, in Supply, either, except to pay her salary. That's all something else the boys got up."

"Why is it that they got all this against you, Colonel? Is it like this at some of them other places?"

"There's some of it everywhere," the colonel said. "Maybe not as much as there is here, right now. That we can both thank your son for. He was back of it."

"He the only one?"

"He was the main one. The others just took off from what he said. They wanted to believe it. They wanted to believe first about Miss Wick, and then about myself and your son, and the fire. The circumstances just came together that way, and the Air Corps suffered as a result. I can't say anything about the motivation. That's out of my area."

"I can't either. And the girl—the woman—in that hot place, I sure wouldn't go back in there, not if I was you or me or anybody else."

"Why not?" the colonel asked, his eyes a little humorous.

"I was in there twice't," Cahill said. "The air is bad, and the way you hear things is bad. All them dead sheeps, quiet as it is: you can't tell who'll do what, in there. But I don't find no fault, no matter what it might'a been. I'm gonna go back to Atlanta and forget it, soon as I can."

"You can do that," the colonel said, "as soon as you're able. You can go back, but we'll have to send somebody with you. I'll put one of the MPs on TDY. He'll bring you back when we're ready. But you understand we can't just let you walk away from the whole thing. Maybe there'd be some items you could recollect, between now and then. Maybe you could find out some things for us. We need to know what you know. It's not over yet."

"So they tell me," Cahill said, and closed off that part of the talk. "How about you?" he asked. "Where does this leave you? You still the boss man?"

The colonel rocked back. He looked up and then down. "This is more or less sure to finish me as commanding officer here," he said, with resignation and surprisingly little bitterness. "But I don't want any more of the Training Command. They're finished with me; I'm finished with them. I'd just as soon go out to combat. England, maybe. Wherever they send me."

"Could be you'll run into McCaig over there," Cahill said. "He'll be surprised."

"He shouldn't be," the colonel said. "Not all that surprised, anyway."

"He's gonna do everything at night, he tells me. Everything in the dark."

"More power to him," the colonel said. "It's all one war." He opened the door, ready to leave.

Air fanned over Cahill's face and bare arm.

"One thing more, you might be thinking about."

"What's that?"

"Did your son keep some kind of record, as far as you know?"

"No. All I know is what people told me."

"He was supposed to have left a notebook; some things he wrote. Have you read it?"

"I never saw it," Cahill said. "All that's news to me."

"Do you have it?"

"No."

The air on Cahill fanned again; fanned shut.

That's all that'll be coming around, he thought. He was not sleepy, or hungry. He was not thirsty, even; he must be on the right medicine, the right amount. Someone—Gilbeau—took the needle out of his arm. He flexed it and gripped the fist, waiting for the doctor.

Air puffed at him, something like the catches of wind at his face in the cockpit; he remembered those; he checked the steadiness of the bed. "Who is it?" he asked. "That you again, Gilbeau? Doc, is that you?"

Malcolm Shears, his hair wet and combed, had come in, and four other cadets, with him and behind him. "Shears," the cadet colonel said. "I've got some others with me."

"Who?"

"Cadets Spain, Harbelis, Blazek, and Adler. The others will come, if you like. I can send somebody."

"Don't do that," Cahill said, propping up. "This is enough. I'm glad to . . . I'm glad you wanted to . . ."

"We wanted to see how you were. It's not likely we'll be able to get back by, before you leave."

"How'd you happen to get by this time? Ain't you . . . don't the colonel . . . ?"

"We're not under any restrictions," Shears said. "We can't go on open post, but nobody told us we couldn't come over here. They might later, but there're not any orders out."

"What's goin' on? Everything quiet?"

"Everything's quiet," Shears said, "and a little strange. Nobody looks at anybody else"—he waited, and smiled at the others—"except us. We don't mind what we look like."

"You gonna leave when I do? You goin' on to that other field?"

"Not yet," Shears said. "The whole class has been held back, until the board meets. It'll fuck up the quotas, but there's nothing else they can do. That's a situation we don't mind. Not at all."

"Well, God A-mighty, boys," Cahill said, gone good-natured suddenly, bouncing the air at his sides, palms up. "Where's it all gonna end?"

"It's not," Shears said. "This is only the beginning of it."

"You should have seen Lieutenant Foy," Blazek said impulsively, touching the bed near Cahill's knee.

"What happened to him?"

"He was out at the parade, when the whole thing started. He was standing with the other instructors, the check-riders, and when the first plane jumped, and things got to banging around, Neilson cut; Neilson cut and went after him."

"Shit," Cahill said. "You don't mean to tell me somebody else got hurt?"

"No such luck," Blazek said. "Foy took off through the basketball courts, with Neilson right after him, goin' this way and goin' thataway, zigzaggin', runnin' him down."

"Wait a minute," Cahill said, trying to picture. "Are you talkin' about the guy . . . the guy I taken holt of by . . ."

"That's him," Blazek said. "He had his cast on, but Neilson wasn't gonna let that stop him. Foy did everything he could to wash Neilson out, and would have, too, if it hadn't'a been for Joel and McCaig. Neilson went after him, right on out through the courts and on to the main field, gunnin' right down on him; he wasn't gonna let him get away."

Cahill swallowed, hearing the roar again, this time from behind. "Did he catch him?"

"He caught him," Blazek said, nodding vigorously and with satisfaction. "He caught him, but he caught him by the scarf, that fly-boy white scarf he always sported around. It jerked him back, almost right into the prop, but it broke, and he fell down; fell under the wheels. He didn't get a scratch. Just the shit scared out of him."

"The fear of God," Shears said. "Or of something else."

"I'm glad he didn't get hurt," Cahill said. "I don't want that on my head."

"You won't have anything on your head," Shears said. "And you sure won't have any trouble with Lieutenant Foy. There was some talk about him preferring civilian charges, making trouble with you about his hand. I don't think he'll do that, now. He got off this time, except for his scarf being wrapped around that prop-hub. He might not be that lucky next time."

"Did you see all this?"

"No. One of the ground personnel, Corporal Phillipson, told me," Blazek said. "He could see a lot more than we could. He said it was wild."

"What we saw, we could just see in flashes," Adler said. "I was never in anything like it. It wasn't just one lifetime that went by; it was hundreds."

"You can reckon what it was like, where I was."

"You couldn't think about anybody else," said Adler, bypassing and concentrating. "Things were happening too fast. I wouldn't of known about Neilson if Phillipson hadn't of told me."

"You want to see Neilson?" Shears bent and asked.

"No," Cahill said. "I don't want to see him."

"There was something else, too," Spain said. "The Eagle, here, says he couldn't see to see, that nobody could. But that's not quite true. I don't know about anybody else, but I got a flash of something. I would swear to it."

"What?" Cahill asked, his heart stirring, coming back.

"I was battling away," Spain said. "Planes were coming at me from the sides, and I could get out of the way but I couldn't catch one to ram him; I couldn't get one in my sights, you might could say. I was after getting somebody, anybody I could. They could all take their chances, like I was doing. I got clear, once; I got all the way off the parking area and onto the dirt, and was clear of the whole place, the whole area where the planes were tearing into each other and all hell had done been turned loose. But I went back in. I hadn't had enough; I couldn't *get* enough. I turned back in; right back in."

Cahill lay tensely; this was not it, yet.

"So did I," Harbelis said. "I wouldn't be surprised if most of us didn't do the same thing."

Cahill's listening built until there was nothing else.

"And then," Spain went on, his voice lowering and intensifying, as though speaking only to one other person, or to himself, "just before I went in on that second pass, I saw a plane that hadn't been hit. I was standing on the brake and turning, and through two props, mine and somebody else's that was there just for a second, just when they came together, one over, one behind the other one, when they"—Spain used his hands, and they moved as though to go over the bed, but did not; the others glanced at him, but turned back to watch Cahill, his eyes closed—"when they kind of intersected with each other, overlapped . . . there was one blur made out of two blurs, and that was when I saw who was in the plane."

"I don't believe you," Cahill said, opening his eyes and shading them. "What are you talking about?"

"I swear it, Mr. Cahill. He was in that blur, but his face was right there, coming out like . . . like a negative in the hypo. Like in that film. I saw it, as plain as I can see you. He had on a helmet and goggles, like the rest of us, but it was him. He had that expression on his mouth, and it was him."

Cahill shook his head, the pillow not softening with the motion.

"He nodded at me. I saw his head do down but not up. But it was a nod, it said yes. It said do it."

"You really believe that?" asked Cahill, suddenly tired, but excitedly. "You really believe what you're tellin' me?"

"I believe it," said Spain. "I'd swear to it."

"And that's not all," Shears came in quickly; very quickly. "You know what plane it was?"

"Believe me, I don't."

"It was the one you and McCaig were in," Shears said decisively. "It couldn't have been any other one."

"How could you know that?" Cahill asked: he must force this; there was no other way he could go. "Don't one of 'em look pretty much like the others?"

"Sure," said Shears. "They're all alike." He stopped, and swept his hand. "You look out there. That one aircraft . . . that one, the one you and McCaig were up in before we started, was sitting out there away from all the others: out there all by itself, at the end of the ramp. It had just been checked. It was all right but it hadn't been assigned. The colonel had just had it gone over, because of McCaig's report." He hung where he was, in what he was in. "You look out there now," he leaned over the bed, almost over Cahill's face. "Anybody here'd tell you." He waited himself out, again.

There was breath; gone, but still saying.

"There's nothing there. No plane. Nothing. Nothing but empty flight line."

"And so?" Cahill said, blocked, supremely blind, himself. They must tell; they can't back off.

"So it was Joel Cahill," Shears said. "It was him, in and out. It was him, with that touch. The touch. That's all it takes, and it's *what* it takes. It comes out of anywhere, but it's what it takes. There's not anybody else that had it."

"For what?" Cahill asked. "Has it for what? What the fuck good is all this?"

"For something the world has not seen yet," Shears said. "For the end of everything that's ever been wrong."

"What's . . . ?" Cahill began.

Fields. Cahill moved among his past, trying to pick them up. Finally there came to him the scrappy openness of Piedmont Park, where he had walked freely, as much as he wanted to, surrounded by the city. But he could put no blue, no purple, into the grass, into the air, into the uneven towers of Atlanta on

"Think," Shears said, leaning intently. "Think, Mr. Cahill." He pulled back, upright, almost too far, then leaned again. "You can probably get it in your mind, right in front of you, better than any of us can. Think of that big purple field, just as far as you can see." He spoke, as though another, like a hypnotist, someone they had seen in movies. "Think of the lakes, blue and clear, glittering: glittering with initials, like Joel used to say. The initials can be anybody's: anybody can belong to 'em: anybody who's there with us, who's made it through, and out

640

all sides. The color of these was gray, and could not be anything else. No matter what sun would ever shine on them, or snow fall, for him they were gray. As for energy, as for the towers he associated with electricity, he could find only one or two in the country, seen from highways, gaunt, mostly air, moving over hills out of sight, tall without meaning. When would he have driven where they were, and noticed?

Cold food. Cold food and waterfalls. Water coming from above him, at his sides—both sides—and falling past him. Continuous. Continuous. Wings. One wing. One, to the horizon, covered with snow.

Picked up. Up from the ground. Picked up into the air. One minute in the air.

White water going down: all white: whiter than anything other than it. White water falling: he staying. He not falling. Rising. One minute in the air.

the other side. Think of our energy source: the one energy, the only energy: electricity. Think of it: really think of it. Clean, quiet, all we need: energy based on a mystery that'll not ever be understood, but that works. Think of the little rivers, and the water moving for us, moving with us. Think of the long music.

"And when the war ends, we'll have what we want," Shears said. "And we'll have *all* we want; we'll have our momentum." He looked around him, and particularly at Adler, who stood blinking, as a person will do who needs glasses, and for his own reasons won't use them. "When the war ends, that's when it'll really start. One of the reasons for war is to make heroes; there's nothing else like it. Not sports, not medical discoveries, not politics. With the momentum we get from the war we can do anything we like, go any direction with it we want to. We can make this fucking world over, and then walk off and leave it. That'll be our answer: to walk away from it. There won't be anything left but the big blue field, some water, electricity, and the ones of us who get there, who knew that it was there, and knew how to get to it. Everything will be simple: simple and deep. There won't be anything else; only nihilism and music."

"Where is McCaig?" Cahill asked unexpectedly. "Is he comin' around?"

"McCaig is gone," Shears said. "He might even be in Canada by now. He left before the parade, even."

"Too bad," Cahill said. "I wanted to tell him good-bye."

"He was sure a good one," Blazek said. "Him and Joel were lucky to get together. He was the right one for Joel."

"Amen," Adler said. "He could've been Alnilam, if he hadn't'a been too old."

"In a way he *was* Alnilam," Shears said, but not emphatically. "He was Joel's instructor. Joel trusted him. He had the right frame of mind."

"It's funny," Spain said. "None of us was ever actually in the aircraft with Joel. That's why McCaig is so important: because he was the only one that was."

McCaig took my dog out into the field and turned him gray. The field was supposed to be black, burned up, and my dog was black, but the field turned him gray. The snow melted off him, but the gray, the ashes, must have stayed for a while. Except just when McCaig came back with him, came in out of the fields, nobody ever said anything about it.

"You're forgetting about Lieutenant Foy," said Adler. "He never rode with Joel, but he talked like he had. He wanted to. He wanted to wash him out. Don't forget about him."

"*You* don't forget about him," Shears said, "what Foy wanted to do, he didn't. And Mr. Cahill took care of him for us. Foy's behind us now, for good. His name don't even need to come up."

"Who?" he asked, catching back into the conversation again, mainly because of the laughter, some mean and some nervous. "What about Willis? What'd he ever do?"

"His and Willis's," Blazek said.

"He did just right," Shears said. "When Billy Crider gunned up, he panicked, and jumped. And I think it was him that ran into Captain Faulstick and killed him. But not right there at the first. A little later on, prob'ly. I think it was him, though."

"They'll find out later, maybe," Blazek said.

"No," Shears said. "They may try, but I don't think they'll ever find out. I doubt if Willis knows, himself. His head was prob'ly down in the cockpit the whole time, with the throttle open."

"I guess I won't be seein' you boys any more," Cahill said, tired and heavier; a lot heavier. "I reckon we can end it up. Good luck to all of you."

"Thank you," Shears said, motioning the others toward the door. "We'll try to keep in touch with you, if you like."

Cahill raised himself on an elbow and tried to brighten, to finish strong. "Remember," he said. "I got to come back up here, when they start askin' all them questions."

"We'll be around too, I reckon," Shears said, as the others left. "They've got to go through

643

the motions, and we'll help 'em." He bent close to Cahill's face. "I'll try to get back by, one more time before you leave," he said. "There're one or two more things. I won't bring the others."

"I'll be here," said Cahill. "I'll be here till I go."

*   *   *   *

The door-air fanned him again; he was not surprised; he had not been sleeping. "Ain't there but one room in this place?" he asked. "Who is it?"

"I don't think there *is* but one room," said Captain Whitehall. "At least not but one private one. Everything else is a big bay, and a tunnel. There's nobody in the bay. I just came through the tunnel. There's not anybody there, either."

"You ain't the doc," Cahill said, "the doc from Charleston, that talks like a crawfish. You ain't him, and you ain't no boy."

"You know who I am," Whitehall said.

"I do by now," Cahill replied. "Come on in and sit down, if there's anywhere you can. What've you got, and what do you want?"

Whitehall turned the slick-painted green chair around and sat on it, leaning forward on the back. "I don't want anything in particular," he said, "but I did bring you a little something, which I'll give you when I leave."

"Is it somethin' to eat? The doc won't let me have it."

"No; it's not anything to eat. But don't let me get out of here and go off with it."

"I don't like surprises."

"I don't think this will be any too much of a surprise to you."

"Does it have somethin' to do with this base? If it does I don't want it. Some kind of trainin' thing, is it?"

"Not this kind of training," Whitehall said. "Only a little, with this kind of training. More with my kind. You can use it on ships, too. Even cars, if you know what you're doing."

"Ships, yet," Cahill said sardonically. "McLendon, back in town, says I ought to get acquainted with the ocean. That what you're talkin' about?"

644

"Maybe," Whitehall said. "You could do that. After the war, you could. Take somebody with you."

"Ain't nothin' that's impossible, I reckon."

"Almost nothing," Whitehall said, jumping the chair forward. "Far as I'm concerned, I like water better than air. When you get killed, it's better; even death is better that way. I used to sail a lot, and I was never afraid of anything. I used to think, you drown and you're still whole. Nobody ever killed in an airplane was ever whole. Not one."

"Maybe you should'a been in the Navy."

"Too late now," Whitehall said, with some regret. "But I can take the air all right, if I can get into it on my own terms. Pilot training they can have. Fighter aircraft they can have. You can't get me off the ground unless they put an office up there for me. Stars, tables, time, and spherical trig: that's my flying. Angles. They work. There's no blood there, no dirt. And not much fear there, either, come to think of it. You're too deep down there—up there—in the Principles."

"You can fall."

"Sure you can. And it keeps coming back to you, that you can." He shifted again. "And you remember the accidents you've seen, the shape the bodies were in, and try to get back into the numbers, quick as you can."

"It'll all be over, one of these days," Cahill said without conviction. "Then you can go back to sailin'."

Whitehall went on as though he had not heard. "The airplane is a mutilation machine. No human body—nothing alive—ought to be subjected to the forces that high-speed metal has, when it impacts. Every airplane is full of death. And the people who fly in them, especially in wars, are the kings of death, the real kings. While they're alive, they are. Then they impact, or someone—some one of themselves—sees that they do."

"You ain't no hero," Cahill said, but not harshly. "You're a damn preacher."

"Every one of these boys is being taught to kill," Whitehall said. "Cannons, thirty-calibers, fifty-calibers, antipersonnel bombs, general-purpose, napalm, white phosphorus—you name it. All these innocent-looking kids. That's their stuff. They're being raised on it. That's their toy pile, their sandbox. They know what to do with those things, but they don't know what they mean."

"I guess Captain Faulstick, your buddy, found that out."

"What did he find out?" Whitehall asked, unexpectedly indignant. "How do you figure?"

"What he was tellin' us about; when he was in the glass bomber. You ain't forgot that, have you? It was only the other night, that he was tellin' us."

"I know," Whitehall said, now very still in the chair. "I wasn't sure what you were getting at. You mean that spark from the yellownose, the ME-109, over France."

"Right."

"What he called the 'spark of creation,' life and death at once, creation and destruction, in one blink? One flash from a nose cannon?"

"I wonder if he ever saw it again."

Whitehall looked away, decided, and then looked back. "He never saw it the first time," he said.

"What?" Cahill said, struggling. "I don't get . . . ? He didn't . . . ? How . . . what do you mean? He just sat in there the other night and . . ." he settled on what he would say; grasped it. "How could you know that? You wadn't there. Now *that's* the damn truth. You wadn't there. How the hell could you know?"

"He never saw it," Whitehall repeated, more slowly.

"You're shittin' me. There ain't no way you could know."

"Yes there is," Whitehall said. "The ME-109 doesn't have a nose cannon. That's just fiction. Even some of the guys in the ETO believe it, like Faulstick. But it's not so. That propeller hole is part of the cooling system. It's an air backup for the coolant. That's all." He stood up, his legs held apart by the chair, and sat back down. "Think of that: the beginning and end of everything, life and death by propeller hole, where there's not even any gun."

"I can't take that in," Cahill said, rubbing his elbows on the sheet. "I can't take all that in."

"I've seen the tech orders on some of the reconstructs. I repeat, there's not any nose cannon in the ME-109."

"Then why . . . ?"

"It's a war story, Mr. Cahill," Whitehall said evenly, and with patience. "They're all over the place. And every one of them has to have some kind of moral to it. I never heard one that didn't. A lot of them are deliberate mysteries, because people want to have something to set against the realities they're in. Hell, they tell me that in the First World War the soldiers said that an angel came up over the battlefield, somewhere, over the trenches, over no-man's-land. A whole lot of those poor fuckers believed it." He smiled and shook his head. "Some angel, eh? Made out of barbed wire and sandbag sand. Made out of slime and snow and shit. It had rat's eyes. I'm sure it did. I'd feel better about it if I knew that was true. An angel with rat's eyes over no-man's-land: that'd be appropriate. It's the only one that belongs there." He sighed, and gestured; his hands fell. "But then that's *my* war story. I just made it up like somebody else did, back there in that other war."

"But that flash from the other airplane, when he . . . when Faulstick was up there in that glass place . . . I mean he seemed to . . . it seemed to me like . . ."

"It was just something that Faulstick had," Whitehall said. "Something he needed. In the end he probably thought it was true. After all, like you say, he was the one that was there."

"Out of the propeller," Cahill said, foreign to himself. "He found the propeller, all right."

"But not the hole in it," Whitehall said. "It was a void, an illusion. There's nothing in there. Only air for the enemy's machinery."

"Why was it him? Why was it Faulstick? What'd he ever do?"

"He talked too much, I think. The boys knew how he felt. It's my impression some of them—that Spain kid might have been one—filled him full of panic stories. They primed him, figuring he was weak, that they could get to him. They knew the Air Corps was carrying him, like that football player, Knocker Nicholson. They were embarrassed to wash him out."

"I know Knocker Nicholson," Cahill said. "He got a lot of Chinese people killed."

"That's right," Whitehall said, surprised, even gratified that Cahill had heard, and that he remembered. "The Nips wiped out every town that'd saved his life. They all died. Nicholson is still around, doing publicity tours. He'll recruit many a kid."

"The people here, the colonel and them, should'a got Faulstick out. He wouldn't'a minded. He didn't like to fly; he'd tell anybody."

"He sure would. He told everybody that would listen."

"They should'a got him out for his own good."

"Well, he's out."

Someone knocked. *"Now* what is it?" Cahill said. "Come on in, for God's sake. Let's have us a convention."

"How's the sugar?" Major Iannone asked, his hand on the bed-foot rail, balancing and looking down.

"It's simmerin'," Cahill said, "but it's fallin' off. It ain't makin' me feel bad. I might could eat somethin', pretty soon. I wouldn't have no objection to that."

"We'll bring you along," Iannone said. "We'll time it and weigh it and measure it, and your blood'll get the message."

"Many thanks," Cahill said. "Thanks again."

"It's not just your fouling up your dosage, old-timer," Iannone said. "You bring a lot on yourself you shouldn't have to put up with."

"What's that?"

"Exhaustion, for one thing. Your body's a dead wreck from trying to do what it can't do. You got exhaustion," he said, counting on his fingers for his own benefit, "you got what I'd call emotional strain. You've been drinking too much not only for a diabetic but for Primo Carnera. You haven't been getting enough sleep. And there's one other thing that the medical journals don't talk much about: confusion. Turning this way and that way. Physical attrition from that, from not knowing which way is right, for what you need to do. Confusion, Mr. Cahill. Confusion is bad news. We've got to get you back to your own doctor. Go home and get together with him."

"Soon as I can."

"They'll have to call you back up here for the board, the investigation. They'll tell you when; it might be a while; sometimes it takes months to set these things up. You don't want to be around here all that time."

"I sure don't."

"I want you to be in good shape, the next time I see you."

"I'll do what they tell me." Cahill moved his feet and crossed them. "That all?"

"More or less," Iannone said, making no move toward the door.

Whitehall got up from the chair and offered it. The major nodded and sat down, rubbing the heels of his hands together and staring off into the corner. "There are a lot of things that can go wrong with you, you know. You've got to cut down on the ones you can deal with; you got to cut 'em off at the pass."

"I said I'd do what they tell me."

"You know, Mr. Cahill," the major continued, "the world is jampacked with secret little evils. Germs, microbes, bacteria, they're nothing to the other stuff that can get after you. As far as the bacteria are concerned, there're plenty of 'em, all right, but in a certain way you can understand 'em; you can get to know 'em and live with 'em. Your teeth are full of 'em, just to bring in one illustration. You can't kill 'em off fast enough; they come back right away. But you can kill some of 'em for a while, and keep the level down. Even so, your teeth stay full of 'em no matter what you do, to say nothing of your skin and your guts." His face changed. "But you take your boy." When Cahill had repositioned his ear, he went on. "His trouble was not infection. He had that psoriasis bothering him, which is a matter of chemistry. An enzyme deficiency, so far as anybody knows. The trouble is," he winked at Whitehall, "what anybody knows, so far, ain't so far."

"Your man was tellin' me about that," Cahill said. "The man that keeps the papers from blowin' away, in this indoor wind you got around here. I know all about my boy's . . . my boy's skin. Your man said you had to paint him like a telephone pole. Said it turns you black; at least if you've got blue eyes, it does."

"He tell you that?" Iannone said, startled enough to be angry. "Gilbeau tell you that? It don't make you black. No such of a thing."

"Then . . . ?"

"You'd think it would," Iannone said. "If somebody told you about it, you'd think that if you put that stuff on a human being it'd make him black like a telephone pole is black, or at least mighty dark, like bridge pilings, or something. But it doesn't do that. It's just a clear glaze, like any other water."

"I'll settle for that," Cahill said. "I'd just as soon he never did turn black. I couldn't get used to the idea."

"That's one thing you don't have to worry about," Iannone said. "He was a good-looking fair-skinned blue-eyed kid, full of energy and enthusiasm. He had more of what young boys ought to have than all the rest of them put together. And they tell me he was a damned genius in the air." He held back. "But I reckon you're getting tired of hearing that."

"I don't never get tired of it. It's like everybody tellin' you you're rich and famous. Even if you are, it don't hurt none to hear it."

"Flying," Iannone said, spinning the chair around on one leg so that he could sit in it and use the back, "this flying is something strange and wonderful for these kids. The war makes it all possible for 'em; it's like an enchantment, a spell. A lot of 'em know something about engines, about how machinery works; a lot of 'em, probably most of 'em, have messed around with cars. They can tell you about carburetors. They know the firing cycle of the internal combustion engine."

"They don't know much about gas, though," Cahill said. "But the teacher's not bad. He used to live under the ground, he told us."

649

The major smiled, and glanced at Captain Whitehall, who had moved to the window and was staring out into the grayness.

"They may learn, then," Iannone said. "I hope they do, because they ought to know everything about what carries 'em, what totes 'em up there, where nobody'd ever been until forty years ago."

"What you're sayin' is the truth," Cahill agreed. "I know *I* ain't never felt nothin' like it."

"When these kids get carried up in the air in that thing they've put themselves into, when they see that they're actually on wings, and feel it, feel the air all around them, the moves, the motions of the air moving them, and they have that wide view, that purple view that most of them have never had before, they're not thinking about the tolerance of cylinders. They're in some other kind of place. When they get up there for the first time, it's not the pistons dancing up and down and the gas exploding in a little round hole. It's being lifted up, and staying up, and in a way doing all this by yourself, by your own means and your own body. A lot of them forget there's an airplane involved, they're so lost in this other thing. They're not the same people they were on the ground. They're not the same people they were when they were growing up, when they were playing games and chasing girls around. You could say that everything that's young and excitable about them is brought out, everything that has to do with danger, and newness, and they're right in the middle of it. Nothing is the same. When they drink that air coming through that open cockpit they're drinking something more powerful than any liquor ever made. They're in the middle of something that's brand-new, and it's endless. That's the part of it I'd want for my boy, if I had one. If there's ever been a kind of situation that's made for youth itself, that satisfies every need that kids have, and creates some new ones, it's up there." He pointed to the ceiling. Whitehall, at the window but not looking out, propped against the wall in the opposite of any military position, glanced at the major, and turned again to the outside.

"The feeling's like the air," the major went on. "The damn air itself. It's unlimited every which way. And to have that just given to you, like these kids have"—he shrugged and shook his shoulders in middle-aged wonderment—"and then, for one of *them*, in the situation just like all of them are, not these tired old farmerish instructors, or these career military hot-shots, these grown-up people just looking for their flight pay, like I am, like Foy and Manetta and Guignard, and probably the colonel, if you won't tell him I said so"—he hesitated, and ran his hand over his hair, as thick as Brillo—"but for one of these boys, one of their own, somebody who seems like he belongs there, belongs up there in that strange new element that's like nothing ever experienced before, who seems to almost everybody almost a . . . a . . . an inhabitant of the air, and that maybe *came* from the air: who might've come down to them, to live with them, to live like they do, for . . . that's what you've got here, Mr. Cahill. It's your boy we're talking about."

"So?" Cahill asked, wondering if Captain Whitehall was still in the room, but had some reason not to talk. Or had he gone out? The door had made no more air, and he was sure he would have felt it.

"So he raises some questions."

"I don't have none of the answers, if that's what you're talkin' about. Not a one."

"That's not what I'm talking about," the major said. "I thought you might like to have some of *my* answers. I've been mulling this over." He stopped and pulled at his face again. "It's pretty unusual."

"Go ahead, Major," Cahill said. "What is it you're gettin' at?"

"Well, first of all," Iannone said, engaging the chair-back with his side and shoulder, "you've got your son"—he looked closely at Cahill, who lay as he had been—"you've got your son in this immense playground, and you've got him in a life-and-death activity that's the most exciting thing in the world, a real airborne drama full of kids and men hardly older than kids, and you come to find out that you're the master of it, the magician. You're what everybody doing it wants to be. Everybody tells you you are, and everything that happens bears it out. You think you can do anything you want, when you get into an airplane, and so do the others. You are exactly what's needed, and you know it. If you don't know it at first, you get to know it right quick. And you're the kind of boy that thinks—that gets to think—that more than flying is involved, and that you can be the center of that, too, whatever it is." He leaned forward. "Or whatever you *make* it to be: whatever you say it is. You think that there are a whole lot of new laws to be made; that the old ones are no good, and maybe never were."

"That ain't somethin' I got any ideas about," Cahill said. "I ain't the center. Maybe that's the reason I don't know."

Iannone went over his hair again, this time with both hands.

"These kids haven't run into the death part of it yet," he said. "Except with your boy, Mr. Cahill. And now with Captain Faulstick. Before this it was all magic. Most of them have never been off the ground any higher than they could climb up a hickory."

"Once is enough for me," Cahill said. "I'll take the next tree."

"I hate flying myself," the major said. "Every time the god-damned thing turns, every time the colonel goes into a bank, or whatever they call it, I feel like I'm falling out. It's a thing some doctors do for half-again pay. It ain't that way with these kids. For me, it's too lay-ut for the magic. Not for them. You got to remember: half of them will be dead in a year; maybe more than half."

"He . . . Joel had a bunch of friends here . . ." Cahill began.

"Let's cut all that, Mr. Cahill. You know what his 'friends' did."

"Say what you want," Cahill said strongly, and feeling strong. "You think it was them that busted up all them airplanes. That what you think? You think my boy was behind it?"

"It all has to be weeded out. They'll get to the bottom of it, in a few weeks."

"Why would a few boys want to break up a bunch of airplanes, Major? Even if they had somebody they thought was the greatest thing that was ever in one of 'em? That don't make no sense. That don't make no kind of sense. Why would they do that? Why would they do what he said? You tell *me*. Would they?"

"Sure they would," Iannone said, nodding vigorously. Whitehall, now in the far corner of the room and behind the major, frowned, and moved again.

"Sure they would," Iannone repeated, when Cahill did not reply. "I keep saying it. You've got to remember that these are kids. They may be pilot trainees, but they're still kids. If it weren't for the war they'd be in college, most of them. Fraternities. Societies, some of them 'secret.' Skull and Bones. Porcellian. This bunch is in a way the equivalent of that, except that it has other things mixed in." He paused, and located Whitehall, now at the blue medical dresser. "Things like life and death. That gives it a dimension that Skull and Bones ain't got, even with that name."

"But, shit," Cahill said, "this bein' a pilot is a real big piece of what you want, what these kids want. Why would they fuck it up? They tell me they wear silver wings, and that's the biggest thing around. Why would they go in for somethin' like this? Wouldn't they want to go on and be pilots, and all?"

"Some would. Most would."

"But this," Cahill said, "it don't lead to them silver wings. It don't lead nowhere. Who would go in for somethin' like this?"

"A few would. A few. That's all it takes."

"You mean to tell me," Cahill rose in the bed and said, "that somebody—some kid—could just get all this up out of nothing? Nothin' but gall and talk, and bein' good at flyin' an airplane? Out of nothin' but an old book he had in school, and bullshittin' these other boys, and a few guesses, and some luck? You mean to tell me that these were just some things that happened to come together, and because of 'em a man is dead? A man is dead and the war effort in North Carolina is fucked up, as far as airplanes have got anything to do with it? You mean you can knock a thing down that easy?"

"Depends," the major said. "If you have a group, an outfit, a person —if there's a force of some kind that nobody knows is there, that just comes out of left field, it can hit you pretty hard. If you're blindsided real hard you can get the shit kicked out of you. It can be all over before you ever knew it was coming."

"And this is the way Joel . . . this is the way he wanted to do? I still don't see how he could make a thing like this happen. How'd he do that, Major?"

"Timing," Iannone said. "There was the climate made up by the people he was with. Things were right for Joel Cahill to come into. He created part of the atmosphere; he was good at that, they tell me. He created part of it, but not all. When it was there he could feel it. So could the others. He made Malcolm Shears, and the others, Cadet Spain, and that poor dumb Greek boy, feel as though they had been waiting for him; that he had just come along to take his rightful place. Like I say, they were waiting for him." He pointed a finger at Cahill, singling him out for himself and Whitehall. "And they were waiting for you, Mr. Cahill. It's not so much that you became part of it; you were already part of it. You were always part of it, and your coming up here nailed that fact down for these boys. And I'm not sure that it was nailed down just for them, either. It seems like there's more than an element of chance in it. Not just coincidence. Some other thing." He put the back of his left hand on his right cheek and rubbed it. "You know, sir, that you're not only part of what you do, you're part of what's done by means of you. If you want the meat out of the lobster's claw, you've got to know where to crack it, and how the cartilage runs through it. If you don't, you can't get the meat out whole, which is the way you want to put it in your mouth. Joel knew where to crack it. He knew how the meat lays in the claw."

"You can sell some of that, Doctor," Cahill said. "But I'm not buyin' it all. There's no way in the world that that boy could'a knowed I would come up here. He didn't know I was blind, either."

"No," the major said quietly. "I don't think he did know that."

"He didn't know I was blind, and he didn't know I'd come."

"But you are blind," Iannone said slowly. "And you did come."

"You mean to tell me that you think he got himself killed in order to get me to come up here? What the hell kind of sense does that make?"

"Putting aside the question as to whether he's dead or not," the major said, "you can consider, if you want to, that children will do ingenious things, desperate things, to get together with their parents, if the regular ways are not working out. I'm just saying that this is very ingenious, and very desperate. But I'm also saying that there's a 'call' psychology working here, whether you know it or not, or whether he knew it or not. I'd give you big odds on it. Why *did* you come, Mr. Cahill? In your situation, everything was against it."

"I came because . . . because I wanted to know what the hell was goin' on," Cahill said lamely, and then picked up, as he felt himself coming nearer the truth. "I came because I thought maybe it would be hard . . . it would be hard for a man in my shape to do, without nobody helpin' him, without nobody but him and a dog. I felt like I could do it, and I wanted to do it, and I felt like it was somethin' that couldn't no other, couldn't no ordinary man do. No ordinary blind man, anyway. Them's all part of the reason. I just got it into my head that I could do it, and I did."

"That's honest," the major said. "What did you expect to do when you got here? What did you think would happen?"

"Now how in the name of the Devil and the Lord put together, how in the name of death and damnation was I goin' to know *that?* I ain't a fuckin' mind reader. I don't read nobody's hands, or the wrinkles around their eyes. What happened happened. You know more about it than I do. You can see. Why don't you go with that? Why bother a damned blind man?"

"I don't know more about some things than you do, Mr. Cahill," Iannone said. "I don't know as much about the group of boys that followed your son around, and now follows Malcolm Shears around. That you can tell me, and I wish you would."

"That ain't your business, Doctor," Cahill said. "That's somethin' between them boys and me," then added, "and between my boy and me."

"The military is going to do their best to get to the bottom of this. It'd be mighty useful if you could help."

"All this talkin', Doctor, all this here talkin' you're doin', seems like it

654

would show anybody that wanted to listen, and I mean *anybody*, that you know a whole lot more about everything than I do."

"Alnilam," the major said slowly. "Al-nilám. String of Pearls. The middle star of the northern winter constellation Orion. Orion the Hunter." He turned one way and did not find Whitehall, then the other and found him. "That right, Captain?"

"That's right," Whitehall said, smiling, but more to himself than to the major. "Low magnitude, and not much used in navigation. There are lots of better ones. But it can be used if you like. It'd be easy to find. It's in the Almanac, and *Selected Stars.* But his dog, Orion's dog, Sirius, the Dog Star, is a lot better."

"But not central," the major said. "Not the middle of anything."

"No; he's out in the dark, by himself."

"Doctor," Cahill said, setting up his moves like a checkers player, a new thing for him, which he liked immediately. "You ask me to level with you, and now I want you to do the same thing, with me. That seems fair."

"It is," Iannone said. "I don't have anything to hide. I'll tell you what I think."

"Do you believe that all this was got up because one star is in the middle of some other ones? That ain't much to go on."

"It doesn't take much, if you've got imagination, and the ability to make other people's imagination work. If you can fire up that part of a person, you've got him. He wants more; he don't want that to die. And you're the only place he can get it; you see to that. After all," he sat back, and put his hands behind his head. "After all, what does Mussolini have but a bunch of sticks tied together? Hitler's got a cross with the ends knocked flat. New England had a snake that said not to step on it. Jesus had a fish. All America has is a mangy bird. By the way, the bald eagle has an unusually high incidence of lice. Did you know that? It's true."

"You mean you believe this was all just some school-kid thing? That tore up all them airplanes? That killed my dog? That killed a man, and god-damned near killed me? That what you think?"

"Yes," the major said. "It is what I think. But I also think that the same things could be said about all these so-called leaders, Napoleon and Julius Caesar. Huey Long down in Louisiana. Most of the time they don't really offer much. They give people the notion that they can make life different in some way, and that the people who help them, who join in with them, will be different, will be made different, will exist in a new way, a way they couldn't have thought of by themselves. If you can sell people that notion they will do what you say; not anything on earth will stop them. There's not a person in the world who really likes himself, the way he is; anything at all would be better for him than the way he is. Most men wouldn't say that in so many words, but deep down they feel it; they know it's the truth."

"That's the answer to everything? That your notion?"

The major nodded. "Tell 'em you can make 'em different, and you got 'em. Put 'em in a black uniform, or a red uniform, and tell 'em they *belong* to something, that they're special, that they've been picked out. Not by a government, not by a school; not by anything official. Something else. Something that comes out of nowhere. Out of left field. Out of the blue, you might say."

"Special," Cahill said. "Who's special, Doctor?"

"People who follow leaders think they are," Iannone said. "They've never been special before, in any way. But their specialness exists because of you. They're not going to turn loose of it. Jesus, they think"—Iannone pushed both hands overhead, in gratitude to the ceiling for revelation—"maybe it's even true!"

"Your notion is that you can take just a few things, that somebody could just take a schoolbook and a . . . a knack for flyin' a airplane, and a few crazy words about stars that can't nobody understand what he's talkin' about, and he could set all this up? He could fuck up this whole base? He could get somebody killed? All that? And all over nothin'? *Nothin'?* Just a whim? Just a wild hair up his ass?"

"Could be done," Iannone said. "It's been done with less than that. A lot less. If a person has enough personal force, and conviction, he can do a lot. And mystery; he has to have that. He gives it to himself, and he encourages other people to build it up. They don't mind. Don't mind a-tall. All along the way, they'll add anything they can; anything they can think of, that'll make the whole thing more fascinating. The more fascinating it is, the more effective it is. And the more power you've got."

"You talkin' about *any* mystery? Any at all?"

"No; some mysteries. Some mys-teries in the hands of some people. That's as far as I've ever been able to get."

"It wadn't nothin' but a game, then," Cahill said. "That's all it was. Right?"

"There was a lot of that in it," Iannone said. "All these aircraft were toys to your son, Mr. Cahill. They could be made a part of an eleborate personal scheme." He leaned forward and this time touched the bed, but not Cahill. "A *central* part, the point around which the other elements group."

"Still, still," Cahill said. "It still ain't much to go on. It's just . . . what do you call it? It's just a kind of . . . it's just a smatterin'."

"A smattering is all it takes," the major said. "In fact, a smattering is *what* it takes. People who want to follow someone don't have time for learning a lot, or really going into a subject. Most of 'em don't have the brains, either. What you need is an attitude, a suggestion, something that flashes across." He demonstrated with his hand, in front of Cahill's unmoving head. "Something that flashes across, and something that *makes* it flash. The more outlandish, the more outrageous it is, the more people want to believe it. Especially boys. They want in on it. Would you believe"—he tapped the bed again—"that there was some kid a hundred, a hundred and fifty years ago, that thought he could save the world by sailing pieces of paper out the window of a hotel?"

"Would they stay up a minute?" Cahill asked, unexpectedly. "Any of 'em have a minute in the air?"

"It's not recorded," the major said, looking curiously at the man on the bed. "He didn't really make the difference he wanted to, but there were some people that would'a followed him anywhere. He was drowned in Italy, as I remember, and they burned him up, and some fellow couldn't stand to see his heart burn, and pulled it out of the fire." He grinned and relaxed. "Damned if I know how I remember that."

"My boy had more sense than him."

"Yes, he did," the major said, nodding. "More sense, and more effect. You know"—he shook his head with dismay, and also with satisfaction at his analysis—"when something like this, some bunch of people with the same ideas, get going, the followers put a lot of things onto the leader that they didn't even know they had to give him, and also that *he* didn't have. Joel Cahill was them; he was the cadets, with one more twist. A twist they had in 'em somewhere, but that they couldn't give themselves. They could recognize it when they saw it, but they couldn't free it up. He had a way, he *was* a way for them to do that."

"That ain't anything new."

"That's just the point. It's not. It's happened plenty of times before, all over history. And it'll happen again, over and over. Your boy was just the form it took, here."

"Form? Forms?"

"Sure. The ones that were in with him felt that they had something that nobody else had. That's a powerful inducement for kids. It'll pull hard on anybody. Hell, look at the Masons. Look at the Elks and the Shriners. Look at the Ku Klux Klan, if you want to. I'd just as soon not, myself."

"They don't kill people. Except the ones in the white sheets. The Elks don't do nothin' like that."

"All these organizations are all right," the major said, "if the element of fanaticism doesn't come in. But for some of them that's the thing that makes it go: At first it's fun, and then it gets fanatical. If you're in it, you're locked in, and the only way you can behave is to be more fanatical than the others. That's when the blood starts to show through, starts to show up. And the worst thing about it is that it gets justified. The bunch that sheds the blood can give you plenty of reasons for it; to them, they're the best reasons you could ask for."

"Too much talk," Cahill said tiredly.

"What?" the major said, not offended. "You mean me?"

"No," Cahill said, though he did, at least partially. "I mean Joel and his buddies. They got too many notions."

"Yes, but they get hold of you," Iannone said. "They sure do. About the Alnilam notion, it keeps coming back to me that something like it might work. A lot of things more crack-brained than this have been tried; all kinds of holy men, prophets, kings, cranks, you name it. It's not just Hitler, even though he ought to be crazy enough for anybody. All of those folks are cranks, if you ask me, Jesus Christ included. Some of them have come to plenty, though. Plenty of good, and plenty of bad."

"We won't get rid of them kind, I reckon."

"No; they're built into us. You get some kind of imaginative notion going, it can come out of anywhere. Some notion, some comparison of one thing to another, some new way of putting things. That's your power; and the control. That's your centrality. And if you can back up what you see, they'll believe not only what you say about the thing you can do, and that you can show them that you can do, but they'll believe everything you say, no matter what it is. And if there's a mysterious twist on it, they'll believe in 'superior powers.' Superior powers is what it's all about. Not everybody wants to have them himself, but he wants *someone* to have them; he wants to believe that they're possible. And if they come from left field, that's even better. Left field is as good as God."

Cahill blew so that his cheeks swelled, then flattened. "Maybe it'll end here," he said. "I reckon the Army'll cut 'em off at the pass."

"I don't think so," Iannone said, getting to his feet. "Those boys are too full of the idea of power, now. Blind power. Of all power, blind power is the most powerful kind." He stopped, realizing. "I'm sorry. I didn't mean to offend you."

"You didn't do that," Cahill said. "I wadn't even thinkin' about it. Blind power's the only kind I got."

"When you have it, you're beyond everybody. Beyond them, behind them, underneath them, above them. You sit in judgment. These boys have been there, now. They'll go on from here. They've got it all. Everything. They've got a martyr, everything they need. All the Army's got to stop them with is laws. Laws can't do it all. There're some places they can't reach."

"Is there any way out?"

"What do you mean?"

"Out of . . . of that bunch of boys? Out of what you tell me they're in there with?"

The major shook his head. "There doesn't seem to be any," he said. "Not without some kind of violence. Pain, blood, betrayal, and the rest." He rubbed the back of his neck. "Betrayal: that's the worst. The worst of all. There ain't no worse name than Judas. But there'll be one in there somewhere. There always is."

"You takin' off?" Cahill asked, hearing the voice coming from higher.

"Yes. I'll leave you and the captain, and maybe come back before you go, one more time."

"You got a lot of ideas about my boy," Cahill said, raising himself on his elbows. "I've only got one or two." Cahill took a breath; a lot of it. "It was an act," he said. "It was all an act. That's the way I see it."

"OK," Iannone said, "if that's what you want to call it. You can look at it that way. It'd be maybe a little too frightening if you didn't."

"It was an act," Cahill repeated. "It was somethin' he . . ."

"I wouldn't sell your boy quite that short, Mr. Cahill. He had something. Something that nobody can figure out, but it wraps around people. It gives them a place to be headed. That makes a big difference, Mr. Cahill."

"My name is Frank, to tell you the truth."

"All right, Frank," the major said, with a kindness that no one could doubt. "I'll leave you and the captain in the big dark, out yonder

659

between stars. Do what you can with it." He laughed, and the door shed air. "It ain't no place for me."

The door air quit, with a click. Beyond it Cahill heard two footsteps, and then no more. He reached behind himself and rearranged the pillows, then stretched out onto them, blew his cheeks again, and relaxed.

"I'm still here," a voice said.

"I know you are, Captain," Cahill said. "And you can quit roamin' around. I been knowin' exactly where you was at, anywhere you was, in this room."

"How'd you know that?" Whitehall asked, smiling as he wished, and taking the one chair.

"I got my ways," said Cahill. "I ain't givin' away no secrets." He smiled, himself, but with no teeth. "The major's got all of 'em: them things."

"He can talk," Whitehall said.

"He don't mind it. I'm just as glad he's got somethin' else to do, right now."

"He means well enough," Whitehall said. "He's trying, like everybody else."

"Was you payin' attention to all that stuff he was goin' on about?"

"Some of it," Whitehall replied, and then, his tone changing, "but it was just conventional. You can take this as a preview of what the other conventional folks are going to be saying when the investigation comes up. What Major Iannone says is pretty much what the others will be coming up with; their explanations will be like his, or maybe not even as good. They may satisfy themselves with them. Nobody's liable to think of anything better." He sighed. "But it won't do. There's a lot more to it than that. There's a deep bottom on this thing. Real deep. It comes out of the caves, and it'll go on out beyond the planet, when it comes to that. It has to do with . . . with what's part of the nature of people, and the ways they influence each other. There are ways you can get hold of somebody else's mind. Blindside it and catch it. You give somebody's imagination something it didn't have any notion existed, and he'll do what you say. And not just one person. More than one. A lot of them."

"Don't *you* get started," Cahill said, meaning it.

"Don't worry," Whitehall said. "That's the last thing I want to do. I've had enough catechism already, same as you have. That's not what I came around for."

"I forgot what it was," Cahill said. "Did you tell me?"

"Yes; I want to give you something."

"I'll take it," Cahill said, "whatever it is."

"Here's something that maybe you don't know about," Whitehall said, placing the calculator in Cahill's big, half-open hand. "What this tells you, you can believe."

"I do know about it," Cahill said, holding the E6B in one hand and with the other turning the dial on one side, slipping the plate through, back and forth. "I done had holt of one of these before, out in the snow. This is the way you boys get from one place to another, up yonder." He grinned, this time so that his teeth felt the air. "Didn't do me no good."

Whitehall's face filled with gentle memory, with concern and intelligence. "I'd like to tell you that this was Joel's, but it wasn't. The same principles are working in it, though. Day and night and all the time. It'll get you home."

"Hell of a thing," Cahill said. "Just the right thing for a blind man." He realized that this did not say what he felt, and added, "I do thank you, though."

Whitehall leaned, drawn to the bed, eager to speak.

"One thing you might like to know," he said. "It's the one I had on the Rabaul raid, that I was telling you and Faulstick about the other night."

"No shit?" Cahill said, running the plate through the calculator face again, and once more. "It is, really?"

"It is, really," Whitehall said. "That and the sextant are parts of my best life. I can't give you the sextant, but you can sure have that E6B, if you want it."

"Sure I want it," Cahill said, his hands quiet on the calculator now, the instrument still. "Sure I want it." He turned toward Whitehall's voice. "I guess the other captain didn't have nothin' to give me, but that gun flash, that blink of light he said he had, that didn't happen, that wadn't from no gun. The one he just made up."

"You keep that, too," Whitehall said. "I believe he'd want you to have it." He stood up. "As far as my calculator's concerned, no matter whether you can read it or not, it's full of one thing you can always use, the same as the tables are, the same as the sextant is."

The circle of rubber around his eye came to Cahill, and he realized what it pointed toward; that he had been, that he was looking at the sun. "I remember," he said.

"The sextant's for triangulation," Whitehall said. "That's the game.

It takes triangular eyes to see heaven, somebody said. The navigators believe it, whether they know it or not."

"Maybe I got the next thing to it," Cahill said.

"You hold on to that thing," Whitehall said.

"I will," Cahill said. "But you never did tell me what it is that's in it."

"Where you are, is in it," Whitehall said. "It's the only sure way to know."

"And then what've you got?"

"Just that much."

"Well, I ain't sure," Cahill said. "I've had about all I can take from the stars."

"That may be," Whitehall said, "but that's not the end of it. You've had the sextant in your hands, and that changes a man's life. I know. I've been there. I'm still there. Remember this about the stars: they're just waiting for somebody to do with them what was built into them, that they don't even know about."

"I'm obliged to you," Cahill said, "but I don't see how all that's goin' to help me, in my shape."

"The actual instrument maybe won't," Whitehall said, "but what's behind it will. The idea—the truth—that there is a place that the universe can't deny you. The stars get together on you; there's no other way. They can't help it. And numbers are the same."

"All right," Cahill said. "If you say so. I got it."

"You're damn right you got it," Whitehall said, taking hold of the front of Cahill's shoulder with no fear. "The universe will confirm your place any time you ask it. It'll back you up all the way."

"You're standin' up," Cahill said, "so you're leavin'."

"I am," Whitehall said.

At the door he paused. "And good luck for the rest of your life. Keep hold of that thing, like I told you," he said. "I may meet you some day on the ocean." He grinned again. "Out of sight of land."

"What ocean would that be, Captain?" Cahill asked, but the door had closed; the air had fallen from it.

*　　　*　　　*　　　*

More time. An hour? An hour and a half, maybe? "There ain't nothin' for a blind man to do," he said to himself. "You're supposed to wait in these-here beds till you heal up, but there really ain't nothin' wrong with me. I ought to get out of here and get on down the road." There

662

was the question of when, though, and he waited, shifting this way and that, one face after another floating in front of him: Shears, the colonel, Spain, Harbelis, as he had made them be. And his son as well, as personally real, as much imagined, as much made up as any of the rest of them.

Another knock came. "Who is it this time?" he asked before the door opened.

"Stathis Harbelis, sir."

"Come on in," Cahill said. "You're one of 'em I don't mind."

"Shears is outside, too," Harbelis said when he was in. "I asked him if I could see you by myself for just a minute, and he said it was all right."

"I'm glad he don't mind," Cahill said. "Next time, do it like you want to, yourself. He ain't your father."

"No, sir, but we're together. We understand that things have to be a certain way."

"Well," said Cahill, "I guess we can say good-bye without him."

"I'll say that now," Harbelis said. "I'm very happy that I got to know you. Everything about it was good."

"Thanks, son. I hope you make it through the war. I hope somethin' in the air don't get you."

"I want to say something else, too," Harbelis said, swallowing and looking straight ahead. "I killed your dog. I was the one."

"Somebody sure as hell killed him," Cahill said. "I picked up his head. That was all I could find."

"I couldn't help it. I ran over him with the prop. He jumped right into it. Until the prop hit him I thought he was going to tear me apart, and the plane with me. He was really coming."

"That'd be him," Cahill said. "He'd get after you."

"I sure am sorry," Harbelis said, now looking at Cahill.

"That's all right," Cahill said. "It wadn't your fault. Don't worry about it."

"Can I do anything for you?"

"No; I'll be all right."

Harbelis brightened. "I'll bet there *is* something. I'll bet I can give you something you can use."

"What'd that be? Your navigator done give me something it's gonna take me quite a while to figure out how to use."

"How about some new dark glasses?"

Cahill thought. "Well, sure," he said. "I could use 'em. I'm used to havin' some. You must'a broke them others when you was runnin' over me and my dog. If you're thinkin' the same thing, we could both figure you owed 'em to me. Sure, I'll take 'em. And much obliged."

"They're issue, sir," Harbelis said. "They're Ray-Bans. The best the Air Corps's got." He put the glasses, in their curved case, on the bed near Cahill's hand, which slid and found them.

"These'll do," he said. "I can already tell."

"I've got to go, now," Harbelis said. "Colonel Shears wants to see you."

"Are you goin' on with it, son?" Cahill asked, tilting his ear.

"Going on with what, sir?"

"With what you . . . with what Joel . . . with what Shears wants to do?"

"Yes, sir," Harbelis said. "I've got to, now. Besides that, I want to see where it goes. I want to see how far Joel can take us. I mean on out past any place he's ever been, himself." With his hand on the knob, he said, "I'm in at the beginning, just as much as Shears or any of the others. That's going to matter a lot. More and more. It's not just something you'd want to throw away."

"Good-bye, sand-runner. Sand and snow. Slows everybody down but you. You can run fast. I could hear it. Hear you comin'." He waited himself out. "Watch your feet, son."

"I'll watch everything. And thanks for coming up here and being with us."

Steps came through, came forward; different ones, as though closing in: too quick; and stopped too abruptly.

"Good afternoon, sir," said Malcolm Shears. "I'll be the last cadet to come in. I wanted to see if you needed anything."

"No," Cahill said. "I've got all I can carry."

Without any hesitation at all, Shears asked, "Has the colonel been here?"

"Yeah, he was here. I liked him this time better than I did."

"Did you tell him anything?"

"What would I tell him?"

"Anything about us?"

"No, but he may ask me again when I come back."

"Use your head," Shears said. "If you don't mind my advising you. The colonel will do everything he can to find out about us. He's trying to save his ass. Don't let him do it."

"We'll see," said Cahill. "That'll come later."

"How about Major Iannone? Has he been in here a lot?"

"He's been here. And yeah, I guess you could say a lot. More than anybody else, anyway."

"The colonel sent him, Mr. Cahill. They're all in this, against us. Don't tell him anything."

"He did all the talkin'," said Cahill. "I couldn't hardly get a word in edgeways."

"Let him keep talking," Shears said. "The more he explains things to himself, the farther off he is from us." He thought a moment. "Anybody else?"

"The Navigator was here."

"He's all right," Shears said. "But I wouldn't trust him, either, all that much."

"How is this turnin' out? How much trouble are you in?" Cahill asked.

"No trouble," Shears said, smiling. "They're the ones that're in trouble. They'd play hell washing out a whole class. It'd make too many people look bad; the Air Corps couldn't live with it. And we've got our system, we've got Alnilam set up in the other bases, now. We kicked it off here, and did it right, and the others'll want to run with it. If they stop us here—and they won't—Alnilam will still go on; it's going right now, just as we sit here. The lines are drawn. We've got what we want here, and later on we'll have *all* we want. That I'll guarantee you."

"Would you tell me just exactly what you did? How you went about the whole thing, out yonder Sunday?"

"We panicked Willis. Billy Crider did it. Just like Joel set it up; we followed it through. We panicked Willis and he panicked Faulstick, and then ran into him."

"Killed him, they tell me."

"Yes. We didn't intend for him to be killed. It just happened that way."

"He was a good man, don't you think?" Cahill said quietly.

"He just got in the way. Willis broadsided him."

"He was a good man," Cahill repeated. "He's done been in the war. He's been over there. Been up there," Cahill pointed up, with his elbow on the bed. "It's a hell of a thing to come back from what he's been through, and end up bein' chopped apart at a kids' trainin' base. That ain't right; there ain't nothin' right about it."

"Regrettable," Shears said. "I agree with you."

"That all?"

"It happened. It might have been avoided, but right now I don't see how. The situation was fluid and unpredictable; those were the main qualities we wanted it to have. It was every man for himself. Any one of us could have been killed, too. We were all in there with blind chance. Except"—he smiled and shook his head with self-agreement—"that all the Alnilam people were safe. We were all relaxed; when you relax enough you can react almost before the thing that's going to happen, happens. When you don't think, you can move before it does. We could've been out rolling baby carriages."

"A man's dead."

"That was maybe not necessary," Shears said, with a little irritation that Cahill picked up. "But maybe in the long run it was. They want life and death, we'll give it to them. The main thing is that we're under way. It's exactly like Joel said it would be. Alnilam has started, and nothing on earth can stop it."

"I can stop it," Cahill said quietly, noticing how relaxed his forearms were, bare against the cool sheet.

"Not even you, Mr. Cahill," Shears said almost immediately. "What you should do now is go home, and leave things to us. Your part is over. You showed up when you did; you were the proof of what Joel said would happen. You even hit the basketball shot, the 'unusual thing' that was required. Harbelis said you swished it on the third try. Imagine that; a blind man. Now you've got your own legend, and it's connected to ours. You're as much of a symbol as Joel is, if you want to call it that. What other blind man could have gone out there like you did, with those planes and props all around him, ramming and wrecking? Who else? Who would've been out there across the field, in the first place, but you? Who could've come through that high wind of blades, all that confusion, all those hits and misses? All that chance? All that blind chance, all over the place and going every which way?" He waited. "Nobody but Joel Cahill's father. Nobody else on earth could have got through there. Do you think it'll be lost on anybody who ever hears about it? Do you think this won't be all over the Air Corps, all over the service, all over the country? All over the world? Do you think it won't stay in the air? Do you think it won't grow, and keep on growing?"

"It was just luck," Cahill said, carried with Shears in spite of himself. "It was just luck, all my p—"

"No," Shears said emphatically. "Everything you've done up here has locked together; everything you do feeds our effort. The Link Trainer, the flying with McCaig, the strut wire you found, out there at the crash site, the zipper, Joel's tooth: everything. All those things were right in there, right in line. Standing up to the colonel and backing him down, busting Foy's hand: all that. None of it could have been better. But when you went through all those props—a blind man, stone blind —all those aircraft on no track but pure chance: when you went through that, and did it like you did it, and came out the other side, that topped it; that was the icing on the cake. It was not only what we needed; it was *more* than we needed; it was almost too good to be true."

"All that . . . all that, and the other stuff, like the basketball. You can't tell me my boy . . . I mean what did he really *say?* Did he tell you I could throw a basketball? I ain't never picked one up but once or twice in my life."

"He didn't say anything about basketballs," Shears said. "He just said that anything we gave you to do, you could probably do. He said that you could do anything."

"Some things," Cahill said. "The rest is just luck. I wish I could tell him."

"You got through it," Shears said. "He set it up. I think he might've controlled the chance of it, in some kind of way. Maybe he was looking after you. A spell, maybe. It's not impossible."

"What now?" Cahill asked, not wanting to encourage any more talk on this line.

"Now all we want you to do is to drop out of sight. Go back to your old life. Do what you want. Go where you want to go. Wherever we are, you don't need to be anymore, ever. I might even go so far as to say, stay away from us. Wherever we are, don't come." He paused, gathering. "Don't come, because you'll already be there. You're in the story, now. Nobody will ever forget it. The beginning's done; it's made. This is going to be your immortality, if you want one. Nothing you could ever do from now on could be this important."

"No more dead people," Cahill said. "If I hear about any more, I *will* come where you are, no matter what. I'll come after you."

"There won't be," Shears said. "You have my word on it."

"Are you like the others, Shears?" Cahill said suddenly.

"What do you mean, sir?"

"Do you believe my boy is dead?"

"Well, he's . . . his spirit is surely . . ."

"That's not what I asked you."

"I think he's out there, and that he'll show, one way or the other. You asked me what I believe. That's what I believe. He's out there, and if he's out there he'll show up. When the time comes, he will. Everybody believes it."

"When will that be? If I'm supposed to be in on this all that much, you can sure as hell tell me."

"I would tell you, but I don't know. That one's not for me to say. It depends on a lot of things. Everything else I'll have to do for myself; I'll have to figure out the ways. But that one I don't have any control over. He still controls that. And if he's out there, he'll turn up when he thinks it's right. It's up to him, though. It's still up to him."

"I could stop you, Mr. Shears," Cahill said, not moving. "Maybe not them others, at them other bases you're talkin' about, but I could put a end to you and your bunch, right here and right now."

"You wouldn't do it, Mr. Cahill," Shears said, with confidence, but not entire. "You wouldn't tear down your own boy's thing, the thing he's built up with the rest of us. You wouldn't do that. You wouldn't turn on the spirit of your own boy, your own son. Some fathers might do that; a few, maybe. But not Joel Cahill's. Not the man who went through those runaway propellers on guts, luck, or whatever you call it. On spirit, maybe. Raw spirit. You won't go back on us. It's not possible. This is the thing of your son's that goes on; the thing that's still alive and will go on God knows how far, and for how long. And I'll guarantee he knows it, too, wherever he is, whatever condition he's in."

"You poor kid," Cahill said. "You're in too deep. I think it's done got away from you. They'll catch up with you. All of you. They don't need me. They'll catch you. And when they show that you meant to do it . . ."

"No they won't," Shears said. "No one will break. Not one. And if that one person does—and he won't—it won't make any difference, because the idea's already going; it's in the air. We don't matter all that much, here at Peckover. This is just an insignificant little place. But what's happened here has happened. And now they can't stop Alnilam any more than they can stop Orion, any more than they can stop the Hunter from crossing the sky." Shears grinned. "From crossing the sky, with his dog."

"Joel didn't know I had a dog."

"You did have one, though. How do you explain that?"

"You, I can stop from killin', Shears," Cahill said, implacably, ignoring him. "I can do that."

"Listen," Shears said, closer now. "Millions of people are going to be killed, and nothing will come of it. We don't want to kill anybody, from now on, but Germans and Japanese. In the Air Corps, in the places where we function, we will infiltrate, just like we have here; just like we infiltrated at Peckover. In an underground way, but known in exactly the ways we want it to be known, we will take credit for various things that happen. Credit, but not blame. No matter how scattered we are we will be in close communication. For as long as the Air Corps issues E6Bs. And you, too: you can read—get somebody to read the newspaper to you, as the war goes on. More than once you'll be able to tell where Alnilam is, where it's been, and maybe even guess where it's going to be. I can't tell you that Alnilam will win the war, but in some ways we will shape it, and above everything else we will gain from it. And at the end, when it comes, we will be in the position we want. The leader will have to come from someone who was here at Peckover; there has to be an original witness. It may still be me, if I make it through the propellers."

"I hope you do," Cahill said. "It ain't no fun there."

Shears cleared his throat and spoke impulsively. "I knew Joel; I shook his hand. I might even a flown with him, if they'd'a let two cadets go up in the same aircraft."

"Who'd be the head, if somethin' happened to you? Harbelis?"

Shears smiled indulgently. "No; not enough steel. Spain, maybe; right now he's the best second in command there could be. Adler? No; he's too much like Joel for what we'll need; he looks maybe too far off. What we need now is organization. Joel was never interested in that, only in the young charioteers drinking the wind of their own speed, and the big purple field where we won't fly anymore, but that we get to through the airplane, before we leave it behind. Now we get practical. All those planes out there in the parking area, all that scrap metal and fabric they're cleaning up now with bulldozers, that's practical. That's the sledgehammer side of Alnilam, and not the cloud side. Let Joel Cahill look down from his cloud and see what we did, with what he set in motion. And let him keep on looking. We won't give down. Not now."

"While they were cleanin' up out there," Cahill said, coming painfully to his elbows, "amongst all that other stuff, did they . . . what'd they do with Zack? I had his head there, for a while. I think I did. What did they do with him?"

"We have him, Mr. Cahill," Shears said, changing. "We buried him."

A great thrashing roar without color went over Cahill; involuntarily he reached down. "I mean . . . did you . . . was he . . . ?"

"Yes," Shears said quietly. "We didn't leave anything. We got all there is, Mr. Cahill."

"Where is he?"

"We buried him out in the pines, off the road, just where it loops around. The colonel said it was all right."

"Well," Cahill said, a little satisfied. "He used to play out there, you know. Used to play in the snow. You could feel it all over him, and you could tell he liked the hell out of it; you could feel it, before it melted. That was a beautiful thing. The way I imagined he must'a looked was prob'ly better than it really was. All white, with the sun on him. A dog made out of snow, just like that, just for a second, when you taken holt of him." He paused. "He liked to get stuff all over him. He must'a rolled in them ashes, out where Joel got killed. I felt that, too, but it wadn't as good. But I've had a dog made out of ashes, and another one made out of snow. That's enough for me. No more dogs."

"He's in a good place."

"I'm glad you did that, son. That was a good thing. I thank you. I do thank you."

Shears hesitated. "Some of the fellows—I won't say which ones—thought we ought maybe to have . . . to have one of his teeth, but I didn't think that would be right."

"Shoot whichever ones they was," Cahill said. "Shoot 'em in the balls."

"I will," Shears said. "And you do something for us, too."

"What's that?"

"When anybody asks you about us, don't tell him anything much."

"I'll tell him what I remember," Cahill said. "But that ain't much. What can a blind man tell anybody?"

"About Saturday night, just say that we showed you the film, the movie with Joel in it. You can do that. We showed it, and described it to you. The ceremony and the rest, you needn't say anything about. Don't tell them about 'Rejoice O Princes.' Don't give the words away; don't give away any of the words. Don't let them have the words."

"I don't remember any of 'em anyway," Cahill said, though this was not true. "What was that about comin' through the desert?"

" 'As I came through the desert thus it was,' " Shears said, and then slowed his words down and emphasized them. " 'No hope could have no fear.' "

"Who said that, in the beginnin'?"

"His name was Thomson, but for some reason he called himself B.V.

670

when he wrote things. That, and what we say together, is all I know about him. He lived a long time ago, I think." Resuming his normal voice, Shears said, "Keep the words. Let's keep all the words."

"After you'all got through, there in the shed, and all, what'd you do then, Shears?"

"I . . . we went back. Back to the base. It was over."

"Did *you* go back to the base?"

"Why yes . . . sure . . . sure I went back."

"Somebody said that some of the boys stayed in town, and that you was one of 'em. Is that the truth?"

"Yes, I did," Shears said, holding himself. "I forgot. I did stay in town. I had an overnight pass, and I stayed . . . I stayed with some people I know. But I went right to sleep. There was nothing else to do."

"There was a lot of wind that night, Shears. You wadn't out in all that? You wadn't out and around in it?"

"No, sir," Shears said. "I went straight to bed." Picking up momentum, he added, "Civilian beds are very nice. I don't think I turned over, all night."

"Good enough," Cahill said. "I wondered if you remembered all that wind. I didn't sleep all that well, myself."

"Did you stay out there in the shed? Must have been cold."

"Yeah, I stayed out in the shed. I told McLendon I might go back up to my old room. But I stayed in the shed." He listened for changes in Shears's breathing, but he could not find what he wanted.

"I have to go now, sir," Shears said. "All of this counts, and all of us are grateful."

"Take care of yourself. I'll prob'ly see you in a couple of weeks."

"It's likely," Shears said. "But hold on. 'No hope can have no fear.' "

"No hope," Cahill said. "I never had none." He paused, with his own kind of emphasis. "But can't nobody tell me I can't have it. That's my business."

"You bet," said Shears. "You're the man."

*   *   *   *

Cahill sat in the room chair, his suitcase beside him, dressed, shaved and showered, his mouth sweet with toothpaste. "I'm ready to go," he said to Major Iannone. "Do I have to sign out?"

"No," said the major. "I'll take care of all that. All you've got to do is remember what I told you, and follow through on it. Stick to the diet I

671

gave you. Get your doctor in Atlanta to give you a new glucose tolerance test; until that, stay on one hundred units of insulin a day, without fail. Inject at the same time every day. Morning is the best. And get some exercise. I'm not talking about stationary exercise, like lifting weights. I mean something that keeps your heart active for twenty or thirty minutes at a time. Walk. Get somebody to walk with you. Every day. Or swim. Can you swim?"

"I might learn," Cahill said. "I've got lots of water, where I live."

"Buy yourself another dog, and have him trained properly."

"I'll look into it."

"You could go for walks with him. It appears to me that you haven't been giving your heart enough to do. It needs more activity, maybe even a little more development than it's been getting, than it has."

"At least I don't cut it, Major. I don't cut the heart." He stood up.

"Who said anything about cutting it? I'm asking you to work it. You'll live longer, and do more, if you do. And don't drink so much. See if you can cut it out, speaking of cutting things."

"I'll take up with the idea," Cahill said. "But there's somethin' you don't want to sell short."

"What's that?"

"The blind drunk. See, when a blind man goes on a blind drunk, it ain't like any other man's blind drunk. That's when what you remember gets good. It gets better than it was when you could see. It's somethin' you'd just as soon not give up, if you was blind."

"Well, try to hold it down," the major said. "Hold it down as much as you can."

"We'll see."

"Like I tell you," Iannone said, "move the body." He patted Cahill on the shoulder as he rose. "I think you like being immovable."

"Maybe so. The other things have got to have a place where they can come; they got to know it's there; they got to know where it is."

"One other thing," the major said. "Go back through everything that happened here. Rethink it. Get the uselessness of it into your mind." He hesitated, as Cahill's face above his own grew stony. "The war and the world are hard enough situations for anybody, without making trouble that don't need to be there."

"Mr. McLendon from town's comin' after me. Maybe we ought to go see if he's here yet."

"He's not here, Mr. Cahill. And don't change the subject. Think of the cost. Think of the losses your son's wild notions have brought on this place. And a man's dead, too. Don't forget it."

"My boy wouldn't kill nobody," Cahill said. "Take your big mouth and your insulin and the rest of it and shove 'em up your ass."

"He killed Captain Faulstick just as much as Tim Willis did. He cut him in half, from the right side of his neck on through the lower trunk. Remember that when you come back. You may want to remember some other things, too. A case needs to be made against these other boys."

"Make it, then," Cahill said, reaching down for his suitcase. "It's all yours."

"Too bad you have to go out of here like this," the major said.

"I don't mind," Cahill replied. "I would like one thing, though."

"What is that, hard knocker?"

"Could I talk with your other man for a minute? The one that works for you?"

"Gilbeau? Sure, I'll get him."

One side heavy with his suitcase, he stood straight. The boy was not far from him.

"Could we go stand in the wind you got here?" he asked. "Couldn't be too far."

A trapped look on his face, Pfc. Parris Gilbeau stood facing the big solid figure in the olive drab overcoat with the service insignia cut off it, the old suitcase, and the new sunglasses.

"Yes," he said after a moment. "It's only a few steps from here."

In the new subtle movement of air Cahill put down his suitcase, took off his hat, and folded his arms across his chest. "This where it was?" he asked. "This where you said it was?"

"Yes," Gilbeau said. "It was here, a foot or two one way or the other."

Cahill gave himself to the air.

Gilbeau stood at parade rest, watching the blind man turn his head carefully, in stages, turning and then stopping in what gave the impression of a preset position, then turning more, stopping, turning once more, shifting his feet slightly and repeating the small, strong moves.

"You try, too," Cahill said impatiently. "Don't just stand there. See if you can get anything. You told me the other day you heard somethin'. Told me you heard somebody's voice. Said it was telling you all kinds of things. Where is it now? Where is it, God damn it? You said it was here."

"I am trying," Gilbeau said. "But I can't hear anything, either. I can't hear anything this time."

"You didn't hear nothin' the other time, neither," Cahill said, breaking his slow rhythm, destroying it, picking up his suitcase. "My boy never said nothin' to you. And he never turned black." He put out his finger.

Near tears, Gilbeau started back from the finger lifted not toward him but the wall of the tunnel, then moved so that it pointed at him, into his chest.

"And," Cahill said suddenly, "he didn't have no ugly mouth, neither. Nobody ever said that but you. Them others . . ." he went this way and that for words. "Them others said he looked all right."

"I couldn't tell," Gilbeau said. "I can't tell. Maybe my imagination about him got too strong for me." He bit his lip; the upper, not the lower. "But those were all things he could have said."

"Well, he didn't," Cahill said, standing motionless again, heavy on one side, straight, listening once more, briefly, before he broke from the air and left it unsteady and the same.

* * * *

"They done moved where the bus comes, Frank," McLendon said, driving evenly toward the town. "They got 'em a little cubbyhole between two stores, and done put a sign over it. That's where we're goin'. We might be a little early, but you ain't got no problems."

"I feel OK," Cahill said. "I'm glad to get out."

"Them military doctors take care of you?"

"Yeah. Got me straightened out, with my medicine, and all. And some of the cadets came around. So it wadn't too bad."

"Friends of your boy's?"

"That's right. Five or six of 'em. I wonder why the colonel . . ." he stopped, anxiety touching him, and not leaving as he thought more. "If them boys . . . if the colonel is wantin' to get after them boys for . . . for bein' friends with my boy, I wonder why he . . . ?"

"What?"

"I wonder why he didn't keep 'em out? Keep 'em away from me? Why wouldn't he do that, if he had somethin' against 'em? If he wants to try to prove somethin' against 'em? They come right in, right in my room, and there wadn't nothin' said about it."

"It might not be all that hard to figure," McLendon said after a minute. "If he wants to make trouble for them boys—all of 'em together —and maybe make some of it for you, too, he couldn't do no better'n to let 'em get together with you, like you was all in on the same thing. The same thing before the airplanes run together, and the same thing after."

"If that's so . . ." Cahill said slowly, and whistled, a slight whistle more breath sound than a tone, ". . . if that's the truth, then Shears walked right into it. Him and them other boys, they didn't come to me, they went right to the colonel. He won't have no trouble provin' they was over there with me."

McLendon smiled and glanced at Cahill. "They must figure you're the key to this thing, Frank."

"Well, I ain't," Cahill said. "They'll play hell layin' that on me."

They entered the town, slowed, turned off half a block from the highway and stopped.

"We're here," McLendon said, "but the bus ain't. You want a beer or somethin'? I might could get you one."

"No," Cahill said. "I don't need no more beer. I'll just say good-bye and thank you for everything you done."

"Good-bye, Frank. I'm glad you was here."

"I was here," Cahill said. "I'll prob'ly be back; it ain't like I was dead. If you want me any time soon, just holler like the rabbit, and I'll come. I'll come if you can make it sound like that rabbit is really dyin'. Then I'll come. I'll come swoopin' down, and take your head apart."

"You ain't gonna get me to do that again," McLendon said, lifting Cahill's suitcase from the back seat. "When I do it, it'll be me that's dyin'."

"I'll be listenin', whenever it is," Cahill said, standing now beside the suitcase, as McLendon's gears engaged and the car moved off from him.

"Well," he said to himself aloud, feeling the warmth of his breath blow back in his face from the words, "you can be cold standin' up or cold sittin' down."

"It's all cold," a voice, a woman's voice, said. "This is a cold-ass place."

"Who are you?" Cahill asked, grimly but not forbiddingly.

"You know who I am," said Hannah, slouching near him, with her hands in the pockets of her oilcloth coat.

"What the hell're you doin' around here? You goin' somewhere?"

"No, but I knew you was goin' somewhere. I know when the bus leaves, and I know this-here new place that the bus comes. There ain't no puzzlement to it."

"We just gonna stand around here?"

"There ain't nowhere else. The bus'll be here, direckly."

"Tell me when you see it."

"I'll tell you. I hope you don't have no trouble gettin' back. You gonna be all right, now?"

"Sure, I'll be better than that."

"You gonna get yourself another big dog?"

"No; I don't think so; no more dogs. I think maybe I'll go with people, if I can find me the right ones. Or just by myself; for a while, anyway. Down yonder, I got somebody, this Mexican kid. He can sing from down under the ground; did you know that? It don't sound like no other kind of singin'; he can do it. And he can swim . . . he can swim like the moon." He was surprised that he had said this, and grinned, straight ahead. "I used to see him, in that green lit-up water. Shit," he said, seeing the black figure lifted in green, "I might even learn to swim, myself. It's my pool, by God. It damn well is."

"Might be the bus," she said. "Somethin' with some lights on."

"You done good for me," Cahill said. "You was good for me, and you was good to my dog. You're the only other one that he ever . . . that he could ever . . ."

"He was a awful good big old boy," she said. "He could eat the world."

"I got that, you know," Cahill said. "You talk good about eatin'. I got that out of North Carolina, and that's about all I got."

"What're you talkin' about?"

"I know what the best taste in the world is. I done found it up here. That ain't such a little thing, I'm tellin' you. The best taste in the whole world. There ain't none better. There couldn't be none better. If God's made anything better, he would'a kept it for his self."

"What was it?" she asked, looking up, her expression plain and vivid.

"Honey and well water," Cahill said. "This is the only time I ever had it. You get holt of some of that, if you can. You'll know, just as soon as you put it in your mouth. It's the best thing . . . the best thing that . . . that you could get."

Her expression changed, but not to sadness. "You might find somethin' better."

"The hell I will," he said irritably. "I just done told you: there ain't nothin' better."

"You might find somethin' better," she said, "on your way home. And you might remember somethin' better, when you do."

676

"Come on, now."

"I might could find me a way to give you somethin', on down the road a piece."

"I think you already done give me somethin'," Cahill said, having with him the early morning, and the beginning of a sharp wire being pulled decisively through him; he felt it there now, and did not want to think of draining again before he got on the bus. "I think you did."

She sighed. "I reckon there ain't no way around it. I was afraid you'd end up with what I got. That's somethin' else you can thank your boy for. Couldn'a been nobody but him." She pursed her lips and socked him on the arm. "But you can get rid of that. There's doctors in Atlanta. I mean, on your way back, I mean, you might just find somethin' you're gonna like. Somethin' like the good side of blood. You'll see."

"I reckon," he said, shifting his loins, trying for a better position.

"Bus's comin'," she said. "I can see it now."

"You wadn't never in no prison," Cahill said. "Tell me the god-damned truth."

"No," she said straightly. "I never was in one. I was in a fire, like I said. But I wadn't in jail. They let me go, before I was ever in."

"And all that stuff you . . ."

"That was just somethin' he liked," she said. "Somethin' Joel Cahill liked. He told me what he wanted, what came in . . . what came in at the right angle for him. He told me what to say, what to talk about, what to put up there in front of him while we was . . . while I was . . . he told me what to say, and I went on from there; went right with it. I just took off with it, and it was dead right. I could tell it was right. I just made it up when I . . . well, like, as I went along, and all."

"And all that about them girls bein' cut up with scissors . . . ? All that?"

"It just come to me, out of . . . out of what we was doin'. I don't know exactly how. He liked all that; it was just right for him. It kept buildin' up. That's the best; that's the best of all. I don't know how I come by it. Don't ask me. But when you get down to it like that, you know that's where you want to be. There ain't nothin' like it, anywhere else. There ain't, and you know it."

"Ain't nobody around here told me the truth," Cahill said, blowing out much white. "But I got it, anyway. Or most of it. A lot of it. They come to me. I was in the middle. I got some of it."

"People are loadin' up," Hannah said. "Let me put your grip in, where it's supposed to go."

"You do that," he said, and stood. She came back; he could feel her take up her exact steps in front of him.

"Can you swim?" he asked suddenly.

"No."

"You could swim."

"Why?"

"Why not?"

"Can you?"

"No, but I just might get into it. Dive, too, maybe. I got a lot of water. All mine. Comes from the city, but when it's in the pool, it's mine."

"I don't b'lieve I'd take to it. Too late to learn, prob'ly."

"I bet you could take a tan real good," he said, feeling for her face in the cold air; finding it and feeling it. "You got high cheeks, like a damn Indian."

"Everybody around here's got Indian. Some of 'em don't like to talk about it." She smiled, again plainly, but shyly, giving secrets. "I know one Indian name. It means, 'We crossed this place.' "

"What's the name?"

"You be good, and I might tell you some time."

"Come go with me," he said, with just those words, understanding that there were no other ones. "You could do it. Right now."

"You just want somebody to lead you around."

"You'd play hell leadin' me around," he said, and then took it slow. "No; that ain't what I want."

"What do you want, then?"

"How the hell do I know?" he said. "Maybe some more rice, with that stuff. I liked it as much as Zack did."

"Some more playin' on the dulcimore?"

"Why not? That the broom? Them broomstraws?"

"That's what I was doin'," she said. "But I'm not so good off. I'm sicker than you might want to fool with."

"A sick one and a blind one," he said. "A sick one and a blind one. And a dead one."

"A dead one ain't all that little of a thing. Not that dead one, anyway. He's somethin' we both got different parts of. He ain't goin' to wear out."

"So . . . come on. Let's go; let's get on. I'll buy your ticket. Come on with me." Though the idling of the bus did not increase in sound, he began to talk faster, and a little louder. "Listen. I got four towers. I got a crazy house about half built, and right in the middle of it is a snake named Buster. He'll get after you, but he could be your friend, too. He would not be a bad snake at a weddin', if it was to come to that; if you'd want'a ask any snakes. I might even go back to skatin'. I got a rink I made, all tongue-and-groove hardwood. You can even get to feel the turns with your legs; I'd bet on it. Everything just goes around one way, around and around, and keeps on goin'. I could get to where I could do that again, know just as sure as I'm standin' here. I used to skate a lot. I could do it again. You better come on and go."

She said nothing; he could not get her to speak. He took his hands out of his pockets. "Well," he said, "you can say that you 'us the one that gave the clap to a blood-drinkin' blind man. Done come from his own son. Ain't many can say that."

She was quiet. He felt for her, touched her, but there was nothing she said.

"And maybe," he went on, as memory came back and hit hard, "maybe you could say that you done give it to this man . . . this man whose son was fixin' to rise up out of the fire. Let 'em wait for it."

"He won't do it," she said. "He's gone."

"All right," Cahill said. "I think so, too." He stepped toward the panting of the bus. "But you could come. You could come down there. For a while, anyway. You might have to get to likin' nails, because that's what I'm goin' back to. And finish my house, and maybe some other things.

She went silent again, but stayed.

"Well, write to me, anyway," Cahill said. "Willow Plunge, Cumberland Highway, Atlanta. That'll get to me."

Nothing.

"I can write, you know. Ain't nothin' says I can't write." He thought. "Shit, all you gotta know is where the paper gives out. A man . . . a man can write all he wants to. Write anything."

"I'll read it," she said. "Or I'll read *at* it. And that's the truth. You write at it, and I'll read at it." She drew breath, and had more than he did. "But I can't go with you."

"Why not, God damn it?"

"Ah, shit," she said. "I don't want you lookin' after me. I'm used to lookin' after myself. And you sure don't want me bleedin' on you no more. There ain't no way you could want that."

"You already done bled on me," he said, without thinking. "You don't hear no gripin' about it, do you?" He changed his feet and grinned down, but away from in front of where he believed she was.

"Anyway, you don't have to get up there . . . I mean you don't have to get up there on me, if you don't want to."

"I would want to, prob'ly," she said, and then was quiet so long that despair came back over him again, but worse. "I can take better care of myself than you could do it."

"I'll bet you," he said. Then, "Come on, and bring your broom. I like all that racket. That's kind of a quiet racket, you know; it's got somethin' to it." Then, "I'll make a big bed out of a tree. I'll put in my own sawmill."

"Just right to cut off your fingers with."

"I might cut off my dick," he said boldly, white with air.

"Don't do that," she said. "Don't let me catch you doin' that."

"You don't have to get up there no more. We could do somethin' else, if you wanted to. Or we don't have to do nothin'. But gettin' up there again, that sure ain't somethin' you're gonna have to do."

"If I 'us to come, I'd be up there," she said. "A whole lot. I just don't want to run my blood on you no more. That's all."

"You done run it," Cahill said. "It wadn't all that bad. I ain't dead. I ain't dead from nothin' you done."

"I don't take too much stock in my blood," she said. "I don't trust it. The doctors, they don't trust it. They don't know what to do with it."

"Mine ain't so hot, either," Cahill said. "It's full of sugar. It is, or else it ain't got enough. Like to 'a got my fuckin' head chopped off. But I got it straightened out. I could look after mine and yours, too."

She shook her head. "You don't want it all over you."

"Shit," Cahill said again, louder. "I done had it all over me. What're you talkin' about? I done had it all over me."

Two men came to them, the bus driver in pale blue and an MP staff sergeant with white piping at his shoulder. The sergeant said, "Mr. Cahill, my name is Sergeant Shellnut. I met you back at the colonel's office, when you had that . . . when you had that situation with your dog."

"Yeah," Cahill said. "You showed right up, when the colonel called you. It was real fast, but as it turned out you didn't have nothin' to do."

"I've got something to do now," the sergeant said. "I need to go down to Atlanta with you and . . . and more or less keep you in sight, until you come back for the investigation, when the board meets. I hope that's all right. I'll try to keep down low."

"Sure it's all right. I don't have no dog; I might as well have me a soldier. You come right along."

"We're fixin' to move," the driver said to Cahill. "I got a seat for you."

"Come on, Hannah," Cahill said. "We can talk about it on the bus."

"You don't need me," she said. "You already got everything you need."

"That ain't so," Cahill said. "I need more. I'd like to have more."

"Blind, strong, and wild, Cahill," Hannah said. "They ain't gonna take none of that away from you. You don't need Zack. You didn't never need him. You don't need me, neither. I ain't feeling the best, you know. Another one dyin' on you, that might break you down some."

He went into the seat, all the way over, against the metal, and palmed the glass slick. He turned and said, "Don't nobody sit here till we leave." He faced to the outside again, and raised his hand.

Sergeant Shellnut worked along the bus, and reached to touch the blind man, who sat large and rigid, his head leaning. "Shellnut here," he said.

"Don't sit down," Cahill said. "Go on in the back somewhere. I ain't gonna get away."

"I couldn't anyway," the sergeant said good-naturedly. "Somebody's done left a package in the seat."

The doors ground; the bus lurched and subsided.

The smoke of the exhaust hazed, eddied in a half rise; dispersed, was added to. Except for the bus, the street was empty; an unexpected car cleared past, and it was emptier.

Cahill cleaned the glass again, and reached, almost dreaming, with his other hand to the seat beside him. Paper rustled coarsely; the bag was not closed. "This must be mine," he said, taking from the bag what was in it. "Might as well be."

"Shit," Cahill said, feeling the cold metal with both hands, worn, brutal with function: the screw-grooves, the level-hand

Though it had not yet begun to snow, the driver started his wipers, and moved himself and his people forward, away from their smoke. The gears gathered, smashed and crowded, found

grip. He wound the handle until the press narrowed onto his finger and held it, then gave it half a turn more, so that it truly clamped his nail, and hurt it, and he could feel his heart beat there, as the sound of the engine went up, and was hoarse and large. each other; the bus straightened onto the highway. Little by little and then quickly the town dropped from it. The highway came to exist in the bodies of the passengers, as the driver brought it into himself, and with it made the engine hoarse and large.

Winter took it.